AVENGER :

a swords and skulls fantasy

CHRIS TURNER

This is a work of fiction. All the characters and events portrayed in these stories are either fictitious or are used fictitiously.

Map: Trevor Porter
Cover Art: Battle mage

Published by Innersky Books
www.innersky.ca

ISBN-13: 978-1-927117-92-7

CONTENTS

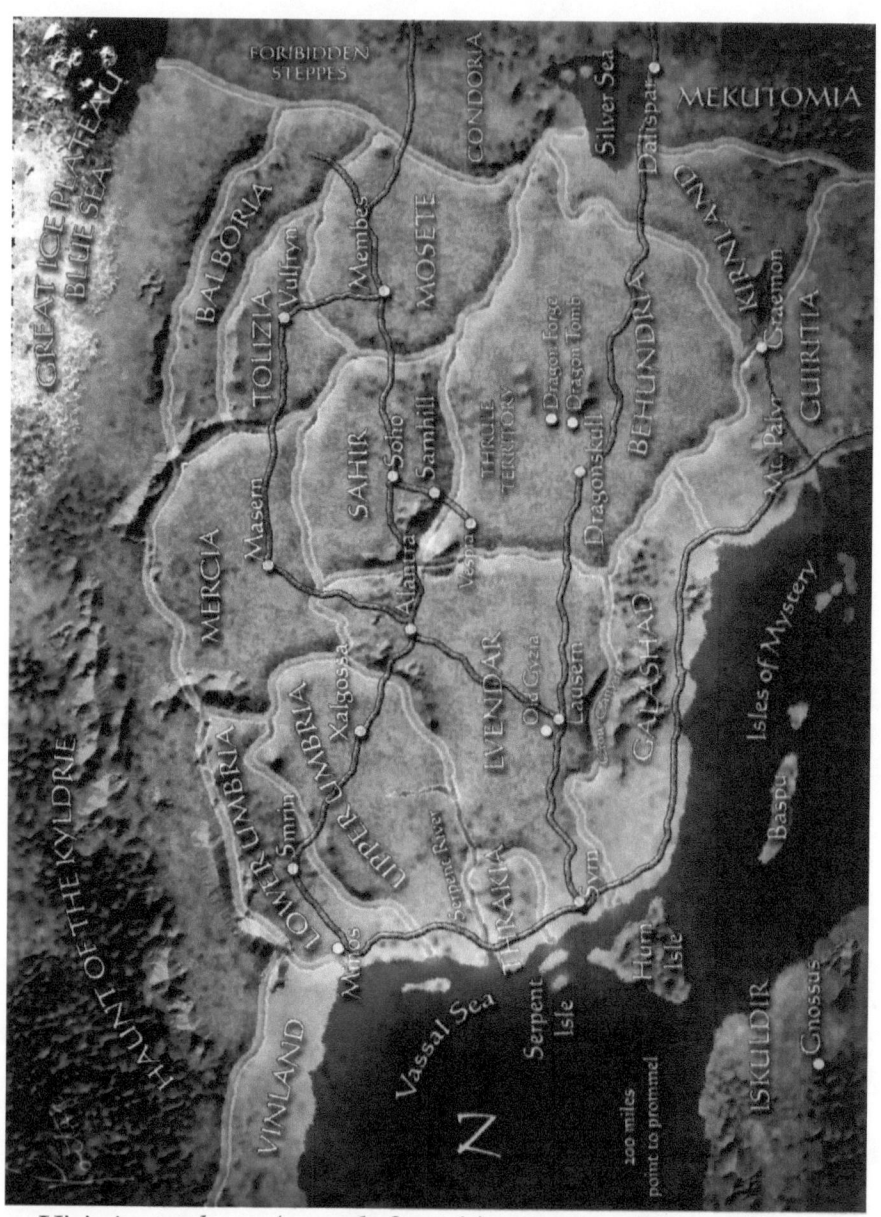

Visit *innersky.ca/swords* for a hi-res map of the world

FLAME OF EROS

CHAPTER 1

Below the Hall of the Mages dwelled a warren of catacombs and ancient halls rich in murk and mystery. Who built them or for what purpose none knew. Legend says by the hands of some bygone race. It might have been the slave-wards of the mad king Marizon or the race of beings who lived far below the earth which had tunneled up. Skirl the apprentice thought not. Just myths to prevent adventurous thieves like himself from looting the place when it became abandoned after the reign of the sorcerer priest Hunak or some such figurehead. He only knew that if he were caught here, slinking and creeping about the stygian dark with his spitting, fast-dwindling candle, he would face a harsh punishment, if not death. The end thus of his masquerading as a 'wizard's apprentice'.

With the love jewel of Eros clamped in his other fist, much was at stake. Indeed, kingdoms could fall or be born. Such was the power of the charm he held in his fingers. He alone knew the far-reaching implications of it in the wrong hands, be it monarch, wizard or thief, let alone stealing it out of the wizards' circle. That the talisman was much coveted by the head Archmagrix Taranis herself was another matter.

Taranis. What a piece of evil hatchery she was, and the most splendid specimen of vixenish flesh imaginable. The ultimate desire of every man.

A wily smirk spread across Skirl's chiseled features, roughly handsome in good light. In the prime of his youth, a young schemer, he was just past his twenty-first year and reveled in the fact that he was likely the youngest of the apprentices to have ever reached this far in the catacombs.

He stole forward down yet another set of wide, broken

steps. Far beyond his years in cunning and lore, yet still green in many phases of life, in his brain existed a fledgling logic which had barely saved him from being skewered on a spit or roasted over a royal fire. That, or being stretched thin on a rack in the king's dungeons.

The pads of his fingers walked along the smooth curve of a dolomite colonnade that formed part of the ancient passageway's walls.

It was risky skulking around these subterranean ruins but the husky murmur of the Archmagrix, dallying with one of her apprentices in the upper tapestried chambers, had unnerved him. He could not be caught anywhere near her inner sanctum, and so had taken the easiest escape route possible: the open door leading to the crypts.

The steep staircase that cascaded down into untold depths had not been an easy one to navigate. Indeed, the molder was intense, and stifling murk and stale air smote his nostrils like an ogre's club. He had ducked his head under cobwebs thick as yokkle stalks to come to a surface level with the Hall far above. It formed the beginnings of this wide passageway and led into a sepulchral underground hall. He had counted the steps—99 to be exact.

Skirl crept by an area in the wall where blocks of stones had been stacked in a crisscross fashion, some removed, revealing dark spaces beyond. They formed a kind of grate to an inner chamber where the stench was overwhelming. Rotten meat? Worse?

Such was the lightness of Skirl's movements and stealth of his passage that he had slipped unnoticed by whatever might be living beyond that dank stone. He sensed no movement. Yet he felt a living presence there. This foul reek of unwashed hide signified something far worse. But he dismissed the idea as fanciful imagination as he hurried on.

The dust ran thick in this wide, eerie hall. More thick webs pocketed the upper grouting and tiers of stone and it looked as if not a soul had ventured into this mausoleum for a century.

The passageway that his light-footed boots trod now opened up and led to an even more immense hall. He raised his candle high. In three directions ran the ruins of ages.

Along a footworn, flagstoned path he threaded his way. Among loose bricks, chipped flagstones, fallen statues of kings and overlords: one which looked like some horned statue and still leaned on a drunken angle. A horrid thing, pocked with age, bearing a face most disturbing. A sprawl of desiccated bones, what might have been half elk, lay at its feet. The statue's face, a grim, two-fanged visage, half bestial, humanoid with dog ears stared at him. He could not repress a shudder. Was this a giant shrine, or cryptic fane, or some bestial homage to a long lost god or devil? The sight of such statuary brought another round of shivers prickling his back. He escalated his pace. Trepidation and wonderment chased him in a circle as his young mind imagined all manner of rites, rituals and sacrifices that had been practiced here in years far past.

Expelling a slow breath, he could feel the blood pulsing in his ears.

A soft crunch of brittle stone sounded under his boot heel. He winced. As catlike as his tread had been, echoes as these carried far and he wished to alert no creature of his presence. Creature? Why would he even think that? He stifled a nervous cough. These haunts hadn't seen the light of day for years, so how could any life form exist?

A drip-drop echo sounded from faraway down the hall. An ominous plink into a still pool. The sound conjured up nightmarish things in his mind's eye.

Into the gloom he squinted. Pocked columns piked drunkenly to either side. Another crooked stair of broad steps beckoned at the far end which rose to dusky heights somewhere above. But the main passageway continued on, or seemed to go on in its buckled, crooked way to a lower level. Places that harbored yet stranger mysteries and dooms: a square-cut shaft like an old mine.

Skirl paused, prickled by indecision. Lofty heights of arched darkness reached above him which the small candle would not illuminate. Somewhere above, the elegant marble halls of the mages dwelled where he had recently run errands for Keren and Voydred, resident mages bearing titles of beastmaster and spellcaster.

The ghost of a smile quirked his thin lips, spread across his sharp features as he recalled the circumstances that led up to his journey to this eerie, disquieting place. A rare moment had presented itself. The Archmagrix, not in her chambers, had left on some business. Five quick strides and he had seized her famous necklace draped over the tall chair before the gothic mirror. He had stripped the Eros jewel from its twine of leather hide, replaced it with a clever imitation he'd had wrought by a gemsmith earlier. Now he meant to steal off with the jewel, and be rid of this band of arrogant spellcasters who called themselves mages. The ones who thought they ruled Umbria, or at least the capital, Xalgossa.

But no, a sound had unnerved him. He'd fled beyond the iron-bound door to the side that had been left slightly ajar, admitting the faintest, coolest breath of dank air into her tapestried quarters lest he be discovered by the Hall's guards.

Why had the sorceress been so careless? Perhaps she'd been caught in a moment of distraction? What dwelled down here that might interest her?

He licked his lips. Dissatisfaction bit at his heart. For the second time he swallowed the sour taste in the back of his throat. More unanswered questions. They only added to the pile that escalated his unease and the pace of his thudding heart.

The jewel's reflection stung his eyes. He turned it over in his palm, bringing the candle ever closer to the sapphire-like surface.

A gem of great worth and beauty, the size of a fallen chestnut. A living flame wavered within the red glow, scarlet as a rose, but at odd times it turned ultramarine in a queer way. Even he could sense the gemstone's emanation of power. It oozed of mesmerism, an eldritch, eerie love feeling, warming and melting the heart, bringing with it rapture alternating with an odd feeling of dizziness, if such were possible from an inanimate object. It was a mystery that both frightened and thrilled him. Indeed, it left such a discord in his mind that he tripped and barely caught himself in time before he smashed his teeth into a jutting wedge of loose brick.

With a cursing grunt, he plunged the jewel back into the pocket of his loose apprentice's robe. Already the cuffs of his robe were grimed and soiled. The voluminous fabric draped around his ankles swished and itched his sweating skin.

His heart skipped with anticipation. He knew his chances of escape dimmed with every passing minute spent in these nighted crypts. How long had he been wandering about these murksome halls? An hour? More?...and yet, something told him he had only a certain hundred or more steps to take before the dank corridor ended and led to safety up and away from the Archmagrix's private quarters.

He did not know for sure; he just had a sixth sense that there existed another egress back toward the Mages' Hall.

The thought was still skidding about his brain when the clink of a boot heel had him nearly jumping out of his skin.

Footfall? Voices?

A flicker of torchlit cut the eerie shadows.

"He must be down here," came a muffled voice. "Look. Footprints in the dust! A skulker's size."

Skirl bit back a soft moan. He ducked back in the wavering shadows. Sweat pooled under his robe, dripping down his dust-caked brow into his eyes.

Hold forth the jewel! Let the sorcerous light spill into their eyes, smash their brains. Bend their will to yours.

The commanding voice spoke in his mind. But no. The sight of their glinting blades, the memory of the ferocity of those blades in the outer courtyard while training, unnerved him. If the jewel's magic should fail him...

A better idea surfaced. His lips curled in a sneer.

With the desperation of a cornered rat, he doused his candle. Swiftly he nestled his lean frame behind the nearest object he could find: a bronze gargoyle, standing chest-high. The leering face was squashed like a pumpkin. In the dimmest of light the claw-like fingers were outstretched, beckoning any who trod here like an underworld ghoul. The head was missing one rat-like ear. He crouched, breath held, his back to the cold stone.

More gruff voices drifted from ahead of him. Or was it behind him, a trick of deceptive echoes in this loathsome place?

Capture was inevitable lest he come up with some plan. The area below the Hall of Mages was forbidden to novices. He was no swordsman, or master magician. With a last huff of defiance he stuffed the red-flamed sapphire into the cobwebbed mouth of the moldering gargoyle, in the hope that he could retrieve it later.

None too soon.

A torch hissed and flared not twenty paces away. Four of the Mages' Guard stood illumined under the fleeting, feral light.

"There he is."

He flicked his fingers outward. The approaching figure, torch in hand, suddenly stiffened as Skirl sent a push of magic on him. *Poof.* Like the breath of wind, or an invisible creature of the night, the flame flickered out. The guards were left blinking, the ancient hall cloaked in darkness.

There came a weird whistling sound from somewhere above...then a bewildered exclamation.

An anguished cry rang out in the dark. Then a scuttling of bodies and a scrape of boots as men scurried desperately to get away from some horror.

While the guards bumbled about, grunting and cursing, Skirl grinned and made stealthy steps away from the crumbling path and the gargoyle that now hid the Eros stone.

The laugh froze in his throat as a torch lit up and a familiar figure strode out of the murk.

Taranis!

CHRIS TURNER

Chapter 2

The sorceress stooped and lit the smoking torch lying in the molder. With a vehemence known only to her, she thrust it into the hands of the captain of the guards. "Go, you fool! Capture him!" Her eyes blazed with wrath.

Skirl turned and faced them.

The first guard that came at him, he deflected with a wind push that sent the man reeling back on his heels.

A bulbous creature that had shimmied down on some slimy rope of web scuttled across the lifeless body of his peer. A temple spider.

"Pin his arms, you fools!" Taranis cried. "Let him make no more thaumaturgic gestures. I'll strip this wretch of his powers ere the moon sets! The witch-shields and incantations of Dal Sagoth shall see to that!"

Terror seized Skirl's heart. It was one thing to stymie a few bumbling guards, but to go up against the Archmagrix... No... He ran and ran until he thought his heart would burst. But his feet and vision at last failed him as he tripped over a fallen block of crumbling stone.

The disgruntled guard at his heels made a wild lunge and tackled Skirl. With the wind knocked out of him, he had no ability to spring to his feet.

Skirl flailed about but to no avail.

Strong arms hauled him up, rough hands slapped his cheeks and pinioned his arms behind his back. The caching of the jewel had been his undoing. His devious scheming likewise with the wind magic. "What are you doing here, scoundrel?" the captain bellowed. "The Lady told us somebody had broken into her chamber and had taken to the secret ways below."

"The door was ajar," Skirl protested. "I was curious. Take your hands off me, you louts. I'm an accredited apprentice of the

Order!"

"No, you're an intruder who's gadding about in forbidden territory. Search him!"

The closest guard gave a rusty snort. He padded down Skirl's loose robe with no gentle fingers. He suddenly came across something solid. He plucked out a strange bone. Smoothly varnished, about six inches long, a pale blue-gray color, inscribed with arcane ruins and script and swirls. The grinning-eyed man held it up in the light for all to see.

The captain of the guards snatched it out of his hand. "So, you're a proven thief. In a place you shouldn't be. Archmagrix, over here!" he called.

The other two hauled Skirl away. At times when he resisted, they lifted him bully-puppet-like a foot off the ground, his feet pedaling in midair.

The troop was not eighty paces down the passageway when there came a clicking sound and faint whistling from above. Eyes beetled upward. A familiar black-haired gangling shape sprang down from the murks above on some slimy rope-loop of fiber. It was the size of a coconut. Skirl's mouth gaped. Another of those temple spiders: a cross between a giant black widow and a wolf spider. Deadly in these climes.

It sank fangs into the neck of the leftmost guard. The man buckled; he let out a hideous, bloodcurdling scream. He loosed his hold on Skirl. Skirl toppled back like a marionette while the man gurgled another incoherent cry. He took six stilted steps before he convulsed and fell, his mailed body arched in a grotesque V. The captain of the guards pushed forth his torch. Under the flickering glare, the man's parched white face lay creased in a rictus of agony.

"Dergath's devils!" He crabbed back, shoving the others out of the way.

Taranis emerged out of the stygian gloom, unafraid of murks or beasts. "Kill it, you fools! Are you so inept not to dodge one single clumsy spider?" In a clenched fist, her stave came whistling down to swat at the hairy thing as it crouched over the body of the dead man. She sent it scuttling back into the shadows on three broken legs. A horrible clicking sound echoed in the coils of darkness in its wake. Angry. Resentful. Brooding.

"My lady, we did not realize that there was only one—"

"Silence!" Her darting eyes flicked across the space at the apprentice. Her shadow fell over him like icy winter. "Skirl! I should have known. Get him to my chambers. One of you can fetch the fallen guards later."

"Yes, Archmagrix."

Taranis stood brazenly, legs spread wide apart. "What have you seen?" she demanded of the cringing man.

Skirl sucked in a breath, trying to straighten his spine to his full height, two inches shy of six foot. "Shadows and murks. Loathsome smells and vulturish spiders. What should I have seen?"

She scanned him through her hooded eyes, assessing the truth of his statement. Not an easy task with a dissembler such as he.

She loomed larger than life, her broad cheeks flushed with anger. The sorceress was lean and slinky as a black panther, her bronze skin oiled and gleaming in the dim light. Chestnut-blond hair dyed to the roots spilled down to the sides like wings. Regal, awesome, intimidating. A dominatrix, in all her domineering majesty.

How to describe the seductress? A figure who struck awe in the bulk of the citizenry, terror in the rest; promiscuous to the core, a student of black magic, arcane and forbidding, recognized as a power unto herself in all respectable wizard circles.

The top of her chestnut hair was ruffled and a puffiness remained around her eyes and cheeks, as if from a recent love play. No more the sultry murmurs and husky laughs of the boudoir from her throat. A feral gleam lurked in those eyes, as if a black widow had just devoured her mate.

The captain of the guard edged back cautious steps out of her shadow then motioned roughly to his two remaining men. "Leave Farl's body where it is. Watch out for those damn spiders."

The group resumed their journey. Flickering torches cast monstrous shadows on the ancient walls and pillars.

Taranis led the pack back to the moldered staircase; Skirl gazed in a rueful daze at the sway of her hips…seductive under the glare of her snug, skin-tight gown revealing every ripple and muscle clench. From her near-perfect curves there emanated a waft of the unmistakable spoor of animal hide he'd sniffed earlier.

Odd. Down by that criss-crossed stone-block grating. Considering she'd spent no more time down here than he had, was she dallying with beasts now? The thought repulsed him.

As if sensing his obscene thoughts, she whirled on him in sudden suspicion. "How did you get down here?"

"I came to call on you, Lady. To discuss the intricacies of a moon spell. The door in your sanctum was open."

She gave a mild snort of exasperation. "True, it was my fault. I must not have secured the portal's bolt properly. It will not happen again."

The captain of the guards gave a derisive grunt. "Caught him with this on him." He thrust forth the gleaming bone.

Taranis snatched at it. "That is Keren's wish bone," she muttered. "A femur of one of the young Kyldrie beastlings he used to raise. An obsessive pastime. Mind you, one of his lesser talismans. What else have you pilfered, thief?" She glared at Skirl. "Speak up!"

He gave a diminutive shrug. "Keren, our beastmaster, was not using the bone. It lay in dust for many years. I thought to try an apprentice's spell or two, to see if I could coax more magic out of the talisman. Is that a crime?"

Taranis laughed, not a pleasant sound. "You speak in

euphemisms. An attempt to brush off your theft and trespass."

The captain snorted. "I've seen this thief loitering about the beastmaster's trunk of trinkets. Hoping for a bone or two."

"He's a meddler and a snoop," said Taranis. "Make no mistake, Grindar, he will be punished. The question is, how?"

"Maybe cut off a hand, my lady?"

A cat-like murmur purred in her throat. "Crude. But there is a certain poetic justice in the recommendation. Still—" She frowned and her eyes grew duskier. "The matter merits thought. And yet, something is still amiss. The obvious confounds us, a slinking weasel putting his nose where it shouldn't be, skulking in the murk his trademark. I've had my eye on you, Skirl. You must think I'm stupid."

His breath drove quick and sharp against his clenched teeth. *Yes, you are, you dumb wench. You still haven't figured out the Eros jewel is a fake.*

She fixed him a sultry glance then pierced him with eyes that seemed to bore holes right through his skull. "You're holding something back, aren't you? My psychic sense tells me so. You thought to steal another treasure." In a moment of doubt, she clutched the leather strip around her neck. Long fingers touched the amulet. She examined the crimson flame deep within the contours of the jewel, which albeit didn't seem to gleam as brightly under the flickering torchlight. But she did catch the characteristic deep blue flame that was the jewel's taint as it morphed from scarlet to ultramarine.

"If you'd tried to steal this," she said, "I'd have cut off your head and had it shrunken and pickled."

Skirl licked his lips. The sweat pooled down his back. He tried to mask his anxiety but was unsuccessful. "I wouldn't think of it, Lady."

"Don't 'wouldn't think of it Lady' me. You are a filthy liar! You'd steal this talisman in a trice. You're a mendacious conniver. One who seeks to con me at every step and everyone else in the academy with the most forked of tongues."

"I'm distressed that you have such a low opinion of me, Archmagrix," Skirl said unconvincingly. "Were you not enamored with me enough to lay naked at my side the night of the last full moon?"

"Enough of your knavery! For your impudence, you'll serve as an example at tomorrow's prisoners' trials. I don't care if my cousin holds your child in her belly." She snatched at the iron ring to her chambers and shouldered the door open, her last words gusted with such venom that Skirl shrank back into the arms of the guards, trembling.

They all repaired to the sorceress's chambers. Up the last uneven steps and into the welcome light of sconces and guttering candles, Skirl was happy to be out of those murks. But not in the clutches of the witch. Everything had gone sour. Well, not exactly everything. He'd hid her precious jewel in a place she'd never find. One success. Unless of course, she were to discover that he had substituted the jewel, and went on a mission to torture him for the truth.

Skirl swallowed hard. He must never let that happen. If he survived tomorrow's trials, whatever those were to be, he'd sneak back and recover the jewel at a later time.

No mean feat. If he could pull it off...dear Taranis would have a rude surprise awaiting her, the surprise of a lifetime, and then they'd see what they would see.

Chapter 3

The public market of Xalgossa was a noisy and shoulder-jostling experience. Flanked by square stone towers, weatherworn as the dusty hills, the main road passed through its animal liveliness and the central square. Every manner of trader, peasant, hunter, fishwife, thief, priest, peddler and con-artist in the northern capital of Umbria was present.

Sword-for-hire Vetravincus pushed his way through the throng, hoping to snag a half decent meal and some ale after a long journey. He'd been working for a petty baron on the Mercian border for small coin. That had not ended well and he had taken his measly share of silver and headed south.

There was a wolfish hardness about him that marked the lone and wandering swordsman…and yet, a kinship and empathy for the underdog that was rare in these times.

The city was the oldest of such settlements in Umbria and the northern kingdoms, predated only by Lausern in Lvendar and possibly the seaport Syrn farther south and east. Priest kings had given way to hereditary kings and satraps leading up to the 2nd age. The real power lay with the mages who held the stronghold to the west. There, on a low hill within the city boundaries rose the octagonal tower complex of the Magicians. Its bright yellow-white gleam caught the full reflection of the noonday sun, causing Vetra to squint.

The king's castle loomed opposite to the Mages' stronghold on a lower hill east across elegant gardens and shrubberies where stone bridgeworks connected the four-towered palace to the inner city. Slums and dives huddled to the immediate south. Ironworks and smithies, tanneries and brothels ran right up to the southern gate of the city with flanking barbican that protected Alantra from invaders from Lvendar and Sahir farther afield. Here archers stood aloft, keeping watch for outlaws and troublemakers and anyone else who looked suspicious.

To the north lay low brooding hills, topped by evergreens and outcrops of rock, amid the odd slender blackstone watchtower that too looked north for invading armies and protected the winding dirt roads that led to peasant-tilled land, crofts, sheltered woods and at last the inhospitable mountains of the Kyldrie.

The sky was a clear blue and sunbeams traced bright lines through puffy white clouds. A twin gallows stood at the market's side under the watchtower. Already there was activity there: royal guard and city soldiers in red and yellow surcoats over burnished armor milling about and tacking up flags and pennons on long staves and poleaxes, preparing as if for a public spectacle. Not the clear day one would expect for a public hanging, thought Vetra, but this was Umbria after all. Such barbaric spectacles were commonplace. It was nothing that he hadn't seen before. A scar ran down the tip of his left ear to mid chin, mostly hidden by the brown-black hair that rested at shoulder level. Also hidden was the pink scar running from the top of his left shoulder to elbow from a sword slash that had nearly taken off his arm in a border war in Condoria when he was but a stripling learning his craft.

Rutting hogs on one side; on the other, fruit of all colors hanging in baskets in vendors' stalls. Raw meat buzzing with flies, slabs of venison hanging on hooks or wooden slats. Vetra would give that a pass.

Snarls and growls caught his attention past the hanging meat and the butcher's block. Some wolf-baiting was in progress—or some look-a-like cross between a steppenwolf and a wolfhound. A man grinned, let out a squawk of triumph as a wolf yelped, tucked tail and ran to the back of a lengthy fenced enclosure while a larger dog leapt snarling at its throat. The wolf keeled over from wounds. Money changed hands. There came another savage snarl as the same vicious animal sunk its yellow fangs in another's hind leg. The gambler gave another crude squawk as more coins changed hands.

Vetra walked with certain ease toward the fenced-off confines of the wolf-baiting, the gears working in his brain. In places like this he'd walked a hundred times. Never without his hand far from his sword. He gripped the pommel now, a broadsword of crucible steel, of impeccable quality with keen edge. From his shagreen belt hung a Sahirian blade, gleaming and oiled, purchased from a Mosete camel herder on a mission east. The blade was razor sharp, the hilt gilded and thickly scrolled, ever at the ready if his broadsword should fail him. His dark brown hair fell in loose waves upon his gleaming black-scale mail coat over leather-jerkined shoulders. The hair on his head covered by a light bronze helm of matching color, designed for quick movements, lightning fast combat.

The semi-snug leathers underneath the chain mail could not hide the breadth of his broad shoulders, the lean muscle that rippled under the sway of his confident gait as he walked. His thighs were well-formed, his dark brown eyes like a soaring hawk's, wide set in a face usually pleasant but often moody which was his manner of late. Not that he couldn't show a rare mirth at times when the occasion warranted.

His instincts were honed, his eyes sharp, senses alert, ever aware of danger and threat in all cities. Such sixth sense and reflexes had saved his skin more than once. In these rough precincts, the only law was the one a canny man created himself.

A mix of races traversed the market. Lean-shanked Thrules standing no higher than his shoulder in black dusty robes with dusty hoods drawn up around their lean desert faces. With skin as dark, lean and parched as lizards. Pale-faced northerners from Umbria and Mercia. Husky, bearded mercenaries for hire from as far away as Balboria and Tolizia bearing axes, swords, and every weapon imaginable. Hawk-eyed tradesmen with reddish beards from Thrakia. Camel merchants from Membes and far-off Condoria. Traveling gypsies and grifters with slatternly women on pony-driven carts of spice, wine and charms as distant as

Behundria and Guiritia. Galashadians, brown-skinned and grinning, and the odd sea traders with gray-green eyes and characteristic bow-legged strut from the seaports, Syrn and Mmos.

All the color and life one would ever want…if it were color and life one was looking for.

Pickings were slim in the central kingdoms in the sword-for-hire department. War was brewing to the north. Good for business, if it were mercenary work and Mercia he was cheering for. He was not. Already skirmishes had broken out between wandering hordes of looters and wannabe glory-hounds in Upper Umbria and Mercia. But it would be a cold day in hell before he'd fight for the Mercians, the treacherous dogs they were. And the Umbrians?…They'd likely get their asses handed to them if war broke out.

So now, with only a chipped silver talon to his name, funds were running low. The prospect of gambling looked better to his eye than perhaps it was in reality.

A commotion rose. In the lower half of the market jeers and rough calls drifted. Curses and bawdy jests. Vetra pushed deeper through the throng, throwing aside hunger and thirst, though tantalized by the smells of frying meat in oil and spice. An interesting, if not brutal tableau was brewing at a rude pen of chicken wire strung on wooden stakes. Wild dogs of mixed breeds and colors in individual cages were thrown in to fight it out, some perhaps to the end. Those in cages or those roped at the back of the pen, paced back and forth, snapping and yipping, some which looked half-starved. The flagstones were stained with dark umber and there was the sharp tang of piss and wet dog in the air. The pen ran flush to the high stone wall that enclosed the market, and served as a backdrop to a butcher's shop and a weapons' dealer.

A thin man with black, oiled mustache and tapered goatee called out wagers. He strutted in front of the pen calling challenges in a brassy voice. Fingers on one hand beckoned, fingers on the other clutched coins. The gamesmaster. Gaudy opal earrings dangled from both ears. He wore a dirty purple caftan and bandanna as if he were some pirate from the high seas. Yet he bore a wicked-looking whip at his side, ends flecked with metal barbs to chastise the dogs if they grew unruly.

"Come one, come all! Betting is open! No one with a dog or *wolfshen* here worthy to challenge my own champion? Be not faint-hearted, friends! Are you all lambs? A bunch of wafflers and chicken-hearts?"

This bravado generated laughs as he crouched low, waddling around like a hen making *bok, bok* sounds.

Very droll, thought Vetra.

A voice spoke in his ear. "That black-furred wolfling there is the one to lay your money on, friend." A heavy hand latched on his shoulder.

Vetra looked into the chiseled face of a tall, muscled traveler in mail like himself with a grin on his face and a scar that ran down the left cheek to his chin. Twin curved blades were sheathed and tucked on his back in a leather dusty baldric.

A soldier-of-fortune, like himself, Vetra thought. The battle wounds showed it—scars, chiseled face, worn leather jerkin. A badly-trimmed, matted beard speckled with the faintest white hairs ruffed his square chin. Vetra guessed his age at about forty. Ten years his senior?

Scar-face gave a small frown and impatient tug on Vetra's shoulder. "Well, what are you waiting for, friend?"

Vetra muttered. "If you're so confident of your dog, why don't you bet your own money?"

"I would, but I can't," he explained with a rueful shrug and twiddle of his badger beard. "My love for ale and women has got the better of my finances." Again, the disarming grin.

Vetra examined the animal in question. It was a shaggy halfbreed, still young, now being roped and yanked into the pit by the comedic gamesmaster. But, would grow into something to be reckoned with. "The runt looks as if he couldn't make it to the next butcher shop."

"*She*, friend," said the stranger. "And looks are deceiving. I've got a nose for this type of thing." He tapped his flattened nose that had seen many a fist fight and taproom brawl.

Vetra rubbed his chin. He set himself to pondering. While he dithered, the fight was on and the runt charged to send the larger russet male back on its heels. There came a flurry of snaps and bites as the larger dog struck back. But too late. It was over before it began. The runt had ripped the other's throat out.

"Told you," the man chuckled. Big blue eyes glinted under bushy brows set underneath a rough mop of black-gray hair.

Vetra made a wry face. "Bet-master!" he called in an impatient voice. "Put three shekels on the black runt. On the next round!"

"Which one?"

"The one with the white line under his throat." Vetra lay down his last talon.

The oily-faced bet-master snatched up the coin in quick, greedy fingers. "As you wish, Sirrah."

"Where's my change?"

"You'll get it after the fight. And more if you win. Stakes are high. I'd estimate 6 to 1 against Wolfsha, the runt. Are you sure?"

Vetra shrugged. "Sure as rainbows lie flat in the rain."

The betmaster grinned. He shook his head. "It's your money."

"Just place the wager."

Chapter 4

Men thrust their noses in and there came much elbow jostling and mutters, such a stir the bet had created. More prospects pushed their way forward like packbeasts, champing at the bit for a piece of the action. Many wished to take bets: a mix of grifters, idlers, practiced gamblers. Bets were accepted. The black wolfling was clearly not the favorite. The next wolfshen up, a wolf youngling, was almost twice as large and looked mean as a snake.

"I'll put a crown on the white wolf!" cried a bloodshot-eyed Behundrian.

"Another on the white mutt," said a smith whose breath stank of grog.

"Three Mercian pennies on the black!" bawled a squinty-eyed Mercian.

The lone mercenary who'd befriended Vetra chuckled, grinned, as if proud of the ruckus he'd created.

The wolflings were set in motion. A blur of flying fur, a vicious frontal attack. Barks, snarls and flashing teeth. The rivals leapt at each other's throats, fangs glistening under the sun as they snapped and lunged for any purchase of flesh.

The smaller animal with the black fur got a piece of the enemy's nose and ripped. The victim cowered back, set up a hideous yelping. Blood ran from its jowl onto the flagstones. Saliva and foam flew.

Vetra winced, licking his lips in distaste. This was not a spectacle he liked. Ordinarily he didn't go in for this kind of crude brutality—but he was down of coin and somehow he'd gotten himself sucked into the madness of it all.

Despite his disgust, his face brimmed with appreciation. The runt was a clear winner. The fight was as good as over and the coins in his pockets.

The gamesmaster did not look happy. The outcome seemed

to surprise even him. Vetra could read from his features, the down-curl on his thin lips, the muttered oaths, that he had saved this runt as a sacrifice to gull in chumps like himself to scoop up spoils when they lost and his poster animal made mincemeat of the other.

But it did not. The gamesmaster bit his nails. He darted shifty eyes left and right. There came an imperceptible tug of sweaty fingers on his left bangled ear.

Almost at once, a hunk of pig flesh came hurtling over the heads of the spectators to land in the pit beside the rearing dogs.

Vetra's head turned. The entrails had been thrown by an accomplice. He caught a brief glimpse of fleet feet, a hooded figure bustling off into the crowd.

The white dog's teeth went for the meat, despite his bloodied muzzle. The black wolfling took opportunity to snap at the dog's belly. She missed, but her teeth went on to snap at his heels. Vetra winced at an audible crunch. The white dog yelped, limped away, tail tucked between legs.

The betmaster snorted his disgust. He leapt over the chicken wire and kicked the black wolfling in the muzzle with his heavy boot.

Vetra started forward, his fist balled. "Hey, leave her alone!" He did not abide by wanton cruelty to animals. "She's done nothing wrong except defend her life. Give me my money, you bullying shyster! You owe me 18 shekels at 6 to 1."

The bandanna-man growled, "Sorry chief, but that meat thrown in declared a foul. Outside interference. The game's forfeit."

"To hell it is!" Vetra blared. "Dergath's cocks! You mean to vouch for a lackey of yours?"

The gamesmaster blinked, but Vetra could see the sly smile behind the narrow face. "You knew you weren't going to honor your bets the moment you started losing, so you had some schmuck toss in meat to throw the fight."

The gamesmaster shook his head. "You're seeing pink elephants, outlander."

"No, you're running a racket here."

There came a rumble of discontent from the onlookers. They looked sullenly and ominously at the betmaster, ready to take fists to him.

The man swallowed but reached for the whip at his belt. He gave another quick signal. A not-so-subtle clench of fist with knuckles brought up to his left ear. From the crowd came a stir as four rough-looking bravos pushed through the mob, wielding knives and clubs. Each had tattooed ears and necks.

Vetra quickly sized them up. Thugs. Hired goons. Likely Mercians. The knobbed clubs and gleaming blades had the capacity for violence in the hands of these burly brutes. They looked mean and meaty, just another routine messy cockup that needed mopping up. The problem was, they'd done it once too often. They had a look of complacency about them. They shoved people out of the way without a backward glance. Those who didn't move fast enough were kneed in sensitive places. The first enforcer plowed his way in to menace Vetra, a two handed grip on his wooden club raised to the right side over his head.

Vetra did not flinch. He treaded slightly to the left out of the line of the club, reading the man's movements. His body moved with a fluid ease, instinctively, automatically, his rippling muscles mirroring the years of training under various sword masters and his father. He pivoted sideways in a crouch to allow minimal surface area and less of a target on his body should the club, by quirky chance, jerk sideways and snap up into his face. Ordinarily it would be foolhardy to face four ruffians like this in close quarters. Better to avoid such encounters altogether. Too many bodies, no room for maneuvering. It reeked of the stuff of broken limbs and cracked skull. Yet no fighter was ever given ideal conditions. Anything could go wrong. One smack in the wrong place with that club or the thrust of a sword and it would be all over.

These thoughts were just bees buzzing in Vetra's mind. Arrogant swine like this cockerel were just begging for a beatdown. These cocky bastards had piqued his blood lust. The game had been rigged which meant the loss of his last coin. He couldn't back down now; someone needed to teach these bullies a lesson. Obviously the town guard did not give a shit. Out of the corner of his eye he could see a few stiff figures fussing about by the gallows off in the fringes, looking busy but doing nothing. They probably pocketed a percentage of the cut that the corrupt betmaster had squeezed out of the people.

At the last minute Vetra feinted left. He drove his elbow with the iron studs into the man's jaw.

There came a crunch of bone. A delayed yelp of substantial pain as the man doubled over, clutching his broken jaw. At the same time he barely ducked the hissing sword of a second man who had a slaphappy, showy style to him.

Hoppy little bastard. He bobbed back and forth like a jack-in-the box.

Vetra was unperturbed. On the balls of his feet, he moved and slashed steel into their comfort zone. Hoppy leaped back with a foolish grin. The third man charged, his blade whirling in time with Happyjack's hops and bobs. With a hog's roar, Hoppy skipped in and Vetra let him advance. Vetra was an old hat at this type of game. He shifted stance, rocked on his heels, jerking head back in time to slash out his blade unpredictably, drawing a thin line of blood on Hoppy's sword arm.

The crowd had spread out, sucking in breaths. Now they moved closer, jeers on their lips. The fire of blood was in their eyes, excited by the prospect of fresh blood with that of the dogs'.

A crude chant had sprung up. "Fight, fight, fight!"

"Three shekkies on the swordmeister!"

Vetra roared over his shoulder, "You owe me 18 shekels at 6

to 1!" He ducked another clumsy strike from Hoppy.

The gamesmaster looked on with an amused simper. "You don't look in any position to claim it, outlander—Think you can get past Dokin and Joki?" He sneered and crossed arms on his thin chest.

A short burst of speed and Vetra sprinted in. Sheathing sword, he picked up the betmaster by his scrawny neck and hindquarters and hurled him into the dog pit. He hopped the fence, unsheathed sword, and came marching toward him, a grim craziness on his face.

The dogs went wild, snipping and biting at their ropes and cages, nipping at the betmaster's shins. One sank its teeth into his lower leg.

The betmaster gave a howl of dismay. He crabbed back on his haunches, spitting curses, much to the amusement of the spectators. Apparently, the animals had no love for their cretinous master, the animal-baiter.

"You bloody boor!" he shrieked at Vetra.

Vetra nodded and did a mock bow.

The victory was shortlived. The third thug had hopped in and rustled up behind him. Now a wicked club came arching down at Vetra's helm. Vetra rolled, but caught the hair's edge of the club on his right ear, a glancing blow that sent a hollow echo ringing through his brain. The club came down for a second, fatal strike but the black wolfling leaped in midair and chomped at the attacker's arm. The man yowled, beating at the dog with his other fist.

The dog would not let go. He dropped his club. The dog ripped and tore, snarling like a maniac. He started to drag the dog around in a circle but couldn't get her wretched teeth out of his arm.

There came laughter and hoots. A new chant had arisen. "Dogfight! Man-fight! Dogfight! Man-fight!"

Vetra's mercenary friend with the scarred cheek laughed. He

sauntered into the pen, spread his arms and boxed the ears of the third man wrestling with the wolfling. The man fell to the ground with the wolfling tugging and dragging at him still with her teeth. The scar-cheeked mercenary ducked just as a fourth man, a blond giant Mercian in a steel cap, took a swipe at his head with his curved blade.

Scar-cheek roared and came charging at him with both swords bared. There came a great clang and clash of blades. Steel met steel. Scar-cheek bulled his head in and butted the blond Mercian hard on the forehead, sending the man reeling back with his eyes swimming.

He kicked him in the crotch, jammed his bootheel in the back of his knee, sending him to his knees. His boot came up, lashed out at the arm, cracking bone.

The last man, Happyjack, decided the odds were against him. He licked his lips and snarled. Three of his companions already lay sprawled in grime and blood, groaning and wheezing. Cornered between the two mercenaries, he now tried to edge his way back toward the fence.

Scar-cheek jerked forward. "Boo!"

The man hopped the fence in a panicked leap and turned tail and ran.

Scar-cheek bounded after him, shoving bodies out the way. He chased him for while then decided it wasn't worth it and came back muttering, "Too many weaklings in this world."

"Leave him," said Vetra. "Cowards can run like rabbits."

"Don't I know it. I think I like that black dog," he said, stepping over to ruffle the fur on her head.

But the betmaster hobbled in toward the black wolfling with his flail. Vetra sneered and raised his blade, ready to split his head. The wolfling backed into a corner, snarled, ready to pounce.

"You going to pay up or what?" he demanded, steel bared. "Where's my money?"

"Get lost, you bastard. You've done enough damage already."

"Not nearly enough."

With a cold grin, Vetra hacked at the wooden fencing with his blade. The wolfling charged and when the betmaster's flail fell, the dog leaped past it as the metal ends clacked on the stone. She leaped over the broken barrier and fled into the crowd before the betmaster could get his clutches on her. Vetra hacked at the ropes of the other dogs and freed half of them before any of his hirelings could beat them back.

The betmaster looked on in horror. His setup was a shambles. On stiff legs he limped in, his mouth gibbering. "You loosed my wolfshen! You lost me hundreds of talons of prime dogflesh," he cried.

"All the price for shystering." Vetra grabbed the man's fist that clutched the whip and squeezed, hearing a bone crack. The whip clattered to the flagstones. While the man sank to his knees, Vetra took 20 coins from his pockets. This was enough to pay for a decent meal and lodging—plus four more for extra measure. He spat at the three bully boys lying in their own blood. These thugs would have slit his throat and the betmaster wouldn't have batted an eye. Other disgruntled gamblers surged forth to extract the rest of what was owing to them while the pirate-fake nursed his cracked hand and bitten shin.

Vetra cast a brief nod of acknowledgment at the scar-faced mercenary who stood by surveying the scene. "Well played and fought, old soldier." He counted out nine coins, pushed them into the other's hand. "Here's your half of the spoils."

"That's mighty generous of you."

"Wouldn't have won anything without your help—or your tip on the wolfling."

"The name's Nog."

"Mine's Vetravincus. Vetra for short."

"A fine day, Vetra. Let's try for something a little slower, shall we? A little less bloody?" He chuckled. "Cups and beads?"

"Lead on, friend," rumbled Vetra. "I'll watch."

The big man hefted his broad shoulders in a shrug. "Your choice. But you're missing out on the fun."

"I highly doubt that."

Nog motioned to where a younger man dressed in a loose, gaudy orange smock sat at a table like a fortune-teller. Three cups lay tipped upside down before him. He was holding up one pea in a hand.

A crowd had already gathered. The young man placed the pea on the table, lifted the middle cup over it, then with dizzying speed, rearranged the three cups in the hopes of stymieing the onlookers.

The young man stopped at a certain point. He put the cups back in a row. Which cup hid the pea? One did, the others did not. He whipped back his hair and called out a challenge. "Anyone, anyone?" Catcalls came from the audience.

"Gather round!" he said in a hearty voice. "Whoever guesses which cup has the pea, gets double his wager. One shekel, a single coin to bet! Place your bets, young and old. Only a shekel. Who's going to match my two shekels for his one?"

Vetra rubbed his chin. Watching with amusement, he gave a knowing smile as he saw the young man laughed when he lost and did aw-shucks faces when he won. He was not wrong to conclude that it was all show to stifle any suspicion of skulduggery.

Nog, after watching for some time, sat down opposite the trickster and threw his coin on the table. He stared at him with grim mirth.

"Oh, ho!" said the young man. "We have a scar-faced brute willing to double his money."

"That you do, young upstart. Shuffle the cups."

The young man obliged. After a time he stopped, looked straight into Nog's eyes.

Nog pointed to the middle cup.

The man lifted the cup. No pea. Nog blinked owl eyes.

"Right cup!"

The young man lifted the right cup. No pea. He overturned the last cup and there was the pea.

Nog bit his lower lip. "Go again!" He laid down two more shekels. The young man tipped his head, matched it with four.

Vetra grinned, hitched in closer, amused by the drama. He stood aside, his arms folded across chest.

Nog lost the next round too, of course, the pea not where he pointed but he laid a hand on the gambler's forearm and shook the voluminous sleeve.

Four dry peas clattered out.

"You're going to retract that bid, aren't you, friend? Give me back my money with interest?"

The youth licked his lips.

One of the tavern wenches, a saucy maid with painted face, baggy pantaloons and sagging breasts, leaned on Nog.

Nog bunted her away. "I'm busy, woman. Can't you see? Look over there for sport, to my strapping friend, Vetra."

With a toothless smile the street woman now seemed to have taken a shine to Vetra. Or more likely to the glint of silver in his hands.

"You in need of a pretty maid to wile away the time, muscle boy?"

"Not at this hour, missy, thank you. It's too early in the day."

She sniggered. "Never too early to any man I know." She gave a speculative scowl. "Unless of course you are one of those…" She gazed down at his package. "You don't look like a eunuch to me."

"Careful with your tongue, missy," Vetra warned. "Could get you in trouble in these precincts."

She gave a wild snort and bawled out a gravelly oath. "Think I've seen all the trouble there is to see, friend!"

It had Nog near laughing. He was still looking for kicks and giggles. After extracting his money from the charlatan, it seemed he was about to try his hand at some gambits with the mettlesome woman, but suddenly a trumpet blew.

Nog's and Vetra's heads turned. A band of eight horsemen had burst into the square, clearing a path for a small cavalcade. The middle rider, a tall, brazen woman, seemed the point of interest. She rode a sizable steed.

Trouble was afoot, thought Vetra.

Chapter 5

The woman's chin was held high, her long, flowing chestnut hair tucked in a leather basinet but coved down the sides like wings. Her horse was a spirited one, caparisoned in red and gold silk with the emblem of the six wizards: an eagle facing a dragon with talons clutching stave and wand.

Behind her rode a scowling prisoner in blue robe, handsome in a rebellious way, with hands shackled in his lap. His smaller roan was herded forward by the rest of the riders who were guards, clad in red and black jerkins, plumed morions and high black boots. All were armed with swords and daggers at their hips, maces at their saddle-bows.

Nog gave a soft roar and lifted his bulk from the stool. "What are these bumpkins on about? It's either whores or cheats. Now pompous wizards and royals."

"I'd guess a hanging's about to go down," Vetra mused.

"But why the wizard's templar?"

"They probably run the town."

"That young man looks like he's not enjoying much of this."

Vetra snorted. "You think?"

"Off with his head!" cried members of the mob, piking fists in the air.

"Hang him!" expostulated another.

The crowd's thrum grew to roar as the lead rider, the captain of the guards, dismounted and dragged the prisoner off his mount and up onto the scaffolding. The solemnity of the ceremony was further reinforced by guards and leathered officials who stood by watching impassively.

Nog uttered a low growl in his throat. "Barbaric ritual. They haven't even heard the prisoner's crimes yet."

"Does it matter?"

"He doesn't look like a knave. If I were a better man, Vetra, I'd save his skin. But I'm not."

Vetra exhaled. "None of us are better men. We're just pretenders, Nog. Always leaving the tough jobs for someone else."

"Isn't that the way of it? Still, I don't like to be witness to a hanging. Let's go."

"Me neither, but wait. Let's hear the woman out. She looks like she's the queen bee."

Nog scoffed. "That's Taranis, queen witch of the wizard's order. You're right, I hear she rules the city."

"With a body like that, it doesn't surprise me." Vetra's eyes flitted off her contours with rising interest. "There's a challenge for you, Nog, old boy. Why waste time with these dumpy, pock-faced whores?"

"Don't tempt me, please, Vetra."

Taranis removed her helm and whipped back her lustrous hair. It dovecoted outward, giving her the semblance of some predatorial hawk. She dismounted, touched a brilliant red jewel that hung round her neck.

As the captain of the guards hauled the man up to the gallows, the woman set her black-clad hips sashaying up the stairs to stand beside him, face carved in triumph. She held arms wide to address the crowd.

"This man is a thief!" she called in a husky voice. "A former apprentice of the Xalgossian Order, Skirl Atherlai. He tried to rob the Mage Order of our most sacred magic."

"Not true! I merely borrowed a second-rate talisman from our own beastmaster, Keren. 'Tis you who have stolen the Eros Flame." He lifted shackled wrists to the sorceress. "Look, everyone! As we speak, the Archmagrix flaunts it around her neck. See how it glows blood red even in the noonday sun! An omen, plain to see. I dug it up with the oldest wizard of our Order, Senesch, but two moons ago. The Archmagrix stole it from us and claimed it for her own."

"Infidel! I should cut out your tongue. Your weakling magic

is a testament to your guilt. Look! Does the accused, a mere apprentice, dare suggest that as false founder of Eros Flame, his power is superior to ours?"

The young man had nothing to say. He fumed, his long face flushed with humiliation. The dark veins on his neck bulged, now circled by a stout rope. The hangman, a bald, beefy man dressed in gray robes, stood hawk-like nearby with leather sack ready to drape it over the victim's head on the lady's signal.

Another rider on an elegant roan came galloping into the throng: a woman with the likeness of Taranis but not as supple or beautiful. A golden braid in her blondish hair hung full-length upon her shapely back. Slender arms dropped loosely at her sides past her silver-gray gown. Her concerned face was creased in anguish.

For a moment the prisoner held a gleam of hope. But not for long.

"Come to see your paramour off?" Taranis mocked.

"Belgra, tell them!" the condemned pleaded in a hoarse voice.

"Call this off, Taranis," the blond woman said. "Skirl's a sneak and louse, who's betrayed us both, but he's not deserving of a death like this, Taranis. He's served faithfully the Order for two years at Dormoth."

"Stay out of things you have no concept of, cousin," Taranis warned her.

"I will not, cousin."

Taranis hissed, pushed her palms outward in the direction of the defiant woman. "Go, Belgra! You are not welcome here."

There came an odd gust of wind. Belgra's lips twisted, her hair seemed to fly straight back, as if stricken by a freak breeze, or waft of some more unpleasant magic. She did not waver and countered with a flux of her own, a whistling, forest-like sound that caused her cousin to grimace and cover her ears. But Taranis shook off this wall of spell-sound and pushed harder, outward with her palms, as if pressing against an invisible wall.

A pale green bubble manifested in her outstretched palms. The orb wavered in the sunlight like a soap bubble blown by a child.

A strange warp clutched the air. The faint ting of chime, then the low ring of a gong came from farther off.

The transparent bubble whistled through the air and struck Belgra square in the chest, with enough force to send her toppling backward over her horse. She sat dazed on her haunches, her face waxen, her brow beaded in sweat. A cry was on her lips, terror writ in the slant of her eyes. Slowly she lifted her slender weight, the golden braid slipping from her hair to the flagstones. But Taranis had lost interest in Belgra. To her, the fight of wills was over.

Vetra's mouth pinched in a grimace. Ever distrustful of magic, he was one to wish all magickers to Dergath. His hand wandered sullenly to his sword. Two women mages fighting over a lowly apprentice slated for the gallows? He sensed darker overtones to the history of these bickering vixens under the surface and he did not care to find out more.

Taranis beseeched the crowd, "See what happens when misguided forces attempt to stop justice! But because I am lenient and serve as Archmagrix of the Dormoth Order, and because you, dear Belgra, are my second cousin, I will only have this cur whipped." She turned to the prisoner. "Skirl! I sentence you to fifty lashes, administered by Derk here, our executioner. " She flashed sultry eyes at the plump, ugly punisher at her side. "Derk?"

The hangman chuckled a mean laugh. His lips curled and he snatched up the whip at his belt. He snapped it on the oak slabs at Skirl's feet and his hairy hand reached over to tear away the dust-caked robe, exposing naked shoulder and back. Skirl saw his chances diminishing to zero for an escape. He lashed out with his tongue, "You can take your whip and shove it!"

Had the prisoner been smarter, he would have kept his mouth shut and accepted his fate, for, as most men would agree, a flogging was better than a hanging, but Skirl was churlish and not one to accept any punishment or humiliation.

The hangman's fist wiped the surly words from his mouth.

The prisoner spat out blood. His pride was shattered, his honor smirched. Never would he be able to walk in the public market again without the ridicule of commoners in his ears. Even as the executioner's lashes came stinging his back, laying bare his youthful skin, he wished he had not been so prideful.

As he howled and writhed under the lashes, fighting the guards' grip, trying to bite at their bare hands, he cried, "You faithless, conniving bitch! Do you always whip the men you lay with…as numerous as fleas clinging to a dog's back? You're no more than a common tavern slut."

Taranis teeth showed white. Her eyes glinted with a dangerous fire.

Skirl spat further, "Belgra there, the woman you despise, is a woman a hundred times better than you. Let it be known, I shout it out to the world!"

Taranis shrieked, "Off with his ear! Now! Grindar! Derk! I don't care which of you does it."

Grindar, captain of the guard, held Skirl while Derk flashed a knife. The apprentice's blue-black hair was drawn back and a quick stroke and the left ear was sheared off.

Blood dribbled down his neck, staining his torn robes and the planks. Derk held it up with a hangman's flourish for all to see. He threw it out in the crowd with a laugh for the dogs to chew.

The mob chanted for more blood. Taranis's lips curled cruelly, as if a black part of her heart was fed. She could endure shame no more than Skirl could.

The spectacle gave Vetra cause to grimace. He turned away.

"Now, thief," intoned the sorceress, "consider yourself

exiled. If I or one of my guards sees your smirking face again in this city after sundown tomorrow, it's off with your head. Do you understand me?"

The prisoner gave a sullen yowl. His shackles were removed from his wrists and he nestled his head against his shoulder to stop the blood rolling down his cheek.

"Withal, you are hereby ejected from the Mage's circle. You are an embarrassment to this Order. Your magic has been stripped. That I saw to earlier today with the Eros stone. Go forth and redeem yourself, then come back no less than two years hence when you feel you are worthy."

Taranis and her riders mounted and rode out, leaving Skirl tottering and trembling on the dark-stained planks. He clutched at his head as blood dripped. Someone threw him a rag which he snatched up and pressed against his ear. Belgra looked at him in despair then with tears of rage and frustration in her eye, she hopped on her mount and abandoned him too in the dust.

The apprentice moved weakly down the scaffolding's stair. He stumbled and fell, picked himself up again before he tottered amid the crowd. Others avoided him, as if he were a leper. He glared around at the many mooning faces about him, sulfurous curses on his lips. He seemed to be in a trance, a red daze, looking for someone to blame, someone to unleash his aggressions upon...or perhaps someone to champion his cause. It was an odd juxtaposition of emotions, considering his state and condition.

Vetra frowned and felt some kinship with the wretch, if not some pull of fate beyond mere curiosity.

Their eyes met.

Nog gripped Vetra's arm. "Let's get some ale, Vetra, call it a day. This drama has soured my zeal for gambling."

Vetra lifted his arm from Nog's clutch. "Hold on."

The riders were trotting under the east archway back to their hillside stronghold. The trumpet blew again. Vetra stared after them with reflection. What need for a public spectacle? The woman was grandstanding. Obviously flexing her muscles in the absence of the king. Easy to make an example of a rebellious apprentice and a rival sorceress.

Standing five paces before Vetra and Nog now was Skirl, his chest heaving. His eyes burned like oil-fired lamps. The look and thought behind Vetra's musing seemed not wasted on the apprentice. He gazed at them not without some wiliness and interested motives. "You are a mercenary?"

Vetra afforded him a curt nod.

"I sense you hate them as much as I do."

Vetra shrugged. "What of it?"

"Just this. I have a proposition for you...the two of you." His tawny eyes narrowed on scar-faced Nog.

"What, that you'll travel along with us to shine our boots? Sorry, boy, we've no time for miscreants. There're many ale games and young girls to entertain yourself with down at the *Goshawk Tavern*. They don't mind a man missing an ear either, I hear."

"Very witty, mercenary. But no. Ale rooms are for drunkards." He glanced at the lean layers of sinew rippling under Vetra's leather and accouterments. "With your swords and my magic, we can go far."

"Oh?" Vetra leaned on his blade in amusement.

"We can take revenge on these upstarts...these arrogant implings who call themselves wizards."

"You might. We wouldn't."

"Vetra and I are here to drink ale and win money, aren't we, Vetra?" Nog emphasized.

The apprentice's eyes gleamed through his winces of pain. "There's wealth to be gained."

Vetra gave a grunt of some interest.

"We strike at night, raid the wizards' coffers. We steal their magical talismans then take off with the most fabulous of all, the

Eros Flame...a sapphire old when Sarkala, the sorceress-priestess, made charms to ward off the dark gods."

"Aye, and what if they strike us down with lightning bolts and fire bombs?" Nog asked.

"I will create counter spells to thwart them."

"With your stripped magic?" Vetra snorted. "Sure you will. The same that saved your ass from getting your ear chopped off."

"I can spite them," Skirl hissed. "If we can sell the jewel in the black markets of Lausern or Alantra, we can split the profits."

Vetra looked him up and down, musing. "You could be one of those magickers, masquerading in the form of a trap. Why should I trust you? "

"Because you could be filthy rich..."

Chapter 6

Vetra turned, was about to take Nog up on his offer of ale when Nog gripped his arm. "Hold on, Vetra. Let's hear the wretch out." He motioned toward the east gate where horse caravans were moving on to Alantra before the afternoon grew old. "Let's walk. Too many prying ears about this place."

Vetra shrugged. He examined the bloody-eared apprentice for another time. What did he see? A youth of tousled hair the blackest of black, a narrow face, jaw, small trim mustache, the beginnings of a trendy scholar's goatee. A wide, smiling mouth affected with an oily tongue, a charmer who may or may not be inclined to tell the truth. Like at the present instant.

"Those robed cretins have disfigured me," the apprentice muttered angrily. "Now they'll pay." He gritted his teeth against the pain of his shorn ear. Luckily, the rag he pressed against the side of his head had somewhat staunched the flow of blood. Though Vetra was not sure if it was enough to stave off infection.

The mercenary gave a sad smile. "I admire your spirit, boy, but you must know, you are one, they are many, with more means at their disposal than you. What chance do you have?"

"No matter. I will strike when they least expect it. I will roil them with spells, I will—"

"You are capable of no such thing," Vetra scoffed.

"Since we're short of funds..." Nog said, grabbing a cheap shawl from the rack while the garment-monger was looking the other way. He tossed it at Skirl. The young man nodded and unpeeled the rag gingerly from his ear then wrapped the shawl around his head.

"Stealing from the locals?" Vetra inquired.

Skirl clicked his tongue. "Such pure-hearted rogues." He shook his head, a sardonic grin on his lips.

"Get moving, you thief," Nog growled.

Vetra frowned at a sudden thought. "How did you raise the malice of those two squabbling vixens? That was one of the most spiteful displays I've seen, never mind that bit about your ear."

Skirl raked at his prickly goatee. "I impregnated the woman with the blond hair who came riding in after. I got seduced by Taranis, the witch, and her Eros stone at about the same time. Belgra found out I'd lain with her and well, you can imagine the rest, me almost getting my nuts cut off. The two initially opted for castration, but Taranis opted for something more lenient, a hanging."

Vetra rolled his eyes. "You sure know how to piss off the ladies."

Skirl's lips pursed in a scowl.

Vetra jerked a thumb back toward the wizard's stronghold. Four towers rose ominously among high domes in the fading light. "Why did the mother of the child do no more to save you?"

He lifted his shoulders. "I think Belgra stews and broods upon my betrayal." He closed his eyes and hung his head in something of penitence. "She sees me as the cause of her problems when really it is that tyrant Taranis."

"What of this Eros Flame?" Vetra pressed. "What in Hades is it?"

"'Tis a love charm, but more than that. An elixir of power. One of old relics of the Age of Magicians. Sarkala, the sorceress, kept it as a periapt of the 3rd Age, to be precise. One gleam of the amulet's light, and the first suggestion the bearer speaks, becomes the recipient's desire to fulfill."

Vetra frowned. "I didn't see any of that back there at your ear-cutting."

Skirl's lips curled. "That's because I hid the real jewel. Taranis flaunts a fake. She does not know it."

Vetra and Nog both blinked.

"Sounds a little farfetched to me," said Nog. "You don't look like the type to be running after any love charms."

"You insult my honor, mercenary. There is nothing more important to me than love."

Nog gave a bark of wolfish laughter. "You're in the wrong world then, friend. The mage-sisters or cousins look like they rule over Xalgossa—no lost love there—and the curvy chestnut-hair looks like the winner. No doubt they have the ear of the king."

"And more."

"Listen, boy," Vetra began, "I appreciate your offer but we're fighters, not thieves in the night. Better suited to bashing skulls with sword and axe on the borderlands. You're better off hiring a poisoner to deal with the witch, if it's vengeance you seek."

Skirl hitched in with a murmur of frustration. "Listen! My father was a soldier. A swordsman like you. He died splitting Mercian skulls. War pigs. Brigands. In the end, he was slain by a Mercian hetman. I know who you are and what you are about. My mother was a beautiful woman, exquisite beyond belief. Golden hair, the most tawny amber eyes, lissome as a sapling in the wind. The army came and sacked our village. The war was savage, brutal. Umbria and Mercia have always been at each other's throats. They took her away. She was taken into the seraglio of some southern kingdom, I don't know where, sold likely for a few coins to a rich scum lord. I was a boy of 7 years old. Nothing I could do. A tousle-haired, rowdy guttersnipe. Having to fight my way among the other urchins for scraps of food.

"An old conjurer, Nistis, hobbling on a crooked leg with a varnished gnarled cane, took me in. There I learned the arts of gray magic, secret arts. First in prestidigitation, then in higher forms of spellweaving. Then, to a craft more secret and darker. By 12, I became his equal. By 18, I was his better. Nistis had ambitious plans for me. How wide his grin split upon seeing me grow and flourish when he realized I was to become his champion—to fight for a place in the Mage's Circle at Xalgossa.

"But he died, stricken by a rare illness of the spleen. I suspected he was poisoned—by certain jealous individuals within the Circle, and I was left on my own again, pondering, brooding, leaving me with a thirst for magic that I'd never known. I dabbled and delved deep and sought that which was unseekable—the wisdom of the ancients. Forbidden to mortals. I dug for the serpent, the golden apple—the philosopher's stone—the eros of the lost kingdoms...and I failed.

"I was close but far," he sighed, "and to my bitterness, I knew that I had scratched only the surface.

"I wandered the regions far, seeking out country witches, tarot readers, philosophers, spellcasters. I was taken in by croftworkers, wine merchants, alewives, blacksmiths, only to return to Xalgossa as bereft as a wandering vagabond. I applied to the Order at Dormoth. I showed them tricks they hadn't seen before, I answered their questions: 'Who was the archmage of Titon? How would you create a spell to ensnare a conjurer and deflect his magic of the Winds? Who is the maker of the Magic Mirror?' Things like that. The Order accepted me as a lowly apprentice as I showed promise.

"I learned many things. You are right, mercenary. The two cousins rule over Xalgossa. Or should I say the one cousin, Taranis.

"The great library of Linderlore became my home during the day. I crammed every bit of lore, sorcery spells, incantations I could into my brain, till evening when the great iron door was closed. But because of my zeal, I was granted permission to stay on after hours, poring over old musty scrolls, tattered tomes, screeds of the philosopher-historians to my heart's content. I worked uncountable hours into the night, taking notes, pondering, scribbling, pulling at my beard which grew ragged and unkempt. My eyes were red-rimmed craters...

"And then I stumbled on something... Yes! The hidden key to which many a philosopher and grizzled mage had missed over the centuries."

Nog shook his head. "You're either obsessed or crazy."

"Both, mercenary," croaked the apprentice. "I am a cursed man. I drank the potion, and bit into the poison apple and swallowed. Born under a dark star, a shadow living among men haunted by an illusive dream. But with some strange purpose I still cannot yet fathom."

"Cephala's tits, Vetra!" Nog cried. "We have a poet in our midst."

Vetra slapped his arm. "Quiet!"

Skirl scowled. "Do you always take up company with boors, Vetra?"

Nog pushed the shiny blade at his belt under the mage's chin. "Mind qualifying that statement?"

Skirl coughed. "I only jest. No hard feelings. Withdraw your blade, if you please."

The brawny Nog reluctantly sheathed his knife.

"All fine and nice this history," muttered Vetra, "but what does it give us? A disgruntled, disfigured mage, thinking more with his embittered heart than his brain."

"The jewel's worth a fortune!" Skirl hissed. "Unloading it to the right merchant or ambitious wizard, we can live as rich men for the rest of our lives. Do you not see? Taranis has maimed many on her path and now I will thwart her for the rest of her days."

"Revenge, eh?"

"The dish best served cold, as a man of the sword like you, can understand."

Nog's mouth twisted. "If they catch us, it will be all of our necks they will slit, not just an ear."

"Life's risky, mercenary—" Skirl showed a thin smile of fine white teeth and upturned palms. "I need muscle to deal with the guards in and around the Hall's exits and entrances. From there, I know the way to retrieve the jewel."

Vetra gave a skeptical murmur. "No spells? Potions? A big, bad, powerful magician like yourself can't even get past a couple of guards?"

"You heard her—" Skirl flourished icily. "My magic has been stripped. The witch Taranis so brazenly bled off my powers and boasted about it to the crowd. I am missing an ear! I'm in rags and penury and half starved. What more can I do? I have not many props to fall back on. One glimpse of a leper-like beggar at the gates of Dormoth and sure as Aramis's tits they will lop off my head."

Nog frowned, pulling at his beard. "Risky, clubbing down a couple of grubby guards at the castle, Vetra. More'll be prowling around the interior of the apprentices' hall. They'll cut us down in instants. I've heard the Order is well protected—like a Knight's Templar or Crusader's Haven."

"You make a good point." Vetra stroked his chin. "If the jewel's as valuable as you say, it could be worth the risk. We'll need some well-wrought plans."

"Get young Skirly here to turn us into mice then," Nog muttered. "We scamper through a hole, change back to fighting men, grab up the jewel and bust our way out."

Vetra rubbed his chin. "The idea's not as preposterous as it sounds." A wide grin settled across his face. "If we appear as harmless as mice to them, we might be able to make it work."

"I didn't mean it literally, Vetra," Nog protested. "You've been smoking too much poppy."

"Fool! I mean, why not apply to the Order as guards? A couple of strapping fellows like us, we'd be snapped up. We'll sell ourselves cheap, give the impression we're down on coin. We get in there, dress our mage up as some harlot or cripple, sneak to his hiding place, recover the Eros jewel then off into the night."

Skirl's eyes widened. "This is the spirit, gentlemen! I knew as soon as I saw you across the crowd, you were my man, Vetra. I don't even have to go into Dormoth. You two can get to the gargoyle statue in the combs, then——"

Vetra shook his head. "Not going to happen, mage. We aren't doing all the heavy lifting while you sit back on your laurels sipping wine and collecting the spoils."

Skirl gave a stiff wave. "As you wish."

"It boils down to this," Nog said with an impatient flourish, "we need lodging, a good rest, a good start tomorrow. If we are to sneak our prodigal black-sheep magician into the wizard's lair, we need to set our heads together."

Chapter 7

They were half way across the footbridge over the canal when the half wolfling came snugging up behind them, giving a happy bark.

Vetra knelt down and gave her a good pet. Her matted fur was caked with dried blood. The bloody wound on her back would be long in healing where the other dog had sunk its teeth. "You sure are a scrapper, aren't you, Wolfsha?"

She whined, licked Vetra's face. His lips curled in a smile. The first genuine smile that day.

The magician looked down at the wolfling. "Seems to me the half wolf and I have something in common—fresh war wounds."

Vetra gave a brief mutter. He seized the dirty leather collar with the iron spikes and used his sword to saw through it.

"There you go, Wolfsha, whatever your name is. You're a free wolf, your own master."

The animal gave an excited bark and circled around Vetra, jumping up at his waist. Her tail wagged as if it would fall off.

Vetra looked at those around him: three oddball loners, all met under the oddest of circumstances.

The sun was a shimmering orb over the western towers, burnishing stone in crimson. It'd taken till sundown to find a place affordable enough for the three to rent a room. Their searches took them to the *Rat Peacock Inn* on the dingy south side of the canal. Legend said the brick-walled canal had been built centuries ago to separate the slums from the royal grounds and the wealthy landowners and tradesmen. Either way, it was not the most pleasant of surroundings. The sour smell wafting from the stagnant, blue-black waters now emphasized this disparity clearly, but in these quarters the prices were much lower, and neither of them could foot any bill for modest-priced accommodation. Vetra grumbled ever more loudly at his lack of coin. He voiced his amazement anew that after the wolf-baiting they'd managed to walk out of the market without getting their throats slit.

"We can hole up at *Madder's Pike* down the alley for 10 shekels," Nog said, "but I'm not keen about the roaches and bedbugs. This *Rat Peacock* place looks and smells better." He spread his palms, nodded approvingly. There was a convivial glow of the taproom and an aroma of roast venison. Inside, men huddled over tables of dice. "Looks like some easy pickings here, Vet. Perhaps we could throw down a few more coins later in the evening?"

"And attract more attention?" Vetra scoffed. "No. You can gamble your last coins, not mine. I've risked enough already back at the wolf-baiting."

"You an edgy bird today, Vetra? Turning into a killjoy?"

"No, just not stupid. Fool me once, fool me twice, blah blah blah, call me a damn simpleton, Nog, you know the saying—"

"Yeah, I know the saying. It was your choice. You were as eager as me to make some quick coin, so stop your grousing."

Vetra was about to object when a bustling, barrel-shaped figure wiping his hands of meat and kitchen grease squared himself solidly before them. He took one look at their dusty leathers, mail and soiled, blooded garments—not to mention Skirl's bandaged head—and shook his head.

"No lepers allowed—" he motioned to the door.

"He's not a leper," Vetra explained. "He's a friend, in a jam—*Skrill.* His face is disfigured from an accident."

"Sword fight?"

"You could say."

"Axe?"

"Not quite." Vetra licked his lips. "Let's just say a vindictive woman was involved."

"Oh. The worst." The innkeeper grumbled an apology. "Well, we have one room left that'll fit the three of you roughboys, but it'll be a squeeze. It's neither pretty nor clean, but is going for 13 shekels. Includes a meal each."

"High for this neighborhood," Vetra mumbled. "You have any other cheaper lodging—"

"Sorry, fellows, rooms all booked. Only suites left are deluxe, at least deluxe for the Canal District—100 shekels per night—and you boys don't look like rich merchants to afford 100 shekels."

"Grand larceny," muttered Vetra.

The innkeeper cast him a sober look. "It's a supply and demand world, friend, run by complex mathematics."

Vetra huffed a sardonic breath. "We'll take it. Beggars can't be choosers."

Wolfsha had snuck past the door and came creeping around Vetra's legs, wagging her tail.

"No animals either!" the man said testily.

Vetra gave a resigned nod. "Okay. Go on, girl. Get!" He clapped his hands. "Find a home, or at least some dry place safe from flails and baitmasters. This world of men is not for you."

The half wolf whined and seemed to understand the gist of Vetra's words. After some backward hounds' eye looks, she trotted back through the open door and off into the alley.

Vetra shook his head. "I swear that animal knows the human language, Nog."

"You'd have to, fighting those lowlifes for masters, who pit her against wild she-hounds."

The landlord flourished. "Come upstairs, I'll show you your room." His eyes lifted in a wise look and he wound his burly frame up the narrow staircase and down a hallway past the landing. They saw he walked with a jerky limp.

The room was small and stuffy with the lingering odor of sweat and grog. White paint peeled from the walls. A small window overlooked the canal, much as they would have liked a room at the back of the inn. A clink of coins came as Vetra thrust the shekels in the innkeeper's outstretched hand. He limped away with a contented murmur.

Nog flopped out, boots and all, on the far cot. "Only two beds. Someone's got to take the floor. And no way I'm sleeping with mageboy here."

Skirl grimaced. "Fine, I'll take the floor." The apprentice hunched amid the dust balls.

Vetra slumped on the other bed, stifling a yawn. "Tell us now where the jewel is, Skirl, in case we can't smuggle you into this Dormoth place."

"It works both ways, mercenary," said Skirl coolly. "What's to stop you two from getting the jewel and cutting me out of the deal? You don't trust me, I don't trust you."

"Fair enough, mage," Vetra growled. "But you'd better not be scamming us. Be ready. Await our signal. We'll set a light, torch or some candle in one of the courtyard towers. Three flashes when the guard changes. Watch for it—say between midnight and two."

The apprentice grunted.

"I'm going to the taproom to see what I can learn from the locals and get some eats."

Skirl jumped up. "I'll go with you."

"No you won't. You'll stay here and keep Nog company. I don't want you drawing attention to yourself."

Skirl rolled his eyes. "Spare me the sentiment, Vetra... You think anyone cares about a bloody-eared apprentice? I think I'll go mad if I have to listen to Nog's chatter any more."

Nog leaped off the bed, shoved his blade under the apprentice's chin. "Care to revise that statement?"

"Knock it off, you bozos." Vetra shook his head, rolling his eyes. "See that you two don't kill each other while I'm gone."

Chapter 8

To the tune of a lively hornpipe and bawdy lyrics of half drunk minstrels, Vetra drank ale and mixed with the locals. He played dice in the taproom with the last of his shekels. He learned several salient facts. That Xalgossa was in decline and that there was unrest in the kingdom. The king would likely be deposed before long, if not full-scale war to come first.

The bawdy melody was not to Vetra's liking. Though he endured it: three troubadours with lyre, pipe and fife, red faces shining and grinning teeth. He preferred the soft, slow melody that harked of country forests and trout-filled brooks not slutty limericks of dancing vixens and lecherous lords. About twelve patrons milled about or sat at tables in the dim sconce light: a mix of men and women. The smell of varnish and sour wine hung heavily in the room. Notched blackened beams ran along the low ceiling. Various heads of stuffed animals were bolted to the walls: elk, boar and goat, including a large green peacock, inspiration for the pub's name. A plunk of darts echoed from an old warped board not far from where the minstrels sang, along with the clinks of mugs and low laughter, some hearty, some bitter, amid the usual barroom murmur.

A sheep trader sat on a stool next to Vetra, chugging a tall tankard of dark, warm ale. He spoke in a moribund tone, wiping his drooping mustache. "King Grinas has decreed all firstborn males to fight in his army, can you believe it? Outright banned deserters who buck their duty. The Mercian dogs encroach on our borders and have put spies in the city."

"Aye," said another, a sad-faced man with droopy eyes and threadbare cloak. "They use Alantra in nearby Lvendar as a base. Taranis is his new advisor. Probably whips his naked ass at night. She has no love for this city. At least not more than that fancy jewel she totes around her neck can give her. Devil's beards! Like a sorcerer's ring, drawing people googly-eyed to her side."

Vetra recalled how the sorceress had twirled the stone in her fingers while addressing the crowd. "She seemed not to have the ear of the crowd today," Vetra said innocently.

The trader looked away and winced. "That was unusual. I'm at a loss to explain it. Maybe the bitch was having a bad day. Or the magic had deserted her for a space. I hope both."

Vetra absorbed the news with a thoughtful rub to his chin. The trader's words gave more credence to Skirl's story. That he had stolen the real jewel and cached it somewhere in the crypts below the wizard's hall did not seem so farfetched. To have that amount of power... Vetra marveled. The value must be beyond worth.

He spoke in a cautious tone, "From my eye, it appeared the Archmagrix wasn't much in control of that crowd."

The sheep trader grunted. "'Twas odd. The jewel usually turns people into obeisant sheep. Fawning and fumbling over her every word. This time—" he smacked his lips "—I always look away from the thing or turn my head, or better yet, I don't attend any of her pompous public ceremonies."

"A wise policy."

A hunter in a red-and-black-checkered trapper's jerkin sat cleaning his nails with a hunting knife. "War's brewing in the north," he said dourly. "Up Davilnook way, where the hillside barrows separate Umbria, Mercia and Lvendar. Just came from there. Seen it with my own eyes. I checked the rabbit and mink traps while scouting for elk. Border raids, skirmishes in the night. Mailed men with fine broadswords, some with mace and evil on their minds. They slaughtered horses and livestock, set fire to barns and sheds, killing hens and goats, the odd ravage of a farmer's wife. Anything to try to goad Umbria into a war."

"They'd love that," spat one of the barflies familiar with the other two. "Give them more of an excuse to come in and take over our lands. 'Annex' it. For the safety and security of all. Whether they be fighting Umbrians or Lvendarians, it doesn't matter. Let's face it, fellows, Umbria's weak. I doubt she could hold even with our good King Grinas's horse guard and pikemen."

A quasi-fortune teller and palmist put in her two bits. "Mercia's in for a humbling, I reckon. A great flying beast'll come from the west. It'll smite her. I've tossed the bones, I've seen it. 'Tis foretold—in the scrolls."

"And unicorns'll fly," scoffed the innkeeper. "What island world are you living in, Zelda?"

"I've seen it in the cards!" she protested. "The cards, the bones, they don't lie."

There came boos and hisses from the motley mix of patrons in the dingy room.

A man with a red face and purple veins on his nose raised his mug. "Three tankards for the lady! A great winged flying beast! Hearken, all." He waved his peaked hat to the minstrels who stood at the front of the room. "Relph! Can you do us the honors? Ode to the dragon!"

There came hearty roars.

The minstrels obliged; the instruments changed hands. The tall man with the green jongleur's cap sang in a high, jaunty tone:

"There came a dragon from Whistling Woods,
All scaly and glistening with plates he stood,
Hey diddle diddle and play my fiddle!
Flame and feather, whither, thither!
Hi hi ho and a bottle of rum,
To fire the city under a darkened sun,
Hell's fire and ruin. Smoke and cinder. Beyond huntsman's ken,
Came   the   crusty   dragon   from   the   sorcerer's   den!"

Vetra rolled his eyes. "Dragons and kings, wizards and rings," he muttered, "who needs them?" He gave a ragged sigh. Time to call it a night.

A jaundiced-faced drunk bumped his shoulder, scowling. "You don't appreciate our lore, outlander?"

Vetra just shook off his arm. Better he use the time to plan an early attack for tomorrow. They'd have their work cut out for them. He drained his mug, raised a hand to his new friends, pleading fatigue. He was about to saunter off to bed when he turned to see the skulking figure of Skirl stealing down the stairs. The apprentice's face was flushed. A wide grin split his face as he assessed the liveliness and movement in the taproom.

There was a jingle of coins over by the dartboard. Vetra saw the apprentice's eyes narrow shrewdly as they passed over the three men playing darts.

Vetra strode over to intercept Skirl. "Shouldn't you be resting, Skrill? That split head of yours needs some healing." His voice was cheery but gruff.

"By no means, my good man. I feel spry as a dunghill cock! And thirsty too. Ale, bartend! A cup of your finest, if you please!"

The innkeeper finished wiping down a glass and cast Skirl a cool glance. "How will you be paying for it, sir?"

"Put it on my tab. I'll give you coin, plus half more by the end of the night."

"We don't do tabs or honor here, sir. Too easy for unscrupulous patrons to play jiggery-pokery with us." He blinked. "Half more, you say?"

"Indeed."

"Coming right up then." The landlord poured a foaming jack and walked it personally over to Skirl who downed half of it in one gulp and wiped his thin mustache of amber foam.

"Another!" Skirl cried as he sauntered over to the dart board.

Vetra shook his head in amazement. He murmured some unkind comments about apprentices missing ears under his breath. "It's your neck, Skrill."

"My neck is fine, Vetra," he called. "As is the rest of my innards, skull, brain, wits and heart!"

Skirl was invited into the game without question, despite his crude bandage. Apparently he was a man of importance having gained the innkeeper's vote of confidence.

Nog had come down to briefly watch the dart play before he drifted off to the back where he started chatting up a shifty-eyed, slatternly woman in the shadows.

A fat man who did most of the tossing and talking at the dart board, name of Jaksi, swore and fretted and took a furious gulp of his arrack. "These darts seem flying cockeyed! Missed the bull's eye three times now."

"You've missed not only bullseye, but the inner ring and outer ring," laughed one of his lank-toothed pals.

Skirl clapped him on the back. "Tough break, master Jaksi. Those darts seem to be your enemies."

"Damnedest thing I ever saw. As if there are magic elves skittering about this room, magnets turning my points."

Skirl's eyes widened. "Elves? Today the Archmagrix accused a young man of theft and witchery. Had his ear lopped off in the market, can you believe it? Perhaps witchery's in the air?"

"And spooks fly on the full moon," crowed a man from a nearby table. "You dart-mongers utter mere wives' tales. You don't believe any of that mumbo jumbo, do you, Jaksi?"

"Most of it, no, but I remember when old Darv, the carnival-monger, brought in a witch and an ape to the midsummer show. The moon and stars turned red and—"

"Spare me," the man said. He made a cut signal with his hand.

Skirl lost a few rounds then went on to win sizable coinage which he attributed to 'beginner's luck'.

Vetra knew better. He'd seen the apprentice move his fingers in a weird way then mutter some unintelligible syllables as Jaksi and his peers tossed. He wondered just how much of the young man's power had deserted him.

With a happy cluck, Skirl sidled over to Vetra sitting sullenly at the bar. He thrust 4 shekels into his hand.

"There you go, mercenary. Don't say I didn't gift you anything."

Vetra eyed the mage under narrowed lids. After some muttering and small talk, he rose to leave. Skirl elected to stay and quaff another round of ale, try his hand at some more darts. Vetra gave a sigh of moderate exasperation and wished him all the luck.

Halfway down the hallway back to his room, he could not help feeling dissatisfied with the day's events. The feeling puzzled him. Things could pay off well in the long run with this jewel heist. *If* they could pull it off and pawn the gem in Lausern or some city. It could be the best thing to fall into his lap for months. A lot of ifs. No, there were strange things in the works. Trouble was brewing. He was no psychic, but he could feel it in his bones.

He opened the door to the room and in the dim candle-light he saw Nog lying on the far cot snuggling up to the buxom tavern whore he'd been schmoozing earlier. He gave a sour curse. Definitely bottom grade, this unkempt slatternly maid with dirty dress tossed on the floor and cuts on her face. A shekel at the most. And why not? Nog didn't appear to be too choosy about his bed-mates.

Vetra sighed and lay on his cot. He turned his back to them.

There came a half hour of noisy tumult—creaking cot, slap on slap of bare skin and vigorous play before Vetra finally had enough. He launched himself up and marched over to the bed and shooed the woman out bare-breasted into the hall. He bolted the door, oblivious to her curses. There came insistent bangs on the wood.

"Foul mouth on that wench," Vetra grumbled. "You certainly know how to pick them, don't you, Nog?"

"Still had a half shekel's worth from that moaner—Why'd you have to go and spoil the fun?"

"Because I'm tired and need to sleep. Do it somewhere else. You're forgetting who paid for this room."

Nog gave a reedy sigh. "Too knackered anyway." He yawned and grinned. "Probably for the better, Vetra. Dame smelled of fish anyway."

Vetra grimaced.

"Where's our mage?"

"You mean the one you let downstairs despite my instructions to the contrary? Still down darting. Amazingly seems to be winning." Vetra frowned. "With whatever faint whiff of magic he has left."

"Magic, you say?" Nog reached for his jerkin. "Maybe I should tag team with the rogue."

"Be my guest. Just don't be bringing any more of those hosebags up here."

"Sure, sarge." Nog tipped fingers in a salute.

The next day, Vetra awoke at the crack of dawn to the squawk of crows and the snort of hogs outside their open window.

Bright sunshine streamed in, causing him to squint. He stretched his muscles and cracked his joints. In his bones he felt a vague stiffness he didn't remember in his youth. *Dergath.* He was getting too old for this.

He tied the laces to his black leather boots then did his regular fifty push-ups and forty deep knee-bends, a vigorous routine...to the bellow of a fishwife, the various odors wafting from the window, the rolling of beer barrels down the street and the yowl of stray dogs.

Nog had his mouth half open as if collecting flies. The man had dark circles under his eyes and smelled of sweat and sex. He was snoring loudly. Vetra scowled. With a forceful swat, he nudged him awake. The mercenary jolted upright, clutching for his sword.

"Hey, wassup?"

"You snore too loud."

"Sorry for being alive."

Skirl was just rousing, blinking like an owl from his perch on the floor. He groaned and clutched his ear.

"Still hurts?"

"What do you think?"

"A little pain never hurt anyone," Vetra said.

"Sure, I'll trade my ear for yours."

"Let's not get hostile. We've got work to do. If we don't return to the *Rat Peacock* by noon you'll know we made it into Dormoth."

"Or you got your throats cut."

"Fine. But let's not put too much energy into that thought."

Skirl nodded. "I've been doing some thinking of my own, Vetra. I'll meet you two at the north junction of the Hall of Wands where the corridor widens—you'll see the wizard's emblem hanging on the wall, the Dragon and Eagle. At midnight. No later. The tower gong tolls on the hour. If you can light a candle in the North or West tower where I'll see it, I'll know I'm not wasting my time. From there, we'll proceed to the place where I hid the jewel."

"You seem confident, mage," said Nog, "for one with only one ear. How are you going to get in?"

"Never you mind. I'm not without my tricks."

"From last night's dart play, I don't doubt," Nog quipped. "How much did you rake in anyway?"

Skirl gave a cryptic smile. "A wizard never tells his secrets."

Chapter 9

The shadow of the sorcerers' stronghold fell over them in the mid-morning blaze. Vetra squinted up at the high stone wall and the forbidding, blackstone towers. He and Nog had approached the 10-foot spiked iron gate at a cautious pace to find it partially ajar.

Vetra frowned anew. The doubt in his mind grew about this mission. A guard outfitted in steel hauberk, bronze morion and red plume called out a challenge. "Who goes there?" His sword swept up past leather greaves and mail shirt.

Vetra saw the hints of an open courtyard beyond him and the gate. Three mage guard in red and black surcoats practiced with sword, axe and mace. Gaudy coats covered their leather and mail.

"We're mercenaries for hire come to offer our services," Vetra said. "We were impressed by Taranis's speech the other day in the market. Her call for law and order and a crackdown on knavery is a good one. We figured your Order of Dormoth Mages could use a few more fighting hands." He spread his arms, gestured toward the sparring figures who grunted and smashed mace on heavy shields.

The man's sunburned face creased in a grin. "Well, you've come to the right place. The Archmagrix has put the word out for more men-at-arms. I'll pass your request on to our captain."

"Very well. We'll wait here and not disturb your training."

Before long, a tall figure made swift strides over toward them. Vetra recognized him as one who'd helped in the ear-cutting at the market. Grindar. A grim-faced bully with dirty blond curls and weathered war gear.

He looked them up and down for a few seconds then snorted with a practiced eye. "Mercenaries you say?"

Vetra gave a smiling nod. "Of singular quality. We are willing to work for a decent wage." His eyes roved past the iron bars to see that one of the fighting men was down, his shield battered by repeated mace blows. His partner-in-arms lifted a hand to help him.

"Where did you fight and who did you fight for?" the captain demanded.

"Tolizia, Mosete and Condoria. Border wars mostly."

His stark, blue-eyed gaze turned to Nog. "And you?"

"The seaports of Syrn and Mmos. Mostly guarding ships and cargo from raiders."

"What are you doing this far west?"

"What any other mercenary would be doing," Vetra interjected. "Seeking work."

The captain gave a brief mutter. It was something he could understand. "This way then."

The gate was pulled wide and they followed the thickset man into an even wider expanse, a grand octagonal court bordered by arched doorways of shaded colonnades. Plumed winter palms rose close to the inner walls.

The other guards paused for a brief moment from their practice but paid Nog and Vetra no heed. To see mailed men coming and going in this court was not uncommon.

Grindar's quick heavy tread brought them under the shadow of the south tower. Six high-looming towers of black stone flanked the courtyard, two facing each of the four directions. In between each set of towers, gilded domes rose over elegant halls. The southern-facing dome was twice as high as the others. Twice as opulent too. Inlaid with bands of pure silver and crowned with a spiky spire looking like one of the mysterious, stepped pagodas he'd seen in his travels far east in Membes. Atop the walls surrounding the stronghold ran a wide stone parapet where archers could rain fire down in case of attack. Two men walked back and forth across the sun-warmed stone with arbalests pointed downward.

In the center of the court rose a circular stone well. Two

plain-faced women dressed in peasant smocks bore buckets of fresh water suspended from ox-yokes about their necks. Likely to the kitchens, Vetra mused.

Nog tipped his helm with a cheesy grin on his face as they passed.

There came the scurry of feet as a young apprentice dressed in blue robe and conical cap with a spellbook tucked under his arm almost ran full tilt into them as he hurried across the cobbles. He was mumbling words to himself, his mind clearly elsewhere. Grindar swatted out an arm and muttered a curse at the apprentice's lack of attention. Another scooted by in a red gown and loose hood with wand in her hands. She had close-cropped sandy hair, a young maid in her teens. One with short legs and budding hips, making quick steps toward the north-facing, domed hall.

A big place, thought Vetra. A conservatory of sorts? A place that held a small student body and fighting force? Self-contained, independent? Perhaps a cover for the tyrannical reach of the head sorceress? Every cell in Vetra's body told him this was likely so. His mind churned over the possibilities, likewise how the situation could be handled. The gate was well guarded, the courtyard occupied and friend Skirl would have a hard time getting past the watchmen. The apprentice had been overly optimistic. Perhaps a change of plans was necessary? Skirl had lived and worked here for several months. Basic logic would dictate he'd have considered all this before boasting that he could gain entrance on his own. A conundrum that Vetra himself couldn't answer. He sank deeper into doubt.

Grindar led them through an archway into a private, enclosed court. Shaded porticos rose on either side. At the center to the back, a marble fountain tinkled into a small pool. Snub-nosed goldfish lazed in the water. To the right grew a garden of shrubs and flowers. Most disturbing was the squat gargoyleish statue by the pool, a great ugly brownstone mass with scaled wings tilted in flight, hideous bat face, glaring eyes, ratlike teeth and enormous peaked ears. The statue guarded the waters, where incongruously someone had thrown a few rusty coins.

"Wait here," Grindar instructed. He left, tipped his massive head under a low archway and disappeared into the cool darkness beyond.

While they waited, Vetra prowled the perimeter. Nog was content to study the fish.

So, a secluded garden courtyard... Beds of flowering myrtle, rose bushes and faint scent of myrrh in the air. Very pleasant, but all tainted with an unspoken tension...no less, the gruesome and grimacing statue. What was the purpose of this grotesque symbol of the underworld that looked so out of place? In Vetra's mind, one that should be blasted to ruin? The sun slanted down between lazy clouds warming his helm. He rubbed his cheek. He wondered how nuanced Nog's playacting would be during this interlude. No doubt their easy entry was an audition. They may be testing them right now: silent watchers gazing from the darkened, upper windows.

Nog and he traded uneasy glances. All was quiet in the court but for the tinkle of waters and the soft rustle of morning breeze through the fragrant shrubs.

"So far, so good," Nog said. "Everything going to plan, Vet."

Vetra cast him a distant nod. "Let's keep it that way, Nog. Just follow the script."

Nog made an easy gesture. "No worries, Vet. I have everything under control."

Vetra's lip curled and gave way to a scowl. "That's what I'm afraid of."

Bootfall echoed from the arched doorway. Within moments Grindar returned with another man just as big. He was unsmiling, lumbering and rangy and curled fingers gripped the pommel of his broadsword that hung from jeweled scabbard past hips and greaves.

Vetra turned to the sound of a husky voice to the side. "Gentlemen." A familiar feline figure sashayed in at them from a side archway. She tipped her head in brief acknowledgment. With an exaggerated and brazen swing of hips she strode past the two guards and came to a halt before them. A blazing heat radiated from her body.

"Lady." Vetra and Nog dipped their heads in unison.

She wore a skin-tight black leather gown with a silver tiara which held the chestnut sweep of shoulder-length hair. Her oiled cheeks were powdered with the faintest rouge. Dark kohl accentuated the mocking mystery of her gaze. Brass cups adorned her perfectly-sculpted breasts. Her bare forearms, brow and neck were oiled and gleaming to perfection.

Even more striking was this she-panther in the flesh than at a distance in the chaos of the market.

The Archmagrix waved an uplifted, jewel-fingered hand. "I hear you are seeking employment in my conservatory."

Vetra gave a swift nod. He could not help his eyes straying from the supple thighs and camel-toe crotch to the disturbing statue staring out from before the pool, guarding the precincts like a scavenging basilisk. The black glaring eyes seemed to follow him wherever he went; the ratlike teeth threatening to champ at his limbs like a living fiend.

Taranis saw where he was looking and gave a brief chuckle. "Do you like Besemooth?"

"He is charming," Vetra said. "A regular Sarkala's bane."

"Isn't he? He is—" Her eyes clouded and suddenly grew chill at the name. "Sarkala? Where did you hear that name?" she demanded.

Vetra licked his lips. He wished he had not spoken. "I am not unfamiliar with lore," he recovered, knowing full well the name of the sorceress priest had been dropped by Skirl.

"There is more to you than meets the eye," she mused. Her

red ruby lips curled once more into a playful cast. "The statue is a likeness of the one who is the winged messenger of Dal Sagoth, the Elder God. I recently had the statue moved here—from a distant ruin our students were excavating at Cuiros. Not far from Mmos on the sea. The god was transplanted in this garden to commemorate the darker arts and their implications. See how Besemooth's ears peak like an attentive hound's? As if waiting for his master's command...and the wings, so far outspread! Ready to carry him off and deliver a dark message across kingdoms on the whim of a god."

"A fascinating history," Vetra murmured, "and I'm sure you will regale us with more later but—"

She cut him off with a curt wave of her hand. She seemed pleased with Vetra's reaction, as if it were part of her plan to unnerve them. Nog only seemed to give the statue brief notice. His eyes were glued to the vivacious figure of the black-clad sorceress who flaunted herself before them.

Vetra glanced over at the ruthless face of the captain of the guards. The same mean-ass mongrel who had helped carve off Skirl's ear. Whose ear would be next?

For a moment, the two appraised each other, each reading the other's thoughts. Somewhere in all this interplay, they divined there would be a clash of arms.

Taranis moved in closer to Vetra, so close he could feel the animal heat of her. "You seem sturdy and quick, mercenary, and carry good weaponry. Judging from the cast of your sword and its silver guard, I wonder where you hark from? What are your qualifications?"

She came up behind him and traced a slinky finger along the edge of his shoulder then down to waist in a flirtatious, if not provocative way.

Vetra did not like that touch. There was a hint of snakes about it, cold and sinister.

"Well built...handsome, in a rugged, no-nonsense way," she

said.

She circled him the other way as his head turned. "You do not answer me, mercenary? Has the cat robbed you of your tongue? Where did you learn to fight? The Umbrian army?"

"No," Vetra rumbled. "My father's school in Tolizia. He was a harsh taskmaster. We had a riding school there where he trained swordsmen and bred destriers."

"Oh?"

"I was on the road to becoming an elite defender myself. He wanted me to fight for the Royal Guard in Vulfryn. I despise all those powdered nobles and refused. I objected to the fatebringing he proposed for me. We clashed. A vicious argument led to blows. I finally fled my homeland, journeyed east by foot, where I trained under three sword masters, the first, the mad hackman Lu Zu in Mosete. He lived in a tree and ate only papayas."

She let out a snorting laugh. "Very droll, swordsman. How do I know you are not feeding me a bunch of malarkey?"

He shrugged. "You don't."

For a second her gray-green eyes flashed, perhaps taking the remark as an insult. Then her gaze veered on Nog. "What about you?"

"A boring story. Look to Vetra, he's the one with the history, not little old Nog."

She gave an impatient mutter. "Enough evasions. Why come here and appeal to the Order of Mages? You two would do better with jobs as bounty hunters or swords-for-hire at some rough outpost in the hinterlands, as suits your looks."

"I remember your quick punishment of the feckless wretch at the market. He deserved the gallows' rope but got only a cleft ear. We figured it would be less tasking to our hides serving the mages of Dormoth than cleaving heads on the frontiers."

She seemed pleased with the logic and his denigration of the renegade apprentice.

"Can you two fight?"

"We would not be here if we couldn't."

A flash of eyes and a brief tug on her left earlobe had Grindar leaping forth with blinding speed. His mailed bulk hit Vetra like a battering ram. He was smashed sideways. Grindar's blade flashed in his hand and there came an attack as furious and merciless as Vetra had ever faced. Like a well-trained assassin or the deadly assault of a wolverine.

Vetra's sword was in his hand, parrying death. Steel rang left, right, backhand, overhead with Grindar's intent to beat down Vetra before he could lay a single stroke.

Vetra had no shield. He must rely on pure footwork and clever parrying. He dodged back, giving himself enough room, parrying skillfully. All too aware he must allocate his energies optimally if he were to defeat this foe and not get spitted and bleed out before this sultry sorceress. But he could feel his lungs already working, his arms beginning to feel the shock of Grindar's hammer blows on his Sahirian blade. Grindar's blade was half a foot longer and probably three pounds heavier, and he had no doubt the bigger man was his better in terms of strength.

But speed? Vetra gave a cursing laugh. Never.

The captain's attack was iron savage, though he lacked a certain finesse that should have ended this fight moments ago. Somehow it was all by rote. Hammer blows, grunts, cuts and parries.

Vetra, responding in kind, parried his steel and followed all the standard sword moves, feeling the ruffian out, noting Grindar was always a step ahead of these practiced maneuvers, as if anticipating such rehearsed moves. This was good. But it was uncanny. An odd mix of luck, technical skill and brawn that had Vetra for a time hard pressed to keep him at bay.

Grindar spat and laughed at Vetra in glottal mockery. "That all you got, mercenary? You'd be dead in a whore's breath in a real fight! You'll never work at Dormoth. I'm only toying with you!"

Vetra's lips curled. There radiated a pompous arrogance about this man, also some shame in his own performance, for there was truth in the captain's words. If shock and awe and number of strikes were what kept score then he was losing. He tried to convince himself that he'd underestimated this captain of war, that he'd been unprepared for his lightning attack and that he'd not be paying for it in the end, but he could not kid himself.

Grindar grinned, seeing he'd struck a nerve. Doubtless a psychological trick he'd pulled a thousand times on lesser men. He advanced, pushing Vetra back and back until his mail coat was nearly flush to the statue. A quick glance behind and Vetra could almost feel the thing's evil breath on his cheek. *Dergath's hell*...if such thing were living it would freeze the blood of the living dead.

A stone or chip turned under Vetra's heel. He felt himself slipping as his weight shifted from under him. What? This was unnatural, as if something had hexed him. He caught for a moment the cold lazy grin of mischief on the sorceress's face and the sardonic twinkle in her eyes...as if she'd been hatching a spell.

Nog saw it too.

In a blinding spurt of speed, the scar-faced mercenary's twin blades sang forth and his throat rang with a fierce cry.

His three-foot blades scissored overtop Vetra's head and caught Grindar's descending sword and a clangor of tempests rocked the courtyard. It was a ringing blow that would have ended Vetra's life then and there, one that could be heard in the nearby octagonal courtyard.

Panting and gasping, Vetra crabbed back on his hindquarters. His first thought, an unkind one to himself, was that Grindar was the better swordsman. If not for Nog's razor-honed reflexes, he'd be an eye-staring corpse right now lying in a pool of his own blood.

It was a horrible feeling, shame. Vetra felt it worse than anyone. If he had a flaw it was that. Pride.

On a diminutive signal from Taranis, the remaining guard gave a cry and launched himself at Nog. Nog'd interfered with the sword fight and now he was there to fix it.

Such a stream of sword blows had not been seen in the garden for an age. There came a flurry of steel from the guard that would have rivaled Azlek of ancient Mercia. Nog's blades crossed out to block then unfurled in savagery to strike wicked arcs at the guard's head. He fought bent-kneed, in a pirate's crouch, as in the panther style of the Thrakian mercenaries. But he was as surprised as Vetra when he found himself pushed back to the farther wall.

Grindar now worked to the left on Vetra. Denied his win, he gave a feverish bellow and came chipping in with a vengeance, sword seeking any pocket of Vetra's flesh to end this fight swiftly.

Vetra stepped back, parrying calmly. He let his heartbeat slow. It was a skill he'd learned over the years, taught him by his old sword master Thorian, his belated teacher from Mosete, the Ring-gast.

Whose voice from the past now echoed in his ear, *The distracted warrior is dead, Vetra. Stay focused. Stay alive!*

Chapter 10

Vetra's breath was controlled, his mind alert and his senses focused. Beads of sweat pooled down the back of his spine. While the sorceress watched on, her eyes gleamed with a catlike expectancy of a waiting sphinx and Vetra felt the cold thrill of death tickle his back, like a reptilian specter lurking over his shoulder, ready to pounce.

Grindar bulled his way in. An impulsive and risky move. A bold and winning one too, if he could pull it off, were Vetra half the man he was. But he was more than half. His thews flexed. He ducked wide, avoiding an arching sweep and a certain beheading. Grindar's blade kept traveling and the sharp, gleaming tip struck the statue's ear off.

Taranis hissed air past her lips. "Fool!" she cried. "You're not fighting statues!"

But the Archmagrix's outburst had unnerved Grindar. He swatted at air for a moment as beads of sweat dripped into his eyes and Vetra slashed in a wild arc. Sword and steel clanked as Grindar's blade barely made it up in time to stop his strike. A twist of body and Vetra's elbow was in the captain's face. His back leg tucked under Grindar's knee and with a wicked shove, he sent the captain tumbling back on the paves.

The mercenary hovered over him like a wraith. He shoved the tip of his blade at the crook of Grindar's neck. "You yield?"

"I yield, damn you!" Grindar rasped, shaking with rage. Vetra withdrew the blade. The captain scrambled to his feet, blasphemous curses on his lips.

From across the court came a clink of steel. Then a painful cry. Nog's twin blades hovered high in a murderous clench ready to shear off the man's arm as he lay sprawled on the cobbles. A bloody gash marked Nog's left cheek. A look of madness was in his eyes.

His blades whooshed down to take off the man's arm, but

Taranis pushed forth palms. A vague pulse seemed to snap at the air. In one swift movement, there came a blue-purple globe that hurtled toward Nog's chest. The semi-transparent missile struck his chest and sent him reeling back and his swords clattering to the ground.

"Enough!" she cried. "This was to be a test! Not a full out bloodletting!"

"Seems as if you thrive on the sight of blood!" Vetra growled.

"You are not mistaken."

The man sprawled before Nog was lurching to his feet. Sword in hand, he was bent on skewering Nog.

Vetra moved faster. Like a cat, he sprinted in and smashed his boot into the man's face, sending him flying back along with two of his front teeth. Vetra brought back his sword, ready to despatch him.

But Taranis gave a shrill cry and gesture before Vetra could drive the sword tip through the man's brain. "Hold up!"

Nog sneered, shaking the daze out of his head. "The fight was rigged!" He cast her a baleful glance. Vetra, he graced a nod of gratitude. Gathering up his blades, he looked on in disgust at his bloodied adversary. The man still groaned on the cobblestones. He tore a strip off the hem of his undershirt and stuffed it under his helm as a crude bandage. All the while he kept an eye on his defeated opponent.

Taranis stood squared before Vetra. "I just wished to preserve good fighting men." She stared at her desecrated statue, fingers tipped to lip, as if in deep reflection. "A strange synchronicity here. One man wins, one man loses. Vetra clearly the loser, the famous swordster, with a veiled pride higher than a mage's tower... yet he seems to have a guardian angel hovering at his back ready to die for him."

"There's no such thing as guardian angels," he sneered. "Fate and the gods are all crocks of shit."

"A heretic?" she crowed. "I'll have you a believer before the night's over."

"You think? Like your two dogs here?"

"Sword fights are like cards overturned on a tarot deck," she lectured enigmatically. Her brows rose. Her eyes took on a dreamy cast. "This pantomime today—it is enough to stymie the most astute tarot reader." She gave an uneasy laugh. She cast a moody gaze at her shorn statue. "An omen, and a desecration, which the captain must answer for."

Grindar hung his head. He was unable to meet her eye, and unwilling.

Vetra wiped his mouth and frowned. He liked not this truckling and pandering to this sorceress. Was she a deity that everyone must bow to?

She swung her inscrutable gaze upon his truculent stance, then Nog with the blood-dripping face, as if pondering whether to kill them outright.

Then she smiled. Her cat-like ease was back. The spring and lithe immediacy of a seductive monarch working in full form. "Well fought, gentlemen. Welcome to Dormoth!" Like a royal courtesan she sashayed over to each of them, gave them both sensuous kisses on the lips and a full embrace.

Vetra tottered slightly backward, immediately struck by the woman's sexual magnetism. Nog stood frozen, his square jaw hanging agape. His tongue lolled like a lovestruck schoolboy.

Taranis licked her lips clean of Nog's blood. She smiled. "Now, to business."

CHRIS TURNER

Chapter 11

Vetra was not overly pleased with the way things had turned out. Yes, they'd survived the audition, but they both'd almost got their throats cut. Unless Vetra missed his guess, Taranis was a woman who got a kick out of men scrambling about bloodying themselves, while she wasn't shearing off the ears of those who irked her. Cordiality would always be the operative word during this mission. He would trust this she-vamp no more than he would a grass adder.

Taranis gestured. "We run a tight ship here, gentlemen. A school for young talent to develop their skills. A place our practicing mages can explore their craft and build on the wisdom of their forebears. It is for the security of Umbria that we offer this service and not for our own ends."

Vetra could barely refrain a sardonic laugh. Really? The vindictive, ear-shearing she-mage, a philanthropist? A protector of the realm and the common interest of her citizens? Hardly.

"No shenanigans here," she said. "No roughhousing, no abusing of the women of the compound. If you see anything suspicious, you report it. Including aberrant or unseemly behavior, unfamiliar or unauthorized persons. You understand?"

"Clear as a bell, your Excellency." Nog saluted, two fingers at his brow.

Her lips curled in a scowl. "Wipe that snigger off your face, mercenary. This is serious business here."

Vetra gave him a nudge hard in the ribs. "Nog had a bit of a rough night with some mettlesome maids and a cask of ale."

A husky murmur rumbled in Taranis's throat. "There'll be no consorting with harlots here at Dormoth," she warned. "I can see that's a regular pastime of yours. Drink is strictly regulated: a dram of wine and a half flagon of ale per evening, no more."

"What is this, a nuns' convent?" Nog cried.

"It's a place where we adhere to strict discipline.

Punishments are meted out accordingly for breach of conduct to maintain our integrity. To both guards and apprentices."

Vetra heeled Nog in the talus and passed his mouth close to his ear. *"Don't push it. You trying to blow our cover? Keep your mouth shut."*

Nog gave a sullen grunt.

Taranis made a lithe movement. "Keep a watch on your dog here, Vetra. He seems the least sensible of you two." She swung her gaze back on her captain. "Outfit them, Grindar. See them to the barracks. Clean up that reverse thrust of yours too. Today it was a bit slipshod."

"Yes, my Lady." His teeth clenched with a sullen sheepishness that Vetra did not miss.

She turned on her heel and disappeared through the archway from where she'd come.

Grindar glared at Vetra and Nog as his henchman slunk off to deal with his bloody teeth. "I'd slay both you here now if the Archmagrix wouldn't skin my hide first. You'll stay in the barracks with the others. Cleanliness and etiquette is our watchword. Slobs and boors will not be tolerated. Pay attention—particularly you, Nog. Slobs'll be beaten. You are part of the Knights Mondalar. The wage is two silver crowns per week. Training maneuvers progress from 4 to 6. Dinner in the Guards' Hall at 7. Got it? Can you ride?"

Vetra masked a grin. He'd been riding horses since he was six. "I can manage."

"What about you?" His hard eyes swung on Nog.

"I know a black one from a brown one."

"Well, you'll be put on training detail bright and early in the morning. Six bells."

"Why not 5?" Nog suggested. "I'll be all ready and saddled."

"Is that being a bit smartass?"

Nog gave an impudent shrug. It did nothing to alleviate the captain's resentment of him.

Grindar led them out of the garden back into the main courtyard. His boots clopped noisily down the colonnaded walkway parallel to the main court. He motioned to the nearest gold-chased dome which caught the bright glare of morning sunlight. "That is the Hall of Wands. You'll not need to go there. To the south, are the Hall of Mages, to the east the Hall of Winds, to the north the Hall of Mystery. You'll become familiar with all the Halls as the days pass."

He led them down a stairwell into the outfitter's room, a miniature armory cut into the stone. It was unadorned, permeated with dampness. Weapons, helms and various gear hung on hooks, including crooked staves, polearms and maces.

The captain plucked one of the helms down and thrust it into Nog's hand.

Nog stared at the plumed morion with wonder. "I'll pass."

"You?" He thrust one at Vetra.

"My helm's fine."

"Suit yourself. But the surcoats are mandatory. We need to be able to recognize our guards from enemies should it come to a skirmish."

"Understandable," Vetra said.

Nog and he withdrew coats of appropriate size and slipped them over their mail. They had the Dormoth Mage's emblem of red dragon and yellow eagle on the front. Both were of good quality, the wool trailing just past waist.

"Do you have a mirror?" Nog asked, batting his eyes while peering over his shoulder.

Grindar gave a curt grunt. "This way, clown. The dining hall's across the hall. Supper at seven…and ends at seven thirty. If you miss the window, too bad. You go hungry for the night."

The irascible man had given them only the briefest tour and the most hurried one. He seemed eager to secure them cots at the barracks then hand them over to one of his underlings to see them to their posts rather than waste time coddling them himself.

He sped off down the shadowed hallway to the barracks, but Nog lagged and stared through an open arched doorway.

"Over here, ape face," Grindar called back at him. "Barracks are this way."

Nog paid him no heed. He stumbled in, jaw agape, on curious feet to wander about the sunlit Hall of Mages, much to Grindar's dismay.

The captain strode after him and Vetra was on his heels, a grin pasted on his lips.

Vetra's eyes widened at the grandeur of the place. Crusted jewels banded the upper rim of the cavernous dome: carnelian, rubies, emeralds, rare crystals. Many magical creatures etched in soft, colored stones were depicted on the high dome, itself like a hallowed chapel—of dragons, mages, trolls, witches, crowns, wands, swords. There soared a pantheon of battle scenes. A slain wild boar with hunter tipping a chalice to members of the hunt; a wizard with yellow conical cap tapping a wand on his apprentice's shoulder; a fierce dragon swooping low over a castle, razing it to the ground with tail and fiery breath. Each scene told what Vetra guessed was an epic story of the myths of the lands far and wide. Below the crusted gems, ran a band of high engraved runes. The symbols circled the hall, citing the stories and parables of the heroes of old, in some forgotten tongue. Two stained-glass windows faced the court. These were crafted in the shape of two mighty dragons, from which filtered rainbow hues—blue, red, green and yellow. Dozens of sconces and candles lit what otherwise would have been a gloomy hall, but for the double doors that were thrown wide open, admitting light from the courtyard.

"Nog!" Grindar called. "This way please." His voice echoed across the marble floor.

Nog was not listening. He was more interested in the figures huddled to the side, particularly the slinky Taranis who was bent over, offering one of the young apprentices assistance with a wand. Eight of them gathered in various garbs of robes, hats and wands while two of the older mages stood by, arms crossed on their chests. One was snowy-haired and hunched in an old brown monk's robe, the other was tall and saturnine in midnight black with a cadaverous face and hollow cheeks. Taranis gave the young apprentice they'd seen earlier in the blue robe a caress on the cheek and a wink. Then a husky laugh as she let one of the bluish-purplish globes drift up to the domed ceiling.

The apprentices cooed and cawed. They waved their hands, flapped their wands. The sorceress materialized another globe from her agile fingers. One of the other apprentices seemed hopeful of snagging the Archmagrix's attention. He made a fancy leap up to grab the globe, as a dutiful hound might bring a thrown stick back to its master. The youth fell back with a shriek. What seemed to be a lightning-like tinge had charred his fingers. He rolled on the marble floor, groaning in anguish.

Taranis seemed unmoved by the accident. She did not offer assistance. Instead she muttered under her breath. "Fool." She did a strange leap in the air to catch the transparent globe, catapulting herself catlike six feet up, before it could do any more damage.

The other apprentices took deep breaths. The two mages watched like owls.

"Harpies Horrors! Did you see that?" Nog grunted. His eyes widened into pools. He nudged Vetra. "Imagine her snug in bed showing you a trick like that?"

"Are you insane?"

"What's that, soldier?" Grindar rasped, striding over.

"Play the dumpling, you fool," Vetra hissed at him. "Remember the plan."

"I asked you a question, mercenary," Grindar bawled.

"I heard you, Cappy," said Nog. "When you start saying something worth listening to, maybe I'll answer."

The captain's face reddened. "You and I are going to get into some skull-bashing before the day's done."

"I'm shaking in my boots," Nog jeered. He pushed thumbs in his ears and twiddled his fingers.

Vetra hissed at him. "Don't antagonize the rascal."

A man-at-arms strode up to give Grindar instructions. It distracted the captain from further violence. It seemed reinforcements were scheduled to arrive on the morrow at sundown from King Grinas's garrison. Grindar and he talked for a while in low murmurs, leaving Vetra and Nog to their discussion.

Nog was still staring at Taranis's body as if the wench was all he could think of.

"Dergath, man!" Vetra muttered. "You're like a lank hound chasing a bitch's scent. Get over it. Get with the program. She almost got a yard of steel shoved into your guts, remember?"

"I know, Vetra, it's messed up," Nog said, flush-faced. "But it's like I can't get the wench out of my mind. What I wouldn't give to hop in the sack with that luscious—"

"Why, when you can have any of those ugly mutts down at the *Rat Peacock*? Cheaper and less chance of getting your throat cut."

Grindar turned their way and pushed irascibly in between them. "Talking to yourselves again?"

Vetra cast him a chill smile. "I was just commenting to Nog how fortunate we are to be in such venerated company in a hallowed hall. With local men of such high repute. The view is extraordinary from here. The inlaid jewels, the lush art, the panoramic scenes, the—" he extended an arm which swept over to Taranis.

Nog grinned and mouthed the word, 'bedroom'.

Taranis clapped her hands, sending echoes around the hall. "Enough play, apprentices! Jemin has had his finger burned, but he will survive. I trust this is a lesson to all." She drew herself up to her full height.

She turned and scowled on sight of Grindar and the two new recruits. "Why aren't they at their posts?" she demanded.

"The big one," Grindar began, "snuck in while my back was turned."

"I don't want to hear your stupid excuses, Grindar." She stroked her chin, as if musing further. "Well, now that you are here, I may as well introduce you to our other mages. But first! I have called you all to this assembly to alert everyone to certain changes. Upon Skirl's insubordination, I have no choice but to enforce stricter security. No one enters or leaves Dormoth without my permission. All suspicious activities and movements are to be reported. No matter how innocuous or benign."

There were grumbles, but everyone agreed.

"I have requested more guards from King Grinas. A dozen will swell our numbers by tomorrow. This is important timing. Five of our own guard will escort Yarne and Hodus to protect the archaeological caravan that travels to uncover more relics at Syrn. A goldmonger, my agent from the moneylenders' guild, has alerted me to recent discoveries when the new silver mine went up. I have no doubt Senesch, our elder mage, will wish to tag along and oversee the operation." She glanced inquiringly at the old man with the snowy white beard.

"I think you are correct," Senesch said with a serene nod.

Taranis looked on with approval. She lifted her hand to Vetra and Nog. "The resident mages, five of us in total, have their own workshops. Each of us is adept in a particular aspect of thaumaturgy. Senesch here is our eldest mage. A guardian of history and philosophy. He is a hundred and four years old. A loremaster." She gestured. "One cannot miss this long, white-haired gentlemen with the philosopher's face, grinning so astutely at Zena, our youngest and most attractive apprentice. His specialty is arcana of the magicians of the Third Age and the overall gamut of spellcraft. Once a powerful spellcaster himself, he considers himself now retired, and devotes himself to the esoteric study and classification of magic—and its unification into a cosmic whole. Whatever that means." She gave a facetious laugh. "Senesch's only mistake has been to take a traitorous thief named Skirl under his wing and dutifully scour the old tomes for lost tombs, relics and amulets."

Senesch pulled at his beard, "I'll remind you, Archmagrix, that the search bore fruit."

Taranis fidgeted with the stone on her neck hanging from its leather strap. "Yes, it is you and Skirl who discovered the Flame of Eros—in a forgotten tomb fifty leagues from here between the sea and the old acropolis of Nespion." Her fingers hooked into claws around the red-shining gem.

Senesch raised his brows in curiosity. "Does the stone make you itch, Lady?"

"No, it is just functioning in an odd way—" she frowned and glared at the old man.

"You are always twiddling it like a child with a broken toy. It seems to have a hold on you."

Her eyes bored into Senesch shafts of ice. "Meaning? What is your interest in the gem?"

Senesch shrugged. "Nothing. Only that such things and objects of power are not without dark histories and have the tendency of corrupting human souls and bringing ruin to those around them."

"A pessimistic philosophy, Senesch. I'll say that as crude as that assertion may be, it is not without some truth. Please, let me continue my introductions."

"Proceed as you wish."

"Voydred over there, is a similar scholar, though more gloomy in temperament. He is a wanderer, thaumaturgist, and the closest to a warlock you will find in the lands. Do not look to Voydred for humor. He is dour. He specializes in incantations and pentagrams. Look to the tall, sallow-faced fellow beside Senesch, dressed in the black satin robes and the skull cap and you will see Voydred. Many have likened him to a black-robed heron on stilts."

Voydred did not appear to care for the joke. He muttered words under his breath from a language long dead and seeming unintelligible to Vetra's ear, lost as they were in the echoes of the hall. But all of a sudden the mage seemed to grow taller and an inexplicable wind entered the hall, tousling everyone's hair. A low moan came from the shadows and the keening cry of what might be witches, frightening the apprentices. The ghost of a smile touched the man's waxy, cadaverous lips. Taranis merely smiled.

"Keren is our resident beastmaster," she said. "There he is over there. His specialty is falcons and hawks. Look! Even now he tries to tame that feral goshawk and teach it not to gouge out his eyes on a bidden command."

Vetra peered off to the side and saw a short, beefy, ruddy-cheeked man garbed in a hunter's vest and peaked cap. He seemed of no determinate age with flat nose and large, slightly balding head. On his left shoulder a large falcon perched, staring serenely. On the other arm, a goshawk, wild and feral as the wind, clutched the leather grip with ever-tightening talons. It eyed the falcon aslant.

The beastmaster tipped his arm. He muttered a gloomy set of words and the bird took flight, sweeping up to the very dome of the ceiling then came swooping straight down at the mage.

The beastmaster did not flinch. Even though the hawk came within inches of his glaring eyes, the breath of wind from its wings only tousled his hair, flipped off his hunter's cap. The bird flattened out its dive inches from the beastmaster's staring eyes.

"Old Keren is a martinet," Taranis exclaimed idly. "It is said he can take the form of any bird, the best of birds, and fly to all corners of the lands. But he hides his magic and no one has seen him take the form of a beast for an age, though he speaks of events and things beyond the knowledge of men. Chiefly in the border kingdoms and faroff lands which none could know without a waft of sorcery.

"There are others. My cousin, Belgra. How could I forget her? There she is now, at last making an appearance to stand beside Voydred, our wandering thaumaturgist. Belgra is the closest to a master herbalist you will find." Her voice took on a mocking tone, a barbed resonance that Vetra did not miss. She flicked a hand toward an unsmiling blond woman who Vetra remembered from the market, still wearing her gardener's apron overtop her white woolen gown. "She dabbles in herb lore, potion-making and healing salves, the lowest of the thaumaturgical arts."

Why they were lower, Vetra did not know. He thought to ask, but stayed his tongue. He was more curious to hear Taranis's take on her cousin.

"She deals with plant medicine and nature lore and is a dear student of woodcraft. She reads the signs of the trees, the bend in the boughs, the cast of the leaves, the play of winds, skies and clouds. Her nickname is 'Skywatcher', though I find the title pretentious."

"And you, Lady? What is your specialty?" Vetra asked.

Bedroom. Nog mouthed the words, grinning.

Vetra gave him a hard nudge, though fighting to stifle a chuckle.

"You ask the most frank questions, mercenary. In reward for your bluntness, I will answer this: I encompass all. Whatever the mages of Dormoth come to know or attain, I siphon that power from them."

Vetra blinked. "A most fortunate skill, Lady. I commend you for your resource. While you hold the keys to the castle, binding all the power and talent of your peers to your will, you, as head of the Order, can capitalize."

She peered at him with a tang of coldness. "Is that a sarcastic remark?"

Vetra gave a faint smile. "You read too much into my words,

Lady."

"Perhaps." She brushed a pale tongue over her lower lip. She drifted over to look at him with shrewd deliberation. Her penetrating, gray-green eyes did not hide their travel to his muscular thighs, his groin. She took Vetra aside.

"Since you express such 'astuteness' and interest in the subjects well beyond the ken of a layman, I invite you to our conclave this evening after dinner."

Vetra hesitated for only a brief instant before nodding.

"I am sure you will find it intriguing."

"I'm sure I will, Lady."

Nog was about to utter a cheeky comment but Vetra dug fingers into his shoulder. "Nog would like to attend too and he promises to be on his best behavior. Isn't that right, Nog?" He shafted him a meaningful glance which the mercenary seemed to heed for once.

While the dim afternoon light drifted in from casements tinted light purple from age, the score of men from the Mage Guard sat at the long, scarred table in the Guards' Hall. Some ate their venison greedily, like trenchermen while others quaffed half flagons of ale frugally, occasionally glancing at the two new recruits and muttering the odd remark or uncomplimentary jest.

Vetra and Nog ignored them. The dusky plumes of their morions dipped as they tucked noses into stew and venison. Vetra could hear the scrape of a chair, the noisy mastication of meat. Not a lot of idle banter among these men, for hired guards with no women about. No doubt a result of Grindar's constant watchdogging and queen Taranis's tyrannical strictures hanging over their heads. He would be happy when this mission was over. A sentiment which Nog shared.

Though the venison was fine.

Chapter 12

The five mages of Dormoth sat on grand chairs in a rough semicircle. These were heavy, ornate seats like thrones of carven oak in the high-domed Hall of the Mages. Taranis sat in the middle upon a larger, more elevated seat to emphasize her status. They all wore ceremonial robes and heavy ornate rings and medallions and charms on necks, wrists and fingers, as was the custom of their ilk. Per usual, Taranis wore the sapphire jewel round her neck. It gleamed like a sinister beacon, announcing its presence to all. It hung on a leather thong, heralding her championship of the Eros Flame.

Nog and Vetra shifted from foot to foot at the back of the hall. Grindar stood, feet planted beside them, indifferent to the mages and their ceremony. His eyes were lazy but watchful, his enormous broadsword slung loosely at his back.

The flickering candlelight lit the crusted jewels, adding rainbow hues to the hall. The band of engraved runes glared with an ancient power of their own.

Across from where Vetra stood, the heavy brass double door adjoining the inner courtyard was barred and bolted. The only other exit lay at their backs through which Vetra and Nog had entered the Hall of Mages under Grindar's command. This exitway led out to a corridor that branched into various other areas of the complex, the main branch which ran parallel to the octagonal courtyard.

A gnarled hand lifted from the man seated to the left of Taranis. Senesch. "Why are they here?" he demanded.

"Because I asked them. They are new additions to my Mage guard detail. As a reward for their besting my two best captains in a sword fight, I thought to give them an insiders' view of our council. Vetra, as you recall, is the one to the left. He seems to know a thing or two about thauma-history and lore, also, to have a good head on his shoulders."

"Really?" snorted the blond woman, Belgra at Taranis's other side. "More like another concubine for your bed?"

Taranis brushed her cousin a cool stare. "And are you jealous, cousin?"

"Hold off," Voydred intoned. He gestured idly, shaking his head. His dark, saturnine orbs of eyes peered curiously at Vetra. "You claim astuteness in the thauma-arts? Where do you hark from?"

"Tolizia."

"Many magicians have come from that land—a stormy, moody place, faraway to the east. So who is the most renowned sorcerer of old from the 5th age of Tolizia?"

Vetra held up a hand. "Alas, lord, I am no bibliophile or history adept. I only know from the priests of the old tabernacle of Sot, who mumble prayers before candle-lit altars, that they laud Nerut of Tosthumus. He is spoken of in the apocrypha written on lambskin papyrus."

"You would be correct in that... And you subscribe to what teachings?"

"My views are syncretic, lord. I merely observe the world around me. I make deductions based on what my eyes and ears see."

Senesch nodded thoughtfully. "That is a wise response, mercenary. I see why Taranis holds you in high esteem."

"Can we cut the chatter?" Keren griped. "We have things to do." He waved an impatient hand. "My falcon has sprained a wing. She dove too fiercely upon Elgrex, my goshawk, and now is in pain."

"You and your birds can wait," Taranis said curtly. "I have called this meeting for various reasons. As you all know, the Wizard's Exhibition is upcoming on the Eve of Valgon. The Time of the Whispering Winds. This year they will be held at Alantra."

"Yes, we know that, Archmagrix," the tall, thin man

Voydred said with annoyance. "It is common knowledge. Do you wish to beat your breast about it? How we will win it with flying colors under your tutelage? I daresay we won't. We are too few. Our powers are too weak."

Taranis spat a mage's oath. "I hold the Eros Flame!" She jumped from her seat. "You are one of the last-living, old-school spellcasters, Voydred. Senesch is wise beyond his years. He has studied more tomes than can fill the Linderlore library. Keren is beastmaster of renown. He has traveled the far kingdoms and talked with the Weremarks of Kyldrie, the—"

"One jewel," interrupted Senesch, "and a few over-the-hill mages are not going to match the might of all the wizards of the Eight Kingdoms."

"I have to agree with that," Voydred said.

Keren gave his own grunt of acknowledgment. He stroked the feathers of his goshawk perched on his shoulder. "A traveling beastmaster or not, I find your vision overly ambitious, Taranis."

Senesch gave an affected sigh. "I'm not one for pomp and ceremony, Archmagrix. More important is another excursion to the ruins of Gotha, where our ex-apprentice Skirl discovered your talisman before he was excommunicated. The project is a worthy one. I think that is the only one I can fully support at this time."

Taranis sneered. "You're all a bunch of pusillanimous lack-wits. It seems you have all already given up before you have started."

"Nay, Archmagrix!" stormed Voydred. He slumped back in his seat. "We are merely fatigued and practical."

Taranis stamped her foot. "I shall not be daunted. I mean us to be well represented at the exposé. It is an important event, a hallmark milestone, so it is for this reason I call these weekly gatherings. That we can share our resources and help encourage each other to strive for better, more puissant magic. The judges are the kings and queens of the realms—King Xilos of Mercia, Lord Ragnum of Lvendar, Queen Barbassa in Galashad, to name a few. If we win this exhibition, or at least score high enough, we can expect the royals' patronage in the exploration of our spellcraft dominance in the future. It is a boon which cannot be overestimated. We'll put Xalgossa back on the map! As an ancient seat of power, where she once was and where she belongs!" In her slender fingers, she twiddled the amulet around her neck such that its reflected light angled in each one of the mages' eyes. And yet it did not herald the same adulation or luster as it once had, judging by the amount of scowling and murmuring therein.

"A nice speech, cousin," Belgra intoned jeeringly. "What are your real motives? To seduce as many nobles as you can once you get your cheap ass in there?"

Taranis quirked an eyebrow. "You are as suspicious as a paladin badger. What eats you? Did your dainty day lilies die? Did the deer trample your precious begonias? Horse-weeds choke out your secret garden? I was chosen as Archmagrix, you were bypassed. All here know the fact. It is no secret you hold a grudge against me when your closet lover, the apprentice Skirl, turned cuckold and seduced me instead of you. I can understand your bitterness."

Belgra's face turned red. It was not as if she could deny what Taranis said.

Taranis gave her a patronizing smile. "Go ahead. Show us what miracles of herb and plant you've discovered this week." She spoke not without three degrees of mockery.

Belgra smoothed out her dirt-stained gardener's apron still wrapped around her waist. "I have only this to share, cousin. 'Tis what I call the *Star Ruby*. Cultivated in my own 'secret' garden."

From her satchel, she withdrew an odd flower with drooping rosy head. "What looks a simple sunflower is one graced with mystique and mystery. Watch!" She blew a soft breath on its rosy petals. She murmured some words to it in an odd tongue while tapping away at the drooping head with a gray wand.

Instantly the flower began to bloom into a taller sunflower that came rustling out of her grip. The stem rose, the stalk extended, as if given fresh life by rain and sunlight. The petals opened in a wild rush. The central bud pulsed with a strange fervor, then came a humming sound and a murmur in the air as of a swarm of bees.

All looked around the hall, but there were no bees. From its effulgent, vital bulb emerged a magnificent silver-backed hummingbird which hovered for some time before the mages then rose higher to survey the hall.

Belgra's face glowed. The hummingbird dropped lower to linger before the nose of each mage, to greet them with formal courtesy.

Taranis swatted her visitor away. "Very pretty, cousin. But of what utility is such a toy-like oddity? A flower that births quaint birdlings? Pah!"

Belgra's face fell and her lip quivered. "Can't you see, cousin? 'Tis only the beginning. This bird demonstrates the transmutation of one species to another! It suggests a whole new branch of magic! If I can unlock the secret, I can…"

Taranis held up a hand. "Spare us your fantasies, Belgra. If you had produced a war-bred condor that could fire bolts of flame from its eyes, I would perhaps be a little more interested."

"Always scheming," Belgra hissed. "Always dreaming up new ways to harm people and maim. Any form of megalocracy to fuel your incessant power-mongering."

"Is that a new word, megalocracy?" She gave a mocking chuckle. "How can you claim that I am a 'warmonger' when I wield an amulet that casts only love and admiration in the viewer?"

"Because—" Belgra clicked her tongue "—it is something quite far from that."

"Let us not bicker," Keren said. "We are all friends here. United in a common goal."

"Of what?" Voydred grunted. "At times I begin to wonder."

Taranis gave a sullen shrug. "What can I say? Biggest wolf gets the choicest meat."

Senesch intervened. "The feat is unique, Belgra, and you are to be commended. Despite Taranis's criticism, it is an accomplishment to be written about in the spell tomes. In all my years of poring over magical scholarly works I have never heard of such a spell. While not earth-shattering, it shall surely turn a few heads at the exposé during the competition of wizards." He gave a brief pause and frowned. "I have had some revelations of my own to share among the gathering—"

But his words were cut off by a fluttering of wings. The hummingbird, which had floated too near Keren's goshawk, gave a frantic chirp. In its inbred feral instinct, the goshawk gave a shrill, savage screech. Up it flew to sink talons into the hummingbird, unheeding of Keren's shrill commands. Down jabbed the goshawk's beak in its side to tear bird flesh from its victim's defenseless hide.

Belgra gave a cry of dismay. "Stop your bird of prey, Keren! It is devouring my hummingbird!"

Keren muttered commands at the disobedient bird, to no avail. "It is too late." He shook a fist. "Your bird is good as dead."

With a whimsical gesture another sinister globe appeared in Taranis's glowing palms. She lobbed it on high where it engulfed the goshawk and its prey, encaging both in a transparent prison. The globe floated down to halt before all, eight feet in the air.

Taranis tilted her head back and gave an exultant cry. "Carved in living light, cousin! Framed like a picture. A gruesome snapshot of mother nature at work."

"Save him!" Belgra pleaded. Defeat loomed heavily on her pale face. She was unable to watch the ghastly sight and turned her head. Nor could she stand to listen to the savage squawking and carnage.

"There is no saving your bird, cousin. 'Tis the law of the jungle. Big fish eats little fish. As the goshawk flies, so it feeds." This Taranis spoke even as Keren's bird of prey tore Belgra's hummingbird to pieces.

"This spectacle gives me an idea," she mused. She rose up to her full height and cried, "Watch!"

Her arms lifted. They manifested a giant ball of blurry wonder. Swirling within the ball were the chaos of distant galaxies, forming and reforming. Magical clouds of dusts and planets swirling amid myriad stars.

The eyes of the mages stared up in wonder. The globe floated up, magically, miraculously to reform into something hideous, something unnatural.

"Picture it!" she brayed. "A strange magical plant gives birth to new life. Feral falcon gets jealous. He attacks the bird, angry as it steals all the attention. Another scavenger flies to intercept, wanting a piece of the action itself, smiting the falcon. The jealous master of the falcon, resenting its death, manifests and unleashes a demon. The creators of both beasts, join the drama of their creations, just as the gods are wont to meddle in the drama of mortals. There ensues a full blown mage war!—Keren, me, Voydred and Belgra. We launch fire bombs and beasts at each another. There is an epic battle!—it showcases our talents. Only one survives. Can you see the artfulness, the beauty?"

There came blank stares.

"It strikes all the emotional archetypes of the human psyche!" she cried. "'Tis brilliant. Epic. We cannot fail!"

Voydred spoke after a time. "Aye, you are quite the macabre genius, but you are most definitely mad."

"Mad you say?" the sorceress rasped. "This is mad." The globe grew bigger, darker, pulsing with an eerie light. From within, the ghastly blueish ball morphed into a basilisk-like monster—half gargoyle, half bat in the likeness of Besemooth, Dal Sagoth's messenger carved in living stone in the nearby garden. And yet it was still in its birth, a youngling, not much larger than the goshawk.

"I too have been practicing my arts of transmutation. If you will not participate in my exhibition, then let us play pattycake in a drama right here!"

"What are you raving about?" Voydred cried in a hoarse voice. "The Hall of Mages is not a forum for summoning demons. 'Tis sacred grounds, for displays of benign magic and intellectual discussion."

"Don't you see?" Taranis implored. "This is the perfect tableaux to present at the exhibition. To showcase our talents and entertain the judges. Macabre and unpredictable! Unique! Twists of violence, jealousy and gore."

Senesch mumbled, "'Tis the mark of a diseased imagination." His lips crinkled in a grimace.

Voydred grunted his agreement.

Taranis gave a resentful jeer. "And you, Belgra, what think you?"

"I cannot abide by violence to animals. It smacks of the same cruelty you unleashed on Skirl shearing off his ear. Call off your spook, cousin! Whatever you are brewing."

"I might have guessed," Taranis murmured. The Archmagrix spat an old oath. "You are a bunch of sissies. Goody-goody simpletons pretending to be mighty magickers but beneath, nothing more than lambs. The stuff of weaklings. Even you, Voydred—I am disappointed, one who I thought entertained an ounce of backbone in his body. You would have us all presenting little hummingbird fantasies, whispering and humming sweet little rhymes in the judges' ears. Pah! This is my answer to that."

She repeated an old ancient evil spell that even confounded the ear of Voydred. She channeled the might of Dal Sagoth.

"Garshrak mi an hia globan!"

The beast within the globe swirled and grew to a monstrous size. It widened and bulged into a giant of what it formerly was, a bat-bird, like the sinister gargoyle in the garden court.

The mages drew back, strangled gasps catching in their throats. They leaped from their seats in horror.

CHRIS TURNER

Chapter 13

Even Voydred was slow to mutter his ancient incantation. Harsh, guttural vocables spilled from his lips to counter the monster that peered evilly down upon them, *"Agrak Nor Sensum Auditus!"*

But it did nothing to penetrate the nimbus of power surrounding the demon. The flux of word-bombs only clattered harmlessly against the shield of energy surrounding it.

In fear and surprise, Voydred lifted a bony hand to summon an even more fell puissance.

To no avail. The pulse clattered against the shield of the monster's armor and rebounded off to strike at the band of jewels surrounding the hall. Several gems fell clattering to the marble floor.

Taranis's magic channeled from the dark well of Dal Sagoth, reigned supreme.

In a raucous voice, the mage uttered an even more terrible spell that must blast the invader to bits.

Taranis lofted another of her grisly globes which blocked the flux, absorbed it and sent it showering into a thousand sparks.

Vetra stared on in morbid fascination. The demon flapped wings and sprang on the beastmaster who had cursed it with a hex of the elder beasts.

The man gave a bewildered cry and ran, shielding his head with his hands as it threatened to tear off his head. Voydred had failed. Upon seeing the impotence of the mage's word-magic, surely more powerful than his own, Keren the beastmaster must wonder, what chance had he?

For the first time in witness, the beastmaster assumed the form of one of his own minions, the goshawk. Lips a-murmur, eyes closed, he became one with the goshawk, though one more massive, the size of a hulking condor.

The transformation prompted a rapturous cry from Taranis.

This movement of magical energy seemed all part of her plan, as if in the blink of an eye she saw her vision manifested—how her four fellow mages could be part of her mad impromptu stage play. Something darker too—them being used as props and pawns to play their roles from this day evermore. Not only in her fabulous drama which would win them the contest of the Mages, but at Dormoth.

Eyes dilated, her husky breath panting in almost sexual ecstasy, Taranis stood tall, like a female titan. She was black-clad, leather knit, a black-hearted demiurge, awesome, terrible, beautiful, all at once, and yet absolute in her power. Even without the real amulet ringing her neck, the power of Dal Sagoth radiated from her pores like hot steam from lava.

"A gift of Dal Sagoth!" she cried. "He sends his wishes."

The monster flapped around the spellstruck hall, diving upon the mages. From its vile beak jetted a noxious gray fluid, dousing them with generous sprays, fetid to the senses, even as the creature vented shrill chitters.

Vetra cursed. He ran forth, his blade swinging. The gleam of its silver hue attracted the demon. It dove. With an ungodly chitter, it swept upon his head. Vetra's blade twanged hard on its beak, hard as horn. And yet it was not horn. His blade bounced off it as if it were a mass of luminous energy rather than living tissue. He blocked only in the nick of time as the talons came clutching for his face.

The quick move saved his life. The bat reared up and screeched. Midnight black wings flapped as its left claw dangled from an ugly stump.

No blood flowed from such a wound, for this creature was not of the three dimensional world; it was of the sepulchral mists of Dal Sagoth's crypts.

Nog ducked, dodging a fang...then flailing claws that would have gouged trenches in his back. But the swipe knocked off his helm and stripped him of his bandage.

In undisguised glee, Taranis clenched her fists and howled. From foot to foot she danced as she watched the delight of her creation. "Marvelous, marvelous! More, more! I must record these scripts! These can be modified for the exhibition to create a show of horrors!"

The Hall tingled with madness. The hair stood on end on Vetra's scalp. Keren flapped in close, to hover in opposition to the demon. His hooked beak clacked open, ready to sink into the bat's neck. Beady, burnt-umber eyes stared forth from an ugly, bulbed head. Wattled skin hung from his neck like a turkey's.

On a sudden whim, Taranis stayed her bat-minion which hovered ten feet in the air, glaring at them all.

"I am Archmagrix. I call to see who is loyal! All who are for me, come forth. Stand at my side!"

She held her arms aloft, her thick chestnut mane whipped back. Her long black-painted nails beckoned. "All those who are against me, stand over there." She twitched a jeweled finger to an eerie circle of light that had manifested some twenty feet distant.

Her chest heaved. Her fingers clenched.

Belgra was first to move. In utter defiance she stood in the circle of light. Senesch broke the spell and with a tired, aged scowl, doddered his way over to stand beside Belgra. She smiled grimly and put her arm around the old man's shoulders, her lips firmed.

Voydred made jerky steps toward Senesch, but then stopped with an odd curl of lip. He seemed unable to look his friend and mentor in the eye. He muttered an incoherent word then moved quickly to stand at Taranis's side. "I stand by our leader. Twenty moons ago we elected her Archmagrix of our Circle. I honor that pledge."

Senesch snarled in disgust.

Taranis's teeth glinted in the candlelight. There came a nod of vindication and a feral glow radiating from her cheeks.

An uncomfortable silence fell over the gathering; an

awkward standoff tainted the hall.

Keren who had now alighted on claw-feet somewhere in the middle of the hall, shimmered back to his human form. Dazed and starry-eyed, he croaked in a rusty voice, "I cannot stand against both Voydred and Taranis. I ally with the Archmagrix." On shaky feet he moved to stand on Taranis's other side, but stayed out of reach of her outspread arm, as if it were the touch of a viper.

Grindar moved like an automaton toward Taranis and stood in front of the group, his back to the mages, sword upheld. Now there were four.

All eyes turned to Vetra and Nog, who stood transfixed under the shadow of the hovering bat-beast and the glare of its burning eyes.

Nog drew Vetra aside, his swords gripped, for once thinking twice before making an impulsive move.

But Vetra had no counsel to give him. A dry sour taste lingered in his throat. A dangerous situation presented itself. One slip and they would both end up dead.

In a calm voice he addressed those in the hall, "We are new to Dormoth. We are not interested in getting caught in the middle of any mage wars. We come only to guard Dormoth's walls against thieves and intruders. We choose to stand on neutral ground."

Taranis's eyes narrowed; she smiled. "Very well, mercenary, you can play the part of the cautious man."

Then, as it had all appeared, all came to an end. On a casual flick of hand, the bat-beast shimmered and dissolved into a thousand motes and disappeared. The hall was plunged into silence. Belgra and Voydred's arms relaxed at their sides. Keren's eyes blazed with a timeless rapture and a lack of memory of the somnambulist, as if he were still in a trance of his own making. The sinister globe faded into nothingness and released the goshawk. The bird flew free to land on Keren's shoulder. But

Belgra's hummingbird was no more, nothing but feathers and gristle in the belly of the goshawk.

Taranis's ruby lips parted in a jaunty leer. "Friends! Let us put aside our squabbles. This was only theater. A rehearsal for our big show at the exhibition. What do you think? Are we not stars? Are we not heroes?" She laughed aloud. "We will go down in history!"

Vetra gave a cynical grunt. He did not trust her. Nor did the other mages. He did not miss Belgra's silent sneer, or the twitch of doubt on Senesch's lips.

Snakes and curses! The intrigue among this brood of vipers was thick enough to cut with a knife. The machinations of these mages was little to his liking. They all seemed to bear some grudge against each other, except maybe the old man who seemed the wisest of them all.

Taranis's eyes narrowed. Long jeweled fingers strayed to her talisman, twirling its facets so its reflected light beamed into the eyes of each of her peers. But nothing seemed to happen, at least to any visible effect.

"Must you always shine that silly bauble in our eyes, Lady?" grunted Senesch in annoyance. "The thing's magic is weak. My guess, tainted. Every good mage worth his salt knows that true power does not come from objects—it comes from within."

Taranis looked on him in cold disfavor "Pretty words, Senesch. Old school rhetoric pales in face of real power."

The old mage's eyes flashed with discontent. "It seems that you alone were selected leader of this esteemed Order. You are strong, fearless, even adept in some of the arts, particularly the dark arts, but you harbor an arrogant cruelty and sinister cunning in your actions. It follows the very steps you take, the air you breathe."

"Are you following in the jealous footsteps of Belgra here?"

"No," the old man replied haughtily. "But do not forget that you used to be one of us not long ago. You were at our level it seems but yesterday before you achieved this exalted status as Archmagrix, to replace Elgress our leader who mysteriously disappeared. All of this suddenly happened after the Eros Flame was uncovered. Skirl and I dug it up, under the death-shroud of Sarkala. I wish to Dergath we'd never found it!"

Taranis laughed. "And yet you persist in digging up more trinkets in the hinterlands. Ere the caravan rides out to Gotha once more, you would jump on it as nimble as a goat. You are a hopeless addict, Senesch. Admit it. A hypocrite no less."

The loremaster looked away. His age-cracked lips muttered something unintelligible. "I see Dal Sagoth has given you a clever, forked tongue as well, Lady Taranis, always beguiling the ear and spinning endless deflections and counterarguments to hide your basic evil and lack of morality."

"Boo hoo."

"This bickering is useless," snarled Voydred. "Let us reconvene with clear heads."

"Silence!" The old mage's jaw worked. "There are words long overdue that must be spoken. I denounce Taranis. I call for a new leader."

"Who are you to request such a thing?" Taranis jeered. "What do you know, old man? You spew lofty ideals about good and evil that are but whiffs of vapor in face of hard reality. You speak words that have no play in the real tenets of power and spellcraft, the power of Dal Sagoth. I hear only pretty maxims that cater to feeble minds gulled by idiots' compassion and the watchwords and parables of the fading past."

"Perhaps, but there is a higher order to things which you seem oblivious of, where those things I speak about carry foremost weight."

"And what's that?"

"It's beyond this forum and conversation," Senesch intoned. But his brow clouded and his lips pursed in silence.

Taranis loosed a mocking breath. "You cannot even name it,

can you? It is as I thought. All talk and no substance." She turned on her heel. "This meeting is over." She sauntered out, her chin high, her hips a-sway.

The other mages watched her disappear and they departed in slow fashion to their own corners of Dormoth, dismayed by the cloud that had fallen over them and the awful potential of the magic they had just witnessed.

Grindar motioned Vetra and Nog along the adjoining corridor, now chased with shadows and the dim glow of guttering cressets.

Vetra's mood was dark. He set himself to musing. He and Nog needed to get this wretched jewel and quit this jackal's den before they were caught in the crossfires.

Only three hours remained till midnight. Skirl had better get his ass here quick-time.

CHRIS TURNER

Chapter 14

Skirl had been busy. He'd concocted some combination of false beard and mustache which he'd shaved from an unlucky sheep in the market. He'd smeared his face with some goose grease from the landlord and pasted on his new facial hair with a flourish. With a tattered slouch hat perched on his crown at a jaunty angle, a false stoop and feigned limp on a gimp leg, makeshift cane pressed in hand, he was all set to go.

Noon had passed and the mercenaries had not returned to the *Rat Peacock,* implying they'd made it into Dormoth, or'd perhaps gotten their throats cut. He'd find out soon enough. He hoped they had the resource to maneuver themselves into position at the rendezvous point near the Hall of Wands. Vetra was clever enough, but the other, Nog, the scar-faced brute... Skirl frowned. He had his doubts, though he thought the two had the potential to be fierce, if not capable.

The mission would not be an easy one. He hadn't described in great detail how perilous their task would be, or how dangerous the Archmagrix was, should she get wise to their ploy. That was their problem.

In his jerry-rigged disguise, he trod the nighted streets of Xalgossa to Dormoth, on a circuitous route through the dives and the distillery district. He kept to the main streets as much as he could. The cane would serve as a weapon against footpads should it be needed, though he would not count on it. He had other tricks up his sleeve.

Skirl's mind was a hive of ambitious and conflicting thoughts...

A sinking feeling crept over him. Was he a dilettante, like Keren had accused him of the other day?...trumpeting it before all at the conclave in the Hall of Mages? Words like 'washed up wannabe without talent' had come up.

No. He would never accept that. The mages were jealous of

his abilities—abilities he once had. He had talent. He was going places.

Skirl calmed his nerves. He let the angry images of their mockeries subside. *Fools.* What were they but a bunch of codgers dabbling in weak witchcraft? All this paled in comparison to what could be, if he could tap into the power of the Eros stone.

A lot of ifs there, Skirlie…

No matter. He had bigger fish to fry. Greener pastures to graze.

As for the jewel, should he succeed in retrieving it, escape from this adder-ridden stronghold with his neck, he could never let it pass into the hands of a grubby market merchant or gem dealer. The jewel was priceless. He could never let his new allies know his true thoughts either. Better to use them as pawns in the overall scheme of things. He was a better guardian of the jewel, not Taranis or any of the other mages. When he had it in his grasp, there would be hell to pay.

He reached to touch his ear, or lack of one, and winced. The wound still throbbed like a devil. A fierce rage burned in his chest. He promised Taranis a reckoning more violent than the eight kingdoms had ever seen.

He took comfort in that thought as he plodded on with his fake limp, grimed cane and goose grease, down the cobblestone way.

The hour was near midnight and an awkward time to be calling at the gates of Dormoth. But no matter. He had great faith in his abilities as a dissembler.

He halted before the high gate. A single lamp burned from the spiked iron. Atop the south tower, all was dark, but from the west tower he could see a small torch wavering in an open, square window.

Skirl's lips curled in a grin.

"Who goes there!" came the guard's challenge.

Skirl put on his squeakiest, old man voice. "A half blind

beggar, master watchman. One wanting crusts for his breakfast."

"Hardly a time for a breakfast, beggar! Go away. The hour is late. Dormoth is closed. Jungar and I are in a game of dice."

"Spare a few scraps of meat then? A bit of watered wine?"

"Begone, I say! The abbey and soup kitchen is down the way. Call on old lady Mildred to ladle you broths, not me. You'll find no pity here."

"Mind your manners, young grump! You do yourself no favors. I know people here. I have friends in high places. Like Keren, the birdwatcher. Where is the old coot? He's an old friend of mine."

"Sure he is," the guard jeered. He flashed his blade through the bars under Skirl's chin. "I said, begone, beggar. This is your last warning."

Skirl pushed the blade aside. "Peace, ruffian! Call on Keren, if you are in doubt. The beastmaster! Him and me, we go back a long ways. He'll vouch for me. Tell him his old friend Arkovitrix is here, to pull his beard and trade a spell or two. Remind him about the little mole on the left side of his buttocks, if he doesn't think it's me."

The guard paused, lips parted, as if fearing that this old man perhaps spoke the truth. Did he face a magician? With a grumble and a curse, he turned the key in the lock, mumbling under his breath. The gate jerked open a few inches to let the gaffer pass. "Keren's workshop is first on the right, past the Hall of Wands. But I'm sure you know that already, don't you? Dally not, or I'll have you whipped!"

Skirl gave a cheeky salute. "Thank you, young whippersnapper, and I'll pass on your friendly regards too."

The guard pursed his lips. Even he paled at the prospect of Keren's wrath coming down on him.

Skirl hobbled swiftly across the courtyard, a cagey grin etched on his face.

CHRIS TURNER

Chapter 15

Five men awaited their orders in the bare, limestone guards' command post adjoining the barracks. Vetra and Nog were among them. Grindar gestured a rough hand at the first two stubble-chinned sentries. "West Tower duty for you. Yes, you, Dakin, don't look so surprised." His steely eyes settled on his two new recruits. "Get these two clowns on kitchen guard duty, patrolling the scullery staffs' quarters. It's very exciting down there, especially this time of night on a six hour stretch."

Vetra feigned a sigh of relief. "Anything away from heights, captain. Nog and I are a bit leery of high places, aren't we Nog?"

"Quite right, Vetra. Anything with parapets or lofty towers gets us queasy."

"Queasy of heights, you say?" Malice shone in Grindar's eye. Vetra nodded.

Grindar jerked a thumb. "Get them to take the West tower then. You boys can start chipping away at your fears tonight."

Vetra put on a wild-eyed look.

Grindar held up a hand. "No buts! Who's going to show these mutts the ropes?"

"Garfu's your man," Dakin the red-bearded man with squint said, jerking a thumb at an ape-like figure with underslung jaw and lopsided morion. The man looked half asleep.

"Let Garfu alone," Grindar grunted. "He's paid his dues. Too many of them. I'd say it's like you're a bunch of old hens, chicken-pecking the one easiest to peck."

"Guess I will then, Sarge," a curly haired man said, polishing his plumed morion.

"Good man, Macdem. Tower's not too high, should these two babies fall and break their arms. You can relieve yourself at midnight. Call on Janos."

Vetra masked a grin. Better this than sneaking around the guards' barracks with these soldiers watching and ready to snitch on them.

Macdem made a gruff acknowledgment. Torch in hand, he led Vetra and Nog across the nighted courtyard to the west tower's lower door. He pulled open an oaken portal and beckoned them inside.

The landing was dark. Only a few spare weapons and gear hung on the wall: mace, dented helms, wicked looking polearms. Up the winding steps they tramped.

"I heard how you got the drop on our friend," Macdem said. "Danys looked a veritable mess. Would have loved to have been a fly on the wall, seen the look on Grindy's face when you busted him up."

Vetra gave a brief shrug. "It was over before it began." The echo of his voice gave way to the ghostly echo of boots on stone. The smell of dust and spider webs hung heavy in the air.

"My advice, keep your head down. Grindar's not the type to let down grudges. He's going to come after you."

"Thanks, we'll keep that in mind," Nog said.

The guard shook his head. "Surprised old Grindy even allowed you up here, instead of putting you down to clean the latrines." He gave a ribald laugh. "Must have a soft spot for outlanders."

Through the arrow slits, Vetra saw the murky glower of lamps from inns and the odd temple settling over the city. At another landing, Macdem led them out onto a high parapet, torch held in hand: nothing more than a narrow stone walkway where two men could walk abreast. Crenelations rose to waist height. The domes of the Mages' Halls loomed below. Commanding views could be seen of the surrounding area. Stars wheeled in the sky, the moon had not yet risen, lending a dark, humid feel to the air. Sound carried from a perch this high. A low hum of voices emanated from the city: drunken shouts, the high piping of musical instruments, the beat of a drum, the bawdy laugh of a tavern harlot maybe in a mud-hemmed kirtle hunting for a mark.

Torchlight shone from the main gate now barred for the evening. Vetra could hear muted laughter and jeers of the watchmen from this direction as they won and lost at dice.

Macdem pushed the torch under Vetra's nose. "Say, you don't seem too scared of heights?"

"It's not as bad as I thought at night."

Macdem gave a low grunt. "Not much to show you boys here. Just a lot of waiting around. You watch, make sure no skulkers come to breach the tower or over the parapets. In fact, if there're any movements at all, you yell first then beetle down to the courtyard with your swords ready. Now, it's harder to see anybody because there's no moon. Ordinarily no one can cross that open space without getting spotted. If you squint real hard you can see, Harfar, lean as a spring gopher, traipsing the parapet. Orders are he's not to keep a light. Makes him a sitting duck for archers. As I said, just a fearful lot of waiting around here. Maybe that was Grindar's way of punishing you." He gave another coarse laugh as if it were the funniest joke that evening. "Any of you fellows play dice? If so, I hope you're good at it. There's a lot of that goes on among us tower watch." He pulled out a sack of dice from his surcoat pocket and emptied four skew-faced stones in his hand. "We usually play double or nothing. Sigs and Sags. You play?"

Nog's brows rose in interest. "You play a lot?"

"As much as I can," he said proudly. He took off his helm. "What about you?" His beady eyes glinted, trained on Vetra.

Vetra shook his head. "I'm not a gambler."

"Pity. Well, keep your eye on the courtyard then, friend. While Lord Nog and I have a friendly game of Sigs and Sags, we'll swap duty in good time. Nice to have some company for a change."

Nog and the watchman settled in with gusto, squatting on their haunches, rattling their dice on the dusty parapet, jeering when they won and clutching ears when they lost.

Vetra smiled. This was almost too easy. Almost like clubbing a bunny.

The gong struck dully from the opposite tower. The moribund note echoed across the desolate courtyard. Fitting for the place, thought Vetra.

On Vetra's barest nod, Nog moved closer to his gambling mark.

His first punch came hard and heavy.

A quick mallet fist that clubbed the guard in the face, sending him toppling back. He gave a squawk, reached for his sword.

Vetra was already there, his blade tipped at the man's throat.

"Nothing personal, friend. Just business."

"Sure, just business."

While Vetra kept the man at bay, Nog tore strips from his breeches and bound his wrists and ankles.

"What are you two bullies up to? If it's thieving on your mind, you'll never get past the gate guards. Grindar'll skin you alive, cut your throats to ribbons—Hey, why you taking off my boots?"

Nog pulled off the guard's left boot, ripped off the sock and grinned as he stuffed it in the man's mouth.

"Clean, and neat." Vetra stepped over and pushed the sweaty rag deeper into his mouth.

"He'll have a sore head for a day or two, I reckon." Nog scooped up the man's morion, looked at it, tried it on, found it too small and tossed it back on the slumped body.

"Let's not piss around, Nog," Vetra warned.

"If our friend's not at the appointed place?"

Vetra shrugged. "We'll just bust our way out of here. No worries. No use lingering around getting drawn and quartered." He nudged the slouched figure with his toe. "How long we have to sit here with our hands tied is another matter—"

"Wait!" Nog lifted his bulk, nudged Vetra in the ribs.

"There's our man. Look! Visitor at the gates."

Vetra peered and caught a vague glimpse of a lean figure standing outside the iron pales.

"Here, pass me the torch, let's give our friend a signal." He waved it slowly for little while, then set it leaning up against the parapet. "Let's make like rabbits, Nog."

Nog glanced at their prisoner. "What if chatterbox tries to roll his way down the stairs and alert the guards?"

Vetra gave a mirthless grunt. "Let him if he wants to break his neck."

"Should we go down there and help our one-eared mage?"

Vetra studied the scene for a few moments then shook his head. "No need. Look, the gates are opening. Looks like Skirl managed to wheedle his way in. Incredible. Let's stick to plan."

"The torch?"

"We'll need it. Take it. How's your night vision?"

"Not good."

"Then I'll take it. Let's go."

* * *

Skirl passed from courtyard to portico under an archway then into a wide corridor flanked with ghostly statues and dimly lit by sconces. He paused. His fake beard and mustache itched like the devil. He pulled them off, cast them aside like one would used dishrags and wiped his face clean of the goose grease. His skin smelled rancid. No matter. Fifty paces to the Hall of Wands, another hundred to Taranis's quarters. An estimated 5 to 7 minutes skulking and eluding sentries, should nothing untoward occur.

He'd make no more than twenty steps past a darkened cross-corridor when a shadowy figure jumped out at him.

"The Hall is off limits for the night. Don't you know curfew's at 9?" He squinted in the sconce light and frowned.

"Wait, I recognize you."

Skirl recognized Brezel, one of Grindar's roughboys, who had manhandled him on his way to the gallows the other afternoon. Skirl kept walking, hoping the problem would go away as he tried to come up with a plan.

"Hey, wait up, you skulker!" The guard caught up to Skirl and whacked him on the arm with the flat of his blade. "'Tis as I thought!...Skirl, the banished apprentice."

Skirl licked his lips and slowed to a halt. Catching his breath, he gave a conspiratorial wink. "Brezel...quiet down, come here. I have something to show you." He beckoned the man closer as if with an insider's tip. "You're a keen man, one with good senses and quick eyes. This is your lucky day."

"How's that?" The guard's suspicion grew. "What do you have to show me, a bloody ear?" He pushed his swordtip at Skirl's chest. Crooked teeth glinted in the sconce light.

Skirl pressed a hand deeper in his pocket. He withdrew a coin, one of the misshapen shekels he'd won at the dart game back at the *Rat Peacock*. He flipped it in the air. "A rare coin of Dergath," he called. "I found it in the crypts at Gotha. 'Tis worth a king's ransom." He caught it in a quick palm then held it up.

The guard peered, squinting under the dim light. His hand reached for it. But Skirl flipped the coin in the air again before he could grab it and while the guard's eyes hungrily watched it somersault, he thrust his hand into the other pocket and flicked a yellowish dust in the man's eyes.

The guard staggered back, a shrill cry in his throat.

Skirl grabbed at the sword, snatched the weapon out of his grasp. He reversed the hilt and jammed the pommel in the guard's face. The metal smacked square on his brow. The guard gave a cursing cry.

Already blinded by salt dust, the man swung a wild fist and staggered forward. He flailed now, groping for Skirl's body.

Skirl jogged backward as fingers came clawing for his face.

The guard heard the scuff of Skirl's feet and roared, rage in his heart. Skirl was too close. He had no room to sidle away. The guard grappled him around his torso, clinging to him like a monkey.

Skirl tried to break free. He could not. He squirmed, desperately struggling to free his sword pinned under his armpit. His efforts were in vain. There came a grasping and heaving like a comical dance of monkeys and Skirl felt the air whoosh out of his lungs. His ribs started to crack. In a desperate panic, he wormed the sword up and jammed the tip under the man's chin. There came a gurgling as blood slopped onto Skirl's face.

The man's body relaxed. Skirl wrenched the blade free and arced it back for a strike. Fearing another assault, he swung with all his might and let blade bite deep into shoulder and neck striking bone. Brezel collapsed in a convulsive heap.

For long seconds, the apprentice stood there, his chest heaving. His blood pounded in his ears. He could hear his heart flap like a songbird chased by a hawk.

No sooner had he swallowed the lump in his throat when he felt his wits returning.

This was the first man he'd killed. A rusty gasp rustled past his lips. An empty feeling pressed in on him.

Being an apprentice, he was used to energetic movements of magical force and spirits. Now it was as if a disembodied entity, the life of Brezel, floated over his body and would demand a blood price at some later time when he desired it, calling from the grave.

He shook off the curse.

A nasty, dirty work.

Skirl stepped away. But not without a contemptuous look at Brezel's corpse. The bastard got what he deserved. That would teach him for dragging an innocent man to the gallows.

He grabbed the body by the heels and dragged it into a storage area off the hallway. He tore some fabric off the man's surcoat and hastily dabbed the blood off the stones, hoping the trail would not be noticed too soon.

With a fretful glance up the corridor, he scooped up the man's sword and hurried off down the hall.

Chapter 16

Vetra and Nog crept on stealthy feet under another archway and up the corridor that ran parallel to the inner court. On the rightmost wall, a giant sigil loomed, entwined with snakes heralding the emblem of the wizard circle—dragon and eagle.

Vetra motioned. "This is it."

A familiar figure limped out of the shadows bearing a blood-drenched weapon. He wore a blue robe and was gnashing his teeth. "What took you so long?"

Vetra glanced at the figure's weapon. "You been busy? We had some fancy footwork to do ourselves. Enduring Grindar's murderous swords and Taranis's intrigue. You could have warned us that auditions to the mage guard would be wrought with treachery and throat-cutting."

Skirl lifted his shoulders in a careless shrug. "I didn't want to discourage you."

"Pipe down," hissed Nog. "Where's this passage of yours anyways?"

"This way."

As one, the three crept on noiseless feet down the hallway. The mercenaries gripped their weapons with anticipation as they stole through the dimness. Vetra held the flickering torch; Nog dogged at his heels. Iron wall sconces barely lit the hallway's gloom. Vagrant drafts snuck in through small windows that opened high on the court side.

Skirl hissed a frustrated oath as he motioned to a figure up ahead. "Damn, there's a man guarding the door to Taranis's chamber. I expected no less. This hall loops around the back. It meets up on the other side behind the guard. I can distract him while you two creep around the back—"

Vetra pushed Skirl aside. Nog, grinning, followed on his heels.

Vetra strode up to the surprised guard.

"Hey, what are *you* doing here?" The sentry's blade moved to strike him down. "You can't come in here—"

Vetra blocked the steel that came flicking at his neck and twisted adder-quick to smash his elbow into the guard's face. Nog came sliding in and kneed the sentry in the groin and sent him to the flags.

Nog stepped over the inert body. He bunted the magician toward the door. "Inside."

Skirl dusted off his tattered robe and swallowed hard the knot in his throat. He pushed the door ever so slowly ajar. Vetra pulled the slack body inside. He cached it from sight behind a chest in the shadows.

The faintest murmur of voices reached their ears.

Across the dim-lit space a heavy door to an inner chamber was open a crack. From within, came the sound of a brief grunt of exertion. A man's. There followed a woman's soft moan then a husky sigh. Taranis. Now it was the man's turn to groan. Despondence? Fatigue? Duress? Vetra was at a loss.

Nog cast Vetra an impish grin. "Should we break up the party?"

Vetra shouldered him aside, warning him to silence. The two crept across the room to a shadowy iron portal where Skirl was beckoning them. Vetra had the crawling feeling that they were heading into a pit of vipers. But they'd come this far. To turn back now would be a waste…

He thrust the rogue thought from his mind.

As the sounds of pleasure escalated in cadence, the details of the room started to take shape. Rich tapestries on the walls. Dramatic, sweeping scenes—a demonic queen sitting on a throne, monsters on smaller thrones atop snow-peaked mountains, a prison below them with iron walls in the shape of a coffin. Skulls and swords intertwined. Dragons flying in the sky, breathing fire on the villages. Troll-haunted forests in the mix. A glut of cryptic runes and sigils interspersed throughout.

Before an iron-wrought mirror sat a heavy chair and scarred wooden desk bearing quill and stylus with ink and parchments crammed with crude symbology. A gold censer burned pungent incense, releasing a heady smoke, purplish in color. A pile of worn spellbooks lay stacked at the foot of the chair. Nothing Vetra could read, unless he was a rune-master or could decipher hundred-year old script. To the side sat an ancient iron-strapped chest, containing who knows what relics or magic talismans. The mirror looked as heavy as sin. Crude-carved gargoyles not dissimilar to Besemooth peered down from the top corners. What was a little reminder of Dal Sagoth in one's private space between friends?

Passing the desk, he caught a reflection of himself. One he did not like. A stalker, grim and sheeted in mail, tense as a tiger, with scowling face, a dark wanderer wondering what he was doing in a sluttish sorceress's den, one inch away from getting his throat slit. He wiped his lip and the crude thought away.

Nog scratched at his stubbled chin, nudged the mercenary's elbow. "This is getting tricky, Vetra. Even if we get this jewel, how are we ever going to get out of here?"

Vetra hissed back at him, "We'll figure it out, Nog, when the time comes."

"Not so loud." Skirl pressed finger to lips.

The heavy candelabra that dripped wax onto the desk's wood lit the space with a dim eerie glow, more of which came beyond the cracks of the open door twenty feet away, and from where more heated sex sounds drifted. Now a sexual battle. The man appeared to be losing. Vetra licked his lips. "Quick mage! Show us this passage," he hissed.

Skirl gave a grim-lipped nod, drew back the bolt, grimacing as it scraped.

With no more noise than weasels, the three slipped into the darkness and shut the door.

CHRIS TURNER

Chapter 17

The three plunderers navigated the stone stairwell on wary feet. Skirl led, Vetra stalked behind, his torch spitting from time to time. Nog took up the rear, a strained grimace on his face. The narrow way seemed to plunge down deep into the earth, perhaps to its very core. At times Nog nudged into Vetra, his boots seeming to slip on loose stone, and only reaching out a hand at the last minute to stop his weight from pitching into Vetra's.

"Watch it, fool!" Vetra growled. "Sending me face first to my doom isn't going to help us, is it?"

"Relax. You're wound too tight." Nog wet his lips. "Not used to all this stale air and stench. What is it?"

"Who knows? Dead rat? Stagnant pool? What does it matter?"

Vetra peered down at the steep, crumbling steps that dropped ever deeper into thick gloom. His unease grew. "What else is down here, Skirl?" he demanded.

"Nothing, mercenary, just gloom and must...maybe the odd spider."

"Spiders? You said nothing about spiders!" Vetra gripped the magician's shoulder with fingers like claws. He had had a frightening experience when he was a boy, trapped in his father's cellar full of webs and wolf spiders.

"Must I describe every creepy crawly? Beetles, mice, rats, bats. Goblins maybe?"

"You didn't tell us about spiders before you got us into this caper."

"Why should I?"

"How big are these spiders?" Vetra demanded.

Skirl drew fingers about three inches apart. "Maybe a bit bigger than normal." He had underestimated the size by several inches. "Nothing we can't handle."

Vetra rubbed his jaw. His eyes darted to and fro at the walls of dank limestone as if expecting one to leap out. Sweat glistened on his brow.

Nog grinned, amused to see some chinks in Vetra's armor. He clapped his friend on the back. "Come on, boy, toughen it up. What we can't see, can't hurt us, can it?"

Vetra shook off Nog's hand. "How much longer, mage?" he griped at Skirl.

"Just down here. Look." The stairs had come to an abrupt end. At right angles to the stair ran a narrow passageway that cut crudely into the damp bedrock. Skirl ushered them down the rightmost branch which at first only allowed a man to walk single file but soon opened up to two then three abreast. He led them on unfailing feet for a fair distance where the smell of animal hide only worsened.

He slowed, a frown growing on his face. "Not far now," he mused. "Or is it?" He halted, head cocked, foot in midair like a hesitant hound.

Vetra cast the mage an impatient stare. "Look, it's either here or it isn't. You leading us on a wild goose chase?"

"Dergath's hexes, Vetra! Everything seems so different in this witchlike darkness."

Nog balled his fist and got Skirl stumbling forward quick enough. "Move it!"

"Wait. I remember!" Skirl hissed. "This block of fallen stone…it has an odd shape to it. The smell has changed too."

"What, from hideous to unbearable?" Nog said.

"Over here," Skirl motioned. "Past the stone grate, then on to the leaning gargoyle. I remember the way. I cached the Eros Flame in its mouth."

The mage plunged on with deft steps, his boots tramping on the flaked flagstones. The two mercenaries followed behind with dubious strides.

It was in those halting steps that their destinies would change forever.

For they came to what looked like a crosshatched stone barrier to the right, through whose six-inch gaps admitted glimpses into a cavernous space beyond.

Vetra paused. He frowned. There appeared to be movement in that black gap beyond. His lips parted while Nog snatched at Vetra's torch to get a better glimpse.

"What the—?" He peered between the stone blocks that formed a kind of crude but ancient barrier.

A massive reptilian shape sat crouched on all fours in the thick darkness. A thing with talon-like claws and scaly hide glistening like plate-like armor. The tail was eight feet long if it was an inch and snaked along the molder like a twisted trunk; the hooked claws scraped into the stone itself. A gigantic eye opened, large as a gong, and a pale saucer-like light gleamed in the torch's reflection.

Nog pushed his nose in closer, spellbound.

"Don't—" Skirl reached.

There came a skin-crawling rustle—of leathery wings then the ratchety movement of scaly flesh as a violent mass bounded out of the blackness. The great jaws snapped open and a torrent of fire came belching through the gap, whistling past Nog's face. The force sent the mercenary flying backward on his heels. He lay prostrate on the dank stone for some time, slapping at his singed hair. He cast off his helm, tamping at the once dark fringes that had caught fire. The tips of his fingers still tingled from where they'd touched his helm that had the devil's heat to it.

"Loins of Dergath's whores!"

Vetra hissed, bared his blade. He crouched, ready to spring at the thing should it burst through the wall. But he ducked to the side instead behind the protection of the flanking stone. He peered sideways at the grate, breath held.

"What other stygian horrors aren't you telling us about, mage?" he hissed. "Do the wizards hold dragons in these catacombs?"

"I—didn't—I d-don't—" Never did Skirl imagine such a creature existed down here.

"One of these wizards' pets, no doubt," Vetra spat.

"He's young, no more than a lizardling—" Skirl stammered "—if anyone can call a beast that lives a thousand years 'young'."

"I don't care how young he is," said Vetra. "Let's get to this gargoyle of yours…and try not to get crisp-fried in the meantime."

Nog picked up his smoking helm. He rubbed at his scalded ear.

Skirl gestured to his own ear or lack of one. "Looks like we're a pair now, eh Nog?" he quipped, trying to dull the stress with some humor.

"Good joke, mage. Now button up, unless you'd like some white teeth knocked out."

Skirl stared at the middlemost stone and crouched for a better look at the grate. A star-shaped runestone with four parts like some quasi diamond, glinted with an eerie light.

"I don't recall this rune on my last tour here," he mused. "Funny how things get muddled."

Recovering his wits, Nog reached out a hand, feeling he was protected by the protective stone, and made a funny face at the dragon that peered through the gap.

There came a roar and another gust of fiery breath that nearly scorched Nog's skin. The winged dragon, or whatever it was, moved fast as a greased eel and smashed its crusty head against the grate, threatening to bring down the very rock around them. The stone barely held.

Dust and rubble fell from above. Vetra arched arms to shield his head. The creature reared back, charged again, rocking the very foundation of the bedrock.

He and Nog wheeled away, grabbing Skirl at the waist and scrambled past the barrier and up the passage. The stone blocks still held but had shifted a few inches.

"Dergath's bane, we've roused a hellspawn!" Nog cried.

"Move!" Vetra bawled. He shoved Skirl forward up the passageway while the beast turned to thwack its tail now against the grate in regular rhythms.

"Find this jewel, mage!" Vetra cried.

Skirl scuttled ahead, nodding as if his head would fall off. He stumbled on tender feet while the flickering torch sent monstrous shadows leaping across the walls, showing ghostly pillars, stelae with carven figures and glyphs, slanted slabs and crumbled masonry.

Vetra gave a colorful curse.

They scrambled down a set of six broad, crumbling stairs into a vast forum of ancient columns. Around them reared fountains, altars and shrines amid sunken walkways. The only sound was their boots crunching on rubble with the echo of the dragon's freakish malice dwindling behind them. The ceiling soared above, lost in a cloud of darkness in what seemed the vague curve of a dome.

A broken hall of statues and pillars, Vetra mused, a temple or forum from ages past. The grim, staring faces of statues and their uplifted arms symbolized pagan rule, ritual, power, torture and enduring darkness.

Skirl drew them to a halt in order to recoup their bearings.

A crypt-like silence fell over the ancient ruins but for the distant thud of the dragon entombed in its stone prison. Indeed, a feeling of death hung over this eerie place like an ancient curse.

Vetra peeled back his lips in a strained grimace while Nog swallowed hard. "I hope this gargoyle thing of yours is nearby," he said.

Skirl pointed a shaky finger into the murks ahead. "It's this way."

CHRIS TURNER

Chapter 18

On shaky feet the three threaded their way across an expanse of rubble and broken stones fallen from the ceiling or flaked off the statues.

They stepped over two toppled columns crisscrossed in an eerie configuration at the entrance of what might have been a ruined courtyard. At once Vetra leapt back as the scuttle of a black shape, the size of a small rat but could have been a spider, nearly had him jumping out of his skin. "Dergath's shades, mage! Could you have picked a less perilous place for your jewel?"

Skirl made no comment.

When Vetra thought the mage was utterly lost and leading them in circles, he stopped short and gloated with triumph. "There! As I told you."

Vetra saw a disturbing bat-like statue shrouded in the gloom. Frozen in some frightening stony repose between crumbling slabs of rock that may have been altars, it loomed with a face carved of an obsidian leer. One of the bat-like ears was missing. The rest of the face was worn, hideous: a snub nose, toothy maw and outstretched claw-like digits.

Skirl crouched and withdrew a chestnut-sized shape from the gargoyle's mouth. An improbably large sapphire. At first it gleamed dully, but when Vetra lifted his torch, he saw that it radiated an unnatural lambent glow.

"Look how the flame swirls within!" Skirl hissed to himself.

Vetra saw it change from deep crimson to ultramarine then back again. It suddenly dawned on him the improbability of faking such a jewel with its play of light.

"I hired a master gemsmith to create a replica of the original jewel," Skirl explained. "To mimic its living fire! I paid the woman handsomely for it. By clever design she carved the flicker of light to appear as a moving flame. When anyone peers from a different angle, the stone changes color. Look! Reflection and refraction. It's intricate. Enough to fool the witch."

"Very interesting," Vetra mused. "Time's wasting. We need to get back past that dragon."

Nog muscled his way in. He snatched at the jewel. "Here, let me see it."

Skirl pulled the gem away in one jealous motion. "By no means! I am the keeper of the Eros stone. This is an object of power, unfit for layman's hands." He shoved it deep in his pocket.

Nog's face lit with a hostile grin. He advanced with menace.

"Cool your heels, Nog," said Vetra, laying a hand on his shoulder. "We've got what we came here for. Let's not squabble. We've got to get away from this loathsome place—"

A faint clink echoed from behind them. The jingle of armor, a slivering scrape of a sword being unsheathed.

"Dergath's wrath!" Nog hissed. "Can they have stumbled on us so soon?"

"Maybe," Skirl murmured. "With all the ruckus we stirred up with that youngling."

"No use going back that way," Vetra grunted. "Quickly! Let's push on. We can hide somewhere, ride out this storm then sneak back with the gem."

There didn't seem to be any other plan. Quick as rats they hurried deeper into the gloom. Vetra cursed the torchlight that would give them away if the guards saw it.

They mounted another set of broad steps and came out of the eerie ruins only to scramble deeper into more of the same. Vetra liked this turn of events little. Things were getting out of control. More molder, more crumble. Dergath! More grim looking statues and now an even more stagnant waft lingering in the air.

They hurried along a sunken pathway and mounted another set of steps.

The sound of bootfall echoed louder behind them. Vetra

heard the murmur of men's voices somewhere back the way they'd come. His lips formed in an oath. "Douse the flame."

"We can't!" Nog rasped. "How are we to find our way back?"

"Better that we're not seen, Nog. Douse it."

Nog winced. He went to swat out the flame, but then shook his head vigorously. "No, Vetra. We do it the traditional way. We fight! What are we, pansy asses?"

Vetra gave a curt nod. "You're right, Nog. Let's head deeper into these ruins and find some higher ground. The torch we can use as a decoy."

Somewhere ahead of them, a dull plink sounded, like the drip of cool water cascading into a pool.

"What's that?" Nog rasped.

Vetra perked his ears. He moved ahead. He shone the light. His eyes discerned a rectangular pool of black water, about 50 feet long by 15 wide. A foot-high stone curbing framed its perimeter. They'd come to its long-side edge and, it seemed, the end of the cavern.

So, a dead end. A dank smell wafted from the waters. Across the pool, a barely-discernible bat-like statue as macabre as the one Taranis had cached in her summery garden, perched on a time-eaten pedestal. The effigy was reached by a ramp of broad, ancient steps. This statue was thrice Besemooth's height. The ruins continued across the water, but the sight prickled Vetra's scalp. What new chilling surprise would they discover in this eerie, creepy place?

"Just our luck," Vetra grunted. "A pool of sorts. A reservoir maybe? You've seen this before, Skirl?"

Skirl shook his head. "I remember a plink of water."

Nog reached down to slosh his hand in the water. "Care for a drink?"

"Not just now." Skirl lifted a hand. "Let's move on. This place is evil."

"I think we've come to the end of the line, Skirl," said Vetra.

Skirl's brow furrowed. He crouched to trace a finger along the crumbling ledge. "A cistern is my guess. Old beyond belief. See the cracks on the stone?" He pushed his nose closer. "The glyphs of winged creatures, faintly engraved. Look, mythical sea beasts too. My guess, Marizon the Second's reign when the great dragons flew—"

"Enough," Vetra snapped. "It does little good citing history—"

"Sh! Voices."

The clop of boots came louder.

Vetra stifled a curse. He knelt, poked his sword down in the inky black water. It did not touch bottom. Even when he pushed as far up to his shoulder.

He withdrew his blade and muttered sullenly. No chance to swim across this pond with their heavy gear.

He motioned them back behind the pillars that fronted the curbing.

Their pursuers had sighted them. Many of them. Shouts drifted across the gloomy rubble. Then the clap of boots came on stone and the flickering dance of torchlight on the walls and the time-eaten masonry.

Vetra counted eight figures, all with swords and maces drawn, their teeth glinting in the uneven torchlight. A third of the Dormoth garrison, he guessed.

Eight in hauberks and helms came leaping and snarling out of a near-distant circle of crumbling columns.

Vetra bared his sword. They were all doomed unless they could take down these new foes. But how, trapped at the edge of this dark water?

Vetra leaned the torch up against a broken column and motioned Nog and Skirl to take cover. They spread out behind the broken columns. Skirl and Vetra flattened themselves behind ones about six feet apart; Nog crouched at the base of a column whose top half had been smashed off. Vetra clutched his hilt. In his mind's eye, he mentally counted the moments when he would leap out, uncoil his thews and rain bloody ruin on these vermin.

A familiar voice echoed out of the darkness. *Grindar.* "They're here. I can smell them. Spread out."

As the first helmed guard came within six feet of Vetra's hiding place, he lunged and chopped down on the man's helm. There came a grunt and clang of steel. His morion was dented but the wearer only dazed. Vetra swung his sword again and the edge ripped through the man's throat.

The man fell to his knees, gurgling, clutching at his neck.

He ran to the torch and thrust it in the mage's hand. "Quick! Guard the jewel! Stay behind us! If we fall, run!"

"You traitorous bastards!" Grindar spat.

He lifted his blade and Vetra parried as another man came sprinting in at him. Nog was five feet away, twin blades scissoring, crouched in his Thrakian war crouch.

The clash of steel rang loud in the dimness and sent strident echoes arcing about the once silent hall. Dusky echoes disturbed the spirits of this desolate place. Spirits better left in slumber. Vetra moved back as another attacker came slashing in at him to replace the dead man.

To his side the water spread like a dark mantle of clouded glass. Uttering a coarse oath, he sped across the curbing even as it crumbled under his feet. It was only twelve inches above the forum's floor, yet a perilous path to take. From the corner of his eye he caught a glimpse of Skirl darting away from a man twice his size with plumed morion. How this mission had gone sour!

He turned and slashed at the stalker behind him, then ran on ahead. The guard gave pursuit, others behind him, seeing that Vetra had nowhere to go. Twenty feet down the curbing loomed a cold dank wall. Vetra turned with a snarl and bared his sword at his attacker.

The man lunged. His foot gave way as part of the crumbling

shelf disintegrated. Teetering on his heels, his arms pinwheeled, and Vetra helped him along with a sudden kick. The man fell into the water with a cry thick in his throat, vanishing beneath the glassy surface, pulled down by the weight of his helm and mail.

There came a glooping from below. A viscous surge of lighter-colored liquid?

Blood?

Ripples broke the surface and with it a broader stench. Not what Vetra would expect from a single man plunging to his doom into stagnant waters of indeterminate depth.

From the ripples came a writhe of movement. Vetra's mouth sagged. A dark mass lifted…an octopus-like head. Except it wasn't an octopus—it had a frog-like face with salamander snout and mottled skin that might have been boils. Vetra did not want to stay and examine the fine details. A single eye burned from the wrack of a face, glaring like an evil moon at him.

Dergath. He leaped off the ledge, almost staggering to his own doom into a thicket of steel.

He parried blades as three mage guard hacked and slashed and were hot on his tail. They would have slain him then and there had not a strange, whistling tentacle flickered out from behind him. It whipped across his line of sight, curled about the snarling, cursing man in front of him. The obscene thing latched onto the man's ankle and pulled him down on his back. He slid across the molder like a possessed man as the tentacle wheeled him toward the waiting frog-like monster perched on the curbing. The man cried out, lashing at the tentacle, severing it nearly in half. Before he could lift himself, another coil whipped about his waist and lifted him high off the ground. It pulled him toward the waiting monster and the water.

A horrid gob-slobbery maw snapped open. The frog-like head reared and while the man dangled like a fish on a hook, its fanged teeth clipped off the man's leg, as would a boy in cruelty tear off a fly's wings. There came a horrid screech as an arm was snipped off next, gobbled whole.

The guards reeled back in horror.

"Get back!" Grindar bellowed.

Time seemed to slow. In the darkness of a dead hall, fangs of nightmare sank into flesh and Vetra's ordered world turned into one of nightmarish fantasy.

In a moment of inattention, Grindar's blade chopped down at his helm. Vetra reeled and twisted about as blackness threatened to engulf him. He shook off the daze of death, caught Grindar's next blow on his upheld blade. He did not relish fighting amid such horror and against such a foe as Grindar. Only too fresh in his memory was the opponent who had bested him in swordplay in Taranis's eerie garden.

"Die, thief!" Grindar cried.

Skirl stepped forth. "No!" he brayed. "It is you who will die." He brandished his jewel like a sinister beacon.

Grindar shrank back in the wake of the light that stung his eyes.

"Look me in the eye, you rogue! Behold your doom. Bow to your master!"

Grindar paused in the shadow of wrath before them. For a brief instant logic slid sideways. The magic held sway and the men of Grindar's company could lift no steel against the tentacles that whipped forward like snakes. In its sphere, Vetra himself felt his limbs heavy as if fettered.

Skirl stood sorcerer-like in the darkness. The Eros jewel lay lifted in his claw-like grip, a haunted look on his face. His ferret eyes gleamed; his limbs shook and he waved the pulsing gem like a fiend himself.

The mage seemed oddly oblivious to the monster lurking in the water not twelve yards away and the flicking tentacles that could seek his neck any moment, as if they were but small intrusions on his world. This bore testament to how deep and all-encompassing the power of the jewel was, when a man could not see danger when it treaded on his shadow.

"My fear lost me the jewel days ago!" he raved. "Now I will rive you limb from limb!"

A tentacle-arm whipped through the air and curled around his waist. The member whipped the mage three feet off the ground and sent the jewel slipping from his hand to land at Vetra's feet.

The spell was broken. Two of Grindar's men hacked at Vetra. Others came at him tooth and nail.

Nog surged forward, a savage cry on his lips. His twin blades sang melodies, cleaving flesh, chopping the waving tentacle in two before it could drag Skirl to his doom. The magician fell to the moldering stone, clawing, squirming, drenched in gore. From the severed member oozed a black, viscous fluid. Skirl skidded back, his feet kicking convulsively at the fetid loops that still quested his limbs. They were slackened now, but pulsed and jerked about mindlessly.

On the tentacle's tip piked a four fingered claw—of bone, horn or flesh, who knew—was this used for some crude form of navigation underwater or afoot, in some improbable way?

The monster's frog-like head reared up and leaned over the curbing, with hungry glassy orb eyeing easy pickings. The creature seemed oblivious to a few maimed tentacles. Black water dripped from its grotesque snout. The only saving grace was it appeared unable to venture beyond the well of its captivity. But the reach of its cursed tentacles was long.

Vetra thrust steel into an exposed leg of an attacker, prompting a scream. He blocked a strike, then another. In a moment of indecision, he crouched to snatch up the jewel.

An impulsive move.

The upturned jewel gleamed brightly in his eyes. It stymied his brain for a brief second. He felt a languid, dizzying rapture in his skull. No oversized toy marble was this, but some instrument of power. His fingers clasped its egg-like smoothness. It burned there with an unnatural warmth. Like Skirl, he fought its jealous grip, and he plunged it in his pocket.

"Vetra, behind you!" Nog cried.

He whirled in time to twist out of the way. A mace, swung by a big-boned, heavy-footed guard, angled for his neck.

Vetra jerked back. The spiked ball skidded hairs' breaths from his face and smashed against his helm just above the left ear. For a moment he saw stars, then his vision clouded and the world became a sea of dead calm.

Chapter 19

Nog and Skirl staggered off on a path parallel to the edge of the cistern, at right angles to the melee, trying to get as far away from the horror as possible. Behind them came the din of men's cries, the thwack of steel on flesh. All faded. Now only the muted slap of tentacles on stone as Grindar and his men fought to keep the frog monster at bay.

Ahead a wall of damp stone reared before them. But on the rock face of the giant cavern was etched a darker blot: a square-cut passage.

Down this murky tunnel they scrambled, plunging into shadowy mystery. Skirl led the way, his torch in hand. Nog lagged behind, watching their backs, making sure that no one followed them.

After several twists and turns they slumped down in exhaustion where the tunnel forked into two equally dark passages. Skirl's torchlight flickered. It cast uneasy shadows across the walls, but the fugitives could not be seen by anyone from the main tunnel entrance.

Nog stared about, not without some unease. The two black tunnels burrowed deeper into the rock at a steady downward grade. The walls looked hewn by giant hammers. Stranger, deeper scoriations marked the bare rock, as if hewn by giant claws.

Nog licked his lips. A sprawl of bones lay scattered at their feet: human, animal? He was past caring. They were parched and desiccated and old beyond belief.

He kicked at a broken femur and stared at the apprentice and heaved a heavy sigh. His last image of Vetra was his slack body being hauled away by hostile hands and a wall of guards threatening to leap after them if they pursued. The jewel was lost. There had been nothing he or Skirl could have done. They too would have been caught and dragged back to the sorceress Taranis.

Skirl muttered curses at the loss of the Eros Flame. "I had it in my hands, Nog!" A fresh claw mark lay imprinted across his left cheek where the frog-monster had lashed out with the end of its tentacle. "Then *poof*, a swamp thing comes out of nowhere and clips it off me."

"You're lucky not to be in its belly," Nog grunted. "What were you thinking back there, just standing gawking like a loon? How many times must Vetra and I save your miserable hide, mage?"

A hoarse murmur caught in Skirl's throat. "You don't have to keep mentioning it. But yes, I should be more careful, and be grateful. I owe you two my life."

"You owe us more than that," Nog said, teeth clenched. "Vetra's still back there! Because of that stinking jewel, he's as good as dead." His fists bunched, tightened on his sword.

"We've got our lives, Nog. That's the good side. I say we lay low for a bit and—"

"Let me think!" He waved off the mage's babble. Too many gaps in this story. He was addled and frustrated. He flashed another apprehensive look up the tunnel. "How can creatures live down here so deep sealed off from light and air?"

Skirl lifted his palms. "Who knows, Nog? How deep did the builders delve? How deep did their underwater channels run to connect to the cistern? That well is hundreds of years old. Did they know what they were digging into?"

"What about the dragon?" Nog rumbled. "What does it eat? How did it get here?"

Skirl spread his palms. "I have no answer for that. Nor the origin of these cursed ruins."

"What of Taranis?"

"What of her?" Skirl spat. "She's a witch, what more do you want?"

"How'd she get so powerful?"

"She comes from a long line of powerful mages, is all I

know. And wealth. From Smrin in Lower Umbria. More than her cousin, Belgra, she had skill in thaumaturgy, taught her by her master, the Warlock of Tharax." The apprentice gritted his teeth. "If I had the jewel, I'd rive her limb from—"

"You'd do no such thing...shekels to peanuts you'd whimper like a cur and get your other ear chopped off too."

"You don't know the half of—"

"Fat lot of good that jewel did you back there!"

Skirl turned on Nog angrily. "You'd sell the Eros Flame for a whore's pleasure when we could have the power to—" Skirl bit his tongue, realizing what he'd just said.

Nog snarled and lifted him by the throat and slammed him up against the damp wall. "No more lies, you miserable trickster. You didn't know about the dragon, you didn't know about the water monster. What else haven't you told us?"

"You're threatening to crush my neck," Skirl croaked.

"Good. Now shut up and listen. I'm not going to sit back and let Vetra die at the hands of those apes and that ghoul-witch, Taranis. We have to get him out of their clutches then make like bunnies out of here. First, we have to make sure we don't run into more dragons or serpent monsters."

"A tall ticket, mercenary. We're holed up in a dark cave with nothing but a sword. Better we save our own hides," he said hoarsely.

Nog grunted and lifted Skirl higher. "There may be other exits or hidden escape tunnels out of this warren. Where?"

"I—I just discovered this place for the first time a few days ago," he gasped, "to h-hide the amulet in the gargoyle's mouth."

Nog shook his head in hopeless frustration. He clutched the mage's neck tighter. "You're not saying the right things, mage! Give me something, anything at all! Think harder!"

"I can't. It's hard to think—" he croaked "—when someone's crushing your Adam's Apple."

Nog relaxed his grip. "Better?"

"Not much," Skirl gurgled.

"You'll be the first to die, mage, if you don't tell me the truth."

"We'll get your friend Vetra," he gasped. "Just let me down! They're probably dragging him back up to Taranis's chambers."

"No kidding." Nog let the mage fall to the ground where he slumped in a heap, massaging his throat. The mercenary paced back and forth, murderous hands clenched behind his back.

He picked up the fallen torch and flashed it in Skirl's face. "Take this." He hauled Skirl to his feet and thrust the torch in his hand. "Lead the way, pretty boy. If you steer us into any traps, you'll be the first to die." He bunted the apprentice back up the passage where the lingering darkness only waxed deeper. "Part of me thinks you'd be happy to see me gone. No tears either if Vetra got his throat cut."

Skirl stumbled on marionette feet, refusing to answer the unasked question. Several empty, muddled curses hung on his lips.

They mounted the set of broad steps they'd passed earlier then came at last to the passageway that housed the dragon.

Nog saw four figures moving quickly down the darkened passageway, less terrified now that the dragon had quieted down. They were all that remained of Grindar's guards: two muscling Vetra's loose bulk along the passageway, gripping heels and shoulders, another taking up the rear while Grindar led with a torch.

Nog gripped his blade and made motions to press on, but Skirl held him back. He made a cryptic signal across his neck indicating to hold off and wait.

From behind the stone grate came a rattling gurgle ending in a snuffling roar. The dragon.

Nog heard one of the guards mutter, "That's a mighty big rat back there."

Grindar motioned his sword. "No rats, soldier. Move along.

There are devils in these murks you'd rather not know about."

The guard lagged. He uttered a nervous laugh. Grindar sheathed his sword and smacked the man a heavy wallop with a massive hand. "You heard me, fool! Move out!"

The three shuffled off past the grate. The stench of unwashed dragon was fiercer than ever. The guards trod down the crumbling way, muttering and grumbling.

Nog and Skirl followed at a more leisurely pace. They lagged behind on weasel feet as the company made their way to the steep stair that angled up into the gloom back to Taranis's chambers. Nog cocked an ear, listening for danger. Only the echoey tramp of men's bootfall, their grunts and heaves as they bore their heavy load.

Now there was only one left. Nog forced a grin and nudged Skirl forward. A single sentry had been left to guard the crooked stairs. The man bore a single torch. He whipped back his sword in a trembling hand when he saw Nog approaching out of the gloom like a wandering vagrant with steel in his hands.

"Back, I say!" the man cried.

Nog blinked and laughed. He advanced with slow, easy steps, a funny, cattish grin carved on his grime-streaked face. "Nice day for a head-stomping, isn't it, mate?"

CHRIS TURNER

Chapter 20

Vetra came to. His head throbbed to a splitting headache and a thick sour taste welled in his mouth. His left shoulder ached to the pulse of ten drums. A dozen bruises plagued the rest of his body.

A soft but familiar glow lit his surroundings: of dim-lit candelabra that rose above him. To his side, the gothic mirror on the wall and the stack of spellbooks toppled beside him, wafting a faint, musty scent. Hands gripped his wrists and ankles, pinching into flesh; crude, unsmiling men whose breath smelled of ale.

He groaned as the memory of past events flooded back to him.

"Sick of lugging this brute," snorted a familiar voice.

"Leave him here." One of the two red-coated guards let Vetra's bulk fall unceremoniously to the floor.

"Here he is, Lady," Grindar said, "as you wished."

Taranis's cat-like form stood over him, her legs braced, arms folded on her chest. "So...we have a traitor and a spy in our midst. Where's his peer, the one with the ox-like face?"

Grindar frowned but did not answer.

Vetra rubbed the back of his neck. He shifted to a crouching position. His helm was dented. Two sword tips immediately flicked down at his throat. "Stay where you are, scum."

Vetra grimaced, but complied, still groggy.

"He was clutching this," Grindar growled. He held in his open palm the sapphire they'd plucked from the gargoyle. The real Eros Flame emitted a sullen radiance.

Taranis's eyes blazed. Her trembling hand snatched at it and her flawless face pinched with madness and fury.

"A thief! You stole the stone and tried to replace it with this fake!" She ripped the bauble from her throat. "How you got it off my neck and its leather cord, I can never guess. Maybe you are a magician like me. Yet I detect no magic about you."

Vetra remained stone-faced. Anything he said would incriminate him. Nog and Skirl must have either been slain by Grindar's men, or gotten pulled down by the frog monster. Slim chance they had somehow escaped into the warrens of the ruins below.

"I don't know how you got in here or what you and that other impostor's game is, but when I find out, you will all roast."

"There's nothing to tell, Lady," said Vetra in his most convincing voice, struck with a sudden ploy. "One of the guards planted the gem on me, perhaps even your star, Grindar. Look for your traitor among your own conspirators. You said yourself, your own organization required more security."

For a moment Taranis's eyes flashed with spite. Then she mumbled a curse and stared hard at Grindar. "That may be the case, but you are still up to no good here, creeping around the crypts."

Steel flashed in men's hands and Grindar started toward Vetra.

"Hold, Grindar!" Taranis stormed. "I'd have the truth, before anyone's slain!"

Grindar halted in midstep. The man was seething to the bone, a lurid oath on his tongue. "This man is a liar, Lady! I'll kill him myself! I knew on first sight of Macdem trussed at his post atop the West Tower that he and his sidekick from Thrakia were blackguards. I came scouring the compound for them. It took every ounce of my resolve not to slit this weasel's throat when we caught him below. But I heeded your instructions and brought him as he is to you."

"Very wise and good that you did, Grindar, else you would be the one with his throat slit. Others are down there. His treacherous friend is missing. I want to know where they are. I want to know how he got this in his paws—" she shook the gem. "But first, how did his ox-eyed friend escape?"

"My lady," Grindar said delicately, "some horror came up

from the water. We don't know what it was, some mutant from an elder time."

Taranis's face registered incomprehension. "What do you mean?"

"From the filthy stagnant pool at the edge of the ruins of Old Sagoth. 'Twas on us before we could apprehend the others."

"Fools! You woke the guardian?"

"We...I mean—this rogue, he was responsible!" Grindar shafted an angry finger at Vetra.

"How can he be responsible?"

"Gisil, one of the men he was fighting—the rogue kicked him into the pool and Gisil never resurfaced."

"What? Where are the rest of you?"

Grindar licked his lips. "We are all who are left."

"You're an incompetent ninny and fool!" Her gaze shifted sideways upon Vetra, a new awareness dawning in her. "And you—a meddler, almost as bad as that Skirl skulker I banished from Dormoth."

"Speaking of which, Lady—we saw the apprentice down there. How he got his clutches on the jewel I could never—"

"Skirl? Down there in the crypts?" She gave an incredulous bellow of hate.

Grindar nodded. He bit his lips, as if afraid of saying more.

"Now it begins to make more sense," she cried. "Find them! On the double!"

"But Lady, the mercenary, he will—"

"He will cause me no trouble." She held forth the jewel. "With this gem, no man or creature can stand before me. Go now! Find me these infidels, Grindar. Before I have Dal Sagoth blast your brain to mush."

She clapped her hands and from her palms came a burst of sinister energy: a blue ball which came vaulting at their feet, sending blue fumes up which blinded their eyes and stung their noses.

They coughed, swatting at the vapor while Grindar kicked his two men toward the iron portal.

Grindar followed after them.

No sooner had the three disappeared beyond the black gap when two new figures strode into Taranis's chambers, swatting at the smoke themselves. Each man bore sleepy, slitted eyes, mussed-up hair, and scowls on their faces.

Voydred halted and hissed, "What is all this infernal din and booming coming from below?" His loose black cowl draped around a cadaverous face, robe swishing about his ankles. "Hades, but the foundation of the Hall of Mages must crumble asunder!"

Lugubrious, square-shouldered Keren supported his peer's complaint and voiced a querulous oath, clearly peeved at being woken from his slumber.

Voydred, hawk-nosed and gangly, stared menacingly at Vetra, as if wondering, and guessing correctly, what the rogue was doing here in Taranis's private chambers.

"Calm your fears, Voydred. 'Tis nothing. A few thaumaturgical glitches. Nothing more. Everything is under control."

"What do you mean, 'thaumaturgical glitches'? Why are your grim men skulking down into the forbidden passage?" He lifted a bony hand. "I warn you, Taranis. I've heard it is a secret passage leading to the crypts below the stronghold, where you keep secret things. You have kept it long out of the topic of conversation at the Mage's conclave."

Vetra spoke in a harsh and gravely rasp. "Lord, if it pleases you, it is a quagmire of ruins and statues down there. Some beast is entombed, quite likely a dragon. The thudding you heard was its horned head and tail banging against the stone."

The color ebbed from Voydred's face. "A dragon, you say?" His beady eyes glinted in disbelief.

"There is nothing down there, Voydred," assured Taranis.

"Only must and murks. Mice and stenches. This man is a weaver of fables. He is ripe for punishment. I fear we have been struck by an earthquake. A savage one. I tried to counter it with my magic, but failed. It has luckily passed."

"Earthquake?" he laughed. "That is the most ridiculous thing I've ever heard." He nudged his companion in the ribs. "Come on, Keren! Let us see this 'dragon' for ourselves." He strode past the magic mirror toward the portal. His hand reached for the iron grip.

Taranis held forth the jewel in a cupped palm. "Halt!" The ruby light shone forth: a vivid gleam that reflected in both sets of eyes.

Keren sneered. "Must you keep wasting our time with that silly bauble of yours, Taranis? It is tiresome. It has no power to—"

But suddenly his jaw hung slack and his eyes stared glassily. Voydred's hand likewise slumped at his side, as if he had been rendered passive by its sinister shine. Robbed of his senses and wits as if they had been switched off.

Taranis's ruby lips twisted in a ruthless grin. "You two will go to your workplaces and await further instructions. Please, carry on as before. Nothing is untoward. All is under control. There is no disturbance. Dormoth is safe, and secure." She said the words in a wheedling tone, as if toying with a pair of pet cats.

Keren twitched at his rust-colored beard as if fighting a powerful spell. His face relaxed. Then he and Voydred both nodded as one.

Vetra stared aghast, lips curling in disgust. These two fops were the pride and might of Dormoth? Really? The two had basked in the magical essence and now both gazed at her spellbound, in almost boyish adulation. Taranis's luscious curves and magnetic presence held an ultimate mesmeric clutch over them.

Like automatons, they shambled on duck feet to the door

and disappeared, closing the door softly behind them.

Chapter 21

Taranis cast Vetra a most sulfurous glare which gradually, as the moments passed, gave way to a look of grudging admiration. She cooed, a sinister and insolent sound. "As for you..."

She dimmed the candles and set another incense stick burning in the censer. She closed, but did not bolt the heavy, corroded portal from which dank odors crept, leaving the two alone in the quasi gloom.

"Let us move to more comfortable quarters," she suggested. She led him by the hand unresisting to the open door of her inner chamber where Vetra caught a glimpse of a low altar and candelabrum by a satin-sheeted bed. He did not like the look of the obtrusive effigy jutting out from the wall. A half elk, half bat monstrosity overlooking the bed. He gestured to the grotesque figure with glaring eyes and a bestial snout. "Should I make a guess as to what that is?"

"That is Yeasaba," she intoned. "Dal Sagoth in different form. He is the great god who watches over me and comforts me, in times of trouble."

A saturnine smirk played over Vetra's lips. "Are you in the habit of keeping quaint bibelots as this in your bedchambers, or do you like to stare up at freaks in the heat of passion?"

Her lips quirked, but otherwise she made no reply.

"Well, are we to play patty cake here in this pretty room? You seem to be in the habit of inviting strange men into your bedchamber."

She gave a gruff laugh. "Is it your wish, mercenary, or just a nervous witticism? Perhaps something more exotic's on your mind, something in which your trained sensibilities forbid you to indulge?"

Vetra narrowed his eyes. He in turn offered no reply. The instinct of the Tolizian warrior told him to ignore her wiles. Not a tavern wench she. Yet his blood burned at the sight of her. She was like a hell cat pulsing with sexual mystery. He was bound like all the men before him by the lure of the seductive female. What was worse, he was not used to sultry, seductive, bewitching women.

"Not tonight, I have a headache," he muttered. "Your bully boys have given me too many raps on the skull."

The pulsing, hypnotic power of the love jewel in her fist had put him in a dreamy torpor as an overall dizziness pressed at the edges of his throbbing head. He felt as if he were drifting at sea, awash in foam-crested waves.

She pulled a small glass vial from her bodice and popped the cork off and shoved it under his nose. "Here, rogue. Sniff this."

He reeled back from the sharp odor. Camphor? Something stronger yet? He felt like retching and yet...his head seemed to clear. It had stopped its infernal pounding. Now a delicious, warm numbness replaced the throb in his skull. His senses swam, as if trying to slip away from him like a fleeting dream.

He looked back longingly at his blade leaning up against the chest by the mirror not ten feet away.

She opened her gown and his eyes traveled to the gleaming line of fresh-oiled woman: the sly, sullen slant of jaw, the dusk-chestnut hair, tangled and sun-streaked, the daring sweep of thatch below the flat, smooth belly and the rounded hips. Was she goddess or demoness? His awakened senses wondered.

It would only take a quick leap, a sudden twist of strong hands to strangle the she-fiend where she stood.

But something stayed his hand, perhaps a primitive survival instinct. Any murderous intent on his part would have him slain.

He had no doubt the witch would blast him with her sinister globes of power where he stood.

Another means must suffice. He had a gloomy premonition this would not be to his liking.

Vetra shook his head, fighting the spell. He drew back from the door three steps into the main chamber and thought to steer her energies in other directions. "This beast you keep down there, is it then a pet you wish to keep secret?"

As she languidly refastened her gown, she exhaled a sharp breath. "Yes, Drako, the apple of my eye. Do you like him?"

"He almost singed Nog's beard and fried us to crisps."

She gave a breathy chuckle. "I had Grindar build a stone grate with the help of some workmen we brought up to Dormoth. The egg had hatched and I needed some pen to contain the youngling. He arranged to have their throats cut so they could not speak of what they saw, or the rare beast encaged. I have leverage against Grindar. A lock of his hair, a fingernail, an old boot. With such items I can cast a powerful spell on him under Dal Sagoth's direction. Should Grindar ever grow loose of tongue or turn against me…his soul would be blasted to such fires of hell that he'd wish he'd never been born."

Vetra licked his lips. "Convenient. As is the place to hold the dragon."

"'Twas an old cathedral or temple of some kind, left unfinished somewhere in the mists of time. Bare walls. No masonry. The reek is abominable down there, I know, but it must needs be worse, if the creature were not one of the more intelligent species. A natural well—a crevice that opens up underneath his chambers—drops to a swift underwater stream. The creature is smart—smart enough to lift tail and defecate there and let the feces be carried off by the current rather than foul his own bed."

"Clever beast."

She nodded. A flush rose in her tanned features. "I have Grindar sneak baskets of meat into my conservatory unbeknownst to the others. Even my fell purpose he does not suspect. Only that I keep a dark creature for my own amusements, and experiments. Which is not far off from the truth.

"I fed Drako deer, hares, scraps of bones and sinew from

the many abattoirs that I patronize. All the time I hoped I could win him over. I must have been mad! Easier to win the moon. And yet, I succeeded somewhat. The dragon could easily have taken me and crunched me in his jaws—or fried my body to crisps with his red hot breath. But when the jewel came into my possession, I shone its dusky light into his feral eyes and I have awoken a trust in the beast, a fierce love for me that no animal in the world has ever known for its master. So much so that he will fight for me to the death if I wish it."

"You are an army unto yourself then."

"The chamber is sealed. Only an entrance from above, which I have had filled with earthworks and garden shrubbery planted overtop the ceiling to hide its existence. I can always dig the earth up and let the dragon fly free."

"You would loose the dragon?"

"A wise woman never reveals her secrets, haven't you learned that? Now what to do with you?" Her long-lashed eyes looked at him lazily, playfully, seductively, as if she had every intent to milk the moment for all it was worth. "You saw my dragon, Drako, then? Or did you only hear him?"

"Both, if you call that scaly creature a dragon."

"He is not just any creature. He is young, a Kyldrie, one of the old ones, a breed thought extinct." She circled him, eyeing him lasciviously from head to toe. "You're too fine a specimen to maim or kill. Nobody must know my secret. Do you understand, mercenary?"

He did, but he chose not to acknowledge her.

"My guardian and mentor, loremaster Tharax, entrusted me with a secret. While middling in age when Senesch was young, he watched the thing for a generation, carried the egg singlehandedly from the wastes of the north... from the Haunt of Kyldrie where came the dragons and creatures of nightmare, and the marshals, the Dragon Lords of old. They all died centuries ago. Only legend and myth remain. Of tombs and ancient resting places where the dragons lie—and the odd egg.

"But enough for now. I seem to be boring you and there're far more interesting things we could be doing ere the night is through, lover."

Her lower lip curled and her eyes glinted mysteriously. "Seeing as you're so obsessed with this jewel, I think you'll be the first to taste its power on this new moon of love. It strikes in an hour, an auspicious alignment of stellar bodies. Are you ready?"

Vetra held up both hands. "Let's talk some more."

"The time for talk is over! The Eros amulet will uncover all!"

She held forth the jewel in front of Vetra's eyes. Before he could react, its throbbing light awoke some inner fire within him. Like a sunbeam striking off a lake's surface that blinds the viewer, the sultry rays seemed to pulse with a spectral energy and dance off his brain, like a thing alive, threatening to pull him with it, like a cascade of molten lava flowing out of a fissure.

He tried to turn his head away but couldn't. For a while he seemed frozen, one step away from becoming her plaything.

Flashes of quicksilver crackled at the border of his senses. The pulsing light was penetrating the deepest core of his soul. Its power and rhythmic movement threatened to make him a helpless automaton to her breathy suggestions.

She did not miss the look of desire in his eyes. A lust so fierce, however masked…for her figure, her heat, her mystery, induced by the erotic spell of the jewel and the sultry setting. Her slim body twisted languidly, her arms arched behind her back, her hips moved with a lazy undulation and the lithe ease of panther.

She leaned in, slipped an olive-skinned arm about his muscled shoulders. Her sleek half-naked flank pressed against his thigh. The jasmine perfume of her dove-tailed hair flamed in his nostrils.

Despite the jewel's mesmeric pull striking at the heart of his resolve, a part of Vetra yet remained aloof and witness to the eerie thaumaturgy at play. He managed to keep a tiny essence of himself intact. But this was only a small victory. When she gestured and stared at him with seductive eye, he felt in his chest battering ramp thumps that beat against his ribcage and sent him into overwhelming passion for this woman. She with the perfectly coved hair, the slinky hips and the full breasts pressing through the tight fabric of her mage's gown. Every fiber of his being wanted to rush over and tear off her clothes, pull this goddess down and ravage her. Vetra started forward on ox-like legs while a lascivious roar rumbled in his throat.

"Very good, mercenary," she taunted.

She slapped him as he bulled forward, a withering blow across his left cheek, then she stood back and watched him freeze like a statue. Vetra, the schoolboy, marionette in a parody of frozen pantomime.

"All in good time, mercenary. I will enjoy you at my leisure. Pleasures beyond your puny imagination. Even you, the simple mind you are, will get a taste of real ecstasy. But through every erotic moment, 'tis you who will be the slave and I the master."

By the hand she led Vetra past the wide, oaken double-door to her side chambers where she had taken many men to her bed.

There, dwelled a small boudoir with high queen-sized bed with elegant satin sheets. Leafy alpadacus plants rose in all four corners of the room, giving a waft of eucalyptus scent to rival many a tropical island. A small fountain bubbled to the side where clear waters fed a small pool and small reddish-gold fish swam, which looked like goldfish but could have been piranhas for all the teeth on their snub-noses. A pungent incense drifted from the altar to the side. Faint purplish fumes, a sickly sweet odor enough to make Vetra's senses swim.

The magic continued to work its way and the jewel latched ever tighter in her fist.

She pulled him down into the bed, kicked off what little remained of the black gown around her luscious hips and Vetra's breath caught in his throat at the sensual beauty of her, her lush figure, her animal vitality, her fulsome flesh pulsing with a radiance that was divine as much as it was evil.

"You are only one of a long line of lovers, mercenary. I take them all to my bed. To test their mettle. Be honored, Vetravincus of the flashing sword! Doff your war gear and make love to me as you have never made love to a woman before!"

And like an obedient serf, Vetra kicked off his clothes and clung to her. Part of him resisted the overpowering, yielding flesh, the red-hot heat of her tanned skin, but her luscious sensuality was more than his willpower could master. Indeed, each clutch of oiled limb, thrust of naked hip, moist tongue licking on hot skin and quivering flesh achieved new heights of ecstasy and meaning in the dusky light of the oil lamp beneath the bestial effigy. And even as her vixenish heat blasted his skull with bursts of pleasure, he felt as if he were entwined with a serpent.

Chapter 22

The only thing more powerful than Taranis's Sagothian magic was the Eros stone itself, which lay clasped in her fist as she straddled Vetra, riding him like an exotic mare, oiled and naked.

In the heat of the moment, amid moans of sultry abandon and slap of flesh on flesh, none noticed the skulking figure sliding like an uninvited shadow at the door.

Creeping up from the dungeon crypts of Old Sagoth, Skirl made three quick strides to rip the jewel from the sorceress's grasp.

Taranis jerked aside; the spell was broken. Her sensuous loins slipped from Vetra's spent body and her gray-green eyes blazed with disbelief and hatred.

"You filthy traitor!" She spread palms wide to launch a death globe.

But Nog grabbed her wrists and the globe went caroming off the wall. He dragged her off the bed, ogling her olive-toned nakedness and curved perfection and the thick black bush shrouding the wet loins.

"What a pleasant surprise," he muttered.

"You're all dead! You hear? Dead!" She lashed left and right like a fiend in his grip.

Skirl wielded the stone in a trembling fist, not yet registering the fact that the power of the gods were now in his fledgling's fist. "Back, witch! I will use this bauble to rend you asunder. Make no move, if you value your skin!" The apprentice looked a vision of fury, though haggard, unkempt and wound tight as a demented clock.

Vetra raised his bulk to a half sitting position, blinking dazedly. Groggily he shook his head.

Nog gave his own head a shake of jealous amazement. "I see you've been dipping your wick mighty hard, Vetra boy. While we've been out fighting an army of hostiles—"

"I'll gladly switch places with you," grumbled Vetra. He staggered off the bed. His lean muscles rippled, poised in all his well-spiked phallic majesty. It seemed the sorceress had waved certain exotic incenses under his nose prior to their lovemaking, thus prolonging his tumescence.

Nog drank in the sight of the gleaming witch, licking his chops…from her sweat-glistening thighs to the dark nipples on her ample breasts, her slender waist, busty hips, rounded buttocks and oiled and gleaming hide.

Skirl seemed immune to the sorceress's allure. He seemed to be fighting some dark part of himself. He'd already had enough of the wench. The mere sight of her repulsed him.

Though the shimmer and gleam of her voluptuous body dangled on a thread within his reach.

Taranis shifted and shafted the apprentice a cruel smile. "Yes, Skirl, you remember our twining in this bed, don't you?"

Vetra struggled to wrench himself from his stupor. With jerky motions, he donned his leather jerkin and black boots, trance-like. He searched for his sword, recalled it was leaning against the wall in the other room. He went to fetch it, paused there on stiff legs and shot fast the bolt to the cursed door that led to the bowels of Old Sagoth beneath the Mages' Hall.

He came back to see Taranis in all her gleaming glory, sweat-laced and magisterial, advancing on Skirl.

Skirl shrank back. "I said, back, witch!" he cried while Nog leered. "Your power is dim without this carnival prize." He clutched the cursed gem tighter as if fearing it would bite him.

Vetra grabbed the magician's arm. "Better not, mage. There's no time. The guards'll be here soon."

Taranis jeered, "Aye, mage, you know not how to wield it."

"Says who?"

"Says me. You're a better bookworm than mage."

He rounded on her hotly. "I found the exact location of the

sorceress's tomb." He shook the gem in an angry hand. "You'd have been fumbling around for ten years if I hadn't pinpointed the exact location of the secret tunnel to Sarkala's mortuary chamber. The jewel lay there on her breast, her body parched and mummified, a thousand years dead."

"'Tis all true, it was there, eight moons ago on the expedition to Mmos we found the Eros Flame, thanks to your hard work and diligent digging, apprentice Skirl. But so what? Only I can wield the stone's power. It has been habituated to my use. 'Tis you who yield to me, the head sorceress of Dormoth."

Vetra snarled, "Ignore her. She's up to her old tricks. How did you get past Grindar?"

Nog gave a cheeky grin. "We disposed of the sentry left to watch the bottom of the stairs. When we heard Grindar and his ghouls clopping down the stairs we dragged the body over into the passage with the dragon for more fun, then hid. From there it was easy to make our way when they passed. Here we find you bedding this she-panther, not in a torture chamber."

Taranis noted all information with a cat-like gleam in her eyes.

Vetra stirred, seeing the witch's devious gaze, one sizing them up as a cat does mice. "Enough! Let us be away from this witch. The more time I spend here in this abominable crib with her and her leering statue, my soul sickens."

Nog stood rooted, staring lustily at her voluptuous, naked flesh.

"Wake up, Nog!" Vetra rapped his knuckles on his helm. It took all of Vetra's prodding to snap him out of his infatuation. Even without the jewel, the woman's mesmeric power was formidable.

"You will burn!" she cried after them.

Nog motioned carelessly. "We can't leave this vixen running free."

Vetra scowled. He reached for the dresser, flung her

garments on the floor. Tearing strips of cloth from one of her gowns, he bound her arms and ankles while Nog stuffed a gag in her mouth. To her sullen dismay, they tied her securely to the bedpost. They shut the door, retraced their steps back to the hall.

Empty, but for the sound of boots and men's murmurs echoing up the hallway.

"Follow my lead," muttered Vetra. "If anyone asks, we're on our way to the main gate, on a mission from Taranis herself."

Nog cracked wide a grin.

They took heel and ran down the hallway.

At the first archway, Vetra halted. A pair of lighted censers wavered to drafts of cool air wafting from the blackness opening on the court. Freedom was close, but it would have to be prodded delicately with stealth and guile.

They scrambled through the archway out into the court, grateful for fresh air and the star-filled sky. Vetra's mind raced. He could hear the rustle of men near the gate, as if divining that something was up. To get out of here may not be so simple…

He hustled them along the portico and winter palms to where a pedestal stood with a bronze gong hung from a chain. He snatched the mallet and beat it against the gong. "To arms, men! To arms," he cried. "Hearken, Taranis is waylaid! She is in her inner chamber. Treason is afoot, men!"

A guard came running, a bewildered look on his face. "What do you mean 'waylaid'?"

"Someone has ravaged the Archmagrix," Vetra said breathlessly. He gestured back toward the Hall of Mages while Skirl tipped his face away from the man to avoid recognition.

Vetra shook a fist. "From her lips I heard her utter the word 'Grindar'. She has banished the rogue while he fled off shamed of his deed. Heed not anything he says. They are all lies! Some men are helping her now. I have come to summon the town watch. Grindar must be caught!"

"What? This is an outrage!" The guard went to scurry off but

Vetra grabbed his arm. "Take this mallet, man! Beat the gong. Warn others of the outrages."

The man gripped the handle and took up the task, nodding, in a feverish sweat.

Vetra chuckled, grinning maliciously as he moved off with the others.

He turned to Nog. "Let us flee this hive. It'll be a swarm of bees before long. They will be out for our blood."

He peered back toward the hall and caught a brief glimpse of Belgra disappearing through an archway in a flash of white robe. Senesch trailed behind her with a cane.

Torches were ablaze in the covered colonnades abreast the Hall of Mages. The sound of men's shouts echoed amid the slithering of blades from sheaths while the gong rang incessantly.

Where were the other mages? Likely huddled in their workshops like obedient puppies.

Vetra did not mind. With a satisfied grin, he booted it with his partners in crime across the nighted court, past the shadowy well toward the iron-piked gate, heedless of any guards they met.

They came to a breathless halt before the watchpost, limned in amber light gleaming down from oil lamps on the gate.

The gatepost sentry leered at them through his wooden wicket. "Where are you three monkeys going to? Can't you hear the gong? No one enters or leaves. Taranis's orders."

"We were told to summon the town guard!" Vetra grunted. "Why do you hesitate, man? Hurry! The Archmagrix will have your head for not letting us out. Grindar has defiled the Archmagrix. We were told to summon the town guard."

"This is irregular. I have had no such orders. And why the three of you when only one need go?"

"Do you doubt your orders, captain?" Vetra rasped.

It wasn't working. The ruse was going sour. Vetra peered into the shadowed street beyond the iron bars and thought to try a gambit. "Hoy, thieves!" he cried. "Blackguards!"

"What? Where?" The guard strained his eyes into the murk but Vetra slammed him hard in the face.

The guard toppled over and fell in a heap on the flagstones.

Nog yanked the chain from around his neck and snatched up his key ring. They unlocked the gate and he and Vetra pulled wide the iron grille.

"Slick," grumbled Skirl as they scrambled out.

"What I wouldn't give for a Tolizian war horse right now," groused Vetra.

"No matter, the *Pauper's Cauldron* is down the way," Nog said. "We can hide our noses in some brews. The sight of that sultry vixen has whetted my—"

"Pick up your feet, fool. There'll be no *Pauper's Cauldron* or *Rat Peacock*. Less ramble and more speed, old man. Run! Run!"

Chapter 23

A faint glow grew in the east over the towers of the royal palace. The clatter of distant carts had already intruded on the passing night: merchants keen on delivering wares to market before the bustle started. Long runners were also on the road: caravans, teamsters, horse-pulled wains. It was to these that Vetra and his two companions looked.

They'd walked for several miles, steering clear of the dives, alehouses and main roads where they thought the Dormoth guards might be looking for them. They stood now before the stone bridge leading out of the city over the canal heading east to Alantra. It had been agreed upon by the three that heading south and east was their best bet as far as fencing the jewel was concerned. Between Smrin to the west and Alantra to the east, Alantra had won out.

They saw the first of many wains clatter by: laden with hay, geese, farmers' cheese, eggs wrapped in straw for protection. Heavier vehicles too with bulky cargoes—metalworks fresh from the smithies.

Wolfsha, the half wolf, had sniffed out their trail and caught up with them. Maybe her bloodhound's nose had tracked them as far back as the cobbled road at Dormoth. Perhaps she still remembered the noble service Vetra had done for her, saving her life from the murderous wolf-baiter. More likely she was just lonely and remembered Vetra for the affection he'd given her.

"We're getting nowhere," Nog said. He flapped his hands down at his side, discouraged by the many fruitless attempts to get a cart to stop for them.

Vetra stepped into the middle of the road with his hand raised, his other hand pushed down on the pommel of his sword at his hip. His red surcoat swirled in the breeze as he pretended to be a member of the city guard.

The next cart driver ground to a halt, scowling into his salt-

and-pepper beard. "What do you devils want? Can't you see I'm busy? Move aside!"

Vetra rambled over to the driver's bench to stand two feet away. He patted the nearest gray mare and squinted up at the surly man who was muttering between his teeth. "You heading to Alantra?"

"What of it?" The man drew a knife. Wolfsha growled.

"You have ample space in the back of your covered wain, I see. We'd like to hop a ride with you east."

"And witches like to fly to the moon," he said. "You can go on 'liking' all you want, friend." He looked them up and down. "Don't see anything in it for me."

Vetra gave a carefree shrug. "At the very least, we can offer protection."

"Protection from what? Your wolf?"

"No, Wolfsha'll keep guard of your wain from footpads. Our swords'll also lend a hand."

He hissed a soft staccato sound through his teeth. "What's to say you don't cut my throat somewhere on the road half way to Alantra, then ride off into the wild blue yonder with my goods?"

"We could have already done that," Nog said cheerfully. "What's so special about half way to Alantra?"

A steely grin spread over the fat man's lips. "Okay, well, hop in then, rogues. Dergath curse you if you betray me. If anything happens to my cart on the road, by Lingara's elder beard you'll pay for it in spades. You're running from something, I can smell it in your breaths, on your breeks, not counting your bloody and disheveled looks. Sure as my name's Marath, I hope my good deed doesn't bite me in the ass."

Nog chuckled. "Unless you keep yapping about it, why should it, old man?"

The cartman mumbled, black front tooth showing in the fugitive morning light. He flicked the reins and the twin mares jolted off, barely giving Nog and Vetra time to jump in the back. They caught Skirl by the arms and hauled him in. Likewise, Wolfsha leaped up in after the mage. They covered themselves under some dusty burlap tarps next to the sacks of flour and baskets of chicken eggs protected in straw. Wolfsha happily snuggled herself in beside them.

The steady clop of hooves came and went on the dusty cobbles. The squat weathered slate-brick apartments gave way to rolling countryside then fields of corn and harvested stacks of wheat. Hidden in the covered wain under tarps, the fugitives caught occasional glimpses of the passing scenery: wisps of gray smoke curling from the flaked chimney of a single-story stone farmhouse, the ruffle of wings of a crow perched on a dead elm, the trudge of foot-wayfarers, goats, geese, lowing oxen, the jingle of tinkers' wagons as they were pulled by donkeys. The occasional clatter of imperial wagons as they too pushed by bearing men and arms.

Skirl peeked up from his dusty tarp and again appeared gloomy. "Taranis will come after us. The Eros Flame—is too valuable."

"Dergath, man!" Vetra cursed. "All this sneaking about and killing, for something that is supposed to make people love each other?"

"The magic was corrupted ages ago," he sighed. "Like everything else in this wicked world. So many good things turn black and treacherous, like the flesh of a ripe apple—at least when too many people get their fingers into them."

"I don't know," said Nog, "I hear some of the women at the *Bounding Boar* in Alantra aren't too shabby. Maybe we can use this black magic, see how many dames I can bag."

Skirl rolled his eyes and gave a dismal grunt. "Such minds of limited capacity in our company, Vetra. Where do you get them?"

A gleaming blade flashed against the apprentice's throat.

"Are we going to go through this exercise again, Skirly? You have a death wish?"

"Knock it off, you two," Vetra rumbled. "This journey's long enough—"

"Okay, everybody out!" a voice bawled from up front.

The wagon juddered to a halt. Vetra peered out to see they were at the dusty crossroads of a main junction heading to Tarnlake.

"This is the last stop," the cartdriver warned. "I head north to deliver my eggs…pick up some hens then it's back to the city for me before nightfall. This is where we part ways." He uttered the words with some relief.

Skirl jumped out and made a gracious bow. "We thank you, cartmaster. Your kindness in escorting us thus far has been only too timely."

The man gave a brusque shrug. "Extra weight slowed us down. Tired Bessy out more than she needed."

Skirl nodded in sympathy. "The mare looks worn."

Before the man rattled off with a jolt, he brought the Eros jewel out and its ruby-rich rays caught the farmer's attention.

"Beautiful isn't it? How would you like that piece of glitter to adorn your wife's neck?" Skirl gave an easy grin.

"I—" The cartman's pale eyes mooned.

"Alantra is not far," Skirl said brightly. "'Tis but a hop and skip down the main road. I'm sure you'd like to ride with us to Alantra, wouldn't you? Gaze at the pretty jewel?"

The cartmaster seemed ready to utter a disparaging comment but then his jowly cheeks slackened, his eyes glazed over and his lips parted. "I suppose I could visit my brother in Alantra. Try my luck at the famous market there. Did you know it's the largest market in the northern kingdoms?"

Skirl clapped his hands. "A marvelous idea, cartmaster." He lifted the jewel higher with an impish grin on his face. Nog and Vetra had wandered over to stare wryly.

"The jewel? Would you offer it in exchange?" he gulped.

Skirl beamed.

His face was flushed rosy red. "It would be my honor to escort you," he stammered. "How silly of me not to suggest it in the first place. Hop in the back!"

Nog, unable to restrain a snigger, murmured, "Pawning our lodestone so early?"

"No." Skirl tucked the jewel back in his robe. "Our friend the cartmonger'll not get it. You saw him. He'll have forgotten the gem by morning. He's putty in our hands. A jay. He'll do anything I tell him."

Vetra scowled, not liking the power of this jewel, or the one wielding it.

The cart rattled forward before Wolfsha and the three were barely back in their usual places. For extra security, Vetra and Nog turned their surcoats inside out so the dragon and eagle emblem of Dormoth would not be visible to anyone peering in the back.

"A bit much," said Vetra after a time. "You didn't have to go that far, did you, Skirl?"

"You heard him," said the apprentice, "he wishes to visit his brother."

"Yeah, sure," Vetra snorted, "go 80 miles out of his way? I don't think so."

Skirl gave a whimsical shrug. "Marath may fare better in Alantra than Xalgossa, for all we know. What's a little venture out in the country anyways? Not going to hurt anyone."

Vetra gestured bleakly. "That jewel is evil and you know it. You're becoming a menace."

"And a fabulous con artist," Nog added.

Skirl tipped his head in smiling acknowledgment.

Vetra inspected the apprentice through slitted eyes. Not for the first time did he have doubts about this venture. "This jewel, magician...it seems to be more trouble than it's worth. How did you say it came into your hands? What makes it so powerful?"

Skirl fingered the jewel in his pocket out of habit. "'Tis said the priestess Sarkala infused the stone with her life essence a thousand years ago. Embedded into the very fabric of its glow is a magic most puissant, most elemental—a stunning sapphire dug from the rugged mines in Kyldrie. The ones bordering Vinland where the dragons once flew. The Legend of the Eros Stone is an old one, known by only a few people. Mostly scholars. Her dying wish was that the jewel be placed at the head of her shrine so that all could remember the charitable deeds done throughout her lifetime. Not for her glory, but that the common citizen could follow her example, practice good will, respect the freedom of everyone in the lands and give more than receive. When she died, such was her power that she could get all who gazed upon the stone to love her and revere her good will and legacy. A rare being in the black-hearted world of today, full of war, strife and hate."

"It seems like an old wives' tale," said Nog.

"It may be. But you have not heard the rest. There were those who were jealous of Sarkala's lingering memory and her renown and her power after death. Those of the crown hired villains of the night to steal the stone and desecrate her shrine. They came in the dark before dawn to pillage and tear apart her shrine and make off with the jewel. They failed. Some bite of lightning singed their hands when they tried. The unwarranted vandalism only angered the people and they rebuilt her shrine. Even though the jewel now had many notches and scratches on it, its inner flame burned with a fire brighter than ever. The hews of the vandals' blades could harm not its beguiling facets.

"They were depraved, and though they defiled it—slapped mud, rotten fruit and offal on her temple, the red flame burned ever brighter than before.

The ruling class who came after, grew ever bitter and conspired to hire a dark magician to curse the jewel and lay a spell on Sarkala's shrine. The sorceress they hired was Arcana.

"'I will do even better,'" she boasted. "'I will taint the jewel with such hexes that it brings an equal amount of darkness to those who gaze upon its contours.'" Skirl, seeing he had a captive audience, assumed the guise of storyteller of grand and animated gestures.

"The king rubbed his hands in glee. He handed over five bags of silver and gold to the evil witch.

"Arcana rived and blasted the jewel with spells from the underworld. The undying flame flickered. It was replaced with bursts of green and blue. But only at odd times. No matter how hard she tried, the sorceress could not quench the flame utterly. Such was Sarkala's power beyond death. For brief moments all that could be seen was the flame turned to blue, as it signaled that the unfettered power of good, once free-flowing and eternal, was no longer pure. The jewel, though still powerful, was tainted now.

"After a dark age, Xalgossa was razed to the ground and King Minos's head hoisted on a pike. The skeletons of towers and temples and market forums fell into ruin. But it was said that Sarkala's mummified body was spirited away to a mortuary temple, and the jewel placed at her breast. It was this very same legend which inspired me to seek the jewel and the underground temple of Gotha where the sorceress lay and retrieve the talisman. Which I did. I believed that if it existed, chances are, in the mists of time long passed, it had not been grave-robbed."

Vetra blinked as if lost in an ancient world. "An interesting story, mage. So real…and yet, I could almost feel the cool stone of her tomb and hear the coos of the citizens as her fane was desecrated."

Skirl held up the jewel for them to see. Vetra gaped. He could feel its warm and ancient power seep into his bones. It filled the confined space around him, even as the cart jolted over potholes. A familiar dizziness once more swam in his head, and with it a tremor of unease.

Wolfsha gazed at the jewel too, cocked her head from side to side as if it were not of this earth. She gave herself to whining.

Nog scoffed. "I don't know, Vetra, I've heard a lot of talk. Seen a bunch of pretentious people dressed in robes and costumes posturing as sorcerers. Even seen a halfwit cartman goggle and moon and offer to drive us to Alantra. But witnessed little proof of its magic."

"You still don't believe, mercenary?" Skirl cried aghast. He pushed it closer to Wolfsha's snout. "Watch as I—"

Vetra slapped his wrist away. "Keep the jewel away from her. I don't like its light shining at the dog...it disturbs her."

Skirl clicked his tongue. "The wolfling loves it. Look, it's a love jewel."

"It's a sinister relic. Probably better off burnt. Or thrown in a deep pit."

"You're harsh, Vetra. You're talking about the thing that's going to make us rich."

"Speaking of which," Nog said. "What's the plan? Do we pawn it at the market at Alantra as soon as we get there?"

Vetra gave a moody scowl. "It's as good a plan as any."

Skirl bared his teeth. For a moment it was as if he found the idea repulsive. Then, catching himself, he gave an affected sigh. "I guess it falls on my shoulders to be the stone bearer."

"See that you don't lose it, apprentice, or misuse it," Vetra muttered.

Nog laughed. "Misuse it? How can it be misused? Give me this jewel and I'll teach some of those young tavern maids a thing or two about the art of love."

"If you're such a stud," Skirl said, "why do you need a prop?"

"You make a good point. Let's give it to Vetra. Looks as if he needs help in the charm department."

"You forget who lay with Taranis," Vetra growled.

Nog's lips curled in half jealousy. "What I wouldn't have

given to have been in her bed back there. Dergath's apes! What was it like laying with that vixen?"

"Let's just say I'd trade places with you any day."

"You can't be serious?" Nog cried.

Vetra's face was dark.

Nog leaned back in the straw, his face a mask of puzzlement.

* * *

The night that Skirl and Nog had invaded her chamber, Taranis had wept in rage and frustration. The freakish twist of fortunes had cast her into a cauldron of misery. That the skulkers had bound and gagged her was imprinted on her mind forever. Shame and humiliation burned in her soul. When Grindar and his men had finally clambered in to cut her loose, she had sworn the thieves all would die in agony and had sworn the guards to silence, on pain of death.

Now she fell to her knees on the hard cold stone floor and dug her nails into her palms, so hard they drew blood. She gazed with hatred upon the sinister idol that she had worshiped for years—Yeasaba, the dreaded one, the grotesque half bat, half elk that would wither the heart of the most hardened dark priest of Umbria.

"Why have you deserted me, O Great One?" she wailed.

A voice came from the bowels of her mind, of pain, torture, a long dank well of ebon depths ringing in her hollow skull.

"Deserted you I did not, dark child. Look to the crescent blood moon on a starry night in the June sky. This setback was but a test. An obstacle only. To test your loyalty to me, your faith in the creed of Sagoth..."

Taranis cried, "A test? A setback? But they have stolen the jewel from me, Lord! From me, the Archmagrix of the Circle. The audacity! The impudence! The brazen insolence. They will all die in lakes of their own blood, O darkest One!"

And with violence in her heart Taranis moved to shatter the

dark effigy hanging above her bed to a thousand pieces.

But with the next message given unto her by her dark lord through her mind's eye, Taranis's hateful sneer turned to a croak of laughter, then a leer of sheer anticipation.

Chapter 24

By nightfall the fugitives'd made the hill station of Ravenknoll: a small village surrounded by high hills on both sides north and south. Noted only for the mighty stone heads of kings with ravens' beaks that lined the overlooking ridge and marked the ancient borderlands of the north with the bird-kings of old. The cobbled road continued into the plains, on to Alantra in Lvendar some 30 miles distant.

The cartmaster rented a room at the *Boarmaster's Rest* while Vetra and the others were content to stretch out in the back of the wain to pass the night in the hay and protect the cartdriver's goods. The canopy had certainly shielded them from any prying eyes that day.

While the cartmaster fed the mares and watered them at the troughs set out by the inn's stable, Vetra visited the taproom with Nog and Skirl to see about some food and ale. The weathered gray oak door, Vetra noticed, sported a husky hill boar's stuffed head nailed to it. A bit of local color to welcome the passing stranger...

Inside the inn was dim, warm and cozy. The three were afforded the usual odd stares expected for a couple of rough-looking mercenaries in mail and a blue-robed mage with a bloodied bandage tied slantwise on his head. They sat at a table apart where they chewed their mutton stew in silence. After downing some watered ale, they repaired to the wagon to maintain anonymity. It was agreed upon that Nog and Vetra would alternate on watch while the others slept: Vetra had still not rejected the idea that some form of the Mage Guard would be on their tails before long.

By noon they passed through the great gate leading into Alantra city. Under the piked walls adorned with ceremonial gargoyles they clattered along the main thoroughfare to the tune of bustling thousands. Archers bearing the yellow eagle of Lvendar on their jerkins ranged the parapets of the high stone walls. Two massive bulls' heads flanked the gates and dwindled behind them. The bulls' round, staring glazed-eyes were plated in pure silver, large as gongs.

The cart creaked to a halt a stone's throw from the market and the old man's voice bellowed back at them. "An uneventful journey, friends! Good luck to you. Nice to have your swords at my back. I hope your enterprise fares well."

"Likewise, cartmaster," Vetra rumbled as he came hopping down with Wolfsha.

"About that jewel now..." The cartmaster frowned, his black eyes glittering.

Skirl skipped out and approached him on nimble feet. "I release you from all holds, bond and obligations."

"What do you mean? Can you not give me the jewel—?"

"Alas, the bauble is an heirloom," he explained, "a family treasure. A memento that must stay in my possession."

"You—" He gave a gulping cry. Then frowned. "A pity. May I see the gem at least one last time?"

Skirl reluctantly withdrew it. The scarlet radiance had the man blinking and sweating, his face lit in a bright, red flush. A last longing look back and the cartmaster gave a wistful sigh and an acquiescent nod.

Had Skirl cast a spell on him? Vetra patted Wolfsha. She circled at his heels looking for treats. "We appreciate the ride, cartmaster," he said gruffly, handing him a small coin. "Do you know any gem dealers in the area?"

"Gem dealers?" He frowned. "Not really. Try the market. You can ask around." He clicked his tongue, flicked the reins and the cart jolted into the milling crowd toward the afternoon market.

The companions took their leave and wandered in an opposite direction, away from the hubbub toward one of the soaring temples fronted with a sandstone sphinx. Vetra noticed that the cartman, upon a quick look back, had tarried and sat in his seat staring back at them. When he saw them peer his way, he shook his head and frowned, then whipped his cart forward with a slap of reins.

Vetra cast a shrewd glance at Skirl. "What was that bit about ties and obligations and whatnot?"

Skirl shrugged. "The Eros stone magnifies the emotional link between wielder and receiver. I merely released the cartmaster of the spell. His memory'll come round, in about a half hour. Maybe he'll feel a tad angry, maybe bitter, no big loss. We'll be long gone."

"More than a tad angry, I think," Vetra muttered.

"We're at the last of our coins," Nog said. "Only enough for a room for one night."

Vetra peered up at the sun as it dipped behind clouds drifting in from the east. It was already late in the afternoon. Maybe rain coming? "Let's follow the old man's advice. Get the word on who's good to sell rubies to. Worse comes to worse, we'll rent a room at one of the dives and pawn it off in the morning."

He strode among the crowd under the shadow of a forty-foot high temple. The sheer face of the smooth-polished blocks were carved with the faces of kings and martyrs, sages and half-human gods with horned heads and half goatish bodies. Vetra kept thinking, so many deities to worship, how could a man decide which to put his faith on? So many diverse kingdoms and people. He kept the apprentice well in sight of him.

Alantra! Most populous of the cities of the northern kingdoms. The crossroads to Mercia, Umbria, Sahir and Tolizia. To the south, Behundria and Galashad. The city of a hundred gods... if not the Temple mecca of all the kingdoms, predated only by Old Gyzia, 120 miles south. They'd crossed the border into Lvendar back at Ravenknoll. There was little need for tolls or tariffs here; Lvendar and Umbria were firm allies. The volume of traffic and goods made it impractical.

Past the temple district, the market was astir with the usual honking geese, clattering carts, roving merchants and peasants. Everyone afoot in one mad jumble of humanity.

The three waded their way through people, animals, carts, merchandise and noise, Vetra noting that festival time was upon the city. Ritual and pomp were the rules rather than exceptions. From far and wide, mendicants, holy men, fakirs, soothsayers and pilgrims had come to pay homage to the pantheon of gods that ruled in this city, or more accurately, the eight kingdoms. The most aggressive were the merchants, eager to sell their tawdry trinkets, homages to Dergath, Azath, Morgot and Aramis, and such stuff. Jade figurines hung from hawkers' racks of staring eyed priests, prophets and alleged holy relics of toe-bones of saints.

Nog muscled his way through the throng, stepping on toes, elbowing touts and hawkers out of the way. Proselytizers and shoe-shiners received no better treatment. Urchins ran in packs, pawing at thighs and waists for coins.

The slender, pale gray-blue slate minarets of the Temple of Lingara reared up in the sky, overlooking amber-colored cupolas where holy men came out to ring their bells. Others came out to shake castanets and belt out prayers in singsong voices to the city. It seemed, this was a competing game among the diverse factions. There came higher and shriller calls and entreaties. Solemn-faced priests moved as one on quiet feet through the crowded streets, their loose white robes trailing at ankles, arms crossed over their chests, hands tucked in voluminous sleeves. Hoods draped their shaven heads. Some of these holy men ran ahead, beating gongs and announcing the presence of the third coming of their god, be it Lingara or Azath. The pilgrims and votaries alike swooned in their wake like swaying cobras.

Vetra stuck close to the spellcaster on the chance that some vulturous cutpurse might try to rifle his robe and snatch their priceless jewel. In their favor, Skirl, garbed in his ragged, torn and muddied apprentice's robe, looked about as wealthy as the next beggar in the gutter. The thick bandage plastered to his left ear gave him the look of a leper.

Grinning, Vetra stuck close to the apprentice, nevertheless, his dark eyes were ever roving like a hawk's.

A grizzle-haired woman intruded herself between the Vetra and Skirl and thrust one of her cheap, soapstone figurines from her basket into Vetra's hand: a mermaid with crown, tiara and trident-staff.

"Only four bits and quarter shill for one, good pilgrims! The festival of Tiara is on. You'll need a figurine to get past the monitors at the Lingara temple to receive your blessing from the virgin!"

"That is good to know, lady, and thank you for the information," Vetra said. He pushed the trinket aside. "Perhaps on the way back. We're visitors here, looking for a dealer in gems. Do you know one?"

"Gems?" She frowned, showed a mouth full of missing teeth. She jerked a shoulder back to where they'd come. "Most well known gemsmith I know would be Zlandar. As for reputable—I don't think there's such a thing in this city." She laughed and flashed him another toothy grin. "Still, Zlandar's your man, if you're looking for gems…"

Vetra nodded and motioned the others to the place the woman had indicated.

CHRIS TURNER

Chapter 25

They traipsed on to a less busy district of shops and taverns set in neat, polished-brick rows. Vetra set his feet toward what looked a respectable establishment with old brown brick and ivy, and ornate iron grilling set in stylish swirls, with fairies and birds laced over the dark-tinted casement. A placard was posted on high, *'Zlandar's Fine Gems'*. The lettering was archaic, perhaps lending an air of respectability to the place.

Nog grunted his impatience. While Wolfsha sat obediently at the steps, her ears ruffled, Vetra pushed through the heavy door into a squarish room with high ceiling inlaid with dark, lacquered wood. Cases of necklaces, rings and bracelets stood under glass in the center aisle.

The gemsmith looked at them with shrewd eyes across the counter—a hunched man with stooped shoulders, hooked nose and heavy gray-brows. It seemed the gears in his practiced brain were already working to size them up. But nothing could be more difficult than to assess this motley group.

Vetra approached, pushing Skirl forward. He motioned the apprentice to lay down his jewel.

"Hoy, sir!" said Skirl. "We are in the business of scouting out the sale of a family heirloom."

The man blinked and for a second seemed to gasp at the size and beauty of the Eros Flame. "Where did you get such a jewel?"

"I recently acquired it from my aunt. Our family is wishing to divide the coins of whatever it is worth." Skirl motioned to Vetra. "This is my brother, Valar, and my brother's friend, Nojen."

The gem dealer lifted the Eros stone in a trembling hand and gazed at its faceted wonder for some time. His bespectacled eyes stared, turning it over in his gnarled fingers. He seemed entranced at its living color, the crimson of blood sage or dahlia and the mesmerizing flame wrapped deep within its contours.

"A fascinating specimen," he coughed. "Let me scrutinize it in more detail in the back. I have magnifiers in my workshop, and salts and solutions that can test its authenticity. I'll quote you a price in a trice, gentlemen." He turned with salamander quickness and went to take the gem, but Vetra laid out a hand and gripped his thin wrist. "No, gem-monger, the bauble stays with us."

The gem-dealer scowled. "As you wish." With a droop of shoulders he wet his lips. "Very well, but I must consult my indices at the very least. Wait here." With a cluck of annoyance, he shuffled into the back room on heavy feet.

Nog grew bored after a time and circled the shop, poking his nose into every nook and cranny he could find, which wasn't many. Albeit, the dealer was gone for an inordinately long time and Vetra began to get suspicious. He suddenly got cold feet about this, recalling the shrewd look of the gem dealer, and he muttered, "Let's go!" He grabbed up the stone and stuffed it in Skirl's pocket.

"We just got here," Nog protested.

Vetra nudged Skirl to the door. Nog followed, shaking his head in bewilderment.

Sure enough, out on the street under the graying sky, Vetra saw the hunchback of a gem-dealer at a far corner where the roads crossed, whispering to a trio of bravos. They had knives stuffed in their belts, bandannas and hoods on head partially obscuring their young, rough-looking faces.

So, the dealer had skipped out the back to inform his network of thugs. Likely they planned to waylay them in the shop or on the street. It mattered little, so long as the jeweler got the gem.

Vetra steered Nog and Skirl down a side street and urged them to haste.

While Wolfsha took off ahead to chase a scruffy cat that had slunk out of a worm-eaten basket, Vetra swore under his breath. "Seems as if old Taranis's got a watch out for the jewel. Even as far as Alantra? Dergath! That conniving wench has a long reach."

"She does." Skirl seemed oblivious to the botched sale, only breathed a sigh of audible relief, a reaction which Vetra found puzzling. But then it dawned on him. Skirl was already getting cold feet about selling; he was far too attached to the gem. In no hurry was he to see it change hands.

His inner voice advised him that things were sliding into dicey territory. "The day's getting old, friends. I fear we'll have to wait another day to fence the jewel. Time to start looking for lodging."

"As long as you're paying, chief." Nog grinned. "I'm fresh out of—"

He did not finish that sentence. A ripple of movement came from ahead. Three hooded shapes leapt out of a darkened doorway. Vetra had been slow in drawing his blade. One of the bravos from earlier hobnobbing with the gem dealer got his mitts on Skirl and smacked him down on the dirty cobbles. The cutpurse snatched the Eros Flame out of his pocket and took off in a run up the alley while his other two accomplices squared off against Nog and Vetra, blocking the way. They kept the mercenaries busy with eight-inch knives and knotted clubs.

Wolfsha had heard the smack of fist and leaped at the fleeing footpad with a growl. She caught the man's bare arm clutching the jewel. He gave an anguished cry. The sapphire clattered to the cobbles while he sagged, trying to shake the wolfling off his arm. Wolfsha released her grip and he ran clutching at his mangled wrist, howling, leaving a blood trail behind him.

The two other cutpurses were less sure of themselves after that cockup.

Vetra parried a sweep of steel as a wicked poniard with curved tip flicked at his throat. He reversed his motion and smashed down hard on the knife arm of his attacker, knocking the blade out of his grip.

In the same breath his mallet fist came angling up to the

man's face and sent him crashing to the street. Nog did a twist, ducked a swing of club and plunged a half yard of steel into the other rogue's guts. He doubled over, unable to stop his entrails from spilling out.

Wolfsha had snapped up the jewel and came dropping it at Skirl's feet.

Skirl knelt down and hugged her with joy. "You are a treasure, little one!"

The wolfling drank deeply of the crimson beams emanating from the jewel.

Vetra rubbed his jaw and debated whether he should kill the man worming his way in the dust. The thief was on his belly, murmuring, pleading, ready to rise in a crouch and flee.

In all practicality it was not wise to let any more of them report back to their masters. With an unsympathetic grunt, he licked his blade out at the man's throat. The man rolled in a gurgling heap and died.

Nog kicked at the blood-stained corpse. "I've a mind to go back there and demand restitution from that treacherous gem hound, Vetra."

"Forget it. He's probably surrounded himself with street toughs. Let's unload the jewel somewhere else, get our money and save playing enforcer for another day."

Skirl nodded vigorously.

Vetra mused, "I have a feeling we'll have similar dealings trying to pawn this bauble through formal channels. The black market may be our only option. Let's find a room and regroup."

With a troubled stride, he took them to the temple district, the *Habar* it was called, where transient men lodged on the cheap, men on the run, men in layover or seeking their fortunes south and east.

They found a seedy room close to the Lingara temple. The muezzins bawled prayers from atop their amber-tipped minarets in loud voices on the hour. A minor inconvenience for the comparatively low price of the room, thought Vetra. Little better than a squalid dive, like the last one at the *Rat Peacock*. But that was the least of their problems. Every hour they spent dawdling in this town, the greater their chances of getting their throats cut.

Once again, Wolfsha gave a soft whine and trusted her luck to the streets. Where she went none knew. Probably she scoured the back alleys hunting for scraps of food.

"Not liking this chase and bait stuff, Vetra," Nog muttered. "We need to unload this jewel as quickly as possible. Nothing but trouble."

"You don't have to convince me, Nog."

Skirl gave a mournful bray. "It's powerful, you fools! We can't just pawn it off on anybody. I'm thinking it deserves better, that we're getting ourselves into trouble unloading it on any dumb schmuck claiming to deal gems."

"And why's that?" Vetra leaned in with some menace. "What of our agreement?"

Skirl thrust his chin out in an aggressive manner. "Agreements can be modified. We need to think this through some more."

Think this through some more. Vetra's fist knotted. Skirl was starting to get on his nerves, and a little too big for his britches. Whether the gem dealer was just plain greedy or murderous, or had been on the watch for an infamous jewel, was irrelevant. Had he to guess, he'd say a bit of all.

With a mirthless grin, he brought the cool edge of his blade next to the apprentice's good ear. "I'm through pissing around, mage. Nog's right. We need to get rid of this thing. We need to find a buyer quickly who's not bought off by the establishment. Sell it, get our equal shares, then we go our separate ways."

"As you wish, swordsman. Don't get so uppity."

Vetra gritted his teeth. "I'll be getting more uppity as the hours go by. Hades balls! You forget who's been saving your ass all these times!"

"And you forget that you're already under the sway of that miserable witch and this gem. You've lain with her, Vetra; she's shone the stone in your face. Somewhere you're still hers, somewhere she will hunt you down. You want to just let this jewel—the relic that has a piece of your soul—pass to any fly-by-night crook who can get their hands on it?"

Vetra frowned. The mage had a point. A shadowy pall descended over his spirit. He snatched the jewel out of the magician's grasp. "I think I'll keep this wraithstone in my possession for a while until we sort this mess out."

He rubbed his red-rimmed eyes. He was bone tired. His back ached.

While Skirl glowered, he unclasped his helm, kicked off his boots and lay on the lumpy cot, eyes growing heavy. Within minutes he was asleep, the stress of the last days catching him up. Nor had he recovered from his taxing hoedown with the sorceress.

While he lay lost in dreams of dragons breathing fire and seductive witches waving jewels, Nog slipped away to the taproom, keen on trying his luck at dice and maybe score some silver bits and extra drinks.

Chapter 26

Vetra awoke to find Skirl gone. And when he patted his side, he found the jewel missing.

"Dergath's tits! Damn to hell that apprentice and his conniving treachery!"

Nog was snoring, nose upturned, lips parted, slack mouth and larynx making ratchety sounds. Vetra came over and kicked him awake.

Nog blinked, wiped at his cheeks.

"Wakey, wakey, sleeping beauty. Our pigeon's flown the coop. With our gem."

"What? Little pissant. I'll whip his damn ass." He wiped his lips, grimaced at the sour taste in his mouth, doubtless the sour ale he'd drunk last night. "Agh, my head hurts."

"We'll walk it off. You drink too much."

"Who doesn't?"

"We have to find this scoundrel."

"What, in a city with thousands?"

"We've a lot invested in that trickster and his little talisman."

Nog gave his head a rueful shake. "True, but he'll be long gone, Vetra. Alantra's a big place."

Vetra rubbed his temples. He remembered the delight Skirl'd had playing darts at the *Rat Peacock*, conning the gamesters with his wind magic. He nodded with a cool grin. "Our apprentice'll be playing mage for a while, Nog. As much as he can, he'll milk the opportunity while he's got the chance. I know his mind. Let's make some inquiries at the local dives, some of the ale houses. Shekels to peanuts we'll find our mage there."

"You want to waste time on that?"

"One day, Nog. It's all I'm asking. It isn't going to kill us. At worse, you get drunk, scout out some of those sluts of the night you relish, then if we come up a bust, we part ways."

"Okay. You're a blunt man, Vetra, but deal." They shook on

it and he pulled at his beard. "Why does life have to be so damn difficult?"

It was well into the evening after scouting out various dives that the mercenaries found their quarry at an ale house, graced with the evocative name, *Birdnest*, a hop, skip and a jog from the Temple of the Sphinx.

Skirl was laughing, spilling ale on himself at the bar stand, a jack of grog in one hand, the Eros Flame clutched in the other. A busty redhead was swinging off an arm.

Nog grinned. He marched over to Skirl's side and pushed aside the redhead and grabbed his ear. He gave it a savage twist.

"Ow! What's the idea of this?" Skirl cried.

Nog pulled his head down to the oak slab. "Thinking to leave us so soon, Skirlie?"

"By no means! I was just thirsty, came in for a swig."

"A swig, at what, six in the morning? Wasn't that when you last left us?"

"One thing led to another. I met Wenda here."

"I'm sure you did."

Nog looked the wench up and down. He liked what he saw. He licked his lips and released Skirl, smoothed his beard and tipped his helm in a convivial manner. "Perhaps I'll dally here, Vetra. You go off with our fink here and let him know about the birds and the bees."

Vetra growled. "Forget it, Nog. Taranis and her henchmen're going to be on us soon. There're probably already here. There're spies and informers everywhere in this town. Probably already got the word out. Remember what happened back at the gem dealer's?"

Nog frowned. "True."

Vetra'd no sooner uttered the words when a ruckus erupted at the door. A giant of a man stomped in, throwing another muscly figure out of the way. The man who was tossed fell as if he were a sack of potatoes, assumedly the bouncer. From the muttering, it appeared the giant had a history of violence and was banned from the bar.

From behind strode a short, goatish man with an oiled, tapered beard. He wore a peaked red cap tucked on a jaunty angle that contrasted oddly with his pale gold smock. The homunculus peered around with large brown eyes of whimsical interest. The towering ape-like figure beside him was four heads taller and had arms that hung down past his rumpled black cloak to knee. A child's simper was carved on the brutish face.

Vetra frowned. Really? Rings graced the brute's nose, sleeveless cape hung to calf, iron-studded bands ringed his hairy forearms, good for clubbing a man or gouging out his eye.

"Skirl!" called the waspish mouse of a man. His voice had a high ring to it, bordering on a warbling shriek. "Skirl? Is there anyone named Skirl in this hovel?"

The apprentice flourished. "'Tis I." He hopped forth. "Who asks? One of my fans?" The apprentice's head was addled with drink and Vetra rolled his eyes.

"Nay," the small wizardish man answered. "'Tis Farbar, prestidigitator and overseer of the Alantra Consortium." He studied the drunken Skirl with a narrow-eyed dislike. "Borknad here and I wish to have words with you. You harbor a forbidden relic, if not a dangerous one, which has come to our attention."

"Oh?"

"The gem is sought by Archmagrix Taranis of the Mages' Council in Xalgossa, our not-too-distant neighbors. We are friends with those in the guild, and thus, are sympathetic to their needs. In fact, we've formed an alliance. Going back as far as the *Hundred Years* when magic was forbidden and Umbria and Lvendar were ruled by the sorcerer-kings, Drail and Smail. In fact, I am a personal friend of the spellcaster Voydred. Perhaps you have heard of him? Yes, I see the name has caused a stir in your faces." He tapped his chin. "We would study this jewel ourselves before returning it to the Black Mage and his master, the Archmagrix Taranis, as is standard procedure."

"I can't help you there, sorry friend." Skirl gave a dismissive shake of his head. "Try the *Painted Dog* next door. There are jackals and thieves by the basketful."

The man stamped his foot. "I am not interested in the *Painted Dog* or any other dive. I am interested in—" and here he blinked "—but ho! I see you clutch the gem in question. Like a beacon of radiance it glows. Do not try to hide it! Bring it forth, knave, for all to see! It shines like a woman's greedy eyes!"

"This?" Skirl held the Eros jewel up high for all to see. "'Tis a heirloom, of sentimental value. Isn't that right, Vetra? Is that so odd?"

"Give it to me!" the wizard cried.

"By no means! I discovered it in the ruins of Gotha nigh a hundred leagues from here."

"Mayhaps, but such things are not for the hands of laymen." The wizard's eyes gleamed a jackalish hue.

"I'm no layman," Skirl roared. "I'm a venerated apprentice of the Order of Xalgossa!"

"Perhaps at one time you were, but I hear you have been demoted, excommunicated in fact. From my vantage, I see a scruffy stripling barely out of his teens. One with a chip on his shoulder the size of Stonetroll Mountain."

Skirl grew red in the face. He was about to commit to a foolish deed when Vetra stepped in. "He's with us, wizard. Take your ape and begone." He knuckled his fist and gripped the hilt of his sword. Nog stepped in beside him, cracking his knuckles. The mercenary wore a huge grin on his scarred face.

The wizard studied them with both curiosity and amusement. "A curious mix of bodyguard and brawn for a lowly apprentice. Two bully-boys for one stripling? Ha, ho. It is irregular, even unorthodox. My...and an insolent stripling at that." His luminous eyes wandered back to his apish cohort at his side. "Borknad! Would you do the honors?"

The giant's lips split in a leer, showing yellow teeth. There was a red lolling tongue under an unpleasant cork of a nose. "Yes, my lord." He lumbered forth, a full head over Nog and reached a brawny fist under his black cloak to snatch at a club. The giant's shadow fell over Nog. Nog tugged at his nose, as if wondering what he'd gotten himself into. A wicked club of gnarled wood, all whorls and walnut, came singing down to lay waste to his skull. Nog leaped back at the appropriate moment to scamper to the safety of a table of ale jacks.

Vetra's sword sang out in a dangerous arc. But the wizard flicked a hand and sent him flying back with a push of his Moosh magic.

Nog launched a punch. The ape-giant caught the fist...even as Nog was trying to hook a sword tip into his eyes.

The giant picked Nog up and twirled him about like a toy. Then with a bellowed grunt, he released him and Nog's bulk came hurtling into a table halfway across the room.

Coins, drink and dice went crashing to the floor. Men were on their feet, cursing, knives in their hands.

Vetra picked himself up, shaking the daze out of his skull. The wizard had written him off and now kitty-cornered Skirl who was flailing away with fists, flinging curses. Farbar snatched at the Eros Flame. There came a schoolboy tug of war between wizard and apprentice.

While the giant stalked forth to finish off Nog, Vetra sprinted forward. But the wizard caught the fleeting movement and pale knuckles lifted and another Moosh pulse came sailing at Vetra's chest.

Vetra ducked, blade raised. The pulse, or whatever it was, caromed off his gleaming steel and struck a nearby patron in the chest, felling him instantly.

Dergath's balls! This murderous bastard is playing to kill.

"Down!" Vetra called. The patrons fell to the straw-strewn floor or fled.

Nog's bull's roar rose above the din. He smashed helm-first into the giant's waist before the ape could get his hands around his head. He jabbed a blade into the giant's thigh then plunged another into his calf. Easier to stab an oak trunk. Skirl managed to evade the wizard's clutch, thanks to Vetra's deflection and took heel. The apprentice was out the door, Eros jewel clutched in hand, the fuming wizard at his heels.

In five quick steps Vetra pounced and kicked the legs out from under Farbar. Vetra's heel came down and knocked loose some teeth. The wizard groaned and slumped down senseless, a trickle of blood oozing from his mouth.

Nog and Vetra turned their joint attention to the giant who had become doubly-enraged at the sight of his unconscious master.

"Master," he crooned like a baby, clutching at his leg wounds.

Vetra sneered. He strode in behind him and cut his sword into the giant's hamstrings.

The ape collapsed on one knee, bellowing like a bull. Nog hit him from the side. Together they hammered him down until he cowered.

Nog jammed his sword into the ape's gut. There came a final wheeze of bloody froth then he fell silent. Nog glared around the astonished crowd. He snatched a mug from a table and chugged it back, spilling warm ale over his beard. He grimaced and spat it out. "This beer is swill, innkeeper! You put more water than ale. Makes for cat piss." He trudged forward, wiped the blood off his sword on the giant's cloak. Vetra gave the unconscious wizard a boot in the ribs and they both made for the door.

Grumbles and groans echoed behind them as the innkeeper and his regulars gathered up the ruin of the taproom amid the broken bodies.

Vetra and Nog took to the nighted streets.

"There!" Vetra grunted, lifting an angry hand toward the

Temple of the Sphinx. The shadow of a fleeting figure was moving across a deeper background of darkness. Massive stone sphinx-paws flanked both sides of the temple entrance; a lion-like head reared overtop. Nog and Vetra hurried across the near-deserted square and up the broad steps before Skirl could duck past the iron-bound double doors of the temple.

Skirl shrilled, "Hands off me!"

"Going somewhere?" Nog rasped.

"I just went out for a walk, got caught up in the night life at the tavern and you persecute me."

"Sure, we know," said Vetra.

"Skirly, Skirly, little birdie," Nog rhymed. "Little birdie likes to flee."

They dragged him off the steps back down into the street.

"Hey, be careful!" Skirl called. "You're pinching my arm!"

"It's a cruel world, isn't it, Skirl?" Vetra grinned.

Nog flexed his aching muscles. A spasm of pain rippled across his face. "Old Borknad did a number on my back, Vet, when he lifted me onto that table." He massaged his neck that had been wrenched in the giant's clutch.

"You'll live," Vetra grumbled. He glared at Skirl. "I should have left you back there for that gray ape to work over."

The apprentice licked his lips. He was sober enough to realize how lucky he'd been to escape with the jewel without getting his neck broken...

Chapter 27

For the past two days Grindar and his men had scoured the ale houses and inns looking for the thieves, but they'd come up with nothing. Only a beggar's garbled story about three figures matching their description heading east on the road to Alantra.

Dal Sagoth's sepulchral hints had prompted Taranis to cram her brain with many, many dark spells for the days ahead. On swift feet, she descended the stairs to visit the dragon below in his den. She threw the runestones before the sphinx-like paws and looked at the angle of their configurations and the symbols they drew in the dusky candlelight. She put a finger to her lip and hissed. Was the time right?

Yes. Her dark master had spoken true, as he always did.

She hurried back to her chamber with a look of satisfaction on her face to pore over her ancient spellbooks.

Not two hours later, Belgra swept into her chambers with an angry step. There was a flutter of fabric about her white-robed ankles that made her appear almost whimsical in light of what she was about to attempt. Her mood was bitter. The conservatory had degraded into sloth the past few days since Taranis's metamorphosis, and yet her resentment was dampened by the pungent smells of the exotic incense that drifted in the air.

"What have you done to Keren and Voydred?" she demanded.

The black-leathered Taranis lounged languorously on her divan, engrossed in a forbidden book of runes written by the Old Ones. She blinked in easy complacence as she sipped a strange tonic of ruby fluid from an ancient goblet.

Belgra went on, "They are like lovesick puppies. They move about on game legs. Slow as turtles, nodding and grinning. They cannot function, or put two sentences together. They come no more to the Hall of Mages or the Hall of Winds to instruct the apprentices. They just grin and nod like foolish children in their workshops. The apprentices are beside themselves. They languish. They learn no more new spells or useful skills. Dergath's hounds, but our own beastmaster and spellcaster have become zombies! The only ones sensible in this dark tomb of Dormoth are Senesch and me, in my opinion. You've spellbound everyone else."

Taranis gave a slow nod. Her smile was as sultry as midsummer heat. "It is that, cousin. You speak truth. Nothing that those two didn't want in the first place. Languorous little puppies—bent on amusing the whim of an alluring woman."

Belgra stood arms akimbo. "I'm not your slave or puppet. I'll never yield."

There was a pause in Taranis's breath. Languid amusement showed in her eyes, then an insolent lift of brows that Belgra did not like, that mirrored eyes as cold as obsidian.

"Your skills as a herbalist are all nice, cousin, but of little importance in the overall scheme of things. I think you have too high a regard for yourself. You think you are above the other mages. I think you will be subverted like the rest. I have just waited for the appropriate time." She gave a husky chuckle disturbing to Belgra's ear. "You come unbidden into my lair. Do you not know what you are inviting?"

"What are you talking about? Is that a threat?"

The Sagothian queen rose and sashayed forth to caress her cousin's shoulder with a sensual energy. "Pretty little thing. Belgra Skywatcher... I can use you, pet, as a love child. Whenever I need to subvert these petty kings or princes like righteous Ragnum or the barbarous lord of Mercia. Even the licentious rogue of Lower Umbria, our silly neighboring count, comes to mind. There is much wealth in the hills north of here. To be exploited and plundered—mines, minerals, wood and resources—if we can ever gain control of those territories, and make Umbria whole again." She gave a sharp exhalation. "We cannot with Nelfban, that silly count on the throne. He is a useful puppet, but a worse statesman. I have not enough manpower to manage all these petty officials and tracts of land. One day I will."

"You are nothing more than an evil slut, cousin."

Taranis sneered. "And so will you be, cousin. You cannot hide behind your uppish sanctimony and good-for-all airs forever. You despise me, yes, but deep in your black heart you secretly desire the same privileges as what I command, a long line of men to service your body and suckle you in bed."

Belgra's cheeks flamed and she looked away. Her lips pursed. A dark part of her knew Taranis spoke truth.

With a twirl of the false amulet, Taranis shone the light in Belgra's eyes. She said some strange words in an ancient tongue and a relaxed, almost listless languor came over her cousin. Licking her lips like a cat, Taranis led her fellow sorceress into the eerie back room that housed the queen-size bed and its pure satin cover, over which the sinister, leering head of the elk-bat idol Yeasaba, surveyed her boudoir.

Taranis stepped forth, limbs a-quiver as with a sudden expectant motion, she ripped the robe from her younger cousin's bosom.

Belgra flinched, but did not resist. Taranis exhaled a husky breath and stripped her naked and herded her onto the soft bed where the two clasped each other in heated embrace.

Belgra caressed and suckled her older cousin with a passion born of the memory of the Eros Flame that lingered in her brain. Their pleasures knew no bounds. The imprint of the stone's power lay so entrenched in Belgra's mind that she became obeisant to Taranis's every suggestion. Every touch of flesh was a memory so implanted in her psyche that even with the false jewel dangling around her neck, its shine could evoke the same response of erotic pleasure and madness. Such was the extent of Taranis's drunken power and current of emotion and sexual heat bordering on brutal lust, that she cared not whether she lay with a woman or a man, stranger or kin. She did not care if there was any right or wrong to any of it, only that she could slake her unlimited hunger for pleasures of the night here and now.

Taranis and Belgra assumed positions of ardor which culminated in domination for Taranis, submission for Belgra. Long through the night there came twin moldings of body, thrusts of hip, arches of back, entangled joinings of loins and breasts in manner and frequency undocumented... accompanied by the sounds of erotic stimulation so earthy and bare to blast the mind of a mortal.

The sensual frolic progressed to orgiastic abandon, until the dark alabaster of the leering, omniscient eyes of the cruel god Yeasaba, or more accurately, Dal Sagoth, glinted with movement, now a thing channeled from the nether spheres, a silent, greedy voyeur of the love play of mortals born of the tainted magic of the Eros Flame.

Chapter 28

Nog eyed Skirl with lingering distrust. "What now? We've got the jewel, bagged our feckless apprentice but half the city and its sorcerers will be out looking for us."

Vetra's features firmed in their characteristic moody cast. Because of the apprentice's foolishness they'd been tracked by the sorcerers' network as far as Alantra. So? Worse things had happened.

And yet, Vetra gritted his teeth. This could not be good. They had little time to act. The impulsive Skirl was a liability, also an asset. Another false move on his part and he'd slit his throat personally. Every voice in his head told him to seize the jewel and flee on his own, but he needed Nog. Better to keep a close watch on their wayward magician too, rather than have him running free, causing havoc.

"I say we head south," Nog suggested. "To Lausern or Dragonskull, away from Mercia and this priests' scumhole."

"Problem is, that's exactly what they expect," Vetra muttered.

"You want to venture north, closer to Mercia?"

"I have a friend of the family lives north of there, Nog, goes by the name, Vrigin. He owns and operates a vineyard. He can take us in. We can lay low there for a while at his estate before we head south."

"What about the jewel?"

"What of it?"

"Shouldn't we—"

"Better we wait till the heat dies down. It'll be easier to unload."

Skirl twisted visibly in his tattered robe. "You're both talking nonsense. I've outlined the danger to you, Vetra."

"Never mind your pretty head about dangers, Skirl."

"But the jewel—"

"To hell with the jewel!" He was sick to death of it. He couldn't care if the damn thing self-destructed. But a ray of hope sparked in his heart, and he secretly grinned, struck by a sudden idea. If all went well, the jewel would burn, and he would reap the rewards from it. He would be rich, and he'd rid himself of this canker on the lands, and a sorceress's magic binding him.

He would not breathe a word of such plan to Nog. Let him blab off at the mouth while drunk on ale or in the arms of some sleazy tavern wench and his plan would be foiled.

"The way is clear," he intoned. "Let's get moving. The night is still young and we have many leagues to make."

"What?" Nog croaked. "It's midnight for Dergath's sake!"

Skirl gave a hoarse groan. "My brain's reeling from that wizard's mooshing and the inn's ale."

"That pisswater?" Nog jeered.

"Onward, you louse!" Vetra gave Skirl a rough shove. They headed up the flagstoned way with Wolfsha trotting happily at their heels.

The gates of Alantra were always open except in times of war. The trio passed under the stone archway, with the steady gaze of the stone bulls upon their backs.

They had little to fear from footpads at this hour. Their surcoats and murderous looks and swords gave them a look of authority. Light was the problem. It was pitch black. No stars showed and only the ghost of moonlight behind thick cloud was to guide their passage. With dogged steps, they followed the cobblestone way where it touched the weeds. They passed the odd cart with glimmering lantern mounted out front, but these conveyances mostly steered clear of them, distrustful of wayfarers at this hour.

At Farwin's Junction the sun was just peeking over the city of Alantra at their backs. They'd trudged all night; feet and muscles ached. Skirl had eventually stopped his whining, courtesy of Nog's frequent slaps.

Wolfsha seemed happier. She'd grown since they'd found her in the market, taken on more protective layers and more devotion. Prancing about on graceful paws, she ran up ahead and came bounding back with her tongue lolling. Her dark pelt was glossier than ever, her blue-black shadow tracing dancing shapes in the dawn's glimmering light.

By midmorning they'd flagged down a hay wain on its way north to Aspenmoor, a hamlet known for its farriers and smiths. They caught a few hours of sleep in the back of the cart despite the bumps and jolts of the road. Many fields of oats and barley and apple orchards passed and the rickety cart ground to a halt near Vrigin's country estate a few hundred yards off the main way.

Fall was in the air and dry leaves rustled in the lonely court that fronted the house and vineyard. They let themselves in past the wooden gate. No more than half way across the flagstones they'd stepped when a middle-aged man with the beginnings of gray in his short-cropped hair, looked up, fumbling for his blade and shouted a challenge. He'd been trimming the first of the grape vines to the side of the house. But his pruning looked haphazard, as if his mind were elsewhere. In the background came the baa of a sheep.

"At ease, Vrigin," Vetra called out. "Do you not recognize an old friend?"

For a second the man squinted, then his eyes lit with recognition. "Vetravincus? Dergath's ghosts! Can it be? You've grown. Uglier and stockier. Gaunter of face."

"I'll take that as a compliment," Vetra said. He gestured to his companions with a grin. "This is Nog, a swordsman ugly as me, and Skirl, a magician of repute."

"I am Vrigin, good sirs." He tossed aside his shears. He held out a hand. "Welcome to my abode, *Vinemoor.* Come gentlemen, inside!" He clapped his hands. "There is drink, good wine from my vineyards and meat and bread. We have much news to catch up on. My home is yours."

The travelers accepted Vrigin's hospitality; they stepped into his impressive atrium overlooking the vineyard.

He clapped Vetra on the back. "What brings you to these parts, friend? When you went off east, I thought you were gone for good."

Vetra's mouth quirked. "It was in my heart not to return, Vrigin—but I did. And you, how much land do you now hold? Looks as if you've done quite well for yourself since you moved." He gazed about the rich furnishings, the massive fireplace and its stone hearth, the stone-cut walls and their rich, wine-colored wood paneling.

"I have, Vetra. Fifty acres—" the man's expression darkened. "My heart is heavy though. Tatla, my only daughter, has gone missing. Snatched, I fear, right out from under my nose. You may remember her from your younger days? A fair maid with light brown hair, amber eyes, not small, not large. A fine girl. Though now she's all grown up and quite a beautiful woman. Three other girls were taken too. The youngest, choicest maidens of the region. Who knows where they have gotten to?" His lower lip quivered.

"This is sorry news, Vrigin."

"There have been several abductions of late. Have you not heard?"

"I've been in Alantra for but two days," Vetra said gruffly.

"My guess, it's a local gang who call themselves the Ravenclaws," Vrigin spat. "They ship them to various cities: Masern, Soho, Syrn, Lausern. I fear your own sister has been taken too."

A startled breath caught in Vetra's throat. "What? Minas?"

"Did you not know?"

"I have been east for a long time," Vetra said in a hollow voice.

"A month ago, snatched from her village Tarnwold, a few hour's ride north of here. She and Tatla were friends. Three other maids were taken from various hamlets around the region by these cursed, murderous bandits. By no coincidence either. All the fairest of the fair."

Vetra licked his lips. His heart thudded in his chest. He felt as if part him had been ripped out. He croaked in a hoarse whisper, "Minas settled here three years ago. When I was away, she ran off from the family riding school. No more relishing the fate my father set up for her than I did. But how——?"

The vintner shook his head. "In the dark of night, she was snatched from her bed, like the others. I fear for their lives, Vetra. Their souls."

Vetra hung his head. Clutching at his temples, he choked back his grief. "This changes things."

"And you? What brought you here?"

"We were on our way south—in transit—seeking respite from trouble that has come down on our heads at Xalgossa."

"Ever the wanderer and disruptor, eh Vetra?" he said. "Always stirring the bees out of their hives." His lame attempt at humor was shortlived. The smile quickly faded, replaced with a hollow-cheeked sigh.

Vetra pictured Minas in his mind's eye: a tall, sensitive girl, slender as a willow, graceful, elegant with blue eyes and a simple grace she'd inherited from his mother. Where he had been dark and stern like his father, often moody, brutal and volatile, she had been his opposite.

Now she was gone. Likely sold to some cheap lecherous lord for a handful of shekels at the slave markets. Vetra's fingers curled into claws.

A deep sorrow struck him. "The local sheriffs?" he croaked.

Virgin gave a wolfish bark. "What do those ringworms care of a few maids gone missing? This is backwater country, Vetra. To them the villagers are like serfs, poor downtrodden cattle, to be exploited. We live richly in the country compared to most folk in the city, but to the lords of the capital, we are but chattel."

Vetra knew this to be true. His mood was bitter.

In light of Minas's capture, the Eros Flame became less important. If anything, it could be used as a stepping stone to acquire funds to launch an expedition to track down her oppressors.

"They carry the pennon of the raven with a red skull behind it," Vrigin said sullenly. "Merciless killers. Plunderers. Ravishers. They've been growing in numbers since Mercia pushed fighting men across the Lvendarian border. Launching skirmishes against her southern and western neighbors. A mix of Mercian outlaws and rogue mercenaries consorting for fun and richer spoils. More freedom than their tyrannical masters could give them."

Vetra rubbed his jaw. He recalled the golden triangle of hills bordering Umbria and Lvendar. A no man's land and maze of canyons, gullies and caves ideal for thieves. Lvendar and Mercia formed its eastern tip. "Clever," Vetra mused. "They have easy access to the borders of all three territories. Vulnerable if not defenseless villages are the only settlements on the hinterlands."

"The royals turn a blind eye. What is it to them if a few farmers' daughters get nabbed and sold into a distant seraglio? As long as the number is within reason to evade notice of the general citizenry. Young boys are taken too for sick pleasures. Older ones sold into slavery, the mines, rough labor or worse. 'Tis a lucrative trade."

"'Tis a vultures' world," Nog rumbled.

Vrigin gave a grim nod. "To make matters worse, war brews. There's talk of a Mercian invasion on our northern borders. Already raiders have crossed into our territory to push southwards. My fear is they're but forty miles away from where we stand."

Nog licked his lips.

"Lord Ragnum launches horsemen by the hundreds to lend

aid to those from Alantra as we speak."

"What? This is fresh news." Vetra's face darkened. He recalled the wagonloads of soldiers passing by in the temple district and those on the east-west road on their trip to Alantra. It seemed his hasty plan to push north had not been a wise one. And yet, if he hadn't, he'd never have learned this grave news of his sister.

Shifting from foot to foot, Skirl clutched the Eros Flame in his pocket. "We will use the Eros stone to help your daughter, Vrigin. Also to help Vetra's sister, if we can. The gem's power is ancient and profound. It fills men's hearts with love." He lifted it with a fierce determination and the man's eyes for a brief moment were set blazing.

"Thank you, friend. But what can a mere jewel do?"

"Much!"

"Put it away, Skirl," Vetra said quietly. "It is no toy to comfort distressed men."

"If you find Tatla, you will find Minas," Vrigin said. "I am not asking much, old friend. If you are heading that way anyways, to escape the law or some other demon that harries your heels, I only ask you to keep your eyes and ears open. If you can find these rogues, discover who they are, where have they taken her, perhaps I can petition for her freedom, at the very worst bribe the lord or lords, or whoever has taken possession of her."

"I will do my best, Vrigin. I owe you for the help you gave me and my father in times of trouble when I was young. Though I can promise nothing."

"Your honesty is enough, Vetra. You're a good man. A trustworthy one." He tipped his head. "If you can get her back, there's 100 gold pieces in it for you. It's all the wealth I have." He left and returned with a small, dusty sack. "I'm an old man, beyond my fighting years. Twenty in advance for expenses." He plopped the sack of jingling coins down on the table.

Vetra murmured. He took up the coins. "I'll not fail you,

Vrigin. I'll return with good news or bad either way."

Vrigin nodded. He left by a side door to fetch supplies for their journey. Vetra and his two companions wandered out into the courtyard which was made even emptier with the man's sorrow. Leaden skies crowded down on them. The first cracks in the clouds showed rain.

Nog took him aside. "Look, I can understand your grief for your sister, Vetra...but our necks are already on the line without running such risk."

"I owe the man, Nog," he explained. "He was like a second father to me when I was growing up."

Nog shrugged, resigned to Vetra's moods.

Skirl had been contemplating the words spoken and his mind fell to churning. "I can defeat these slavers, Vetra. With the jewel in my grasp, nothing can stop us. Once we return Vrigin his daughter we will use the jewel to defeat Taranis," he rasped. "You, Nog and others will be my prime bodyguard."

Vetra blinked, not sure whether he had heard the apprentice correctly.

"Listen to me, Vetra! I can defeat this vile witch. The one who holds power over you—and me too, for I have lain with her. You've nothing to lose by joining me in my quest."

"Except our silly heads, boy," Nog grunted. "Still, these sorcerous freaks have rubbed me the wrong way. When have I ever turned down a challenge, eh Vetra?"

"You can do as you wish, Nog. I only go north to set Vrigin's soul at ease, then to find my sister if I can. Like Skirl's mother, Minas has been taken by slavers, perhaps these same filthy traffickers who nabbed Tatla. I have no love for these Mercians. They strike secret deals with the slavers, that is my belief. They are a warlike people who push their empire ever south, east and west to create misery for the rest of the world."

"So. What's your plan, Vetra?"

"To look for Tatla. To find my sister, if there's hope."

"A tall ticket. The trail is cold. Even if you could find which harem she was at, a few men against an army'll achieve nothing."

"It doesn't matter, Nog. I must try. My conscience will never leave me in peace if I abandon her."

Nog grunted. It was something he could understand. "You realize we must pass through war territory, if what Vrigin says is true? Mercia's king is at war again with Lvendar's. Not a pretty scene."

"These cursed lands are always at war, Nog! Jealous kings, petty monarchs, pitching feuds against one another. Peasants and mercenaries used as pawns to fight their endless wars and to shed their blood. It will never end. It's gone on for centuries."

Vrigin returned, carrying two horse saddles.

"I can give you horses. I have two to spare. Come." He led them beyond the courtyard to the pasture where three fine mares grazed. They came drifting over, heads bobbing, their manes swishing. Two black mares, one chestnut. Vrigin fed them oats from a shaky hand through the fence.

They passed through the gate and Vetra stroked the mane of the youngest black mare, a mettlesome animal, self-willed and proud. Nog and Skirl picked the larger chestnut-hair with a quick, prancing step and a milky white eye.

After outfitting the mounts they filled their saddlebags with what food Vrigin could spare: stone ground bread, strips of dried venison, bladders of water. Within the hour they rode off at an easy canter. Wolfsha tagged easily at their heels. The three took to the dirt road north, with the wolfling happy to be out in the fresh air, frolicking at will away from the stink of the cities and her cruel masters.

They wound ever north through rolling country, the potholed road muddy in places, at times heavily hemmed by copses of young hemlock and alders that showed a mauve color this time of year. They saw mostly orchards and vineyards like Vrigin's, maybe not as lush or well-maintained.

The leaves of aspen had yellowed from their summer green and a fresh wind pushed at their backs, warm and soothing.

The ground became steadily hillier. With an omenish cast, an old rook with a gaunt beak flapped down from a high perch to squawk at them for invading his territory.

"This is lonely country," Vetra murmured. He rode in silence beside Nog. "I can see why my sister Minas chose it. It reminds me of home."

"'Tis not my choice of homeland," Nog muttered. "Give me the seaside any day."

They passed through the village of Smildren and halted to water their horses at a communal trough. The villagers gave Wolfsha wary looks. They seemed spooked by the wolfish look of her loping in plain sight. But they relaxed when Vetra stroked her and let it be known that she was a pet. The three kept their ears open for news. Riders had been sighted, with the devil in their hearts. They flew a black pennon much like Vrigin had described.

Vetra urged his party on with grim fatalism. Toward the village of Tarnwold where Minas had been taken was but an hour's ride away.

"This is insane, Vetra," Nog murmured. "We cannot stand against a band of raiders with only three."

Vetra stared moodily at the thin track ahead that wound through the silent lands. "If we can locate their hideout, perhaps we can find a way to surprise them. The advantage of stealth and speed is on our side."

Nog gave a stony grunt. "A small one at that, Vetra. You're too much of an optimist."

As bad luck would have it, a small group of riders, bandits, blackguards, whatever they were, had spotted their company from a distance, and now spurred across the open fields to confront the fresh prey on the road.

Vetra gave a sullen curse. He wished to Dergath he'd not

been so impulsive. The burning rage he'd felt at Minas's abduction had addled his wits and stoked his need for swift justice.

"We can't outrun them," he muttered. "But perhaps we can outfox them."

"How?"

"Stay your ground, Nog. Follow my lead." He gripped the hilt of his sword. He rode on to meet the band. To his squinting eyes they looked to be about eight.

"Are you crazy?" Nog cried. Shaking his head, he rode on after him.

Vetra only turned his head to peer back at Nog, his face lit with ghoulish vengeance.

On fleeting paws Wolfsha shot off at their heels with a growl in her throat. The hair bristled on the back of her neck; her high-peaked black wolfish ears piked straight up.

Vetra weighed their odds. The outlaws knew the territory, they did not. He and Nog were strangers to the land, riding double on unfamiliar horses. If there were bowmen among the riders…Vetra did not wish to finish that thought. Either way, he vowed that he'd not sell his blood cheaply. The thought of his sister reigned foremost on his mind.

Chapter 29

As the horses came pounding in on unshod hooves, there came the sound of wild whoops and men's yells. Vetra saw their mounts were strong and fit, and of fine quality. Thoroughbreds, if he knew anything about horses. Nostrils flaring, the beasts were much used to the long runs of the outlaw, the sudden quick spurts of charging a quarry or escaping the law.

They clattered to a sudden halt before the vigilantes, circling them, snorting loudly. Their lean flanks were lathered with sweat. The mounted men spread out around them, in an ever tightening circle to prevent their escape or sudden flash of violence.

A mixture of rascals and roughnecks, Vetra surmised. Living in the rough in the hills and on the blood and spoils of honest folk. Eight rag-bearded outlaws, two with slit noses, one with ear bangles, all bearing scars of battle. Men with nothing to lose, only the wild wind in their hair, the pulse of malice in their hearts. Blood-stained leathers clad their backs, cruel blades armed their fists. Black hearts in their breasts bent on thieving and murdering, dark fire in their eyes to carry them through the day. Fine steel lay strapped at their hips. Two carried maces and bossed shields. None wore armor, only tough leather jerkins and matching bowl helms topped with two-inch steel tips.

One bowman rode in their company, a lean, hatchet-faced rogue with a round black shield strapped to the back of his saddle. A pennon stood piked at the horse's rear, marked with the emblem of the raven's beak over a human skull. The crossbow tip pointed down, aimed at a spot in front of Vetra's horse should it be needed.

The leader of the pack flicked eyes off their torn surcoats and frowned. A tall rangy man with scarred cheeks, steely gaze and a draping, gray cape who said, "You some kind of high lord's guard?"

"We fought as part of the Xalgossian Mages' Order," Vetra

answered.

The man wetted his lips. "You're a long way from Xalgossa, if that's what you call home. Running from something?"

"Maybe we like the country air," Nog replied carelessly.

The leader did not like the quip. He tugged at his brown beard, the man they called hetman, and crowed, "So, a trio of wayfarers on a lonely road?"

Vetra ignored the remark. "Have you seen a young woman? Young, fair, daughter of the vintner."

"Maybe we have, maybe be haven't," the man crooned. "What's it to you?"

"She was snatched several nights ago, by men looking much like you."

"Fancy that." He leaned on an elbow tucked at his saddlebow, his mouth partially open as if catching flies. "A maiden taken. What are you going to do about it?"

"We mean to get her back."

The leader stared in disbelief at him. "You heard that, men? You and what army, chief? That pipsqueak in the blue robe yonder with the bandage over his head? Looks as if he couldn't fight his way out a gunny sack. And your ugly bully with the crooked teeth and ox smile? Couple of beat-up rats if I ever saw any."

A low growl rumbled in Wolfsha's throat. She backed up, took two steps forward and snarled at the rider, spooking his gray stallion. His horse reared.

"She doesn't like you," Vetra said, smiling.

"And I don't like her," the man rasped. He got his mount under control and gave a small jerk of head.

His mate at his side, a heavy-set man perched on a sleek roan, lifted blade and heeled forward to slash steel down at Vetra' skull.

Vetra parried. He flicked blade off the descending steel and set it flickering up in a reverse thrust to send the man reeling off his saddle.

There came a flurry of horseflesh moving in and about and a thicket of swords flashing around Vetra's head.

A horse reared. Men grunted in anger. A crossbow lifted. Vetra felt a bolt whiz inches from his ribs to thunk into a man's saddlebow behind him.

The thrown man came sprinting in at him, sneer on his lips, trying to hack him off his horse.

Vetra cut down at him. Wolfsha leapt, sank teeth into the man's sword arm, sending him screaming back in a fog of pain. She dodged another rider's blade and leaped up, caught the mounted man with her teeth, playing a vicious tug of war with his leathered leg. The man's sword came slashing down on her and slit a three-inch gap along her back. She wheeled, yelping, spinning in circles. Her spine was laid bare. A great spurt of blood soaked her thick black fur.

In some quixotic act, Skirl jumped down from his place behind Nog and scrambled toward the crippled dog, lifting the Eros Flame high. "Stay back, bullies! One glimpse of this gem and it will blast your skulls wide open. 'Tis riven with ancient powers! Look deep into its contours!"

For a moment, the riders sat stunned on their saddles. One lean rogue with black eye patch, unaffected by the spell and only half registering the magical light, spurred forward and smacked the jewel out of Skirl's grasp with his shield.

Swords came flickering in at Skirl. He dodged. Vetra reined in, drawing his horse in a wide loop and blocked the first savage blow that came at Skirl. Arms swung. Swords clanged. Blades hungered for flesh. Vetra's mail absorbed the excess sword strikes, his sword parried the rest. His agile ability to twist in his saddle out of harm's way was his savior. Nog swung in to shield him, swearing as the blows came hard and heavy while Skirl scrambled to snatch up the Eros Flame from the bloodstained grass. An unhorsed rider kicked the mage in the chest, sending him flying, the wind knocked out of him.

There came a flurry of steel. Vetra dodged and drove murderous blows into his flailing assailants. But he felt a mace graze his helm and knock him off his saddle.

He was up on his feet in time, shaking the blood out of his eyes. He was breathing husky gasps. He leapt aside before the horses' hooves could trample him. He bellowed a war cry, parried four sword thrusts whistling over his head. He struck, blocked another strike that would have taken off half his face. Nog scrambled in at his side, unhorsed. The two fought side-by-side, spitting and cursing. They were hemmed in by a pack of enemies. Of the eight outlaws only six remained.

Vetra turned in time to send a spiked ball of a mace skidding off his blade. He slashed a mighty backhand that took off the bandit's sword arm at the elbow. The man screamed. Vetra twisted in to plunge cold steel into his gullet.

The spilling of blood had brought a communal rage upon the outlaws. A storm of bodies fell on Vetra and dragged him down. Nog was next.

A shouted command rose up over the din. The hetman's. It had been their blades that had hewn Wolfsha. They expected it to be theirs to dispatch Vetra and Nog. But it was the man's voice that had their blades halting their course of death. He sat back on his horse with a brooding look of distaste. Up till this moment he'd let his cutthroats do all the hackwork. Now with two men dead and one without an arm he was not so cocky.

He leapt off his mount and stared down at the bloodcaked corpses. "Peace, brothers." He made a savage flourish and slew the man with the severed arm where he lay on the ground. He marched over to Vetra who struggled in the grip of three captors. The hetman lifted his blade for a killing blow, but his face relaxed. His eyes took on a tranquil quality. "You're quite the sword meister, aren't you, rogue?" His lips curled in amazement. "A rebel? A scrapper?" He laughed, spread arms wide as if beseeching his fellows. "Look here, rascals! In this man's dark heart lives the true spirit of the outlaw! See? A killer, reaver, a braveheart among rogues, a courageous soul. I praise you, swordsman, even though I hate you for slaying Mest and Duar. Two of my finest men. No, I'll not kill you. I may have need of you... But as for these other mongrels..." His eyes lingered on Nog and stared at Skirl as he fingered his blade.

From the side came a flash of cold steel. The hetman whirled and blocked the murderous downswing of one his men that meant to put an end to Vetra's life. The hetman lifted a knee and kicked the man back, an oily-haired raider, with a rumbled curse. "You defy me, Jarno? Trolls' heads! You miserable skulker! Back! You forget who's the leader of this rascals' band. Brule of the Ravenclaws!" He gave a mighty ululation that had the air tingling with menace.

The four other riders stared with vicious contempt. Sour leers crept over their leathery faces. Malice and expectation played in each black heart while white-knuckled fists strained at their sword-hilts to kill and avenge their clansman. They loved the random law of the outlaw, these rogues—the blood, death, and fickle swing of power. Tension crackled in the air, thick enough to be cut with a knife. Indeed the fate of the clan hung on a spindly thread.

The man Jarno gripped his sword. He took two steps toward the hetman with a murderous gleam in his eyes.

The hetman sprang back on his heels and parried Jarno's first strike. He called out in a throaty drawl, "We're all blood brothers here, aren't we, Ravenclaws? Say it! Say it!"

The others raised a muttered cheer. Two lifted swords and moved to fend off Jarno.

Jarno dipped back and his sword arm fell, his lips moving in mutters of disgust. The spring-coiled event had turned in the hetman's favor, as it always did. To a rogue, one crafty as an adder.

The hetman's brooding gaze fell on Vetra. "You gallop up, draw swords against thrice your numbers, knowing full well you would lose, and sit there smug as a bug. Why?" He squinted at the mercenary in puzzlement as if he'd never seen such a brazen display of foolishness.

Vetra allowed himself a tense chuckle. He licked his bloody lip. "You only live once, reaver. Better to die courageously and have lived valorously than survive a week with one's tail tucked between his legs, wishing he'd tried this or that."

"Pretty words for one who's already half step in the grave."

The hetman stooped to snatch up the glittering jewel lying in the bloody grass. He squinted at it with curiosity, then he tossed it to an ugly hound-faced man with a sloping brow, jutting mouth and hangdog look.

"Take it, Igir. The bauble'll adorn your neck. You like pretty things, don't you?" He laughed, a coarse guffaw. "That, or sell it. I could care less. Probably a fake anyway."

The skew-jowled man grinned. For a moment he tested the stone with his teeth as if for authenticity like some gimcrack jeweler.

"Their weapons are of good quality," said another, the ragbearded man with the squinty eye and eye patch. He bent to gather Vetra's and Nog's blood-stained blades.

"We'll take them for our own then, Halfhan."

The man smiled. "I think I'll take this ox-faced rogue's beard cutters." He hefted Nog's short swords. "They have a sleek, murderous feel to them which I like."

"All the power to you. The world's your oyster. So long as you keep these knitting needles to yourself, away from my new pups, you hear? That goes for all of you slew-faced rascals." He glared at Jarno and the rest of them.

There were grumbles and a few muttered curses. Jarno seemed content to claim Vetra's sword for his own.

The hetman made a curt gesture. "This here dark hair's got

some piss and vinegar in him. I think he'll do fine at our game of Ranks. What say you? Bind 'em, boys. Hoist 'em up on their horses!"

The raiders left Wolfsha where she lay bleeding out. Vetra, biting back his dismay, shook his head in sorrow and anger.

The dark fringe of trees ringing the north was where the dirt road meandered. But they did not take it. To the west across green plains they rode, toward low grassy hills which rose with faint gray-blue rocky outcrops. Further beyond lay bare crags, wind-carved and skull-domed, crow-haunted and mysterious peaks that delineated the range separating Lvendar from Umbria.

Thither the raiders whipped their mounts and Vetra felt himself jerked forward, wrists bound on his own mare while Nog and Skirl trailed behind, hog-tied on theirs.

They left in a flurry of hooves, back the way they had come. Vetra shook the blood out his eyes that dripped down from the slit on his brow. A fierce fire burned in his coal-dark eyes. He promised to make every one of these cutthroats pay in buckets, choking on their own blood.

Chapter 30

Down below the Hall of Mages on the narrow passage that led to the ruins of Old Sagoth, Taranis held a candle in hand. Her fingers pressed an engraved rune on the center-top block above her head. She whispered ancient words.

The lower blocks shifted. With a grating screech, the centermost ones slid almost effortlessly aside.

She ducked under the mantle of darkness into the deeper blackness within—the lair of the dragon. She strode with confidence toward a moving shape, a shadow darker than dark, unheeding of the fearsome reek of the thing's scaly hide, that of young dragon.

A slither and scrape of scales echoed off the towering stone walls and she glimpsed armored plates, of tail and belly as massive as a small whale, as an enormous shape reared before her, a bastion of sinew and strength. The lizardish head rose twice her height in the cavernous murk. A drip-drop of water fell from unseen heights to splash on the beast's glistening back. The giant claws scraped the wet stone underneath its bulk in its quest for freedom.

"You have the rut of lust of a young buck on you," she murmured. "Good. But good luck in finding a mate in this unhappy world, Drako. All your kind are gone. Poor dragon! You have only me. And in truth, only a face which a mother could love. For who else could love such a beast as you, nurtured from an egg that birthed you to dragonhood?"

The dragon, as if understanding her words, opened its huge jaws and returned a foul breath, showing rows of serrated teeth. From each fang dripped foul thick drool. The creature loosed a fledgling roar as if to char the sorceress. But the slim, black-clad Taranis did not flinch. Nor did the dragon exert further energy to fry her. The love jewel had seen to that. The Eros Flame had worked its magic on this demonic beast, even though the real jewel was not in the sorceress's possession. Only the fake one, collared about her neck. The memory of the moons of programming and subtle, soft words spoken in ancient tongues and the shining of its eldritch magic into the huge, lamplit eyes, had bedazzled the dragon. Even the sight of the fake Eros stone was enough to stimulate a response in the beast of renewed devotion. Such was the gem's power, and such was Taranis's confidence in its lingering hold. She cared little whether she wielded the original or a replica.

Taranis gave a wolfish laugh. She was the dragon's master and she thought to herself how she could exploit this fast-growing minion. The might of beasts and men were hers to command! It only remained for her to secure the real Eros Flame, and dominion over the eight kingdoms...and Drako was her ticket to this goal.

"We will ride, young dragon!" she roared. "Ride! To the ends of the earth where the sunset has no cease. We will conquer the eight kingdoms. We will send the proud and petty kings back on their heels!"

The dragon rumbled. Fire huffed from its huge maw, claws pawed at the rubble, digging trenches into the moldered stone.

Budding horns curled from its ridged brow and yellow eyes peered forth from dim slits.

Taranis set down her candle on the dank stone and lifted hands above her head: in a U-shape that wielded some thaumaturgical significance.

From her palms lofted blue-gray orbs into the sepulchral darkness.

The orbs bit into the ceiling, at a particular spot, and sent hefty chunks of earth and rock falling down into the narrow chasm below where an underwater stream flowed.

The dragon watched in curious fascination. A stray hope grew in its febrile brain. Indeed, a fearful intelligence lurked behind those eyes that was much in sync with the sorceress's ambition.

On quick feet Taranis fled up the steep stairs back into her chambers; then out into the corridor that ran past the Hall of Mages. She came to the garden which housed the eerie bat-statue, Besemooth, messenger to Dal Sagoth. For here was a spot she'd marked days ago directly above the fresh tunnel she'd just bored. A narrow space only separated the dragon from freedom. With lip curled in delight, she launched more of the sinister orbs upon the heavy flagstones at her feet, blasting them and laying bare a cone of darkness that connected the two tunnels. Here the two shafts met, releasing with it dank airs from Drako's den of Old Sagoth.

The dragon wormed his long, flexible body up through the conduit as a rodent squeezes through spaces many times smaller than itself. Greedily his five-inch talons clutched at the rock.

The furor had alerted the Dormoth guards and now a troop of them came clattering down the corridor abreast the Hall of Mages with shields and swords.

Eight stood in unison, gaping in terror at the hide of the ponderous dragon that lifted above their heads on wings of crusty sinew to hover there like some bat of the underworld.

"Slay it, men!" a doughty man-at-arms cried. He waved his sword and came in bent-kneed at the monster.

Only he and another dared come that close to the dragon.

Mace and sword licked out, as if to sting the winged devil's crusty hide. Fresh from the nether depths, the dragon was in no mood to be re-confined and it bared its scissored teeth and blew a raging fan of fire, charring the two men where they stood.

The other guards recoiled in horror.

Taranis stepped out of the shadows, warding them back. "Fools! You would oppose this juggernaut of the earth? Stay back, or be singed!"

They cowered back, swords and mace gripped in trembling fists.

More figures arrived: Belgra and Senesch. They stopped short to glare at the beast thus summoned from the murks by Taranis. Its black mass hovered, horned head tipped in a menacing direction their way. Voydred and Keren too had now come shuffling down the hall with the captain Grindar, to gaze on the mythic beast.

"Stay back, you fools!" she ordered Voydred and Keren, who particularly had shambled close to the dragon like a pair of zombies.

She lifted arms and the dragon landed on its clawed feet and clattered toward her as would a pet hound.

"Rise, you dumplings!" she cried. Her eyes blazed at Voydred and Keren. "Be warriors! Fight for me. Fetch me my jewel!"

She approached and muttered arcane words in their ears. Tracing the forbidden sign of an arcane rune on their brows, she then snapped her fingers and hissed a final word, *'Erunk!'*

Voydred and Keren seemed to rise inches higher, like knights of Umbria. No more the automatons of the past but transformed of mind and spirit. They shook their heads and gave vengeful cries and vowed to serve Taranis unto death.

"Good!" Taranis cried. "Now Voydred, you will take a steed and search for the traitors who took the jewel. Keren, you are my eyes and ears." She gestured with a jeweled finger.

Keren gave a quick acknowledgment and his body blurred and shimmered into the form of a giant condor, a bird of majesty.

His outspread wings flapped, his gray beak opened and dim slitted eyes blinked as the bird took flight northward.

Voydred took himself to the stables and mounted the fastest steed. He sat with ramrod-straight back, his fierce gaze straight ahead as he spurred the black stallion through the gates of Dormoth. Grindar and a dozen mage guards likewise took horse and clattered after him down the torchlight cobbles.

Taranis's glittering eyes fell on Senesch and Belgra at last.

"You two will remain here and guard Dormoth in my absence."

They rose to object.

"Silence!" She held up a preempting hand.

"Rise, Drako, rise!" she crooned at her dragon. She climbed on its back. "Follow the bird, Keren. Whoever finds it first, Voydred or the beastmaster, we will be there to claim it."

The dragon lifted its crusty wings and soared into the darkening sky. Senesch and Belgra watched with growing dismay as the laughing sorceress clung to its scaly back with a clenched grip on the budding horns, then disappeared, a dark blur crossing the moon, like an omen out of the lost chronicles of Sahir.

CHRIS TURNER

Chapter 31

The outlaws' horses cantered across the green fields and angled upward until they were lost in the hills. Brule led them down secret ways and wild-goat paths that twisted among scrub and bush.

Two of his men dismounted to lift a screen of foliage, cleverly disguised to conceal what would appear to be an overgrown trail. They put it back up as soon as the riders passed then remounted their steeds and fell in behind the grim cavalcade.

After a time they came to a narrow horse trail only wide enough for two mounts abreast. In double file they trotted in silence. Pools of water puddled in the deep ruts of hooves, testament to the recent rains. Bare stone slopes rose high above them on either side. Verily this was the wild hill country of ibex and bighorn sheep.

The trail opened onto a small clearing backed by another protective hill. Smoke rose from the embers of a stone-circled fire pit. A rude shelter stood off to the right, a stockade of sorts, about thirty feet square. Human figures were contained within. The crude pen was crafted of tight-knit wooden stakes, sharpened at the ends. The farthest edge was flush against a sheer wall of rock. A dozen young women huddled within that Vetra could see, in various states of distress.

A massive guard dog came bounding up to greet the hetman. It was all wide drooping jowl, corked snout, bat-like ears and shade-gray fur. He reached into his saddlebag, threw down a hank of beef. Ravenous teeth gnawed the morsel—some breed of a half mastiff—which was gone in seconds. The dog surveyed the new arrivals with distrust. Under hooded eyes, it took a proprietary piss at their horses' hooves then trotted back to guard the padlocked gate of the women's stockade. Its teeth were bared.

"How do you like my beauties?" the hetman gloated at

Vetra.

Vetra saw the maids were lean and mud-streaked from teens upward. Wild, desperate looks showed in their eyes which peered from behind the wooden bars. Hands of those who sat in the dirt were clenched with arms wrapped tightly around knees; others clung to the fence with fingers bunched like claws. All had hollow, pinched and tear-stained faces. The odd moan or forlorn whimper came from the group, pleading for mercy.

But no mercy would come from Brule and his black-hearted rogues.

Somewhere Tatla was among these wretches, Vetra thought. Minas, he noted, was nowhere to be seen.

His keen eyes took in the rest of the gang's hideaway. A sheltered lee on three sides by steep grassy slopes pocked with rounded outcrops and boulders. Above climbed stony hilltops, piked with aspen from where noisy ravens squawked. Some vultures circled oddly farther afield.

The black mouth of a cave gaped in the hillside dead ahead: a cavern eight feet high. The hillside to the left gave way to a narrow footpath flanked by sheer rock 40 feet high. This path ended in a heavy door drawn with a bolt and seemed some trapdoor to doom. Blue-gray stone arched overhead many more feet.

The place was quiet but for the low moan of wind and the shuffle of the listless women in their pen. The clearing would be difficult to attack from above. Indeed, as difficult to escape from. The only way out was the way in—through the narrow pass of rutted track.

The lonely encampment appeared to be deserted but for the penned women and the vicious dog, pissing on everything it came across, including the corners of the stockade much to the women's dismay.

The riders dismounted, forced the prisoners off their mounts then sat them before the embers. The hetman milled about with his men, muttering, deciding what best to do with them. Riders in groups of eight or more arrived, bringing in fresh spoils. Two new women were thrust into the stockade to add to the dispirited souls huddled within. The numbers of the outlaws swelled to forty now.

Two of the ragbeards lingered to ogle their new prizes, muttering crude jests and making insinuating gestures with hands and tongues, one even gripping the stakes to get a closer look.

The hetman came loping over and slapped the first man with the flat of his blade. "Get away from there, you cur! Any ideas of night play or deflowering and Malfar'll make short work of you."

The hulking half-mastiff, hearing its name, came trotting over to raise its hackles and growl, sensing the displeasure of its master.

"Our buyers'll give us half and less for dames with any hint of virginity spoiled. Go to a whore's tavern in Alantra and get your pleasures there, if you feel an itch."

They grumbled and slunk away. Brule returned to the fire pit where his indifferent gaze swung back to Vetra and Nog.

From snatches of conversation, Vetra divined that a slave agent from faraway Guiritia was due to arrive on the morrow to negotiate the purchase of up to six women.

His fists knotted. A keen rage curdled his blood. Maybe this was the same scum who'd spirited off Minas?

"What about them?" Brule's lieutenant inquired, jerking a thumb.

"They'll fight in the pit," Brule said.

Halfhan's squinty eyes gleamed. "And the jewel?"

"Pawn it somewhere," Brule intoned in a bored voice. "In the cities, as I suggested to Igir." He waved a brusque hand.

"Yes, hetman."

Skirl gave an agitated yelp and struggled to his feet. "You can't pawn it!" he shrilled.

"And why not? Who is this popinjay?"

"An insolent pup, sir," Halfhan said. "Calls himself an 'apprentice'."

"An apprentice? He'll be apprentice to my ass, cleaning it out with his tongue if he yaps any more." The hetman gave a signal and Skirl was smacked down into his ungraceful squat again. "He'll fight with the others, Halfhan. No, wait." The man's lips curled in a baleful grin. "Let Igir have him. He has need of pretty boys, doesn't he?"

Halfhan laughed.

Skirl's eyes bulged. "No, you can't! This is inhuman malice!"

The hetman turned his back on Skirl as would a lord his lowly slave.

"Put these other two mongrels in the hatch for now."

Jarno, Igir and two outlaws seized Vetra and dragged him and Nog to the mouth of the cave.

With a grim and restless glower, Vetra strained against the hemp that bound his wrists. But he and Nog were pushed mercilessly into the murk. Behind them the sun sank behind the hills.

The hetman gave a sphinx-like smile, stirred by the prospect of some fresh sport.

Vetra caught a glimpse of a natural cave of high rounded walls smoothed by the rush of mighty rivers eons ago. The outlaws' living quarters? Primitive but serviceable.

Pools of shadows lurked everywhere. In the spider-webbed nooks, the ratlike crannies, around the pillars of rock that may have been stalagmites at one time, hung a feeling of longtime decay. Oil lamps burned from crevices in the walls, emitting a dim orange light. An odd, musky smell hung in the air—of old rags and frayed garments that should have been long discarded. That and unwashed bodies. Vetra saw tunnels and crawlspaces where rough-and-tumble men could sleep.

Igir dragged them to a low wooden door set into the rightmost wall of dark rock. One of the foul-mouthed rogues got it creaking open before they were thrust inside into the murk. A small rank cubbyhole greeted them: with the smell of mice droppings and bats. The crack under the door let in just enough light that Vetra could barely make out Nog's hard-chiseled face. It was etched in a vindictive grin.

"Well, we're going to have to bust out of this place somehow, Vetra. Wonder what's happened to our mage?"

"Don't know, Nog, probably warming Igir's bed."

The other laughed but then seemed to cringe at the precariousness of their situation. Vetra could hear him shuffle restlessly in the dark.

Those poor women.

He thought of Minas and the terrors she'd face, trapped, desperate, without hope. Used like a breeding mare by shallow, lascivious men. It made his blood boil and he paced the confines, exploring every nook and crack with his fingers. Nothing. Only sheer rock. Cold, damp, unyielding. The door was three-inch oak and strapped with iron. It was already getting stuffy in here. How much air had they used up? It seemed not much leaked through the small cracks under the door and around its edges.

"It'll be sealed tight, Vetra. Forget it."

Vetra gave a sulfurous curse. "We can't just sit here and be used as entertainment, Nog. They're going to barter off those girls."

"What can we do? We're like two rats caught in the hold of a sinking ship. Are we going to gnaw our way out of here?"

"We have to come up with a plan. Think!" Vetra smacked a fist in his palm.

But no plan was forthcoming. Vetra sank back on his heels. Even if they could surprise creepster Igir or any of the guards, there was small chance they'd win free of this motley horde with no weapons at their disposal. They were but two, unarmed and vastly outnumbered.

Time ticked by.

At last Nog's murmur intruded on Vetra's gloomy speculations. "Wolfsha...she was a good companion, Vetra. She didn't deserve what they did to her."

Vetra gave a gruff acknowledgment. An old memory flashed in his mind: of her running up ahead while he and Nog prowled the streets of Alantra, then she'd nip back, tongue lolling. "She helped save our skins, Nog. That's always going to be our memory of her." He recalled Wolfsha's glossy pelt, her happy bark, the sharp whiteness of her teeth, the ones she'd sunk into the street thugs without a second thought. He exhaled a bitter sigh.

"A life for a life," Nog murmured. "You saved her, she saved you."

"I think she saved our skins a lot more than we saved hers."

Nog's rusty exhalation echoed as grim confirmation. In it lurked a guilty overtone.

"Her courage reminds me of a story, Vetra," Nog said. "When I was a young buck, haunting the wharfs of Kablin, I made friends with an old dog, a sheephound or some cross of white retriever. I was looking for work, or trouble, I don't know what. The hound only had one eye. Sailors and stevvies used to call him, 'Old Cyclops'. For laughs and kicks. One of his canines was yellow, the other black. He was half lame. But he could fight. By Dergath, he could fight! He could hold his own among the other mutts that prowled the docks looking for scraps. They left him alone.

"One day a new dog came to town. Came off a black-tarred ship sailing up from Syrn. It flew the black flag of the Vassal Privateers with a witch and skulls. A mean Hortooth Hill Hound with a touch of the Bearhusky in him. The buccaneer, Chivano— Roost, they called him—captured the dog and put in to port. He was a notorious pirate who sailed as far as the Mystery Isles and Guiritia. Been running spice and gold and silver and whatever else he could get his hands onto from all the carracks he'd sunk and sent to hell in the Vassal Sea. Him and his crew of sea dogs had sailed the Vassal before I was an itch in my pappy's pants. Past Baspu, past Mt. Palyr, as far as the Gray Lands. He came in like a sea lord, causing trouble in the town with his mates. They smelled of tar and sweat and blood, some with missing teeth or an ear. They swaggered about the inns, practically took them over. The innkeepers were forced to keep them busy with whores and free ale. There was no law there in Kablin, only the town watch, which was afraid to walk the streets at night down at the wharfs. But I'm getting off topic. I was working the fish nets just out of my teens, cleaning and gutting the catch of the day, setting billhooks and mending and repairing nets, but ended up getting mixed up in a fair deal of privateering myself before it was all over. But that's another story.

"This black giant of a dog whipped the other street dogs and sent them all running. Last to face him was Old Cyclops. He just stood there among the piles of fish scraps the sailors'd tossed out, munching his meat as if nothing were untoward, as if he could care less about any new upstart dog in the neighborhood. Only a sullen stare on his snouty face and a low growl in his throat matted with dirty yellow fur. The black hellhound charged. Near sent Old Cyclops five feet back. They rolled and snapped in such a flurry of fur, teeth and claws, I thought Cyclops was doomed.

"But he was a smart dog. After a time he lay as if dead, pretending to be beat, licked like a torn rat. While the other slavered over him and bit into his bloody fur, took a chunk out of an ear, as wild dogs would do, he didn't move a muscle. The bigger, meaner dog grew bored with such weak prey under him and he looked away, and in that time Cyclops leaped up, spry as a gazelle, sank those yellow teeth into the other brute's throat. He hung on for dear life, like a rattlesnake. Took some mettle and courage to do that, Vetra. I witnessed it all myself. The other dog couldn't break free. He collapsed and bled out. Old Cyclops lifted himself off the limp dog and staggered off as if it were just another day in the streets. Damnedest thing I ever did see.

"When old Chivano found out, half drunk from sousing at the *Whistling Sandpiper*, he near tore up the town, looking for the mangy yellow mongrel that people called Cyclops. I hid the old battlehound in the room I'd been renting on the cheap in the slum district south of the docks. I knew Chivano, the skulduggerer. He'd slit Cyclops ear to ear when he found him. I grew fond of that dog. His courage and cleverness moved me. And so, with a young man's idealism, I planned at night to stow us aboard on a carrack that set sail the next morning."

"So did you?"

"I did, and I tell you, Vetra. I never came back to Thrakia for eight long years! Managed to weasel my way aboard as one of the crew. The sights I saw... The daunting 100-foot stone palaces at Iskuldir, the golden domes, the cupolas of the Shemir, the wild beauty of their dark-eyed women. The wild, haunting fastness of the Isle of Baspu and its petrified forest. The colorful and exotic fruits and spices of the faraway markets. From Graemon in Guiritia to Kirnland. Mouth-watering olives and figs the size of apples. Three-humped camels carrying ingots of gold across the sands from faraway kingdoms. Coconuts the size of gourds. The roll of the sea, the emerald wake, the ever-changing moods of her waters and skies, from tempest to midsummer squall to calm blue. Hairy fights on the seas with only scimitar and cutlass...

"I'm telling you this story, Vetra, because I think life leads us down strange paths. Whether we're sitting in shackles in a dungeon like this one, or we're up to our eyeballs in sorcerers, outlaws, dragons and hellhounds, something tells me we got a lot of Wolfsha-ing and Old Cyclops-ing to do. If we're going to get out of this pisshole and send these bastards to Dergath, we'd better do it fast!"

Vetra gave an explosive grunt of rekindled vigor. "I like your spirit, Nog! You say some dumb-ass things at times but some wise jewels pop up. When I met you in the market, I thought you might have been one of those blowhard grifters, but I'm glad we crossed paths, even if it was under a dark moon. Even if we may not live past this night."

Nog gave a rumbling laugh. "Let's make a pact then, Vetra!" he rasped. "We fight back-to-back to the end. Whatever surprise they spring on us with this Ranks nonsense, we protect each other, watch each other's back…When the time comes, we kill. We take down as many of these mangy rats and butt-wads while we draw breath."

Vetra's lips curled in a murderous sneer. "Deal!"

They both clasped hands like brothers…and thus marked the fellowship and seal of bare-knuckled camaraderie that was to change history.

Chapter 32

Igir had gained special privileges being longtime goods-peddler and watchman; he was granted a small chamber to himself, a pot of silver and a maid. The chamber, barely fifteen feet square, was adequate for his needs. Only the hetman and Halfhan enjoyed chambers as large.

It was in here, in a nook off the great cavern that housed the black-hearted outlaws, that Skirl had been shuttled and was now confined in a small, iron-barred cage. Here he crouched disconsolately in the dim lamplight. It was a space not dissimilar in configuration to Vetra's, but one with light and the feel of living beings in it.

A brass-bound chest sat beside his cage. A few weapons were tacked to the wall behind him: mace, sword and shield, before which sat a wooden chair and a wolf-skin rug before a small hearth in which a tiny fire could be lit and meat roasted if the master of the house should desire it.

Another figure crouched in a cage of similar size to Skirl's about six feet away. A young boy from the look of him, with long ruffled black hair. The desolate lad squatted and stared zombie-like as if escaped into a world of his own.

All this was extraneous to Skirl's focus. His burning eyes rested on the crimson jewel that sat atop the brass-bound chest. The Eros stone! It glowered a deep crimson under the dim flicker of the few oil lamps that graced the chamber.

Igir sat on cushions before the fire pit, now dark and dead and smelling of old embers. He examined his prizes with small beady eyes.

"Pretty boy in a cage, pretty birds with clipped wings," he crooned. "I like pretty things. There's Mizron now," he gestured idly to Skirl. "The boy's been with me for several weeks. Raided on Mistletoe's eve at the village of Voken. Cheer up, boy," he rattled on to the lad, "things can only get brighter."

Skirl's eyes turned in dismay toward the tousled-haired youth squatting in his iron bound cage. Several weeks he'd been here? The boy had tears staining his face, his knees were scuffed and his dark eyes were dull pools of lead staring into nowhere. He seemed oblivious to the words being traded.

"A pretty thing to light a middle-aged man's heart!" Igir mused. "Sometimes to sit at my side on a rainy night by the fire. Oh, lucky me, lucky me!"

Skirl cringed. The man was obviously deranged—like all these outlaw freaks whom he had overheard, drank human blood around campfires on the full moon.

Igir snuffled and yawned. "I shall return with your suppers soon enough. Have a care not to commit any mischief!"

He lifted his bulk and sidled to the door, stepped out, closing it tightly behind him.

In the silence of his cage, Skirl was left to his own devices to meditate on his turn of fortune. Who knew when the madman would be back?

* * *

It had been more than a day that they'd been confined in the dark and Vetra's gut crawled with hunger.

What seemed like hours later, he heard a key rattling in the lock. The heavy wood banged open, clapping hard against the copper-colored rock. Igir sauntered in bearing a gnawed bone and some soupy slops in a big pewter bowl. Dusky light poured in from the main cavern, stinging their eyes.

"Something for you boys to fight over." He threw a half gnawed stag bone at their feet. He set the slops in the bowl down nearby. They squinted in the half gloom to see it had a dishwater color; the chunks of meat that floated could have been cabbage as much as horseflesh.

"Wouldn't want you to get too frail before the festivities," he laughed, an evil echoey sound that intruded on the thick silence. He retreated, latching the door tight, plunging them into darkness again.

They shared the bone, eating like savages in the dark with fingers and teeth. Food was scarce...but food was food even though it tasted horrid and practically made them gag.

Nog swore. "There're going to be some heads to roll for this, Vetra."

A time came when the door burst open again and Igir stood with Jarno and two others bearing swords and knives. They snatched the two out of their lethargy and herded them back to the communal area with steel points at their backs. They prodded them down the narrow path and past the wooden portal set in the side of the leftmost hill, the one that Vetra had thought led to hell.

From there they walked them cautiously along a narrow ledge that overlooked a stone pit roughly 20 feet by 40 feet. The pit was enclosed on all sides by sheer rock. No getting in or out of the pit without assistance from above. From the ledge, natural tiers of stepped stone ran upwards on which the outlaws squatted or stood while Igir and his mates held the prisoners at the pit's edge with a knowing and conniving look on his vole-like face.

The hetman came down the narrow path with slow ceremony. He seated himself on a flat rock overlooking the pit. This perch was like a miniature throne that gave him prime view of the pit. When all were settled, he gave a brisk signal of hand.

Even though daylight still lingered in this late hour of the day, torches burned on either side of the pit and sent smoke curling down into its eerie confines. Vetra saw the stone-worn path continued on to an open vale and hills beyond: an escape corridor perhaps should the bandits' lair be compromised?

"Anything goes," the hetman intoned, "from weapons to opponents. Our boys like wild fights. With some funky surprises along the way." He gave a ratchety laugh and looked up, a devious glint in his eyes. "To honor our new guests, let's give them a big cheer, boys! We're all good sports here."

While the outlaws snorted and jeered, chugging wine from heavy incised mugs in their hands, the lieutenant Halfhan gave Vetra and Nog a strange salute. "The men who die in this pit are tied upside down at the heels, drained of their blood." He lifted an arm in a practiced ritual to bond with the rogues up in the stone seats. "Blood which we drink on nights of celebration!—" he brandished his cup and took a big swig. "We've two new recruits to raise the stakes in the games of Ranks, lads!" He pushed the cup under Vetra's nose. "Would you care for a drink, outlander, before you die? These mugs are filled with the same blood which we slug back as part of our old tradition. The corpses are tossed to the wild wolves in the hills. Blood for longevity! Blood for the men which makes them strong and keeps the clan battle-ready!"

Vetra swatted the cup away. The red liquid slopped over the man's jerkin. "It's a perverse and disgusting rite, bordering on cannibalistic."

Brule lifted his heavy bulk from the throne and strode over. "It's an evil world, mercenary! Ruled by evil people. I proudly joined their ranks decades ago." He gave a tired laugh. "Black-hearted deviltry lurks in the public markets. Behind velvet tapestries, the golden doors of the capital. In palaces, fortresses, merchant's bedrooms. In the hypocritical hearts of the priests, the greedy governors, the self-serving magicians. Who are you to lecture us about villainy? We're no more evil than any of them."

Vetra exhaled a bitter breath. The words held a note of truth in them, as his life experiences had shown. Either way, he wouldn't lower himself to reply.

On a signal from the hetman, Igir pushed Vetra into the pit. Arms pinwheeling, Nog followed. They both landed on the balls of their feet, rolling, grunting, clutching at their ankles.

Vetra staggered to his feet, peering about wild-eyed. The sand was littered with old spilt blood and refuse, from discarded boots to half gnawed bones. The rock walls were sheer and smooth, eight feet high, no handholds, grips or indentations. Forty roguish Ravenclaw-clan faces peered down at them. Vetra counted three crossbow-men in their ranks.

Muttering to himself, Igir left the prisoners to their devices and skulked on quiet feet back the way he'd come, a restless look in his eye as if he had unfinished business to attend to.

Chapter 33

Skirl examined his cage. Bands of iron framed a four foot cube with three-inch checkerboard gaps. He shook the bars. To no avail. It was quite impregnable; he sat himself down, teeth bared, head in hands. Shuttered like a caged bird, to spend the rest of his days. A pretty keepsake to a mad monster, Igir.

"It's useless," said the boy in a listless voice. "Igir keeps the door locked and our cages tight."

Skirl gripped the bars, peering out. "Where are your kinsmen? How long have you been here?"

"I don't know." The boy shrugged. "The days slip by without my counting." He did not seem to hear Skirl's other questions; only to drift off in his own fantasy world, probably a barrier he'd created to keep himself from going insane in this gloom.

Skirl slumped back on his haunches and sank into deeper misery.

After a time the door creaked open and a figure entered: a maid wearing a blue bonnet and a blue-gray dress. She had buck teeth and heavy-jowled cheeks. A woman who looked neither young nor old.

"Who are you?" Skirl croaked. He crabbed over to the bars to get a better look at her.

"I am Igir's charwoman. I come to dust and sweep while the men play at Ranks." She blushed. "To keep him company when he feels the need around the fire."

Skirl muttered wryly. "I see."

The woman was not pretty, in fact, quite an oddity. A dumpy, lank-limbed, buck-toothed maid come to dust chests and Igir's weapons.

"You are new here," she said in a bright voice. "Mizron has been here nearly two months. Igir likes his charladies plain lest the other outlaws make eyes at her."

"I see," Skirl remarked. "But it seems as if our good friend Igir likes to collect pretty things."

"Like me!" she cried, twirling her dress, fluttering the blue fabric around her ankles with such a flair that Skirl blinked.

As she swept around the room, dusting, sweeping and humming a nonsensical tune, Skirl noticed that the maid kept making eyes at the Eros jewel posted on the chest as if she could not help herself.

A crafty thought began to brew in his mind.

"I see you like the jewel," he said.

She nodded discreetly as if ashamed of the fact.

"How pretty it would look round your neck."

"You think?" Her cheeks flamed.

"On a fine necklace inset with pearls and opals, I think," Skirl mused. He rubbed at his chin. "Bring it here and we'll see. You have a mirror over there to admire yourself in." He motioned to the aged glass on a crooked wooden frame hanging on the wall by the weaponry.

The charlady made a whimsical step toward the mirror to look at herself with shy regard: beaked nose, underslung lip, lumpy figure, moony, half-wit eyes. She shook her head almost forcefully. "I mustn't disturb master's things! I am ugly! Igir will beat me—he will do terrible things in the night if I don't—"

"Hush," soothed Skirl.

"Once when I went to sneak a bit of raven pudding from the larder, he...but I mustn't speak of that."

Beads of sweat budded on Skirl's brow. He whistled, a soothing breath between clenched teeth, "What is your name?"

"Zilda."

"Well, Zilda, Igir is gone for many moments, I daresay. An hour, maybe more. We will see that the brute doesn't harm you. For one, I am a powerful wizard."

"You are?" Zilda's lips parted. She stood arms akimbo, peering at him askance. "Why are you in a cage then?"

For a moment Skirl's mouth hung slack. Then he licked his lips and gave a hearty laugh. "I am merely pretending to be imprisoned, dear girl! A game I play with those around me to see if they are paying attention. You, on the other hand are not so easily fooled. You have keen wits and the sense and courage to talk to me. In my estimation, these are excellent character traits, all guaranteed to win boons and favors from an Archmage of Xalgossa!"

"Boons and favors? Really?"

"Of course!"

She grew emboldened by Skirl's logic—a skewed logic which even Skirl was having a hard time keeping track of. She took five hesitant steps toward the chest on which rested the jewel. She tucked it in a palm and with a conspiratorial wink at Skirl snuck over to the mirror where she admired herself, twirling her dress, with the gem placed smartly at her throat. "It does set off my eyes!"

"Of course it does!" Skirl gave a happy laugh. He clapped. "Now fetch the key, Zilda. We will go off together and get more jewels like this one."

She blinked in startlement. "Really? How many?"

"More than you could ever imagine."

"You're teasing me!" She gave a dreamy sigh.

"We will depart today and leave Igir behind and go someplace safe where we can sit round a warm fire and eat raven pudding to our heart's content!"

She clapped her hands in delight. "Goody!" She smoothed out her bonnet. "I wish no more of Igir. He is a mean man. Harsh and cruel. He grabs me at night with his pinching fingers. See these welts on my arm?" She pulled back her sleeve and glided over to the brassbound chest. "He keeps the key in this chest."

"I know, I have seen him stow it there. Go ahead, Zilda, retrieve the key. It is but a hop and skip away. It is yours for the taking."

She mustered the courage to pry open the heavy lid then rummage around the bottom, searching for Igir's keys. There came a rattle and jingling and finally in triumph, she held up a corroded key ring. On the feet of a somnambulist she glided over to Skirl's iron-barred cage and fiddled with the lock for several moments. The bars parted; at last Skirl was free.

Skirl wrung his wrists in glee. "You have earned your reward, Zilda! The jewel is yours. It was mine which I now freely give to you. Your master stole it from me and he means to sell it. For now, let me keep it in my safekeeping so that we—"

The door burst open with a crash and an owlish, hulking man loomed. A pair of mean eyes glared forth.

"What is the meaning of this, Zilda?" The outlaw's fists knotted. "Have you been up to mischief?"

"No, Igir, I—"

"Consorting with thieves and prisoners? I will tan your hide within an inch of your life!"

Her face flushed in terror.

Skirl snatched the jewel from the maid's fingers. He lifted it high in his left hand. "Stay back, you rascal! This gem harbors arcane powers!" He thrust it closer to the blackguard's face.

Igir drew back. "I've heard that before. You cannot gull me, ninny. I've been lenient before but my patience is wearing thin. Prepare to die!"

Zilda's eyes mooned; she fled past the outlaw, escaping his long, grasping fingers before they could grip her.

Igir's icy eyes prickled and he advanced, knife in hand, with a smiling leer and dusky menace on Skirl.

The boy heard all. He blinked, squatting in his cage, wearing a look of dull fascination.

Skirl's eyes darted about the chamber, looking for a means of escape. There was only the weaponry tacked on the wall: a mace, a knife, shield. If he could get to them…three quick steps…

He lunged, making a mad grab for the hanging knife with his right hand.

Igir reached out to snatch at the apprentice's neck. Skirl twisted aside and grabbed the first blade off the wall.

Igir's long knife flashed. In the same motion, Skirl thrust the Eros stone in his face with the speed of a viper.

The villain gazed at it and faltered. He shook his head and croaked…giving Skirl enough time to lash the blade at the exposed face and neck.

Igir teetered back, clutching at his slit throat. He gave a startled gurgle, then sagged to the ground.

Skirl's knife arm fell limp…

He panted, chest heaving. The jewel was still clasped in his nerveless fingers. This was the second man he had killed…and it felt no easier the second time round.

He stepped over the lifeless body, blood pooling around the villain's dark silhouette. Skirl swallowed the bile in his throat.

The whole scene hovered like a sordid shadow over his soul. The boy had witnessed everything. His wide-eyed gaze replaced the dull one from before.

Skirl scooted over and unbolted the boy's cage. He scrabbled out, his doe eyes rounded with horror as if he were in some nightmare.

"Take heel, lad," Skirl whispered in his ear. "Find your way back to your village. Minutes from now this place is going to be vipers' nest. You'll wish you were nowhere near it."

Head nearly bobbing off, the youth scuttled out the door into the shadows. Skirl made a more leisurely retreat, gazing both ways when he came out into the cavern with its high-ceiling. Nobody was about. He was confident that nothing could touch him now that he possessed the Eros jewel. The warmth of the jewel spread up his palm, his arm, into his chest. His heart beat with erratic fervor. Every time he wielded the Eros Flame, he could feel its ancient power. Now he was lord! Power once stripped from his bones was returning in spurts to his veins. He felt as if his wiry frame had grown taller, stronger than before. No doubt the ancient magic at work of the priestess-sorceress Sarkala…

Now there would be a reckoning. A fierce reckoning…and a heavy blood price to be paid.

Chapter 34

Vetra looked up to see a ragged prisoner being prodded along the ledge at swordpoint. On a curt nod from the hetman, he was pushed into the pit to join him and Nog.

The man flailed and fell with a cry. He rose to his feet in a crouch not dissimilar to Vetra's, wiping his sand-flecked lips. His face was grime-streaked. A thin-boned wretch from one of the villages, Vetra surmised, with washed-out blue eyes, pale straw-colored hair and cheeks hollow as spoons. No doubt snatched on a whim for sport in the game of Ranks.

The newcomer assessed the two broad-shouldered men before him, and quavered at the sight of what he faced. He decided he was no match for their brawn and backed away on spindly legs.

Crossbow bolts thunked at his feet. The nearest archer reloaded to point steel-strung weapon at the man's chest.

The wretch cowered back.

"Fight them, damn you!" the hetman roared. He leaped up from his throne, fist clenched.

The wretch froze; his Adam's apple bobbed. A look of wide-eyed fear grew on his grimy face.

On a signal from the hetman, another bolt came whishing down. It struck him in the left foot. He screamed, a raspy wheeze from parched lips. He hopped around in anguish. With madness in his gaze he came half-shambling at Vetra.

Vetra swatted him away; the man went sprawling on his hands and knees, nose in the blood-streaked sand. Another bolt clacked at his side. He upped himself and frog-hopped toward Nog. Nog leaned in less leniently, amazed at the wretch's resilience, and hammered him down. The wretch stayed down for good.

Vetra and Nog looked up at the hetman. Brule nodded in gruff acknowledgment. "First kill goes to the outlanders. Rank goes to two!"

There were sniggers, as if Rank 2 wasn't much of an achievement.

An old boot came flying down and smacked Vetra in the chops. He rubbed his jaw, muttered and stared up, looking for the culprit. Nog was slow to move and a bucket of slop landed on his head: rotten cabbage and chicken bones. He wiped off the refuse with a sulfurous oath. The hetman slapped at his belly in mirth. Loud jeers came from the spectators, indicating they thought this funny too. Nog grabbed fistfuls of slop and flung it back at the drunken oaf who'd upended the bucket. The rodent-faced man bawled a curse of his own and drew his scimitar, a wicked curved blade. He took an exotic leap into the pit. He bobbed to his feet, his sword with hilt of scrolled brass flashing in his hand.

Vetra and Nog circled the man warily. Their arms dangled loose at their sides. Cheers and catcalls waxed from above.

Things could go badly in this arena, Vetra thought. The outlaw was armed. He and Nog weren't. A vicious sneer rolled across the man's pasty, nose-ringed face. A gaudy bangle dangled from a half-torn ear. He fingered his two-foot blade, did an acrobatic twirl, thinking to impress his mates with some bloodletting. What could the outlanders do? He laughed, and lunged.

A mistake.

Nog feinted and drew Sir Ear Bangle aside on a nod from Vetra. The vicious weapon slashed at empty air inches from his nose and Vetra slipped in and hammered the drunk with both fists in the throat.

The outlaw crumpled and Vetra stooped and snatched up the curved blade. Now they had a weapon.

The rogue shuddered as he struggled to get up. Nog smacked him down and stomped on his throat, thus silencing him for good. Now two motionless humps lay on the blood-soaked sand.

Crossbow-man trained his weapon down at Nog's throat.

The hetman swatted the weapon aside, fouling his aim. "Hold up, you dolt!" The bolt went wide a few inches from Nog's thigh to thump into the fresh corpse near the far wall.

"They're resourceful. These rogues deserve a better challenge." The hetman rubbed his bearded chin. "Second kill goes to the outlanders. Rank is now three! So...we're having some rich entertainment tonight, aren't we, boys? Villy! Smoge! Get your hides down in there and teach these pretenders a lesson. As members of the Ravenclaw clan, you're both at Rank 6. If you win, your rank rises to 7. If the outlanders win, their rank goes to 6. Be warned! An opportunity to rise and shine and win! Show them what you're made of!"

With a rumbling cheer the two rascals hopped down in the pit. Landing cat-like on their feet, they were up, clutching weapons.

The two killers were determined not to lose this fight, their cockiness reinforced by the grim weapons at their disposal: small bossed shield and mace, and a four-foot broadsword. They approached with casual ease, if not murderous anticipation in their eyes. Coarse jests wafted on their breath. The one with the Mohawk cut twirled the spiked ball on chain and faced off against Nog. The squatter, roguish brute with the bully-boy grin, rounded on Vetra with sword extended.

Vetra smelled the grog on their breaths...an advantage they could use. Nog cast Vetra a knowing glance.

The Ravenclaw pair came at them in a sudden rush of flashing steel. War cries were on their lips, teeth glinted in the dancing flames of the torchlight.

Vetra wielded the only weapon and he cut at the yellow-toothed weasel with the broadsword. He parried and kept moving back at an even pace, matching his attacker stroke for stroke, making him use his forward momentum to keep coming at him.

When he was almost pressed to the stone wall, Vetra scooted out along the rock face, ducked a strike and flicked out his scimitar, drawing blood from the man's thigh. The man gave a grimacing cry.

There followed a vicious play of flashing steel: cut and leap, dodge and slash, as filth fell and crossbow bolts thudded at men's heels making the entertainers dance like cobras in a fakir's pipe dream. The blood-red gleam of the torches cast monstrous shadows on the walls. The reek of rotten vegetables and meat and unwashed bodies were enough to make one retch.

How many men had died in this grisly arena?

Nog ducked a spiked ball and lured the mace-wielder away from Vetra. He was not foolish enough to try to wrest the weapon from him, but rather, focused on staying out of the reach of that deadly spiked ball. He taunted Mohawk Hair and succeeded in getting him to flail away and waste energy. One strike of that globe on the head and it was game over.

The steel spike clipped the stone wall, taking chunks with it. Nog darted over to the opposite wall. He snatched up the old boot that had been hurled and chucked it in the mace-wielder's face. Like a mad bull he charged. The weapon came down at his head but Vetra caught the descending ball on his sword before it caved in Nog's skull.

In a split second reversal, Vetra launched a backhand strike that pushed his attacker back. He lashed out two quick strokes but got too close and the man's brass-knuckled fist smacked him on the forehead, a cheap shot that ripped off some flesh and sent a seashell ringing in his ears. With a snarl, he struck a volley of crosscuts that had the swordsman crabbing back. The man fell backward over the old boot. Vetra pounced. He thrust the tip of his curved blade deep in the man's throat. Reversing his forward momentum, he slashed at the mace-fighter's ribs, ripping an ugly seam across the man's waist that let out a trail of steaming guts.

The man sank in a crouch, holding his own entrails, mace

slipping from his gory fingers. Nog leaped in, grabbed the hilt of the mace and sent the ball singing into the man's skull. Brains and bone flew as far as the nearby wall.

A deadly silence descended over the ragged company.

Now four corpses lay sprawled in the filth. Pools of crimson oozed on the blood-strewn sand. Nog's chest heaved. He and Vetra stood as one, their faces grim as death.

The hetman licked his lips. He held up a hand, scowling. "Outlanders rise to rank 6."

Brule twirled his mustache, perhaps wishing he hadn't sacrificed two of his cruelest scrappers for this no-win outcome. The Ravenclaw bullies didn't like it either and booed and hissed, stomping their hob-nailed boots.

The gash on Nog's cheek had reopened and now blood trailed down his grinning face. Vetra's forearm was slashed and his brow leaked blood, adding to the bright red on his surcoat emblazoned with the dragon and the eagle.

The hetman had reached a decision. On a quick signal to his crossbowman, his archer took aim.

"Wait!" Vetra cried. "Have you no other wannabes to fight us? We've won weapons so at least you'll get a fair fight." He stared up at the faces of the reavers peering down at them. "No? Are you all a bunch of chicken hearts who must hide behind the skirts of your bowman?"

The taunt raised angry sneers. The Ravenclaw bullies, perhaps pleased less by the insult than the death of their comrades, rapped the pommels of their blades on the stone terraces. Vetra's words had a ring of truth to them.

The archer was about to loose a bolt when Vetra motioned his head toward the wall to Nog. Nog moved in a lynx-like crouch to hunch underneath the ledge as Vetra tucked his blade at his belt. Vetra took a long running leap and vaulted on Nog's back and sprang up as Nog lifted him, giving him extra buoyancy. Vetra clawed his way up onto the ledge and grabbed at the archer's ankle. In his surprise, the archer fumbled his shot. Vetra pulled him down into the pit where Nog made short work of him with mace. Vetra continued his charge along the ledge and ran straight for the hetman. His scimitar was now blood-drenched and gleaming. The hetman sprang to his feet, parried the strike that would have sheared off half his skull.

At the same time, a lone figure came striding down the path onto the ledge. *Skirl.* He wielded a strange object in hand—a blazing ruby that cast a surreal, if not ominous hue over the grisly surroundings.

With an exalted gleam in his eyes, the apprentice made for the hetman, as if he'd heard whispers from the gods themselves. Now he exulted in his glory. The Eros stone, raised high like some sacred runestone, cut rays of light through the half gloom and spellbound all who peered upon it.

Vetra reached down a hand and pulled Nog up onto the ledge.

Unlike the time in the crypts under Dormoth, Skirl was not afraid. He held the Eros Flame in a steady fist. "Look into the light, knaves! Drink deep your doom!"

Nog's lips parted. His eyes glazed over.

"Don't look at it, you fool!" Vetra rasped.

Nog squinted and looked away.

The last two archers turned wicked crossbows down at Skirl. Their target was now an upstart who dared to preempt their sport. But when they took aim, they found they could not draw bolts. The mystical light stung their eyes. Their draw arms sagged. Their tongues lolled.

"Shoot, you fools!" the hetman bellowed. For the moment he alone seemed unaffected by the eerie magic.

Skirl backed away, hedging his way along the ledge. The jewel dispelled the blood-darkened carnage of the death pit. His cheeks burned with a rebellious heat, his face radiated an otherworldly glow. The full force of the Eros magic seemed to course through his blood.

While the reavers' jaws hung half open like village idiots, Vetra slit the throat of the first man, the leather-faced Jarno, thus reclaiming his trusty sword and knife. Nog snatched back one of his short swords from Halfhan, the next nearest cutthroat, and plunged it deep into his guts. With a vicious snarl, he slew the first archer he saw. He snatched up the man's crossbow and put a bolt through the last bowman higher up in the stands.

Nog aimed for the hetman's chest.

"Wait!" Vetra cried, catching the bow's stock.

The cutthroats hunched transfixed, eyes dilated like mesmerized acolytes. At any moment these dark-eyed cutthroats could break out of their grip of enchantment and massacre the lot of them. Vetra admired Skirl's concentration to hold a spell of power that kept almost forty of them in thrall. Perhaps the jewel was doing most of the work?

No, he thought not. He recalled how easily Taranis had ensorcelled him back at Dormoth while now the fledgling struggled with all his might to keep the bare minimum of the spell going. Beads of sweat had sprouted on his brow.

Skirl backed up, shielding his companions from the hetman's blade. The steel of the murderous but spellbound outlaws looked ready to erupt in a riot of slaughter.

On vengeful feet Vetra strode forth and faced Brule. "Tell me, reaver. There was a girl you took about a month ago—a fair-haired, slender maid from Tarnwold with not a mean bone in her body."

The hetman gave a swinish grunt. "I remember her. Golden hair, golden eyes, skin soft as down. What about her?"

"What did you do with her?"

"We sold her to Tork, the slave dealer who rode in from Soho or Sarnhill. Claimed to be an envoy to the Emir Jasir in Kirnland. She and three others we sold were taken off our hands. No quibbling. Silver paid at double the price."

Vetra gave a fatalistic nod. "Then it is too late."

The hetman gave his neck a rueful twist, suddenly paling and wetting his lips. "I have done bad deeds, mercenary. This ruby—" he said in an odd voice now, as if the magic were seeping into his bones "—has given me new hope." He swallowed and peered into the scarlet light. "I-It has filled my heart with a love...a love I've never known! I shall go forth and take a straighter path, mend my ways."

"That's a noble sentiment, hetman, and I laud you for it," Vetra said, "but there's still another matter."

"What's that?"

"This." With a snarl of indescribable loathing, Vetra snatched the hetman's hair and with three mighty hews, hacked the man's gibbering head off. A gush of blood slathered the stones. "Send my regards to Dal Sagoth!" he rasped.

The corpse fell and Vetra wiped the filth from his blade on the man's jerkin. He tossed the head into the reeking pit where it bounced like a rotten melon. The staring men below glared as if half possessed.

A look of deadly earnest settled over Vetra's face. Into his smoldering eyes came a look of calm. As if vindicated, he breathed a desolate sigh, knowing that one good deed had been done for the day.

The Ravenclaws rushed at him as one. Had Skirl's magic slipped? Vetra's blade flew in cleaving arcs, a whirl of murderous thrusts and slashes. He hewed men like corn stalks under a scythe, and men died in agony, their throats ripped out or bellies torn asunder. Nog bunted others dead or alive down into the pit and did his fair share of slaying. Others crammed up on the uneven tiers above the ledge halted in their tracks. Nog swung the crossbow up on them.

Then he trained it down into the pit. "Stay where you are, you filthy pigs!" He turned to Vetra. "Shouldn't we slay the lot of these miserable scum?"

More of them were snapping out of their daze as Skirl's hand that bore the Eros Flame dropped.

"I'm sick of slaying for one day, Nog!" With a vicious grunt, Vetra snatched up the crossbow from Nog's hand. "Stay back, Raven-scum!" he cried. "The first to come creeping out of that pit or sidling after us, gets a bolt in his guts!" He loosed a warning quarrel among the wretches in the pit. By lucky chance, steel thunked into a man's thigh. He hopped about, cursing, condemning all outlanders to Dergath.

"Come!" Vetra snarled. "Let's quit this vipers' nest."

Nog and Skirl snatched up a sheave of quarrels. Vetra and Nog passed along the ledge to the oaken door that gave way to the clearing while Skirl took up the rear, hefting jewel. Vetra turned to cast the apprentice a thoughtful appraisal. "Come to pay us back for all the times we've saved your ass?"

"I heard the brutes carousing in the pit and came to see what all the fuss was about."

"Where is that ghoul, Igir?" Vetra hissed, peering past Skirl's shoulder. "Haven't seen his ugly face among these vultures since he crept away on skulking feet. Still have yet to slit that bastard's throat."

"I spared you the trouble, Vetra," said Skirl.

Vetra cast him a sharp glance. "Well, one less outlaw to send to Dergath. You've been busy I see." He kicked open the door to the communal area.

"I told you, none can stand before the Eros Flame."

No sooner had they passed through and Nog shot back the bolt when there came a thud of steel and swords on the other side of the heavy wood. The tumult echoed across the clearing. Vetra sneered. He turned in time to recognize the low growl and the pound of heavy claws on stone as the murderous mastiff leapt for his throat.

Nog's blade lanced forth. The froth-jowled killer skewered itself on the tip. While it thrashed and yelped, Vetra hacked hard at its neck, silencing its frantic leaps and whines forever.

"Is there no end to fiends?" he murmured. He gripped his hilt in rage. He wiped his bloody blade on the beast's thick fur. "Let's see to the women. Come on!"

Chapter 35

Restless, red-eyed figures shuffled and whimpered behind the pales of the stockade. Passing the fire pit, Vetra saw the charred carcasses of several deer and many broken casks of beer. A degree of feasting and ale-drinking had been enjoyed by the Ravenclaw rogues during the mercenaries' captivity.

Vetra examined the padlock and chain. Hopeful, tear-stained faces peered out between the slits, calling out, while white, trembling fingers gripped the bars.

No use blunting their swords on the chain and lock, Vetra decided. He and Nog slashed at the stakes around the lock. Those that splintered, they wrenched free and jerked the gate open. The captive women scrabbled out in a half mad rush.

"Tatla! Who among you is Tatla?" Vetra called, scanning the faces.

"I am, lord!" Vetra turned to a hollow-cheeked maid about eighteen with matted chestnut hair. In her narrow cheeks lurked a resemblance to the skinny, sloe-eyed child of eight he remembered from his youth. But he saw her features had matured nicely. She had a fine-boned, attractive face and her bedraggled look and grime did not diminish her slender, gorgeous figure. Vetra grimaced. All the better for fetching high prices at the slave auctions. He motioned briefly, "Come with us, your father awaits."

"Papa?" Glad tears sprang in her eyes. She stared, as with disbelief.

Vetra took her hand; they set off at a run to the roped off horse corral; many horses already whickered with the excitement. Some were saddled, most not.

"Take what horses you can," Nog said. He snatched at the reins of Vrigin's milky-eyed roan.

"Can any of you, ride?" Vetra peered at the huddled group.

There came ready nods.

Half could, so under Vetra's direction, they doubled up on the horses, six with saddles, while Vetra nuzzled the nose of his black mare with a grim nod.

"You ride at my side, lass." He pulled Tatla up behind him.

One of the taller, more mature women who'd been eyeing Skirl's weapon laid a hand on his arm, "Give me that crossbow. Any of those lowlifes comes near me, I'll plug iron bolts down their throat."

Vetra smiled with appreciation at her warrior spirit. He saw she was a tall, fair maid with light brown curly hair. Eyes steel blue. She raked back a rebellious lock and held his gaze without flinching. "Take it, miss. You'll not have use for it while they lie dazed and jerking each other's beards in the pit."

The woman gave a hoarse laugh. "There're always more. These brutes come at all hours of the night. Drunk sometimes, at the crack of dawn, always with more spoils."

Vetra gave a bleak nod. An uneasy thought gripped the back of his mind. "Then let's go. We don't want to be trapped in this devil's pit."

Tatla cried, "Wait."

Vetra turned and saw a tousle-haired boy scrabbling toward them. He was all knees and elbows, wide eyes. He'd been hiding behind the horse corral, in a pile of straw.

"The lad I released from one of Igir's cages," Skirl cried.

Nog reined in. He was about to scoop him up when the woman armed with the crossbow reached down a hand and pulled him up herself, settled him on the saddle behind her. The rest of the women had gained their mounts and seemed capable enough to ride, Vetra thought. Dergath help them.

Vetra swatted the rumps of the remaining dozen to get them scattering. No sense leaving them for the outlaws. He heeled his black mare ahead. Behind him, Nog rode with Skirl clutching his talisman. Together in semi-organized fashion they trotted past the horse pen, across the grubby communal grounds, down the scrubby slope.

"You're a sight for sore eyes, sir swordsman," Tatla whispered in Vetra's ear, "or should I say Master Vetravincus?"

"You remember me?" he said incredulously.

"Yes, I remember you from my childhood. The horsemaster's son. Vetravincus of the moody tempers and the flashing sword. Always the bee in everyone's bonnet, the restless rover."

A smile crept over Vetra's lips. She clung to his back and he could feel the soft press of her breasts against him as she murmured again in his ear. "I remember when you thrashed one of those bullies harassing young Domlin's brother. That story was popular for a month!" She clung to him tighter. "When you first came to this cursed place, a hope flared in my heart, that there was justice in this world. But when I saw you all trussed up and bullied by them and taken to the cavern, my hope fled with it. Now I am on the back of a horse with you, and your friends are like gifts from the gods."

"We're not out of this yet."

"I still feel like I am caught in an evil dream," she gasped. "Still trapped in that filthy pen. Where are those other villains?"

"They lie blooded and dazed in their loathsome pit. How long they stay there, I could not say. Some had already crept out and were banging hard at the door." He left that thought unfinished. A rogue fear gnawed at him. Maybe he should have slit all their throats while he had the chance? Had he not vowed to send them all to Dergath?

Dull yellow bands of cloud hung over the hills behind them. They rode through the screen of foliage the outlaws had erected to conceal their path. No need to restore the sheltering branches. Dusk was coming, and was but an hour away. It would bring with it a coolness to the lands and the threat of night discovery.

No sooner had they wound their way out of the foothills when specks of black shapes emerged from the dark fringe of trees to the north.

"What more foul luck to add to the day?" Vetra cursed. A stray arm of the Ravenclaw band now returning from their hunt laden with their spoils…and fast moving toward them.

They'd spotted them. Like the wrath of a blistering wind they now came galloping across the fields at a breakneck speed.

"Ride!" Vetra cried. He urged his mount to double speed. Nog dug his heels into his own roan. The women gave their horses free rein. Anxious cries spilled from their lips, drifting across the lonely countryside.

Vetra squinted ahead. The north-south track was but five hundred yards away.

It may as well have been five miles. The raiders were swift. They knew their craft. The women who lagged behind were headed off by rearing stallions. Half of them waylaid as rag-bearded men leaped off their mounts and onto the saddles of the women. The mettlesome maiden with the crossbow drew back a bolt and shot one in the face.

Vetra swore under his breath. This venture was not going well.

Already cross-bolts were raining down upon them, whistling by his ear and rattling like snakes about the horse's heels.

He could not save them all. Their only chance was to get to the road and try to escape into the protection of woods.

Nog slowed, his mare bucking with a quarrel in her rump.

Riders were all around them now. Nog hacked while Skirl spat out threats. The Eros jewel clutched in his hand seemed useless under the bucking, heaving madness.

Vetra circled back and lay steel into the first outlaw with upraised sword who was half way home to plunging a blade into Nog's throat. Tatla clung to his back. The outlaw toppled with a bellow of agony, trampled underfoot by beasts charging at the rear.

"Ride faster! Follow my lead!" Vetra called back at the

panicking women. There were too many of them. "Don't try to fight them!"

The warrior-woman with the bow and boy in tow paid heed. So did one other.

The three hurtled toward the road with Nog and Skirl struggling to keep up on their wounded roan. Vetra turned his mount on the dirt track heading south, aiming for the trees around a bend in the road.

Shouts and jeers echoed behind him. Raucous wails, the thunder of hooves, desperate cries.

A startling sight lay around that bend. A massive column of riders bearing the Lvendarian flag.

Vetra huffed an explosive breath. Was it a mirage?

The column's standard-bearer bore the pennon of Lausern with the blue and yellow griffin.

So, the rumored expected invasion was real…

The soldiers heard their cheers and came at full gallop to strike terror in the black-clad riders' hearts. A strident blare of a horn announced a hundred armored swordsmen with glinting shields…and more were coming.

On sight of the mounted soldiers, the Ravenclaw riders turned their mounts and fled. Terror of the Lvendar army had them whipping their horses to a frenzy.

Vetra gave a smile of triumph. Perhaps the day had not been lost and Dergath had not deserted them completely.

CHRIS TURNER

Chapter 36

The rush of thunderous hooves and armored flanks of black stallions mingled with the swish of arrows and the cries of dying men. The Lvendarian guard charged forward. Men leapt off their horses and skewered four of the downed outlaws with poleaxes.

In total, Vetra estimated they were 400 mounts strong. Knights who wielded axe, sword and mace on prize destriers dressed in blue and green aprons over mailed flank and belly. The pride of Lvendar.

A stocky man in a blue-plumed morion piked his sword and kneed his horse forward. "Back to your ranks, you rascals!" he yelled at his riders. "There'll be more to kill later. We'll rout out those scum on our way back. Pressing matters loom. Let us ride!" He was a muscly jowly man with flint-gray eyes, high cheekbones, and a hard-bitten air of authority.

The courageous woman of Vetra's company with the crossbow cried out, "There are others back there, captain! We must save them." She waved her bow at the outlaws on black horses streaking off with six of the women she'd rode with. Her breath was a husky echo.

"They're going nowhere," the captain called back. "The outlaws' slavers' route is through Masern, which is where we go to break the approaching army."

"You must stop them!"

"Damn it, woman! There will be no Lvendar left if we don't halt this invasion. An insolent horde bent on splintering our borders. We must think priorities." His stony eyes flicked off her onto five of the other women his riders had brought forth. They all stared comatose, grime-streaked, cringing in the arms of the soldiers. "Take her and the boy and the others back to their people," the captain ordered.

The woman struggled in her saddle as the men-at-arms tried to escort her back to the end of the column. Vetra scowled. He reined in, but did nothing to stop them. He tried to convince himself that the maid didn't realize how lucky she was to have escaped the slavers.

But something did not sit right with him. "Hold up!" he rasped. "The woman fought valiantly. She slew at least one of those raider scum who were after us. Without her, many of us would have died."

The captain glared at him. "You giving me orders?"

"No, I merely suggest the woman deserves more than what you're giving her...to be heard and leave her her horse. I stand in her defense."

The captain rubbed his jaw. He muttered into his beard. "If you're so hell bent for leather, woman, take up a sword and fight with the men."

"That I will, and gladly," she cried.

His lips grew wide in appreciation. "Tell me then, what's your name, lass?"

"Caradwen.... Dwen for short. I come from Cairnhill, a village two leagues east of here."

"Dwen, you are hereby promoted to rank of mounted knight. Man-at-arms of the Lvendarian guard."

"Woman-at-arms, sir."

He waved his arm as if it were all one. He turned to his lieutenant. "See to it."

Caradwen was fitted in a spare hauberk, bronze helm and handed a decent sword. Vetra gave a nod of satisfaction.

The captain looked to Tatla and motioned to his lieutenant. "Go, take her home too before dusk sets in."

Tatla twisted in her saddle. "When will I see you again?" She clutched at Vetra, blinking back her tears.

"I shall pass by Vrigin's when this is all over." His words sounded hollow even to his own ears.

"We'll make camp within the hour, before dusk—" the captain gestured. "Ahead, past that round in the trail on higher ground." His gloved hand indicated the brow of a hill. "The aspen and hemlock'll give us shelter. No fires are to be lit."

"As you wish, Lord Onas." The captain's lieutenants gave stiff nods. They rode back to give orders to the others. Nog replaced his disabled mount with one of the larger horses that the soldiers had rounded up. Skirl too rode his own horse. The company moved on sure-footed hooves up the nearby slope to spread out and make camp.

The captain took stock of Nog and Vetra. "We have known about this band of cutthroats for a while. They have lived too long...A slaver band led by a man called Brule."

Vetra grumbled. "We know. Trouble yourself no more, captain. I slew him myself."

The captain stared at him, licking his lips. "Then you've done a service to Lvendar. You're from where?"

"Tolizia."

"Tolizia? And you, sir?" He turned his piercing gaze on Nog.

"Thrakia."

The captain shook his head in wonderment, a low grumble under his breath. "Tolizia and Thrakia? Wanderers? Mercenaries?—serving justice in Lvendar? Surely this is a strange world. What next? Balborian strumpets giving lectures on chastity in the public square?"

His men-at-arms laughed.

"Five hundred yeoman infantry to be wagoned in from Alantra on the morrow! Six hundred more riders to follow from Lausern with archers. This will swell our numbers threefold. Lord Ragnum sent us in advance to check the Mercian incursion, to slow down the march on Alantra."

A soldier slapped the captain's arm and pointed high in the sky. Onas turned and frowned up into the dying light at an odd shape.

A black speck in the west was growing larger with every passing breath. A thing of jagged wings, crusty body and sharp pointed snout. Taranis's dragon, if Vetra knew anything. Who other than the Archmagrix herself riding its back, her chin held high like some sorceress queen. The dragon was already enormous. He shuddered to think of how big it would get when it was fully grown.

"Lord, the devil rides!" croaked the man-at-arms.

"No, it is Taranis," Vetra murmured. "Sorceress from Xalgossa. She rides Drako, the dragon hatched from an egg."

"Dragon?" the captain snarled. "An egg? Are you serious? What know you of such a beast?"

"We stumbled across it under the stone stronghold of Dormoth, lord. The Hall of Mages at Xalgossa. We have fled from there these past days, evading the sorceress's wrath."

"Dergath's bane! What other imbroglios have you gotten yourself into? Outlaws, witches and now this dragon?" He shook his head violently and spat an oath. His eyes narrowed to slits as superstitious fear now crinkled his cheeks. In glided the dragon, sweeping lower over their numbers in wide circles. The batlike wings stretched wide, a duskier crimson than the burnt-umber body. Its ugly horned skull dipped and its basilisk glare swung upon the gathered horsemen. Jaws parted, revealed twin white fangs and now the puff of its smoky breath blew, as if waiting to belch a stream of fire to char them all.

"Shields up!" the captain bellowed. Horses whinnied and four hundred knight's shields lifted in unison. "Dragons! I did not know such things existed."

"They do, captain, and you see proof with your own eyes."

"What does this sorceress want?" he demanded. His blue-gray eyes gazed up past his shield as the beast continued its arc of reconnaissance then tilted its snout to the north.

"She seeks the jewel of Eros," Skirl said, reining in closer, "the Eros Flame—" his voice pitched louder than necessary.

"Which our doughty mage guards in his robe's pocket," Vetra murmured.

Skirl held the jewel up for all to see.

The captain blinked and blocked the light from his eyes with a hand. "Put it away, you oaf! It blinds my eyes, even in this waning light."

A sea of swords piked around Skirl's neck. He quickly stuffed it back in his pocket. The swords retreated, dropping like feathers in the wind.

After a time the dragon faded in the distance as if to scout out the Mercian army to the north. For what reasons, Vetra could not guess. The sorceress, it appeared, had not spotted them among the ranks of horsemen. Or perhaps she was just toying with them.

"You say she is Umbrian?" the captain asked. "They are no friends of the Mercians. Let us hope she harries them, not us."

Vetra's thoughts were doubtful, thinking there'd be little chance of that.

"You two fight well," he said, "I may have use of you. Will you join our forces?"

Vetra shrugged. "What say you if we pass?"

The captain bared his teeth. A chill smile ran up the line of his rugged jaw. "We could also send you packing back to Alantra with the females... For a long interrogation at the bailiff's office inquiring as to why you are in Lvendar."

Vetra moistened his lips. "We'll ride with you, captain, only if you add the mage to our company."

"What, this scrawny pretty boy? Look at him, half an ear, ranting about a magic jewel and a dragon-riding sorceress. I've seen dozens of raving lunatics on the streets of Alantra. Street cats too less battered. What need have I of a jackleg magician?"

Skirl piped up in a voice of hauteur, "You have Taranis, and a dragon pitted against you. I can weave counterspells to thwart the witch and her magic spells."

"Aye, and get mixed up in a private war with the Xalgossian mages? No thanks."

"You're already entwined," Vetra intoned. "The sorceress has marked you and your army as she's marked us. You've nothing to lose. I say, take up the mage's offer." He gestured to the restless soldiers who were looking all too uneasily skyward even after the dragon's shadow had passed. "From where I'm standing, you're going to need all the help you can get."

The captain rubbed his cheek. "Perhaps you are right. But it's on your head if this goes sideways. Make sure the mage gets us in no trouble."

Vetra gave a brief nod. He didn't care about trouble, just as long as they rode in protected numbers. Nor did he care to mention that the apprentice was at best a tyro, if not an outright fraud. What the captain didn't know couldn't hurt him. Vetra's instincts told him he had to stay close to Skirl. He needed to protect him, and the mage needed to protect them, if that made any sense.

Vetra mumbled to Nog at his side. "We've got plunder-happy Mercians to the north, angry Lvendarians to the south, now a mad witch flying on a dragon out for our blood. To the west, a band of cutthroats who would ride out of the hills to slay us for fouling their nest. What more could we ask for?"

The riders settled in and made camp on the ridge as the sun sank behind brooding crags that bordered Umbria and Lvendar. Fresh loaves and cold mutton were brought out from saddlebags. The men sat in a clearing under tree cover, munching and trading stories in companionable groups. Tents were erected under the swaying aspen with their falling leaves, the horses fed and watered at a small stream running down the other side of the hill and hobbled to prevent any loss.

After they'd made camp, the captain motioned Vetra and Nog to sit by him, seeing that they sat apart. "You'll need shields, lads. Go around back of the tents to the weapons' stores and take what you need. There are daggers, mace and greaves."

Nog grinned and patted his hauberk and swords. "Got all I need right here, captain. These blades are my shield." He unsheathed the swords slung on his back and crossed them before his chest.

"Suit yourself, crusader. If dying's your wish then run with it. We move out at dawn's light. We'll meet the horde that wishes to sack Alantra and it's not going to be pretty."

"No war or battle is," Vetra muttered. He remembered his father's words long ago and missed the old man's presence more than ever.

Skirl selected and donned a steel cap, then fitted silver mail over his soiled robe. The accouterments gave his frame a bit more substance, though not much. He took a dagger from the spread which he shoved in a thigh pocket of his tattered robe. Vetra's lips curled into a wry smile. Garbed in his war gear, the mage scarecrow looked a veritable warrior but not one to strike terror in the hearts of an enemy.

Onas left to inspect the camp. He gave brief instructions to his sentries while Nog took Vetra aside. "Why do you hate these Mercians so much?"

A dark cloud came over Vetra's face. "They burned my father's gladiatorial school, raped my mother and slaughtered our finest horses."

Nog swallowed. "Who?"

"A band of Mercian raiders. As a lesson to my father who defied them. I learned of this travesty after my travels east, Nog. Those long wandering years, lost, footing it through Condoria, Mosete and elsewhere. Rumor had it, the deed was done under the orders of the mad King Aethrith of Mercia at the time, the jealous snake, as a lesson to my father, Menicus, who had trained so many good warriors to fight against Mercia. He fought against imperialism. I'll kill every one of the vermin I get my hands on."

"Understandable. But not all Mercians are evil."

"No, just the ones that matter, Nog. Crooked men working

under a king who endorses crooked policies. I hate Mercian imperialism as much as my father did. They were jealous of the number of quality fighters he churned out to destroy the march on our borders. I have no doubt Minas's kidnapping had something to do with this vendetta Aethrith had against my father. Even these scum outlaws had blessings from Mercia."

Nog firmed his lip. "That's a tall accusation. This is all news to me. No matter, we will kill them all."

Even as darkness fell, Vetra glanced up into the black velvet sky through the wavering branches with a wary eye. He did not like the fact that Taranis was so near. "I can almost smell her," he said. "I feel a quiver in my bones."

Skirl drifted over to stare up beside him. "'Tis her power, Vetra. The power she wields through the Eros Flame."

"Dergath's hell!" Vetra swore. "Am I to be forever the pawn of this she-devil?"

"If the originator of the spell is slain, the spell is broken."

"So I am to be a woman slayer then?"

Skirl lifted his shoulders. "You can conclude what you like."

Vetra bared Skirl a toothy snarl. "I rue the day I joined up with you, mage. This zany quest has caused us much grief."

Skirl tried his best at a grin. "But what fun we're having, eh Vetra?"

Vetra grabbed him by the scruff of the neck and propelled him toward the trees. He looked ready to give him a beating.

Skirl called out in protest, "Wait! Peace, brother! The only way forth is forward."

Vetra halted and patted the mage on the back. He gave a reluctant grin and shook his head. "Come on, knave! Let us see to this mutton they're dishing out. My guts ache with hunger."

Chapter 37

Dawn had risen far too red and early for Vetra's liking. A thin mist blanketed the camp and the shallow vale to the north. His bones ached from the abuse of the past days, not to mention the rough ground and chill dew on which he'd slept. Nog seemed spry, his black-gray mane sticking up in places like turkey feathers. He patted the spikes down and slung on his helm and stretched his long arms with a yawn. Caradwen had been given a tent of her own by Onas's tent that evening and she'd passed the night in safety.

A clatter of hooves heralded the arrival of a scout riding into the camp on a steel-gray stallion. He reined in beside Onas who was gearing up in silver-scale mail and gaudy, plumed morion. The rider dismounted and bent a knee. "Sir, I have come from the head of the Mercian march. Thousands of soldiers!" he said breathlessly. "Bearing swords, mace, axe and at least 200 archers."

Onas exhaled. "This bodes ill for us, Baldir."

"It gets worse. The Mercians have recruited a tribe of giants—from beyond the norther border of Balboria, the haunt of the Kyldrie."

"Giants?" The captain blinked in astonishment. "What in Dergath…are such things possible?"

"I have seen them with my own eyes, sir. Huge juggernauts. With steel caps like drums and wooden clubs like trunks. They take strides as men would take running hops. Perhaps fifty of them, serving as rear guard. At first I thought they were misshapen trees, or strange siege engines, but then I saw they were men of enormous size. Eldritch things brew in the haunt of the Kyldrie, sir, the place from whence the dragons came."

The captain shook his head in dismay. "I fear we are hopelessly outnumbered, Baldir. We will fight anyways! And we will die like men. Dergath help these invaders who marshal against us! The bigger they are, the harder they will fall." He rounded on Vetra and Nog who'd ridden up with Skirl on their horses. "Mercenaries, if your mage has any power, let him wield it now. We ride to war! Let us be off!"

Horns signaled the march to arms.

The company was not five minutes into their canter when two robed figures came riding up behind them. Three outriders veered off to intercept them and escort the newcomers to the captain's place at the vanguard.

Vetra recognized them immediately, inauspicious mages of the cloth of Dormoth.

"Who are you and what do you want?" the captain demanded.

"We are mages of Dormoth at Xalgossa," the first figure in white said. "I am Belgra, this is Senesch, come to secure the Eros Stone. 'Tis known as *Arkmida* in the tongues of old of the Sahirians."

"More mages?" the captain cried in exasperation. "Dergath, will I ever hear the end of this silly jewel? Is it that important?"

"It is. And scorn not our assistance," Senesch chided. He clutched his robe ever tighter about his thin frame in the chill of dawn. "Taranis, head sorceress of Xalgossa, has uprooted the garden over the crypts of Old Sagoth. She has unleashed a dragon on the world. Doubtless you have seen the foul fiend pass over at some recent time?"

"Aye, we have, old man. What of it?"

"Taranis rides it into dusky dawn and fiery sunset. She ensorcelled our fellow mages with the Eros Flame before we could intervene. I fear she has plans to enslave the entire north and become dark queen of all the lands—if she wins this battle for the stone. I fear she has learned of the location of the Dragon Lords who kept the dragons' last eggs, and will rouse them to unleash an army against the free kingdoms."

"Wizard, is there nothing but woe in your news?" Onas clutched at his beard. "All of what you speak is foul, wizard, foul!"

"Alas, captain, there's more. Our kindred mage Voydred has fallen to the Archmagrix's spells. Even now he rides behind us on a jet-black stallion. He calls himself 'The Black Mage'. No more than a few hours away. For Taranis he would wield black magic against you. You and your men will need all the sorcerous help you can get. Keren, our beastmaster, has also fallen. Once he was wise and canny, now he is under the grip of her tainted magic. He acts as her eyes and ears. A conduit some say...a scout who's taken the form of a great condor with all-seeing eye, and armed such, he can sniff out the stone bearer and its magic at a distance."

The captain rocked back in his saddle. "Is there no one who can give me favorable news?" He dragged his knuckles across his plumed morion.

Senesch shook his head. "Better to hear words of truth than false whispers, my Lord."

Onas gave a bitter nod. "You speak truthfully, old man." He scratched his head, his battle cunning at work. "Can we not devise a truce with this witch?"

Skirl made a derisive sound. "It is said she goes up to her secret observatory in the Hall of Winds on the night of the full moon...to gaze at harvest time on the blood-red moon and dream lusty dreams of Dal Sagoth. She cut off my ear on a whim." He tilted his head and its bandage. "Does this sound like one with whom you can deal truces?"

Onas shook his head.

"She will destroy anything in her path that bars way to the stone."

After a time Onas frowned. "How came you mages of Dormoth so quickly upon our company?"

"I threw the bones," said Belgra. "I asked the gods where

goeth the stone, and in the pattern that fell, the shades told me that the Eros Flame would be here in this lonely corner of Lvendar on the eve of the waxing moon. And so—my divination has proven true."

"Witchcraft," the captain grumbled.

"You disapprove?"

"I don't approve or disapprove, milady. I merely dwell in the world of the living. I follow things I can see with my own eyes, not shades, spirits and heathenish magic. They are not for me or to my liking."

Senesch gave a disgruntled snort. "Then you are sorrily deluded, captain. This world is ruled by unseen forces. We are part of a whole, as wind is to air, water is to the sea. There is much mystery in this world which we will never see, or hear or understand."

"Riddles and gibberish," the captain muttered. "Which I care not to dispute with you. 'Tis time we move on. Stay back out of the way of my riders if you wish to accompany us. Wield your magic, if you must, but only if it will help us win this battle, or eliminate these fiends of whom you speak."

The four hundred riders moved on only to be met by the forces from the south, swelling their numbers three-fold as the captain had predicted. Up the dirt track they rode, many dozens of men abreast as the terrain allowed it. The terrain here, mostly open fields, pastures and scattered copses of aspen and oak turning yellow in the changing season, was pleasant country and easily navigable.

They at last mounted a hill and looked over a golden valley. The morning mist was barely clearing. The Mercians had taken up on a knoll across the valley. There the enemy armies stood separated by an open plain down which the north-south road ran. The warriors contemplated each other. Like ravenous wolves. The sun glinted off their burnished weaponry, their bronze helms and steel hauberks. Their horses finery and accouterments clinked in the distance.

"Fine day for killing," Nog remarked. He peered at the rows of mailed riders and the enemy pikemen. The standard of Mercia rose high from a polearm on a lead rider's horse—the black war wolf on a green background. A grim insignia which fluttered in the gentle breeze from the hills to the west.

"For you, every day's good for killing," Vetra said. His voice held no humor. Every time he'd had to face a wall of mailed men in a full scale battle, his stomach had churned. The notion that war is a glorious thing is a misnomer, that it brings purpose and strength to a warrior's body and soul. Pure codswallop. It may cleanse him of illusion, if there is any gain. Blood and death, the taking of lives, senseless destruction and the rape of land and women, it is a dark stain and taint on the human soul. So too the burning of crops and peoples' dreams. The whispering rush of shades of the departed is no proud thing to experience or the bristling of hairs on the back as one walks the battlefields of the dead.

Yet the poets and sages, and the pundits and scholars, would sing and scribe about it forever in many a heroic verse. They would wax on till the cows come home, in their myths and their anthologies, never lifting a blade once themselves in their valiant careers. Yet men would fight on and men would die deluded with the same thrill of battle in their breasts as the curse of war had given them since they were apes rising out of the jungle.

Both sides, the enemy nearly three thousand strong, were ready to slay each other and claim northern Lvendar for their own. In ranks of hundreds, the enemy riders poised, blue-green jupons draped over silver-scale mail, swords tipped now in a wild battle cry. Both kings were strangely absent, as if this theater were but a mere exploratory skirmish for a greater battle to come.

Vetra was puzzled. Were more troops and horses held back to pour from the heartsprings of Mercia and Lvendar at a later time? Siege engines and war machines? The puppet monarchs being content at having their ambassadors and generals do their dirty work for them seemed odd, but then again, odder things had happened in this age.

On the horizon was something that was not so puzzling—a hideous lizardish shape that come winging from the west—all burnt umber and mottled crimson. It hovered above the opposing armies out of arrow range.

Taranis's black-robed figure sat astride her pet in all her gleaming glory. And a new surprise, a gigantic hook-beaked bird, a condor half as large, but with brownish wingspan nearly as wide as the dragon's. It hovered in the dragon's shadow like some minion goliath—the ensorcelled beastmaster, Keren.

The warriors massed below. Committed thus, they heeded not the double omens. Men shuffled and roared and clacked their swords on shield. What was a freakish condor and a fabled lizard hosting a luxurious rider to them in this do-or-die moment?

The captains shouted their orders. Horns blared. Then the horses thundered forth as one as the sun lit their burnished armor aflame.

Vetra rode with Captain Onas in front of him. Nog was at his side with hundreds of mailed riders surrounding them on either flank and behind.

Behind the Mercian ranks a phalanx of foot soldiers knelt and took aim in the dewed grass with their arbalests. Volleys flew like a flock of black hornets. They arched over the Mercian ranks to find targets among the Lvendarian horsemen.

The lead riders ducked behind their wooden shields. Vetra heard a murderous thunk of bolts as they plunked on wood and some smashed through men's shields. Two score mounted riders fell, pierced through throat or breast. The rest of them thundered ahead.

Vetra and Nog spurred their mares, roaring war cries, keen to slay as many of the enemy Mercians before the next volley of arrows could punch through their numbers.

In a thunderous rush the two forces met. A clangorous clash of steel that smote the air as blades of fury met in the middle of the valley still bathed in fresh morning mist battling the golden rays. It was like the crack of divine thunderbolts sent down from the sky. Horseflesh smashed into iron. Tortured cries rang up and down the valley, curdling the men's ears.

Vetra closed with his opposing rider, his shield up. A vicious spiked ball came for his head and he blocked the blow while he jabbed and slashed at his opponent's ribs. His enemy misjudged—a bearded Mercian with glaring eyes and horned steel cap—and Vetra drove the blade forward and cut through a rent in his mail and slewed into his vitals. Blood gushed and Vetra kicked the man off his saddle. He muscled his mare in to take up the space.

No sooner had he done this than he crossed blades with another bearded foe. Nog pushed into the gap while arrows flew thick and furious. The Lvendarian archers had been slower to shoot. Smoke seared across the sky as some of these shafts bore flaming ends which set men's surcoats aflame.

Horses wheeled. Many bucked and fled in terror, free of their riders. In the maelstrom of licking blades and spurting blood there was no logic, sense or order. Any man who went down was not likely to get up beneath that roil of stamping hooves. Horses milled, jammed together. Men reached and stabbed with swords, slashing murderously at limbs and torsos. All was pandemonium.

The Mercians had not come unprepared.

CHRIS TURNER

Chapter 38

Skirl rode somewhere back of the confused line. As keeper of the jewel, he clutched the precious Eros Flame like a jealous maid. Belgra and Senesch flanked him, riding no less fretfully. Skirl looked to them for support, but they seemed distant, faraway, as if absorbed in their own dark ruminations. Skirl's face grew pale, his mind troubled, his eyes darting every which way. Never had he expected to be in the press of such deadly forces.

Belgra hissed, "Do you have the stone?"

Skirl gave a slow nod.

"Let me see it."

He reluctantly pulled the stone from his pocket.

Belgra gasped, as did Senesch, for the gem's starlit radiance had increased, almost stinging their eyes, degrees beyond the fake they'd remembered adorning Taranis's neck.

Belgra gulped and licked her thin lips. "Better you entrust the talisman to me."

"Why?" Skirl demanded. He withdrew the stone jealously back into his pocket.

"I garner sufficient magic to defend it. Yours was stripped, remember?"

Stonier than basalt was this Belgra who held his gaze through narrowed lids, the same who carried his child in her womb. The sorceress seemed too eager, all too grasping for this piece of magickery.

Skirl bit his tongue. A sudden swoosh and arrows came whizzing at them. He ducked, cheating again death's sting.

Belgra spoke in low murmurs, like a breeze rippling through the high treetops. The crossbow bolts seemed to shiver and warp in their flight and thud into the ground at their horses' hooves. She made a furious gesture, "We'd better hope the Lvendarians don't fall, Senesch! If the jewel passes into enemy hands—" she let the thought dangle even as Skirl's eyes traveled to two brawny figures in red surcoats hacking and slashing a stone's throw away in a knot of blue-clad enemy horsemen.

Belgra heeled her horse forward. Her intent was to stop more Mercian arrows from piercing the Lvendarian defenders.

Senesch rode in beside her. "Belgra, wait! We must counter Voydred. Look, he rides!"

Their eyes turned. Behind them, a mounted figure in black, surrounded by a dozen mage guard, galloped their way.

A wicked pike came jabbing up at Vetra's horse then through his mare's ribs. The animal gave a last painful scream and threw him. Vetra rolled and staggered to his feet, shaking the daze out of his head. His sword, blood-dripping, swiftly lifted to ward off a hive of enemy blades. In the confused fray, Nog crouched a dozen feet away unhorsed. They both gave cursing shouts and joined the foot soldiers, now a milling wheel of hacking and stabbing men hemmed in a circle of snorting horses and enemy riders.

The Mercian plan was simple…To strike hard and fast at the heart of the enemy. Kill the leader and create a rout. They had not yet killed Onas but had inflicted terrible casualties on the Lvendarian riders. The hovering dragon provided no wrinkle in their plans—yet.

Arrows flew upward but either skidded off the dragon's hide or went spinning wide. For all those who sighted on Taranis, she sent down blue globes of death to smash them to bits.

The bulk of Mercians heeded not the dragon. They at last unleashed their armored giants at the Lvendarians, who for a time thought that their scouts had exaggerated the might of these mythic beings.

They had not.

Figures of nightmare, twice as high as a man, they loped in on bare thighs the size of hemlock trunks. Their faces, grim under their horned helms, were carved like oak. They gripped massive clubs in brawny fists. Though their legs were bare, their chests were burnished with cast iron that curved around their torsos like tortoise shells. They swatted men and horses aside as wanton boys would pesky flies.

Mounted bowmen peppered the first eleven of these monsters. They began to slow, finally to sag to their knees. The raging pikemen gathered and slew them to a man, hacking their heads off and sending them to Dergath.

But other giants had broken through the clot of men and horses and now lunged forward to take down Onas and his main vanguard of defenders.

Three came roaring in, knotted clubs swinging in fists, their lips frothing with spittle. They would take down the Lvendarian commander and his horse, crush and stomp him and his lieutenants to oblivion under their iron-shod boots.

The riders formed up a shield wall.

The horses reared and neighed in terror. Mercifully, they held. One giant crashed through the wall and brought a massive club smashing down on Onas's steed's skull. In a limp heap, the horse toppled, kicking up dust and gore. Onas rolled, his sword up, cursing and frothing at the ruin of his horse. The giant's shadow bore down on him like a harbinger of death.

Vetra blinked at the sheer horror of it all. He sheathed his sword and drew his knife…he clenched it in his teeth then took a running leap to vault on the back of the attacking giant. Into the nape of his neck he stabbed the blade again and again.

The giant reached a ham fist back to try and get a grip on his head but Vetra jerked back in time to slash at the giant's probing fingers. He leaped off as the giant staggered forward. Uttering war cries, Onas and his bodyguard surged forth and hacked the giant to pieces.

Onas flashed Vetra a grateful, blood-dripping salute. A tribute to his good sense in recruiting Vetra from the start. But even as the token gesture was exchanged, two more giants broke through the captain's bodyguard and swarmed the hapless riders. Vetra watched in dismay as they were pushed back and Onas's head caved in to one fell swoop of a log-like club. His limp body was pulverized under the sweep of oak and mammoth feet.

The two juggernauts rose in their glory, piking clubs in the air. Their heads were tipped back in ghastly battle cries. The commander of the Lvendarian forces was slain!

Taranis watched all this with lip-curled interest, as if entertained by the gore on both sides. She gave a husky howl and urged Drako lower and lower for a better view. Arrows flew at her, but none found their mark.

She barked a harsh syllable and bade her dragon swoop down for sport. To balance the scales, she directed him toward the Mercian commander three dozen paces away amid his knot of bearded, blood-thirsty warriors who rained sword blows upon the Lvendarian defenders' shields. The dragon caught the steel-helmed commander in its jaws, lifted him high off his steed and crunched his ribs. Then it dropped one of the blood-stained halves down on the warriors' heads below. The other half it devoured, a quick morsel to nourish its growing body.

Hovering on her dragon, the sorceress bade the winged lizard breathe fire on any who aimed arrows up at her.

Witnessing this travesty, Skirl bravely spurred forward to face the sorceress. He shook the gem in a raised fist. "Go back to your slime pit, witch! Take your dragon with you! Behold! I hold the Eros Flame. I turn it freely against you. Even its crimson light despises your sluttish hide!"

Taranis quivered in her seat, speechless with rage. Upon a furious gesture at the hulking condor at her side, she willed the hooked beak to turn her way. "Down, down, bird of faith! Seek this squawking infidel. Fetch me my gem!"

With a low guttural croak, the condor flapped mighty wings and angled its sinister beak toward the defenseless Skirl.

Skirl held the Eros jewel high, undeterred. The magical rays shone forth with a rare brilliance, straight into the descending condor's eyes...eyes that were Keren's.

Under the witch's spell, Keren was safely immune to the sway of magic while he assumed the form of this hulking bird-shape. With a flap and buffet of wings, deadly talons tore the jewel from Skirl's grasp...and unluckily, two of Skirl's fingers with it.

A spray of blood watered the grass. Skirl stared down at his missing fingers and an inarticulate cry caught in his throat. He clutched at his forked stump of hand, whimpering in grief as he slid off his horse.

The condor flapped back to where the sorceress perched on her dragon. She snatched the jewel from its upraised claws while a flurry of arrows whizzed around her. But she pressed her slim body flat to the dragon's hide. Thus clinging to its neck, the sultry witch made herself a near impossible target. "Go, good Keren!" she bawled. "Make sport of the Mercians, and the Lvendarians, I care not which." Even as she snapped the order, the brown-winged condor gave a shrill croak and dove with talons raking the helms of the fighting men below; it carved deep ruts through mail, flesh and bone.

Riders were unhorsed. Mayhem descended upon the ranks of both Mercians and Lvendarians. Vetra looked up to see chaos everywhere. Hordes of men hacking each other. Blood spraying from men and beasts.

Taranis's scintillant eyes glowed with rapture. An almost sexual heat radiated from her erotic figure as she twined her fingers about the Eros Stone. A soft moan rumbled in her throat. She caressed the gem, as if thriving on the spilling of men's blood, the blood of warriors who painted the battlefield with their life force. It was as much a thrill as the excitement of the stormy, loin-on-loin encounters with upteen men in her boudoir...under the voyeurish eye of her underworld demon, Dal Sagoth.

Arrows lanced up from all directions, but clacked harmlessly off the dragon's hard-scaled plates. Those who sighted on her were smitten by the power of the love amulet. They either sat or stood slack-mouthed, dazed in the vortex of the scintillating gem's magic.

Not all the arrows missed. One whizzed up and caught the giant winged Keren in its breast. The condor gave a mournful caw, outspread wings shredded as more bolts flew. He batted head back and forth, beak plucking at quarrels embedded in his flesh. He plummeted to the earth, crashing into mailed men, steel pikes and swords, breaking neck and crushing scores of soldiers. The beast shimmered out of existence, leaving only a naked, twisted figure of a man amid a sprawl of torn bodies.

Angered by the demise of her servant, Taranis shouted down, "Fly, Drako, fly! Let us avenge our knight!"

The dragon swooped low, and as he did, he opened wide his maw and breathed gales of fire upon horses and men alike and laid waste to hundreds in the fray.

Blackened humps lay behind her. Only a scorched ruin of charred flesh.

The dragon bore down now on Belgra who sat alone a-saddle her gray-white mare while Senesch sat three horses away, lips compressed.

Taranis cried from the back of her steed, "You would rebel against me, oh faithless cousin? No hummingbirds or enchanted begonias to take down my dragon?"

"I cannot tolerate your megalomania, Taranis!" Belgra shrilled back. "You have brought nothing but disgrace to our Order and death to countless innocents."

Taranis clicked her tongue. The shadow of the lizard fell over the slim figure of her cousin, though she rode off like the wind, her eyes white with fright.

The servile dragon swooped, smoke puffing from its nostrils, oblivious to Belgra's shrill shrieks of terror as scaly horn and sinew hooked around her waist and lifted her off her mount.

Skirl gave a mad cry of grief. He came running after her as if he could catch up and free her from the dragon's clutch.

The dragon circled and at Taranis's whispered command, caught the apprentice too in its opposing talon.

Now the two struggling figures lay clutched in the dragon's claws and Taranis gloated vindictively. The dragon rose once more to peer down upon the host of fighting men. Many hundreds milled below in disarray, many charred.

The sorceress tilted back her head and gave another dusky laugh, which rang across the assembled warriors like an evil chime.

Dragon and rider settled above the armies. Taranis held forth the jewel, her eyes slits of blazing wrath. "You faithless curs! You would fire arrows on me, Archmagrix of Xalgossa? Look within, what do you see?"

The dragon clutched Skirl ever tighter in its right talon. Skirl cried out in anguish. Belgra, constricted in its left, squirmed desperately. Skirl's face was a mask of pure misery. He looked on the verge of weeping. He peered over at his love Belgra, in the early stages of pregnancy, clutched as tightly as himself in the dragon's foul grip. Fresh blood spurted from his wound. But this was the least of his concerns.

"Off your horses and bow now, slaves!" Taranis shrieked. "Perhaps I will spare you!"

She crouched on the dragon's back. One hand was gripped on the dragon's neck. The other hand clutched the Eros Flame. Her head was tilted back, long chestnut mane trailing behind, mouth roaring a mantra-like spell.

"Garageis Umpheunt Karwezs!"

The love jewel, twined in her fingers, burst into a flare of brilliance more vivid than ever before, its sapphire radiance blinding the eyes of all who looked from below.

The willful dragon swooped low; it breathed fire and death

on the swath of those directly under his path. It swooped and rolled with the delight of a juvenile of the Kyldrie wastes allowed free reign in the sky, and carried Belgra and Skirl aloft again.

Taranis, drunk with her power, laughed, amused at the antics of her pet.

The sorceress's cruel gaze fell upon Vetra and Nog who struck and parried the swords of blood-soaked warriors below.

"Stop, you two faithless hounds!" And such was the power of her bellowing voice that their sport ended abruptly. "As punishment, you will fight to the death over me. The winner takes all! I will lie naked with the one who is still standing. Ere the rising moon this evening, I will then slit the winner's throat! Commence!" She clapped her hands and like a thunder burst, so it was done. The two began their pantomime of death. Like cobras swaying to a snake-charmer's pipe, Vetra and Nog dropped their hewing and scrambled over heaped bodies in a mad race to meet each other in mortal combat. Blood-caked swords clutched in fists, gleaming under the sallow light of the sun, with snarls on their lips, they turned on each other and steel clanked on steel. And such a fight was not to be seen on this gory battlefield that day...

Chapter 39

Even after the first clash of swords, some dim part of Vetra's brain registered that this was but a dream. A sorcerous parody of tainted magic.

But his body would not obey his reason. His muscled thews danced, like a strumpet at a bazaar; his heart beat and soared with love for this beautiful evil, black-leathered witch who hovered in the sky above him.

Nog too, caught up in his lust for the witch, possibly the chance to mate with the black widow herself, charged his closest friend and rained such a flurry of savage blows that Vetra was hard put to defend.

Vetra backpedaled, parrying, grunting. He saw an opening where Nog had overextended. The man's murderous twin blades had completed their circuit: the one clutched in his right hand was at the end of its lethal downswing, the other was drawn back ready for another strike. His left side was completely exposed. One quick thrust and he could drive cold steel into Nog's throat.

But he couldn't. Nog had saved his life on at least two occasions.

The hesitancy cost him.

Nog redoubled his fury, slashing left and right, his face beet red, lips frothing, and Vetra was pushed back to the line of enemy riders. The flickering blades of Mercians flicked out at his back to the snorting of horses.

Nog. Don't do this!

But Nog was not listening. He was beyond help, his senses completely addled by the thaumaturgy of the sorceress. He saw only red where Vetra walked, a barrier to his ultimate prize, Taranis lying naked on her satin bed.

Vetra ducked a swipe from a Mercian rider's blade. A horse's rump bunted his left shoulder and sent him sprawling forward.

Nog struck. Vetra's sword arm was slow to defend. The

blade went spinning out of his grasp as Nog's weapon hit square on. Cold steel traced a dizzying arc at his head. Vetra ducked, Nog's blade sweeping hairs' breadths from his head. He scrambled sideways, snatched up a fallen shield just in time to catch Nog's raised sword as he rained blows on the Mercian wood, nearly deafening his ears.

Voydred had made better time than Senesch had estimated. On his black stallion the mage sat a stone's throw from the heart of the battle, protected by a ring of his mage guard. Three had fallen, leaving only eight to protect him, including Grindar himself, grim-faced and leering, sword dripping blood. The Black Mage cut a grim figure himself: tall, resolute, head crowned with black morion and black plume, a sightless stare on his thin pale face, eyes pits into nowhere. His was a heart of malice tainted by the Sagothian magic, without pity or remorse. With fingers outstretched, he hurled spells as fatal to the Mercians as to the Lvendarians, as if now that the jewel was in the sorceress's hand, he had no further purpose in life other than to punish all around him and unleash his dark pent-up energies.

Horses fell and men dropped from their saddles, clutching their throats as he launched incantations, sonic pulses and dark blasts of every sort. Voydred cared little who he slew, as long as they died and he could channel his destructive energies on someone.

Taranis paid little heed to this juvenile play. With the jewel in her grasp, all else was incidental. She feasted eyes on the slaughter like a drooling jackal eyes a wounded antelope, or like the old crow waits patiently for the other younger ones to fight over bits of carrion, then swoops down to peck at the spoils.

With Voydred, Keren and Belgra out of action, Senesch, eldest and last of the Xalgossian mages, stood alone against Taranis. His horse was slain and charred by dragon fire. He shook a fist up at the black-clad sorceress. "You cannot do this,

Taranis!" he shouted. "The gods forbid it. They govern the scales of balance. The future of sorcery lies in peril, dangles on a thread. The balance must not be skewed toward evil."

"The balance already tips this day, old man," she crooned. "'Tis the start of a new age."

"Unleashing a dragon on the world is unthinkable! It is sacrilege! The beasts are unpredictable and dangerous. There are reasons why the Scaled Ones were entombed by our forefathers in the earth, cast to the lower realms."

At this insult, Drako, who seemed savvy to the old mage's threat, gusted a fiery breath that near singed all Senesch's hair off. He fell back with a feeble cry, tamping down the gray strands on his singed pate.

Taranis gave an unsympathetic chortle. She pushed out a hand and sent a sinister, blue-gray orb lancing down to blast the dirt at the old man's feet. He went flying face-first to land in the dirt like an old blind beggar.

"What are you but a useless geriatric?" she called in contempt. "An old bookworm groveling like a worm in the dirt. I could squash you like a bug. But you have no powers left. I can see it plain as day. I'll let you live only for my amusement, so you can scribe my glory, 'Taranis the great!', 'Wielder of the Eros Flame!'"

Upon the fall of the last mage of Xalgossa, the giants of Balboria gripped their clubs and stared helplessly into the sky. Their brows poured sweat, their limbs dripped blood. To a half dozen their numbers had been whittled, courtesy of Drako, the fearsome dragon. They saw the inevitable, the unbeatable witch and her ruthless minion ready to pounce and unleash more fire-breathing rampage upon the battlefield. Dire warnings from their ancient myths clutched at their hearts. Four of them loped off into the grassy fields, leaving only two behind clutching their clubs to stand against the onslaught. The others had broken their vows, deserted the army and earned the curses of the Mercians.

The dragon, seeing this as a game, dove down to blitz the giants, perhaps wishing to grind their heads to pulp in his jaws.

Taranis hissed. She smote him with the edge of the stone. The dragon turned and huffed smoke of displeasure at her.

The game had become tiresome for the dragon. *Fetch the stone and puny humans and puff out fire and do as you're told.* His mistress had become a bore. Rather would he be free of his ornery black-clad albatross and fly off on his own to wreak havoc on the humans which for time immemorial the dragons had hated.

He swooped lower over the soldiers and fleeing giants and dashed and buffeted the sorceress to and fro, as if to tease her off his back. This only earned Taranis's incontestable wrath. She called strident curses and rapped the Eros stone against his horns, so that when the heavy lizardish head swung about, the lurid crimson light was again in his face to plunge him into a dream-like compliance.

Vetra scrambled to snatch up a shield, to replace the last which Nog had shattered. He stumbled, crouching, hard pressed to protect himself from Nog's incessant and ensorcelled rain of fury.

While Senesch crawled like a worm amid the mounds of bodies, he came within earshot of the Black Mage and the old man's face paled in light of Voydred's macabre incantations.

The witch had been wrong about Senesch and his powers. Like all wise men, he had kept some of them guarded. Masked like an artist's motif in a complex oil painting, they lingered in abeyance. A guiding voice in his brain had told him that one day, when it most mattered, he'd have to call up every trick he knew. Even if it killed him.

What Senesch said or did on that fateful day, even the gods do not know for the scope of his magic had been kept hidden for many decades.

An injured soldier, downed by sword thrust to his abdomen, lay moaning in the dirt and saw Senesch inch his way closer to Voydred. He caught only a brief flash of light emanating from the old man's hands, a blueish glint in his eye, as some miraculous form of star-spangled dust seemed to move from the old man's fingers and flutter about the Black Mage's head.

For a moment, Voydred teetered. Then he shook his head as some of the demonic madness seeped from his brain. The spell of the Eros Flame was splintering. Voydred saw things clearly— the slavering dragon hovering in the air, the black-robed sorceress riding its back, the crumpled and torn bodies all around. He gave a wild cry in the midst of the carnage and lifted his magisterial arms and uttered thunderous words:

"Auschkag, Vellum, Vohor!"

Voydred's lips worked and strange syllables flew like hissing snakes about the fray, sending a hollow shriek like the wind over pike and shield; men on their saddles clutched at their ears.

The dragon jerked and reeled, almost upsetting his rider, tortured by the whistling, gale-like tumult.

The magic discord rose in pitch as Voydred's spell gathered weight and his concentration brought beads of sweat on his brow. Like the sound of an incoming tornado, the wind grew and grew.

The eerie whine broke the spell of Taranis's enchantment over the gathered hordes. Vetra and Nog shook their heads, liberated for the moment of their bewitched daze. In unison they turned their eyes to the sorceress and the enemies surrounding them.

The dragon circled over the battlefield, seeking the cause of the disturbance. Drako's keen sense pinpointed the source of his torment as the black-clad mage and he came hurtling down without Taranis's bidding, talons outstretched. He dropped his cargoes, Skirl and Belgra, then reached. Talons grappled the mage's helmed head to tear it off in one blood-wrenching sweep.

Skirl and Belgra went skidding to the soft grass amid mounds of bodies. Vetra turned his head, his senses restored, and lifted his shield to block the energy of the light from the Eros Flame that grew to a blinding, blazing ruby brilliance. The reflected glare shot back up at Taranis, straight in her eyes. For a moment she blinked, her brain stymied, smitten by her own magic.

Clutching his blood-drenched prize, the dragon swooped low.

Too low.

The last two giants lunged and swatted at his hide as he passed, even as they were fire-blackened to crisps in one huff of the dragon's foul breath.

Yet knotted clubs had clipped the left side of the dragon's hide near its tail, unseating its cocky rider. Enemy soldiers piked blades up to slash at the dragon's limbs. Drako whipped his lizard-like head back and forth.

A thousand shafts rained up at close range to pelt the dragon's scale-plated body. Most missiles merely bounced back, but some cracked through the armored hide and brought fresh blood dripping down on their heads like warm spring rain.

The dragon jerked side to side and reeled. One wing flapped wildly. It tipped dangerously earthward and dragged on the ground, slicing a score of men and riders to ribbons. Meaty flesh flew.

The sorceress who'd been thrown clear, lost grip of the Eros Flame. The gem went flying into the jumble of men and horses. Yet even her lithe body was not quick enough to escape the doom fast upon her. The dragon plummeted, and as it made one last spasm, its bulk rolled on her, crushing her from toes to hip.

Taranis died in an instant, a look of frozen horror on her white, bloodless lips.

Surprise was writ there, how fate could be so cruel to deal her such an ignominious end. It seemed her dark gods had finally deserted her.

The soldiers fell on the floundering dragon. Arrows rained from all sides like a hail of hornets, penetrating eye sockets and vulnerable areas of underbelly. A new awareness moved among the awakening hordes. Thousands had died in the senseless slaughter. The bravest warriors of both sides mustered forth, now in union rather than conflict, to slice off the beast's head, even though it was already as good as dead.

Vetra caught sight of Nog who stood blinking nearby, rubbing at his brow as if not knowing where he was. Vetra snarled and came charging at him in a fit of rage. He knocked him flying.

"What's the idea of trying to kill me, you dumb ox!"

Nog rose to his feet, shaking his head in bewilderment. "I've only a vague memory, Vetra—of hewing and slashing. You were stealing something from me. I felt like I was in a dream...having no meaning, like I was in a watery realm. My heart pounding with a passion for some prize I can't even recall."

"Well, maybe for the witch lying there crushed. I guess you were not in your right senses, Nog. I suppose I can forgive you."

Skirl and Belgra had drifted over, bleak-faced and grimed, Skirl with his mangled hand tucked under an armpit, Belgra with scratches and welts on her face.

Gruesome sights had Vetra and others grimacing with distaste. Even in death, the Sagothian witch's face was beautiful, even though her lower body was crushed under the savage weight of Drako, the dragon from the Kyldrie.

"The witch is dead," Vetra muttered. "Even her devil Dal Sagoth couldn't save her."

Senesch who had hobbled over, lay a hand on his shoulder. "This is the steep price for those who dabble in forbidden magic." His milky-gray eyes swung to the broken, twisted bodies of Voydred and Keren lying not far distant. "'Tis a foul day, Vetra. Both men and gods have forsaken each other. They've decreed it a day of death."

Vetra looked on the ghastly slaughter with unconcealed repugnance. Wincing, he wiped his chin and neck of blood with the flat of his hand.

"Dragons cannot be allowed to live," the old man continued. "They are a breed of dangerous killers, a scourge on this world that will always contrive to lay waste to kingdoms." He limped several steps away from the stench of dragon and death. "It is for this reason that the Kyldrie was purged centuries ago by fearless warriors of fable and legend. All that remains are the myths of the Dragon Lords."

Vetra was entranced, and yet only half his brain registered Senesch's words, for his eyes had turned away to stare at a point where scattered humps of bodies lay…and a familiar glint.

An object gleamed blood red amid a pile of bodies. The Eros Flame!

With a choked cry, he scrabbled for it, knocking several men out of the way.

Skirl and Belgra had seen it too and took chase.

Vetra got there first. He snatched up the mace of a dead Mercian lying nearby and brought it down hard on the jewel. The gemstone split neatly in two, to a resounding crack that echoed like the champ of dragon teeth up the valley. Both fragments showed jagged edges where they had once been joined.

Skirl gave a yelp of anguish. He leaped over to stare in horror at the two pieces. One lay near his feet, the other had skidded off to Vetra's side.

Vetra heeled the chunk behind him under an upturned helm. He stared bemused while Skirl scrabbled for the larger half that had landed near him.

Feigning a spasm from a battle wound, Vetra crouched down and snatched up the piece that he'd hid. He stuffed it in his jerkin. The bauble would come in handy when he needed it. For now its magic was dead, just the way he preferred it.

Skirl peered left and right. "Where is the other half?" he cried. With his good hand he clutched his hair in grief and scrabbled about like a frantic schoolboy who'd lost a marble. Crouching on hands and knees, he burrowed about in the rubble of bodies. "Maybe it can be resurrected?"

Senesch hobbled in closer. "Not likely, mage." He looked on with a genuine air of pity. "The Flame of Eros is not a toy that can be repaired like a broken toy sailboat. It'd be like trying to mend a piece of wood from ashes, or string a sorceress's soul together that has been sold in pieces to the nether forces."

Skirl bared his teeth. "You speak in riddles!" He shook a fist at Vetra. "Look at what you've done, you cretin! What the devil did you have to go and crack it for?"

"It's caused us nothing but pain," Vetra growled. "Look at the ruin and death around you. The thing's evil."

Skirl clawed at his hair and sank into a miserable crouch. He rocked on his heels, his words bordering on snivels. "I despise you, mercenary, I despise you! You're a bane to sorcery... And yet—" He lifted his head, grimacing with despair at his missing fingers.

Nog had wandered over to frown at Skirl and shake his head. "Stick to love, boy, like you once told us back at the market before this crapstorm came our way. It's better for one's health. Little good the magic did you." He gestured curtly at his stumps and missing ear. "Little good it did this wench either." And he kicked the hide of the dead dragon under which Taranis lay crushed.

Vetra exhaled a sickened breath. "If the legend speaks true, then this Sarkala priestess who birthed the stone would have wanted it destroyed, or at least hidden so that none could use it for nefarious purposes."

Senesch gave a slow nod. "'Tis too easy to pervert its use, Vetra. I believe you are right."

The last flicker of blue from the half fragment in Skirl's hand grew dim. For brief moments a red glare flared up, a pure scarlet burst that nearly blinded all gathered around the dragon, then it fizzled out forever.

There came a mighty gust of wind that swept down from the hills to the west and with it a gale-like roar which nearly knocked all those standing off their feet.

Senesch muttered something that it was the sorceress's last breath.

"Dergath!" murmured Vetra.

For some time Senesch spoke words that might have been protections spells against further evil...words spoken in a forgotten tongue, the last of which Vetra recognized as the name, 'Dal Sagoth'.

Chapter 40

Vetra picked his way through the battered hulks of giants and mangled horses. In his ear he was barely conscious of the clink of harness, the tramp of boots and the shift and mutter of brooding men. Carrion birds had come to circle and eye the battlefield: large noisy ravens and turkey vultures with small, black heads that vented raucous croaks. He saw Caradwen among the survivors. He was glad of that. She was picking her way among the ruins of bodies while other of the riders helped gather up Lord Onas and his fallen lieutenants to be burned. She walked with a limp and had a dent in her helm, also a cut above her right eye but otherwise looked intact.

Vetra made a slow salute and she returned it with a ghost of a grin. She was as comely as ever, in her grimed accouterments and gripping her bloody blade. In happier times he would have paused to dally with this courageous maid, but he had other business to attend to. He knew where she lived, Cairnhill, and could always return to pay her a visit.

Half of Onas's riders had been slain or lay broken amid the heaps of horses and men. Of the 5000 soldiers, Vetra estimated two-thirds lay dead from sword, sorcery or dragon fire. All the commanders were slain.

The survivors began the long trek back to their homes, with tales of grimness on their lips and of dragons and sorceresses to regale friends and family at many a hearth gathering. Whispers of an unspoken truce rustled in the air, declaring neither side a winner.

Skirl seemed to have forgotten the pain of his missing fingers temporarily, or perhaps he was in shock. He'd torn a strip of a jupon off a felled Mercian and wrapped it around his bloody stump.

Senesch groaned, suffering stolidly his many aches and pains. He lay a gentle hand on Skirl's shoulder. "As wielder of the Eros flame, I think there is a future for you at the head of the cabal, boy. I am too old. Even if Voydred were alive, he and I would be at each other's throats—" he laughed "—like dogs, squabbling for the seat." His hollow chuckle faded and a tear rolled down his grimed cheek. "I've no taste for ruling now in my hundred plus years. Keren too had his head in the clouds and would have had us all turning into birds and worshiping hawks, or carrying falcons on our arms. And Belgra? Well, you and she are good complements to each other. You'll keep the balance of power at Dormoth. I hope. What's left of it, anyways."

Skirl nodded sagely. "What remains of the Eros Stone shall hang in the Hall of Mages. Let this be a lesson to all, Senesch, how darkness corrupts. I think Vetra's right. The thing's a curse. Evil's taint will always be rooted out! I'll hang this jewel there with my own hands to stand in the Hall forever!"

Skirl's words were grandiose and Senesch, seeing Skirl reach for the half-stone in his robe, shafted him a sour look. "Are you starting to act a trifle magisterial, Skirl? Already? Careful, boy," he warned.

Skirl cupped his gored hand and winced. Belgra fluttered over to his side to bless it with healing spells and incantations. She treated his stump with salves, potions that she kept in her robe. "That was very courageous of you to come to my rescue when the dragon snatched me up," she said briefly. "Stupid, perhaps. And a death wish, but courageous all the same."

Skirl smiled. Overcome with gladness to have Belgra back in his life, he gathered her in his arms. They vowed to rebuild the shattered Order of Mages together.

"No one person shall rule the Order like Taranis did," Skirl exclaimed with an expansive sweep of arm. "It will be but two and I nominate Belgra and I!"

Nog cast Vetra a goofy look and rolled his eyes. "Double the trouble."

Vetra muttered, "Let them sort out their own affairs, Nog. I head south on the road to Alantra then Behundria. Are you coming with me?"

"I'd like to, Vetra, but no, I've had enough of these warring kingdoms. My place is by the sea. I pine for the briny coasts and the open water. It's back to the docks of Syrn for me. I feel more at ease there than here."

"Suit yourself." Vetra tipped his head. "To each his own. I shall miss you, old friend."

"And I too. You know where to find me. Ask any old sea dog there at the wharfs—if I'm still alive and not with a scimitar in my gullet." He gave a phlegm-filled laugh.

Vetra chuckled wryly. "I doubt that, Nog. You've got a few years ahead of you yet. Here's to a long life." He lifted his blade.

"To a long life, Vetra."

Nog lifted his.

Vetra's mind turned to brooding once more. There was this matter of his sister, captive to some distant lord in a seraglio. He must find her, even it was nigh impossible. The trail led south to a man called Tork, that was all he knew, a trail getting colder every day. He must not let the hope die that yet she lived.

But first he would need funds. This fragment of the Eros jewel in his pocket would be what he'd pawn first. He'd have more luck fencing it in the southern kingdoms like Galashad. Behundria? Maybe Dragonskull? The jewel's notoriety was less known there. He'd be less likely to get his throat cut by agents of the Wizard's Circle or bounty hunters.

Time would tell. The world was a fickle mistress. It was one full of changing dangers and strange dooms. Even as he flashed on the thought, his scalp prickled, for the Eros Flame, or what was left of it, still radiated a sinister warmth in his pocket where it brushed his side.

DRAGON LORDS

I : DRAGONSKULL

Vetravincus, wandering mercenary, was on a mission to fence a jewel. He found himself jostling shoulders among the crowd in the central market of Dragonskull, a lawless oasis in the arid wastes, also famous for dragon bones scattered among the dunes. Less than two generations had passed since a slave caravan of brigands, deviants and cutthroats, bound for King Juna's prison mines, broke their chains and took control of the town. Often a man was beaten for some minor offense, or his throat cut or his valuables seized; worse was done to women.

Of foul play, Vetra was little worried. His broadsword was forged with crucible steel, sharp enough to cut through bone, and hung from his armored back in a shagreen scabbard. His hard features, broad shoulders, sure step and reinforced ringmail were enough to give pause to the most impulsive footpads.

Vetra heard someone cry out and he grasped the pommel of his sword. A boy struggled in the hairy arms of a red-faced merchant. A yam and a cuchri fruit lay mashed at their feet. A flash of steel glinted in the noonday sun; the merchant raised a cleaver to the gaunt-faced boy. Vetra lunged and pulled the boy away.

"What're you doing?" the merchant screamed, his cleaver missing the youthful hand and sticking deep into a wooden table. "He stole—"

Vetra smashed the pommel of his broadsword into the merchant's mouth. Blood, broken teeth, and curses filled the air. Vetra grabbed the man by his scraggly beard and pulled him close. He could smell the fruit merchant's fear; piss ran down the vendor's leg and rancid meat wafted from his agonized face.

Vetra put his blade to the merchant's throat. "Have you ever swiped a grape? Have you ever been that hungry?"

The merchant opened his bleeding mouth to say something but stopped. His eyes flicked to the side.

Vetra turned and saw a large man approaching. Dragon tattoos rippled on bare, muscled arms, and a dirty blond beard curled low under a pointed chin.

The big man snarled. "Who are you to impose law on us, outlander?"

Vetra sheathed his weapon. "I meant no imposition to your laws." He glanced down at the child and mouthed the word 'Run.'

The boy jumped to his feet and tore off through the crowd, panic-stricken. He squeezed his way through moving carts, tables and milling bodies, eluding the grasping hands of bystanders.

"Stop that weasel!" the big man yelled to the crowd. He put his hand out to Vetra. "Out of my way! I'll not kill the thieving brat. Just put him to work in Berit's smithy, or chain him to a post in the tannery."

Vetra chuckled and stepped aside. "You'll never catch him. His feet are faster than a rabbit's." He shook his head and sauntered up the monger's lane, merging with the crowd. He peered left and right, his dark eyes on the alert for trouble. At least he had saved a young urchin from mutilation, no doubt a better deed than anybody in that motley crowd had done that day.

The aisle merged into a common square packed with bustling traffic. Carts jolted past without heed for people safety; noise and dust were like layers of froth off a devil's brew. A camel came bearing down on him and he stepped aside from the grunting beast, whose rider shook a fist at him. The diversity of the throng fascinated him. Lean Guirites from Amashra swarmed the streets with keen, curved, gold-chased swords belted at their hips.

Thrules, four to five feet tall, wore loose, purple robes to the ankle, whispering among themselves with hoods drawn tight, concealing all but their cat-like eyes. Wood traders from Kamuchaya trundled in by cart; silk merchants from Asban on their desert ponies, whipping their dust-ridden beasts through the throng. Behundrians dominated the scene, swarthy, stocky residents with tempers and arrogance to match, who imposed their law, which was cruel at best.

Spices, jewels, and fruit, along with silk and ivory flowed from the east while fish, wheat, timber, and steel came from the west. The odd caravan of gold came from the south, with armed escort, from as far as Pakshar and then by way of Senesch on the coast. The Kirns of the South, the Mosetes of the North, the Guirites of the East, all plied the common route, some friends, some foes. They traveled the same dusty streets, rubbing shoulders with each other on foot or donkey or camel, drank by each other's side in the seedy ale holes and saloons or rolled dice in the gambling houses that graced the town.

Vetra ducked under awnings and pushed his way through the back curtain of a fabric shop. He gave not a glance at the fine silks and Damir linens, but took a shadowy route through a narrow alley with wet clothes strung up from the railings of the overhead apartments. A particular dealer resided here who could fence these emeralds of his. Pity he had to come all the way to this remote outpost for this. He had learned upon arrival that a recent entry permit was imposed on non-Behundrians. Persons in transit were exempt, but to be caught without one while even entering the bazaar was considered an offense—a hefty ten talon fine, or time done in the stockade. Nothing more than a local collection tax, he thought. Two silver talons, one permit.

He pushed down his disgust and wiped the back of his shiny black hair. He was sweating like a stallion.

The sapphire was the jagged half of a once powerful magic talisman, the fabled Eros Flame—the spoils of his last adventure, withal, nearly the demise of the northern kingdoms. The magic was tainted, fortunately stripped now that it had been split in twain by his own strike of mace. Easier to fence it here in out-of-the-way Dragonskull than be caught in Lausern, pegged as a smuggler by the Vizier's street watch. He had to find the dealer who would move it first, otherwise his trip was a waste of time. As for the permit, well, he was willing to take a chance...

The alley reeked of sour cabbage and spoiled wine. Trickles of noisome gray water ran in gutters. Vetra turned. A man's cry? A scream of pain? His lips parted in a scowl. Best to keep walking. But he knew he would not.

Down the narrow, littered alley he stole like a thief, his *garbandia* knife clutched in one hand, his other on the pommel of his sword in its worn scabbard. He thought he heard a sound behind him, a stalker, crouching hidden behind refuse heap and crumbled wall. He paused.

Nothing.

A large rat skittered out and down a dark hole.

Angry shouts drifted through a canvas-covered gap in a plastered wall. The sounds rose in pitch, the wheezing gasp of a pleading man, grunts and blows, then various chuckles and throaty murmurs. Hackles raised, Vetra bent his head, unable to overcome his curiosity. He pulled back the canvas flap and peered into a windowless chamber dimly lit by oil lamps. A man was gibbering, spreadeagled on a low table. A dozen figures surrounded the victim, and taunted him with cruel knives and wicked bits of sharp, rusted iron.

"I tell you, Rafa, I don't know where the map is." The prisoner was lashed hand and foot in stout cord and struggled helplessly as he wailed.

"Liar!" cried Rafa. "I saw you chewing the parchment and swallowing it. Only a knave or fool would do that before looking at the map. Nestor! Jangir! Put the tong to him. This rogue deceives us."

Nestor nodded, a brawny ape of a man, with a ragged overcloak, iron wristbands and yellow front teeth.

The sound of sizzling flesh came to Vetra's ears. He clenched his jaw.

Predatory laughs added to the tortured man's howls.

Vetra, for the life of him, could not stand by and witness a defenseless man tortured and killed, even if he were possibly a villain.

He ripped a hole through the canvas and leaped in, sword gripped. He saw they had branded the victim's right calf with a lurid mark: a long knife piercing a dragon skull. The victim was a short man, no more than five feet tall. He looked Thrule, but for his wincing features, thin Behundrian nose and more strongly defined jaw. It was hard to see past his shaggy mop of sweat-matted brown hair.

The victim was struggling anew now, and in a fierce display of strength had to be restrained with force despite the strong cords binding his limbs.

Vetra barreled straight for the man with the tongs. The best attack was a surprise one. Without preamble, Vetra pounced, cleaving skull and jawbone in a spray of blood and brains. The villains around him fell back with cries of horror. Leaning in, Vetra slashed more throats and limbs.

They circled closer, having wits to stay out of reach of his hissing blade. Now they came rounding in, and he was penned like a boar among huntsmen.

A bold young voice called out from the shadows. "Oi! Ugly face!"

The rogues quickly faced the unknown voice, and Vetra took the opportunity to slice the next nearest man's throat. The man staggered into his fellow villains, gurgling blood, a ghastly expression on his face.

Vetra ducked a whooshing blade. Darting sideways, he crouched as another sword edge thumped off his padded leather undershirt, ripping white desert robe. In the same motion, he slashed the victim's cords that bound legs and arms. The prisoner rolled off the table and crawled across the floor out of reach of the scrabbling men. He snatched up the tong while Vetra held off the attackers then hurled it into the face of his captors, eliciting a cry of anguish.

"Get her!" the leader cried.

A flat-faced thug broke from the pack and turned on the intruder who had voiced the taunt, a young woman with cinnamon hair trailing down her slender shoulders. A gleaming knife was gripped in her hand, a dangling scourge clasped in the other.

The aggressor towered a foot over her, sword hanging loosely at his side, sizing her up, as a bull eyes a ripe cow. His leering face bobbed closer to inspect her with more care. He reached a hand out like a snake to grab her wrist.

Her blade flashed and slashed a crimson line across the back of the hand. He grunted in surprise. A knee to the groin doubled him over. Her lithe body then spun with a long leg arching up to crack the side of his head. The man crunched to the floor. The smack of leather on flesh resounded throughout the room. Two more leering figures broke away and came leaping after her, their hoods rustling and white desert garb trailing to their ankles. She sprang forth, whip whirling behind her head. She moved in sync with the rhythm of her foes as they came at her, cursing and grunting.

"A girl? Really, swordster?" Rafa sneered. "You are quite the hero, bringing an entourage from the local bordello!"

Vetra grunted, ignoring the taunts. He twisted to avoid the rake of the grinning man's two-foot *Shamari* blade. He was in the thick of the fray, besieged by foes. Parrying left and right, he swore and swiveled left, evading a one-eared attacker who lunged for his vitals. Blood ran down the hilt of Vetra's naked blade as he cut down hard. A high squeal erupted from a man bowed over in agony.

Meanwhile, the freed victim rolled underfoot. Despite his pitiful state, he hobbled to his feet and grabbed a weapon from the hand of the felled torturer then met an upraised sword aimed for his skull. Vetra laughed, cutting down a man to edge closer to the ginger-haired girl who had saved his neck.

Vetra saw her scourge rising and falling in sprays of red. A wicked weapon of leather strips and rusted nails, meting out an unforgiving punishment. She disarmed the first attacker, lashing out with a shrill cry, to leave a gaping gash on the man's arm.

Rafa came striding in with a howl of disgust, keen on despatching the hellcat. But in his anger he underestimated his opponent, driving in too close too fast. A quick lash took out his eye. His lips gave rise to a screech of a pain. Hand thrust to his bloody socket, the man reeled, trying to stop the jet of blood gushing from between his fingers.

Vetra, summoning a savage fire from deep in his warrior's heart, gave a berserker's yell and launched full on the last four villains who faced him. Sword swung like a mallet, dismembering jaws and bursting brains. But more foes came pouring out from the shadows of a hidden entrance. Many more.

He shook the blood and sweat out of his eyes and edged back, his sword dripping in a white-fisted hand, snarling like a panther. "Quick! If you value your lives!"

The young woman and the freed man wasted no time: together the three of them cleared a path to the back flap.

Vetra squinted under the daytime glare to examine his mysterious aide in better light now. She was lighter skinned and wore a sleeveless vest, short leather breeches, brown belt and soft leather boots. Her shins were bare, and small ornamental bracelets and cheap rings decorated her ankles and fingers. She was in fit shape, with green eyes, provocative curves, and was scarcely winded.

The three staggered out of the shadows, scuttling to the end of the alley.

"What's your name, girl?" demanded Vetra as they ran.

"Jhara. And yours?"

"Vetra. Why did you help me back there?"

"You saved my brother. I was curious about your business in Dragonskull. Not often does a stranger risk his neck for a nameless urchin." Her breath caught in her throat as she kept abreast the mercenary while the rescued man was struggling to keep up, wheezing up a storm.

Vetra laughed, a snort of contempt.

"You seem to have a knack for getting yourself in trouble," she said. "That's Rafa's lair, don't you know? His thugs pay allegiance to Cthan, the sheriff. Are you a daft brute or just a simpleton, going in there and taking on the whole crew?"

Vetra made a brusque motion. "Where did you learn to fight like that?" He halted, peering back down the alley. The Thrule held his branded leg, wincing with every step. Only three of the dozen pursued and they strode with leisure, as if they had all the time in the world. Vetra frowned. Confident swine they were, to saunter with such laziness, as if they had the luxury of kings to ferret out a cocky outlander and a few rebels.

"My father... He never let me use a sword." The girl offered a wry, white-toothed grin, though there was pain in that smile. "Said I would kill somebody."

Vetra shook his head with bemusement. The whip she used earlier was sewn with hooked, rusted nails and ended with a blood-stained wooden handle. "In that I have no doubt."

He glanced at the hectic market scene. Folk and mongers moved about their business, oblivious to the violence that had just taken place. His puzzled curl of lip returned upon remembering the girl's performance.

"One learns to think fast on her feet," she added, seeing his appraising look, "especially a woman, growing up on the streets."

"My advice is get a proper sword," he muttered. "And you,

Thrule, what's your story?" He peered at the man that they rescued.

"I am not a Thrule," he gasped, stumbling up, his chest heaving. "I am a half Thrule. Lehundr. Snatched by those thugs but an hour ago." A flicker of doubt passed his eyes as he debated whether or not he could trust the swordsman who hulked before him. "I have desert ponies waiting in the stables of the Prospector's Inn. My uncle runs the place. Not the fastest steeds, but sturdy ones and reliable. We can be out of here in short order."

Vetra considered the prospect while rubbing his jaw. Recent events had gone awry and suggested it was time to quit Dragonskull. His gems would have to wait till another day. They were not worth his life. Though he liked not the prospect of delay.

"The fools, they thought I was eating a map," Lehundr continued, croaking out a harsh laugh. Again, a doubtful hesitation, but he continued. "It was but a decoy. The real one is weaved into my caftan here." He lifted his torn cloak for an instant and Vetra caught a fleeting glimpse of two dragon heads facing each other—a mystical and sinister sign if he ever saw one—the beasts poised as if a cleverly woven part of the fabric, evoking mystic terror in any who saw it. The fabric was ancient and the pigments dyeing the wool were dulled and faded by years of sun.

"They wanted the map and were ready to kill for it," he explained. "The rest you can guess."

Vetra grunted. "Those killers are not going to give up their hunt to lynch a few ornery trespassers. We got lucky. And I don't know why they haven't pinned us down and gutted us already."

Almost as if in answer, his keen eyes detected five grim figures on the other side of the market, blood trailing from their cheeks and arms.

A quick glance over his shoulder showed four more

stumbling out of the adjoining alleyway.

Vetra pulled the two into a nearby back alley. "Quick, girl! Make yourself scarce. You, Thrule—or half Thrule, whatever you are—follow me!"

"What about the treasure?" Jhara demanded. "I heard about the map. We're all going to be rich!"

"Are we now?" grunted Vetra. "Recall, we just narrowly escaped getting our throats cut. Look yonder, what do you see?"

"A market and a bunch of bustling fools."

"No, death. Go take care of your brother. Begone, this is my last warning."

"That's not how this is going to play out—" She gave lip to a rush of words, but seeing the mercenary's inflexible face, her mouth curled in a sullen scowl and she turned and dashed off. She disappeared down the alley in a flash of gleaming brown leather and bouncing hair.

Vetra shook his head with perplexity. Her appearance was certainly one of the more bizarre things he had seen in a long time. He had a hunch yet more bizarre things were to follow.

Lehundr stared in awkward fashion, wiping his bloody blade on his torn garment.

"Where did you get that map?" Vetra demanded as he forged his way through the market crowd.

"Off a wandering Guirite, who knew not what he had. He was selling knickknacks and memorabilia from his market stand and I happened to notice it hanging there, pinned to a hide, as an emblem or decoration. He said it was a good luck charm. I recognized it for what it was—the mark of the Dragon Keeper. My father had schooled me well in the legends of the Dragon Lords. He said their treasure was an ancient secret woven into a map."

"Well, you paid a hefty price for that bit of fabric." He motioned to Lehundr's quivering leg.

"Help me get to the Thrule district. I have healing ointments there."

"I doubt any salve is going to fix that burn too quickly."

"You don't know Thrule medicine."

Vetra's eyes darted about. What to do about this Thrule? He was in bad shape and likely would not survive another assault if the band of ruffians caught him again.

Almost as if in answer he saw a garish sign to the trader's post looming like a sore thumb: a wooden slab with carved-out pickaxes and shovels crossed together.

Another reckless camel came veering in, the scowling man cursing from its saddle. Vetra was deafened by the animal's grunt in his ear. He stumbled into a wizened merchant, carrying a load of silk bales, who rang out some Mosete words at him for being in his way.

"Quick, in here!" Vetra growled, annoyed with the overloaded street. The oppressive heat was getting to him. He pushed the Thrule on through.

They plunged past the swinging wooden door. A wall of noise, confusion and impatient voices assailed them.

Figures moved every which way in a bright-lit open pavilion. Sunlight streamed from the long windows that ran along the upper gallery below an arched, bricked ceiling.

Weigh scales lined the nearby wall, men measuring vials of silver dust, gold nuggets and ore chips, others wielding heavy sacks of precious metals. A few gripped freshly signed deeds and land rights. The depot was a central hub where all the traders secured their commerce, signed trade deals, filed mineral claims, and lodged complaints.

An open area at the back of the depot fronted a sprawling cobbled courtyard rich with milling folk who toted sacks of grains and other goods to the weigh stations—barrels of precious water, crates of Thorian metal, rolls of silk, or linen, baskets of dates and coconuts, raw leather, rugs, amphorae of wine. The heaving, jostling men swarmed about like ants. Vetra stared past the figures and tethered horses at the temple of Dergath and its forked spires and shiny jade dome rising into the white-washed sky. To its side rose the great curving bulk of the stone reservoir of water that kept the town alive.

Shaking his head at the chaos, Vetra strode to the central area. Straightaway he was accosted by a uniformed man selling trading permits at an alleged discount. The man rattled clay tokens in his fingers with confident ease and pushed one in Vetra's hands. Vetra squinted at the disk with skepticism, then, seeing it bore a true Dragonskull seal, flipped a silver coin at him, thinking it could come in handy if they were accosted by the town watch. The hyena-like cackles of men came from behind and he turned upon the three grubby traders who stared at him with obvious amusement.

A sudden suspicion dawned on Vetra and he stared at Lehundr who straggled behind in a daze, in no shape to call out a warning. Leaning back, Vetra shifted, realizing he had been duped and reached out to grab the vendor. But the smiley-faced con was gone.

He herded Lehundr up ahead and they inserted themselves in a line leading to a main counter, trying to appear as unobtrusive as possible. Lehundr's darting eyes and burn on his leg marked him out.

The trade-clerk of the depot shouted across the nearby counter over the din of voices. "You'll get your blasted silver dust, you damned rogue!"

The fuming, red-eared figure on the other side of the wicket glared. "I doubt that! Give me back my coins, you jackal. All five hundred. Shipment was due a week ago, and it still hasn't arrived out of Dalispar. I've been swilling Jirrir's sour ale and eating stringy mutton with my bully-boys for the last week, itching to carve out someone's liver."

The trade-clerk snarled. "Hire yourselves some trollops then, down Smeldra's way. Amuse yourself for a few more days. Your silver'll come, by Dron, or I'll cut off my beard and eat it."

"Well, you'd better get a knife because—"

A loud shout pierced the air. Then a thud and clash of arms as a dispute over a transaction gained momentum.

Wood flashed in a fist and a brute cracked his club over the head of a lean desert man with a rat-face. "That'll teach you to backbite, you lily-livered Kirn."

The brute's aide grumbled, "Well, Onast, any more of your bullies got a beef with us?"

"Ah," the tradepost-clerk grunted. "This place is a barn." He turned to Vetra, who had thrust himself next in line while a long line of men were distracted. "Well, what's your complaint, outlander?" The clerk glared at Vetra, and the mercenary casually loosened his outer garment to better disguise his rugged physique.

"No complaint," Vetra remarked. "I came to get a trader's permit."

"Trader's permit? That's that office down the hall," he barked, jerking a thumb. "Why waste my time here?"

"I was ripped off by your so-called assistant who carries no more than a few trinkets of pretty clay."

"Say what?"

Vetra gritted his teeth, his anger not allowing him to let it go. "I said, the impostor claims he was the one I should pay money for a permit." He held up a faked token stained with yellow and red.

The clerked grinned. "Well, if you were fool enough to give honest coins to that good-for-nothing—"

"You!" burst out a voice. Vetra whirled to recognize an oily-skinned man wearing a turban from back at the market "—you were the rascal who Vilivet was talking about, some foreigner who thought to flout our market law."

A rustle came from behind the clerk. A tall, broad-chested man came out of the back office, his ears pricked. "What's this I hear about Vilivet?" There was a dangerous glitter in the man's eyes, as a lizard eyes a cringing mouse. "Is there a problem here?"

"No problem, Cthan," mumbled the trade-clerk.

"Aye, no problem," grunted Vetra. "I just suggest you teach your clerk better manners." He recalled the name 'Cthan' dropped by Jhara and noticed that Lehundr seemed to shrink in the presence of the hulking lawbringer of Dragonskull.

The oily-skinned man piped up in anger: "The outlander's a sword-trickster. Took a thieving urchin from under our thumbs and stared down Vilivet."

Cthan snorted. "What do I care of your little squabbles? If Vilivet can't handle one grubby foreigner, then he deserves his hide whipped. Serve the man and be done, Sabias, before I wallop you. I get enough complaints about your surliness as it is."

"As you like." Sabias growled. "And you, Thrule," he grunted down at Lehundr, "what are you looking at? I should have you thrown out and whipped. Thrules go in the other line!" He clutched his writing stick in a white-knuckled fist.

Lehundr had been staring in fascination, still dazed from his near encounter with death. A line of drool slithered down from the corner of his mouth, a detail which had likely triggered the clerk's dislike.

Lehundr, whose natural habit seemed to be to look down, let the flap of his torn hood hide his face. His noiseless movement of upraised hand with open palm seemed a gesture of implicit subservience. Yet Vetra could see by his resentful shrug he was not pleased to be insulted.

"Leave him out of this," Vetra rumbled with impatience. "The half Thrule's with me."

"And what's your claim in this affair?"

"First of all he's a half Thrule, not a Thrule, and he's got your blood in him too," reiterated Vetra, "and if there's any thrashing or bullying to do, it'll be done by me. He glared down at the clerk who was starting to irk him.

The trade-clerk bristled at the outlander's insolence. Seeing the merciless fire in Vetra's eyes and the glint of steel rising out of his scabbard, he grumbled an oath and crashed a fist on the table. "Your door's down there, big man. Take your Thrule with you."

Vetra marched away like a lazy cat, earning the appreciation of several onlookers. He and Lehundr pushed past several grumbling and jeering men, tired of waiting in line.

Vetra motioned to the Thrule. "Don't like you, do they?" He stared down at his companion's five-foot height.

"They don't like anyone here," muttered the shorter man. "The Behundrians, I mean. A word of advice, friend, not that I don't appreciate your grit in sticking up for me, but watch your step. One man and a sword isn't going to take on a whole gang of villains. You don't know them like I do."

Vetra gave a sinister laugh. He pushed his gleaming blade back in his scabbard and sauntered through the throng. "I see you are eager to be gone, and for that I don't blame you. Best be on your way, Thrule, before those bullies target you again."

At that moment two riders thundered up to the depot's back station, kicking up a dust storm. Their mounts were lathered with sweat and looked to have seen some heavy riding. One cried out in a hoarse voice, "The main water pipe is down again. No breaches for a league or so, we checked. But 'tis the Thrules! They've taken the pipe somewhere further up the line. Rebels from the north—the Thorian mines have been hit too."

The booming voice of the sheriff rolled over the general noise. "Damn those nomads! They've likely sabotaged the main water head at Sunswatch. Outback rebels, I wager. Round up your swords, men—and your camels. We've a rebellion to quash."

A chorus of vengeful shouts and murmurs rose from the gathered men.

Vetra frowned. That the Thorian mines were compromised

meant there would be a major movement of militia eastward. Large coin was at stake. The rare mineral Thorian, the magical element from which the wizard Slune had figured out how to manufacture the finest steel, was a lifeline of the Sahir trade. The Dragonskull constabulary, as their purpose demanded, would have to protect the common interest.

Cthan swore, grimaced at an arguing deputy, fit to be tied. "I'll send word to Thraxen's force at Menihem. We'll meet them and rout out the vermin and put an end to this little rebellion once and for all. A round of stiff arrack for the lads."

Vetra forewent his trader's permit. He slipped out the back of the station with Lehundr close on his heels. This place was too conspicuous. While a hubbub of desert mounts being saddled and packed for war reigned there was no better time to escape unnoticed. Even so, Vetra paused. The excited jabber of men's voices aside, he had not liked the suspicious retreat of a particular squint-eyed, curly-haired man upon mention of 'outlander' earlier. He had no doubt there were more of Rafa's spies about.

* * *

The mid afternoon sun blazed down like an angry furnace. Vetra and Lehundr crouched outside the stables at the back of Lehundr's uncle's Inn, for fear of being seen. The smell of dung lay thick in their noses. Three sturdy ponies swished tails at the pesky flies in the shade of the alley behind the stables. The inn rose several feet over the horse stalls: a two-storey clay and stone dwelling with arched doors and painted gumwood typical of the region's desert dwellings. Few folk were about these quarters. The air was hot and heavy and would not be cooling down for some hours. Not fast enough for Vetra's tastes.

"We should be traveling by night," Vetra murmured, "for reasons of stealth and coolness." He poked about in the dusty shadows and gathered what extra supplies from the stable he thought they needed: lantern, rope, extra wicks, a pickaxe.

Lehundr gave his head a decided shake. He fingered the salve he had acquired from the stable. "Rafa will learn that we were at the depot and come hunting for us. So we can't wait until nightfall. In fact, they will be coming here before long." To his burn wound he applied more of the ointment, a mixture of cactus and eucalyptus leaf.

"Nothing we can do about that," mused Vetra. "Better pack up and go."

"Come with me, Vetra!" the Thrule urged. "I need a good man on this job. A fighter! A swordsman. You're a man of mettle. We'll split the spoils. The map is genuine, I know it!" He lifted his outer robe again in excitement.

Vetra stared critically at the folds of fabric which showed the dragons and some crude, cryptic sketch of valleys and temples and skulls. It seemed to point to a hidden tomb, delineated by a dragon rune stone, north of the place where the pipeline snaked, if his bearings were right. "It follows the line of the pipe."

"So—we'll give the invading rebel Thrules wide berth."

"Meaning, you think I'm going to hunt down this will-o-the-wisp of yours? Get knifed, and die with gold in my hands? No, we'll get out of town, hide our heads for a while, but that's all I can guarantee. This treasure seems too much of a longshot."

"Why, though? The girl was not stupid—she could smell the promise of riches."

Vetra ignored the remark and noticed the short, gleaming falchion Lehundr had tucked at his waist. "I see you favor the shorter blade."

"Yes, it's lighter, quicker and more versatile in battle."

"The reach is shorter and you could get yourself gutted by a better fighter with a longer blade, especially on horseback."

"You would know."

Vetra chuckled. "Well, I hope you know how to use it. My experience with treasure is that plenty of blood flows alongside it."

Lehundr gave a furtive grin. He draped the soft woolen scarf about his neck to ward off the daytime flies. Adjusting his coiled turban, he chuckled. Vetra thought he looked less like a Thrule, and more like a Behundrian.

"Daytime could be dangerous," Vetra commented. "The deserts are populated with nomads, like tics on a dog's hide. I don't know what tribes are out there but their allegiance may not be to our favor, nor their temperaments. The region is unfamiliar to me, but I've heard many a tale of wayfarers and traders alike, pulled down by grasping hands, ambushed by desperadoes."

Lehundr clicked his tongue. "Relax, I know the terrain. I can guide us."

Even in daylight hours the sounds of men's shouts and laughter drifted from a nearby canteen. Vetra heard loud coarse music, the odd bray of a donkey or the whinny of a horse. Not even he noticed the slim, covert form who had snuck up alongside Lehundr's extra packbeast while the men stood conversing in the heat, downing some cheap ale at the stable's gate before their jaunt into the scrublands.

Vetra winced and shook his head. "Bah, this tastes like tar."

"Only the best Thrule stock," scoffed Lehundr. "What, don't like my uncle's mix? Drink up, friend. It may be all you'll get for a long time."

Vetra peered around, the smells and sights registering only as blips on his consciousness. The day had unfolded in unexpected fashion and now his senses prickled with a sense of danger. He upended the tankard on the sand by the stable. "I think I'd rather die and go to Dergath than slug down this swill."

The mercenary loosened his caftan, itching with the sweat that soaked the soft wool and made it stick to the back of his neck. The sour ale sloshing in his stomach did him little favors. He scratched at his stubbled cheeks, brushing back his shiny black hair under the coiled desert cap that he had chosen to stave off the desert heat. He was glad he had decided to 'go local', wearing lighter, airier garb, to downplay his real status as a mercenary. No small number of enemies had he made in his line of work, even as far as Dragonskull. Eyes and ears and noses were no less sharp in this town. Under his flowing white caftan, the boiled hide and ring mail protected his chest and vitals. One could never be too careful, even while not on the job. Time for him to skip town.

Vetra's eyes widened at the size of the half Thrule's saddlebag. Lehundr was now adding a sieve and trowel. "What? I thought you were talking about a few day's trip, not a five-year hunting mission? Lighten your load. And what's with all the cooking utensils and mineral-hunting gear?"

"One can never be too careful," the half Thrule argued. "The desert is a dangerous place. Besides, we need some story, some alibi. There are many prying eyes about."

Vetra shrugged. He saw that his companion's stride had greatly improved.

Lehundr, catching his expression, showed a wide grin. "We Thrules know something of healing."

"You're a half Thrule," Vetra reminded him.

"Does it matter? I still have a nomadic heritage."

"You seem proud of it—also ashamed."

Lehundr looked away. It seemed the Thrule kept more than one dark secret.

A disturbance gripped the nearby inn—cries, broken glass, the distant thuds of fists and crashing furniture. Vetra tensed, gripped his blade, while Lehundr's troubled hiss rasped between his teeth. He tightened fingers on Vetra's arm. From the open window drifted hoarse demands, whimperings of pain, and the screams of tavern wenches.

Four turbaned figures in dirty caftans burst out of the inn's back alleyway, dragging Lehundr's uncle by the ears. They thrust him out into the yard and kneed him down. His face was a bloody mess, his lip cut, eyes wild and puffed, cheeks dripping with blood.

Vetra drew his blade. He strode to meet them. The ponies started at the clamor, nostrils flared at the smell of blood; they yanked at their tethers.

The foremost man flourished a long scimitar at Lehundr. "Both of you are liars—" he thundered, referring with disgust to Lehundr's uncle. "Who's this then? Your map-bearing rat?"

They kicked the old man rolling in the dust. He clawed at his torturer's feet, hooking fingers into the baggy folds draping their shins.

"The map, or your life, Thrule," threatened the lead thug. He ignored Vetra and pointed his curved blade at the map bearer.

Vetra brought his sword high and gleaming steel crashed toward the man who was pressing his foot on the innkeeper's neck.

The thug swung a silver falchion and nearly chopped the innkeeper in two, but Vetra's stroke caught the blade. A rasp of metal and Vetra's weapon shimmered in a blinding arc. The sweaty grin froze on the swarthy face as three feet of glittering steel plowed through his chest and up out his back. He crumpled in a bloody heap.

His colleagues gaped at the sudden violence of the attack and scrambled back in horror. Two circled in to lay swords to their new enemy.

Vetra dodged his foes, parrying strikes which would have impaled him like a hog. He stepped over the body—then smote with savage strength. He followed up with a lightning-fast riposte, a bellowing roar on his lips.

The half Thrule scurried out of the fray to help his uncle, but was drawn into a vicious sword fight with the fourth man. They circled and shuffled around like barbarians, grunting, clashing, muscles bunched and triceps straining, while Vetra contended with his two foes.

Vetra's temper grew. The heat burned down on his head, tapping wounds of raw rage and frustration. He hewed and smote like a wild man. His temples throbbed; every muscle in his body rippled and stood out like lumps of iron. Ever since he had come to this wretched hub, men had been trying to kill him, and it made his blood boil. He grunted and whirled about, ducking, stabbed steel at the figures. They grew warier, their eyes widening at the efficient skill of the enemy they faced. His closest attacker feinted, a crafty, drawn out lunge. The man was a lean, hawk-faced fighter, and pretended to fall while his comrade came in leering with upraised blade.

Vetra saw the plan in an instant. He crouched low—and before his head went rolling across the sand, he twisted, surprise registering on their faces. He jammed an elbow in the kidneys of the jeering man that Lehundr now faced.

The half Thrule ripped blade across his attacker's throat.

Two down.

Vetra was bowled over in the rush by the two others in the brief moment it took him to make that rippling thrust. He staggered across the dirt, narrowly avoiding a mortal jab and follow-up boot heel in his face. A grisly vision of death swept across his mind as a desert rogue's blade slipped past his guard. But Lehundr came in grunting with weapon raised and swinging two-handed over his shoulder. The blade met the assailant's and the gleaming steel only glanced off Vetra's arm, slicing his forearm. The mercenary winced, but he shot his blade out to meet the man's desperate counterstrike even as he felt the throb of the wound up to his elbow.

Vetra's blade rang without mercy, a flurry of cuts that were too fast for his foe to follow. The groaning man fell to his knees, choking on his own blood. Vetra put his boot on the dying figure, pulled his blade free and used his left heel to mangle the man's face.

While the other bled out on the sand, the remaining rogue fled wheezing and grunting up the alley, holding his flayed ribs.

"Coward!"

Lehundr sought to chase after him but Vetra pulled him back. "Forget that scum, we have to leave!"

"But he'll blab to Rafa—"

"Forget Rafa! Dergath weeps, but warm blood runs everywhere your cursed map goes!"

The half Thrule grimaced, acknowledging the truth of it. He stumbled over to his crawling uncle.

"Go," his uncle croaked at him, pushing him away. "These swine will bring more with them. Better for you to be far away from here. I'll close the cursed hostel and hide away in Cyr-Down."

Lehundr hung his head. Vetra gathered the ponies and barked at Lehundr to get a move on.

The half Thrule struggled up onto his mount, blinking, squinting back his rage and frustration, muttering at the ill choices he had made.

Vetra sat his pony, a figure of silent wrath. He bandaged his arm, wrapping the sleeve of his caftan in a rude sash around his bloody wound.

Lehundr and he cantered back out the alley with the packbeast in tow. The great eastern road, now a ribbon of white satin shimmered in the drowsy heat through the gaps between the plaster homes. They left the rowdy sounds of Dragonskull behind.

II: The Ring of Pain

Their progress was stalled by the presence of a bearded rogue watching the eastern gateway: two flanking walls of loose sandstone blocks piled one on another, crossed by a wooden gate. Not much of a barrier, Vetra thought, but it was what Dragonskull had to offer. The man leaned on a spear, fingering a long blade clutched in a brown fist. His eyes were trained on the horizon. Vetra recognized the thug from the alley, so he signaled Lehundr to a halt.

Quicker to split the man's skull and be done with it, Vetra mused. But that would leave a clear signal to Rafa and his gang where they were headed. No, better to double back through town and dispose of the spy who was predictably stationed at the western entrance, thus throwing off the scent. But he rejected the plan: too risky. It entailed a complex detour and chance for a run-in. Easier to make a roundabout route and escape by stealth, winding around Dragonskull.

He and Lehundr ducked low in their saddles, and threaded their way back through narrow alleys and deserted service yards, leaving by another unguarded exit that Lehundr knew of. On the way they passed the stone water reservoir and its snaking pipe which swung out over its wide, glaring lip.

Vetra recalled that Dragonskull had once been a thriving mining community named New Thoria after the famed metal Thorian. The mines had dwindled since and Dragonskull would have become a ghost town, had it not been for the trade route, and ultimately the discovery of a water source.

Where water would normally gurgle from the pipe to fill the reservoir's basin, the spout was dry as desert bones. Vetra saw men clustered at the reservoir's base trying to sort out matters about the stopped flow, arguing and gesticulating, and the local constabulary was having a tough time trying to stop panicked locals from climbing the rungs up the vessel to fill bucket and barrel and drain what was now a scarce resource. Not a trickle came from its stony mouth; the work of the rebel Thrules, if the informers were to be believed. How they pumped water that distance was beyond Vetra. He shook his head, figuring it must by sorcery or some esoteric science.

Breaking through a rickety fence and a stand of eucalyptus swaying in the afternoon breeze, they took a goat path north and east that crossed the dusty highway, not two bowshots away.

Past the edge of town, the well-worn track led to the Great Highway, a twin rutted path that snaked in a straight, lonely line for leagues to come—as far as Dalispar in distant Mekutomia.

The oasis that graced this ore-rich area had dried up, much to the disappointment of the early prospectors who pumped water from the nearest water source—a massive oasis some five leagues out. It was here where Vetra and Lehundr fled, and turned their treasure-seeking eyes.

They passed wagons, driven by camels, sometimes teams of desert bullock, many a mean-eyed blue-black ruminant with huge horns and flaring, flat-faced snouts. They snorted and bawled, swinging heads back and forth in their yokes, nursing bellows deep in wattled throats.

They were no more past these when the white tips of bones appeared, peeking up from the sand. A gigantic dragon skull lay on its side, twisted askew. Eye sockets gaped like empty pools.

From where the creature had come, Vetra could hardly guess. He only knew that the beast was one of the great winged fliers that came from an age well in the past when dragons ruled the skies. This parched region had been a dragon haunt.

But now the ignorant Behundrians had affixed wooden signs and crude placards on the magnificent beast's brow. Carven characters were etched on its gleaming white skull: "*Dragonskull. Now entering the golden settlement: Dragonnook, of old.*"

"Why'd they scribe the old skull? Nobody around here can read."

Lehundr shook his head, muttering his distaste for the lurid script. "The old ones would roll in their graves if they were to witness such sacrilege."

Vetra's brows rose, wondering what attracted the half Thrule to dragons.

He saw only a few of the larger vertebrae of the dragon peeking through the sand, indicating the creature's massive girth. The rest of the bones he assumed were scavenged long ago by the locals to be made into souvenirs.

He could not help but marvel at this awesome creature that spanned twenty wagons' lengths.

"It's the largest in all of Behundria and Sahir," remarked Lehundr. "So was the town named, *Dragonskull.* Whether they could fly is not known. What is left of their wing bones are shrunken parodies for beasts of their size."

Vetra rubbed his sweaty brow.

"It was said their empire stretched as far as Lausern in Lvendar to Mekutomia in the far east. That their lords were half human, half dragon with bodies of men and feet, head and necks of dragons."

"I am glad to live in this age, rather than theirs," muttered Vetra.

"Are you sure?" challenged Lehundr. "What makes you think this age so much better?"

Any argument he realized would not alter the Thrule's opinion. What did he really know about the dragons anyway? Their lords, half man, half dragon? He was about to snort out a response when Lehundr added:

"'Twas their half human-dragon lords that held a reign that lasted a thousand years. Legend says they came from a faraway world. I don't personally believe it. There are as many tales of their existence as there are grains of sand in this desert. A certain chilling legend speaks of a time when dragons flew to earth from a distant world beyond the moon. Others say a band of wizards created the lords and morphed with the dragons themselves through wizardly agencies to become the hybrids we see in the crumbled statues poised before us."

"If the old dragons were so masterful, why did they die? Why would a dead race have treasure?"

Lehundr gave a sullen shrug. "Their empire was vast. Their riches as lavish. Dwelling on earth so long, they lost their powers, 'tis said, and the dragon-men came to lord over them in their weakened state, and thus become their masters. The new dragon-lords were fortunately somewhat of a benign force, as far as lords go."

Vetra struggled to control his contempt at such a concept. "Men masquerading as dragons. Putting on headdresses and dancing around a fire in the dead of night. I've seen it from tribe to tribe, temple to temple. Men or dragons, if either had such treasure, they would have kept it well hidden."

"Perhaps, but as to which age is better, if you live long enough here," said Lehundr, "you come to believe otherwise."

The miles passed, the sun a beating scourge, and the clop of ponies' hooves a monotonous beat on the packed sand. The old dragon ruins jutted more frequently out of the scrub, and the dunes took on a shimmering quality—sheltering half-fallen fanes, monuments and temples carved in crumbling stone: eerie statues of dragon men, or weathered full dragon, carved with uncanny skill.

A rambling cart with rickety wheels carrying silks and olives from the east came trundling in a cloud of dust: turbaned Guirites driving a team of desert horse. The outriders stood in their high, leather-padded saddles and colored caftans, with crossbows raised. Vetra lifted his hand in greeting.

Seeing no threat from two lone wayfarers dawdling along the road on their ponies, the caravan men lowered their weapons. "Akzam San!" they chorused in a lively shout, meaning "Peace go with you."

Vetra and Lehundr tipped heads in respect and moved off the road to let them pass.

They drove their ponies in a leisurely trot, squinting into the bright glare off the sand, a hot dry breeze in their face bringing sand flies and dust into their eyes. Alongside the road and twisting through the desert came the stone pipeline that carried the lifeblood water to Dragonskull. Vetra stared at it, shaking his head in curious wonder. He marveled at the human engineering and ingenuity that could create something of this magnitude.

They encountered various traffic, from single caravans, to long trains of covered wagons and bulls with camp-following doxies and footmen wielding pikes. But never solo travelers or even packs of two. Two lone wayfarers with their light packs and blood-stained garments and blithe salutes caused many a suspicious look—and interest.

A painted harlot approached Vetra who had paused to rest his pony, her hips swinging, and cheap bangles tinkling on ankles and wrists.

Vetra scanned her long bare legs and her inviting, full lips and quickly declined the unsaid offer. "Business over pleasure, princess. I'm sure you'll find many a dog in Dragonskull that'll lap at your well-mounted behind."

"Not nearly as manly as you."

"Perhaps."

"What about your little friend?" the trollop followed up with a suggestive wink, her smirk hardened around the edges. "Half price for him."

Vetra laughed. So did the trollop. But Lehundr did not laugh, miffed as he was at being compared with such harshness to the mercenary.

Vetra reached over and slapped Lehundr playfully on the back. "Don't take it so hard, Thrule. These sluts are ignorant." He gazed in amusement as another of the doxy's painted friends slunk by. "I know better wares in Lausern who would practically give it to you for mug of mead."

A ghost of a grin touched Lehundr's dry lips, and he shrugged off his sudden resentment.

They made progress east with their sweating hides and panting mounts, the sun glaring at their backs.

No sign of Rafa or any headstrong, galloping host of his. It was a bare, desolate place, these outlands. Sand-scorched and dust-swept, as wild as the wind, with animal tracks zigzagging every which way across the parched landscape. The moan of the wind around carven rocks or twisted gumtrees caused Vetra a lonely shiver. His keen eyes saw the odd footpath of nomads, a distant low ridge strewn with boulders and dotted with the spiky azenia shrub, brown and faded green, and some faint yellow desert flowers.

Not a bowshot off the roadside, the remains of a stone dragon's tail curled around a huge sandstone man-shaped god with bicorn crown and hooked stave. The symbolism implied some form of an alliance perhaps—denoting a period when men and dragons had been at peace. Flanking the other side of the thoroughfare teetered a gigantic toppled statue with a dragonish head and tail, fangs and detailed scales, but the legs and torso of a man holding a trident.

It brought an eerie chill down Vetra's back, for reasons he could not name. Lehundr and he rode past the monument in solemn silence, the Thrule bowing his head in honor of the old lords of the desert.

Vetra frowned. "Why do you bow?"

"Why not? I pay obeisance to the ancient ones, like all the

Thrules do."

"The Thrules—a people without a leader, beaten down and treated like curs by the Behundrians."

Lehundr grunted, "I could say the same for a dozen races across the lands."

Vetra shrugged. He rubbed his eyes while Lehundr rode on in silence.

They stopped an hour or so later off the beaten caravan trail to rest the ponies. Both were tasked by the late afternoon heat and vigorous ride.

Dismounting to stretch his legs, Vetra gazed around warily at the desolate surroundings. "I almost feel as if ears are listening to our every conversation. Though we are nowhere near that hive of Dragonskull. Are there sprites hiding behind each cactus waiting for their chance?"

Lehundr gave a chuckle. He leaned elbows on thighs as he crouched. "You have a tall imagination for a fighter of your standing, Vetra. Still, it pays to be vigilant." The Thrule darted his own wary glance over his shoulder.

The heat waves shimmered with a wanton fury. Cactus and low, spiked shrubs merged to the eye on the horizon to dance with the rhythms of the hot, dry wind. The land of the ancient dragons was a harsh environment, thought Vetra.

He gained his mount and heeled his pony on, taking only a sparing draft of water from his canteen. He was grateful that Lehundr had packed extra water bladders on the packbeast.

A band of five horsemen riding hard for Dragonskull, slowed and on a signal from their leader, reigned in and surrounded the two men.

The leader squinted with curiosity at the mercenary and Thrule. "Afternoon, outlander. Mighty hot for a pilgrimage. You bound for Sunswatch?"

Vetra said nothing, sizing up his questioner, sitting his mount in easy, carefree manner. Lehundr stared hard at the men: cruel, sardonic bullies with iron at their hips, whips in their hand, axes and water bladders strapped at their mount's sides. The Thrule's pony backed up a few steps.

"The desert's a dangerous place," the tall Mosete continued in an easy drawl. His finger twirled his sandy-colored mustache. "Man can get his valuables robbed, his throat cut. What do you say? Me and my deputy Needs here can protect you—for a fee, of course."

Vetra gazed on in amusement. "Funny, I was just going to extend the same offer to you. The oafs we killed back in Dragonskull were slow in accepting our token of friendship."

The man's scarred face went hard. "Really? How many?"

"A dozen, I reckon."

The rider snorted. "Well, I think you're a liar." On a signal of his leader, his deputy Needs came charging in, blade swinging.

Vetra leaned back in his saddle. A vicious sweep, too fast for the eye, slashed into the rider's shoulder, slitting flesh from neck to ribs.

A ghastly spray of blood wetted the sand, and the man toppled off his brown bay, writhing in blood.

With a malicious roar, another rider came reeling in. Lehundr pulled away, his falchion gleaming, but Vetra was faster, and his blade hissed out, parrying sword, and Vetra's left fist crashed into the man's jaw, breaking teeth and bone.

The man slumped in his saddle. Vetra turned hard and drove steel through the man's chest. The bandit's horse fled off into the desert, dragging the dead man by the heel, whose foot had caught in his stirrup.

The leader took off his cap and wiped down his brow. "Well, that's an unexpected turn of events. What to do, what to do..." With an ugly scowl, the expectant looks of his men hot on his back, he urged his mount forward, hand reaching for his hilt.

Vetra glanced sideways, as if the lizard at his horse's hooves was of more interest than the man's approach. Their eyes locked, but the attacker seemed fazed by the mercenary's unflinching gaze. A sudden perturbation crept over his face, like a shadow fleeting by under a passing cloud.

Vetra had stared down men like this before, and he knew the man for the bully he was: a callous, condescending brute who had won perhaps too many well-picked fights and had a knack for preying on weaklings which by uncanny luck had boosted his confidence. He had judged his marks by the size of their ponies. But for all his cowardice, the man was not completely daft, for when a cloud of dust rose up the trail, he reined aside.

"You've just been saved, outlander, by luck."

Vetra laughed. "Sure, keep on believing that."

The leader snarled and the survivors rode off in a cloud of dust, mouths full of foul oaths.

"Cowards," spat Vetra. "Is all this backhill country full of villains?"

Lehundr shrugged, dabbing at his brow. "No shortage of ruffians and bullies here, I'm afraid. It gets worse."

Vetra shook his head. "Well, it's good that I am a tolerant man, Lehundr. Have a care, Thrule, and don't sweat so much."

They slowed their own ponies, to let the oncoming riders and their guarded caravan pass. Even as he stopped to check the jewel was still there, Vetra frowned at Lehundr's packbeast's cargo bag which seemed heavily laden and bulkier than normal. Something didn't seem quite right about it and Vetra stared at it for a long time, as if it had moved in the shimmering heat. Finally he shook his head and muttered some words about the desert heat getting to him.

The miles passed in a blur of dust and heat. The soil tended to a slightly reddish hue, and sometimes white sand would form dunes, caked with twitch-weeds and low shrubs like juniper. Always the tall, smooth-boled gumtrees dotted the landscape, arching their pale gray and green limbs skyward. Such giants offered welcome shade when they passed by. The only creature that dared the daytime sun were the tiny lizards that darted around the trees' trunks.

Lehundr lifted a hand in warning before long. "The great oasis is fast approaching. See how the pipe runs up the hill alongside the road? We should be on guard for hostility."

They moved with more caution now, well off the dusty track. But not as far as Vetra would have liked for he saw a ravine drop sharply to their left.

The sun pushed its somnolent face lower in the sky, turning a slightly more jaundiced hue. The wind had died, and Vetra brought his pony around to climb a low hill, north of the one where the pipe ran.

Commotion echoed from the valley below. Vetra pulled his mount out of sight, before crouching in the warm sand atop the high dune. He hissed at Lehundr to do the same.

Vultures circled above. He smelled the strong scent of carrion. A battle had raged here recently, for he could see the dark sand below was stained blood red and bodies lay strewn everywhere, both Thrule and Behundrian.

A cluster of Thrules in wine-colored robes and loose hoods milled about a strange wheel, or some gigantic gumwood ring. The wheel lay flat on the sand, fifty feet in diameter and turned slowly under the desert heat. Its movement was aided by eight heaving bullocks with upturned horns, yoked to the ring's perimeter. The mechanism powered a conveyor system up the slope, consisting of large buckets attached to chain and pulley. The conveyor drew water from the nearby oasis up the hill into the great pipe which ran from the summit down the hill's opposite side and alongside the eastern road. Now the pipe lay broken at a lower point, pierced by pickaxe and hammer, and Thrules collected the spouting water into barrels and water bladders of their own, which they hauled with their packbeasts to a roped-off area.

The oasis was surrounded by giant gum trees and billowing

palm with branches laden with ripe dates. A line of ruined stone columns reared up at its center. The site was ancient, Vetra recognized. Flanking it were two stone, gaunt dragon-men, the lords of the time, holding wine cups up to the air as if to catch the rain.

At least a hundred Thrules swarmed the area. A central leader, waving falchion, gesticulated at the others. A red shawl flared around his shoulders. A score of hooded figures scouted the dead, scavenging the bodies for supplies and weapons. Vultures continued to wheel and to drop down with hungry cries to examine and plunder the corpses with parted beaks thick with flesh. Vetra saw some animals had been killed too. Bloated bellies of bullocks lay upturned, exposed to the sun, their hides teeming with flies, and an awful stench. Whether they had died from sickness, or purposeful violence was not evident. Around the wheel, some of the brute beasts' places had been supplanted by Thrules who were chained at the leg to do the task normally done by bulls. They were being unshackled with growls of disgust and anger.

Vetra's lip twisted in contempt. Likely the Thrules had taken revenge, had come to liberate their kin.

"The Ring of Pain," muttered Lehundr. "The symbol of our brothers' bondage. This time they have not been idle."

"A pump?"

"That wheel down there is where our people have been enslaved ever since I can remember, to draw water for the precious Behundrians. Look at the chained oxen which drive the capstan. It pumps water to the Dragonskull traders' post. Sometimes when the bulls die, 'tis only Thrules who drive it. Their oasis at Dragonskull dried up long ago, and some engineer had the clever idea to pump water from this oasis, which is as you see."

Vetra rubbed his jaw, frowning in reflection. Like the spokes of a radiating wheel had the oxen been stationed. Where one of the yokes was empty, a great plank of wood had been strapped to outfit what looked ten Thrules to take the brute beast's place. He saw the Thrules had taken axes to the chained shackles that held their remaining brothers.

He shook his head in marvel. His lip pressed in a grim line.

Some of the mystery of the water's propulsion was dissipated in the course of his scrutiny. Gravity more or less pulled the water down the stone pipe toward Dragonskull. It was just a matter of getting the flow started, which the great pump with the wheel powered by the bullocks, provided.

Vetra caught the glint of vats and screens by the oasis shore. A thin tributary pipe drew water from the sparkling waters. The pump also served a parallel purpose: to draw out emerald-speckled water which when dried, left a precious Thorian residue. Slune the wizard-alchemist had long ago discovered such sediments could manufacture the hardest steel.

Vetra and Lehundr crouched, studying the proceedings below from the nearby hill, squinting against the glare of the sinking sun. "The way I see it, we have to get by this pump site to get to your tomb or dragon fort, but this ravine below us makes it treacherous. If we can skirt its edge maybe, slip by them without—"

A sudden sound of a rock tumbling down the hill had him whirling toward the bushes behind him. Five dark-robed Thrules scrambled out of the cacti grove, training crossbows at them.

"Down!" One motioned with his weapon to Vetra and Lehundr. "Now! Move—down the slope! No tricks!"

Vetra glared. The offender was a young bowman, of more than average height who he sized up in a glance. His swarthy features and thin hooked nose lay shadowed behind a hood. Fingers twitched on a mechanical trigger bar.

Vetra knew they would riddle him full of bolts before he could take two steps to cut them down. With a rumbling curse, he jerked about and made his way down the crumbling slope.

White-knuckled, he gripped his sword. That they had let him keep it was a sign of inexperience. Lehundr scrambled behind. The other Thrules snatched up the reins of their ponies and led them down toward the encampment, prodding them with the ends of their bows. One nudged Vetra a little too forcefully and Vetra turned about snarling, swatting the crossbow aside with a sputter of rage. The bolt flew wide. The other Thrules came running, sending Lehundr sprawling forward.

"Down!" they cried. The lead Thrule, sweating and quivering in rancor at Vetra's truculent manner, pushed and prodded him on, while two others stepped in beside him, bows trained at his midsection. One Thrule tried to tear the sword from Vetra's iron grip, but the mercenary laughed at his pathetic attempt. That they hadn't riddled him full of bolts meant they wanted to keep the prisoners alive, probably because Lehundr himself was half Thrule. He pegged his young captor as an unschooled and unseasoned pup, a new recruit whose heart was probably hammering in his chest.

Vetra let itchy fingers play on the hilt of his sword. The chance that he could gain advantage in this situation was slim; with reluctance he forewent a quick skirmish. Not the right moment...

Surprised shouts came drifting from below. The captain of the troop came marching up, curses thick on his lips at the intruders who dared approach the wheel. The lead bowman ordered the five who held Vetra captive to a halt.

Vetra saw some gripped falchions in their hands, others short curved blades with ends wider than their middles. No taller than chest-height, these Thrules had polished gumwood boomerangs strapped in small packs on their backs. Their loose hoods showed only their eyes and mouths; their bare hands, browned by desert sun. Plump ponies laden with supplies stood a pebble's toss away near the bullock ring, swishing tails to keep away the flies.

Vetra thought hard how he was going to outwit these

offenders. Lehundr, rigid as a board, uttered no word, but his black eyes darted wildly about and passed over Vetra with meaningful fervor. He and Lehundr exchanged glances.

As the leader approached, a great cry went up among the Thrules. Vetra could only assume they thought that more of the enemy Behundrians had been caught spying.

He noticed the relaxed stance of the bowmen, and the weapons slackened in their hands. At the moment of the first cry, he struck with instinctive ferocity. Fists and hilt flew out, then he ducked in a protective crouch. The Thrule next to him dropped like a stone.

Bows came up. His Thrule captor gave a choked cry.

Vetra pulled the body of the nearest bowman toward his own. The struggling Thrule took the other's bolt square in the chest.

Vetra threw the body aside while Lehundr stumbled in a limping dash toward his pony. He seized the animal's reins as the bolt of a Thrule whizzed mere inches from his ear.

Vetra grunted. He sprinted to take out the next man between him and his horse. Blades came up to lock in feverish clangor with a competent Thrule, dancing on his sandaled feet. The robed man swirled close to his back, ready to arc a murderous backhand sweep across Vetra's throat. Vetra twisted around him and lifted a knee to plunge his boot in the small of his back. He pushed him savagely to send him rolling down the slope. Vetra threw himself to the ground, while bolts sped overhead to smash into the foliage.

"Stop this madness!" a booming voice rang over the clangor and thunk of bolts. The commanding figure pushed aside one of the aggressors while wrenching the weapon out of the young Thrule's hand pointed at Vetra. He rounded fiercely upon the mercenary. "You look like no friends of Behundrians."

Vetra grunted. "You think? Maybe we're dragons? Out to spit fire at you and burn up your water—an ugly sod of an outlander and a half Thrule? Dergath weeps. Muzzle your dogs!"

Something in Vetra's sarcasm caused the other to pause and break out in a scowl. "Who are you then?"

"I'm Vetravincus. This is Lehundr. I'm a trader and a sometimes mercenary."

"Well, what do you do here? This is sacred land. Don't you know it is a time of war?" He gazed with rising anger at his dead kinsman.

"That we know. We heard it all the way back in Dragonskull." He spat out a gob of phlegm. "We came in search of—"

"What he means to say," interrupted Lehundr quickly, "is that we're prospectors—in search of new lodes of silver and iron. You'll see our tools on my pony, picks and screens, and more strapped to our packbeast."

"Is that so? Then I expect if I search your belongings, I'll find more of these gold-hunters's wares?" The man strode over toward the mounts. "Zren, Yuel, Munan, go search—" he jerked his head.

The surly youth who had escorted Vetra down the hill pushed past the two other Thrules, thumbing his thin, hooked nose to rifle through the packs strapped on the packbeast. One quivered under his touch and he cursed it, but he jerked back with a sharp cry as a lithe form came springing out of the large bag, bowling him over. The figure sprang back, her hair matted with sweat, wielding a crude knife and a strange knout, with wicked metal barbs.

The Thrule's cry rang with choked surprise as steel gleamed in her hands.

Others poised ready to attack. Jhara stood with her legs braced, blinking in the sun, eyeing the three hooded foes who circled her with curled lips. Her face creased in wary appraisal, then amusement, crouching on the balls of her feet like a she-cat.

The younger Thrule came at her, underestimating her puny weaponry. "Come to me, birdie!" She round-house kicked him in the head. He fell with a crunch, clutching at his head, moaning.

The other came in, swinging a curved blade high.

She grunted and ducked, elbows out, fists clenched and landed a fierce punch. Springing up from her crouch, she was ready to lash into flesh. The young Thrule was rising to his feet, shaking his head and groaning.

"Is that all you got?" she taunted. One hand clutched tightly on her curled dagger that gleamed in the noonday sun. The dangling whip in the other traced shimmering circles and drew blood and bits of skin. Already it had snagged black cloth and blood was flowing from it.

Vetra could not hold back a strange surge of admiration for this spunky girl, in spite of his surprise.

"Stealing young girls now, are you?" grunted the Thrule leader, disgust clear on his face.

"I had no knowledge of her," Vetra growled, miffed at the chief's quizzical, cold stare.

Creeping like cats, many Thrules moved to surround Vetra. Others blocked the girl's path and Lehundr's prancing feet found no avenue of escape. Vetra drew his blade. Snarling through his teeth, he stood bent-kneed and dared any to take him.

Lehundr gibbered attestations in Vetra's defense, but to no avail. "He speaks truth. I came with him from Dragonskull, escaping the persecutions of Behundrian thugs."

"Do not listen to them, Zaln," hissed the young Thrule guard who had prodded Vetra down the hill. "Ulra lies dead with a bolt through his chest because of these pigs' aggression."

"No thanks to your stupidity in holding us under crossbow threat," growled Vetra.

Zaln, the leader, paused, nodding silently to his scout. He turned to Lehundr. "And we should listen to you, why? Because you lied to us earlier? Coming from a half Thrule, this means nothing. Take them!"

"Peace!" uttered the girl. "They speak the truth. I emptied out their cargo bag and stowed away when they were swilling ale at the stables. They had nothing to do with me and are not 'women stealers'. I merely wanted to follow them—this rogue in particular." She waved her bloody whip at Vetra.

The leader frowned with wonder. "And why should you do that?"

"Because this big ox helped save my brother—and because of the map."

"Map? What map?" Zaln growled.

"Stupid girl!" shouted Lehundr. "Shut your mouth or I'll—"

"No, you'll do nothing—so hold your tongue, half Thrule!" Zaln ordered his men to keep the half Thrule constrained, who had rushed over to the girl's mount.

"I ask you again, what do you do here at the Ring of Pain?"

"It is as we have said," muttered Lehundr stubbornly. "Prospectors."

The leader sneered an explosive sound. "A girl who fights with knives and scourge, and a limping, lying half Thrule and a sullen mercenary? I doubt it. I hardly think the word 'prospectors' applies to you. What's your game?"

"Let it go, Lehundr," sighed Vetra. "Sometimes it's better to tell the truth."

"But—"

Vetra waved him off. He pushed past the scowling Thrules, and ignored the wicked crossbows trained at him. He pulled up Lehundr's caftan and exposed the vest beneath. "Because of this, we are here: an ancient roadmap. It shows where the secret hoard of the Dragon-lords is." There was a leaden pause as dull murmurs passed through the awed group. "It could mean immense riches. Not that we're expecting anything," Vetra added with a cryptic grin. "The reality is there's no way we're getting past armed men, or your own patrols and camps. That's why we were skulking so close, and that ravine is not helping. It'll be seething here by sundown with avengers from Dragonskull.

Either you help us, or let us go."

"How be we just kill you?" piped up Zren like a surly badger. "Like we did these Behundrians, and take the map for our own?"

"What? And be just as treacherous and base as your enemies?" said Vetra with comic irony. "That's exactly what the Behundrians tried to do."

"Cool your head, Zren. You're much too hot under the hood. I'm in charge here," murmured Zaln. "Nothing is decided yet."

"Perhaps you could help us?" suggested Vetra, half sarcastically to the young Thrule. "Unless you're all just as shifty and treacherous as that blackguard Cthan and his Behundrian scum at the outpost? I don't think you're as cold-blooded as that lizard and his cronies like Rafa, otherwise your whole rebellion is just a sham, a web of hypocrisy."

"You do not know all," said Zaln through clenched teeth. "We defend what is ours."

"You broke the pipe they made," argued Vetra. "You incited their wrath. How can you not expect retaliation?" he growled.

The leader turned on him, his brows bristling. "They kidnap our women. They sell us and use us as slaves. They breed us for more slaves to work for the cruel lords of the east—Eustan, Daranthia, Gattrland and other parts. You do not know all, outlander. So, do not judge us through the eyes of your own biases."

Vetra frowned, licking his lips. "It seems Cthan has severely misrepresented your cause."

The leader spat out a contemptible wad of phlegm. "Cthan is no more than a lying desert snake and double-talking torturer. He promised us our lands back under the last treaty—that we may pasture our goats and llamas upon the lush oases. He waves instead a charter of forged signatures in front of our noses, saying that we agree to forfeit our lands to his prospectors and overlords."

The Thrule chief's eyes flickered with fury, but then he pulled back his hood to reveal wisps of long steely gray hair. His eyes softened into wide pools as he crept closer to examine Lehundr's map. "Maybe. Can it be...? Yes. It must." He traced his gnarled fingers across the ancient fabric. "This looks more like the inner sanctum of the old temple, that of the ancient Dhraken. A tomb of exotic mystery."

"It is," assured Lehundr with triumph.

"There—" Zaln stabbed a finger "—the key in the tomb." His eyes glazed, passed swiftly over the ancient dragon script, as if he knew the gist of that ancient dead language. "A key that would open the great fortress, Dragon Forge?—one closed for an age."

Lehundr wagged his head; a hushed whisper was on his lips.

"I don't know if anyone's been up to the fortress for years. 'Tis hallowed ground—"

"Some say it is cursed, but 'tisn't," Lehundr cut in. "The dragon-lords were wise; they hid their treasure from the likes of greedy, ambitious overlords."

Zaln wasted no time in arguing. "Take captain Dunon and Gefzad along and five others. Assemble packbeasts with water bladders to head north. The rest will stay here to defend the Ring of Pain and the Oasis from our foes."

Dunon motioned around the scattered bodies and still burning wreckage. "Are you sure we should split our forces at this time? The Behundrians will be on the move soon enough."

Zren shook his head like a wild dog. "Aye, I say we slay this rabble, take the map, and search for the treasure at a later time."

The chief laughed sharply. "There's enough death here today. I'm sure you can see that."

Vetra shrugged, casting a sad look around him. As much as he despised the pesky Thrule, he had to agree with him on one point. They had enough on their plate without watering down their forces. Somewhere he had a bad feeling that these resistance fighters were living on borrowed time.

On cue, the attack came sooner than expected.

No sooner had Gefzad organized the team when the hoofs of enemy horse and camel came raising clods of dirt and the chorus of vindictive wails of men came howling like wolves. A team of camels came pouring over the rise; men were pointing and gesticulating and sabers swinging in their hands. Others loped on foot, wielding crossbows and maces.

The Thrules jolted to attention, raising weapons and forming ranks.

Vetra swore. "Down!"

Bolts came whizzing by. Crossbow men from the attackers were kneeling in the sand, ready to arm and shoot again. A volley of lethal iron whooshed by and thudded into date palms and Thrule flesh like the swarm of many bees.

Camels burst out of the dunes with snarls on their lips. Men atop the beasts hacked down on the surprised Thrules.

The little robed figures scrabbled on their knees, ducking strikes and stabs and hacking at the legs of the cantering camels. Thrules died under those hoofs, but three of the ornery beasts fell hamstrung, spilling their riders to the sand where they were quickly despatched with glinting, gore-flecked Thrule knives.

"Stay back! And follow my lead," Vetra roared at Jhara.

"Fall back!" Dunon cried. "Take cover in the scrub, damn you. Use the cacti as shields! Rake them with bolts!"

In the melee Vetra recognized such rogues as Rafa and Vilivet and several other rough-looking characters from the depot—the bullies and cutthroats who ran the town.

Vilivet snarled, spittle flecking from his fleshy lips: "It's that damn bitch from the market," he cried, "the same whose brother has been stealing from our honest merchants. Get her! She carved up a bunch of Rafa's men."

Cthan and his men gave gusty curses, made the quick leap that Vetra and the girl had joined ranks with the rebels, seeing him rubbing shoulders with Zaln and Lehundr.

A cry came from a sandy-haired ruffian waving a broadsword with leather helm flapping down his cheeks. "Aye, and it's that meddlesome outlander. Take him alive! I want him alive."

Vetra gave back an insulting roar. "Only in hell's last inferno will you take me alive."

They charged into the Thrule huddle. Vetra and the others scattered. Jhara scrambled forward to grab a saber from a fallen camel rider. Cthan rose in his stirrups and looped back with a snarl, smashing down blade to send a Thrule running alongside to oblivion. "First the Thrule leader, you jackleg fools," he bellowed. "The girl'll be spreadeagled on a mattress before long." He arched out a swinging strike and ran a Thrule through the mouth who scrambled beside his camel. "We're here to slay the oasis robbers, not some ragbag trio of thieves."

Cthan pushed his camel through the defenders. The Thrule charge had lost its momentum and the sheriff mowed down Thrules like wheat. His sword raged up and down taking cuts and parries, hewing crimson bodies with it. Bolts whipped around him. Two of his henchmen fell from their beasts pierced through the hearts, but not him. Rafa at his side rode one-eyed with a patch over his left eye. His sleek roan bucked and snorted in battle lust. The sands bloomed red. Footmen of the oncoming host chopped and stabbed down at bodies that lay twitching and bleeding.

Jhara wielded the two-foot saber two-handed. She blocked a cut, ducked, and a Behundrian's whistling blade glanced off her forearm, drawing a thin line of blood. She wailed, and shrank back.

"That young slut with him is an accomplice. Take her! She's a dervish with knives."

Vetra, fighting whistling cuts of his own, smote alongside her, shouldered his weight in to block the slash that would have taken off her head. He jerked a hard, disemboweling thrust that lay the Behundrian attacker howling in his own blood and entrails.

Lehundr gasped and flailed with awkward mobility. He stumbled on his branded left leg. He struggled in an arm lock with a Dragonskull guard who tried to twist the short blade from his hand. Thrules came clambering up and plunged their knives into the aggressor's back. Lehundr rolled free.

Vetra winced as a glancing blow from the flat end of a Behundrian's sword laid open a gash in his scalp. He shook the blood out of his eyes. He and his allies were hopelessly outnumbered and it looked as if they were all dead men. Like it or not, he was caught in a war which he wished no part of. In his dim vision, he caught a glimpse of the unmoving Ring of Pain and the raging beasts trying to escape, terrorized by the stench of blood.

It gave him an idea, albeit a risky one. He staggered to the ring, spurred by a sudden inspiration. The bulls were pawing at the dirt, snorting, ready to tear the whole harness and hitch off their heads if they must. With vicious hacks of his blade Vetra loosed the first yoke and the bulls stormed out, razor-curled horns lowered in offense. They shook their heads and bellowed while Vetra hewed the yokes off two more of them.

These were wild bulls, chosen for their powerful pulling ability and their dogged endurance to withstand the extreme heat of the Behundrian wastes. The dreaded bullocks were mean creatures in their own right with eight-inch horns and powerful hindquarters. They went mad, kicking hind legs and rearing with foam on their muzzles, drunk with the delight of freedom.

Four more Vetra freed, and he leapt aside to avoid their goring horns and trampling hooves. He roared at Jhara to get down. She narrowly jerked aside in time, as a raging, bucking beast fled by and aimed straight for the warring Behundrians. Four more beasts were stampeding their way into the Behundrian fray, mowing down Thrules who could not get out of the way fast enough. In a bloodlust frenzy, the bulls' natural instincts to gore and trample was whetted.

Smashing horns into camels, the beasts plowed on like battering rams, toppling anything in sight. They were unstoppable. Men fell shrieking, dying, gored and bowled over only to be trampled by the hoofs or the wild rush of the camels.

Bolts flew and felled two of the monsters. But not before other bulls had broken through and done significant damage. A dozen camels had been gored or lay groaning in streaming, blood-drenched heaps.

Two younger bulls fled into the scrub, bloodied and rearing with wrath, while the remaining three beasts, still caught in the fray, kept heads down and charged anything in their path.

Cthan's camel, impaled by horns, lay in a twitching heap, bleeding out in the sand, while both human and bullock trampled over its belly and the other corpses littering the sandy plain.

Vetra's steel split the skull of a charging Behundrian. He turned in time to clash swords with Cthan who came charging at him like a bull. The sheriff's strength was phenomenal, uncanny in the suffocating heat and the stench of blood as the fighters struggled in a death dance. Their leg muscles knotted, swords quivering in deadlock over their heads. Cthan, the near bald giant, heaved Vetra back and he staggered away from the broken length of pipe. Vetra looked up as in a dream, dwarfed under the shadow of the dragon-lord statue tipping his cup in mocking salute. He shook the haze from his head and parried Cthan's strikes as his obstinate enemy came in again, roaring a curse. The strident clang of their swords resounded but was lost in the noise of the jostling bodies and dying shrieks of men who slashed and hewed, oblivious to the baying and bleating of brute beasts and the roar of battle and thunk of their horns as they found flesh.

In a sudden burst of volcanic strength, Vetra plunged forth and forced back Cthan's advance. A surprised grimace fled over the rogue's face. Wide-eyed, he careened back, but with a grotesque laugh. He was actually enjoying this, wallowing in blood! Vetra thought with amazement.

"So, you have some fight in you after all, outland scum. Thank the gods! I thought you were just a spineless imp like these Thrules."

"Come and find out," spat Vetra. He twisted sideways and lashed out, kicked the sheriff and sent him reeling backward into a ghastly pile of dead bodies. The sheriff sprang to his feet and Vetra lunged in to run the lawman through, put steel through his gullet. But one of Cthan's men edged in, brushing aside the mercenary's stroke and raised steel for his own mortal strike. Denied vengeance on the sheriff, Vetra bellowed. He wormed forward, breaking half the protector's teeth with a jabbing elbow before running him through to the heart, blade standing out of the back of his chest like a spike. The glaze-eyed figure fell and Vetra pulled the dripping steel free with a snarl. He kicked the corpse away, blocking in time to parry Cthan's follow-up thrust.

Two Thrules came smashing in to send Cthan staggering. A group of Behundrians joined the fray. A seethe and roil of bodies made it difficult to make sense of who was friend and who was foe, as the fighters were swept away in a tide as a dying camel crashed headlong into the attackers. Vetra plunged his blade into a man's back, wrenching his sword free in a gush of blood. Taking deep breaths, he crouched, looking about. Nearby Lehundr defended against Rafa's whirlwind of blades, beaten back mercilessly like a scarecrow.

The Dragonskull thug yelled, "I'll see you in hell, half Thrule! You'll give me that cursed map now, or I'll peel each layer of skin from your sorry hide and stuff them down your throat! You'll beg me for mercy to kill you."

Despite his loss of an eye, the gang leader was about to carve Lehundr to pieces, when silent and deadly as a viper, a thong laid into his side and he jerked around with a gasp. Jhara pulled the weapon free with its flap of flesh. Holding his ribs, Rafa screeched and doubled over and Lehundr kicked him away, his sword barely moving up in time to block the thrust of another bloody shaft as one of Rafa's bravos came chopping down at him in blind fury.

It was a fierce free-for-all in every sense of the word, where only the rules of the wasteland prevailed. The Thrules, disorganized and disheartened and weaving in and out of the chaotic skirmish like rabbits, were fading fast. The wreckage and slumped bodies were appalling, and without any leadership or direction, the defenders fled in terror.

"Retreat! Into the brush," shouted Vetra over the mad slaughter. "There are too many of them."

Some heeded his advice while others kept on fighting. Those who backed their chief Zaln, parried and blocked saber blows, but were quickly surrounded by howling enemy and put to the sword.

"Fools! They'll die in vain," grunted Vetra. "Why don't they pull back, hack their way through?" Rage and frustration soured his blood lust. "All for some water, and futile moments of holding a doomed position?"

Gefzad cried through his teeth, "We gain victory over an age-old enemy!"

"You die in your glory. Quick!" he pulled at Jhara and shouldered Lehundr back toward the hill. "We must get to cover. We will fight them in the scrublands—on our own terms!" They cut their way through Cthan's scattered flanks.

Up the hill they scrambled—the same from whence they came. The crash of camels thundered after them.

Dunon saw the practicality of the mercenary's plan and hurried after, though he was torn by the image of his chief who fought a valiant fight, a last stand, but for a lost cause. With a bolt shivering close to his ear, he put a hand to a jagged cut on his forehead and clambered after Vetra, Jhara and the others, dodging missiles while Gefzad and his kinsmen stumbled at his heels.

What others of the miserable Thrule band scrambled after,

Vetra did not know, for he was clearing a path up the hill through bush and stump. But a band of blood-dripping Behundrians joined in pursuit.

III: Road to Nowhere

The whine of bolts and savage cries rang long after their headlong escape. Vetra and company weaved their way through stump and scrub bush, in an attempt to lose their pursuers.

Vetra pushed on, panting in ragged gusts, blazing a trail for his allies along the thicketed ridge, hacking spiky fronds and low desert thorn. How he hated to be chased like a wounded animal, but this was the reality of the day. They had been heavily outnumbered. The fact that any of them were still alive was testament to their combined skill. The sounds of pursuit faded. He moved among the company, taking a head count and scanning for injuries.

Lehundr was cut and scratched; his limp had gotten worse. Jhara looked battered and sore, flexing the fingers of her left hand whose wrist bore a raw wound, but she held her head high, her fierce pride shining through. The ragtag of Thrule infantry were in no better shape, scrabbling and gasping with wounds, cuts and injured pride. One warrior's arm was broken, others were torn, disheveled, bleeding and dehydrated from battle and the harrowing escape. Twenty-eight of them stood sullen and bedraggled amid the foliage, dragging two packbeasts laden with gear. Zren the truculent bowman, scowled and cursed, whipping his sword about, shredding cacti. Dunon and Besu conversed in heated tones, spittle dribbling from their lips. Aus, a squad leader and his aide Gefzad kept eyes trained on the hillside, while the magician-priest, who Vetra learned was Samos, twirled his stave and muttered chants to his amulets. Vetra reflected that his magic had done little to protect the beleaguered rebels. Among the dust-bitten Thrules, there were maybe a dozen bowmen, all armed with swords or knives.

From his cacti-strewn dune, Vetra and the others crouched on their hands and knees. They gazed through a screen of juniper at the corpse-littered battle plain below. The party of Behundrians that had been sent out to kill them returned and gesticulated to their leader, the bald-headed Cthan and the sword-wielding Dragonskull constabulary. The Behundrians, washed in blood and grime, assessed the gushing rent in the pipe, and knelt to repair it with what tools they had brought with them.

"They don't know where we are," whispered Dunon with gratification.

"They will soon," grunted Vetra. "Look."

"Zaln!" cursed Aus.

They had stripped and beaten the Thrule leader. Those on the hill recognized him only by his ragged wisps of gray hair.

"They'll torture your leader before long," said Vetra. "He'll tell them of your strategies, secrets and hidden lairs."

"He will not talk," asserted Gefzad stubbornly.

Aus, whose hood had been torn off, gave fierce acknowledgment of his comrade's assertion. His hair was matted with blood and Vetra could see his teeth gleaming white in the sun.

"They'll make him," assured Vetra.

Dunon looked away. He was a man grown old and weary from these desert feuds.

"We'll travel together toward the canyons of shadows, in the vale of Zabenzar," he said in sober voice. "Let me see this map again." He lifted Lehundr's desert robe. "Aye, see the eagle's croft on this left tear above the dragon head? Only on the bluffs could be where tombs lie. They must have been looted or destroyed by tomb robbers by now."

"We'll travel as a group and hope they're intact," agreed Besu. He was one of the taller, leaner members of the Thrule company.

"Well, by Besthra! We might as well head for this ridge to get to the key. It was Zaln's last wish that we set forth. A treasure like that'll allow us to buy an army and crush Cthan and his scum. The dragon treasure is to be discovered by Thrules, not Behundrians."

Vetra grinned at the snarl that spilled from Lehundr's lips. Evidently the half Thrule resented the prospect of splitting the treasure multiple ways.

Aus clicked his tongue with skepticism. "There hasn't been a jackleg prospector come through Dragonskull that tried to discover the treasure and succeeded."

"But this time there's a map," said Besu.

"But likely a fable too," assured Samos, the priest-shaman. His bone-carved femur-staff bobbed in his hand while magical amulets draped on gut-cord around his neck jiggled with his every motion.

"If we don't try," Jhara said, "then nothing is to be gained."

The Thrules looked at her with surprise. Some peered with envy at her sleek, toned body which was glitter for the eyes; the swell of her high breasts pressed in appealing fashion through her tattered jerkin and her head was held erect like a young barbaric queen.

For some reason, her words affected the Thrules in a curious manner. There was a fierce note of passion in Jhara's voice, and her confidence was such that stirred the dispirited hearts of these Thrules who were too used to persecution and failure.

"Best we get as much distance from those vengeful Behundrians as possible," advised Vetra. His warning glance was enough at the Thrules who gazed too long on Jhara. Two had limped over to rummage among the supplies strapped to the packbeasts. Vetra and Dunon joined to take inventory. The company had dried food and grains for a few days, several bladders of water that had not been slashed by the leaping, looting Behundrians and various other necessities: pots, loops of rope, torches, wineskins, blankets and weapons.

Dunon pointed ahead to the waves shimmering in the heat. "East along the ridge then. The eagle ridge is north of here. First break in this ravine we branch off! We cannot reach it today, but maybe tomorrow."

"Then let us move," said Vetra, "lest those fiends rout us out or try to flank us."

They followed a series of wild goat paths along the ridge before the desert scrub broke off and gave way into a flatlands. The road, the Great Highway, ran straight as an arrow and the last shoulder of ridge rose up from the sands to grant views of both sides, particularly the shallow bowl north and into the land of desolation.

Vetra marveled at the vast, breathtaking solitude of the windswept terrain. Nothing but animal paths, red dirt, tumbleweed, and the odd cluster of towering cacti or gum tree. Ridges sprawled in the distances in a sinking haze of twilight.

The east-west road wound to their right like a ribbon of glinting silver. Then branched north.

On Dunon's advice, the pack followed the lesser road north. After an hour's brisk slog up the valley, the sun was a flaming ball sinking on the horizon. They had not ventured a league when signs of human activity became apparent. The pack drew back, crouching under a stand of withered eucalyptus whose shadow cast a dusky blanket over the hot sand.

Enemy soldiers wearing helms and glinting mail bore falchions and crossbows. They walked the perimeter like lords. A fence surrounded the compound with broken posts in places, but these had been stitched over time with wire.

Black smoke swirled about wreckage and bodies. Corpses, mostly Thrule, lay broken and mangled, pecked by vultures which clustered upon the sand dunes.

Dunon, Gefzad and the others crouched in restless groups in the desert scrub, grimacing in hate.

The soldiers had irreverently set up a camp around the huge, chipped and worn dragon statue that marked yet another sacred oasis of the Thrules. It was a small Thorian mine too. The water was pumped by means not dissimilar to the last pump site, the same machinery used to control the working beasts that hauled the ore. A tall, wood-framed rig towered thirty feet high on a small mound, with thick ropes looped over its summit that a dozen oxen pulled through a clever pulley system. It was an operation designed to filter the ore dug from the ground while camels lugged wheeled drays nearby to transport the Thorian ore out to Dragonskull or elsewhere.

Samos gazed sourly upon the enterprise. "The Behundrians blaspheme the old ones, by corrupting this site. You see, outlander, how they take our water? The dragon lords used this water for sacred purposes to lave their holy ornaments and purify their bodies. Much of the ritual is lost in time and beyond our knowledge. We revere these waters; they are life-giving. The spirit of the dragon-lords though deceased, gave us permission to use the lands that were once theirs. So it was said in dream quests by our shamans."

Vetra frowned at such ceremonious mystique. He had not much to say about the glorified devotion, so deigned no comment.

Gefzad, as if he sensed the mercenary's critical attitude, growled his endorsement. "They drain our oases! It's our water. We were here first. The Behundrians forbid us to use our own water, for their own greedy purposes. Can you not see our frustration? Can you not fathom our hate, our anger, and why we revolt against these pigs and take command of the pipe heads?"

Zren had shambled forth, like a moth to the flame of confrontation. His eyes burned on Vetra, who, though now unofficially an ally, he had no love for.

Vetra rubbed his cheek with a reflective scowl. The pumps and the water gushing from the open-mouthed pipe was singular, and the three-score armed guards with their spired helms and plumes who moved about with an air of lordly arrogance, no less.

Smoke billowed up over the low-lying trees to the east. Vetra frowned. Another mine? Doubtless the smoking ruin was that of a site that had been attacked and overrun by invading Thrules, if Cthan's informants were to be believed. Such signs meant that Cthan and his vigilantes would be coming to avenge the mine's capture. Whether they would venture on and track their steps and attack from the rear was another matter. Vetra recalled the wild look of fury on the sheriff's face while he battled him tooth and nail; also his boasts back at the trader's post that he would end the Thrule's little rebellion once and for all. He doubted much he was a man who would give up his vindictive duty.

"Let us storm in and attack the soldiers," suggested Lehundr. Vetra caught the sly look in his eye, as if it were a covert way to ditch the headstrong Thrules and secretly make off to the tomb.

"Best not rile them," urged Besu. "We are tired and wounded. The eagle ridge lies yonder." He gestured beyond the guarded mine.

"They've killed our people!" raged Gefzad.

Samos silenced the argument with a jerk of his stave. He gave an imperial rattle of his neck amulet.

Slinking among pulpy flowering aloe vera, they skirted the miners' camp, Vetra leading, next Lehundr and Jhara, masking the jingle of their weapons.

A wild, angry shout went up in the compound. Vetra turned. A glint off a Thrule sword had betrayed them.

Vetra gave a scathing curse. They burst out of their hiding place, crouching low to the ground. Bolts came spraying from the fence line as bowmen on their high perches took aim. There was a loud thunk then a groaning as a Thrule fell flat, throwing his hands up, a chunk of iron through his back. The skulkers fled like dogs, and the defenders of the mine sent horsemen out to ride them down.

The packbeasts ran amok and some of the retreating Thrules halted, kneeling and took aim. One bolt caught a rider in the throat and he tumbled from his mount in a gurgling mess, clutching at his neck. His body lay splayed in the red dirt. Two others came crashing down with their black steeds through the knot of scrambling Thrules, and more Thrules fell.

Vetra and Besu rushed in and struck up at the horseman. Besu hacked from one side while Vetra ran his crimson blade in a fierce uppercut and caught an exposed leg. The rider screeched and bent over, gurgling in pain, his upper thigh streaming blood.

Jhara had the foresight to snatch the reins of the terrified horse. Any extra mount would give the rebels advantage.

The last rider kneed his horse round after the quick deaths of his peers, then turned in a cowardly retreat, deciding that the small band was not worth dying for.

"Into the scrub, before they send more riders after us!" screamed Aus.

"Frightened sheep!" called Dunon, shaking a fist.

"Never mind them," Vetra growled. Though his brows lifted in surprise, thinking that from the enemy's perspective they too were little more than cowards.

No retaliation came from the guarded complex. Too few of an enemy for the Behundrians to make the effort. The Thrules gathered themselves in a tight knot, death hovering over them like a black cloud.

Vetra wiped the sweat from his face. "A bad turn of luck. We lost five back there. The Behundrians spotted us. Now they have an indication of our presence, and may come after us, if they think us a serious threat."

"Easier now they know the direction we're heading."

"And the packbeasts have fled," announced Besu sourly.

"We'll find them," assured Aus.

"Our pal Cthan will come seeking revenge for the loss of the mines," panted Dunon.

"Are you forgetting the havoc you created back at the pipe?" Vetra questioned in wonder. "They would have to split their forces to repair the pump and defend it while charging us."

Reluctantly, the Thrules left the bodies where they were and melted into the wild foliage ahead of them, a low-shrubbed panorama forming a vast net to the north. The scrub thinned; the weary fighters moved from island to island of sand, along worn trails between strands of brush.

A keen-eyed scout, following a trail of broken vegetation and hoofprints, caught sight of a swish of tail, then he gave a muffled shout. Vetra caught a glimpse of two beasts wandering aimlessly. A moment later a group of Thrules came bursting out of the shrubbery to retake the packbeasts. To their relief the supplies were intact.

Twilight was almost upon them. Many leagues had they to cover before an organized pursuit caught up with them.

Besu, the old Thrule, suggested that they find a place to camp.

On Vetra's lead they crossed a low ridge, placing more distance between them and the enemy who guarded the mine.

A soft blue haze hung over the gumtrees and cypress, casting the lands in muted shadows. Samos, versed in such things, selected a cleared area to camp for the night, protected by spirits and barred on the east by tall gumtrees.

They unpacked their supplies and tended to the wounds of their company, wrapping cloth around bloody arms and cut thighs, disinfected scratches and gashes with dampened cloth sprinkled with herbs and potent grasses that Aus and Samos had gathered.

The tenting gear was unraveled and laid out on a flat sandy area near the trees. The extra horse Jhara tethered to the tall gumtrees by the packbeasts. Both beasts hung their heads in gloom and swatted tails at the last few flies that buzzed in the dusk-laden air. There was some argument over whether they should light a fire. In the end, they decided light one, Dunon believing the Dragonskull men would not venture out for a night attack, or even face the hazards of the desert at this hour. His feeling was the Behundrians had suffered enough losses, and had not the Thrules' instinct or skill of surviving the desert. A watch was posted on the hills, to look for sign of invading enemies.

Several Thrules under Samos' direction laid stones down around the campsite while the magician sprinkled drops of sacred water in the four directions, North, South, East and West—an offering for protection, as was Thrule custom. Water, precious as it was, was the life-blood of the desert gods. The Thrule magician, sinister in his jingling, bone-sewn garb and his mud-caked hair, dug an inch-wide trench and poured sparing drops in ritual fashion from his canteen. A long flexible sapling was arched over to create a crude portal under which everyone ducked to cross the trench and enter the campground.

By a small fire they dared to cook broad beans and mutton. Others still, created crude lean-to style shelters, with hides and blankets strung overtop, using the trees as braces.

Losses had been heavy. Despite the lack of gaiety among this group, they sat around the glowing embers, humming folk songs and staring into the gloom.

Dunon raised his hands for attention. He gave encouragement to their flagging spirits: "Stand tall, you doom-mongers! A score of us are left, so let us be happy for that. We've survived an onslaught and where others fell, we live and should rejoice at our fortune. Do not forget that we are Thrules and hold the map to gain us Dragon Forge!"

Vetra lips curved in a smile as he saw Lehundr squirm in his seat on the fallen log. Jhara squinted in boredom.

Murmurs of approval rose among the surviving Thrules. Only a few retained their solemn and gloomy faces, among them Zren who did not feel uplifted in any way by the lecture.

The discovery of the map had prompted a lighter mood.

Many wished to forget the death of Zaln, their leader. Camaraderie and a united purpose made the Thrules come alive while the night deepened and the whine of night insects grew. Even Dunon believed they had lost pursuers and no enemy roamed within leagues of their hidden camp.

Some wineskins were passed around, and the stiff kick of the desert mead burned hot trails down their throats. They did not stint on it. Before long, tongues were loosened and feet and hands began to move.

The half moon was already a golden globe rising over the low ridges and the desert glowed with an eerie light. Akin to the gloaming on the misty downs Vetra recalled, of his native Tolizia; it was a moving sight. One Thrule brought out a small battered zither from a saddlebag and strummed a few tentative, plaintive chords. Others soon joined up in a refrain and a slow dance. Men were whirling in high-kicking dances, toe to toe. Vetra wondered what it was like when their women were with them.

The mercenary gazed around him. These nomads were people who were always prepared for transit, in grief or celebration, with ponies laden with supplies and cured hides ready to become rude shelter or whisked back on a pony when enemies came upon them. The nomad's life was one that few dreamed of, sleeping under the stars, moving from place to place, locked in an endless movement of caravan and packbeast, seeking out food and shelter, water and safety, never having any designated place to call home.

Vetra smiled gamely. How was he any different? The last time he had stayed more than three days in any one place had been back in Trallgate and that had been brief, on recalling the altercation with Rufus the smuggler and the scandal which ensued with a certain noble's daughter. He frowned at that and brushed the memory aside. True to form, here he was in a band of vagabonds in the middle of a war...

Vetra sat like a carven idol, grim and moody in his restless thoughts while the Thrules and their blood-grimed companions drank. His eyes roved constantly in the desert, alert for shadows and movement where every clump and bush looked like some cutthroat creeping from the wilds ready to leap out and hack out his throat. He sighed. His muscled strength lay dormant under the tattered, grimy desert garb of his, but he was ready to uncoil at the slightest sound of danger. Such wariness had kept him alive for more years than he could remember...

Jhara had come to sit by him and he shifted with grudging welcome. His eyes stared in moody intensity into the fire and fled off into the moonlit knolls.

Jhara's voice intruded on the peace. "So many weak men in Dragonskull. You're strong and noble."

Vetra grunted. "If you want noble, think of Bekr the Berserker. He fought the Brusites across the Rouge banks at Brine-Halt at the cost of their own lives."

The girl chuckled and clicked her tongue. "What do I care about Bekr? You were noble enough to save my brother. Fight a war that is not yours. I think that's noble."

Vetra grumbled at that and rubbed his jaw. "Why do you care anyway?"

"Decent men are hard to come by these days."

"Come," he muttered. True to his word he fetched swords and positioned her in front of him, moon over his shoulder, the dying fire to one side. It was time to teach the girl some art of swordplay.

"Like this," he said, coming behind her and taking the hilt in his hand and placing his hands over hers. He lifted the sword, blade pointed down. "Watch your flanks, protect your vitals with a strong block." He swung with authority. "Watch for feints and quick flicks, like this!—" He twisted sideways on the balls of his feet, facing her, letting shimmering steel batter her sword. It nearly knocked it out of her grasp. "Develop a rhythm, girl, don't waver!—" He sped back behind her and crossed over nimbly.

She stumbled, trying to keep up with his feet that moved like those of a panther.

By Dergath, she was going to be a force to be reckoned with, thought Vetra. But he didn't want to let her know. He knew, give her too much praise, and somewhere it would sabotage her growth, perhaps end up getting her killed.

He remembered his own trial-by-fire training by the old Grayhurst, master and soldier in his own right, whose bloody campaigns had been without number, and at whose hands he had faced trials at best grueling. His father had taken Grayhurst into his company to train his son—or knock some sense into him. The many bloody bashings and thumpings he had received at that badgering hand—to 'temper his stubborn pride'...he preferred not to tell.

She fixed him a coy glance. "Do you find me fair?"

Vetra narrowed his gaze.

Pressing herself close to Vetra's muscled girth, she smirked. Vetra, slightly taken aback, could feel the warm pulse of the girl's heart in a completely unexpected turn of events. Without warning she pushed her lips full on his.

Vetra loosed a gusty breath. Without preamble, he grabbed up the quivering girl and herded her into the bushes, much to the surprised exclamation of the Thrules. The mercenary found a cleared area not far away. He spread her on a mat of sand and leaves. Before long, the sounds of their passion rose to animal heights, raking the stillness with its primal beat.

Jhara's languorous moans and cries of laughter burst upon the glade as she followed his muscular shoulder, along his rippling arm, to his strong hand that moved from naked thighs to buttocks.

There came a skullish face peering through the folds of foliage, then the rattling of beads and murmuring curses that spoke of outlanders soiling the protection on the very soil he had blessed with magic. The shaman lurched back on a snarl from

Vetra's lips. The mercenary's gleaming blade flashed violently. The shaman disappeared back in the shrubs, and Vetra went back to his pleasures, his passion undiminished. Nor the girl's, whose pale skin gleamed in the soft moonlight streaming through the twisted branches of the gumtrees. Their passion escalated to a new rhythm in tune with the distant howls of the desert animals.

The moon rose a notch higher. Two flush-faced figures finally emerged from the brush. The shaman was nowhere to be seen, nor was Zren. Facts which did not bother Vetra.

A feverish heat rose from Jhara's sweaty skin and sultry curves. Her dark, burning eyes had the potential to enslave a man.

"The Kirns say drink helps a man overcome his fears before battle," Vetra remarked distantly, swaggering forth to swig a gulp from the wooden cup on the fallen log. "More the act of love, in my opinion."

Jhara made a husky avowal.

"Keep my extra sword. You'll need it. You've earned it. I'll show you how to use it properly later."

"You mean it?" Her eyes lit up.

"Of course! You'd think I'd joke at a time like this? We're in the midst of war. Come on, let's dance." He gave a hearty grunt, a sound deep in his throat then offered his arm. "That'll get the rest of that minx-energy out of your loins. I see it has no end."

She laughed and grabbed his arm and he pulled her up to the dance area, a squared section of cool sand that felt good on their bare feet. Makeshift drums were beating with hypnotic rhythm. Many Thrules had joined in dancing. A lively melody, unknown to Vetra's ears had him reminiscing on days of youth in many a tavern on his journeys. He thought he had heard all the strange melodies and rhythms of the lesser-known tribes.

Vetra failed to see Zren's burning gaze fall on him and the girl, gyrating in the heat of merriment. The Thrule's eyes were sullen and looked with resentment that an older man, an outlander had captured the girl's interest.

Later that evening, Zren went off to a quiet, private place while the embers glowered, to lash himself with a thorn-tipped branch and in a fever of murmurings, recount his vows, taught him by Samos the shaman, to remain pure of spirit and redeem himself of sins. To pray also to Turga, the quiet, wrathful dragon god for revenge on the shame and humiliation caused by the outlander and his female harlot.

When the moon rose higher still, Vetra spoke in low tones to Jhara. "Your father did well."

Her face fell. "He passed away a year ago. Cast out of the league of protectors. He came to Dragonskull an innocent Mercian trader and died penniless. Someone murdered him. My brother Aeke and I have been on our own since."

Vetra frowned. "You're worried about him, aren't you?"

"Much so, I admit. I left him with friends of mine. I hope he's well."

"Likely he's faring better than us," grunted Vetra.

"If he keeps his hands off the vendors' apples," she muttered with a laugh. "Hold me. It has been a long time since I felt the touch of a strong man."

Though the hides spread unevenly on the ground, she came next to him and thrust her warm back against his bear-like chest. He roused with a grunt, surprised at her unfettered way of showing her need. He clasped her in gentle arms, his fingers tracing suggestive lines down her thigh, and he thought with a wry breath, "Let us enjoy this interlude. Tomorrow may not bring such gentle tidings."

IV: Tomb of the Ancients

The way to the vale of Zabenzar was cut with dry gullies and boulder-strewn ridges. A strange range of sparsely populated woodland rose up in their path—a deadlands in its own right. At one time the blackened trunks must have been healthy eucalyptus. What had killed them, Vetra did not know. Dunon suggested a blight had passed through these lands long ago. Besu, who was more knowledgeable about such matters, remarked that fires had ravaged the area, taken the trunks and hollowed out their cores. It was apparent that over the years, these trees had developed a resilience to fire. Some still showed green leaves in the tops. Smooth, ghostly limbs twined from stem, like withered bones of skeletons. The odd lizard darted underfoot with long tail, sliding behind one of the trees, or down a hole of one of the blackened trunks. Overhead the squawk of a desert bird came as an eerie intrusion; likewise the shadow of a circling buzzard, appearances which set a forlorn mood over the company in the sweltering heat of the noonday sun. They broke out of the trees and stood panting at the fringe of the wood to see a rugged canyon wall facing them.

"Call a halt!" Vetra wiped sweat from his brow. It had been two days since the attack at the mines and his eyes burned with a vengeance, squinting under the yellow glare.

"I think we're lost," called the old Thrule Besu at his side. His bowed frame slumped on a charred log.

"I think that landmark is familiar," muttered Lehundr. He lifted a finger to the canyon face. "Is that not the eagle ridge crest depicted here in this hill mesa?"

Dunon stirred; Jhara hissed an excited breath.

Eyes scanned the area; indeed, the shape of the hills and its eagle-winged formation resembled a section of the ancient fabric at Lehundr's ribs, all purple and gold, with its cryptic collection of images

"It's the only place remotely looking like any place for a tomb," Aus said. "We might as well investigate."

A trail wound up the cliff, cut crudely in the form of a ledge into the crumbling rock.

They set feet up the path, though there were many grumbles among the company. Like outcasts on a singular mission, the Thrules trudged up the desolate track, boots crunching on pebbles, the sun beating down on their backs.

Vetra looked over the edge. A sprawl of boulders and prickly foliage promised a quick doom should one fall. A queasy feeling crawled in his gut at the sight.

The trail curved around the far side of the cliff, veering away from the valley. The ravine was quiet, save for a soft sigh of wind brushing the cliff's sides. The path widened to twenty feet. Ahead in the narrow gully loomed two rounded boulders rising three times a man's height in precarious poise. Both looked menacing, balanced as they were on sinister angles. Positioned to ward off intruders? Vetra scowled. Or only a natural formation?

Regardless, the boulders nearly blocked their path, only a narrow gap between them.

Samos gushed out a jabber of warnings about the cursed nature of such boulders. "They're jinxed", he cried.

Vetra rubbed his jaw with great weariness. He had not expected such a timorous reaction from the Thrules. It seemed even the shaman was doubtful about treading here. An omen— likely men would avoid this way believing it was cursed. What better place to hide a tomb? Vetra allowed himself a grin. Possible tombs that had not been rifled in these long ages? He flourished a fist. "A small team and I will go on ahead," he muttered. "Dunon, Besu, Lehundr and Jhara."

Zren's red hot face pushed forth. "Why shouldn't the rest of us go? We've come this far."

Vetra shook his head. "Cthan and his dogs could be marching up the valley soon to liberate the Thorian mine. I need you here to watch the valley and signal if necessary. It's not hard for them to track us here."

Besu gave a grim nod. "Aye, better to take no chances."

A flicker of resentment flashed in Zren's eyes. "Why not keep back your precious girl then?" He spat at the outlander's feet. He flung a finger at Jhara and glared with envy at her.

Vetra's mouth curled in a sneer.

Zren capitulated, shrinking in the mercenary's shadow.

Despite the shaman's gibbering and amulet-waving, Dunon waved them through.

They left the packbeasts behind, and the majority of Thrules were invested with instructions to make traps, triggering piles of rock to fall down from the steep trails and defend the gap on the other side should enemies be sighted.

Jhara and the three Thrules slipped through the crack. It was all that Vetra could do to squeeze sideways between the two mammoth boulders.

He stared up the valley and turned warily to Lehundr. "I don't like the fact that we can't see the valley from past this barrier. With a Behundrian army on our tail—" he left that dangling.

"Nothing we can do," the half Thrule muttered. "As you said, we have the scouts."

Jhara struck light-footed up the trail with inexhaustible energy.

Vetra called her back with the others. "Slow down. We don't know what dangers lie ahead."

Jhara reluctantly dropped back.

Eagles made their nests in the low crags rising to either side of the canyon and screeched at the intrusion to their domain. The canyon was well-named. Vetra looked down at the rough crumble of shale and chips at his feet. He had a feeling no one had been in this corridor for hundreds of years. The whole canyon had a dead, eerie feel to it, as if it were separated from the rest of the lands and sinister eyes watched them from realms unseen.

Before long a daunting cliff rose to their left. Sculpted out of the rock jutted a fearsome, weathered face in full relief. It might once have been that of a dragon with its great gaping mouth and hollowed-out eyes rising head heights above them. At one time the entrance had been sealed but the giant snout had cracked and toppled, maybe from an earthquake, leaving only a crumble of boulders at the foot, blocking out the dark path that led into the stony maw.

The three Thrules regarded it with spell-struck wonder. Besu muttered while fingering the oil lamp he had brought along. Primitive, old beyond imagining, the gateway to the tomb was awesome and mystifying—and creepy enough, thought Vetra, unable to stop the shiver that crept over his flesh.

Lehundr crawled past the boulders and made two steps into the dark interior. The four plunged after him into the darkness. Lehundr led with bluff confidence. The entrance opened up into a small domed cavern. Vetra's eyes widened in the gloom, his blood quickening to the echo of booted feet on smooth stone and the mysterious weight of ages.

The sprinkling of daylight from the entrance revealed a massive stone sarcophagus looming at the far end of the chamber. Besu lit the lamp with trembling fingers. Any jewels or gold which had lain strewn about the chamber had long been pillaged. The crate-like sarcophagus lay flush to the far wall and was flanked by serpent pillars. Draped in shadows under the flickering light, a hulking animal statue with a dragon's head and leopard's body sat watching, eyes glued ahead like an unforgiving sphinx. Vetra felt his blood pulse; he heard others' sharp breaths as they squinted in the gloom.

The sarcophagus's head was mantled with a carven dragon skull. At the foot stretched a stone tail into a darkened passage. All looked with dread, loath to enter that passage. Lehundr, for all his mettle, feared to tread over the vile, serpentish tail, as if it would come to life. Vetra reached down a finger tip, driving back the apprehension that inspired such irrational superstition. Cold, dead to the touch, the ancient stone was smooth carved and painted yellowish green from what weak light shone from the lamp or in from the entrance. He could not help but shudder at the thought of groping and stumbling down into a crevasse or some sepulchral pit of doom.

The floor gave Vetra cause for reflection. The polished paves were crusted with bones and ancient remains which altogether seemed abnormal, for no reason availed such mangled flesh. The paves showed rough scratches, but the ceiling was bare. No chute for boulders to tumble from upon high to crush a skulking thief. Dragon carvings raked the walls, wings lifted in majesty, jaws agape, eyes burning, as if portals to some inside knowledge beyond time and space. In the same panoramas the rightmost wall was smeared with ancient blood and bits of gristle and bone, unless Vetra missed his guess.

He kicked a clump of sinew and the bones rattled like fiendish dice, sending ghoulish echoes and dust around the chamber.

Jhara's teeth chattered. "Would you stop that?"

"Aye, it's disrespectful," muttered Lehundr, "not to mention jarring on the nerves."

Vetra grunted. He thrust his head into the tunnel, calling his own name. The echoes died in a dull murmur. Tink, tink. A drip of distant water—and a wash of dusty vapors, sediment and musty layers compiled from the ages. "Goes on a long way, I think," Vetra mused.

"This must be where the dragon lord who was buried in yon sarcophagus once walked," whispered Besu.

"Aye, probably where he went to feed his faithful protectors," said Dunon. "'Tis said the oldest dragons lived in caves, dark and deep, that stretched to the center of the earth."

Vetra snorted. "Or perhaps it's just some old underground cave carved by water and time. I think you two have vivid imaginations."

Lehundr frowned. Folding arms over his chest, he gripped his cloth-sewn map like a beggar would his last morsel of food.

Jhara spoke, "I heard that the dragons were gatekeepers to the world below. They were used to judge human souls when they passed the river of death for their deeds, good or evil. Men fought and died to tame them because they thought that they would have victory over death. So my father told me."

Vetra uttered a laugh. "Or how about it's all a myth? And that men built this tomb, not dragons. They dressed it up like a dragon tomb, and inside that stone crate there's at worst some moldered human bones, of a petty lord or forgotten king?"

Lehundr scowled; his mouth was drawn tight. He refused to accept that the treasure was not real and that dragons were anything less than magical.

Dunon tested the slab. "The lid's heavier than a mountain. We may never know. None of us could lift that."

"Unless we all get our swords under it and pry it off?" suggested Besu.

Vetra shook his head. "We'd bend all our blades."

"Maybe the dragon things were not the mystical creatures with untold wisdom and the wealth of ages past we think," argued Besu.

Dunon's eyes grew solemn. "Those with dragon heads and bodies of men were ancient before the stars were young," he whispered. "The dragon lords tamed the dragons and became their masters. This is one of their tombs."

The group fell silent and edged their way along the far wall.

By the arched way they could make out the tunnel which stretched off into murk. None wanted to go down there, not even Lehundr, for all his keenness.

Maybe they didn't have to. Glyphs and symbols were carved into the wall around the door. Possibly the makings of a map, and there, at a place below, alongside carven knobs and levers, lay a foot-long, sharp and hard thing, pointed like a claw, a great dragon claw.

Besu gaped. "Can it be? A real dragon claw. They're rarer than finding the gilded elephant tusks of the Kirns!"

"Now do you believe me?" gasped Lehundr with triumph. "Here are signs. This must be the key!" The half Thrule gingerly lifted the claw out of its cradle.

While they murmured and argued, none recognized the shadowy figure creeping over to the sarcophagus.

"This dragon claw must be the key to opening the portal to the fortress," cried Lehundr. "Though I can't understand the script, it's some form of dragon runes."

"Why didn't thieves take it?" demanded Vetra.

"They were looking for gold, not claws. They wouldn't have known it was the key either, unless they had the map."

Besu pointed. "I've heard the dragon fort's never been opened since it was sealed by the curse of a dragon's death, or some old dragon magic. Many a plunderer has tried to and all have failed."

"Aye," said Dunon. "Most died. It's leagues from here out in the middle of the desert."

Vetra suddenly felt a chill crawl over his skin. He peered up and blinked. He felt an unknown presence in the chamber. A razor-sharpened sense of danger told him trouble was near. He reached for his sword. There—a shift of movement near the sarcophagus. Some thin, skulking shape. Something else caught his attention—the perfectly polished wall at his side, almost too polished, and there were those vertical seams forward and back that ran suspiciously up to the ceiling, as if they were—

He gave a harsh cry. "Watch out! Fall back!"

Sliding stone sounded from underfoot. In the moment that the skulking Zren had passed his hands over some hidden lever behind the sarcophagus, the floor suddenly sank a foot lower.

A sharp choking cry rang out. Jhara somersaulted backward, landing on her feet like a cat. The floor gave way several more feet and with the others, she clawed with desperation for something to hang on to—to no avail.

Vetra fell and was knocked on his back, gasping for air. Zren tumbled into the pit too, his fall cushioned by Dunon and Lehundr who gurgled out surprised oaths.

Twenty feet up the sheer walls of the twelve-foot square prison, Vetra peered and heard a sound more terrible than the hiss of vipers—the grinding and scraping of heavy stone on stone. Two parallel walls of massive construction writ with dragon insignias, one which slowly advanced toward them with ominous implication. With savage energy he tried to mount the walls, but they were too sheer and high.

He stared in mute astonishment. Someone had triggered the trap, likely the Thrule, or perhaps it was the girl taking hold of the jeweled lever? No, it couldn't have been her. She had been tracing fingers on the map. Jhara's fingers had not yet touched the ancient runes. It was that wretched Thrule lolling at his feet. "You idiot!" He kicked him in the ribs. Zren sprawled in pain.

"Quick!" Vetra snarled. "Up the wall. Climb on my back!" He crouched and motioned Dunon to climb on. The Thrule wasted no time and Vetra yelled a harsh command at Lehundr next. Putting backs to wall and boots to the advancing opposite wall, they formed a human ladder, Vetra on the bottom, Dunon and Lehundr next, and then Zren. Jhara scrambled last over, legs and arms pinwheeling while others palm-lifted her up to grasp the rim. She heaved herself up over the lip.

Falling dust from the ceiling caught the weak sunlight and Jhara's sweat-grimed face peered over the ledge.

Vetra tossed the dragon claw to her. She caught it and set it aside, then continued to help each man out of the pit. First pulling Zren up, his fingers groping thin air. Reaching over the edge, she just managed to grab Besu's fingers while Zren kept her from falling. Besu scrambled over the top, gasping into his beard; together they formed a backward chain.

The wall was inching slowly closer. Vetra, last in the pit, bared his teeth in a growl. With no less than three feet to spare, he jammed his blade lengthwise between the constricting walls. The steel quivered, buckling fast. He hated to see his only weapon compromised—but it purchased him a few more seconds...

He squeezed himself part way up, pushing with boots on one wall and inching spider-like with back against the other. Barely had he hooked fingers over the edge when hands hauled him up and over, and the walls clanged together like jaws.

He squatted in a pained crouch on the cold stone, staring at the pit of death below him. The sound of machinery died. His sword and the lamp lay mashed down there somewhere. He cursed sore words at the loss of his sword.

Doubtless the trap had been ingeniously constructed, operating in some mysterious pulley and lever system beyond the feet of stone.

Clever minds were at work here and somehow he doubted they had anything to do with dragons.

A trap...to foil who? Would-be treasure seekers?

Vetra craned his neck, looking back toward where the crushing wall originated. A hidden chamber behind the wall?

He stooped and peered wolfishly down into the gloom beyond the wall where a passage disappeared off beside the massive, battering ram that powered the slab.

Another dragon claw was fastened on the inside of that wall

in ceremonial fashion, like pieces of a puzzle. Almost fearful to touch the cursed thing, Vetra hesitated, then gripped it and tore it off its brackets. Nothing happened.

"So, now we have two of these claws," he muttered. "Like parts of a toy. So much for your key," he scoffed.

"Any one of them could be the key," Lehundr objected. "I'm guessing it's probably this one."

Zren clambered forward to have a look; the others glared at him.

"Your curiosity nearly killed us all," Vetra said through clenched teeth.

"Yet if Zren had not tripped the mechanism," remarked Dunon, "we could not see the exposed chamber behind the wall."

Lehundr weighed the truth of the matter.

An uncomfortable silence gripped the group. Jhara went to examine the lethal dragon levers on the wall behind the sarcophagus.

"Can't see what's down there," muttered Vetra. He squatted to peer down, straining his eyes in the faint light streaming from the entrance. He saw shadows of strange statues huddled in the murk farther up and more carvings on the wall. "Dergath's ghouls, what is this place?"

"We're going to need a light."

"Maybe if you use the small brand I brought along," Zren muttered with thick irony. He rifled through the sack tied at his waist and produced torch with flint and tinder.

While Besu grunted and Dunon snatched the items and lit the torch, Vetra turned to the others: "We've come this far, so we might as well explore the likes of this treasure." He pushed his legs over the edge and jumped down with the torch. "Anyone else coming with me? I'll have a look around and when I'm done, you can help me back up again."

Besu was the only one who volunteered. But Zren, blood

dripping from his lip, gave a sullen grunt and on impulse jumped down, as if to redeem himself for his impulsive act.

The pit looked like a chamber out of legend, a crude, cobble-stoned dungeon laced in thick cobwebs that spread amid dense shadows underneath the floor above. The three groped their way about the chamber, Besu and Zren creeping behind Vetra. Unease had him padding like a wolf and blinking into the murk, straining eyes to see what demon or horror would jump out at them.

Vetra's keen eyes discerned a dark opening in the floor some twenty paces to the side. It was crisscrossed with cobwebs, something resembling a stair descending to unknown depths.

The cylindrical stone ram rolled on wheels and was crudely chiseled and affixed to some large stone mechanism. The ram itself was cold and rough to the touch, a work of monumental proportions.

Vetra moved on, transfixed. Following it back under the floor above, he trained the torch up.

A dragon statue loomed out of the darkness, towering heads above them on its hind legs. Clawed feet were outstretched and hands cupped in a gesture of offering—its toothy jowl carved in an austere grin. Vetra gave the thing wide berth, circling round it with bared teeth. His toe snagged on something rough and he realized his foot passed over a long seam dividing a false floor from the real one. He figured the falling floor of stone was powered by a similar mechanism hidden underneath the tons of stone underfoot. Why the elaborate engineering to ensnare a few thieves?

A large disc above with pulleys and chains hung down to fasten on the stone ram. A chute allowed a trail of boulders to fall and power the wheel. The boulders had already spilled, powering the ram to do its bloodthirsty work. Ingeniously constructed, thought Vetra. His hairs stood on end. How floor and walls retracted was beyond his knowledge.

They inched along like mice in a snake's lair, passing one springy cobweb after another and ever-present molder and frightful shadow. The chamber narrowed to a dingy tunnel underneath the floor above. They followed it for about sixty feet.

The passage ended in a sheer wall, edged by supporting pillars, old as time.

Besu pointed. "There! Over by that column, the wall!" They stumbled on to stand gaping aside a closed-off arch. Two skeletons lay sprawled in layers of dust and filth by the wall; one still clutched a corroded pickaxe in its hand. The wall was gouged with crude strikes. Obviously, the figures had been hewing a hole, digging for something—or perhaps digging to get out? Vetra rubbed his jaw. "These wretches likely starved to death before completing their mission."

He held the torch up to the wall. A grim pantheon of dragon faces and scenes met his eye: men, dragons, beasts, weapons, expectant armies and mesmerizing symbols.

Zren peered at him, his face a wild mix of angst and wonder. Besu looked like an old hunted owl, his wings clipped. They retraced their steps underneath what would have been the chamber's wall above.

A harsh grating of massive slabs sent hackles rising on Vetra's back.

"What are Jhara and those fools up to? Do they want to kill us?" He raced back down the tunnel, torch guttering dangerously close to extinction, the others at his heels. "They must have jiggled the controls!"

They came stumbling back to the death-dealing wall. But this time the stone slab was moving back toward them at an alarming rate. Jhara was leaning over the edge up top, whimpering, her face white with tension and a wail stuck in her throat. "Get up, now!" she cried. "Grab my hands!" While Dunon held her legs and lowered her down, she snatched at Besu's wrists and together the two hauled him up.

Besu scrambled to his feet then helped Dunon lower Jhara to attempt to get Zren and Vetra up.

Vetra glared daggers from below.

"We didn't cause it," Jhara protested, answering his vitriolic stare. "The slab started moving of its own accord. Lehundr is trying to reverse it now."

"Well, tell Lehundr to get a move on," Vetra thundered.

"It's starting to close over completely. Faster now!"

The Thrule looked up with fear that he would be the last left behind.

"Get up there!" ordered Vetra. Dropping the torch, he hoisted the smaller man up on his back, pushing him up with a grunt.

No sooner had the Thrule been hauled up when Vetra felt the slab push him back. He caught a brief glimpse of Jhara's look of absolute horror as the wall slapped shut.

The resounding smack of stone echoed about the chamber. Jhara's fading, sundered wail echoed about the chamber and Vetra blinked—to silence. The beat of his heart.

"They'll flip the switches and spring it open," he assured himself.

But no such welcome scrape of stone came to his ear.

Likely the mechanism had a mind of its own. He grimaced.

He stared around his gloomy surroundings, struggling to contain his frustration. The torch would not last forever. Already it sputtered at his feet, smoking and hissing. He stooped to clutch it in a sweaty palm, eyes wide. A square chamber stretched off in the distance perhaps thirty feet.

Something told him he could not depend on his comrades' efforts. These wretched traps! He should have known where one was sprung, another would follow.

His mind sprang back to the ancient pickaxe. Could he chip his way through the wall? It was at least a foot and a half of solid rock. Not easy. Perhaps a work of many hours, if not days, if the corroded metal didn't give out. What of the poor fools who tried to chisel their way through? Could he chip at the movable slab above? Perhaps where the stone joined the ceiling it was less thick. He studied the dragon statue and imagined poising on its neck and shoulders and striking upward at solid rock. He frowned. Only to have stone chips blind him? It seemed a foolhardy plan.

He prowled his prison like a caged lion. Retracing his steps back to the two skeletons, he crouched on his haunches and pulled the tool from the molder. Why? Where? To what end? What had these fools been hewing for? Did they have knowledge of what lay beyond?

Vetra passed fingers along the wall. Rough, cold. It was both inscribed and embossed with relief.

The arched door was five feet wide and sealed to perfection. The seams were tight enough to be hardly detectable. What lay beyond? Had the diggers been trying to get to an adjoining chamber?

He weighed his options and fingered the rusty pickaxe, peeling off the layers of flaking metal at its head. The tool had a stout, four-foot wooden handle; the iron was flaked with orange on the surface, but it was black and strong underneath.

He concluded that such men, despite their evident failure, had embraced a worthwhile mission. At least they carried tools, so they likely had some purpose. Hand on chin, Vetra sat engrossed for several moments in some lip-chewing thought. Were there other options?

Nothing seemed of immediate interest in the vicinity of the tunnel wall. No chance of scaling the chute. The opening was too high, and it looked dead and dark up there. What he wouldn't give to have access to the tunnel he had shunned earlier near the sarcophagus.

Off toward the far wall, a wide staircase in the center of the hall wound down, now cracked and sunken with age. He was almost afraid of what he might find there and crept on cautious feet over to investigate. Drunken steps trailed down into the gloom, perhaps thirty feet. But that was not what held Vetra's attention. They were flanked with low-riding dragon statues, of most familiar design.

Insanely lifelike! Almost like monster lizards, but with the bodies of leopards and the heads of dragons—not dissimilar to that strange, sphinx-like guardian lurking by the sarcophagus. He saw that more of them crouched, on the level below.

Vetra forced himself to walk down the steps, on the odd chance that something might offer an avenue of escape.

No such luck. More of the repulsive things lurked in the periphery, head to tail in what seemed random postures. Some were flatfooted, other poised in mid-step with necks bent and eyes glaring, as if frozen in time.

He stared. The chamber was like an insular menagerie, of size and configuration to the one above, circular, and admitting no exits, save but one corridor which ended abruptly. The walls and ceiling of this chamber bore no carvings or bas relief, unlike its predecessors, only simple smooth stone, as if it were a chamber to house only these repugnant things. Dergath, but they swarmed around him so life-like that he had to catch his breath. Every swell, lip, crack of bared fang and sharpened claw was depicted in startling detail. The things waited in an attitude of frozen menace for what was untold centuries.

Vetra thrust the torch into the face of one of the creatures, better to study its features. The flickering light showed the black-eyed face of a dragon and sleek torso of a jungle cat but sporting the scales of lizards and an alligator tail. The legs were stubby like those of a lizard's. Though the eyes and horns were dragonish, it sported the wide snout of elder amphibians with razor-sharp serrated teeth. The stone was glazed over with red pigments. Like sleepwalkers, the watchers poised in a frozen prowl, as if they were in an induced trance. Jaws were slightly agape as if ready to mouth a toothy roar, and Vetra frowned. Such pantomime reeked of an ancient mystery impossible to decipher after so many passing centuries. He tugged at his chin. The whole place stank of menace and decay, as if upon the dragon-lord's bidding, or perhaps his death, all had come to a standstill, frozen in time.

Vetra had heard of old tales spoken by the Kirns and the Guirites, of incredible life-like statues secreted in tombs. That they were watchers of the deceased, that they had been cast in stone, or iron, or some other form by arcane wizardry too old to name. That they could come to life at will to protect their deceased masters from unwanted intruders.

He brushed aside such thoughts with a wry grunt. These hobgoblins certainly had not come to life upon his entering this tomb. Mere fables. The stuff of myth.

Yet Vetra's finger reached out to stroke the leafed stone of the massive gargoyle in front of him. Instantly he recoiled. The thing had a peculiar rubbery texture, as if made of old moldered clay. Dead but alive—? Hard but yielding? His mind reeled. Too many incredible things lurked in this forsaken chamber to make sense of. He backed away.

What was that? A sound? He retreated to the broad stair. A wretched slithering? No, nothing. Just one of those many uncanny moments when a man lets imagination get the better of him. One of the repulsive dragon statues stared at him with its eerie, sightless gaze. A sudden swish of movement, as of a tail had him whirling. He crouched, drawing his pick. A tongue flickered out and a soft sibilance... The torch guttered and hissed. Vetra blinked. His imagination again. He relaxed, loosed a breath. The sound had played havoc on his nerves—it was a product only of his hissing brand and the elusive shadows in this dim, otherworldly place.

His torch would be burning down soon. How much time had he left? An hour? More? Why was he wasting time here?

Hurrying back to the skeleton tunnel, he propped the fragile flame on the wall. Time to pursue the digger's cause. Taking up his tool, he began hewing at the hole where the others had failed.

Flakes of rock chipped on the rude paves.

Before long a pile amassed at his feet. His long-reaching hope was that the iron head would last long enough for him to hack his way through this barrier. How long had it lain here in the dust and silence?

The minutes passed. Sweat oozed from his pores. His muscles stood out like iron bands as he strained under the flickering flame. Should that light go out... The clinks landed like blacksmith's blows and the tinny smacks rang in his ears like bells with every strike. Ghostly shadows played on the tunnel walls.

All the while he felt a strange presence weighing upon his soul. He felt the intolerant dragon statues glaring over his shoulders and their visionless eyes scrutinizing him and his movements with disdain. That he was trapped here underground with them he sensed they knew and had waited for. Who knew what sinister purpose they guarded?

The minutes passed; Vetra cleared the pile of rock away with his boot. Minutes of life remained in the hissing flame. No sound of help from his colleagues. Surely they could hear his tapping? He had the sickening feeling they had failed and were forced to move on.

The torch flickered and died. Vetra slumped, back to the wall, arms and shoulders sagging. The first vestiges of panic began to crawl over his limbs. The bones of the diggers rattled at his feet. He kicked them away. A bleak feeling of failure washed over him. What a fate to die here in this darkness with these skeletons! He lurched to his feet, a snarl on his lips, rejecting such a demise. It was getting hot in this chamber. The air was less potent, less breathable. The sods had likely died of asphyxiation; two mouths breathing the same air. His head swam, his bloodshot eyes burned, and now his throat felt clogged with dust.

He pounded on without pause, merciless stroke after stroke,

every muscle feeling the battering shockwave of steel on rock up his arm. There came a different sound to his swing. A thunk versus a thwack. Had the blunt head hit air? He smashed with all his blind fury. A tremor of hope bloomed in his chest. He pulled the iron free and passed fingers through a small notch. Yes! Air! A tiny finger-sized hole.

Like a prospector striking gold, Vetra hacked with zeal, surrendering all restraint, flakes of rock flying at his feet. He knelt and heart pounding, passed a hand through the arm-sized opening. The air was cooler there. A glow, very faint, almost imperceptible, drifted from behind that hole. The presence of air meant some fresher source and possibly an escape route out of this stifling burrow. He chipped some more rock and squeezed his sweaty head through and snuffed a mouthful of welcome air.

A two foot hole was gouged out, and he crouched, peering through.

Some natural light shone from a slit in the rock from high overhead.

Solid objects loomed in the dimness. More statues? He could not be sure.

He crawled through, eyes widening pools in the murk, pick raised. The hall was huge; his scuffing boots echoed cavernously. It was like a great amphitheater here, with lofty ceiling lost in gloom. The air was pervaded with an ancient grandeur and the uncaringness of ages.

He crept forward like a man in a trance and in front of him at the hall's front stood a dragon lord statue, eight feet high. On either side crouched two guardians, miniature versions of the ones in the adjacent chambers. Draped on the statue's chest was another dragon claw similar to the others but worn as an amulet. The look on the lord's face was one of solemn wonder and sublime reflection. Yet, a sadness, which struck Vetra as odd.

The statue was not dissimilar to those he had seen in the desert. Was this the last lord of a dying dragon realm?

The lord faced the outer semicircle, as if addressing a vast crowd. A proprietary hand was placed on one of the small leopard-lizard's heads like a pet hound. Vetra turned to see benches spread and tiered on high, row after row, rising from floor to domed ceiling. He shook his head in wonder. What a hall of the ancients. His head swiveled in full circle. The acoustics were perfect here, and he could hear the scuff of his boots and his heavy breathing amplified three-fold.

Wait. There—a light gleamed in the dead dragon lord's eyes. A chill crawled down his spine. The glint vanished, whatever it was. Only a glister off his tool perhaps from the pale sunlight streaming through the shaft above.

He went to stroke the claw-amulet. Two or three of the precious gems encrusted in the ornament rattled free of the ancient collar and clattered to the paves. With swift ease he picked them up and put them in his pocket.

Almost with reverent grace and trembling hand he lifted the chain and amulet off the lord's jeweled head. Why, he did not know. Perhaps all Lehundr's talk about 'keys' and treasure had affected him. This was the third dragon claw, and intuition told him it was more important than the others.

Vetra turned to peer in suspicion. Rows of spectator-seats rose up tier by tier along the back wall, connected by aisles of stone steps at some ancient time. It was a vast auditorium, a honeycomb-shaped dome, hollowed out and built like an amphitheater into the cliffside.

The vents above were too distant to make out—but had all been long sealed with stone slabs by expert masons. All except one had crumbled. Vetra wondered if these vents admitted light when the dragon lord was alive. Perhaps this was his oratory.

His eyes flicked back to the statue.

Another glint in the thing's eye?

No sooner had this flash of light dawned, than a slither of movement disturbed the silence. He wheeled around. What was it? A distinct set of glowing eyes peered from the gap he had crawled through. Teeth gnawed at the edges of the rock. Wild fear stung his gut. It was one of the reptilian leopard statues— struggling to squeeze through. What eldritch sorcery was this? A thing come to life upon the robbery of the dragon claw? Fool! How could he have been so stupid to think he could snatch an item like the dragon claw and not be punished? Frantically, he cast eyes around him for some avenue of escape. The rock he had hewn through would hold the creatures for now. But there were more of them, sawing and biting their way at the edges of the rude opening, like hounds digging for a favorite bone. The hole widened with every gnaw and bite. A snout was almost already out, and with it a bellow and snarl.

Besthra take him for sacrificing his sword! Could he put the claw back? Hardly—the guardians were awake, and likely deadlier than vipers.

He took up the pickaxe and raced over to hew the creatures back. He smashed the iron tip into the skull of one of the slavering beasts. It died, thrashing, but the first guardians of the tomb burst through, waddling on all fours like lizards. The monsters blinked and made small hissing sounds and glared at him with repellent eyes. They spat a foul black liquid that sizzled on the stone like acid and scored holes in it.

With a gasp of horror, he hopped back, scrambling for the stairs heading up to the semicircle of spectator seats. It may be his only hope, the high ground. Some globs came shooting at his chest and he jerked aside and narrowly avoided getting splattered by it. He lurched, struggling to stay erect. He could not help but tread in a pool of acid before the first steps. The sticky goo stuck to his boot and melted part of it away before he could fling it off. With a ghastly moan he leapt back, clawing at the air, aghast at the nightmare around him.

Up the stairs he bounded.

One came at him up the crumbling steps, maw agape, tongue

ready to lob another foul, sizzling dollop at him. He swung—the pickaxe smashed straight through the thing's ear. He pulled his axe free, eyes burning with satisfaction that iron tip had passed through claylike flesh and pierced the brain. The leopard-lizard jerked in a bray of bellowing agony, then slumped to the stone. It gave a final spasmodic shiver then lay sprawled on the steps, tongue splayed. Vetra turned and blundered up the steps past the first tier, leaping like a deer, though he bashed his knees on fallen rock that lay obscured in the murk. Others came shambling up, tails sliding over their dead brother and rustling the crumbled heaps of stone blocking the steps.

The curve of rough-hewn ceiling where the vents glowed must be near the cliff face to afford such light. Years of erosion and quakes had loosened the rock.

Vetra scrambled up the steps where the middle section lay in ruin, stomach reeling from the heights. At one time this auditorium had been packed with dragon folk listening to a lord's speech, or being entertained with some other performance. He had to squat and catch his breath. How he hated high places. Dergath was always putting them before him! He bit back the bile that crawled up his throat, grimacing at the cruel irony of the god.

He mounted the steps, two at a time, pushing through dust and molder. He groped this way and that past fallen rock and cracked benches. His blundering rush had started a cascading tumble of rocks and debris underfoot. A whole section of seats gave out, heaving up a maelstrom of dust.

Vetra lay there clinging to edges of benches, legs dangling in space, while chunks of seats fell underneath him. His lungs heaved to the smell of dust and decay. More creatures were scrambling up after him along alternate routes. It was lucky for him they were more lizard than leopard and that their climbing was limited. The range of their spit balls was no more than eight feet, else he'd have been peppered full of holes.

Dust motes drifted like listless fireflies. He pulled himself up and checked the racing of his heart. On he crept, pick clutched in hand while the dragon-lord from far down watched with impassive deliberation.

Two guardians had now cornered him. They had sidled up from nearby stairways and flanked him, licking jowls in anticipation. Vetra hacked and slashed, snouts and claws flying, black goop spraying everywhere and him ducking the slime. He watched, heard it lap into the other beast's face, blinding one of its eyes. The thing bellowed in agony. Some sprayed on his desert cloak and sizzling smoke clouded him, momentarily blinding him. He tried to brush it off with his sleeve and nearly gagged at the rank odor. He sprang upward to the next tier in a nail-clawing attempt to save his life. An eyeless head came lurching up, fangs seeking to rip into his arm. He smashed down on it with the pickaxe. The dragon creature fell back, its face and neck still sizzling with goo. The shelf of seats gave under the monster's weight, and the rock crashed down, crushing a half dozen of the brutes that struggled to get at him. Bestial whines filled the spacious arena, highlighting the madness of the scene.

Scrabbling with the best of his speed, he crawled through the rubble. At last he made it near the vents. Every stumbling step up those crumbled, haunted steps was like a herculean effort. Sunbeams traced dust-streaked rays in the air. He leapt up on the carved, polished backs of the highest stone benches. Bracing his feet, he began chipping with mad fervor at the cleft that admitted welcome sunshine. It was not wide enough to let him squeeze through. His muscles burned with the effort. The precipitous drop showed the ruined section of amphitheater yawning below like an abyss that made his senses swim. Clang! He struck again with mighty swings. Ever did the dragon beasts below slip on the rubble and blocks of masonry, unable for the moment to edge their way higher and closer to flank him. He could hear the sinister rustlings among those shattered, broken, clogged steps, slipping and sliding on debris and emitting ominous bellows.

Should they clear a path... Vetra shuddered and smashed at the flaky sandstone. His tool sent hard flakes and chips flying. He closed his eyes to avoid stray fragments. At last he cleared an area large enough for him to squeeze through. With a grunting gasp he pushed his way through. At the same time he dragged axe and feet, ducking the black spitballs of beasts that were at his heels.

A wash of blazing sunlight stung his eyes. He could make out a patch of white clouds somewhere greeting his beleaguered sight, and he hauled himself on through the gap, his feet wriggling in air. The hisses and red snouts and black teeth came angling up.

They could not get past the narrow gap.

He crabbed his way on hands and knees down the slope, gulping breaths into his lungs.

He hung on the side of the cliff, up higher than where he had entered the dragon tomb. Below the familiar canyon spread like an engorged snake. He blinked, squinting into the sun. Untold relief flooded his body, and yet, the feeling of height sickness still clung in his gut and would not abate.

Farther below he could see the vestiges of a steep, crumbled stone trail that connected to the path in the ravine. He wormed his way on his belly down toward it, pickaxe lodged in crooks to brace himself should he slip.

After painful effort his feet touched the gravel path. Approaching the mouth of the broken dragon that marked the tomb, he heard not a sound. Not a soul.

Quite a different space than before. A pall of death hung over the sepulchral chamber. The floor was up—and the wall was back to its regular place, exhibiting no sign of having moved at all.

New bits of gristle and bone lay clumped in ghastly heaps in the floor's center, now awash in a thick pool of blood...

Vetra grimaced. The sphinx-like guardian lurking by the sarcophagus had vanished. Bloody crimson pawprints stained the floor where it had walked...on towards the eerie, ink-stained tunnel at the back of the sarcophagus. Where had the Thrules gone? What had happened to Lehundr and Jhara? He shuddered, his mad thoughts reminiscing on who or what it had dragged to that moldering corridor.

He reached down to touch the warm substance staining the rock, and knew before he touched it, it was blood.

He heard a spine-tingling slithering of non-human feet from the eerie tunnel and he backed away, feeling a shiver up his limbs. A suicide mission should he go back there.

A hundred grotesque thoughts swarmed in Vetra's mind. Likely whatever had created that heap of flesh had dragged the victim or victims down that tunnel. He would be next if he lingered too long. Ill would he fare against such a grisly guardian. Could ancient iron continue to prevail against demons that came back to life to haunt the living?

He dragged himself away from that gruesome chamber. His fingers clutched the dragon-claw in a death grip.

Not a hundred paces down the trail he knelt and swayed dizzily. He let fingers pass over what looked like crimson drops on the dusty soil. Another fresh blood trail—maybe two hours old. A hope flared in his chest that there were survivors.

V: Dragon Forge

Vetra squinted south with longing. The sun's flaming orb had swung significantly westward since he had taken up his peers' trail. From his wobbly crouch on the hillside his weary eyes struggled to discern movement. An endless plain of red dirt and sand lay before him, lost in a shimmer of haze. A blur of something else: dust clouds on the horizon, caravans and camels wheeling in a long line. Supply caravans of war? Whether Behundrian or Thrule Vetra could not tell. All practicality screamed at him to leg it back to the great eastern road and hire passage back to Lvendar. He should give Dragonskull wide berth. With what money was a concern, considering the jewel was still back on the pony. But the thought of Jhara stayed his hand. She could be wandering or enslaved by cruel lords, likewise, Lehundr.

Yet without food and water he would not last long. He looked down at the dragon claw. The fort was far to the north of this desolate valley. That's where they would be heading, if they were still alive and if they held the other dragon claw keys. Should the Behundrians catch them, that would be another matter: the scum would either kill everyone on sight or take them prisoner, or force them on to the Dragon Fort to unlock the treasure. Rafa knew about the map and Vetra was under no illusion that they would torture them for the truth. Vetra took a calculated risk and pushed on, past the cacti and windscarred shrubbery, ever north.

The road that he had come up on with the Thrules was nothing more than a narrow, dusty track, winding up the broad, shallow valley dotted with small boulders and husks of ancient eucalyptus. He staggered on, feeling the fire of thirst, keeping a path well off, but parallel to the road.

A disquieting stillness lay over the land. Only the low moan of wind that crept around crumbled rock forms. He gazed into the distance. At his feet trailed a vague set of prints, lightly dusted over.

Before long his lips were parched and split from the heat and his legs burned, but he stumbled on despite his half-mangled boot.

Black smoke—perhaps phantom mist for all his delusion—rose over the low hills to the east. More fires? Vetra guessed the Thrules had been busy burning the Behundrian mines to the ground. He swept a hand over his sweat and blood streaked face where a claw had raked his brow and torn his left arm above the wrist. He shook the fatigue from his mind, shook out the throbbing in his arm. His belly ached with a fierce hunger and his tongue scraped around his dry mouth.

The grunt of a condor intruded on his thoughts—merging then back into the background thrum. He stumbled on a loose stone, collapsed, got up again, stumbled again. A scorpion scudded across his path, a foot from his head. He cursed, staggered up to his knees, slashing at it with his rusty pickaxe. His head spun in a dizzy spell of heat.

His vision blurred. What was this? Puppet figures in the distance shimmering of heat? At least fifty of them—ragged nomads, no more than five feet tall.

Thrules! No mirage.

Vetra stood to his full height and seemed a giant. He squinted in amusement. The desert Thrules either lacked ponies or preferred walking on foot.

"Where go you?" one demanded brusquely.

Another strode forward and passed hands over Vetra's empty scabbard. Vetra saw that they kept scimitars belted at their hips. A group of them fanned out, covering him with bows.

"Kill him if he tries anything."

Vetra weighed the advantages of trying to conceal the truth of his mission and realized there were none. Bluster would not hurt. "Fools!" he snarled at the leader. "Would you slay the bearer of the Dragon Claw?" He took a step, wielding the claw. The Thrules shrank back. "What would your gods think of you then? Slayers of the holder of the key to the Dragon fort—Dragon Forge!"

The Thrule's eyes widened. "Where have you learned that name?" With fascination they stared at the claw and suspicion swarmed over the Thrule's features. A murmur of astonishment rose from the gathering.

"He lies!" sneered an angry voice.

"'Tis a mummer's trick," others cried, lifting bows and weapons.

The archaic pickaxe with wooden handle seemed to disturb and fascinate the Thrules at the same time. He lifted it with its dried black blood. They rotated around him in a circle, murmuring in awe and indecision.

"Where have you come from? Why do you trespass on our lands?"

"Water," croaked Vetra. "Some Thrules and I, from Dragonskull, we entered a tomb back in the valley. Give me water." A familiar light-headedness threatened to have him swaying and sinking to his knees.

"We have water, but you may not get any, outlander," snapped the leader. "At least until we discover more about this sacred relic you hold. You came from the Valley of the Dragons you say. Maybe you stole this dragon claw from some wealthy collector and are fleeing the law, feeding us a lie, only to slit our throats in the night and steal our gold."

"Aye, Nhfer," affirmed another, "but so odd is the tale that it may be true. Look! Here are tracks of the band that he talks about. The prints head toward Dragon Forge."

The one called Nhfer gave a grudging assent.

Vetra snorted. "If you believe anything of slitting throats and stealing gold, you're as simple-minded as those damn Behundrians. Help me find my friends."

The leader scowled.

"What was in this tomb?"

"Guardians, blood, secrets of ages past. It's guarded by ancient creatures—dragon leopards. Their skin was black and they came to life from some foul magic."

The Thrules looked at him in wonder. "You survived the Guardians?"

Vetra grunted.

The Thrule leader fidgeted. "I knew there was some truth to the old tales. You are lucky to have seen them, outlander. Only the aged mystics who induced visions by chewing the sacred mushroom have claimed to have been graced by their presence. They crawl into caves for months on end."

Vetra shrugged, a lackadaisical droop to his lips. He was hardly thinking straight, after being hunted by dragon-leopards, yet he was used to the blind reverence with which these people clung to the long dead race of their dragon people.

"And the others?" grunted Nhfer.

"I don't know what happened to them. I was trapped in a lower wing of the tomb. One of them was surely killed as I saw bones and fresh blood. You haven't seen sign of a band of twenty, travelling light with a girl?"

"No."

"She may be wounded," mumbled Vetra. "I must find them." He turned to leave.

The Thrule blocked his path and trained his bow. "You smell like lizard piss."

Vetra recalled the thick black acid that had almost engulfed him.

"There are hot springs not a league from here. You can soak

your dirty hide." He gazed at the dragon claw with kindled interest. "If there is a chance, we will take it. There could be great riches to aid us in this wretched war. We must go to Dragon Forge."

Grumbles and mutters ensued and several raised their bows and shook their heads with animosity.

"Listen, you fools!" said Nhfer. "The long lost key is legendary. Many have died, starving and perishing of thirst in the desert looking for it. I will call for the brothers in the north. We have stirred up a hornet's nest here in these parts. We will need reinforcements."

Vetra saw that Nhfer sent no scout but reached for some beat-up instrument in his pack. "With what?" Vetra called. "Talk into the wind?"

"No, with this." Nhfer produced a lackluster horn from his back. "Zaln from Sunswatch gave it to me, should I need it."

Vetra stared at the horn—it was small, sleek, archaic, coiled with antique tubing, like a bugle from a far off time.

The Thrule climbed to the top of a boulder and pushed the unimpressive thing to his lips. Vetra frowned, for it made no sound, but a hollow whooshing of air, yet it was strangely lit in glorious gold when he blew into it.

"'Tis done. The Thrule bands will come before sundown tomorrow."

"Are you sure?" Vetra shook his head in doubt. "How will they find you?"

"An old Thrule secret, which you would not understand."

Vetra shrugged, indifferent to the truth of it. "I came from Sunswatch, the pump site. 'Tis lost, and Zaln is dead. I saw him tortured before my eyes."

The Thrule bit his lips. "Dead? Sunswatch fallen? So are the mines. We came from Maniswaning, and it was taken. Though we made a ruin of their precious Thorian rigs. It will take them weeks to rebuild it."

Vetra shook his head. "Not the wisest move. Unless you plan to defeat them utterly, you have made your deathbed when they come after you. These petty skirmishes and acts of vandalism accomplish little."

Nhfer rounded on the stranger in anger. "What do you know? Do you suggest we sit back and let those Behundrian pigs dominate us like serfs and take our land and our women?"

"I suggest nothing of the sort."

"Then hold your tongue, outlander. Give him water." He flourished a hand. "Cut him a piece of leather to tie around his cursed boot." A Thrule snapped to attention and brought a canteen from his pack. Vetra snatched the canteen out of his hand and chugged warm gulps of water—nectar of the gods!

"Then we head north—to the fortress. 'Tis but eight leagues away. To Dragon Forge!"

An hour's march later, with the dull ball of the sun arching a sweltering arc over their sweating skulls, they stopped at a low thicketed wall of foliage.

Vetra frowned, wondering what this place was.

Nhfer led them through the thicket, cutting bramble with his short blade, revealing hot springs camouflaged in a net of green *alphanel* fronds. A bubbling pool gave off an acrid sulfurous scent. Following with grinning anticipation, Vetra shambled on to strip down and clean his grimy skin and cleanse his wounds. Others bathed and took fresh water. It had a sulfury taste to it, but Vetra felt better.

They made camp shortly after. Though they had no packbeasts, the Thrules were efficient, but taciturn.

This company was not so merry as his own, and for this, Vetra felt a pang. No song, or merriment carried over the light wind, only grumbles, stares and solemn predictions by this crew of nomads. After a time, milling around a low, glowering fire, Vetra lay down to sleep. But Nhfer's slightly slurred speech and fumes of mead from his breath caused Vetra to stir. "All this blood and fire, and woe. When will it end?" Other members mumbled their commiserations.

Vetra spoke, "Do you not feel satisfied with your accomplishments, Thrule?"

The leader mused for a long time. "When I was young I thought there might have been some purpose to it all." He heaved a heavy sigh. "Some cause to our fighting. But seeing the cruelty I have, the sorrow that man inflicts on his fellows, I started to lose hope. Now, I just scurry about like a rat in a cage trying to survive, to fight the cretinous swine who push over noses deeper in the sand and every day creep closer to my backdoor. Running, hiding, fighting... It seems an endless loop."

"You think too deeply into purpose, Thrule," grunted Vetra. "You expect too much from your neighbors. The bad ones are swine, and there are all too many of them. Things seem not what they are. They will not change with your restless expectations."

The Thrule exhaled a breath. "You may be right, outlander." He stroked his beard under the loose hood, and his thoughts were faraway, as were his eyes.

"Sleep easy, fellow. Tomorrow we will reach Dragon Forge, and then we will test this claw of yours. Maybe something *will* change. For all our sakes, I hope so."

* * *

Dusk was well advanced and the stars twinkled like a web of sparkling jewels. The cicadas were out and chirping in the dry desert weed.

Vetra lay dreaming, and in his dreams came Jhara. She stood in a frost-glittering field, a maiden fair as the dawn, wielding sword, with a forest not far off, dusted with ice. He grinned, threw down his own crusted blade and caught her up and bore her down and they writhed in love in the welcoming onset of winter, and there was no feeling of coldness, only warmth, their combined heat melting the ice crystals around them.

He tossed and turned. A vague recollection gripped him of

sleeping on hides under the stars with the Thrules, hearing the call of the jackals, and the answering howl of a rival pack. He woke in a sweat, the moon glaring overtop like a sinister runestone. His thoughts were heavy with the lingering question if any of his party had survived. He thought of Jhara again and a guilt pricked his heart. It left him with a sadness that had no relief—that he had failed to protect her and the others of the Thrule company.

*　*　*

The company of Thrules trudged ever north up the valley. Vetra followed in their wake. Shimmering waves of heat hovered always out of reach, merging with the low shrubbery in the flat distance. The Thrules gritted their teeth to the growing heat, trodding on with single-minded purpose as the sun rose in the morning haze. There were few places to hide in this open, sweltering bowl of desert scrubland if enemies sprang upon them from behind.

A faint wind came from across a nearby salt marsh, carrying with it a dry, tangy odor. The pale green desert plants faded in the distance. It was not until noon that the ruin of a mighty fort loomed like broken teeth on the horizon. At first only jagged stumps or spears of rock showed themselves, then a domed mesa, gray and blue, thrust itself out of the haze like the molar of a prehistoric beast.

"Unexpected, isn't it?" remarked Nhfer.

Vetra offered no comment.

A group of white-hooded Thrules moved about the plain, clearing rocks and arranging wooden totem forms. Vetra guessed they were preparing for a ceremony. As they neared, he saw that some were women playing with groups of children. Several of the clanspeople moved in a solemn line up the hills toward the caves to the left, dragging bundles tied with string or carrying baskets.

Twin hills ranged to the north, blocking access to the valley. On both hills reared Dragon Stones, huge megaliths, shaped like twin forks, which rose like enchanted spires in the yellow afternoon light. They glinted like ancient, cyclopean earth talismans. Casting long shadows down on the plain below, they intersected mysteriously to play mischief with the eye, as if defying natural laws, and held some astrological or zodiacal significance. At one time an ancient river had flowed between the hills, but now was dry. Stray boulders and seashells populated the pebbly earth.

Nhfer pointed to the hills surrounding the left flank of the valley. "There is water in those caves yonder. That's why the temple Thrules go there—to fetch sacred water. It was a precinct revered by the dragon-lords."

Dressed in flowing ceremonial garments, with colorful braided designs and brilliant white hoods, the temple Thrules were a stark contrast to the dark rags of the hill Thrules. Vetra noticed complex beadwork showing emblems of dragons on their breasts and backs.

He also saw the low sandy plain looked blasted as if by huge rocks hurled down from the hilltops. The whole area at their feet was a jumble of masonry and sprawling sand-filled ruins. Dragon-headed temples lay carved into the cliffs. At one time it had been a majestic city, that much Vetra could see. Metal doors and architraves had been forged by fiery breaths; he imagined such from their exotic tints. By such unusual means, metals had been melted and reformed into fabulous shapes: of dragons and giants and lords. Fluted columns and dragon-headed turrets rose like broken masts out of the ruins, teetering in drunken unison, and the lines of ancient walls and stone pathways were but the skeletal remains of what was once a great, flourishing center under the rule of titans.

As for the actual fort, Vetra's eyes strayed to a long white-washed limestone portico rising up the mesa's front with a line of columns and four great dragon lord statues. *Dragon Forge*. There was an elemental beauty and stark vibrancy to this place which seemed incongruent with its age. So remarkably well-preserved it was for something so old.

Nhfer pointed. "It was cited that the desert giants built this fortress to protect their realm, though they died off as a race. They fought here and were turned into stone, by the mighty dragon-serpent Ermgen's fire. It was said a star fell from the sky and became the avatar that was Ermgen. Dragons and their lords fought giants and took over the old kingdoms. Thus the giants languished. That is why everything is so monumental here. See there—those gleaming columns—" he gestured to the sprawl of massive pillars in the ancient city beside the fort "—they are intact—as is the great dragon hall."

The Thrule approached the other curious clan members who blinked and stood gazing. Many dropped whatever they were doing. Nhfer lifted Vetra's hand that held the claw. "All hail the finder of the Dragon claw!—the Claw Bearer!"

"What do you mean, Claw Bearer?" one Thrule cried out.

"Can it be?—the talisman to open the gates?" another hissed.

Vetra tensed in recognition of several faces, startled. A ginger-haired beauty with sun-bronzed limbs stood out like a beacon in a sea of shadows. Jhara! She was entertaining a group of Thrule children and had them enraptured, singing in her melodious voice of the legends of the lands that her father had told her.

Vetra exhaled an explosive breath, feeling the weight of days slip from his shoulders. She and others must have caught up with these temple Thrules.

Lehundr was conversing in excited tones with Thrules under the colonnade of the Dragon fort beside the great dragon door.

A circle of domed-shaped yurts stretched to the side, past the ruins and shattered columns and time-eaten stumps of masonry. This was once the dragon-lord kingdom. Houses? Dwellings? Communal halls? Vetra was undecided. Others came running from the small caves up the hills; several were hurrying down a well worn trail, tents and yurt tarps draped over their shoulders. Samos, the shaman, roved among them, directing, whispering blessings.

Knots of Thrules moved in and about in animated conversation and Lehundr had taken pains to gesticulate his theories about the dragon claws to the people who sat on the steps, their downcast heads in their hands.

When Jhara caught sight of the dustworn mercenary, she jumped up and raced over to wrap clinging arms around his neck. She hung on him with her knees bent and small feet angled to the sky. "We thought you were dead!"

"Good to see you," he said with a smile. The familiar smell of her brought back pleasant memories. "I thought you were lost out there, or worse."

Lehundr came sauntering up and gave him a brisk handshake. His cracked smile split his sun-browned features. "Old dog. How did you survive?"

"I found a hidden exit." Vetra quickly told his tale. Others approached, Aus, Gefzad, Dunon, eyes blazing with surprise.

"Incredible! We've been looking for sign of you—and gave up, I fear. We failed in releasing you from the tomb as we had our own trials with the Guardian. But you have survived—"

"Everyone says that this must be the key to unlock the door." Vetra displayed the claw trophy.

Lehundr gasped in astonishment. "So you found it. Small wonder the others failed," he mumbled.

A low, soft female voice spoke from behind, "I am Sebju, leader of the Dragon Forge People. We are the Dragon-Thrule, keepers of the Dragon Lords. You claim to hold a relic. Let me see it—"

Lehundr grabbed the claw before the woman in the white robes could examine it, and caressed it avidly in his fingers. He passed it on to the middle-aged woman who frowned, her long graying hair curling out around her shoulders. A grunt of child-like disbelief passed from her lips. Tracing its contours with trembling fingers, she uttered a startled gasp and swept back her hood. "It seems genuine. Old beyond belief."

"Then let us try the doors!" Nhfer cried with impatience.

Lehundr held up a hand. "Hold! You need this. The map speaks of three dragon claws. We have two." He held up the other scored and ancient dragon relics.

"You brought them?" asked Vetra in a hushed whisper.

"Who is this?" barked Nhfer.

"The one who had the map that led me to this—" Vetra lifted the woman's hand that held the claw.

Nhfer passed eyes over Lehundr with a frown. "What would a half Behundrian want with dragon claws, and why have half a care of our heritage? Except to steal our treasures?"

Lehundr objected to the accusation but Jhara clutched his arm. "He has everything to do with it, Thrule, and we would not be here, if it were not for him." Her features clouded as if struck with a sad thought. "Besu didn't make it," she told Vetra quietly, hanging her . "He was snatched by something hideous and dragged off and mauled. It was horrible! The leopard-sphinx, or Guardian of the tomb, came to life. It got to him before we could—"

"I know," Vetra consoled. "I saw the crimson remnants of the struggle." He looked around at the hollow-eyed group. "Where is that rat, Zren?"

"Gone," snapped Dunon. "Disappeared after our escape from the tomb."

"You mean after all the trouble we went through trying to save his hide, he up and leaves?"

Dunon nodded. "He was ashamed of what he had done, particularly to you, and couldn't stand our cold glares. I would have done the same thing, if I were in his shoes. We shan't see him again."

Vetra shrugged with indifference.

"The Behundrians will be coming up the valley before long," warned one of Nhfer's aides.

"Right, I heard that hound Cthan boasting that he would take an army up and strip every flab of flesh from our hides," murmured Aus.

"Let him try. We laid waste to plenty of their mines," rasped Nhfer. "Though many of us died in the doing. All of what you see is what's left of us, barely fifty, when we were three hundred!"

One of the Thrule women consoled a crying child in her arms. "Why do you bring this evil upon us?" she wailed. "We don't want your wars! This is sacred land to us, and the old ones—they ruled the dragons."

A chorus of sympathetic protests went up among the clan women.

"War is war, woman!" Nhfer shouted back at them. "We cannot control or predict what and where it will strike. Pack your belongings. Delhas! Nesthu!" he snarled at his assistants. "See that the children are prepared for travel. At dawn's light they will go north with you, to seek a place of safety. The Behundrians must pay for their insolence!"

Shocked murmurs rang among the women. "This has been a peaceful haven for years! We are the caretakers of the dragon lords."

Another hissed, "If you force us, so be it. But why not flee to the hills with us?"

Nhfer snorted. "And tuck our tails between our legs like whipped dogs?"

"At least you'll be alive," returned one of the more influential women. She was taller and more composed.

"Do you have that little faith in us?" Nhfer asked with sad incomprehension.

"No, it's because I have too much faith in you, captain. You will give your life to support our independence. Knowing that, I'm sad that you will spill your life blood on sacred soil, if that is what is asked of you."

Nhfer growled, but he curbed his tongue. It was clear in his gaze that he saw the possibility of it and was moved by the genuine concern in the woman's eyes. His lip firmed into a sullen scowl. "No matter. If death is to be my fate, then that I must accept."

Vetra saw the hopeful faces vanish and the feverish whites of their eyes glint underneath their monkish hoods.

"Take the girl with the others." Nhfer jerked a hand toward Jhara.

Jhara stepped back, steel flashing in her palm. "The first one that touches me, dies," she hissed.

Nhfer blinked, raised brows in surprise, as did others of his company. Low, nervous chuckles spread through their ranks.

"The girl stays with me," grunted Vetra.

"As you like, outlander," muttered Nhfer. "But her blood will be on your hands."

"Let us focus on the effective things we can do," said Vetra. "If the Behundrians fall on us, then those high pillars over there are an ideal place to put your best marksmen. We can dig pits to ensnare careless invaders. This narrow tract of sandy plain is a perfect ambush ground." He snarled. "The Behundrian host must pass through this vulnerable neck to get to the dragon hall. We will trap them here! Pick them off like ripe fruit. We will hide up in the crags with our spears and bows and rain holy terror down on them. We used tactics like this when I was stationed in Sarnhill, on the Sahir border."

A flicker of resentment passed across Nhfer's face, as if he disliked being counseled on strategies of war, but he held his tongue. Perhaps the Thrule was afraid of looking inexperienced in his men's eyes. With a wave of his fist, the Thrule leader ordered his men to comply with Vetra's wishes and assist him in any way they could.

Despite the unhappy faces of the retreating group of women,

and the crying children, and the wails of the angry wives, Vetra closed his ears to their tears and sobs. Many would not see the men of their family again. He had witnessed this all before.

"I need a sword," he muttered.

Nhfer motioned to Euth who pulled an extra blade off his packbeast.

Vetra examined the weapon. It felt light in his grip. The blade had a wide end—too wide for his tastes—but it was a wicked instrument, nonetheless. The broadsword was always his weapon of choice. But the curved falchions of the Thrules would do just as well if it came down to a fight.

Down wide avenues of fine sand, Lehundr and the temple Thrule leader, led Vetra through the ruined city over to the Dragon fort, accompanied by various other Thrules. Dunes sculpted by winds curled over the gleaming white vertebrae of dragon tails. Vetra and others pushed deeper into the ancient sprawl of tumbled blocks and walls. More often than not, his keen eyes saw more: scattered bones, a monstrous skull tilted in barbarous fashion, half submerged in sand, or shattered by a broken column, or an elongated snout protruding out from a grave of sand. It was a place that snakes and lizards made their playground, scuttling among the scattered stones and dried earth.

They mounted the steps of Dragon Forge and began a long march down a marble terrace, a few hundred feet. White limestone, buffed smooth as glass, glistened in the intense sunlight. Tall, proud statues of dragon lords stood in a long line at intervals down the court with austere dragon faces and arms cupped in offering in front of them.

Vetra stared at the entrance to the temple, and could not help but be engulfed in a sense of wonder for the construction that spanned ages beyond his imagining.

A thousand years had passed of lashing wind and sun, and still the structure bore a look of gleaming vitality, unbroken and true, something which could not be explained by natural upkeeping. Surely it must have been forged under the protection of advanced sorcery! Its shadow cast a somber hue over the plain, as if steeped in a memory of ancient antiquity.

Sebju spoke in a whisper, "Long ago dragons warred with men over land and the precious water supply of the oases. As you see, bones lie strewn over the plain that was the last Dragon Lord outpost. We temple Thrules call it the *Temple of the North*. Bleached and sun-dried by centuries of sun and wind, it now lies mostly covered by dust storm after dust storm, and their secret was forgotten, by all but a few."

She continued in a proud voice, "The Dragon Lords sealed up their secrets and treasures in their dragon mesa. It was once a great covered fortress, of iron and stone. But it had been battered by invading armies, forgotten but for the low, squared-off vault that shows now. Still the portal stands, invested with carved, copper double-valves, initially fired and cast by powerful dragons' breath."

It was lined and coated, as Vetra now saw, with their own gleaming white bones, the most resilient things in the world, withstanding the test of time over rock, and the legendary Thorian. Vetra gazed at the key in his hand, supposedly a talisman existing to unlock this portal, one that had been lost for ages.

Vetra followed Lehundr toward the middle of the colonnade, his bootfall echoing off the polished stone. The dragon door, unlike the gleaming walls, was reddened as if bathed in the ancient blood of dragons. Massive ringed handles faced inwards like great ox-yokes, for equally massive hands, as if the doors were handled by giants.

Vetra rubbed his scalp. A score of paces away, an ancient dragon lord statue stood fixed in timeless majesty. Palm held open, the giant stood enthralled, riveted in a gaze of sublime contemplation. A tall man with a dragon's head carved in stone, it sported a bronze girdle about his waist, a sculpted boomerang tucked within.

No keyhole was apparent in that solid door and Vetra paused, puzzled. There were no visible seams or signs that indicated whether it opened inward or outward. The temple Thrule leader solemnly passed the dragon claw over the smooth face of the door. The door neither budged or wavered. Lehundr grabbed the talisman from the elder's hands and moved it in different directions, jamming it in faint grooves that showed on its massive face.

"No human hammer will break that gate, half Thrule," the wise woman said, chuckling, throwing back her weathered white hood. "None knows where such stone was quarried from, or how such metal was forged. Some say the eldest, most powerful dragons, breathed fire and brimstone on them and blasted them with their fiery breaths, making them indestructible."

It seemed probable, looking at them now. Vetra stood back, impressed.

An hour later, feverish, fruitless efforts had failed, resulting only in disappointment and no budging of the door.

"Maybe we should think of trying something else," grumbled Nhfer.

"Or adopt some other profession than grave robbery," murmured Vetra.

They had gained no more access by late afternoon and they sat slumped, chin in hands, scowling in dissatisfaction. A shout came up from the plain.

Those whom Nhfer had summoned came marching over the gap where the two hills to the north met.

Vetra blinked in surprise. He saw their numbers approximating the order of a hundred, a welcome addition to their war band. He felt a twinge of relief, for they were a hundred more than he expected. A weary bunch too, for they had traveled much distance, non-stop and in haste, he guessed.

Nhfer greeted them with warm words and exchanged

embraces with Vasuth, the leader, and nods of head and broad smiles with certain of his peers. He introduced his companions to Vetra, Sebju. They nodded and clasped arms, the Thrules clutching boomerangs, with only a few spears and bows among them.

Vetra gazed with curiosity at the newcomers. When he saw their meager, limited arsenal, he winced and massaged his temples.

"Not enough bloody bolts," he muttered.

"Boomerangs will serve us," asserted a proud member of the new company.

"Boomerangs will do you no good against those savages of Behundrians and their camels in close-quarter fighting," argued Vetra. "Make spears from the deadwood at least. They lack the metal heads, but are better than no weapons at all. I'd advise sharpening and hardening their tips well. Twirl them in open fires." He motioned to a zealous, gleaming-eyed Thrule, who gripped a prime example of a spear in hand.

"Aye, Claw Bearer," said the Hill Thrule.

Vetra did not care for the title, but let it pass. A faint strain of condescension edged the tone: an unnecessary attitude, considering he was helping these vandal Thrules who had gotten themselves in a mess through no fault of his own. A part of him wanted to walk away from this dusty plain and never look back, and let them fight their own misguided battles. But he always fought for the underdog, and that was definitely these nomads. And there was always the spoils. But the thrill of the chase was his real inspiration, as was it the heart's drive of any mercenary.

After instructing them on spear-making, he went on to set up archer hides atop the pillars, also lead in digging snare-pits. These turned to be shallow ovals hollowed in the sand upthrust with pointed stakes. They covered them with withered branches, goat hides and a false floor of sand. He went so far as to oversee some crude catapults operated from the caves, and collect larger stones to roll down on enemies from the craggy hills and crumbling pinnacles of rock. He sank wearily on a broken stump of column, squinting against the sun as it sank in a weltering sea of red.

Lehundr sat down aside Vetra some moments later. "We'll not see a gold speck of the treasure once these Thrules get their share. It was me who found the map. 'Twas me who had the vision!"

Vetra shrugged. "We haven't even penetrated the blasted vault yet."

"Which is why I think we should work through the night, crack it open, carry out what gold we can and steal off under the stars."

"A brilliant plan, Lehundr, but it may be these very Thrules who keep us alive, if the Behundrians are haunting the desert to the south. Unless you are thinking of crossing the wastes north into Sahir? With an armload of riches and nosy Thrules all the way? All the gold in Behundria won't buy you water out there, or food."

Lehundr clenched his fists with fury. "It was unwise of you to give up the claw. The old woman has it now."

"You already have two claws!" grunted Vetra.

"I don't think they're the right ones. Decoys maybe. Your claw is different from the others. You said you found it draped around a Dragon Lord's neck, hidden in a secluded chamber. The others were in plain sight, too easy to snatch."

Vetra gritted his teeth. "That claw didn't work." He shook his head in incomprehension. "Take whatever claws you must and do what you like with them. I'll not have part in your plots."

* * *

Before the women had left with Delhas, several of them had prepared a feast for the defenders of their lands who stayed on: dates, mashed figs, dried mutton. The threat of battle lingered heavily on Thrule shoulders. All felt that tomorrow would bring red maelstrom and slaughter to the hallowed grounds.

In the early evening Vetra further trained Jhara in swordsmanship by the ruins of the dragon-lord's hypostyle hall. "Use the same motions as you would with the knife," he instructed her. "Better not change your technique that much. Just use the shorter blade, remembering you have longer reach."

"It's all new—but I'll adapt." She clutched Lehundr's blade with zeal, nodding with a grunt of raw vigor and came at him in a rush.

"Easy girl!" he chided. "You'll exhaust yourself." He parried her short, aggressive thrusts. "Feint in like this—" he made a quick sweeping motion "—then draw back." He drew her into a defensive crouch and turned in an unexpected circle to edge around her lean hide, with the blunt edge of his sword touching her neck. "You see—your opponent wouldn't expect this."

Mouth hanging slack, crouching low, she repeated what she had seen, improving her technique.

"That's it," he encouraged. "Make your opponent waste his energy, not yours."

She gave an exasperated cry. "I always use my cat o' nine tails! If some dumb mule gets too close, whack—" She whipped out the ring-hooked weapon to clash against Vetra's outstretched blade.

Vetra glared. "Perhaps. But don't rely on that thing. It can be thwarted easily. Some 'dumb mule' can come in and snatch it out of your hands, like this." He shot forward, hooked out his sword and her whip lashed around the gleaming flash of its attack. With a lightning-fast yank, he grabbed it and pulled it, jerking her off her feet.

She snatched the whip back in anger. "That's not fair."

He stepped back with a laugh. "Fair? Are we back to that again? Watch that temper of yours. It won't serve you in a battle."

"It could also save me," she argued. "If I see red, I can fight like Mother Dalki, demoness of the hunt. So I was told by my mother."

"Well, she's right, and she's also wrong. You could miss the obvious and end up dead." He wiped sweat from his brow.

Dunon and Nhfer and other Thrules had been watching the sparring, whispering among themselves like adolescent boys, the odd lewd comment inserting itself in their conversation. Both he and Jhara ignored them.

"Come on—it seems we need some privacy from the spectator gallery. We'll wait till dusk when the little boys have gone to bed." He found a shrubbed-off area and lay down with Jhara in his arms, resting, feeling her soft warmness pressed against him, his back to the cool sand, though with one ear and one eye always open.

Twilight brought a salmon glow creeping over the naked desert. The thrum of activity merged into that pleasant bustle and cricketsong that the hill Thrules knew best. Temple Thrules mixed with hill Thrules and men's high voices, laughs and spirited arguments rose over the sounds of desert instruments, zither and palm drum, and the crackling of cook fires. The temple Thrules had rolled out casks of ale from sand-covered holes near the foot of the hills. Samos and the Sebju participated in sprinkling a protective trail of spirits around the common ground, the same spirits brewed from a cactus like plant that grew in these parts. Vetra and Jhara chose to join the company, languid and unhurried of stride.

Scouts had been posted as far as two leagues down the valley to warn of any attack. But none came. The security cushion of advance warning nonetheless lessened their worry of ambush, and allowed the men to relax.

Some of the women had refused to travel north with the others, and Sebju and story-tellers of the hill Thrules revealed tales of their heritage, mostly for the entertainment of all:

"We dragon-Thrule come from an ancient race, long before the Behundrians or the Sahirians came and wrested this land from us, and set us scurrying to the hills—We knew much about the lore of this hallowed land, and how the giants came and founded this city long ago, and died in war with dragons, leaving their treasures with them. Plates of gold and iron meld were then fused on dragons' hides which made them invincible. Stone dragons, colossal statues, piles of bones. The city of Dragon Forge was but a shattered rock when the last dragon lord lay in his tomb..."

Vetra could see the city had been a major center...with its dragon-headed temples carved into rock cliffs, its wide ways and stone-carved avenues that hosted dragons, giants and men at one time.

"It was said a great smoke came over the land when the islands of the sea erupted and spewed filthy ash into the air—and this earthy plain, then a leafy green paradise, turned to dust and cinders, and a coldness settled over the lands. Men turned to war with dragons. They came with a vast host before Dragon Forge. The Dragon Lords raised their hands to the sky, and the dragons dipped down at their command from the clouds to smote the army ranked before them. But the black blood froze in the dragons' veins when the champion of the men, Percias the mad witcher, launched a glowing ball of power into the air which beguiled the swooping beasts as a flame does moths. They flew into its dusky interior, consumed by sorcery, to fall as one, cleaving mighty domes and cloud pillars of the city of Dragon Forge, as you see before you.

"The Lords quivered, their magic fled them, then men with pikes speared them down like marlins...All except one, the most powerful lord—Macemas, who turned within to his abode of power and closed the vault forever."

Murmurs rang through the gathering; many asked how Percias had won favor with the men.

Sebju's voice tolled low and serene. "The Dragon Lords strove among each other, vying for control of the realm. They were not immune to vice. One betrayed his master: a certain protégé and coming lord bound under Macemas. He contracted Percias, the witcher from old Angoram in Mosete, to build him a weapon to usurp his superiors and make him king. The witcher granted it to the aspirant but betrayed him and withdrew his talisman, the magical orb, and he teamed with the men, who he knew could defeat the dragons and their lords, and thus deliver him the wealth of all Dragon Forge..."

There was a pause as many blinked while absorbing the tale. The Thrule magician Samos clapped his hands. He regaled everyone with a few entertaining tricks, letting a hawk land on his shoulder and then outstretched arm, and after encouraging it to clutch up several objects the magician had secretly stuffed up his sleeves, let it fly about their heads, dropping things: seeds, papers, ornaments, from its beak and talons. To the tune of amused applause, Sebju brought out her story tellers, and Nhfer his jugglers and Vasuth, the other hill Tribe leader, let his acrobats perform a comic routine. Some men, drunk on mead early on, fell into the fire and shouts and laughs went up in wild peals as beards and hoods were singed. Vetra gave short shrift to the antics; for all the time his warrior's brain worked on the problems of tomorrow.

Vetra and Jhara and Lehundr enjoyed, or more aptly suffered politely through, the entertainment and conversed some, mingling with the fiery-tempered Thrules and their reckless sports, but Vetra grew restless, as men indulged in ale and grew boisterous, perhaps preparing themselves for the trials and fighting ahead, with its uncertain outcome.

It was easy to evade notice of the two Thrule sentinels who watched the inner perimeter. He did it more to test his powers of stealth, than out of necessity, though Jhara certainly got a kick out of it. Vetra had much experience of getting past guards in his day.

He moved into the shadows, with Jhara at his heels, away from the hubbub, shouts, laughter and song.

The two weaved their way up the hill that hosted the dark

stones and they fought and trained under the forked megaliths limned against the rising moon. Though the landmarks towered like devil tridents under the ghostly light, they paid them no heed. The eerie radiance lit up the sand like molten silver.

At the feet of the nearest megalith a gap opened where a crumbled stairway angled down to gloomy depths. An entrance to another tomb? The passage was half filled with sand, Vetra saw, out of which poked a dragon snout.

"What do you think their purpose was—the dragon lords?" asked Jhara. She wiped the sweat that still poured from her brow after their vigorous sparring.

Vetra shrugged. "What do you think?"

"Why did they die off? I don't believe Sebju's tale about mad dragons and witchers and orbs is true. Did they die in vain?"

"They're remembered still centuries later," Vetra observed. "Our dwarfish Thrules somewhat idolize them, so in that sense, no, they didn't die in vain." He looked up at the garland of stars pricking the heavens and reflected. "It's quite likely, some species altogether more alien than us, might look down on our bones and see our moldered towers a thousand years from now and think the same of us." He grinned at the thought.

Jhara's lips parted in a thoughtful breath.

Vetra caught a sudden glimmer of motion down in the valley. He peered, surprise dilating his pupils. On the terrace before the portal to Dragon Forge, a tiny figure toiled under flickering torchlight, tinkering with hammer and claw. Vetra shook his head, wondering if the half Thrule would ever find his pot of gold. If he did, he'd vanish like a bird in the wind.

He and Jhara slept on the hill under the stars and the warm desert air, their bodies twined in a comforting embrace. Jhara squirmed her lithe body into Vetra's chest while he clasped her tight and drew in the lush fragrance of her hair. She whispered sultry words in his ear and wormed her way closer into the crooks and strong folds of his muscles, and he burned with the feline heat of her. It was all the mercenary could do to keep himself from falling into a torrent of passion, given her pliant advances and strong lust for him. Something he had no intention of resisting. For some moments he forgot the horror of yesterday and the trials to come.

VI: Red Sands

Pale light was spilling over the barrens when Vetra and Jhara sauntered down to find sleepy-eyed Thrules ranged about last night's fires. Sporadic groans emanated from dust-caked lips.

"Up, you fools," growled Vetra. He bared his blade. "The alarm could sound and you hounds would be caught unprepared."

Grumbles and curses passed among the hooded men. They eyed the mercenary with sullen respect as he moved through the camp with ease and authority. The girl trailed flush-faced behind him.

Hardly had the two snatched a few wedges of cactus fruit and handfuls of dates when a shout arose from the shimmering plain.

Scouts came riding in on desert ponies. "They're here!"

Eyes darted to the south. The sign of distant dust clouds rose like smoke on the horizon.

"To your positions," ordered Vetra. He and Nhfer scrambled onto the open plain, drawing their swords. The Thrule leaders rallied each of their detachments and moved them into position. As the minutes fled by, the rumble of hooves grew steadier.

Vetra and Nhfer steeled themselves with their limited forces to face the approaching Behundrians. Jhara and a red-eyed Lehundr joined the main force of Thrules up the sides of the hill breasting the mesa to await and ambush the host at the appropriate moment. Some of the Thrules lay hidden up in the crumbling rocks and peg-like pinnacles overlooking the dragon fort, while others ran up the shale-flaked paths and crouched behind the fallen columns and cyclopean masonry, or barricaded themselves atop the designated pillars with crossbows and bolts. The dust cloud ranged closer; camel riders and foot soldiers took form. Through the haze and the promise of crippling heat, slaughter rode toward them.

Dozens of camels and horses broke through the mirage of dawn. The roans were driven by white-turbanned riders, some Kirns and Guirites, the latter Behundrians from what Vetra could see. The rest, a mixture of races, marched on foot.

The enemy had brought reinforcements—some three hundred strong, forcing a collective gasp from the defenders. The fifty Thrules, for all their mettle, shifted from foot to foot at the sight of the host. Flags and banners flew from the backs of the enemy riders, the blue and red of the Southern Behundrians: a flag much different from the corrupt satrap of Behundria whose reign beyond the northern hills did not extend to these lawless southern wastes.

"Fire!" an enemy rider yelled, and the first bolts peppered the air. The crossbowmen knelt and reloaded.

Curses flew among the arrayed soldiers and those of the Thrule resistance fighters.

Nhfer crouched at Vetra's side, watching the spectacle unfold through grim eyes. He and the Thrule leader had earlier rehearsed a tactic to draw out the Behundrians while others would ambush them from the crumbling slopes. The pits were ready below and the marksmen hunched behind their barricades on the pillars, bolts ready to loose.

"Stand firm," Vetra reminded the uneasy Thrules. Nhfer motioned to his men. They glared at the gathering enemy and whirled shiny blades before them, as if to give them confidence.

Samos, the Thrule magician, readied his stones and his bones of magic.

Cthan, the sheriff of Dragonskull, came riding like a bold king on a shaggy roan at the head of the vanguard. He peered around with insolent self-assurance, like a lord grown fat and cocky with the fruits of success.

"I know there's more of you, you mangy rats!" he yelled. "I can smell your cook fires and taste your rotten meat. I can see your rat prints in the sand. We have your Thrule," he bellowed with contempt. He made a savage flourish and one of his riders yanked a cord tied to a blood-streaked man bound and lashed and sent his heel into his back. The man fell to his knees.

Zren!

"Give yourself up!" Cthan's voice boomed again over the ruin of stone. The impudent tone echoed off the face of the dragon fortress and sent a rumbling anger among the Thrules. "You cannot win. You'll be slaughtered to a man!"

Vetra's fingers clenched on the hilt of his sword.

"If you want this wretch alive, bring us gold and proof of the treasure from the dragon ruin. We know you have it. This scum of a Thrule babbled on about some dragon key, but we had to force it out of his mouth." He rode over and slapped the head that was lolling. He gave a cruel laugh, a wolfish, half-taunting guffaw.

"We have no treasure," called Vetra. "All the keys we sought turned out useless. We have nothing to give you. Go back, Cthan. Go home. There's nothing here for you."

"Liars!" boomed Cthan in a bantering, hysterical laugh. "Do you take me for a fool?" His laughter grated like the slither of a sword from a unoiled sheath. "We'll burn this place down and ferret out every one of your sand-hugging hides. You bed with the weasel, be prepared to have your pelt skinned!"

The arm came closer and a mirthless smile flitted across Vetra's face. Let them walk into the trap. Behundrian falchions glinted in the blazing light and the tramp of booted feet grew louder. Camels grunted in the toiling ranks. Vetra held his breath; he sensed victory, despite the odds.

Cthan rode on, confident in his high saddle. He hurled more

insults at the approaching line of warriors, hoping to rile them into a fight.

One of Nhfer's headstrong Thrules crouching above in the rocks, stepped out of hiding, and in a moment of trigger-happy passion, fired a bolt, taking Zren's captor in the throat. Zren stumbled and fell, then he ran. A cry broke out from the Behundrians. One caught up with the runaway and jerked his rope back with a proprietary tug, as if he were some pet on a leash. It had Zren landing hard on his back.

Vetra cursed. Their position was compromised now; there was no choice but to attack. He wanted to lead them further up into the ambush but the idiot Thrule had loosed prematurely. Dergath, but he would pay! Vetra threw down a fist. The Thrules on the slopes stormed out of hiding and streamed down like a pack of wolves, blades hefted, bows trained.

The boomerangs sang out like strange birds from a far star and swift destruction fell upon the Behundrians. Those that found their mark, broke necks or smashed limbs. Others that missed their mark flew back toward the throwers to land clattering among the rocks. Hands snatched them up, or some were caught in expert flight by Thrules who wore heavy gloves.

The defenders continued to swarm down, as crossbows loosed from both sides.

The unmourned Thrules fought helmless, and for that they suffered losses. The Behundrians wore no mail or iron helms, but their chests were padded with tough leather jerkins worn beneath their loose, light-colored vests which stopped a jabbing scimitar tip or whirling knife hurled from far.

The marksmen, bedded on their high places on the columns, rained bolt after bolt into the seething fray. Some caught camels' flanks and sent riders careening sideways and elicited screeching brays from the crippled animals. As horses rode in, the dragon fort was cut off from access. Horse and camel rode over the sand-covered hides and fell in the pits impaled on sharpened stakes. Footmen also fell prey, shrieking to their doom, while others pushed behind them. The crossbowmen rose with swift assurance from behind their stone barricades atop the ruined columns and released streams of bolts, killing dozens. Riders and footmen alike fell with iron in their gullets and limbs.

The Thrule magician threw his stones and spell bones into the raging horde. With an odd whistling movement they sank into small sinkholes in the sand. Foot soldiers watched aghast as rivers of flame beetles and fire scorpions came burrowing from their holes to crawl up their legs, wherever the bones landed. The creatures came swarming in, and the attackers cried out, clawing at their backs, legs and arms. Quickly the Thrules drove in and cut them down.

Where the last of the magician bones fell, they erupted in a yellow singeing flame that lit up like candles amid the front lines.

Vetra grimaced. He ducked a spear arching through the air which plunged on to pierce Samos's neck. The wizard gave a high-pitched gurgle and sank, bloody froth wheezing from his throat.

"I want that sorcerer's head pinned to my saddle!" howled Cthan.

The hill Thrules fought alongside the plains Thrules as one. Around the Behundrian flanks they circled, to hamstring enemies and plunge steel into thighs or exposed flanks. The Behundrians surged forward. With brute force and greater numbers they plowed their camels through the Thrules like scythes through wheat, despite the traps and crossbowmen the Thrules had posted. One Thrule marksman fell with a bolt through his chest; another slumped, arms flung forward as a spear plunged through his spine. The protective stone shields raised the day before were crumbled, riddled by bolt fire from the ground.

The boomerangs flew true but were less in number, and did not wreak the same terrible damage as before.

Vetra ran into the fray, roaring like a lion. His falchion rose and fell in red waves. He took blood and lives, parrying and blocking thrusts to his vitals, penetrating through leather padding to bare flesh beneath. Blade-wielding Thrules and bowmen poured in behind him, inspired by his fearless assault.

Dunon and Nhfer fought shoulder to shoulder. In a moment of ill chance, Nhfer fell as a Behundrian's saber ripped upward through his chest and he was trampled under the boots of the charging Behundrians. His men gave fierce cries, but kept on slashing and hacking with inhuman strength. Their rage rose and showed in the hewing, steely resolve carved on their faces.

Dunon wavered, blood-stained and torn, narrowly side-stepping a curved sword aimed for his neck. He shook the blood out of his eyes and, helped to his feet by Gefzad, forged into the fray, clanking swords with the spitting, one-eyed Rafa.

Vetra stepped in to block Rafa's strike that would have disemboweled the smaller Thrule, then thrust blade forward to engage Cthan's henchman.

Vetra's corded muscles rippled and lent him strength for his every savage strike. Jhara fought behind him like a hellcat, whipping her cat o' nine tails, taking with it wads of Behundrian flesh. A burly Behundrian charged her, veins popping on his brow. He was enraged at his colleague's death, the man she had just slain.

Jhara twisted like a snake; she spun outward into a crescent kick, smashing his face with the edge of her heel. The man crumpled, and was run through by a nearby Thrule. Jhara's cry rose above the clank of steel.

Vetra saw Cthan in the forest of heads and he pushed toward him like a moving shadow, beating his way with bull-like intensity. If he could take down that pig-headed tyrant, this battle would take on an altogether different flavor.

Such happening was not to be. The surge ebbed sideways. The mercenary was swept along with the mob like flotsam on a sea, as a new wave of attackers entered the scene.

With a dogged fanaticism, Cthan led his charge, thundering orders left and right in the hot wind and thrusting a fist forward. "Forward! Kill them all! Take not a man alive."

The Behundrians roared their war cries and their thundering charge was like the crash of boulders down a ravine. Their combined momentum hurtled them forward like a runaway deluge. It took the Thrules by surprise and hurled them back with fury.

Men screamed and died like corn stalks flattened in a hailstorm. They fought in close-packed knots, the leather-helmed Dragonskull aggressors towering a head over their robed enemies.

The butchery came and went in appalling waves. Steel fell and blades chopped like cleavers; lives drained away as blade lifted and thunked in men's sides. The sands of the Dragon lords ran red that day, not with Dragon blood as men had spilled in the past, but with human blood. Could the Dragon lords witness such desecration to their hallowed land, they would have rolled in their graves, sent their mightiest dragons to hew down the barbarous men who fought here.

The Behundrians with their superior numbers were edging out the smaller force, rallying together in a final pitched wave despite their losses. Their last camels tore through the Thrule line, trampling any who stood in their path. Jhara and Vetra were brushed aside in a flurry of hooves and slashing swords and whirling dust. Vetra was pitched onto his back, scrabbling to avoid the clomping hooves that would surely break his bones. A warning tremor shivered in his head. This battle was lost. He grabbed the girl by the arm and pulled her toward the dragon fort. He twirled his sword, and gave a thundering call for retreat. The camels could not mount the steps; it was apparent that a last stand at the dragon fort was all they could hope for. Vetra and Dunon and Lehundr and others staggered in a dust-choked frenzy, avoiding pits where dead men stared up impaled on stakes. They slid their way through a lake of blood-soaked Thrules and robed Behundrians lying bent and broken.

Knots of Thrules fought still in the dust and mayhem, cut off from the main retreat.

Vetra gave another bellowing roar and he and Jhara and Lehundr and a motley band of Thrules clattered up the central steps, their backs to the portal, holding the one key that Lehundr believed unlocked the mighty gate.

Stumbling backwards down the limestone way, thirty of them, ragged, cut and dusty, beat back the howling mob. They raced for the last stairway edging out on the ruins of the old city where they might lose their pursuers among the dunes and fallen masonry.

Vetra brought up the rear. He smashed his sword on heads, stabbing and hewing limbs, taking cuts and bruises as he retreated down the ancient terrace. The way was narrow, flanked by a low balustrade and intermittent statues, but in their favor while fighting in close quarters.

A quick glance ahead showed a carpet of dead on the blood-drenched sands. Thirty Thrules were already reduced to half their numbers.

The survivors ran along to the dragon gate in a fierce rush of hope.

Lehundr jealously drew the dragon claw from his vest and began scraping it along the impenetrable portal.

To no avail.

Vetra slashed an invader. With a wolfish howl, he kneed another attacker down the steps into the sandy bloodpit below. The howling Behundrians who dared to come near the dragon hall, felt the bite of his dripping sword. A dizzy veil of crimson swam before Vetra's eyes; his lungs heaved. The sun beat down like a scourge. The raging horde had exhausted their supply of bolts it seemed, or their crossbow men would have picked them off like flies. He saw Thrule bodies sagging over the tops of the pillars like straw puppets, pin-cushioned at last by volleys of Behundrian bolts.

"Hold the stair!" shouted Vetra, panting. "If we lose it, we're doomed."

The invaders flanked them, cutting off their escape. They were pinned to the terrace. Vetra hoped to make it to the end of the terrace and lose them in the ruined city, not a stone's throw away. Only three sets of stairs gave access to the temple, one in the terrace's middle and stairs at both ends.

A bloody wretch of a figure came staggering up the step—Vetra sucked in a breath—the figure's arms were bound and a long bloody rope trailed from his neck. Zren. His hood and garments were torn and shredded. It seemed that the Thrule had killed his captor and had managed to scramble his way through the mad melee. How? Vetra could hardly guess. Surely a testament to the Thrule's ruthless craft, no doubt, luck. Vetra winced at the sight of Zren, his hooked nose mashed, one of his eyes fused and swollen shut.

Snarling, Vetra cut once at the cords that bound his arms to his torso and the Thrule gave a gasping sigh, flexed hands and lacerated arms while Vetra severed the rope dangling from his neck.

Behundrians charged in with ruthless force and defenders' blades were hard pressed to keep them at bay.

Zren gurgled out a sound of renewed vengeance. His keen eyes burned with an unquenchable fire; they had not lost their sullen passion. A flash of steel and a chopping thunk and Zren deftly snatched the blood-smeared blade from the dying man's hand that Dunon had slain.

Leaping off his camel, Cthan pushed aside his own men and came charging up the steep dragon-stone steps like a blood-mad bull. His blade met Vetra's in a clash of blind fury. The two strained and heaved, slashing and parrying, until they closed together, fierce adversaries breathing hot air into each other's faces with swords locked high over their heads.

Vetra twisted on his hips. Nearby, Dunon closed with two sword-stabbing Behundrians—"Die, you mongrel curs!" He lanced his blade through the closest man's guts.

Cthan cried out with a piglike grunt when Vetra's knee rammed viciously in his crotch and knocked him down the stairs. The sheriff toppled over into others, sending his men reeling to the sand.

"Open, blast you!" cried Aus. "I'll drag this claw across your throat." He snatched the claw relic from Lehundr's hands and raked it across the glinting stone.

"To hell with the claw," cried Gefzad. "By Dergath. I'll kick this door down. Open! Damn you, open!"

Jhara rushed about in a frenzy. Her eyes narrowed on the statue, then blazed in a freak hunch. The Thrules had been focusing so much on the door that they had neglected the statue. She grabbed the claw from Dunon, and pushed it into the outstretched palm of the dragon lord.

Nothing.

One of Cthan's rogues hacked through the rebel net and knocked the claw off the palm. Jhara howled in frustration. She laid back her whip to slash at him. The man rose, blade gleaming in an angry hand to cut her throat. The rogue fell in a crimson tide as Vetra's sword arched in a deadly sweep and sliced him from shoulder to navel. His blood ran slickly over the fallen claw.

Jhara reached a desperate hand for the claw. More men rushed in to savage the mercenary. Jhara flailed her whip in a fit of panic, snatched up the blood-drenched claw and slapped it back in the statue's hands.

Almost instantly came a rending screech and groan of stone, as if tortured metal and buckling forces from deep in the earth were alive. Then a slither, as of massive gears winding and stone grinding below. The portal slid open.

Vetra's mouth twisted in satisfaction. He drove his sword

through the last of the attackers and pushed ahead. The claw needed only a blood offering to open the door. By what sorcery, he could barely guess.

With a breathless gasp and wheeze of stale, gushing air, the gray slab that hadn't moved for centuries yawned open like some mouth of a prehistoric fish. In their goggling fervor, Vetra and the others pushed through. Spears clattered on the steps behind them. New bolts whined and whistled over their heads. Swords clanked about the opening that was fast jamming with heaving, roiling bodies. Thrule blood spilled, as did Behundrian. Vetra was the last defender through. He grabbed the claw from the statue's hand as the door started to grind shut.

Not fast enough.

Cthan, wheezing in pain, managed to stagger through with a clutch of his fighters and sent steel into a Thrule's gut and kicked the dying man back and away.

The heavy door slammed shut and Thrules and Behundrians were plunged into near darkness.

CHRIS TURNER

VII: Trove of the Forgotten Ones

Vetra stared into the shadowy interior, slack-jawed. Blood trickled down his cheek where a blade had flicked a hair width from his left eye.

A dim watery light leaked around the edges of the portal—perhaps the mechanism in its extreme age had grown faulty. Groans and livid curses rang off the echoing stone of the inner vault. Men pounded at the door, trying to win past the portal with their fists and weapons. Others who were trapped inside slashed in blind desperation at what they believed were enemies, sending sparks along the cold stone walls.

Vetra ducked whistling blades and stumbled ahead through the cobwebs with the others, straining his eyes in the gloom. The hall was about twenty feet wide, equipped with a lofty ceiling running up into darkness. Lehundr, Jhara and Dunon slunk beside him—others he guessed included Zren, Aus and Sebju. All hunched, awaiting his order, their lungs heaving, as did four other Thrules.

Dragon bones littered the long corridor; their boots crunched on them: a twisted mess of dragons and men, helms and swords and shields. A battle had been fought here, that much was evident, a scene untouched for centuries.

Vetra glimpsed the small details of this last stand: a rusted battleaxe, the handle cleaved in twain, a fallen shield held up over a man's helmed skull to stop possibly murderous dragon's teeth. In his mind's eye, a sword poking up from a skeletal hand plunged into the white underbelly of a bellowing beast as its tail thrashed in agony. Ahead, more haunted ruins loomed; even this far in, the thin light streamed from the cracks around the massive portal to bathe the cobwebbed interiors in a ghoulish glow.

Vetra urged his comrades down the hall, his feet crunching on bones and skulls. "There! Make for that back passage."

There came the tramp of men's feet and the rustle of arms from behind.

"Listen! I can hear the Thrule rats," came a nearby voice that sounded like Cthan's. "Follow them!" The voice yelled again, with disgust: "So, you have no treasure, eh? You pack of coward spawn. No key to the dragon fort? I knew you were liars!"

Even then as the sheriff's voice broke, men came clattering after Vetra and his crew. Despite all their spells and wisdom, dragons had died defending their sanctuary against rogues such as the sheriff, Vetra thought with a snarl.

He mounted a short flight of steps and paused at the landing to look back down the stair littered with broken rock and pale bones—only to hear the shuffle and stamp of feet and the angry murmurs of bloodthirsty men.

"Get a light," Cthan yelled from the darkness. Fumbles and shouts ensued, then a slap as a heavy hand smote a henchman.

"This place is cursed," cried a voice that sounded like Vilivet's, the rogue from the Dragonskull market. "Did you see the old dragon skulls, the half man, half dragon bones?"

Cthan spat with disgust. "You halfwit. Curses? Really? Get a grip! We fight these rats to the end and we win. I want that treasure—for the damage to our pipeline, for the deaths of our comrades. I hold them ransom for all these insults." He cupped his hands to his mouth. "Vetravincus! I know you're there. Why scurry and cower like your fellow rodent? Come out and fight, like a man."

Vetra's fist whitened in anger on his hilt. He hated the truth of the bully's words—but it was foolhardy to engage Cthan now, as much as he despised him and being branded a coward. They were thrice his number and thrashing blindly in the dark would only mean death. Better to lure these fools into a trap ahead—hopefully something would materialize—if it didn't get them first. Jhara opened her mouth but Vetra silenced her with a hand over her lips. He ushered the others up the stairs and bade them halt before an arched doorway to their left. He hoped that a last-minute plan would avail itself. If not, Dergath help them...

A faint gleam showed in that passage beyond.

A strange bubbling, almost a gurgling murmur of water echoed about the ancient stone, accompanied by a warm waft of humid air.

To continue past the landing would lead to more stairs snaking down into murk, thought Vetra. Already, faint sounds were stirring down that eerie way—low rusty bellows, sinister croaks and scuttling, things not human. A tingling shot up his spine—rustlings as those were not dissimilar to the leopard-lizards he had heard back in the dragon tomb.

He ducked into the passage where the glow burned stronger. Down a low ramp they crept after him into the bowels of a huge cavern.

They beheld a fantastic scene.

The inner sanctum of the lost dragon empire! Deep in the heart of the mesa, ceilings rose crusted with riches, jewels beyond imagining—countless sapphires, endless diamonds, opals, rubies, emeralds, smatterings of shiny jet, lapis-lazuli and jade which provided garish color to the panoramic maps and designs portrayed there. Dragon gems, the plunder of ages glittered with shameless appeal on high. Treasures fetched from all corners of the world, Vetra saw, anointed in lonely splendor and protected for untold centuries.

Dergath, what a horde! He had seen treasure troves before, but never like this. If it could be quarried, that prospector would be rich beyond his dreams. But how to reach the cavern's ceiling where the wealth shone? The walls rose vertically from the floor without chink or crack where a boot could gain purchase.

Before them spread an enormous bubbling pool, some manner of giant hot springs. It radiated a peculiar brazen luminosity, thus the source of the glow earlier. In the center, accessed by a broad stone ramp, rose a stone island on which stood a crystal-like pedestal of petrified bone, shimmering green, orange and white. Its quality was unique, of an otherworldly radiance, as if activated to life with the fey opening of the portal after centuries. In spite of the countless jewels overhead, here was what the dragons valued most—water!—thousands of bubbling barrels of it.

Vetra glanced quickly behind him. No sign of Cthan.

He edged toward the shore of that strange pool. In the mysterious light cast by it, he discerned the dim, familiar faces he had come to know of late: Aus, Gefzad and Sebju, the venerable leader of the Thrules who had fought alongside the men with sword and survived. But she wore a face set in grim fatality—that she and others would not survive this crypt.

Vetra hissed through his teeth. He turned to the vast pool. A lattice of stone walkways spanned the waters, from one to three feet wide. Like a spider web, these lesser walkways branched out from the central island to intersect each other, like an intricate mosaic.

Each way gave passage across the water in its unique way. A broad stone ramp gave clear access to the island, at first angling down on a shallow grade from where they stood peering in awe, before it spread over the bubbling waters. Almost on impulse, Vetra set feet down this path and Jhara ran close by with Lehundr.

Zren hunched in a defensive crouch like a cornered animal, peering up with his one good eye, the other swollen over, lips pressed in a scowl despite the glistening wealth.

"That eye will do you no good in a fight, Thrule," muttered the mercenary.

Zren grunted. "I can see well enough, thank you."

Lehundr's face lit with greed at the wealth, but dimmed upon seeing the difficulty in chipping the priceless gems out of the ceiling.

"How could anybody build such a place?" Jhara whispered. She turned in surprise. "Where are you going?" She strode after Vetra with darting eyes.

Vetra made no answer.

Lehundr spoke in a voice of hollow wonder. "'Tis surely the heart of the dragon lords."

Great dragon king statues looked down from the far edges of the cavern where their stony feet touched the water. The ceiling was a rugged dome crafted of blasted rock, embedded with untold crystals, and as Vetra's eyes probed deeper, he could see the pattern of the star maps and the legends of the dragons woven in the crusted weave of gems: of faraway kingdoms, glorious and singular, a story of Dragon history told from the beginning. But it was so vast a panorama that Vetra's struggling senses balked, unable to absorb in any single glance the immensity of it all, and he staggered back.

He turned his eyes away. The water had risen over the stone walkways, if these even were human or dragon-lord walkways at one time. To peer down upon and contemplate the pool? Or up at the magnificent maps of ages, and stars? The water's surface seemed in constant turmoil, bubbling with a feverish energy of its own. Why? Vetra did not know.

But the perfectly carved pedestal...and a shining globe hovering a foot over it, about three feet wide, on whose circumference shimmered a veil of transparent water—or yet some type of filmy, magical glass. Impossible, but true.

Vetra shook his head to be sure he wasn't dreaming. Jhara's fingers clutched his arm. Her lips parted in a gasp. The orb defied the mind's reasoning, an apparition of mindless impossibility. It was as if all forms of laws of nature were broken. Inside floated a golden dragon's eye, suspended in some transparent medium. Liquid? Air? Vetra could not say. It was as if held immobile by some incomprehensible sorcery—and fashioned of intricate detail.

Vetra went to reach for it, but an inner voice stayed him. At the pedestal's base on the dusty cold stone sat a circle of small dragon skulls plated with gleaming silver, eyes inset and glaring with flaming garnet. Vetra saw human skulls set in similar fashion at each junction of the walkways over the water, perhaps the gory trophies of past skirmishes between humans and the dragon lords.

The invaders from Dragonskull stormed in, reeling at the sight of scintillating jewels and brilliant color. Three dozen of them at least stared gasping; at the head, Cthan's eyes were lit with rapacity, his jaw clenched in critical wonder. His fingers flexed on a dripping falchion, ready to exact his thirst for vengeance.

Vetra's eyes roved for sanctuary, some strategy to foil these boorish marauders, but before him only the waters bubbled and the steam rose over the long, yellowish pool. The mosaic of stone walkways seemed at best random, some unpredictable labyrinth architected by minds of the distant past. And yet, perhaps this was just what they needed...

A ledge with sections of steep stair switchbacked up the tail end of the cavern to the ceiling, like that of the dragon tomb. For what purpose? A frown curled Vetra's lips. A ritual stair in bygone days? Dragon lords ascending and descending from some hidden entrance or exit? Could they use them to make an escape?

Vetra gave a violent start and lurched back as he nearly stumbled over one of the skulls at his feet. He snapped out of his reverie and murmured under his breath, "No time to probe the mysteries. Let's lure them into the waterways." He motioned a swift hand. "You two, Dunon and Lehundr, draw them away hither—" he jerked his head toward a distant statue on the side wall. "Over there. Jhara, you follow me."

Stealthy as a panther, he skirted around the pedestal and took to the main path toward the cavern's far wall. Jhara struggled to keep up with him.

The ragged, blood-tattered Behundrians charged up to the shore and halted before the bubbling water, their eyes gleaming upon the gems above. They had not yet spotted the scattered band loping down the walkways. With circumspect glares, thirty of them threaded their way along the main waterway to the island where the pedestal stood and the steam rose in ghostly wisps. Several of them murmured in suspicion at the magical construction and the chilling array of skulls set at its foot.

"What's this eldritch fane?" grunted Cthan.

"Worth a fortune!" Vilivet cried. He reached for the shimmering eye in the white-lit globe, but Cthan slapped the twitching hand away.

"Keep your dirty paws off that eye. It's mine!"

Rafa hunched at his side, a hooded figure leering like a jackal with his one beady eye. A bloody patch lay draped over his missing orb, taken by Jhara's scourge back in Dragonskull. Other Behundrians crowded around the pedestal to gawk rapaciously at the impossible treasures gleaming on high. A few ran back to the shore to try and scale the wall and chip out some of the gems glistening from above.

The luminous eye had got to Vilivet's brain. He drew his blade and sneered, "Says who? I'll kill you, you dog. I have just as much right to the treasure." He jumped back, grunting. "Hey, what do you think you're doing?" His eyes blazed as Cthan drew his own saber. "'Twas I who saw the eye first."

"Be careful how you speak, 'dog', and watch your insubordinate tongue," hissed Cthan with danger in his voice.

"Why? You arrogant slug," spat Vilivet. "All the deeds I've done for you? I ought to slice you in two. The Thrules aren't half as stupid as you think. They knew there was power here. They sought out this key that Rafa harped on about, having some fool map that he claimed he almost had in his hand. The eye thing's proof of it. Rafa! Here, help me wrest this golden nugget from its socket, and we'll take the magic for our own, and—"

Cthan upended the butt of his sword into Vilivet's teeth, smashing them back in his throat in a spray of bright crimson. The rogue pitched sideways, staggering back, and slipped into the water. Blubbering, flailing like a fish, he choked out a blood-flecked cry, his sword flashing in a palm aching yet to gut Cthan, but some disturbance came arching over the water.

The Thrules watched in uneasy silence from a safe distance. Vetra couldn't decide whether the foaming roil was some type of jellyfish or octopus, but it wrapped opalescent streamers around the villain's thighs. There came a wretched screaming and terrified thrashing as Vilivet scrabbled to gain the walkway. The thing in the water, whatever it was, must have mutated over the years, Vetra guessed, judging from the elongated tentacles and the ghoulish suckers on each end. Now it pulled down the screaming ruffian to his death into the bubbling water.

The Behundrians recoiled and hopped back from the edge of the water. They sucked in air, brandishing their swords.

Cthan's face wrinkled in corded knots and his hard features locked in a strange sneer. "He was a fool, Vilivet. Serves him right for defying me and believing in the likes of ignorant superstition." He glared about him at the men who still looked on in horror. "Well, what are you waiting for? Let that be a warning to you, fools!" he cried, waving his sword with fanatic displeasure. "Don't get too close to the water. Who knows, you'll end up like Vilivet." His words caught in his throat as his eyes caught a whisper of movement—Vetra and his gang, pushing toward the back of the cavern. "The rogues! Well, what are looking at? After them!"

The ragged Behundrians stared in reluctance at the walkways but hurried forth, cringing at the possibility that they too might fall in the infested waters.

Cthan's hand reached for the mystical eye.

"Beware the old ones," Rafa mumbled in his ear, pointing spellbound at the shimmering globe and what fate it had in store for them.

Cthan's hand stopped inches from the eye. "What old ones? It's a myth. Nothing but outworn statues, old skeletons and fossils dredged up to scare old women."

"You're mistaken," said Rafa in a quiet voice.

Cthan rounded on him. "You too, Rafa?" He glared at him in wonder. "I expected more from you."

Rafa opened his mouth, but Cthan cut him off. "Get them, you idiot! What am I paying you for?" With raised sword thick-smeared with blood, the sheriff stomped after his henchman and beat the backs of three other laggards with the flat of his blade.

A sinister shuffling came from behind them near the back of the chamber. Cthan wheeled about and his twisted features frozen in blank-faced dismay. A curse caught in his throat, one full of regret.

"They live still? It can't be—" His voice trailed off.

Out of the gloom shambled seven primitive-looking reptiles. Dragon-leopards—the guardians of the chamber, like those of the tomb that Vetra had prowled. They crouched on all fours with dragonish heads lifted, the torsos of leopards and clawed feet of lizards. A look of madness shone from those iridescent eyes that darted all ways at once.

With a need for distance, Cthan plunged after his men, abandoning the treasure of the golden eye.

The six dragon guardians fanned out to examine their numerous prey, who they considered invaders of their realm. Already they had cut off any escape and a silent unblinking stare passed among them. A deep-toned rumble echoed from their cavernous throats. Tongues flicked out in unison. With slow, lizardlike movements three of the largest shambled across the water, straight up the main path while the others stayed back to guard the exit passage.

Vetra and Jhara exchanged glances and hurried on; others of their band slunk deeper into the maze of walkways. The guardians reached the isle and fanned out toward Dunon and Aus, and now Cthan and Rafa circled their way like weasels, far from the oncoming brood.

Vetra crouched on his walkway before a human skull, eyeing the waters and the approaching enemies with grave concern. He wondered what sinister creature watched him from below. Jhara hunched at his side, breathless, her ginger hair matted with sweat and blood. "What do we do?" she cried in a strained voice.

"We wait. No choice."

Jhara's fingers tightened on her whip.

From under the tangled mass of his matted black hair Vetra looked to see the gleam of defiance in her fiery eyes, and his heart burned with a fierce pride.

VIII: Jaws of Death

Vetra turned to face the oncoming horrors. One spat a ball of viscous phlegm down an adjacent walkway to affix itself to a nearby Behundrian's vest. Ooze soaked through the man's middle; he slapped at his chest in wild desperation. "Agh—get it off!" His horror-brimmed shriek filled the air. "It burns!" His fingers smoked on contact and the sizzled flesh gave off noxious gray vapors.

Vetra cursed. He sprinted onto an interconnecting walkway just in time to avoid gobs coming his way. Waters bubbled, carrying a sulfurous stench. The chamber was unbearably humid; the air pained his lungs.

"The guardians have increased our chances!" his hoarse cry echoed over the din. "Make for the ledge where their fangs can't get us."

He stared with bloodshot eyes at a distant place across the luminous waters. Shadowy shapes circled closer, glints of wheeling light reflecting off a dozen swords. He bared his teeth.

At places along the opposite shore the steaming pool ran flush to the crusted wall; elsewhere the shore widened allowing room for fighting men to move. To this place Vetra wished to flee, for the ledge wound its way up, away from the pool and the dragon beasts. The shore sloped before the far wall where colossal dragon-lord statues stood in solemn procession, staring in reflection at the sinister waters.

He and Jhara had scrambled as far away as they could from the circling fiends without being flanked, but now steel would have to decide their fate.

"Slay them!" Cthan shrieked in hoarse fury from a walkway not a dozen paces from where they gathered. "Catch them and cut off their privates, you fools! We cannot relieve this cavern of its treasure with these salamanders spitting acid at us. Kill the outlanders! Kill all these wretched Thrules."

"What do you expect us to do?" sneered Rafa. "Pull them in with our teeth? They have feet as swift as wolves."

Cthan scrutinized Rafa with a rancorous grunt. "Fifty gold talons for the first to cut off the outlander's head. Twenty for the girl's. No—take the wench alive!"

A roar went up among the swarming Behundrians and they came charging hard down the walkways at both fugitives.

A quick glance told Vetra that only a head-on assault would make any difference. Throwing caution to the wind, he ran to meet them. Rejecting the odds, the mercenary swung his sword in whistling loops and drove in hard and furious. His blade struck bone in a splatter of crimson; sword met sword in a clanking echo around the skull-littered walkways. Raging blades bit into flesh while steel smashed through sinew, driving the foremost attacker back like a mule into the other Behundrian jackals.

The man died instantly and his guts spilled out on the stone. His colleagues seethed forward, struggling to get around the standing corpse that was wedged between opposing forces, eager to stab at the berserker and win their reward.

Vetra roared and drove his blade more fiercely into the cluster. He could see the bearded dead face lolling in front of him. He could smell the hot rank breath of the men behind. Jhara's whip snapped past Vetra's shoulders and cut into Behundrian flesh. Their fates hung in balance; men's muscles strained and grisly shrieks rent the air. Dragon guardians snapped, gnawing at the enemies' backs. Vetra felt the mass of men surge and a chill wave of horror as the line of Behundrians shivered under the first beast's mauling assault. He released his lock on his attacker's sword arm in a sudden twist and unleashed a flurry of slashes. The next man fell dead, ribboned with cuts. Another took his place, his blade arching, but was soon cleaved to the bone. The mercenary showed no mercy. The blood flew from his blade and boiled in his veins; a battle lust was upon him, and for the moment he was unstoppable.

Fortune did not favor the blood-drenched Behundrians. For all their numbers, they were hampered by this lack of space and the lizard attack from the rear. Despite their initial advantage, another of the brute dragon guardians appeared, lumbering up from a side path like a ravenous ghoul. The thing ripped into their flanks, and the ones in the back screamed and fell, hands outstretched, clawing at stone as they either slipped into the lethal waters or the monster rended them with teeth and claws and dragged them away in its jaws.

Vetra saw a creature shaking its maw like a dog and a screaming victim tossed like a windblown leaf into the pool.

Vetra gave ground, snarling as dying men pushed forward like zombies. They struggled to escape the snapping jaws, the sharp claws and trampling feet. The first two in the thing's path died horribly, crushed and mangled between sets of serrated teeth. Down they went trampled by its clawed feet.

Sandwiched between foes, Jhara fought tooth and nail at Vetra's back. Yowling like a banshee, Jhara kicked with savage force and lashed out her whip at the three rogues who tried to grab her and pull her down.

Vetra abandoned his fight. The wall of flesh was pressing in on him. He pushed Jhara aside and smashed his bloody falchion like a club into her nearest attacker's face. The other he kicked in the stomach and sent him gasping into the waters. The Behundrian reached for the ankles of his fellow man to save himself, only to end up pulling him in too. Vetra ran with the girl, barely keeping ahead of the mad rush of the surviving horde who drove from behind, while the dragon guardian made grisly work of anybody left in its path.

"Fight back to back!" he snarled at Jhara over the din of the tortured screams and eviscerated bodies. "The narrow walkways give us an edge over their numbers!"

Down the walkway they scrambled. Vetra's feet skipped past an intersecting path, his eyes roving for solution, knowing a wrong turn could be their last.

Another ball of black mucus came slapping at their feet, perilously close. He stumbled sideways to avoid it. Not a dozen feet away, three Behundrians crouched on a narrow walkway, weapons drawn, cringing. They realized they had taken a wrong turn several steps back, now they stared into the snouted face of one of the waddling beasts that had swung past a narrow bend and was fast gaining on them.

Vetra wasted no time to observe the carnage. Behind them, yelping attackers wheeled in confusion. Boots rang on stone.

The girl turned and feinted and cut a man just as he was bearing down on her. Vetra marvelled at her fluid skill. She moved just as he had taught her. In a quick follow up lash, another chunk of flesh ripped free from the man's sword arm. He wailed, clamped a free hand to staunch the growing gush of blood. Twirling, she ducked the man's strike, and sent him howling into the steaming water with a swift kick. Immediately a swarm of spidery tentacles engulfed the writhing body. The blubbering shrieks were lost in the hiss of water.

The man's comrade shrank back, the whites of his eyes showing fear, blade hanging limp.

Vetra sucked in a breath. The slimy things must have infested the waters since the demise of the dragon lords. He couldn't for the life of him imagine what had impelled the lords to allow such vermin in their splendorous hall.

He raced on, fingers hooked on Jhara's arm. They clambered for a point along the far edge of the cavern, but a half dozen Behundrians read their intentions. Vetra found the way was soon cut off. "Is there no end to you rats?" he cried, sneering at the enemies who blocked his path.

Cthan's rogues leapt forward and snarled, striving to cut them off before they could get to the next crossway. Too late. They leaped over a narrow gap of water onto a cross path which headed back toward where the men quailed, struggling with the dragon guardian.

Vetra cursed this place. The irregular web-like layout of the walkways made it impossible to predict any enemy's movements for more than a dozen steps. A sudden turn down a crosspath or a doubling back down another could leave a man sandwiched between foes.

A long stretch of open water lay between them and the three Behundrians. The stone path had sagged over time. None wished to chance that water and the loathsome squid creatures that teemed within.

Vetra weighed his options.

The doomed trio slashed at the dragon guardian that was menacing them from behind, trying to keep it at bay. No such luck.

A glob of acid spewed from a gaping maw and hit a man square in the temple. He danced a devil's jig, howling, clawing at his face which melted away in a waxy ruin before the astonished onlookers could react. The gasp died in his throat. Black goo sizzled from his flesh and he sank, twitching, legs draped over the side, his arms the other. In an instant, crawly, green, plant-like tendrils pulled the sightless body under.

Vetra and Jhara halted in dismay. Water foamed over the stone at their feet.

To race across that long sunken stretch invited disaster. No matter—the beast decided it for them. It charged across, unafraid of what dwelled in that frothing cauldron. Vetra stood grimly poised to face the thing. Jhara held back attackers at the rear. Sucker-vine tentacles hooked onto the running beast's forelegs and claws, but these were stamped to oblivion in its angry dash toward them.

Vetra staggered back, pushing Jhara hard into him and onto an intersecting path that sank into water not three strides out. He wheeled and crouched low as the beast's head reared up to smash him from the side. Had he stood where he was, he would have been mowed down by nothing less than the driving force of a battering ram.

A noisome wind hit him as he ducked under that looming wall of flesh and ripped his sword across the thing's throat, and while dark fluid spurted forth, dripping on him and staining the decayed stone, a slippery white tentacle arched from the water to grab its twitching leg. Wild cries sounded behind him.

The thing died with a hissing gurgle, blocking the path.

Vetra shoved Jhara back. Taking a run, they leaped over its humped back. The Behundrians came after them howling. They bounded over the beast's glistening hide with another raging dragon beast snapping at their heels.

Vetra and Jhara leaped between winding paths, the stone lapping with blood and corpses. Vetra's feet slipped in a wide pool of blood. Jhara crashed into him. Her whimper and sob sounded in his ear. "We're doomed! There's nowhere to run."

They pulled each other to their feet, and the blood drained from Vetra's features. Another monster with fanged snout bore down on them. The skin of his back crawled. They scuttled down a cross path and Vetra cringed at the meaty sounds of carnage as the beast tore into fleeing Behundrians. Whatever sorcery animated these brutish killers, it could only have been brewed from the blackest pits.

He closed his ears to more gristle-rending sounds and his hand fled to his blood-matted scalp, a growing lump gathering there where a grazing rake of sword had glanced off his skull.

"Come on," he muttered at Jhara. "We don't want to fall into ruin like those unfortunate sods."

"Cthan's rogues will catch us and corner us!" she protested. "Move!"

They scrambled over corpses and a menacing whoosh flew past their heads. Vetra looked back to see a hill Thrule's boomerang catching the loping beast full in the eyes. It stumbled out of control and splashed into the frothing water. Grinning with satisfaction, Vetra clapped the approaching Thrule on the back. He saw the sweating man had a healthy supply of boomerangs strapped to his back. "Great throw, friend!"

Vetra's sharp eyes took in the scene in a glance: the fleeing figures, the hacking blades, the shambling beasts. His mind registered all. How to win this fight? Lehundr and Aus were knee deep in hewn corpses and cloven skulls. Aus, the Thrule marksman crouched and stabbed and launched boomerangs at advancing foes. Zren raged like a ghoul, his sword gripped and flailing, tossing ear-heavy curses and hacking with unfettered lust. Of the Temple Thrule leader there was no sign; Vetra assumed she had fallen.

His inner sense told him to take a weaving course toward the clotted path where Dunon, Gefzad and Aus battled not a stone's throw from the cavern's edge against a guardian.

Arching and twisting in its confidence, the monster got too close to the water and found its foreleg gripped by a probing tentacle. With a mournful croak, the beast bit at the curling menace, but more tendrils came lurching out of the water. Like sucker vines, they were alive with force. Festoons of the snake-like things wrapped around its other leg, then its neck, and slowly dragged the creature into the seething water. Its head came bobbing up. There it thrashed, seeking release, sending keening moans into the air. But snaking cords soon webbed over its snout, fangs and into nostrils, and it dropped from sight.

Vetra closed with two blood-drenched attackers. His sword found soft flesh beneath the leather. One attacker gave a last sighing gasp and Vetra put a foot on his chest to pull out the blade. He slipped on the spurting blood, lost his grip, was unable to pry the weapon loose from the breastbone in time to prevent the blade from falling into the steaming water. Instinct took over. He kicked the corpse away and winced as his only weapon bubbled away into oblivion.

The mercenary's eyes roamed about the chamber. He felt naked without his sword. Not long would he last amid these fiends without familiar, protective steel. His flesh quivered with the thought of being rended by these foes.

Six feet out in the water, another guardian thrashed, struggling to stay afloat. Crossbow bolts stung its neck. Now its snout and humped back rose above the steaming bubbles. Vetra's eyes caught the glint of scimitars lying not far away on the stone walkway, in the hands of dead men, mauled by the guardians. It gave him an idea.

"Skirt around that way!" he shouted to Jhara. "We'll meet at that adjacent walkway." He stabbed out a finger.

"It's insane!" she cried. "You'll be eaten alive." She saw what the mercenary was planning—and she caught him in a convulsive grip.

"Do it!" cried Vetra.

No sooner had he uttered the cry when a blade came whistling by his head. He made a last savage leap.

Over the guardian's head he launched himself onto its back, now crawling with great, green, slimy tendrils. Even as the shiny, flesh-flecked teeth snapped up to chomp him, his feet were in the air again and he was lunging for the opposite walk. Where was Jhara?

He came slamming down on the crude-cut stone, his boots in the water, and the fingers of one hand clawing on the wet stone. He half expected the creature's lips to vomit out deadly goop.

He pulled himself up and over, legs burning with pain from the scorching water, and the feel of sucker-vines latching onto his leg.

Scrambling to his feet, he jigged around, a frantic fury upon him, smashing boot heels down on the crawly things that wished to twine around his ankles. He grabbed an abandoned sword and beat it against the things creeping up his legs. He shook the horror out of his head, feeling his limbs quiver.

No time to lose.

Sword in hand, he regained his footing and lunged for Cthan and the rogues who guarded the junction. Jhara was alone and against many. He cut the first opponent down in a wave of red, cleaving flesh to the bone, then faced the others.

Cthan darted away, laughing, directing others to take the place of the dead minion. "Hold him! The fool has nowhere to go." He raced back toward the island, where the dragon eye lay.

Vetra caught a glimpse of that fathomless orb, pulsing away like a ghoulish, living thing. It vibrated as if it were of demented, elemental origin, alive and quickening, shining a weird translucent glow.

Cthan had been lucky, or smarter than his hapless men. He and Rafa bolted along a narrow ledge that lapped over with water. Leaping over those sections, with the intent to skirt around the guardians, they closed with Lehundr and Aus, and the boomerang thrower who came rushing up to assist them.

Dunon, Gefzad and other hill Thrules saw the Behundrian enemies storming up to murder Lehundr and Aus. They came at Cthan and Rafa from the rear with howls of rage on their lips.

Cthan gave a rancorous roar. He turned to engage Dunon, who was snarling from lips caked with froth. Dunon turned at a whizzing blade that sliced close to his ear. He stumbled, tripped by a foot snaking out.

Gefzad jumped over and caught Cthan's whickering blade. It would have driven into Dunon's ear. Cthan's blade slid rasping over Gefzad's hilt and Gefzad's finger was shorn off. His blade again locked with Gefzad's. With a quick, snake-like flick, he ran the Thrule through the chest. The gape-mouthed man toppled across the pathway with a squashy thud.

Vetra watched as jelly-like forms swarmed over him, the man's face a parody of comic surprise. Cthan booted him out of the way. The rogue came driving onward. Dunon was inches behind and tried to jab past his man to get to Cthan's jugular, but the path was too narrow and he could do little without suffering damage, nor do much for fear of skewering his own man.

Ten feet in front, the boomerang thrower parried Rafa, and realized that even with a patch over his eye, the man was more than his match. He drew back in defeat.

"Retreat!" came Vetra's pained voice rising across the water. He called to Aus who was spidering his way back with Rafa's opponent to regroup. There both he and Dunon were but two dozen paces away on a parallel walkway.

Lehundr pulled back the boomerang thrower and ran with Jhara, to Vetra's place of cover.

The boomerang thrower slipped and Rafa, seizing the opportunity, ran a sword through his back, his face lit in fierce triumph. Aus gave an agonized bellow.

"Forget him!" cried Vetra. "To the ledge! The beasts can't follow us up there."

Cthan turned and glared at the mercenary. "You're a dead man!" Hearing Rafa's triumphant cry from not far away, he shambled off to the pedestal where gleamed the dragon's eye. Dunon and the two others came spitting curses after him, blades flailing. "Coward! Fight like a man!" Dunon cried with frothing anger at Cthan's back as he stumbled after.

Cthan ignored such insults. He strode with blade hoisted with an imperious grin to carve out any Thrule flesh that would thwart him.

The rest of the Behundrians, crowded by circling guardians, foiled Vetra's plan of regrouping. They cut off Dunon and Aus, with a wall of bristling blades.

"Up the ledge!" Vetra thundered in frustration. He and Jhara reached the opposite shore while Lehundr puffed behind them. Now the shadow of a towering dragon lord statue fell over all of them and they scrambled past its massive stone feet. They reached the ledge that wound up the cavern wall.

Up the crumbling slope they scrambled, a crust of fallen jewels crunching underfoot, sparkling in the luminous glow of the water. Cthan's men saw what they were doing and gave angry shouts. Cthan gesticulated in wild fervor. Half of the forces raced to cut them off at another stairway leading to the same ledge. Vetra clenched his fist grimly and hoped the others could make it in time.

There was an advantage to this route. The sinister dragon lords could not scale the wall, and the Behundrians would be hard pressed to take them on the high ground.

The plan was flawed. Foes were coursing behind them, and up ahead on the straight section of ledge, squeezing past dead bodies, encircling the defenders in a knot. A flash of figures appeared in the dimness and he and Jhara and Lehundr raced to meet them.

They were backed out on a ledge. Below the waters boiled. There was no way to escape.

On the death of Cthan's rear guard, Zren had managed to worm his way through the battle and up the ledge. Panting, with new cuts and bruises, he was like a dripping beast, and Vetra almost cut him down, crouched as he was, lips asnarl and streaming sweat and blood.

"Fight with Jhara and protect each other's backs," Vetra ordered him.

The Thrule listened, for once.

To his credit, Zren had knocked Rafa's man aside and had just saved the mercenary from a direct hit. He was willing to waste himself for the girl whom he eyed with most possessive fanaticism. Young, impulsive fool! thought Vetra. He would get them all killed with his headstrong impulses.

Bellowing a savage war cry, Vetra wheeled and smote in reckless abandon, giving Jhara space and time to crouch and round-house kick, "Die, you ass-licking dogs!" she cried, and she thrust a boot out into a bearded face. Vetra heard the crunch of bone. Rafa rounded in, grinning, lunging in to trip her.

Jhara fell with a thud, crying out in surprise, the wind knocked out of her. Her cat o' nine tails licked out, but Rafa caught the twirling thong as it curled about his sword and he yanked it out of her grasp. She squealed in frustration as Rafa pounced like a tiger, flicking her hateful weapon over the edge.

The girl crawled away but Rafa pulled her up shrieking by the hair.

Zren came stabbing in like a wild man and Rafa snarled with fury at the fierce passion of the man's attack. Rafa gave ground, stabbing wide-eyed, but his men shouldered in and booted the Thrule back.

"Away from me, you stinking cur! Back to the reeking pools where you belong."

Gashed and seething, Zren leered. He swung two-handed frenzied sweeps of blade while Rafa dragged Jhara back into the protection of his knot of rogues.

She writhed in his cruel grip, her face pushed over the ledge overlooking the pool, but he clasped her tighter and encircled her with his ape-like arms, crooning a foul proposition in her ear.

Vetra lunged forth, but too late, blades kept him in check too. Lehundr crowded behind Vetra, his hilt quivering in his bloody fist.

Cthan paused below, a saturnine croak of laughter on his lips like the hyena who has cornered the rat. The smug insolence of the man showed on his face. He stared up at the vise his men had sprung on the rebels while others of his forces contended with the dragon beasts.

Toward the center of the island he sauntered leisurely, a pleased expression on his face. Three of the guardians were down, one guarded the exit and only two remained to harry the walkways, these far away and under the control of his men.

"That's right, Rafa," Cthan called up savagely. "Hold the bitch. She's a she-cat." The sheriff's one eye lingered on the guardian that menaced Dunon and his men at the other end of the ledge. "I'll see what this precious dragon eye is all about."

Rubbing his hands in satisfaction, Cthan paused to appraise the glimmering globe and its treasure. "A fair march to this god-forsaken place", he said in hoarse enthusiasm, "and losses to go with it, but well worth it."

"Aye," gloated Rafa, yelling down from his ragged patch on the ledge. "These Thrules will pay for our losses. And this filthy outlander—" He shook Jhara vindictively as a dog does a rat and flashed her a lascivious smile. "In quarts of their own blood, and in bed favors. Starting with these mangy rebels before us, trapped in this treasure den."

Rafa relaxed his grip, overconfident in his advantage. It was an open invitation for Jhara to strike and with a snake-like jerk, too quick for the eye to see, she twisted out of Rafa's grip, ramming elbow into his teeth. The man howled and Vetra lunged forth, knocking one of Rafa's henchman off the ledge. Vetra cut through another man and ground a heel into Rafa's foot, catching the flailing arm and bending it backwards.

One of Rafa's remaining henchmen grabbed Jhara from behind and put a knife to her throat.

With a savage wrench, Vetra pulled Rafa down to the stone so he was on one knee, gasping in pain, putting blade to his throat. Lehundr vaulted over the two of them, and his curved falchion quivered inches from Jhara's captor's face.

"Drop the swords!" barked Cthan, seething at the sudden assault on the ledge. "Let my man Rafa go free, or my other man will slay the girl. That I promise!"

Jhara protested, struggling with feverish desperation. "No! I got you into this mess, following you here. Don't give into this monster! Let him die, Vetra. Let me die. Kill all these vermin."

Cthan laughed cynically. "He's not that much of a hero, doll face. Besides, that wouldn't be very heroic of him, would it, 'Vetra'?" he sneered. "Our knight in shining armor cannot live with himself, responsible for the slaying of a girl, could he?"

Vetra growled. It wouldn't be easy for him to sacrifice the girl, that was true. Was there another way?

Rafa's henchman now had the screaming rebel over a precipice. Vetra reluctantly released his hold on Rafa. The thug unruffled himself from Vetra's grip and shook out the hurts.

"Now hold her this time, you idiot. I give you a few simple tasks and what do you do, get your eye gouged out."

Rafa snarled and turned in malicious distaste on the girl. "You're a tasty piece of meat. I think I'll take out my pound of flesh on you later." He ogled her sleek body, her luscious curves pleasing to him. He fondled her breasts like a drunken soldier in a brothel. "Do you remember how you gave me this, you wretched spitfire?" He jerked a hand to his eye, lifted the blood-torn patch, displaying an ugly red socket.

Jhara turned her head away. Though she struggled, there was no overpowering that brute who now held her and thrust her arm cruelly behind her back.

A voice from the haunted past, echoing dim and terrible, suddenly smote the chamber. Or was it only in their minds? Vetra did not know.

"So, this is what mankind has evolved to after a thousand years?"

The startled Behundrians peered around in abject wonder. Strangled murmurs hissed through their teeth.

Vetra looked around in no less surprise. But he could discover no source for the mysterious voice that rolled in doomful waves in his mind. A stir began to form in the waters abreast the pedestal.

Scowling into his beard, Cthan reached out with impatient urgency toward the mystical, glowing dragon eye.

Through the ethereal film, his hands thrust with bold intent to seize the eye for his own. A keen thrill of ecstasy rippled through his body and lit up his face.

"A life's fortune," he hissed in marvel.

The iris of the eye was cut like an exquisite diamond. A ruby pupil fitted dead center glared forth. Like a cosmic egg it glowed, solid gold, silver, or both—one could not distinguish. The treasure harbored a shimmering aliveness that tantalized the beholder. Just as Cthan was about to withdraw the prize from the globe, a fierce wave of agony and horror passed over his face. A searing blast of radiance burst from the eye and lit up his face. From a distance Vetra squinted, the flare was so bright.

"I see your bloody past!" Cthan raved. "Dragon wars over eons!" It was as if he came to understand all of the dragons' secrets in that one flash and greedy grasp. A secret not meant for man. The eye lit with the brutal sum of knowledge of the eons that the dragons had lived, and died and warred. All blasted into Cthan's brain—embodied into one blinding pulse, like a hundred possessed lightning strikes.

With a choking cry the sheriff stumbled backwards, his lips mouthing shrieks of pain. The skin of his palms stuck to the white-lit egg, so supercharged it was with heat and mystical energy.

The rogue's eye sockets hung in red and dripping flaps. Smoke billowed from his hands, his eyes scalded by liquid light.

The sheriff of Dragonskull jerked about like a mad puppet, stumbling back in blind terror, as he learned how the dragon lords became rulers of the earth, how all the battles they had won and fought were in vain, and how they had been lords of the sky and the earth ever since the beginning when the oceans boiled and the first islands rose out of the sea to become the fabulous continents on which the first humans stood.

The eye fell from his grasp and hung suspended in the sulfurous air to return in magic force like a faithful sentinel to perch inside the globe.

At the same moment a liquid column of strangeness rose from the pool at the stone's edge. A water spirit? One of the feral jellyfish-like horrors? Vetra was at a loss. The thing was a giant cyclone of raging water at first, then an amorphous mass that bulged and formed the dim outline of one of the dragon lords, tall and imposing, with eyes unblinking, arms folded across chest and staff in hand.

The dragonish head tipped in grave judgment, staring down at the fly-sized humans. A shimmering yellow halo surrounded its watery form, this solemn giant of all creatures.

IX: The Dragon Lord

Cthan groped back blindly, as if aware of the foaming rush of some horror in close proximity. With pathetic whimpers, he pawed for his sword, his senses still intact, but his eyes beyond repair. He found his blade where it had fallen and gripping it in a clenched fist, swung wildly at an apparition he could not see. His blade passed right through the will-o'-the-wisp without drawing a drop of water.

The thing ignored him as if he were no more than a gnat.

Vetra elbowed Rafa in the ribs, taking advantage of the moment. He seized the man's sword. While he was doubled over, he sent him reeling into the hot springs. Lehundr ducked a whistling blade just as Zren surged through the pack and rammed his head into Jhara's captor. Jhara gave a wild screech and in a burst of hysterical strength, pulled herself into a ball and brought her assailant rolling over her back. Vetra plunged steel into his throat and kicked the dying man down the slope.

Jhara scrambled past Zren and Vetra felt her shudder pass over his body as she brushed close. She shook with fierce outrage, her fingers digging into his back.

At the same time, words came into Vetra's mind—thoughts forged from the hidden wells of the subconscious, a deep rumbling sibilance like low waves breaking on an ocean:

"None can lift the dragon eye so waste no efforts. 'Tis the jewel of our heritage, the heart blood of our race, the greatest treasure we have known— excluding the water that gives life, for the eye links soul with body, body with earth and air. We are centuries dead, our memory is preserved, and still you

have brought a blight upon us..."

Rafa floundered in the water, quivering and thrashing as his flesh burned. He clawed his way up the shore, his flesh raw, red and seared. Swarming green and white tentacles crawled over the gang leader's shins and began their evil work. He clawed at them with his quivering fingers, tearing clumps of flesh. The things wound tighter about his legs. He pounded his fists with strengthening intensity, tearing with fingers now bloody. His gruesome shrieks were awful to hear as he struggled in vain to get the ghastly things off.

Up the path Vetra, Jhara, Lehundr and Zren clambered, blocking out the sounds of Rafa's and Cthan's wails. They skidded up higher while the Behundrians stared in speechless horror like stunned deer. Vetra bowled through their startled ranks, leaving two writhing on the jewel-crumbled stone. He, Zren and the girl vaulted over them.

Dunon and Aus scrambled up a stair running parallel to Vetra's and now cut down the last resistance from the back even as Vetra barreled through.

More invaders, rousing from their shock, rushed them, grunting and hacking up from behind. Vetra herded the others up a set of steep, crumbled steps and turned, chopping the pursuers down from the narrow stairway. He was getting slowly pushed up, his back to his peers.

"We need to climb higher!" he bawled.

Dunon motioned. "To where?"

"Doesn't matter! They can't surround us on the narrower ledges."

The voice from the ages boomed again:

"People from this far age—feast thy eyes on Naklion, our Dragon Heart. I am Macemas, last lord of Aslante. But only in memory do I impart this message. Take your wars and skirmishes elsewhere and wrest no bauble from our tomb, lest my curse befall you!"

All gaped in wonder as the voice reverberated through their

bones.

"We, the lords of the dragons, have languished; our reign passed a millennium ago. Yet all must live together in this world. Leave in peace! Whether in life or death that you understand these words, take this memory with you—that whether dragons or their lords live or live not, you are the masters of your own destiny. Nothing comes to pass that is not a form of your own doing…"

Dunon gasped and clambered up higher behind Vetra. "What manner of creature is this water devil?"

Vetra grunted. "Something to mash our brains."

"The dragon lords have left a remnant of their past, you fools!" snarled Lehundr, "—a living, conscious memory! None heeded the call for peace ages ago."

"Get higher!" Vetra yelled.

In the midst of clanking blades he gave ground inch by inch. A long, ghastly line of guardians advanced like hungry predators from the exit tunnel. The mercenary grimaced and gripped his blood-stained blade tighter. Doom crawled at every corner of this forsaken pit.

The water god seemed to watch them with detached interest. Vetra expected it to kill them all in an instant, and drown them in lakes of quicksilver. But it just rose higher, a shimmering tower of judgment.

He craned his neck upward. The crust of jewels glinting like fireflies to the senses was tantalizingly close. While he slashed down at the Behundrians still fighting for a cause without a leader, the dragon pool seemed to cool, and billows of steam flattened in peculiar fashion. An ominous scrape echoed from overhead, like a heavy stone slab lifting off an impregnable tomb.

Vetra's eyes narrowed. He saw a patch of open sky above them, pale sunlight momentarily blinding him. The water lord shimmered and compressed its liquid form into a long, rippling spiral, up around Cthan, who flailed blindly with sword raised like a madman as the dragon guards advanced on him. Up it rose, like a living cobra, swirling like a whirlwind to disappear in the opening and was gone.

Vetra's senses reeled. He shook off his dizziness, a fear of heights returning in full. Sweat streamed off his face; his stomach heaved with nausea.

The rush of booted feet came from below. He edged back and struck all the harder at a leather-helmed skull that bobbed up. He pointed to the opening, then at the sky, and his parched throat gave voice to a hoarse shout. "There! Our only chance out of this burrow. Quick! before the portal closes."

Like harried rabbits they crawled up the stairs, quivering fingers reaching for the opening. The Behundrians came roaring after them, scrabbling at their heels like bloodhounds.

"Cthan's dead!" blurted one. "Our reward is gone."

"Let's kill these rogues and be out of here!"

Water hissed in the pool below and the Behundrian's wild curses were lost in the wrathful echo of the dragon lord's exodus.

Through gritted teeth, Vetra held the throng back, his blade whistling wild arcs of death. Dunon helped Jhara up the hole, while he and Aus and the others pushed Zren and Lehundr through. All were up and out and Vetra leapt, fingers clutching the opening's rim. Feet dangling, he kicked at enemy blades that licked out at him like vipers. His friends snatched at his arms while hands from below sought to use him as a ladder. Vetra smashed these with his boot heels and a tumultuous wail rent the air as a man plummeted to his doom.

He was out, blinking in dazzling light. The open sky yawned above them and the searing heat of the desert beat down on his skin.

The stone slab was too heavy to pull over to stop the snarling Behundrians who seethed up in a mad, feverish wave. Vetra and Dunon hunched over the opening like vultures, slashing at fingers that tried to hoist themselves up. Dying shrieks echoed below; more fell to crash down the stairs and to the cavern below.

Vetra stared about, his eyes wandering to the place where the dragon lord had drifted. He shook his head, saw only a film before his vision. His eyes stung as he looked into the overwhelming, golden light.

The dragon lord glided like a solemn wraith across the skullish, scar-topped rock of the mesa.

Halting at the summit's edge, *he*, or whatever it was, traced circles in the air with its slightly clawed hands. It had shed its watery body, yet its skin glistened as brightly as before. For all intents and purposes, he was now a real flesh and blood dragon lord, stern-faced and regal, and majestically rendered out of thin air. He lifted a hand in the direction of the two megalith fangs perched high on the adjacent hills. An unearthly aura surrounded him like a wizard from another age.

The Dragon Lord stared out over the edge of the cliff rising high above the plain. On the battlefield below, the straw-like figures of Behundrians, drenched in blood and sorrow, gasped and stumbled away in terror at the sight of the apparition. Searing light came lancing from the megaliths, arching out and striking the dragon bones that littered the ruins below at the warriors' feet.

Like ants before the raging storm, the fighting men scurried on all fours, gusting curses. But no such easy escape was given them.

The somber words from faraway spoke, splitting the fabric of the air, the fabric of their minds and the monstrous intonations rose and fell like deep musical waves:

"Fools! Ignorant fools! Do you flee like vermin without a moment's understanding? Die now, and start afresh in your incarnations. Tragic repercussions are in order. Suffer for your actions in face of these Thrules who have struggled to uphold the heritage of the dragon lords. Now they lie broken like dolls on a god's playground. But they die not in vain..."

These words came as not human born, but from an

incomprehensible place beyond the stars.

In his days of life, as centuries ago he had moved in magical ways from hill to hill and tomb to tomb, the dragon lord moved now, the same which had discovered secrets and forbidden pathways far under the earth—the same which had forged the labyrinthic ways under the Dragon fortress of *Aslante* whose vastness and mystery mortal minds could not fathom.

"Time to die..." came the disembodied, almost hypnotic voice. *"Our knowledge is too advanced for you. On your journey of life let you plod in an endless cycle of war, strife and grief until ultimate awakening dawns."*

Maybe he was some great lord or magician, who knew? Vetra stood spellbound. The knowledge of such things was beyond him, and lost in the gulfs of time.

"Dead brothers. Rise again!" Like a thunderclap the voice came over the sunburnt plain. The speech was lost in sand, air and cloud and the last dragon lord's murmurs washed over the shallow valley to end in a final command:

"Rise brothers, rise!"

And the dragon skeletons came to life, bones clattering together in an animated collective, tinkling like a thousand sinister wind chimes. An army of them creaked to life, rippling to unnatural form by some unseen magic the dragon-lord wielded after many ages of rest. The dragons' fierce sun-bleached skulls tilted skyward, seeing a firmament not witnessed for a thousand years; then their necks swiveled to assess the fleeing remnants of the Behundrian army through their empty eye sockets.

A horrific murmur rose through the Behundrian's ranks. Skeletal dragons vaulted the rocky molder of their ancient death beds, springing after routed soldiers who ran in sheer terror. Ageless, undead creatures of bone and teeth rent flesh and crushed skulls, tails sweeping, snouts ramming, soldiers' armor and weapons proving impotent.

These enchanted specters then took to the air, bony wings spread like monstrous bats, flapping at air that should not keep them afloat, and soared low and high, searching for enemies to kill. As they swooped and dove like merciless raptors, they slaughtered in numbers the invaders to their sanctuary.

From his majestic perch the Dragon lord watched all this with no apparent emotion. Perhaps the briefest flicker of understanding fled across that imperturbable face, that the doom claiming these warriors sprang from the same source governing his own demise eons ago.

When the shimmering lord had seen enough, his eyes glowed once more and his pulsing vision sent out the signal to the megaliths on the hill. The animus left the dragons, and like one they fell, their bones scattering like broken twigs over the dismal, corpse-strewn plain. There came a hail of bone on the last scrambling men, crushed and hammered to pulp beneath a storm of undead remains.

Vetra and his company watched aghast.

Satisfied at the death and destruction, the dragon lord walked on solemn feet back to the open slab and Vetra and his ragged fellows drew back with awe and apprehension. Under the natural light of day, the dragon being was a complete replica of one of the old, carven lords of the elder age. The perfect folds of the flesh on his face and naked shoulders and thighs glistened in the sunlight and burned pits in Vetra's memory: the chilling dragon's mane of scales and his corselet of fur, and the clawed feet.

There was no place to run so Vetra clutched his sword, ready to fight or die. "Kill us, if you must, fiend," he murmured. Muscles taut, he shouldered Jhara out of harm's way and faced the menace. Pulsing with instinctive self preservation, Jhara uttered a soft sob. Lehundr gazed in trance-like stupor while the Thrules shrank back, expecting instant death, swallowing dry lumps in their throats, bowing their heads in reverent terror.

The apparition briefly studied the defenders, though those seconds seemed to last a hundred years. Then its kohl-shadowed eyes gave them a blinking appraisal and shimmered back into its watery, mystical form. Like a column of liquid nothingness, it coursed wraith-like back through the black gap and the sad, shrieking cries of the doomed Behundrians trapped below rang out like a gallow-man's song. To a man, their white eyes blazing in desolation, they tumbled back before the unfathomable terror that was the dragon lord of Naklion, and the heavy slab slid back and closed with crushing finality forever.

The Thrules shuddered and shrank back. Jhara gave an exhausted moan of relief. "Am I in a dream, or in one of Dergath's afterlives?"

Vetra gave a grim laugh. He sheathed his sword and faced the Thrules. "So, your dragon lord crawls back in his hole with his riches. Who would have believed it?"

"You should pray to your Dergath that you still guard your head," came Aus's retort, which Dunon and Lehundr endorsed with nods and hoarse "hear, hear's".

"Let us count our blessings then and be gone from this sorrowful place," murmured the half Thrule.

White-faced, they all threaded their way down the side of the mesa, squinting under the unforgiving sun.

Thrule reinforcements were making their way from the north, hundreds of them streaming down like ants from the hillside with rune-scribed boomerangs on their backs as they surveyed the dead. The broken bodies lay strewn from rim to rim in the valley, among the ruined columns and the toppled masonry and the bleached, lifeless bones of the old dragon lord empire. Vultures had already started to gnaw, hunched about the crumpled shapes in the sand, tearing chunks of flesh in red beaks.

Vetra stared dazedly at the dragon temple—an old, silent mausoleum, its facade of stone glimmering in strange, inexplicable mystery. Regal and austere, it stood towering over the dragon lord's last stronghold and the insignificant band of survivors with an ancient, ominous grandeur.

The dragon claw was gone. Gefzad, Nhfer, Samos and Sebju

among others had perished. The great gate was closed, doubtless never to be opened again. The Behundrians were trapped within, like the last unfortunate invaders from bygone days. A chill ran through Vetra's body as he envisaged the horror they must face at the claws and spewing acid of the guardians.

He scratched his head as new questions arose. Macemas had spared them, for reasons which were not quite clear. Was it not by his hands, and his companions, that they had spilled blood on sacred soil? A foul taste fluttered at the back of his throat as he eyed those who lay in mangled heaps before the dragon door, buzzing with flies.

He stepped back with a grim shudder, shaking his head, a hollow feeling in his chest.

His limbs and torso tingled with a dozen cuts. He limped over to where Jhara slumped in an untidy sprawl with others on the steps. Her bare arms and cheeks were dust-caked and smeared with blood; her leather pants were torn, her hair tousled like a drunken doxy's yet she grinned with a lively gleam in her eyes. She had escaped mostly unharmed as had Lehundr, who had a cloth circling his brow and a splint wrapped around his arm, which was either sprained or broken.

The Thrules rounded up the surviving Behundrians to take as prisoners; they helped bury the dead and gave treatment to those Thrules who were injured.

The leader of the arriving company, Arast, approached and addressed the bedraggled group of survivors, "Hail, battleworn. By Zeldra and Dergath! A war of wars you have fought here. I was loath to drive my men faster, lest their hearts give out on them. Pity we could not lend aid. Where is Nhfer?"

"Dead," mumbled Dunon. "Sebju is slain too."

"These are ill tidings!" he cried. He hung his head and wide fingers played idly over the double falchions at his belt. He was a broad and heavy-limbed man for a Thrule and he rubbed his chin with a sweaty hand. "Nhfer summoned us on the magic horn, and we came as quickly as we could."

"Though tardily," Zren pointed out.

The leader flourished a sword. "It is as it is, boy! Men on foot can only travel so fast."

"The last dragon lord has come and gone," announced Dunon with a weary groan, "and will likely never appear again."

The Thrule's eyes glinted. "Macemas, the damned? At this forsaken place? It can't be. Tell me about it!"

Dunon told the tale, motioning to the great dragon fort behind him and tracing measurements in the air describing the size of the guardians. Several of Arast's men gathered to listen spellbound and Lehundr eagerly took up the tale. Vetra and Jhara added their parts when the leader pressed for details. Aus and Zren picked up the story at certain key moments.

After the tale had been told, the chief eyed them with amazement and returned to the battlefield with his men to oversee the cleanup, still shaking his head in awe.

Vetra sighed and turned to face Dunon: "The Behundrians will come searching this place to carve out the jewels when news of the interior reaches Dragonskull."

The Thrule uttered a hollow laugh. "They can try, but the dragons will defy them even in death. You saw what happened to Cthan and his villains."

Vetra shrugged. He could not refute the fact. "That will not stop their thirst for Thrule blood."

Dunon squinted at the dragon fort whose timeless presence had persisted throughout onslaught after onslaught. "The dragons of all beings realized that water was the most precious resource in the lands. More valuable than gold. Or all the jewels of the world. That's why they built this impregnable sanctuary rich with water and gems. They celebrated beauty and life, and presented it in monumental grandeur in the greatest hot spring in all of Behundria and Sahir. They saw the evil that rubies and emeralds and the like wreaked on the greedy hearts of men and grew wary of its lures and perils, and thus hid them away. As the spirit of Macemas pointed out, men like Cthan have still not learned the primal truth."

Zren shook his head in contempt. "The dragon lords are dead, old man, as are all the marshals of Dragonskull, as we all should be. 'Tis a flaming miracle we are standing here right now."

Vetra snorted his agreement. "It's some part of a grander design, which only Dergath knows."

Aus, bursting to get something off his chest, offered an egg-sized garnet to the blood-stained mercenary. "I nabbed it on the way out. You deserve it, I think."

Vetra shook his shaggy head. "The treasure belongs to the dragon lords, not I, at worst the Thrules. Keep it!" He caught the look of painful disapproval etched on Jhara's face.

Dunon shook his head with a laugh. "The bulk of jewels will stay with the dragon lords behind that impregnable wall."

Aus's eyes dropped. "I don't feel right to keep it, Dunon. Cthan learned the error of his ways, when he attempted to steal the mystical eye of the master dragon lord for himself. I have a feeling some doom will come of this." He cast his eyes to the sand.

"Maybe," said Dunon. "You did what you did, perhaps no more than what a nobler man would have done."

"What will you do?" Vetra asked Dunon.

"For now, the captive Behundrians will take the place of the bullocks at Sunswatch and draw water for the Thrules."

"They will rise up," Vetra muttered. "Reinforcements will ride across the desert, ferret you out."

"Let them—we will be ready."

Aus flourished a hand. "We will be ready! We will fight until the end of time. We may die and flee to the hills, but until then, we will continue our vendetta—or retreat north, living in yurts, not the sheltered sacred caves of Zabenzar. We have the map, the garment and a glimpse of the old treasures of the dragon-lords. Their secrets, we know now to be real. The fact that we are alive, tells us much, that the dragon lords are our allies."

Vetra stared and rubbed his chin in admiration for these brave nomads whom he could not help but think were a trifle mad. "Then Dergath be with you!" He laid a hand on Aus's shoulder and gave Dunon a friendly gesture which the Thrules gratefully returned.

With a crinkly eye, Aus pursed his lips. "It'll be sad to see you go, outlander. As far as men go, you're a deserving one."

Dunon murmured his agreement. Zren made no effort to control his grimace and stalked off with cursing grumbles.

"Let us clean up this mess and go," mumbled Aus. "We have many weapons to forge and plans to make. Send riders to the hills on foot to Hruen! Call the other Thrule clans from the north! They will be needing to come down and help us for the aid we have given them in the past. We have offered them sheep for slaughter and supplies when they have had need of it."

The Thrules turned their ponies to the eastern road, but Lehundr hung back from the milling group, pulling at his blood-flecked beard.

"What's wrong, half Thrule?" Vetra inquired with a wry grunt. "Will you not come back with us to Dragonskull, or do you hanker for another shower of dragon bones falling from the sky?"

Lehundr shook his head. His brow creased with warring thoughts. "I grow weary of rogues and swindlers in that dusty town. Cthan has fallen, and an inevitable new order will arise, but the trader's post will decline back into its old habits, I fear. I will head north, my friend, to Vespia, that spire-ridden capital of Sahir. From there? Who knows? A fresh start and a chance to buy some fortune." He scrutinized the mercenary whom he had come to know as a friend. "And you, Vetra? Will you seek more bloody misadventures?"

Jhara broke in sourly, "Aye, will you go with this vagabond and seek out your death?"

Vetra thought for some time, his brows lifting at Jhara's comment, then his gaze drifted to the red glow of the setting sun. "I will take you as far as Dragonskull, Jhara, but no farther, nor will I tarry there. I must return west—to Lausern, the pits and scum dives of Lvendar."

Jhara's lips parted in a desolate look. Her eyes dilated and her lips quivered in despair. "Take me with you," she pleaded.

His eyes passed over her sleek, muscular lines. Keen approval showed in his gaze, but in a brief glimmer of foresight he glimpsed a foul scene: her flesh bloodied and torn during one of his bloody, underground campaigns. "As tempting as it, girl, I fear not." At the look of her crestfallen expression, he added, "The dark places I go are no place for you, as fierce as you are. You're young, inexperienced, have many adventures before you, and many fair men to meet. Maybe you'll take a fancy to one of these hot-headed Thrules." His eyes strayed to a group of hill Thrules digging among the wreckage where Zren stood motioning in heated argument.

She looked away, her sour expression saying all. "They're too short."

Vetra laughed, but quickly stifled his amusement. "Continue your sword practices, Jhara. Find yourself a good teacher, as rare as they are in this world. Dergath's cats, woman, with your skill, you could teach the art yourself!" He paused, shifted, his sweat-draped leather under his mail shirt becoming an uncomfortable burden. "Maybe that headstrong Thrule, Zren, will make a decent swordsman himself one day. He flails like a fish and blunders like a newborn ox, but somehow I see potential in him. You could teach him. Show him how to move and feint. Your zeal and restlessness reminds me of myself in my younger years."

She beamed at the roundabout praise, and a glimpse of the old Jhara came reaching once more in her eyes. There was comfort and protection in the mercenary's gaze, along with the ever-present lure of high adventure, but also the keen promise of death.

"Go then, Vetra. I see where your heart lies. Bloody quests, fighting for the underdog, killing for hire, nothing permanent or satisfying there for me, likely the thrill of a long line of paramours to go along with life on the road. I will remember you, if that means anything. If you remember anything of me, think of a woman who wanted to be at your side, enjoy our trysts, fighting as an equal. It seems you have much to do. Go! I will not hold you back. Nor will I go back with you to Dragonskull—others will make the journey and I will go with them. Return to Dragonskull one day, if you wish. I pray that our paths meet again."

Vetra hesitated, then collected himself, his mouth carved in a crooked grin. "Until our paths meet again then." He tipped his head and walked off. Dergath, but the ways of women were inscrutable.

* * *

So Vetra turned to the dusty road south, but an afterthought struck him, and he halted and turned back to seek out the tearful young woman. The weight of something familiar jingled in his pocket. The others had left, and she was alone on the steps, sitting chin in hands, in despondent self pity. Vetra approached, put on his most amiable face. "Here are three diamonds and rubies that came to me in the dragon temple. They came from about the stony neck of one of the dragon lords." He pushed them into her hand. "Take them and buy you and your brother freedom from the streets of Dragonskull."

An expression of wonder softened her gaze. "You don't want them?"

"I've enough good fortune to last a lifetime." He clapped a hand on his sword, calmly remembering all the death that stalked him through the years, a silent partner treading in his shadow.

She mumbled a dry response. "Nine lives of it. If I could count the times I thought you were dead back in that cavern." Her features frowned and a faraway look clouded her eyes. "Should I be worried about curses and the like cast on these gems?" She flashed them a glance. "Aus seemed serious about that and I heard you agree with him."

Vetra shrugged. "The jewels fell from the dragon lord statue's garland. I see it as an offering he gifted me with, rather than a theft. The spirit of the lord gave them of his own free will. Otherwise I wouldn't have felt compelled to snatch them, and would probably have died back in that dim chamber. It would have been my tomb as well."

Her lips slackened in a grin. "Then go with my blessing, and I thank you. Be gone, mercenary, before I tear up!...a warrior should not cry on a day of victory and good fortune, should she?"

He took her in his arms and her forced veneer peeled away. Her breathless sobs poured out against his chest; her hot breath stormed on his neck, and Vetra, for all his faults in the arena of love, drank in this woman's passion like a stag at the lake, an antidote to the grim business of his trade.

"Come on, Dragonskull's a long ways away!"

CHRIS TURNER

VALLEY OF THE GODS

I

"Hold off, Balir. There's no way we're getting this thing past the bend." Vetravincus halted, his muscles straining, staring ahead down the narrow moonlit ledge where the priest had disappeared. A sheer drop at his side into the canyon below made him wary of his every step.

"It's as heavy as iron," grumbled Balir, his black curls matted in sweat, his swarthy features chased in a grimace. He struggled with the large, unwieldy seashell, all coral-rose and white, that held some mysterious idol, a winged creature of jade coveted by the wizard Caglios. "I curse that priest, Iokru, for tricking us down these wretched paths."

The shell was cumbersome. One man could only carry it for short lengths of time. With two it was manageable. Balir held the strap attached to a brass ring on the back side and Vetravincus the one on the front. Behind them Kalaman trailed: a stocky, steel-helmed mercenary, scimitar belted at his hip. A few feet back was Laskar, the tall, lean crossbowman taking up the rear. Vetravincus, or Vetra as they called him, led the group. He stumbled and cursed on the treacherous path.

"Spare me the grousing," he grumbled. "What's done is done. We have to get this idol out of here before the moon sets."

Kalaman gave a cynical laugh. "The seashell's already enough trouble as it is. High-priest Rojarsh looked ready to slit our throats after we gave him the 'supposed' magic wine cup entrusted to us by your wizard. A commission I wished we hadn't taken from that bloody Caglios."

"You don't have to remind me," said Vetra.

"Don't forget how many gold talons we're getting out of this," murmured Balir.

"It's the only thing keeping me on this fool's errand." Kalaman scratched his coppery beard, loosing a gusty sigh. "Wizards, priests... Who needs them? If we get out of this silly venture alive—" he glanced over the edge into the moonlit canyon below "—the tankards are on me."

"Here, help me fix the strap on this shell," said Vetra. "It's slipping again." He bent to catch it as its spiraled bulk clattered to the stone. Wiping the sweat from his helmed brow, he made a brisk gesture. "We have to haul this thing past that narrowed arch up there. Hard to see much of anything in this gloom. Hope the path widens up again." He stared upward at a sheer cliff one hundred and fifty feet to the blue-black night sky. The ascending ledge carved in the cliff rose up from the base of the canyon. Already they were about a quarter of the way up. The temple city of Old Gyzia lay below, ancient beyond belief. Nothing but a warren of avenues and alleys flanked by carven-beast temples on the canyon floor. Some darkened ways admitted only one person to file through, while other paths were wide enough to walk three elephants abreast. Vetra caught the rustle below of robed priests and their flicker of torches. "Seems as if this place is a rats' haunt. Besthra's teats! This strap unravels again and I'll be breaking somebody's head!" He stopped short, feeling the tug of something alive in his cargo. It was as if the jade idol had a life of its own.

He gaped. The tremor ceased, and he shook off the quivering movement as a product of nerves. "Wonder what the old peacock Rojarsh was doing with it, hoarding this jade piece for all this time? The way he looked at it before it was handed off to us, was as if the the thing was cursed. I'm guessing he was glad to get rid of it."

"As valuable as the thing is, it strikes me as odd," said Balir.

"Who cares?" said Kalaman. His lips quirked in a laugh.

"What of our friend, the priest, Iokru?"

Vetra grunted. "Don't know where that jackal is. Just some stooge of Rojarsh's. So far he's been surly and unreliable. He's so far up the sleeve and cult of the Clam-followers, he'll do anything to appease his master. I've seen his kind before—fanatic, eerie, ready to sell his soul to the devil. I trust him no further than an adder in this swamp of gibbering priests."

"A dangerous snake, if you ask me," growled Balir.

"Looks as if he's not coming back. Deserted us on his scouting mission. We'd better rely on our own resources."

Like a puff of magic—or perhaps having ears on the back of his head—Iokru, a lithe, sinuous figure, came slinking back on long legs. The priest had crept up from behind, not ahead, as if he had looped back through some hidden tunnel in the cliff.

Laskar aimed his crossbow, startled. He looked irritated and dismayed that anyone could appear so inexplicably from behind.

"Back this way," the priest intoned in a dark voice. "The path ahead is too narrow. The junction we passed leads to the *Way of Serpents*. Then it goes down to the lower temples which guard the pool."

Kalaman rolled his eyes. "Snakes, oh joy."

The priest waved a staff which doubled as torch. It was inset with a strange jewel near its tip. Such a jewel matched the disturbing, skull-shaped amulet he wore around his neck. The 'torch', Vetra noticed, had been doused again. It seemed as if the priest preferred the darkness of the night—and the ease to sneak around without notice.

Balir, distrusting the priest, frowned. "Don't sneak up on us like that, shaman. I thought you knew these ways?—'Like the back of your hand', so your high priest said. Now we have to backtrack. Didn't I specifically remember him bidding you to lead us quick as a hare to the pool—some mysterious waterfall?"

Iokru gave a cryptic leer. "My lord spoke the truth. He has great faith in my *abilities*. It has been many years since I've been down these paths..." The priest lifted his stave in airy ease, then he spoke with a serpent-like hiss. "Calm your suspicious minds. To me you are all servants of that head-in-the-clouds traitor, Caglios. I'll get you to the pool. Without fail. All you need do is have trust—" and here he added in an ominous tone "—There you will meet Dapi, your destiny, and you will fulfill your prophetic charge to your master, Caglios."

"Hardly 'my master'," Vetra growled. Yet the mercenary could not help but feel a chill crawl up his spine.

"Bold words, priest," said Balir, but his voice lacked conviction.

The company took to the ledge path again, the passage narrowing to a few feet wide in places. Vetra felt dizzy from the journey down. Now the ascending heights above the canyon floor made him feel sicker at heart. Despite his resilience, navigating high places was not his strength: a handicap while transporting valuable goods, a feeling shared by his hirelings.

Back down in the canyon boulders carved into shapes of gods and beastly things with wings, trunks, strange limbs and faces loomed. From what he could make of it, he saw that the gorge was a long fishbone crossed at right angles with fissures, side valleys and ravines. Temples were cut into the valleys, with crossways and footpaths running high above and sometimes through temples...like the one they trod, which swept up the cliff face like a dark scar.

"Is it really necessary, this circuitous route along this devil-haunted ledge?" Vetra complained.

Iokru stared at him as if he were a simpleton. "No god can be taken from Gyzia valley until it is exorcised, or baptized—cleansed in Otorio, the Waters of Life. A god in limbo will haunt the plane of mortal men for eternity... The proper steps must be taken."

Kalaman gave a sardonic chuckle.

Balir hissed. "What do you mean 'god'? 'Tis a tawdry piece of jade we carry, for Krasson's sake!"

Iokru smiled in condescension. "You know nothing of the power of the gods. Or, how we imprison the essence of our deities in a stone statue in order to make use of a god's power. This idol is jade, which has the power of the moon. It was said that the idol you carry, the falcon-man Dapi, was smeared with moon dust from a magic rock that fell from the sky in a smoldering heap."

"A wives' tale," Kalaman scoffed.

Iokru ignored the remark. "Our god, Meru, is the Old One, the *Great Clam.* He is trapped in a seashell, of some extinct species. His shell covering is like a giant crab's or crayfish's. None really know. His outerbody is secluded in a lower cave. Certain brave acolytes go down to feed it, sometimes to their doom. But should our god escape?" Even the under-priest shuddered in the murk as he seemed to shrink at the thought.

Vetra wondered what hellish world these priests lived in to merit such macabre devotion and constant fear.

Kalaman gripped the hilt of his scimitar and snuffled out a yawn. "All I know is I'm getting paid a hefty bag of gold to get a miserable jade piece out of a canyon where murmuring priests make their home with beast-faced statues."

Iokru pursed his lips; his features clouded with contempt.

Vetra gingerly set down his load. "This 'baptism' as you call it, Iokru, makes me nervous and suspicious. Caglios made no specific mention of any waterfall."

The cleric gave a careless shrug under his priest's vest. "Caglios does not know of our priest-craft here, or the ways of the old gods. He is only a lowly magician reveling in the surface-level powers writ in the common tongue."

"Well, whatever he is," snorted Vetra, "he can still make a serpent turn into a spitting dragon and slither through the air on gilded wings. Such magic I've seen with my own eyes. Let's get a move on. Sooner we complete this mission and get this dead weight off my back, the better."

Iokru's dark eyes seethed at the irreverence of the comment, but he made no reply.

Vetra looked about the shadowy spaces. The cold light of the rising moon stained the stone and dusty ways in an ethereal pall. The god-carven faces on the cliff wall seemed to leer out at him. What the priests and acolytes used for food, he had no idea. Did they hunt buzzards out in the wastes? There were rumors that cannibalism was practiced in these canyons…and things far worse. Kidnappings. Torture and bondage. Victims snatched from the streets of the nearest city never to be seen again. Devil worship. Rites of terrible and obscene nature. Still, people should be free to worship whatever gods they liked. Vetra clenched his hands, sword hefted in a ham fist with a quiver of disgust. Just as long as it did not affect him. Lausern, gargoyle-towered capital of the province of Lvendar, loomed two leagues away from this mad, sorcerer-priest pit—a city of filchpurses and blackguards, vagrants, merchants, farmers and politicians. Yet all were known to kowtow to the priests. Tithing to certain temples, some of the more affluent patrons offered gold and riches to their gods and would wait to reap the reward of their spiritual transactions. These, in the form of more profitable trade, rains for crops, higher yields, success in elections, wine, women and long life. Basically all the trappings that came with the priests' chanting and thaumaturgy.

Vetra bared his teeth. More a black market ring than a service. If one didn't support a certain faction, certain priests would blackmail them with tastes of their voodoo-like curses. An unethical, 'unworthy of the gods' practice. Vetra remained skeptical of this 'fair-trade' agreement. Any god that accepted material wealth in return for blessings was as greedy and corrupt as any mortal man—a force which could just as easily turn on the benefactor and extort more wealth.

He scowled at the realization. He thought of the bondage that had manifested in these 'arrangements'. But yet, it was not his concern. Licking his lips, he curled the fingers of his free hand around his hilt. His role was to deliver the goods and be gone from this degenerate maze. Luckily he had received a third of his earnings already from Caglios. The bloodless wizard had warned him of the consequences of double-dealings. He had shown him what had happened to those who had attempted to take their advance and flee the city without fulfilling their part of the bargain. Vetra shuddered, recalling the husk of a man Caglios kept in chains, encaged in a dome of glass. The wretch looked to have no tongue, gibbering through a set of froth-flecked lips: blinking, staring into space with an idiot's leer, as if his mind had been blasted of all thinking power. All the while the wizard's two subhuman imps tottered around in witless unison ministering to Caglios's every need.

Vetra shook off the chilling memory. Upon more of Iokru's sidelong glances, his distrust of their smiley-eyed guide only grew. "No tricks, priest," he said. "We gave your two-toothed master, Rojarsh, Caglios's gold and a magic vessel in return for our transporting this ghoulish idol on to Caglios. We expect safe passage out of here."

Laskar's endorsement came as an emphatic grunt.

Iokru gave a croak of laughter. He lifted a shell-ringed finger in an attempt to lighten the moment. "What you see below are a series of tombs and crypts which are set at the back of the many temples. We call it the *Way of Temples*. Or the *Alley* for short. 'Tis our main area of worship. Rites and secret communions are conducted on a regular basis. Each sect has its own liturgy and procedures, customized to its gods."

Fidgeting with impatience, Vetra's mind wandered upon the dark tales overheard regarding the horrific blood legacy of dark worship. Nameless civilizations had sprung up and crumbled since the day the first primitive temples erected here had been chiseled out of the bare rock. How old these were was a detail lost in time. All a fantastic blur in his mind, as were those ancients who had carved them. His impulses to take on this mission had been various: wealth, adventure, not a small amount of challenge.

His eyes caught a brief glimpse of Balir behind him, grunting under the weight of the load. Vetra grinned a wry grin. Balir was a good man, a maverick, one to be trusted. His loose-fitting mail did not mask the hard lines of his sinewy body. His hair was dark and cropped short with loose curls along with sideburns slanting down to a bristling beard. Kalaman's crop of golden hair gleamed lightly underneath peaked helm. The merc's strong, surly features and flattened fighter's nose promised a skull-bashing to any who defied him. Laskar's locks were braided and tied back, naturally complementing his amber, catlike eyes. The man, as light as a lynx on his feet, wore no armor. Long, ivory-engraved knives hung from his hips, a leather baldric strung across his lanky shoulders held his crossbow.

Vetra recalled how he had recruited Balir at the *Grand Jackal's Inn* in the laborers' quarters of Lausern. The randy rogue's paws were reaching readily for some wench. Kalaman he had recruited from a ring fight in the city's brewmasters' district—a hefty, hawk-eyed ruffian, handy with knives and prize-fighting for his next meal against the meanest circle of blood-hungry bashers Lausern had to offer.

Like phantoms the company of five drifted through the shadows. Below, a vague world of rustling shapes and flickering torches flitted. To dispel the gloom, Iokru lit his torch with flint and tinder and beckoned them on. Vetra saw the priest wore only furred boots and a thin, sleeveless vest decorated with fur and shells. His naked shoulders were bronzed by daytime sun and flexed not unmuscled. The flat-topped conch for a helm, plumed with feathers, made him look almost like a demon himself. Vetra shook his head, not knowing whether to chuckle or feel pity for the rogue. The ineffective thing would not last long in a battle.

Battle, why was he thinking battle? He reached down to touch the wicked *garbandia* knife strapped to the inside flank of his right calf. Should his sword ever fail him...the curved, hidden blade would prove a worthy backup. He laughed. Why would it fail? The sword was rare, strong and perfectly balanced, the most valuable thing on his person, given by a noble benefactor in return for hunting down thieves who had been stealing gold from him.

Vetra's eyes burned with a calculating flame as he thought of this mission. He shook back his long, shiny, straight black mane with no small unease. Only the sound of boots crunching on stones marked their passing, mingled with the jingle of mail of armed men. Vetra's was perhaps the quieter of those mercenaries' mailshirts, oiled and fitting his battle-hardened body well under a green sleeveless jerkin. He looked less the common mercenary or thief among them as the nobleman in this flaring surcoat of brown and red silk draped over his leather and mail. The leather girdle at his waist was of fine quality. It held a scabbard of no small worth. Those who saw Vetra would see a man not softened by idle living, or plump by decadent eating but one whose lean muscle showed through his fine raiment.

His mind strayed to Caglios and he frowned, recalling the moment when the wayward wizard had given him a relic to bring to the pool. There were very specific instructions on how such relic was to be used to 'bridle' the idol. Instructions which seemed to come in and out of his memory, as if they had been imprinted there by unnatural forces. Vetra's lips pinched in a frown. Something about his last visit to the wizard's workshop raised his hackles...a space of time elapsing of which he had no recollection.

His free hand brushed the relic. A collar of rough metal. Was it iron? What exactly was it? It looked like a ring of strong quality to encircle the neck of an unruly hound. With uncut gems embedded in the once molten metal—gems, serpentine and carnelian, it exuded a presence of magic. He felt its rough contours again in the folds of his vest. He also felt a supernatural danger tingle in his fingers as it trickled on up his forearm.

He recalled accepting it, despite his reservations. He wondered if the collar were a talisman given him by the wizard to brand or track him. Vetra resisted the urge to crush the thing under his boot, or toss it down one of the winding alleys that disappeared into blackness. The thing pulsed with an eerie glow when exposed to even the faintest light. More than once he had seen the dusky, fox-faced Iokru eyeing his furtive gropings in his pockets for the 'collar', while the priest twirled the plumed feather on the back of his headdress as if ambitious thoughts brewed in his mind. How glad he would be to rid himself of that priest and his penetrating leer—and the collar.

Why the wizard Caglios had enlisted him, Vetravincus, for the task, was still a mystery. He could have hired someone else with more experience, and for less gold. The problem was irksome. One which brought Vetra a vision of doom.

Torch clutched in his hand, Iokru led the men with an assured stride. Ahead, before an oval patch of light, two fangs of rock rose from the stony path. They had all the semblance of stalagmites. Treading closer, Vetra saw they looked like the polished incisors of a giant, saber-tooth tiger—a primitive thing carved of stone by hands from an ancient time. Out of the tunnel they stumbled. Lo and behold, out of the mouth of the stone-carved beast, they shambled onto another, even narrower ledge. The canyon spread wide before their eyes. Across the shadowy expanse, a sheer cliff faced them with similar grim visages and carven figures. The glare of red torchlight and voices below bore testament to company.

Vetra peered. Nothing could be seen but indistinct motion. The ledge wound across the canyon face into shadows, where carven faces teetered above them and led, much to Vetra's dismay, to the great looming eye socket of some ghastly monkey face, the shadowy exterior of some other temple. To this disquieting gap, Iokru bid them, with an expression of sinister amusement.

The priest extinguished his torch, and once again, they trudged in semi-darkness. The sky opened up to admit a wash of silver moonlight. Iokru pushed ahead and turned to scowl at Balir and Vetra: "You two had better muffle your grunts."

The monkey god loomed over them, several man-heights in size, crudely carved into the sheer cliff. Bulging lips curled back in a scornful snarl to show a gaping mouth of square-blocked teeth. The god-effigy exulted in some inside knowledge. Vetra knew it. Its grisly eyes were dark pools into another world. To his relief they passed the face and Iokru signaled them down a set of stairs under the monkey's rounded chin. The ledge's curve of narrow rock continued where the stairs left off, looping down to a place only three times a man's height above the canyon floor.

On quiet feet the troupe followed the priest on this exposed ledge, smoothed by thousands of passing acolytes. The avenue below was a natural floor, partly sandy, the rest stone.

Laskar cocked his crossbow, as if sensing the weight of acute danger.

The torches guttered. The sound of chants rose ahead in a low, murmurous thrum that brought the hairs up on Vetra's back.

Despite his eccentric habits, Iokru led the company with an air of stealth. His plumed headdress bobbed in noiseless tribute in the windless air while the red glare of torches gleamed and the first hint of crackling flames came to their ears.

Three priests with bison masks appeared in front of them. These men moved swiftly, casting furtive glances over their shoulders. With brisk grunts, they squeezed past the load carriers on the high ledge in the ruddy gloom. A tense moment passed when Vetra and Balir halted, setting down their load and gripping their swords in their free hands. Iokru indulged the trio with a serene nod, which they returned with a chilling stare. The priests passed by without comment.

Iokru grimaced as the men resumed their heaving. Vetra remained somewhat perplexed by the bison-headed priests' haste. Iokru steered the company closer to a group of forty or more figures massed below on the other side of the canyon. The group was dressed in bizarre animal costumes and rodent-like masks, red furred with pointed ears and black snouts. The figures' backs were to them, and the throng gathered about a glaring fire, observing their ceremonious rite with the absorbed attention of slaves fulfilling a task for an unforgiving master.

"We must pass near them," Iokru hissed. "There's no other way but an hour's detour through unlit tunnels that drop to steep crevasses. Even then, the way is not sure. If you value your skins, utter no word. Do not insult these acolytes or get caught in the middle of their ceremonies."

"Who are they?" inquired Vetra.

"Members of the Rat Fang sect." His teeth glinted. " The *Ratmangers*. A gang of extreme fanatics, prone to blood sacrifice and kidnappings."

"How enchanting," Balir remarked.

Vetra took note of the unpriestly weapons belted at their hips, including knives, hooked bills. Spears were clutched in white-knuckled hands. The muscled guards who moved among them remained stationed at disquieting intervals.

"'Tis the celebration of dark Dathra they hold," Iokru whispered. "To commemorate the five hundredth year of their cult. They resurrect their god every season. Tonight is the first ceremony of the year, spring *yule*, on the full moon."

"Just our luck," muttered Kalaman.

The pungent smell of incense and herbs drifted in the night air, along with the stench of burning blood. Vetra's lips peeled back in distaste. He winced at the cliff looming up in front of him, sporting a gigantic rat sculpture, sixty feet high, rearing upon its hind legs, sniffing the air with ham paws outstretched—the embodiment of the Rat Fang god. The effigy stood on a massive stone dais below which spread a colonnaded court whose flaming interiors teemed with the priests who were conducting their macabre ritual.

Along the far side of the cliff the five crept, with Vetra and Balir taking care not to jiggle their load. Sounds echoed in the valley and Vetra had no doubt the priests had the ears of wolves, despite the low, background chanting and the shuffling feet that masked the company's progress. Vetra caught a faint glint amid the gathering, of chains fastened on heavy rings bolted into the polished stone. The iron loops held back some obscene rat creature, grown huge beyond imagining. The monstrosity had something of an aardvark's body and a mix of fur and iridescent scales on hide and flanks.

The rodent swished its powerful tail and pawed at its furry behind, fretting and gnashing at its bonds. Plumes of flame kept the creature contained in a tight, fiery circle. If the creature could emerge from that circle...Vetra shuddered. Whoever tended the creature was surely endangering his life.

Whenever the creature stalked too close to the flames, its rodent-like snout bore a blast of heat. And when it did, the crowd ululated in a wave of awe. Torches guttered; fires raged around the ring. The acolytes bowed and murmured dark supplications to their flesh-and-blood rat-like god, *"Ratang! Ratang! We worship you in death. With this crimson elixir of life we bathe our souls."* Such glories extended to the looming behemoth that towered above in carven glory. Bowing and falling prostrate in devotional vacuity with each sizzle and flare of the sacred flames, the followers doused their spears and sharp gleaming knives in vats of blood to the side and smeared it on their brows gleaming above the masks. Others smeared their thighs. Several gripped live rats despite the creatures' struggles and gnashing teeth questing their fingers. The throats of these creatures they quickly cut in sacrifice to the great rat poised in hideous splendor above them. The devotees let the blood spill over their grotesque masks. Some stuck out tongues to drink of the rodents' blood. The rodent carcasses were then hurled to the great stone dais before the rat creature which devoured them in noisy gulps.

Vetra felt the sweat bead on his brow. Snuffling and pawing, the creature rose on its hind legs as the devotees' voices rose in a chant of shade-possessed unison.

On a signal to Balir, Vetra paused to wipe his brow. He twisted to get a better grip on the strap, clutching his sword, but the wretched thing had the ill timing of unraveling just as the chant's refrain ended. Before he could catch it, the conch slipped out of his grasp and thudded to the ground.

Vetra grunted a vile curse. A few heads turned from the gathering, alerted by the sharp, echoing clap of shell on stone. On a hissing gesture from Iokru, the men of the party dove headlong and fell flat on their bellies.

Vetra stifled more oaths as he sank in a grim crouch. The toxic glare of Iokru felt like a flaming knife in his back from ten feet away.

The collar he carried slipped from his pouch and lay gleaming in the path. Though Vetra swept a hand out to retrieve it, Iokru's keen eyes glistened in the darkness. The priest's body stiffened. His gaze drank in the sight of the corroded, but magical ring-collar. Vetra did not miss his envious sneer.

"If high priest Rojarsh knew you had the ring of Dapi, the falcon man," he hissed, "he would have gutted—"

"Would he now?"

The priest scowled and bit his tongue. He knew he had said too much.

Kalaman and Laskar scrambled to help Vetra and Balir drag the shell several paces past the ratmen's rite but Iokru jerked a thumb back toward the monkey temple. "Go back the other way!

'Tis safer that way."

The shell's two halves had wrenched ajar and within, Vetra could see the dusky outline of a hawk-like idol. He snapped it shut with an uneasy grimace.

Iokru crept at their heels, his face a ghoul-like mask as he urged them on faster. Whether the *ratmangers* saw their mad scramble up the path toward the monkey's face, or the glint of green and red light off the strange gems on the collar, Vetra did not know. He quickly stuffed the collar back under his belt, glad to hear no swift scud of feet piping after them, and glad that his crew of men was somewhat concealed, squatting in the inky shadows.

Several priests pointed blood-soaked fingers up at them and gave voice to hoarse jeering calls. Spears lanced from below and clattered up the cliff to strike rock and seashell. A steel tip brushed Vetra's mail and skittered harmlessly off, prompting him to curse.

The rat-masked acolytes shambled forward but they could not scale the cliff. The ledge was a dozen feet above their heads. Others were scrambling up the steep stairway farther down the avenue that gave access to the ledge.

"Quick!" hissed Iokru. "Up! Into the eye of the Jeering Monkey. We can outwit these rat-priests in the tunnels."

Another flurry of spears clattered up at them, one jabbing Laskar's boot above the ankle. He plucked it out of the tough leather and hurled it back down at them. A shrill cry came as a man was impaled by a steel tip. Harsh voices sounded in the fiery gloom: shouts and promises of vengeance.

Iokru's eyes bulged. "Now you've done it! You've drawn blood against the *ratmangers*. If they associate me with your aggressive hackwork...there'll be war among the clam worshipers and the ratmen!"

Laskar shrugged, not seeming to mind either way.

Vetra set down his load. He frowned and signaled Balir and

the two edged their way down the path toward their enemies. They drew their weapons. Kalaman, grinning fiercely, was close on their heels. A crew of forerunners had gained the ledge and were clambering up at them. Vetra saw four furred and masked priests come charging up the slope, spears in hand. One hurled a shaft at close range, narrowly missing Kalaman. It slammed into Balir's chest mail just above the left breast. In a rage, he pulled it out and hurled the spear back at the offender. The missile caught the attacker on his bare thigh. He snuffled out a cry and sank to his knees, clutching at his leg. His three rat-masked cronies pressed around him, white teeth flashing in the gloom through their masks.

Iokru moaned. As Vetra and Kalaman rose to meet them, Laskar trained his crossbow and loosed, as calmly as if he were practicing in a noonday meadow. A bolt hissed through the air and took the nearest one in the chest. He fell back howling into the arms of his fellows.

"Stop! Stop!" Iokru hissed. He clutched at his headdress, stamping his feet like a spoiled child.

But there was no stopping. Kalaman twisted sideways and brought back his blade. Ducking a lightning-fast spear tip, he took a two-handed swing. The dusky priest went down in a wash of crimson. He booted the gasping man down the ledge. Vetra stepped past Kalaman's hulking frame and parried the glinting spear that came whistling for his own throat. His blade came fast over his shoulder, smashing down onto the man's spear. The rat-faced man blinked dumbly at his cloven weapon. Vetra ran cold steel through the man's belly before he knew what hit him.

Iokru, jaw-agape, cried out in misery, "What are you doing? Have you a death wish?"

"Shut your mouth, priest!" thundered Vetra. "Or lend us a hand. Do you expect us to sit here and get pincushioned by your cronies?"

Iokru shook his head in frustration. "Don't you see, don't

you know?—Fools! They will flay us alive. The ratmen will feed us to their god. Did you not see the thing? Quick! Into the monkey's cave!"

Sheathing his dripping sword, Vetra stalked back to the shell. He and Balir hauled it on.

The whole episode had taken less than two minutes. More ratmen were on their way, judging from the feverish clamor and sounds of boot heels and men's shouts. But they were a minute or more distant. Iokru grimaced. He shuttled the men up the path in a black mood, herding his charges toward the dark monkey-god face that loomed like a monster out of a ghostly dream.

Vetra's gaze caught the reflection of torchlight on the spears. The flashing of knives. He had a split-second vision of dozens of ratmen crawling up the switch-backed ledges after them…with a shake of head, he ducked back into the shadowy gap of the monkey's eye then staggered on with his cargo.

The darkness closed about them. Iokru lit the torch with shaky hands. He prodded them along with the hopeless resignation of a condemned man. The eerie tunnel reached out like a dusky glove, a passage with no end. Down the smooth stone, they lurched. Balir and Vetra panted with their ungainly load. Many smaller side passages gaped to left and right. Some of these the priest took, others he ignored with a wrinkle of his nose. His choices seemed almost arbitrary—ill-hewn, chill, damp. Depressing passages with no markers or carven glyphs or signs of human hewing to identify them. He weaved down side passages, ones which looked to have seen no human foot for decades.

"What's with all this plunging hither and yon?" demanded Vetra. "Don't we have a destination in mind?"

"The roundabout scramble is necessary, if we wish to survive!"

"We should have taken that hour-long detour," growled Vetra.

The priest said nothing. There were no signs of pursuit. They had either lost the ratmen, or the rat worshipers had given up.

The tunnel widened. To their good fortune, open air rose again above their heads.

The sour-faced priest urged them down another intersecting canyon lit only by dim moonlight that streamed down from a rocky gap. The canyon itself, however, felt dead of life and dark as a tomb. Laskar and Kalaman took up the idol and struggled with their burden. The party came down into a smaller avenue than the last—silent, dry, sepulchral. Only the whisper of a cold draft brushed their cheeks.

They passed under a massive arch that blotted out the moon. Iokru looked back and nodded in new satisfaction.

Vetra's strong fingers closed reflexively about the collar. Muttering second thoughts to himself, he swallowed back a bitter taste in his throat.

Caglios had given him the collar. A thing that made him feel dread. Green gems glowed dimly, yet felt cold as ice in his palm. A voice sprang out at him in his mind. Caglios's? It was as if from a dream he heard the wizard's words echoing like the roar one hears in a seashell:

"Douse the idol in the magic spring. Ring the collar round the winged one's neck. A reward awaits...when I have the idol in my hands, you will be rich men. Be wary! Dapi bears little mercy..."

Vetra scowled at the words. No less the memory of the wizard's imperial way of speaking. He shrugged it off, thinking it no more than apprehension, or some inner noise of foreboding.

Iokru studied the outlander, as if reading his thoughts. His dusky complexion turned a shade darker. "There—" he pointed. "The temple of Dapi resides down this alley, past the winged arch. Inside you will find your god. Be swift!"

"You are not coming?" pressed Vetra.

The priest glanced at him as if he had not heard the question.

A flicker of distrust crossed Balir's face. "Why is it your master, Rojarsh, who worships the clam, possessed something belonging to a competing god?"

Iokru paused, his face inscrutable. "Best for you not to ask such questions. You are priest killers and will all die. I await you here at the entrance to the god's sanctum. Return when you have completed your deed."

Balir snorted out a curse. "You fear the dark judgments of your gods, don't you, you egg-sucking priest? Can't stand a little blood? A coward, like the rest. The mystic mumbo jumbo of Dapi—it's all a front."

Iokru showed yellow teeth in a sneer. "You speak words of a fool."

Balir chuckled at the cleric's reaction. An evil glint pierced the priest's eye. Vetra saw the left incisor was filed like a vampire's.

"I'm not afraid of anything," said Iokru. "Just practical."

"Practical, eh? We'll see," Kalaman snorted. "Not afraid of anything except the ratmen's toothy god."

Iokru stooped to light a spare torch concealed on his person. He pushed the thing into Vetra's hand which guttered in the chilly drafts that wafted up the corridor. Kalaman and Laskar took up the conch and moved on like wraiths.

Vetra's eyes traced distrustful paths into the gloom. A few moments later, he snatched a look back. The priest, like the silent ghost he was, had vanished. With him, his malignant aura.

Vetra glanced about, tracing his fingers on the eerie, porous walls around him. The rock was scored with the faintest markings: cryptic runes and figures. "Something must have spooked our priest."

"Like the rat men and their blood lust?" Balir gusted.

"Well, he's gone now," muttered Vetra. "We'll have to find the blasted pool on our own. He did give us directions to follow."

"Without the priest I don't think we can easily find our way out of here," Balir mumbled, "especially with those ratmen crawling about like beetles. Not to mention if Iokru slinks back to

Rojarsh babbling about some collar..."

"And what of it?" growled Vetra. "By sunrise, we'll be able to see our way about these ravines—ratmen, collar or not. Hopefully these rodent men will have crept back to their burrows by then."

"We're stuck like rats in a maze," observed Kalaman. "Forgive the pun. I never knew these temple grounds were so extensive."

"I would hope to be out of here *before* sunrise," muttered Balir.

"Caglios gave specific instructions on how to 'activate the idol'." Vetra blinked, his mind elsewhere. "*Put the collar on first, lest the falcon's wrath burst.*"

"What's with the banal rhyme?" grunted Balir.

"How am I to know?" Vetra, jarred from his daydream, grumbled his displeasure. "The ways of wizards are beyond me."

II

Side passages branched everywhere but led nowhere. The four mercenaries kept to the main way on the priest's advice, with Vetra pausing at each cross-tunnel to listen for the hostile pad of ratmen. But no sign of babbling voices or bobbing torches came from the dimness. The priest perhaps had lost them in all his taxing twists and turns. As for Dapi's sanctum, they would see...

Vetra heard trickling water up ahead. Also the patter of feet and restless flap of wings. Rats? Bats? The sounds had him shivering. They halted, ears pricked. Eyes darted overhead at a sudden movement. The dark flitting shape of a buzzard passed over the moon. In the open spaces above, dim stars hung in the night sky.

Vetra urged the others on down the cracked, stone-paved path. Balir frowned at the fantastic carvings on the walls: gargoyles, seraphims, the heads of giraffes, turtles, various other wild beasts, all chiseled in marvelous detail by masterful tools. He scratched at the stubble on his chin, eyes seeking any hidden threats in the shadows draping the carvings. Kalaman pulled at his golden hair, fingers hooked on the hilt of his scimitar. Laskar said no word, only his hand clutched tensely at his crossbow.

A lone torch burned from a bracket in the wall. The smell of rank pitch came to Vetra's nostrils. Who had lit it? Other torches had been lit and hung on the richly-hewn walls in niches at various intervals.

On they shambled, each feeling a sensation of crawling unease.

As the priest had mentioned, an arched way opened on the wall to the right. Ahead the path petered out to blackness.

"The end of the line," Kalaman murmured.

Vetra peered through the arch, grimacing as he might look into the lair of a man-eating spider. The trickling of water grew louder. As they passed through the portal, two pools glimmered into view on the far side of the chamber abreast the wall. Twin waterfalls spilled down the cliff facing them to make a small wake in the pools. The waters were of two different colors—dark crimson and yellow umber. Several torches lit the chamber's high ceiling.

On wary feet they advanced, weapons gripped, lips parted in wonder. The pools were deep, without discernible bottom. Vetra took careful steps while Laskar crept close on his heels with one hand gripping a ring on the conch. Kalaman stalked behind him, hoisting the back ring.

Ancient bird statues jutted out in fiendish synchrony from the walls at regular intervals with parted beaks. Hawks? Falcons? The statues had heavily muscled male-torsos and claw-like feet. A few ranged over seven feet tall. In the looming stone above, more anthropomorphic shapes stood carved out of polished onyx and dolomite to leer down with little welcome.

Vetra recalled the inquiries he had made about the legend of the falcon god. Local bards had sung of a prince of Araham who long ago had wanted to fly. He had become so obsessed with the thought that he had sought out a dark wizard to fulfill his wish. Prince Dapi was enslaved by the very magic that gave him his power: his wings and talons. The wizard had forced Prince Dapi to do his bidding and the monarch became like a god, enacting terrible deeds by the light of the moon, worshiped by votaries by day, and thus the wizard gained power and acclaim beyond measure. As to what had happened to the wizard, nothing was known for certain, but it is said his passing was not a pleasant one. The legend spoke thus, and so the crumbling mausoleum of the wizard had writ on its entablatures. The deathless God-Prince Dapi lived on, shunned by man and beast while the cursed mausoleum was forgotten.

The legend was no more fantastic than any of the hundred others that floated on the lips of jackleg bards and skalds about the lands.

Balir fingered his blade with a nervous glance. "I have bad feelings about this, Vetra. All these tons of rock, all these vile faces embedded in the stone...how can they bring anything but a curse upon us?"

Vetra exhaled a soft breath. They did look down on them as if he and his men were no more than mice for the taking.

"And this baneful thing you clutch. What is it?" Balir mumbled.

"A thing to contain and bind the statue."

Balir gave a skeptical grunt. "A cursed relic the wizard gave you for no good, or gain."

"Why don't we just split the talons Caglios gave you?" Kalaman suggested. "Leave the old goat in the lurch. Leave the idol here for Iokru and his ghouls to fight over."

Vetra's eyes smoldered. "After all the trouble we have gone through! What of our oath? The dangers of crossing the wizard are not small." He scowled through his teeth. "Still, there is something in what you say. I promised the spellcaster I would deliver and I am a man of my word—unless thieves and liars double-cross me."

"You're a stupid fool, Vetra," Kalaman snorted. "Your code of honor will get us all killed. I don't trust the wizard. What do we owe him? I like not this chamber. I would not revisit it or this temple for a thousand talons!"

"Gather your wits about you," hissed Vetra. "Are we rodents or men? Let's finish this. Swear on it again!"

With grudging murmurs, they all did. Vetra's eyes probed the dark, shadow-chased ceiling. He thought at one time this place had been a cave; but for the pool and faint mist spray, the chamber was mostly bone dry. He traced his fingers along one of the statues, a horned falcon with long, pointed beak. It was poised on human legs and torso, possibly a depiction of Dapi in elder times. The stone was smooth to the touch, remarkably smooth. The realism was astounding and a chill ran up Vetra's back, for it was carved almost with uncanny skill, as if stone could become living flesh at any moment. He stepped back, expecting the shape to flutter to life. But it did not.

His eyes wandered. He guessed the waterfalls came from some spring higher up in the sprawling mantle of rock. Two hundred feet if an inch were they down in the canyon, judging from the patch of open sky that showed a grudging moonlight. Stalactites pricked down from the rest of the ceiling which had been carved and polished into the shape of sharp teeth. A grotesque, bat-like falcon looked hewn out of nothingness in those shadowy spurs. Vetra gave a shudder.

A swish of feet alerted them. Wheeling, the mercenaries gave ground with cold steel swift in their hands. A hunched form shambled forth from a dimly-lit archway somewhere in the back of the chamber.

A woman...Though this one was no beauty, with her hunch-back, and drooping ears peeking from a wisp of thinning silver hair. She seemed like an old fossil dug from the deep passages. Waist and torso were clad in thick, rough furs. Parched skin was dewlapped on the throat. Apart from some furs wrapped about torso and waist, the rest of her withered body was naked. Though she shuffled like a century old turtle, her lustrous eyes burned with a glare of intelligence.

"Who are you, woman?" Vetra called. He stepped closer.

"They call me Nimeska," she answered. "I was born and raised here in the canyons. So my father, and his father before him."

"You gave us a jolt, sneaking up on us like that," grunted

Vetra. He re-sheathed his blade.

She chuckled, a rich, gravelly sound. "I am grateful for your indulgence. Wherefore do you come to Dapi's sanctuary? Nobody has come into this chamber for years but me. 'Tis not usual to see the like of outlanders—and armed ones at that." She gestured at their bared weapons. Her eyes raked the magnificent conch gleaming under the torchlight.

"We have our private errand to attend to."

"Oh?" Her eyes narrowed in suspicion.

Vetra motioned. "And you? What's your business here?"

"I light the altar, nothing more, as is our custom in this temple city. If any altar remains unlit or untended in Gyzia, a terrible curse will fall on us." Her cheeks flushed the color of old redwood.

"It seems a harsh reward," Balir said.

"Another old wives' tale," spat Kalaman. He struck off, staring with critical contempt at the sinister statues and the two pools lurking by the far wall. The water that trickled down the face into the twin pools tinkled like skeleton fingers on ivory.

"Tell me, why does Dapi sit idle while the other gods in these temples burn with so much oil and fire?" asked Vetra.

The old temple keeper thought for a while then shrugged. "'Tis rumored that a century passed and the falcons flew to the other side of the earth, and with them the spirit of Dapi. The cult died with it." She sighed through her crooked teeth. "Their messengers had abandoned them who were their very sources of power. The oracle of Sarle would have other thoughts on the matter. Yet she hasn't been seen in years."

"I heard the legend had something to do with a prince," Vetra ventured.

Nimeska croaked out a sound of amusement. "Well, your version is as good as mine." Her laugh was hoarse as a crow's. "Do your mysterious deeds as you must, mercenary. I have no doubt it has something to do with a transfer of coin from one man's greedy clutch to another. But desecrate not the altars of the old ones! Nergid, the wizard who gave Dapi his godlike powers, sleeps, but he is not dead. Aye, they both sleep—" she trailed off, her starry eyes staring wild-eyed at the conch on the floor and Vetra believed the old crone had guessed their dark purpose. "I feel a plague in the air tonight," she went on. "This very temple stirs with madness—perhaps an evil waft that you have brought with you."

Balir grunted. "Careful what you speak, woman, or I'll—"

Vetra waved him back. He smiled, gave Nimeska an understanding nod, sensing an ally in this odd-mannered temple keeper. "We have a deed to perform here, as you have no doubt already guessed. I hope you could advise us on it."

The old keeper pushed forth palms. "I wish no part of your rites. Dark purpose lingers in it. I smell death and danger lingering in your presence. This fancy shell you tote—what is it?" Shuffling forward, she patted its curled lid before Vetra could retract it and she leaned over the case, starting curiously at the dull echoes of something apparently large inside.

"I know—" She tapped her nose. "It has something to do with *Dapi*." She gusted a loud grunt. "Be on your guard. Dapi is not a kind god. Ratmen abound. They pad through these dark ways like restless vermin. 'Tis the hour of the rodent. I feel them, skulking and crawling..."

"You're a bundle of joyous news, aren't you, old woman?" chided Kalaman. "Give us something positive to think about in this house of horrors."

The old keeper fixed the mercenary a dark look. With a weary sigh, she shuffled up the passage from where she had come, humming to herself an unsettling tune.

Balir gave a dour chuckle. "Well, so it goes. Shall we slit our throats now, or simply fall on our swords?"

Vetra gestured. "Quiet. Let's get this 'baptism' over with."

"To hell with baptism!" cried Kalaman. "Are you insane,

Vetra? I say we leave this cursed thing here and buck Caglios's charge. Keep our gold."

"The priest Iokru, is gone," mumbled Balir. "I agree. No support from that slinking jackal. Nothing but a load of mumbo jumbo comes from his lips every time he speaks."

"There are merits to your arguments," Vetra mused. He pulled at his chin, but the warning of Caglios brought a cold knot of dread to his stomach, not to mention the priest Iokru's sinister hints. "Let's douse the wretched idol with some of this lighter-colored water and be done with it." Vetra's mouth sagged as he watched Balir start to hack and pry at the lips of the clam. "Are you daft?" he cried.

"I'm trying to get a peek at it."

"You'll damage the idol!"

Vetra strode over to help his impatient henchman. Together they pried open the shell. None of them repressed a gasp of disgust. Teeth clenched, they lifted the statue gently on its side and set it upright beside the crimson pool. The thing was a hideous monstrosity, having a falcon's head, a set of leprous human hands and arms as well as bat-like wings folded over its stone-ribbed back. Clawed feet with four-taloned toes had the squat thing standing at half a man's height, nursing a malevolent smirk with hungry, down-turned eyes and a vicious, pointed beak. It had every look of some stony devil from a primeval time.

Balir examined it with a shudder. "'Tis a repulsive thing."

"You think?" Kalaman grunted, his fingers twitching. "Surely this old mallard won't win any beauty awards." He pressed his palms together in distaste.

Balir gestured. "Now the business with these pools—which one? Over there, one that tinkles red like blood and one slightly less murky over here, which could be old, spoiled egg yolk."

Vetra's eyes glazed over. "The wizard was vague in his hints."

"Just what we need, a nebulous wizard. So we choose from 'rot' or 'blood'."

"I opt for 'blood'," Laskar murmured. He had stepped out of the shadows and hefted his grim, steel-sprung bow with a decisive grin. It was one of the few times he had spoken.

The other men blinked at him, unused to the archer offering any words at all.

Vetra lifted a hand in resignation. "On with it then." He pulled out the collar from his pouch and stepped forward. "Let me cincture this thing around its neck first. My mind seems hazy on the details. The wizard's instructions seemed clear-cut at the time."

"Give me that!" Balir called. He snatched the collar out of Vetra's hand. "I'll sling it around this cursed thing's neck, while you cup your hands under that waterfall and splash it some then we'll lug it back here—"

"Listen!" Vetra rasped, reaching for his weapon. "Enemies are about. Quick!"

Kalaman crouched on the balls of his feet. Laskar ducked, eyes probing the murk. A patter of feet echoed in the corridor. The mercenaries ran fleet-footed to the archway.

Balir wheeled and stuffed the collar in his pocket.

Booted feet thudded in the stony darkness. Hitching forward, Vetra and Kalaman gripped hilts and ducked to either side of the doorway, raising their blades. Four rat-masked priests burst in, howling in frenzy and menacing Balir and Laskar with spears. Vetra and Kalaman hidden to the side plunged steel through their fur-clad chests. They were cut down to a man and fell screaming in pools of blood.

More rat-masks rushed in from behind, tripped unexpectedly over the fallen bodies.

Kalaman stepped in and parried multiple knife thrusts, his scimitar flashing scarlet ruin. He hacked a hissing attacker from sternum to groin, while Laskar aimed his bow and loosed a bolt into his companion's chest. Not before the man had hurled a knife. The missile stuck in the archer's upper arm, the leather from his jerkin catching the knife's point. Laskar pulled it out and hurled the blade back with his good arm into another's throat. A gurgle of pain echoed in the dimness as a tall figure with rat-mask fell like a stone.

Kalaman and Vetra hacked at enemies who pushed through the arch while Balir joined in the melee. Some uttered ghastly shrieks, others died horribly, blood jetting, screaming last breaths to their rat god. Kalaman stumbled dripping blood like a wounded animal from a spear stab just below his shoulder.

A desperate hand grabbed at Vetra's sword. Kalaman turned and slashed, carving an arm off at the elbow. He roared out a foul oath.

Priests were pouring in like moths. Balir smashed a fist into a masked face. A hole tore through the garishly-pigmented wood. Balir rushed through the knot of attackers, but was pushed back toward the pool with Vetra cursing and shouting.

One of the ratmen staggered backward into the idol which crouched, staring fiendishly in the glare of the flickering torches. The falcon of jade teetered and toppled backward into the pool with a great splash.

Vetra gave a lusty cry. He lunged for the thing, but the idol sank from sight in waters glimmering red in the wake of magical currents. Impossible to get the thing out—a commission that was worth three bags of gold. He was too harassed with stabbing foes to make any difference. He lurched back, blade rasping against steel, while dying men reeled about in agony.

Two snarling attackers hustled to bring him to the ground. Balir jumped in, tore the weapon from one's hands and twisted to confront the other. While their feather-plumed headdresses bobbed in waves of blood fury, he speared a gibbering man with his own weapon through the guts. The other he kicked sprawling into the blood-red pool.

Vetra turned, croaking out a low moan of anguish. He saw a strange, nightmarish shape materialize from the water and settle aside the pool—a stocky, brazen, avian-like mass. Could it be possible?—Dapi? The stone idol had come to life, transformed in some way he could not fathom. Bigger and more menacing…and more gruesome. How had the thing—? But he wheeled, the breath catching in his throat. The statue was of solid jade, but the beak glowed a dark crimson and had hooked on a corpse fished out from the pool.

Vetra and Balir watched as the stone god rose before their eyes. So did several of the priests stare. The thing's lusterless wings bore its weight a few feet off the ground, then it brought itself down again on the bloody floor with a delicate precision. Four-toed claws clacked like goat hoofs on the stone. But was it a god or some demon? Vetra backed away with awe. The creature tossed off the corpse with an indifferent croak and shake of its gore-flecked beak. Vetra's throat groped for a cry that would not come. In mute horror, he scrabbled back, thinking to himself he must be in a depraved dream.

The idol had grown a foot higher. Now it was broader and brimmed with a lurid orange aureole.

Vetra drew back his blade. He swung in a wide circle, making ruin of an eager priest's face and another's knife arm. "Quick!" he shouted at the others through bloody teeth. "Snap the collar round its neck. Balir, hurry! The thing has risen. We can't hold off these fiends any longer."

Balir glared at him. "Seriously?" Ducking a jabbing spear, he gripped the collar in a white-knuckled fist. He moved nimbly toward the stone god, dripping crimson from the pool. Bright blood smeared the evil, cone-like beak which had skewered the corpse.

"Here, birdie, birdie, birdie," he called in a mocking tone. He stooped to snap the iron ring around the beast's neck. But there came a sharp movement and the blur of stone and beak. The mercenary's eyes widened in sudden horror.

Vetra whirled in astonishment to catch a glimpse of the thing vaulting in the air. It came to hawk-like life with beak snipping out a hedge-clipper's violence. There came a terrible cry of pain. Two of Balir's fingers thunked to the pavestones. Balir reeled back, barely avoiding the fiend's thrusting beak while holding his hand jetting blood.

The ominous bird floated on spindly legs in the dimness, fresh blood on its beak.

The creature hovered with impossible authority, jade wings flapping with a batlike fury. Half of the collar was seared to its stony neck, still smoking as if it had melted on contact with the jade. The other half was pulsing in brilliant color on the ground. Balir had hooked the thing, but something had gone awry. The relic smoked and sizzled while Balir hopped about, struggling to staunch the flow jetting from his severed fingers. In agony he wrapped his hand under his tunic, ripped off a portion, and struggled with his good hand to twine a leather cord from the hem of his pouch to secure the bandage.

The miniature god fluttered a few feet forward, eyeing Balir and the knot of quivering figures with disdain. The eyes of the thing were lit with an inhuman intensity. As if an alien force had possessed it. The blood water—had infused the fiend with life. But how?

The monster cawed out a guttural shriek. Vetra could only construe it as hatred at the desecration of its temple by the fighting men milling about. With a brisk pulsing of stony wings it gained more height and flew full into the fray. A masked ratman came running at it full tilt with an upraised spear. Dapi jabbed out its beak, piercing the offender through the chest.

The man gurgled out a sickening sound. The stone-carved beast whizzed past Balir, brushing a sharp edge of wing across his cheek, drawing blood.

Wings beat with fury. It tore through the attacking ratmen, transfixing another with its bill and plunging it into the foremost man's mouth, sucking blood. Vetra gaped in flesh-crawling horror. Others fled back in terror.

Dapi's throat worked, as if drawing the man's innards with every spasm. The victim's eyes went dead, as if his soul had been sucked out of his body. Deeper the beak plunged into the man's mouth and worked down the bulging throat until he was a blood-soaked mess. Beak pulled out innards while tiny hands caught up the slop to gulp it down like a ghoul. The bird rammed beak in again and loosed an otherworldly caw which half blew out the man's stomach.

Vetra and Kalaman veered back in horror.

"Get away from it!" Vetra cried. "The thing sucks up men's souls!"

The mercenaries from Lausern howled in dismay. The bird quivered at its conquest, wormed its beak deeper into human mouth and flesh. The defenders clambered back into the shadows. The ratmen followed, aghast at the husk of man which had fallen away like a butcher's slab of beef. The corpse was completely bloodless and white-faced. Dapi, or whatever the demon god's name was, burned with a fierce, vampirish glow.

Balir clutched his blade in his good hand and tottered back. He reeled toward Vetra and Kalaman to engage the small knot of masked foes who scrambled alongside the retreating mercenaries.

Despite his handicap, Balir smote with his sword and sprang lightly on his feet, agile enough to foil the clacking spears and the knives of the ratmen. His muscular sword arm made up for any missing fingers.

Vetra could not understand why the ratmen continued to menace them in the presence of the ghoul. Was so much priestly blood worth that of a few outlanders?

A clang of a spearhead rang on his helm, sending his head swimming in a dizzy fog. The torchlit gloom wavered. Clouds of mist shimmered before his eyes. A priest had snuck up behind him and outmaneuvered him, damn his rat-hide!

Vetra roused himself from his stupor. Flashing stars careened about his head. He plowed on, shoving merciless steel into human guts, parrying forked spears questing for his vitals.

The priests were bold but ineffective in these close quarters. The only advantage they had was their numbers and their long spears which kept whirling blades at bay with their longer reach.

But bodies lay thick in the ghastly splendor. Vetra clashed sword against the spears of the fool priests who still fought him. He wheeled as the god-thing passed within a hair's breadth. The ratmen fled in terrified droves back up the corridor, nursing staggering losses, calling out supplications to their god. The demon bird croaked a grisly, guttural, utterly un-human sound unlike anything Vetra had ever heard.

"Back the way of the old keeper!" A strange compulsion had him dashing over to where the smoking collar lay. He flicked it up with the tip of his sword, caught it in midair before pushing through the knot of wild-eyed rat-men. Why waste time on the relic? His mission was botched. There might be a chance he could bridle the horror that had been loosed. Some other stubborn, sinister reason burned at the back of his mind.

Laskar grabbed bolts out of victims and slapped them in his leather pouch before scrambling up the tunnel after Vetra and the others.

Balir, pressing his hand to his side, winced through his pain while gripping his weapon with fierce defiance in his good right hand.

How the day had gone terribly wrong! Vetra grimaced as he fled up the tunnel where the old woman had disappeared. If the bird did not finish them, there was always Caglios. The old wizard would not forgive this botch-up. Vetra shuddered for the tenth time at the memory of the wretch who had flouted the wizard's authority. Dergath's blood! What fiendish end would come of them all?

The four limped their way along the gloomy passage, trying to put as much distance between the god-fiend as possible. The corridor was narrow, lit only with torches hung at sporadic intervals on polished walls.

"What a grand bungling!" Kalaman raged.

"Aye." Vetra shook the half segment of collar in his white-knuckled fist. He stared at Balir. "Why did you have to snatch the thing out of my hands? I yelled at you to snap it on the thing's neck. *'Put the collar on first, lest the falcon's wrath burst.'* Remember the rhyme? Yet you go and whisper 'birdie, birdie' in its stupid ear."

Balir gave a blood-flecked snarl. "Dergath's three hells about the rhyme! I'm a warrior not a necromancer." He scowled through his pain, pausing to redress his wound. He sheathed blade in his bloody scabbard and tottered up the corridor to keep up with his fellows.

In the torchlit gloom, dim echoes rang: the bloody hackwork of beak thrusting against bodies, chirping cries, the clink and chop of death dwindling to an unreal nightmare. The tinkling waters of the devil pool faded from earshot.

Vetra saw his henchman was now white with shock. He pulled Balir alongside him. "A bad business getting your fingers chopped off like that. It's crazy. Was the thing really stone, or something of flesh and blood?"

"Its beak was stone," murmured Balir in a hoarse voice. "It was like no living thing I ever knew, Vetra." He rattled out a sobbing gasp. "A devil! Not some god. Some cursed thing of the swamps!"

"Quiet down." Vetra ducked his head, trying to see back down the passage. "We've unleashed some barbarous horror in these corridors. Or that swine Caglios has, by his macabre magic. It has something to do with those prophecies and that devil pool…not that everything in this damnable canyon isn't cursed. The god-bird at least is taking care of our masked pests." He grunted and clutched Balir's arm tighter. "You, my friend, drew the short straw."

Balir laughed in sour irony at the fact and coughed up

phlegm. "A hefty price to pay for a blunder. I'll survive. I'll have my revenge on these rat mongers—and that conniving wizard of yours."

"Famous last words," Vetra said. "We have yet to get out of this labyrinth." He turned the collar over in his hand. The remnant was half broken, blackened. Its rough surface gleamed like obsidian as if at one time it had been subjected to high heat. The primitive serpentine and garnet gems glowered with ominous purpose.

"The collar was given me as a countering force. The old wizard said it was a container, should the deity become too powerful."

"A little late for that now," Kalaman snapped.

"I had it in my hands," Balir lamented. "Next thing I know this demon jumps me like some spider. I should have—" He choked back the words, unable to continue.

"Take it easy, Balir," said Vetra.

Kalaman stared at Balir's mangled hand. "I saw it with my own eyes, Vetra. The collar seared into the statue's skin. It was animated by some unknown force, a stone goblin if I ever saw one. Something that should not exist. It whipped its beak round and snapped the collar out of Balir's hand, snipping two of his fingers at the same time as if they were twigs."

"No matter. What's done is done."

"Let's hope the old keeper kept this way lighted," said Kalaman. "The glow seems to be petering out—red as the blood water from that damnable pool. We may be able to get ourselves back to the main path, if we keep our wits about us."

On heavy feet the troupe stumbled up the passage, panting and grunting like pigs. They followed the last path the keeper had taken, leaving blood-stained prints on the floor. The lighted way grew duskier in the smoking torchlight. Blinking in the gloom, Vetra noted the irregularly-spaced torches guttering and casting dancing shadows along the rough stone walls.

The paves petered out to bare rock, which lay buckled and heaved up at places. The two-dimensional wall carvings, worn and chipped, depicted ancient priests carrying offerings to winged gods, also sinister beast-headed deities, suns, moons, and constellations. Walls and ceiling teemed with them, the latter looming a few feet above their heads. No reassuring open sky in this corridor.

"Let's move our feet then," urged Vetra. "We need to get as much distance from that ghoul as possible."

Laskar gave a muffled affirmation. In addition to the shallow knife wound, he had lost part of his ear in the fight with the god-bird. Part of the blood that they left behind was his, despite his efforts to cup a hand over it. Kalaman suffered a great clotted gash bulging on his left shoulder. Grunting, he massaged the wound where a glancing spear had nicked him. Vetra flexed his knee which had swelled since he slipped in a slain priest's blood.

If Dapi hadn't appeared when it did, the ratmen would have likely carved them ear to ear... The senseless soul-suckings of the god were a mystery to him yet burned in lurid clarity in Vetra's mind. How had the pool given it life? What kept the god's essence contained within the stone? Vetra's thoughts did not grant him any peace.

"Demons only exist to kill," mused Kalaman, picking up on Vetra's grimaces. "Being newly-birthed, maybe the thing needs to feed?"

"Or maybe it's growing," said Balir with mounting cynicism.

The minutes wore on. Infused with a tense silence, they did not meet each other's eyes. Like wounded deer the company half limped, half bounded down the corridor, as if stalked by a tiger. A clinging dampness infected the night air, which the few lighted torches failed to dispel. Vetra could see great spider webs hanging from the larger torches in the dimming red light. Snatches of fierce, god-like faces leaped out from the shadows at him. Archways led to various other mini-temples in whose dusky interiors he caught glimpses of winged stone dragons, or simian faces of elder apes of doom.

In a rush, it occurred to him what this place was: an accursed network of temples spanning ages that sheltered multiple, hideous, nameless gods. It was a place where carven facades of temples towered on high—where priests gave themselves over to dark forces conjured by occult means, some monstrous sanctuary where half human, half bestial entities lurked, and very likely used the priests in ways more slavish than the priests liked to believe they used the gods.

Vetra dwelled on the thought while members of the band eased up their pace. At least there was no further pursuit. He pushed back his dented helm, wiped the blood from his brow. Balir's wretched grumbling had them all pondering the twist of fate that enabled them to flee down this musty tunnel. Not two days ago they had all lounged in high spirits together at the Hetman's pub, with Kalaman cracking many a ribald joke.

Vetra's face crinkled, still remembering how he had met the blond-haired Kalaman. Moonlighting as a ring-fighter. How he and Balir had pushed their way up to the front of that mob of fevered gamblers waving coins in their hands one late night in the brewers' district, wagering on who would win the next fight. He had scrutinized the combatants in that sweaty pen—a mixture of ex-convicts, bodyguards and thugs. Confidence, brawn, ingenuity—that's what he had been looking for—someone with the ability to size up an opponent in an instant. Next up was Kalaman—Kal the Dragon. Vetra recalled the stocky brute circling his squint-eyed opponent with casual insolence; then, in a sudden rush and a burst of strength a mallet fist knocked his adversary senseless in less than five seconds, though he was the smaller man, and everyone was betting against him.

Vetra had been sold then on Kalaman the bully-boy and had come striding up to recruit him. Kalaman had looked at him sideways, like a curious panther, with many a scar and stitch around his eye. Kalaman, in his up-front way, had told him of his pub-crawling friend Laskar who was in need of work and that unless the two of them were hired for the job, he would walk...

Vetra shook his head at the pleasant memory. A far cry from the rude, blooded messes they were, scrambling through a ratman-haunted tunnel in the valley of Gyzia.

They stumbled at last upon a candlelit chamber rudely carved in the tunnel wall. Inside, the old crone who was the temple keeper sat cross-legged on a ledge of stone. Her back was set against the rough wall of a cave-like passage whose ceiling was very low. She was surrounded by tiny wicks suspended in oil. Her eyes were drawn in an eerie, somnolent gaze, fixed on a six-pointed star on the far wall lit with smoldering torches.

So absorbed was she that she did not notice them at first. Vetra ducked inside and guessed she was in a trance from the way she sat motionless without a word. The others watched her and looked on, blinking with puzzlement.

Her eyes fluttered a few times then she spoke at last. "I knew ere your coming there would be much trouble in the temple of Dapi."

"If you knew," jeered Balir, "why didn't you stop us? It could have spared my hand."

The keeper gave a long sigh, seemingly unmoved by his wound. "It would not have helped. I only give thanks to the Elder gods of the Five Destinies, lest they work against me. My labors have borne fruit. Twice I have outlived my family. Others are long gone, and so I quit not my devotional practices."

Vetra rattled his bloody sword. "Very comforting, woman, but show us the way out, please."

She demurred. "'Tis said that Dapi would come to life again, and that he has. Risen again, like a demon prince. The old villain would be worshiped by many as a force of terror. I did not expect to see it in my lifetime...Great Dergath, but this is a foul day. Revered Jano! The visions I had in my last meditation...Do you not know what you have done?"

Vetra's lips parted in a cynical scowl.

"I can assist you, but I must have time to meditate." She raked them with a cold stare, her greenish-gray eyes boring craters in them. "I see that you are not bad men, just misguided. Full of blind hopes like most. Seduced by plunder and the misty promise of gold. You have raced to folly. I have no love for the ratmen. Yes, I will show you the way back to the *Avenue of Tombs*, where you can make your way to the gates of Gyzia, and above, to take your chances with the gate-priests and the watchtower."

Vetra raised his brows in sardonic mirth and suppressed the urge to contrive a mocking bow. "Any time soon then."

Showing no pique, she stepped down from her ledge to hobble on stiff legs across the slightly upheaved pavestones. "Come, this way then." She pushed a candle in Balir's cloth-bound hand and pulled a torch off the wall for herself. "Take brands. Pay heed to the wandering priests. They war among themselves; not pleasant are they to cross. The path of the ancients lies long and winding and mysterious, open only to believers. The ratmen cannot pass; their hearts are dark and their minds heavy with the weight of corruption and the sacrifices they have committed. The spirits will not allow them to pass to the forbidden regions, or the higher realms of the afterlife, or offer them any protection whatsoever."

Balir beamed with an ingenuous air. "I always knew I had a halo over my head. Must have been all the prayers I recited."

"Do not ridicule the old gods!" she warned. "They breathe life into this ancient canyon. Possibly the same into your own body. Your life may depend on the gods one day, and their mercy."

Balir glared at the thought, yet Vetra flashed him a dangerous look, warning him not to rile the old woman.

Down a side tunnel she hobbled, leading them with one hand pressed to hip, the other bearing a torch. They passed along a crude passage barely only a man's height in places. Behind a vague veil of dimness, a murmur of ghastly avian croakings drifted in and out of the ghostly shadows. Sound and movement crawled: fiendish shouts, the tumult of fighting men, horrid, unsettling bangs with spears clattering against stone.

Nimeska murmured, "Listen to the sounds of strife among the children of fools..."

Vetra tightened a fist on his weapon, his dark features clouded with unease.

"The night is much alive with mischief." A pale and weary light shone in her eyes. "False worshipers abound in these ancient halls."

The yawning rock opened up into a fissure above their heads. They caught a momentary glimpse of open sky and glittering stars. The mouth of crumbled sandstone then folded over them and the tunnel wound on in silence and murk. Boots crunched on shale. All gazed in wordless unease upon endless fissures and forgotten abysses that dropped sometimes inches from their feet, black as midnight, wafting cool vapors and murmurs of tumbling water. Squinting, they could make out aged carved faces of outworn deities, untended by priest, cleric or wizard—on wall, ceiling and in pit.

* * *

Where they had encountered no foliage before, now battered tree trunks appeared with perplexing frequency in the gloom, thrusting up from the stone like silent ghosts. They were thick-boled things, the product of some unguessable sorcery or diseased magic.

The fugitives squeezed around these dark trunks looming up in their path. Evidently the trees were nourished by the open air, wind, rain and sunlight that streamed from above. But how they could live on in bare rock was a mystery. The corridor seemed inhospitable, and supported little in the way of soil down here where the invasive roots bored through the rock.

"What are these strange trees?" asked Vetra of Nimeska. "They look petrified. Like dead hulks with barely a limb." His sword clanged in dull thuds like Kalaman's when he tested blade on the trunks. Vetra's fingers reached out to stroke one trunk's hard, ageless contours and found it smooth to the touch. He withdrew his fingers, grumbling. The black trunk crawled with a sinister life, something he felt rather than could explain. Though the petrified bark gleamed under his torchlight, hard and dead as bone, there was something else that spoke of malevolence, something tainted by the weight of ages. In the ethereal light, Vetra saw what few branches they bore, lay broken and twisted, ash-gray like bone. Most had snapped off and fallen.

The temple keeper seemed pleased with Vetra's interest in the trees. "These are the trunks of Kaphra. Once living things. A mystic wanderer brought seeds from a distant land, prophesying they would grow to become Jano's children. In the end, these twisted seedlings grew from acorn to sapling to their full height, burrowing down through cracks to suck up the blood of the victims of Dapi's pantheon of violent gods. 'Blood death trees', we called them, whose trunks would ooze rank ichor on nights of the full moon. Centuries of Dapi's sacrifices were buried here in this hall—whose warm blood seeped deep and stained the stone forever."

Vetra shook his head in baffled loathing. "A fiendish heritage you have here, woman."

"Some would call it a hellhole," Balir remarked.

"I grow old," Nimeska grunted, a spooky sound, almost as chilling as her tale. "Not long from now I will pass and these halls will be silent again." Vetra saw a flicker of dreaminess pass in her ageless eyes. "One day I would like to become immortalized like these trees—the magnificent ones. I would become one with their creator, and forever watch over these halls, like the guardians of my heritage." Her voice sank in a hushed whisper. Her eyes lit with the vision of which she spoke.

Vetra shrugged. "One should be careful what she wishes for."

The old woman chuckled. "I know what you're thinking, outlander. That I am a loony old coot."

Vetra smiled, but he said nothing.

Back down the tunnel, the beating of stone wings echoed out of the murk. Something was tracking them. Dapi, it seemed, would not be thwarted.

"The thing hunts us," Vetra hissed.

"You seem to have something it wants." The keeper scanned their persons with suspicion then trained eyes on Vetra, paying particular attention to his clenched fingers fumbling under his surcoat. "Is it your lives Dapi hunts, or your souls?"

Vetra uttered an incoherent sound. His fingers closed over the fragment of collar that burned warmly at his belt. The urge to toss it down the passage was overwhelming. Yet he kept it.

The path curved around a bend and the old keeper stooped to catch her breath before another withered stone tree. With one elbow propped on a knee and the other hand clutching her torch pressed to the trunk, she exhaled a ragged gasp. "I grow weary, outlanders. My bones are not what they used to be. I bid you go!" She flung out a gnarled hand. "Follow the path. Turn at the sigil of the Panther, the Bear and the Hound. If Jano favors you, you will come out to the main avenue of sphinxes. May Jano protect you!"

Vetra blinked, thumbing his chin. "Are you sure you can't accompany us farther, friend? We can't repay your services right now. But we will do so at the earliest convenience."

The old woman smiled at Vetra's offer. "Go!" She shook off his hand. "Dapi is coming for you. Whatever you have done to the god, I dare not imagine. He is not kind, this Dapi, and like all gods, he demands sacrifices to keep him alive."

"And you?" Vetra pressed.

"Worry not about me. I am protected."

The words lingered in the air with strange authority. Vetra

pursed his lips. "As you wish, crone." Fatalistic temperaments always perplexed him. With a grunt, he shouldered Balir ahead.

III

Down the passage the men tramped, their boots sending up a hail of echoes. As the old woman crouched by the blood tree, they caught snatches of her last mumbling prayers to her mysterious god. Vetra was reluctant to leave her behind, yet there was new relief in his purpose, for her presence was somewhat unsettling. Doubt had pricked his mind of his mission. So far, her advice had only been helpful.

He and the others had come out on a bend in the open passage where a cryptic claw-symbol showed in the middle of a three way junction—just as the old woman had predicted. The canyon walls rose up a hundred feet on either side of the split. The left passage plunged down into dark emptiness, the middle corridor wound up and showed promise of light while the right passage was footed with large stones and appeared shielded by a heavy iron gate.

"Which way did the old crone say?" growled Balir.

Kalaman pointed only vaguely at the engraved figure that looked something like a hybrid ape and condor. "Left, toward the sign of the Grinning Monkey—or lewd Owl."

"Numbskull!" Vetra grumbled. "That's no owl." He pushed ahead with a disgusted murmur. "We take the way straight... The high road, always the high road."

From the middle passage came a drunken form lurching, his chest heaving. A priest, of sorts, so Vetra judged by the glinting chest ornaments. The figure spied the armed men and turned on his heels. With a gasp, he scrambled back the way he had come.

Vetra gave a grim nod and they all thundered after the figure, up the murky corridor where they caught a glimpse of his coral-colored conch. It was not dissimilar to Iokru's headdress. While they swung swords and grunted curses, the fleet-footed figure seemed to slip by them into the darkness like a wraith. His footfall suddenly faded out.

Out of the gloom the mercs sped, up a wide, sunken stair whose stones were cracked by time. A circular hall stretched before them like a mausoleum. They caught glimpses of rounded forms of crouching statues bathed in moonlight stationed around the perimeter. The features were eroded by rain and wind of ages past. Catching their breaths, they stood peering with uncertainty, a tiny glow emanating from some place beyond. More torches glowed from niches set along the walls, emanating faint light. Perhaps the doings of another cult like the ratmen? Vetra frowned, suspicious to the core. The old woman had not mentioned hostile votaries along the way...unless, she was so weak of breath to have forgotten mention of them? Other forces were yet to play out in this eerie sanctuary of Gyzia's mystery.

The chamber was rich with carven figures and molder, he noted; bat dung and decay lay everywhere. The space breathed of an ancient stillness, and yet a horror, which lay thick like a curse. Vetra grimaced, not the least at the lurid echoes lingering back in the corridor behind them—human footfall, priests' shouts, dying screams. He gaped at a grisly sight that slowly took the breath from his lungs as it took form under the glare of their torches.

"What the—?"

For a moment Vetra stood completely bewildered—a petrified tree standing ancient and tall with its huge branches thrust up through the hollowed-out mouth of a gigantic stone-carved osprey molded out of the stone wall. Desiccated husks of what were once human and animal bones lay crumpled at the idol's base: sacrifices of some past debased ritual, drained of vitals and fluids—or perhaps what had been chewed off by some abomination like Dapi.

Vetra shuffled back in loathing. The carven image was not dissimilar to Dapi, but this was chiseled in the form of a massive, half human bird, whose beaked face hung pasted on human neck and shoulders and was drawn out in a rictus of intense emotion.

Vetra couldn't decide whether it was anguish or rapture. Not that he cared much to find out.

"Why are all these corridors so grim?"

The thick trunk of the petrified tree, blackened with the blood of victims of past ages, rose from the paves, spreading rocky limbs like coral across the bird face and twining around the neck and crown. Branches thicker than pythons' coils plunged down into the open maw and into the eyes, like some ghastly fungal infection.

Vetra sucked in a breath. There was enough horror here to stop a mammoth in its tracks. The place was a dead end...

The mercenaries peered about in unease. The ceiling rose in a high dome where a cone of moonlight spilled down from a glaring, bat-eyed gap to bathe the ancient floor below in soft, gray moonlight. Where had the priest disappeared to?

Vetra rubbed his jaw in consternation. The priestly footprints were etched in the thick dust. They disappeared at the edge of the far wall. A low, moldering altar lurked to the side, set with twisted candelabra. The altar, Vetra saw, reposed by the hideous god-statue and supported a litter of bird skulls and decomposed candles, shells, furs, glass ornaments, claws and bones.

A sudden scuffling had Vetra drawing his sword.

A tall, lithe figure came shambling out of the dimness at the back of the chamber. The man was wheezing and wiping what looked like a bloody gash across his brow. A rattled figure, at the least—with that harried look of a cornered animal. Stave gripped in hand, the newcomer appeared to have come magically from some hidden exit aside the altar, darkened in the wall.

"You!" growled Vetra with anger. "Skulking about again?"

"Yes, me..." Iokru croaked, looking equally rankled. He stared at the four of them with growing displeasure. A gratified smirk slowly surfaced on his face upon seeing their blood-clotted wounds and their stony glares. "I see you have met your 'god'—" he laughed "—and accomplished your 'task'." Though this last statement was uttered with no small amount of malice.

"No thanks to you," rumbled Kalaman. "Where have you been?" He lifted his notched blade. A score of Iokru's swarthy, Clam-cult priests came gliding out of the murk with grim purpose. This was definitely a hidden tunnel, concealed in the depths of the canyons of Gyzia, with secret hinges and mirror-smooth seams. The priests were tall, unsmiling men, wearing coral headdresses similar to the last fugitive's with glinting knives tucked at their waists. Spears and flickering torches were clutched at the ready.

"One of you," accused Iokru, "seems to have doused your idol in the wrong water...if not your bungling accomplice—" He gestured with insolence at Balir whose bandaged hand tucked under an armpit peeked out like a sore thumb.

"A death wish, do you have?" snarled Balir. "I did not come here to be insulted by a high-priest's lapdog." He lifted his sword and moved to cut him down.

Vetra held him back, teeth bared. "What happened to you anyway?"

Iokru gave a dismissive shrug. "I was waylaid. Isn't it obvious? By those cursed *ratmangers*."

"The rat masks?"

"Who else?" Iokru spat venomously. "What's with the twenty questions? One of them who we passed back at their temple must have put two and two together seeing you carrying that conch." He fixed a glare at Vetra. "Likewise, decided we were planning to raise some god or avatar in secret communion. Idiot!" He flourished his stave. "I curse you for flashing that jade idol and its magical collar back on the ledge! Rojarsh will have my head for this. Dark Carcassis! The Falcon God was never supposed to live again. I'm as good as a dead man."

"Then so be it," snarled Vetra. "The devil with Rojarsh! What do you see, priest? My man's lost fingers. This Dapi thing, whatever you call it, has turned into a fiend. Now it lives, or flies as some demon bird, killing men like lemmings in these tunnels. You're right, it was not supposed to end like this." He winced.

Iokru clicked his tongue. "Settle down. The dark forces prevail. The law of the seraphim, or the handmaid of Fate, foils all. Men's plans wither in her hallowed shadow." The priest's cryptic words stirred the masked votaries who murmured a prayer and other benediction. A group of them huddled closer to Iokru. Vetra could see their gleaming skin and hear their vindictive breaths behind their helm-like masks. Their naked bellies tinkled with the seashells suspended from thin cords while feathers bristled on their muscled arms over armlets of whalebone.

Vetra half turned and the broken collar glinted in his hand. Animosity burned in that gaze. "All for this." He pulled the collar out and shook it like a dog would a rat.

Iokru's eyes almost bulged out of their sockets. "You?—you still guard the collar? But how—?" His eyes gleamed with a malignant energy. "A chosen one you must be, to clutch it while Dapi lives."

Vetra grunted, caring little. "You mean, how is it that this bloodthirsty deity is still living and not some inanimate piece of jade? Ask that of the wretches whose souls it has sucked."

Iokru twitched. He had grown silent and Vetra could almost see the gears working in his diabolical skull. He did not like what he saw.

If Iokru and his weaponed priests decided to strike, he and his men would be hard pressed to defend. They'd have to be fast… A well-timed explosive attack and a quick, gutting flurry of steel would cut down as many of them as they could. Kalaman was in silent accord, as his private nod affirmed.

Iokru gestured in careless fashion. "Look around you, mercenary—these halls were once the old lairs of the priests, the dark dens of Dapi. Forbidden, of course, by the priest-kings, after the destruction of the 'middle path' and the gradual degradation of Dapi. You would shudder if you could comprehend the sacrilege for us to be even treading in this hall. If Rojarsh or any of his high priests were to find us...it would mean treason for us all." His eyes gleamed; his lower lip twitched. "It was only the ratmen and Dapi who forced us here...fitting now that we are here, face to face."

As insulting as the priest's words were, his voice was somewhat strangely disjointed, and prompted Vetra to think that the man was jittery, and possibly as clueless of the events that had passed as he was himself.

Iokru caught the look and the veiled disgust on Vetra's face. His eyes darted to the stone-carved god with its twisted tangle of limbs and he gave a dark, croaking chuckle. "You marvel at Osipres? Look upon the dead god of the Hunt, mercenary. 'Tis brother to Dapi, the Osprey god, a cult which sprang up like wildfire soon after the Falcon God's fall, a century ago."

"What of the invasive tree?"

Iokru wiped his hands on his reeking, blood-clotted cloak. Murmuring some words in a priestly tongue, he made a strange gesture. "As for that, I'm not sure why it was not cut down ages ago. Jano waged war with us and the winged gods. I know followers of Jano, the cursed mother god, worshiped these unnatural things."

He spat with distaste and his fingers bunched into claws. A faraway but delirious glint drifted in those eyes.

"How I wanted to snatch that collar from you the moment I saw it back in the passage of Antali." His eyes narrowed in hungry anticipation. "I could have snatched it. But risk my own neck slitted by your swords. Now it looks as if the tables have turned. I have my warrior-guard at my back. You are wounded and without options. I can wrest the collar from you and your rabble at any instant." He glared at them, his voice rising in a throaty chuckle.

Vetra growled, "Try it."

Iokru chuckled. "Why resist? I shall harness the power of this new bird god, rogue though it is. With the help of the god collar, I'll overthrow the condescending fool of a high priest, Rojarsh. He's mistreated me for the last time, and patronized my abilities."

Iokru gestured to his warrior-priests. A group of them advanced, clutching wicked, single-edged spears barbed with razor tips.

Vetra crept back, gauging the mettle of the tallest enemy. His bronzed shoulders showed a sinewy sheen of slick muscle that was not to be discounted. But then Vetra's own muscles rippled with a pent-up battle heat. The priest, a powerful bear of a man, sprang at him, all gleaming teeth and cool smile. But he betrayed an overconfident grip on his long spear. The presumption marked a man susceptible to ruse, and it was on this weakness that Vetra capitalized.

He sidestepped the snarling lunge and rumbled deep in his throat. "Back, clam-spawn, and you too, Iokru. I have not come to be thwarted by traitor-priests as the likes of you!"

Steel flashed in Vetra's hand and in the dim light, blood flowed. The tall priest thrust his spear forward. Vetra swiveled on his hips, deflected the ill-timed strike and leaned in to strike upward, running bright steel from the outstretched man's groin to sternum. The priest cried out in anguish and his bare flesh was laid open in a blossoming crimson.

"Enough!" called Iokru, glaring at the writhing form of his henchman at his toes.

A commanding voice called from the dim distance, "Aye, enough!"

Heads whirled. Vetra's eyes widened as he stared at a spare form treading closer. Nimeska! How the devil had she found us here...? The temple-keeper had a new spring in her step. A zeal burned in her eyes. As she approached, Vetra could see she was still the same old wandering crone, but new energy flowed in her limbs, as if she had been given new purchase on life by her god.

"You?" Iokru mustered a gasp. "Lowly 'incense burner'! What do you do here?"

"I can ask the same of you, Iokru. I see you for what you are, priest."

"Oh, what is that? A crafty shaman?" Iokru gave a sardonic hoot.

Nimeska's eyes narrowed, possibly in pity. "I remember days when these halls echoed kinder sounds. I remember you of old. Rojarsh, your master, kidnapped and enslaved my daughter years ago, luring her with promises of beauty and wealth into your depraved cult. A raving lunatic, she died, poisoned by your master's foul magic. I vowed to avenge her when I was younger. Now it seems that time has come. I have always loathed your sect, and now fate binds us together. To here it brings us—to the doorstep of Dapi."

Iokru shrugged, unimpressed with the keeper's rhetoric. "It was Rojarsh's way. I was but a boy at the time. Eager to be elevated into the ranks of the clam priesthood. I rose quickly. Rojarsh saw to that. He was not displeased with the potential I showed."

The keeper's face remained unmoved. "You're no different than the other ambitious simpletons of your creed. Your master was the vilest snake of all, an extortionist, a tyrant and murderer—" She stabbed a finger at the cursed, whalebone idol-amulet in the form of Rojarsh riding the sacred clam that hung round the priest's neck. "Beware! Dapi does not forgive, nor does he fear to ride the heels of those and make sacrifices of us all ere the setting of the moon."

"Take her, and these sputtering fools!" Iokru bellowed. The priests muttered and advanced in dark knots. Laskar knocked a bolt to his crossbow and aimed it at the foremost priest's forehead. The three in the front halted, wary of the archer's steady hand and his merciless, unwavering gaze.

"You'll be judged by the gods you worship," warned Nimeska. "Stand back! My deities will protect me."

"Your deities?" Iokru laughed. "Just like your precious Jano? I don't think so." He snorted out a breath through flared nostrils. "They'll drag you through pools of your own blood. Then they'll eat out your eyeballs for breakfast! Dapi will be under my control." He jerked a finger at his underlings. "Seize this wench and take her to the pit of clams! The witch will feed Meru—our great, old clam."

"The old Clam of our god!" cried one of Iokru's faithful followers who shook a fist and hailed his priest-superior.

"First one touches her dies," growled Vetra. His sword raked the air, slashing the man's garment and drawing a line of blood under the rough fur on the man's partially naked brown chest.

A cry rang out. A spear clattered to the stone. Nimeska nodded in triumph, her visage coming alive with wrath. Her priestess-like form seemed to rise a foot off the ground. Vetra marveled at her trust and faith in her god. Another warrior-priest jerked forward, thrusting spear in her face, angry at the challenge and the injuries of his fellows. But she did not flinch.

Vetra sprang forward and turned aside the metal tip of the spear that would surely have pierced her breast. "Knave! Would you kill a defenseless woman?"

"If I must," Iokru grunted. "Kill them all, every last one of them!" His priests rushed forward and lifted spears to hurl at the defenders.

Balir's throat rumbled an oath while Laskar loosed a bolt into the advancing throng, taking the first running priest square between the eyes.

His body fell like a limp rag. A dog-eyed priest thrust his gleaming shaft at Kalaman. Balir barreled into him and kneed the weapon out of the startled priest's hands. He slashed a murderous stroke down on bared flesh, eliciting an agonized shriek.

The hall erupted into a wild melee, men yelling as spears thrust and swords cut.

A lunging priest feinted at Vetra while another, crouching, sprang with a furious yell. A knife stabbed for Vetra's groin. He parried both and booted the crouching man in the teeth as Iokru surged forward, wresting the collar from Vetra's belt.

Vetra wheeled like a cat, evading the first springing attacker then swung out a lashing cut. But the blade fell on empty air. It struck the paves, and as quick as a snake, Iokru darted back with the prize in his grip, gloating venomously.

"With this piece, Dapi will be mine to control!" He gloated, foam dribbling from his lips. "You will feed our clam!"

"Not just yet," came Nimeska's warning. She held her hands over her head. Her dark face grew fierce—then Vetra saw in her gaze something sinister, rising like a terrible wave.

The warrior priests drew back, eyes widening as if sensing something unearthly. Iokru stared at the temple-keeper in awe. A dim understanding dawned in his cryptic expression.

"I am not without magic, priest! Watch!—Nimeska becomes the embodiment of her goddess." And with a sudden stamp of heel, a greenish light coursed around her in a flaring aureole, deeper than all the plants of the wildest jungles of Taro. She invoked the spell and power of Jano, her patron goddess and all the air around her warped.

Iokru gave a snort of rage. "You, the incarnation of the priestess of Mith? Never!" He grimaced in denial. "The treed one has been dead for an age."

Nimeska guffawed, obviously enjoying the rich discomfort of the priest and the intoxicating wave of power flowing through her bones. "My power will make Dapi's look like a worm in the swamps of nameless jungles."

Nimeska's body then glowed yellow and she began to pulse. Her thin body surged upward—growing taller, wider, her rhythmic movement like one of the big snakes of deep jungles. Her legs stood rooted while arms sprouted slender limbs, like those Vetra had passed earlier, with dead leaves crackling on the ends to fall in crisp heaps at her feet. Writhing like vine tendrils, roots displanted toes and thrust in the age-worn stone of the temple, upheaving the pavestones.

The screams of dying men echoed up the corridor from the hidden exit.

Vetra could not decide which was worse, this impossible scene or what transpired in the nearby corridor. He watched as priestly fingers closed on weapons, eyes darted about with wary fervor, men gauging the fragile balance that existed in this gloomy hall of the ancients. None knew what Iokru's henchmen would do. Or what the treed horror would do next, nor what the menace progressing up the secret tunnel was. But it sounded like Dapi's bloody handiwork.

He turned a feral glance at Iokru who gripped the collar with growing doubt. Vetra launched himself at the priest, blade promising swift death.

Iokru ducked under Vetra's strike then scrambled away, dodging the wrathful tree. "Wield your obscure magic, witch! Turn into a tree and regale us with your gaudy tricks for all we care."

As if in response, a newly-budding limb sprouted from the trunk and Nimeska lashed out at him and sent priests flying. It blocked the hidden exit where Iokru pumped long legs, hoping to escape.

Five of his priests were down. The others legged it in a mad scramble to win past Nimeska's thrashing limb and flee the chamber. But the tree-keeper clapped her branches together like hands and the deserters fled back gibbering in awe at the quivering statues hovering over the lintel that fell with a crash at their feet. The priests stumbled around in confusion as a cloud of dust and molder washed over them. Howling and scrabbling among themselves, they groped for safety. Broken masonry now blocked the passage.

Nimeska's plumage was now a violent fan of loose branches, alive and bristling in the air like angry snakes.

Her tree-deep voice boomed over the din. "Sons of Rojarsh! You shall get your wretched wish. Entombed and encaged— protectors of the halls of the damned!" With a gruesome crackling of expanding wood, the trunk bulged and grew. New branches snaked off in unison like vines from faraway jungles, sealing off the entrance forever.

The smile froze on Iokru's face. He held up the collar and strung it around his neck abreast the amulet. "I am not done yet, witch! Pay heed, I guard the talisman. 'Tis I who have power over the god!" These words he croaked with a hysterical vindictiveness.

"No you don't," hissed Balir, reeling up beside him.

Iokru spat. "Get away from me!" He dodged past Balir toward the last passage. Only to come to a crunching halt. Something untoward hovered in the dimness. Iokru's heart seemed to leap into his throat. From the passage that Vetra and his men had emerged, burst a red-eyed ghoul.

For a naked second, the entity paused, with its stone talons clacking on the aged pavestones. Then it leaped in the air, with wings beating a horrendous din.

Dapi loomed over Iokru like a winged avatar. Down it came tearing at him; he struck out with his stave. The bird wavered, did a half roll in the air, stunned by the rod's magic and Iokru gave a rasping chuckle. Without preamble, he reached up, and the pulsing iron collar latched on with magnetic force to something metallic in place around its neck—but which did nothing in the shadow of the falcon god, to the priest's inconceivable horror.

Iokru paled. The segment of collar had failed. He tore it off, staring at it in dismay. His exultant haste had led him astray. Now he realized it was but a half ring in his hand, not the full...that the god had the other half fused to its neck, something he had overlooked.

The red eyes glowed a dusky balefire. A bloodstained beak aimed straight for his throat.

The priest gave a shrill wail. He twisted sideways and lurched as the stony thing sideswiped him by a hair. The talisman went flying from his hand, torn from the priest's trembling fingers like coins in a mob's rush. It clattered against the nearest wall and lay rolling on the floor.

Kalaman made a grab for the fragment. Iokru, dazed but not witless, scrambled for it like a crab. He sank teeth into Kalaman's wrist. The mercenary's agonized shout rang above the din. The priest's strength was three-fold.

Kalaman struggled with his blade and only swung a glancing blow to Iokru's painted face. Iokru parried with a jerk of his stave. Like some screaming banshee, he raced around Kalaman and sank his teeth into the nape of his neck.

Kalaman clawed back, bellowing in agony. He threw the priest to the ground, blood streaming from the back of his neck.

Vetra swore and dodged the assaults of Iokru's minions. He scrambled through the horrified wake of Iokru's Clam-cult priests. He grabbed the collar from the floor, then bolted to the back of the chamber, while Kalaman bled and the god battled Iokru's minions.

Iokru gurgled froth. A foamy shriek rasped on his lips. Distracted by the loss of his talisman, he fell sideways, buffeted by Dapi's smashing beak that came again and again to ram him, but this time full in the face.

The beak pushed through the snarling teeth of the defenseless man and thrust down his throat. The priest's eyes gaped; his jaw cracked and the bird started sucking—blood, innards, the whole works of life out of Iokru. Iokru's back arched. His legs dangled in dancing death over the paves as a gurgle of dark crimson streamed from his wide-stretched mouth. His body went limp, as he hung there like a ragdoll while Vetra watched in numb horror. The god-bird held him suspended in the air, then slung the lifeless body to the side then turned its fiendish attention to the wild-eyed company.

Dapi slowly descended to the ground, eyeing the scrambling men who surged every which way. With impassive detachment, the god-bird watched—its eyes flicked briefly over its brother god-statue, Osipres. The bird burned and radiated a lambent heat, which Vetra felt, its bloody beak stretched wide. Red, inhuman eyes pierced the humans, as if they were but plump hares.

The moments passed in a blinding flash of blood and death as all hell broke loose. The god tore through the ranks of priests and outlanders alike, taking the slowest first.

Vetra pitched backwards, knocking Kalaman on his side. Balir weaved in and out of the bloody fray like a crazed lynx, his foes knocked about like pins. Crimson blade thunked into priestly flesh while he avoided death by instinct alone. A priest's spear snapped on the stone beak as the bird rammed it into the attacker's face. The victim mustered a flesh-curdling cry, before the creature began sucking the life out of him as it had Iokru. The fear-maddened priests clawed their way across the stone, struggling to get away from the monster, but there was nowhere to run. The exits were blocked. Nimeska's magic limbs had sealed them in. The tree stopped its infernal swaying and the face of the keeper, now a misshapen oval in the trunk, uttered spell-ridden incantations.

There came a stony spray of debris showering down from on high as the enchanted trunk raked limbs across the upper half of the chamber. Statues dropped like flies. A beating of godly wings, and the hint of ignoble death, then the monstrous shape of Dapi emerged behind them.

Laskar aimed his weapon for the swooping shape but his

bolts clattered uselessly against the stone-hard body. He raced among the screaming mob, kicking priests away with his spiked boots, or smashing them with the butt end of his crossbow. He avoided a swipe from Dapi's beak, but then his expression turned ashen as the beast veered in toward him. With a flicking wing, it sent him crashing back in a litter of fallen stone.

Vetra could not watch the carnage. In swift panic, he leapt through the throng of dazed, blood-stained priests. Could his stride close the gap to Laskar in time? The archer struck again, the butt end of his crossbow splintering, but it had no more effect than a broom wisp on solid steel. For an instant Dapi came alive, surging at him—a vile fiend of insuperable force. A scrambling, grunting skirmish was in play as the demon flapped forward and back, pressing gore-flecked beak into Laskar's face. The archer's shriek was thick on his lips...then Vetra's blade struck home.

The savage chop had distracted the blood-stained beak from penetrating Laskar's gullet. Vetra whipped aside to intercept the creature and now he smote another clanking blow off its invulnerable beak. The bird turned with an inhuman shriek. It looked more like a man with a hideous beak than a god-falcon. Vetra heeded not. Again his fine Magnelian blade rose and fell until it was scored and notched. Yet the indomitable stone of Dapi's hide remained unblemished. With a hissing curse, Vetra pulled his blade away. Laskar stumbled on through the litter of mangled bodies, freed for an instant from his pinned position while the god-bird turned its wrath on Vetra. The archer shook his head, reached for his cracked but serviceable weapon, but a priest kicked the thing out of the way. Laskar thrust a boot up into the priest's gut and the enemy doubled over. Scrabbling, Laskar retrieved his bow, pulled a bolt from his belt, and loosed it into the fray. A scream died in a rattling gurgle.

Vetra staggered back as Dapi turned, snapping its beak at him. He crouched, blood-dripping, flailing with his ruined sword.

Twice Dapi's reeking beak came perilously close to stabbing into his mouth. But back he beat it with a furious pounding of blade and fist. The murderous bill clamped on the glistening metal and chomped hard. The steel snapped in two.

In dumb fascination, Vetra felt his broken hilt sag in his hands. He threw it back at the bird in snarling despair. He leapt sideways, caught himself in time from stumbling over a dead body, narrowly dodging a soul-sucking lunge. Down he ducked, barely escaping another bout of death.

Lost was his priceless Magnelian blade, sword of a master craftsman, but he was at least alive.

Pulling out his knife strapped above his boot, he crouched behind a chunk of broken statue, sucking in a ragged gasp. He waited for death.

Nimeska's lashing branches had subsided. Her power, it seemed, had waned. Only her face showed, a gnarled oval of aged eye and cheek sunken in the black trunk. But those eyes twinkled with the power of god-like magic. The trunk was scored, riven deep by Dapi's beak ramming it time and again. The roots still drew sustenance from the ancient blood under the temple, as spoken in the legends of old.

The tree-keeper laughed, barely a coherent sound. "Into the mouth of Osipres, you fools! Down the chute of oblivion!"

Vetra ran, knowing that to comply meant survival, though he could not stop the bloodthirsty god that was Dapi. Nobody could.

Nimeska lashed a last mighty limb out at the ceiling and a large mass of stones fell straight on the bird-beast. The creature lay engulfed in a cloud of rubble, pressed into the dust. A follow-up patter of rocks fell from on high, blocking the last remaining passage beyond hope. The bird had already pinned priest and mercenary down like flies. Its ramming thrusts had crumbled the chamber in beat with Nimeska's magical terror.

The dust dissipated. Now the rubble moved, and a dusty wing

knifed up from the ruin. Dapi fluttered free, wings flapping upward, tossing massive chunks aside.

Vetra crouched in the smoke and ruin, staring in disbelief. He watched the thing, a prince in devil's disguise, move about in drunken hops while more debris tumbled from the ceiling. So, Dapi gained the air again.

Nimeska's limbs had writhed to new life. While those gods warred, Vetra grabbed up Balir and the two struggled to reach Osipres' beak. Kalaman and Laskar still battled priests further in; though Vetra called to them, his shouts were lost in the din. Dapi struck over and again and priests fell and lay still. The stone tree that was Nimeska blocked the assaults with more of her wavering branches, while the god-fervor was on her, and she lashed out limbs which hit Dapi sideways and sent the bird careening. It crashed against the wall, crushing another priest underneath it. Dapi had grown stronger with all its sickening soul-suckings and now it coursed to life with new devilry. It sprang airborne and roared, whistling through the air on notched wings to smash a thrashing limb off the treed Nimeska.

Nimeska uttered a dismal cry. A new member grew in its place. Such was the power of Jano and Nimeska's faith burned strong in her one god.

With the exits blocked, only one way existed out of this burrow—through the mouth of the demon god Osipres. Vetra had long rallied his men to gather at the base of the trunk that rose alongside the shoulders of the stone god's likeness. The statue towered thirty feet over them; the older tree's twining branches invaded beak and eyes in symbolic desecration. In its dark shadow, Vetra saw the dusky crimson beak of the effigy hook toward the hall's middle. The open bill loomed several feet over their heads. The petrified trunk was mirror smooth and not to be climbed so easily.

Kalaman gripped Vetra's shoulder. He cupped both hands and gestured savagely for him to slip a boot in the crook of his palms so that he could climb up into the great beak.

Vetra stepped in Kalaman's hands. Grunting, Kalaman pushed him up a foot higher. Vetra, hanging over the lower bill, thrust down a hand to pull Kalaman up. But he was denied.

A spear hurled with terrific force slammed into Kalaman's back. Vetra saw the look of agony cross the swordsman's face. Kalaman fell like an ox, and the enemy was on him, the killing shaft projecting from between his shoulders.

Vetra gave a dismal cry. Balir and Laskar gazed in horror. Desperate priests were trampling on Kalaman's back, trying to scale the osprey's stone face themselves, having seen the only means of escape was via the god's mouth.

Iokru lay sprawled in his own blood, his sightless gaze trained upward. Scattered torches lit feathers and fur and now dead bodies crawled with flame. The clam worshipers were trapped in the chamber, facing gruesome death as the demon god flew about in wrathful abandon, augmenting its power with each being it sucked.

Looking out over the fray, Vetra saw, from the bottom bill of the osprey's parted beak, a fiery maze of smoldering corpses and scurrying figures. Many grotesque, creeper-like limbs of Nimeska slung everywhere. Dapi flew among all, choosing hapless victims at will. The lower bill of the osprey's beak was wide enough for Vetra to maneuver, yet the back part of the bird's throat was hollowed out. Some gloomy passage ran down the beast's throat. Thuds, shrieks, clinks of weapons, the sound of pounding feet and frantic men's shouts echoed about the polished stone.

Vetra kicked priests clambering up the trunk back into the mob to die skewered by Dapi's beak as the god-bird flew back and forth like a ravenous dactyl. It wreaked destruction that knew no end. Laskar helped Balir worm his way up the trunk then struggled to shimmy up on his own, hanging off a priest's boots who was almost already up. Some spears flew up at him, but they whistled wide. The archer kicked gibbering priests in the face who grabbed at his ankles.

Balir heaved a tortured gasp and clung to the osprey's bottom bill, his maimed arm hooked at the elbow over the bird's beak.

A warrior-priest jumped up to hang off Balir's legs. Balir roared in rage and pain, but Vetra stamped down and smashed the priest in the teeth. Bone and broken teeth crunched and sent the man flailing back, shrieking through a mouth of bloody froth into the howling mob.

Vetra knelt to pull the wheezing Balir up. A frantic, climbing priest competed with Laskar to monkey-scramble up the trunk. In blood-fueled lunacy, the priest gained the osprey's lower bill, where its beak hung carved in a silent cry.

Vetra ducked the man's arching blade snatched from Vetra's seashell belt and blocked a quick strike to his throat. He took hold of the quivering wrist and yanked it, splintering bone and tearing tendon.

The knife dropped from the madman's wrist. Vetra gutted him with a disemboweling chop. Dragging out his knife, he slashed at another who tried to hamstring him. Another snarling figure gained the mouth of the osprey. They struggled in the cramped space, elbows hooking jaws, their backs to cold stone walls, grunts and curses loud and echoing off the walls.

Vetra staggered back, drawing gasps of breath in his lungs. Balir crawled on all fours, wincing with the pressure on his mangled hand. The mercenary struck out at a priest's legs which now crowded in to kick at Vetra. Laskar, crossbow strapped at his back, was just pulling his wracked body over the stone-carved lip when a torch came twirling up from below and it rolled at Vetra's feet; he looked at it dazedly, the smoke stinging his eyes. The grinning priest tackled Vetra's legs and loosed a howl, sinking now with Vetra's knife protruding from the middle of his back. Balir wrestled madly at Vetra's side against another attacker, and both felt themselves slipping down, down a smooth, steep grade into the god's throat. All three toppled with cries in their throats down the black gullet of the stone god.

End over end they tumbled—down a series of polished stone chutes, flailing in the blackness.

Vaguely did Vetra remember his head spinning like a kite. Somehow the torch tumbled with them. Vetra caught flashes of beastly images carved in stone, boot heels flashing in his face, hands like claws reaching for his eyes...

Then there came a thud, and an echoing crunch of bone.

IV

How far the hapless men fell, Vetra did not know. Bereft of senses, he tumbled through the tunnels of solid rock down some zigzagging chute to land in a strange, darkened pit.

Wump! A fourth body thudded on the dead priest—was it Laskar? Balir's howl rang out as the latest falling figure caught the edge of his leg.

The bone-jarring impact knocked the wind out of Vetra. He wheezed air back in his lungs. A growing lump throbbed behind his ear. His helm had saved him from a cracked skull!—and by landing on his side.

Two torches dropped next, sizzling the men's jerkins now wet with blood. Swords had slid out of their scabbards during the plummet down the chutes. They lay gleaming in the flickering light.

Vetra crawled to his feet, nursing bruises and a dazed skull. He swatted the flames from his torn coat. Blinking in the gloom, he ran fingers over the ugly dent in his helm.

He glared about him, suspicion rising at the half inch of water that lay three feet from where the twisted body of the priest lay— the corpse's wide eyes stared in ignoble death. Vetra shook his head, amazed he himself was still alive.

Another thought slowly registered in his mind. If Dapi had not taken out so many of the enemy, Iokru and his minions might have overpowered them, taken them as sacrifices to their clam god.

Vetra's shoulders tensed at the grim memory of the

murderous battle and Iokru twitching in his death throes.

The torches on the moldered stone sputtered and hissed beside him like angry snakes. The ends had just missed the water. Vetra snatched one up and caught chilling glimpses of chains coiled in the shadows on the floor strung on the walls. All the rusty iron was draped with thick webs. Corroded vats of stone and bronze cauldrons loomed in the wavering torch-shadows...while the peg-like stumps of columns reared ominously out of the shadows, columns arranged in a circle. Cryptic symbols lay engraved in the circled pit with a seven pointed star, six feet from where he stood. A demon worship pit, if he ever saw one. Now that his eyes had adjusted to the dimness, he walked more boldly among the ruins and perceived sarcophagi ranging about the creepy perimeter. Seven lay on low slab-like pedestals, scrolled with goat's horns and serpent coils. All were inscribed with ancient symbols. A series of glass tubes and metal pipes extended from sarcophagus to sarcophagus in a strange, incomprehensible lattice-work.

Vetra stopped short. To transfer elixirs, fluids and magical airs? The concept seemed unreal. What was this place? Possibly not a worship pit. A wizard's spell-chamber then? A priest's deranged laboratory? Though somewhat indifferent to sorcery, Vetra felt a black pall of death catch his breath in this place of darkness and decay. Most of what was labeled 'spellcraft' was really only mummers' tricks or manipulation of fools' belief and hypnotism over weak minds. But this, and the recent macabre transformation of both Nimeska and Dapi—? His skin crawled.

Oblivious to the stirring of his comrades, Vetra swallowed hard and admitted that part of him could not resist the lure to peel back that lid of one of those dust-caked sarcophagi. He lifted off the broken tube that linked one of the vessels with its silent neighbor. Biting tongue, he chiseled off the lid of a cracked one with his knife.

Holding his breath, he stared within, saw the withered corpse of some vaguely human thing inside, lying like some spider-eaten carcass of a bygone race. The thing was webbed with thick brown crinkled flesh, long dried and cured from ages of settling. Sunken cheeks mantled the moth-eaten face. Worm-withered lips peeled back; the skull was framed by wisps of grizzled hair.

The claws on the end of the shriveled arms was what piqued Vetra's attention—like the paws of a mutant wolf. The legs stretched to the sarcophagi's end, protruding with what looked like talons. There was a monstrous tail that descended from the rump, akin to an alien hawser, curling over the creature's waist. Perhaps this is what those dark-minded priests of old were doing back in distant ages, Vetra surmised—manufacturing god-hybrids to provide the mindless acolytes something to worship and drive their fanatical cults. Through necromancy, they concocted aberrations like this filth, he mused, like the rat-god of the *ratmangers*? Like Dapi?

The ghoulish hulk had died long ago, or perhaps its wretched hatching had gone afoul. Vetra shuddered to think what else lurked under the lids of those other vessels, but he had no time to ponder. The muffled thuds of sliding bodies and shrieks of terror echoed from the oval gap in the ceiling.

He stared up. The chute from which they had tumbled stared back at him in black mockery. The opening looked revered, gilded around its edges and set with massive jewels, shaped like the birth-hole of a female animal. A chill shivered his marrow.

He knew they must have tumbled into some lower section of the temple complex…below the Temple of Osipres, a cave of sorts, or some primordial cavern formed by the ocean when seawater had risen up as far as the chasms of Gyzia. The ceiling, rough-hewn, rose like the inside of a whale's mouth, damp with moisture.

Balir was stirring and Laskar was already poking his bow about the refuse, his baldric hanging loose over his back. His head jerked to the sounds of imminent death above him.

Even in his half stupor, Vetra realized that only through the providence of the keeper's magic had they even survived Dapi's deadly assault. The god beast had meant to finish them all—as Iokru and many of his crew had discovered.

Vetra looked up again at the chute. Should other priests pass through that dark opening, another fight would progress—unless they were to hightail it. A death clash with the flesh-champing Dapi would be inevitable. With clenched teeth, Vetra moved on to the hither wall.

Laskar signaled the others. Vetra hobbled over to where the archer stood, extending a finger at something in the dimness. Chains and bones lay in that filth. A skeletal hand and an animal skull poked up from the debris, and still, something else...an ancient broadsword, leaning up against a fallen block of a ruined column. The weapon was magnificent. Vetra's face lit up with awe. He scooped it up and wiped off the layers of dust and cobwebs. Hefting it, he tested its weight. The weapon was well-balanced, fashioned in the style of one of the old Belarion blades of the wizard-kings. He grunted with appreciation.

Another skull and a headless skeleton lay a few yards away, strewn among lesser weapons—knives and rusted scimitars. These caused Vetra a crawling unease. Perhaps the mishmash of bones belonged to a warrior of some distant age? Not unlikely— nor was it implausible that the fallen man had suffered a gruesome fate like Kalaman. Vetra's teeth glinted. At all costs, he must not fall prey to a similar doom.

The sword lying almost hidden in the molder felt like a gift from the gods. Despite the age and size of the weapon, it had the feel of power in it. Stark, cryptic runes lay engraved in the gold-worked hilt, in a language that Vetra guessed was a lost tongue from the east. The guard on the hilt curled with serpents' heads. The blade, fine steel, was of a silver-color, with a faint shade of green, the like of which had not lost its color or rusted into uselessness after all these years. The stabbing end narrowed to a fine tip. A strange skewering instrument. The ancient weapon quivered with a unique energy, almost mystical, as if wise gods lent force to it when he made mock thrusts.

"That's a fine blade," Balir remarked.

Vetra started at the sound of Balir's voice. "It'll replace my lost Magnelian one," he whispered, frowning at his fellow merc who crept from behind him out of nowhere, "smashed by Dapi's beak in that wretched skirmish."

Balir looked a royal mess, as did they all, torn and bleeding from dozens of cuts. Strained tumult rumbled from above—muted screams and now the clatter of spears—from where the dark chute gaped all the more like an obscene birthing canal. Balir looked up, his spirit looking full of gloom. "If I'd known that our bane Dapi would have caused us this mischief, I'd have tossed that idol down the canyon long ago. Never would I have agreed to the wizard's foolish commission."

"Wouldn't we all," said Vetra hollowly. "If I know that fiend, it'll break down walls of rock to jam its beak down our throats." His lips peeled back in a bleak grimace.

Balir combed his bloody beard. "I don't understand why it has it in for us, Vetra. Are we are not somewhat its fathers?"

"We're as much its birth fathers as those damned ratmen," Vetra growled. "Don't kid yourself, Balir. Didn't one of their cult members kick the idol over into the magic pool?"

Balir grudgingly accepted the logic. He moved around, poking bits of rubble with the rusty scimitar he had dug out of the rot. It looked as if this chamber hadn't been disturbed in centuries.

Vetra watched the proceedings with a sleepwalker's daze. More than ever did he feel like a man in a dream. Should he not be finding a way out of this pit? The thought came as a vague stirring in the back of his head. Besthra's tits! It was if he was ensorcelled. He thought to discern an arched exit lurking somewhere at the back of the chamber. But it was such a wash of murk over there that he wondered if his eyes were not deceiving him. He shook his head, tried to clear the cobwebs from his mind, but he could not shake the feeling of doom clutching at his soul.

There came a smack of bone as a man plummeted through the gap in the ceiling, his leg twisted unnaturally.

Vetra saw the flash of other grisly figures struggling above. Somehow they were all jammed in a great knot in the narrowing chute. Then he heard the shriek of a god.

The man who had fallen cried out in a pitiful voice. "'Tis the pit of Ocelos! Kill me now, before the ghost of the warlock king comes to rip my heart out! Or that beastly bird comes to rape me of my soul!" His fingers clawed desperately at the clammy rock, pulling his body away from his dead peer.

"Gladly, priest," grated Balir. He staggered over to where the man crawled. "Any last prayers?"

"Just to Meru, my clam god. You must pray for me—without Meru, I will—"

Balir ran him through. "That's better. The man's keening was starting to irritate me."

Vetra grunted. "Come on." He started to pull Balir away from the corpses, then had an idea.

Hunkering down to strip the dead men of their priestly capes, he cursed. They could be used for subterfuge if they ran into more of their kind. Laskar winced at the blood. He donned the most tattered and filthy one. Balir slung the other over his shoulder. The shell helm one wore, was cracked and of limited utility. A brownish face gazed up vacuously under the mask.

The tangle of men caught in the jam above twisted and writhed with terror, unable to free themselves. A muffled cawing reverberated through their tight clot.

Vetra and the others stumbled back in horror, almost overcome by a blast of Dapi's bloody reek as the creature skewered priests and attempted to squeeze past the trapped men.

Vetra and his henchmen scrambled to the archway, hoping

for a connecting passage. Into a large chamber they fled: one equally dark and sinister.

"Dapi will strip our souls if it catches us," cried Vetra. They pushed their way through the molder and the refuse. Laskar, crossbow nocked, trailed behind, weapon slung over his shoulder. From behind they could hear the thud of more bodies smashing on their fellow priests. The fugitives were not a few hundred yards in before the echoes of falconish shrieks rattled in their ears. Vetra shook off the images of that chilling bird and its horror of death: victims forced up a ramp and plunged down the osprey's maw to fall into the wizard's pit, never to see the light of day again.

While the moans and screams of doomed men faded behind them, he edged fingers around the collar, feeling a pang of guilt over the vicious slaughter of Kalaman. Had the thing caused his death by his keeping the sinister half ring? It seemed to bind the bird-god in some inexplicable way. He could not jettison it; he had already tried that. Every time his fingers curled around its broken edge, with the aim to hurl it far away, a quivering palsy stayed his hand. Every intuitive fiber of Vetra screamed at him to get rid of the thing. Why hadn't he? He could only cling on to it tighter. His tongue, swollen when he tried to talk about it, felt like a beggar's cloth were wrapped around it.

The passage split and the brush of fresher air on their cheeks had them choosing the rightmost passage. Out they came under a low, crumbling arch. In his haste, Vetra almost toppled to his doom, for the path ended in an abrupt drop. One of the cross canyons loomed below. The night sky reared above them. Now they felt naked and insignificant under its vastness. A narrow ledge ran along the cliff at their feet. It was cut starkly in the rock face. Torches winked in the wells of darkness below, lighting more of the various temples which Vetra believed connected to the main *Way of Temples*. At least they had some semblance of direction. A buzz of activity stirred below, some low murmur of priestly voices which morphed into a drone of devotional chanting. Vetra grimaced. The priests had not yet been alerted to the horror that was Dapi at their doorstep. He looked down in bleak contemplation. He guessed the canyon had once hosted a raging torrent, but had not seen a flash flood in years.

The moon, far in its sweep across the sky, stained the crumbling landscape a ghostly gray. They trudged up the shale-flaked path with heedful steps. Any misstep meant doom, a swift tumble down a headlong drop over fifty feet below. The world that they knew loomed yet a hundred feet higher still: tantalizingly close, but no way to reach it by way of those sheer, ominous cliffs.

Sweat poured down Vetra's cheeks. The prospect of eluding Dapi's lusts for yet another hour was too horrifying to ponder. The bird evidently had no intention of abandoning their flesh; recent experience spoke that it would pursue them forever, at whatever cost, and for what—this collar? Besthra's sluts, but he had to get rid of it!

Balir and Vetra groaned. Not forty feet ahead along the ledge rose another impasse: iron bars meshed for untold feet up the side of the canyon, at whose feet sat some sort of chained gate.

Vetra gave a sour grimace. He strode up to the barrier and halted to glare with sullen distaste. The chains were sturdy—chains which he seized in his fists and rattled like a prisoner. The lock was cast iron, not to be shattered with any easy hewing. The gate was only twice a man's height, but the iron mesh riveted into the rock rose up into the gloom, lost from sight. The barrier was meant to keep wanderers or curious priests out. A forbidden zone? Likely. Ocelos's work area, however long ago that dreaded figure had lived. Half way up the cliff, they could see another ledge running parallel over their heads. It intersected the mesh at a high point. A dark, rough-hewn entrance showed in the cliff several yards down the ledge. A cave? Some tunnel into the canyon face?

"We could make for that ledge," suggested Balir.

"We could," Vetra agreed. They could climb up the iron bars like monkeys, except for Balir. Dapi of course, could fly, and they would all be ripped to pieces.

"Well, nothing to do, except get up there." Vetra sighed.

Balir's eyes glowed surprise. In all practicality the other two should have left him behind.

Sheathing their swords, the three craned their necks up to the height they must ascend. Laskar ensured his crossbow was snug in his baldric. Balir secured the knives and sword at his hip. Leaving the stubs of torches burning on the loose gravel at their feet, Vetra and Laskar took to the gate, heaving their bulks up. Cold to the touch, the heavy iron rattled and creaked like a castle's rusty portcullis.

Some feet up, the two paused to hang with one strong hand on the mesh while grabbing Balir's arm and pulling him up, while he clung awkwardly with one hand.

Balir muttered words of resentment at their assistance, but his pride gave way. Panting and sweating, he secured his footholds then pulled his weight up with his good arm, hooking his elbow over the higher bars. Vetra saw the man's injured hand trembled. "Keep steady," he said.

Vetra saw the ledge grow smaller underneath them after many painstaking efforts. Smoke stole through the canyon like cloud mist below. Ritual fires glared, like fireflies of doom.

Laskar hissed, "Should we rely on luck and try to climb higher, over the top of the mesh, or should we go for the ledge within sight on this side?"

Vetra peered down at a struggling form of Balir and the distant glare of torches. "Take the ledge," he told Laskar. "No time for climbing higher. I can hear that hellish flapping not too far away. I feel that beast is within killing radius. How its cawing haunts me! We may have a chance to lose it in the tunnel."

Laskar grunted acknowledgment of the plan. He pulled

himself higher.

Barely were they arm-lengths from the ledge when, as Vetra had predicted, the sweep of frenzied wings came slashing at the air like a miniature dragon's. Terrible croaking sounds echoed down the valley.

Laskar choked out a strangled gasp. Vetra jerked his head to the side and discerned a gruesome shape set vaguely against the moon. The thing was coming straight at them. It had obviously made bait of many more victims, judging from the blood and flesh on its beak.

Laskar gained the stony ledge and crouched there with a breathless grimace. Fingers fumbled to arm his crossbow. The beast came angling in on him.

Balir howled, steeling himself for death. Jerking sideways, he slipped down several rungs. But the action saved his life.

The bird smashed into the iron bars inches from where his head had been. The fingers of his right hand caught the bars, saving him from plummeting to his doom on the sharp rocks below.

Dapi circled the air above, dripping in blood. With a tumultuous screech thick in its throat, it fluttered in a wide loop then swooped down for another pass. A stir came from the priests far below. Vetra swung down like some spry monkey to pull Balir up.

Balir hung from a quaking hand and shrieked in his ear. "Leave me!...And curse you, Vetra, let me die—and you, you wretched falcon ghoul! Die, why don't you just die?"

Vetra winced. He cursed their folly at not climbing the iron gate faster. The bird had caught them in plain pecking distance out in the open.

Laskar hung over the lip of the ledge and frantically reached on his belly for Balir's palm. Fingers met fingers. Laskar gave a mighty heave.

With a savage cry, Vetra pushed his shoulders up on Balir's

behind from below. Balir rolled like a bear over the ledge. The rogue was up!

Dapi attacked from the air, swooping and cawing in expectant petulance. Laskar pushed away from Balir, rolling on his side. At the same time, he loosed a bolt. Dapi, whose wings were beating the air in menace, had looped in for a second strike and the iron missile clattered off its wing. The bird swerved, targeted Laskar, and dove headlong toward him, its red eyes glaring.

Laskar abandoned his weapon and rolled away down the path. The bird crashed into the cliff face behind him, shattering flakes of rock. A jagged crack grew in the surface.

Vetra recoiled; he gained the ledge and stumbled with awkward frenzy toward Laskar, pulling him to his feet. "Get away from the thing. Move! Down the ledge!" He staggered again. He grabbed Balir by the arm and they scrabbled in a crouching shamble to safety, while the stone bird hopped in a groggy daze behind them. Its claws slipped on the rubble of loose chips it had created.

The bird sprang at them in flying hops and bounds, snapping at them in an attempt to gore them. Vetra flailed blindly. The ancient blade caught an edge of Dapi's wing and grazed crown and neck to knock the bird back. The god-bird glared in surprise, crouching back on its short legs. Its princely features seemed stretched in a ghastly leer. For the moment, it was stunned by Vetra's assault.

Vetra croaked out a laugh. He swiped loops at the menace, inspired to new confidence by the blade's power. The god-bird hopped sideways, wings outstretched in a cloud of wrath. On clumsy impulse, it leaped, missed. Vetra ducked and the horror spilled drunkenly over the edge into empty space down the cliff.

Vetra swore in triumph. So, the fiend was not invincible, it could be hurt—or at least stunned. A cascading wave of hope lifted his spirits. His blade had somehow disoriented the thing, as had the crash against the cliff face.

The three ran helter-skelter across the ledge, not daring to look back or down. They scrambled toward a dark, arch-shaped entrance into a protective overhang of rock. The burrow would offer some protection at least from the airborne menace—for now.

The men lurched under the overhang. Plunged into momentary darkness, they gained some respite. But an oval shaft of moonlight appeared before them, and the rocky canopy petered out and Vetra saw that they would be left in the open again to Dapi.

Vetra cursed. They would be exposed on the ledge to assault from above.

He gritted his teeth. They couldn't linger here. The bird would just follow them in. But what hope was there ahead?

Down the narrow path they raced, stumbling. He saw more dark openings and caves gaping out of the cliff. He turned with wild ferocity on his face to his comrades. "We've got to make a run for it! I'll stay back, keep Dapi at bay. Quick. Let's muster a charge!"

Under the moonlight they staggered, clenching swords and knives, for what little good it did them. Far below, on the deep drop at their side, the shale-flaked ledge wound. Farther down, rat priests ran like stricken ants. Dapi's calls drifted like distant, forlorn warnings in the air.

A small bend appeared in the trail. With pebbles crunching under their feet and rattling over the side, they fled past a cave with iron-gridded gate. This one was man-high, held with lighter chains and an ancient lock that opened into the cliff face.

Vetra hissed the others to a halt. He was struck by a sudden idea. "Swiftly! Strike down the lock. We can lure the fiend in and close the gate on him."

Balir yelled, "And if we can't?"

"Do it!"

Like barbarians they hacked at the chains. Swinging with all their might, they hewed and cursed. Sweat dripped from their naked brows. They took turns raining blows while glaring in a grim ring. It became clear those chains were not going to give without a fight...

Balir's scimitar arced along the iron loops. The fingers under his blood-caked bandage clenched like claws. Some links splintered. A segment of chain fell away, but not sufficient to allow Vetra to pull open the gate.

Vetra swore. "Can the day be full of any more ill luck?" He drew back a pace and smote the lock a gargantuan blow. The ancient sword's impact had the valley ringing with a bright clangor.

The iron held, but sparks flew from the metal and more links spread in submission. The air seemed to whine with a mystical hum of the sword's every stroke.

Dapi had gained the air again. The god-bird soared abreast the canyon, momentarily confused. Its ghastly prince-like head swung to and fro, wondering where its charges had disappeared. To their dismay, the god-bird had heard the din of blade on metal and came vaulting over the overhang, searching for them. Its falconish eyes burned. It loosed a vengeful shriek, then came pelting down at them with a blood-gored beak.

Balir roared a bitter curse. "Do something with that fancy sword of yours, Vetra. Now! Or we're doomed."

He muttered between parted lips, "We all must die sometime, Balir." With fanatic force, he hewed at the lock. The sword's hilt burned in his hand. Laskar bashed with the blunt end of his crossbow. Only through the providence of gods did Vetra's magical blade strike through the last loop. Loosing a gasp of triumph, he pulled the chain free. Eager hands seized the bars, wrenching open the gate.

The rusty gate creaked inward. With glorious shouts they all tumbled into the cave. Like prisoners freed from a dungeon they scrambled with relish. The bird-god pressed its awful weight against the bars and beat its way in before they could swing the heavy door shut.

"Get out!" cried Balir. "The thing'll rip us to shreds!" He ducked, howling, side-swiped by Dapi's sharp wing against the bare skin of his arm. The creature was inside the cave, somewhat of a lofty tunnel, flapping around with violent confusion, creating a fearful din.

Vetra thundered, "Back through the gate! We can trap it here."

Like madmen, they scrambled past the open mesh and clapped the gate shut.

Balir and Laskar leaned their full weight against the bars, digging heels in the loose shale, struggling to keep it from bulging outward. Vetra fumbled to wrap chain link around the bars. The bird rammed beak and talons through the mesh, almost mashing Vetra's fingers in the process. He pulled his bloody hand away, wincing, amazed he hadn't broken any fingers. The last loop he had coiled held and the beast smashed in vain against the gate.

Frustration radiated from the gargoyle-carven thing. Between the bars its hateful rictus took on a perverse cast, a stone-falconish demon gobbed with the flesh of dozens of victims. The hideous beak thrust through the bars, questing for souls. The thing was hungry for flesh. The horn-hard bill reeked of blood and offal. The death and sorrow of the dozens of souls it had sucked weighed heavily on the air about it. The bloodthirsty tales of the prince were confirmed in the presence of this brute. The avian face had changed—from a stone carving of a beast to one of living, manlike semblance. Vetra saw an aristocratic nose, piercing eyes with black bushy brows, a philosopher's chin. But of these features he registered little. If not for the unruly beak it would be a strong-featured prince, the princely Dapi of old. Yet its croaking roar echoed vaguely human speech:

'God bearers, die!' A rasp of reeking breath fouled the air.

Whether it was the face and voice of the prince Dapi of long ago, Vetra could not say. In all its soul-feeding, the great god had started to become possibly more of the *man* it once was.

Dapi hovered there like some perverse specter in between its aggressive smashes on the rungs. Vetra paled. The thing was getting larger, as if the very stone were soaking up the soul flesh it sucked. A foot taller and its shadowy form rose over them, bigger and more menacing than ever when they had lugged it as a stone idol.

The beast could not drive its weight through the bars. Though it crashed against the gate, denting iron and leaving gobs of blood and flesh stuck on the metal, the iron bars held, and the three hobbled away down the narrow ledge in a stitch of dazed confusion. Benevolent spirits had favored them that day.

The bars would hold, Vetra told himself. He felt a wave of relief. Clenching his fists in exhaustion, he stumbled down the crumbled path with Laskar and Balir at his heels. His black fan of hair was damp with sweat and his chest heaved.

He chanced a look back. The bird was contained behind the grate, yet the creature seemed to study him with a malevolent interest. Up and down his spine chills crept, the crawling sensation of being watched by a fiend not of this world. And yet, a thought struck Vetra. What was to stop the bird from backtracking, discovering a way back through the tunnels, catching them by surprise in the open ground?

Vetra shivered at that and thrust the grim worry from his mind. Wrapping an arm around Balir's shoulders, he steered him down the ledge. The bird was restrained. *For now.*

V

They wandered for what seemed hours through the dimness. The ledge dead-ended in a tunnel carved in the cliff face which fanned out to a network of tunnels. Vetra and his crew tried to keep a straight path parallel to the cross canyon, but this was no easy feat. Many winding side passages veered up in silent defiance of their efforts. Their senses were soon disoriented by insufficient markers. They groped their way in complete darkness—inching along for fear of some lurking horror. At times the rock would open up to expose a gash of night sky, admitting cold moonlight playing down on a swath of carven rock.

Who had made these pathways? The priests? It seemed doubtful. The tunnels looked hewn by savage forces—even some of the cuts hewn by sharp teeth. The chipped shale at their feet seemed evidence of it. Likewise the rough-hewn walls. Carved by some power older still? Vetra gave up guessing.

The bones of rats crunched underfoot. Bats flitted overhead. Booms and sinister thuds caught their ears, the sounds of distant activity: the ceremonial beat of a priest's mallet on a deerskin drum. Then the faraway screams of fighting men, coupled with monotone chanting. Whether Dapi's work or some other frightful rite, Vetra shuddered to speculate. The trickling purl of water reached his ears. They forged their way along, and he held out his hand to feel cool water strike his fingers as it spilled down a rough, cold wall.

A glow appeared in the tunnel ahead: a soft moonlit oval. The tunnel wound down to a ledge, presumably the one they had quit long before. Vetra, grateful to see the end of this lightless passage, breathed a gust of fresh air and took to the narrow path. The moon showed as a gargantuan orb on its downward arc; the stars wheeled above in shimmering profusion. Commotion reigned in the canyon below: voices of excited priests, doomful drumbeats, flaring torches, the hectic scrambling of figures who wore curious masks—bear, rat and bison—but mostly buzzard visages or the garish plumage of parrots.

Vetra guessed they worshiped *Wausulo*, the great buzzard god of the Four Winds, seen in obscure temples on the little-trod streets in Lausern.

Priests moved in and out of arched doorways and the colonnaded terraces in the canyon below—like ghosts, conducting their dark rituals. Vetra felt a crawling chill up his back. The unearthly terror that had struck in the dead of the night had inspired these men. They knew what terrible and unnatural things were about in the air—omens of foul breeding. The same that signaled times of change, and shifts of power...So the priests and their priest-lords chanted their dirges and they mumbled their hymns, then to consult their star charts, and heed the wisdom of the black shamans who told them to pay dark homage to their patron gods.

Vetra's face twisted in a wry grimace. A stir of fierce hope struck him as his eyes drank in a familiar sight. Fires burned in the great crenelated stone watchtowers at either end of the wide avenue stretching far below...the *Way of Temples*. The way out. The battlements atop the blackstone walls flickered with torchlight. Men stalked those summits; whether they held bows or such weapons, Vetra did not know. The canyon was up in arms while furred, masked and robed figures prowled below like beetles bringing food to nest.

"There seems to be a stir among our buzzard men," rasped Balir. The fire was alive in his eyes. He seemed numbed to whatever pain he had suffered from his past mutilation. Vetra saw the remaining fingers were wrapped under the bloody cloth with a fearless defiance.

The ledge veered down at a steep angle toward the busy avenue and the canyon floor.

Vetra beckoned his men. They would have to expose themselves to danger. But there was no other way to get to the watchtower.

Acolytes moved in stolid groups down these ways in their buzzard garb. Their masks were embellished with curved beaks, their waists and torsos pasted with bristling feathers while thighs gleamed nakedly in the torchlight, feet outfitted with claw-tipped boots dipped in oil and blood. Those devotees melted back into patches of gloom and eerily-lit cones of light from the fires. Some chattered excitedly among themselves in disquieting priest-tongues.

The three fugitives did their best to keep to the shadows, hiding behind the priestly garb they had accumulated as disguise. Balir and Vetra wrapped the clam-cult capes around their torsos, Laskar held the broken clam-cult mask to his face. But even as he did so, a priest clad in a bear mask strode up the ledge straight at them. Curious, priestly eyes took in their company. No time to turn! They could take out the man, Vetra thought, but if the bear-mask cried out and alerted others...

Laskar ducked back in the shadows, readying his weapon. He tossed Balir his mask. Balir hastily snatched it up and donned it. Feigning an easy manner, Balir lifted his hand in salute as the priest drew closer, the same as Iokru had done, placing a proprietary grip on Vetra's shoulder. He did this as if escorting the mercenary as an outland prisoner. The acolyte passed by with an expression of stern acknowledgment. But he stopped, his expression now edged in suspicion. He thrust out an accusing finger. His throat gurgled with the beginnings of a cry.

Vetra plunged his dagger in the cleric's throat before the priest could react, thus silencing the warning cry. The victim slumped to his knees, uttering a strangled gasp. He and Balir hid the body in the shadows where Laskar waited with his crossbow. Laskar stalked forth, weapon trained, frowning at the bleeding corpse.

Vetra crouched, listening for pursuit. He donned the dead man's bear mask and set his own helm down next to the corpse. The man's gasp had gone unnoticed, thus the priests below remained absorbed in their ritual debasement farther up the canyon. Vetra was reluctant to discard his own helm. He gazed at it with reverence. It had saved him many times. But if its absence could fool a few priests at a distance... Two disparate masks, one clam, the other bear and Laskar with his clam-cape, moved with stealth up the path. Probably not an entirely believable scenario, but it would have to do.

A dismal shriek pierced the air. Vetra and the others whirled. The men of the buzzard cult below looked up while out of the air came a horrible, beaked shape dipping out of the sky.

Dapi! The fiend flew over the canyon floor. Like some blood-caked gargoyle of nightmare. It was as if the thing had been alerted by some disturbance beyond Vetra and his companions' knowledge. Now it rose to the tops of the temples, honing in like a falcon of prey.

Vetra ducked and pulled Balir down. They thrust themselves flat on the ledge, keeping their heads low. It was as if the bird-beast knew their every movement. Dergath! How could it have backtracked and sniffed them out so quickly? Vetra stifled a curse. Either it had torn its way through the bars or looped back through the tunnels, as he had feared...maybe to an adjoining passage that led to the *Way of Temples*. Either way, they were in a nasty predicament.

Spears clattered up and smote the swooping bird.

Dapi gave a ravening shriek. A thrum of screeching voices coursed from the throng. The bird dove toward the offending priests, eager for souls. Squawks and the snapping of spears came to Vetra's ears. The thunks of stone into flesh.

What drove the beast? Vetra searched for an answer, but received none. His mind worked. Surely they had not been in the tunnels that long?

Squatting here in the dark shadows meant death. The way back was an inky crypt, full of violence and savagery. The way out was through the shadowy canyon and on to the watchtower. There, a steep stairway wound alongside and up the canyon wall...

Vetra picked himself up and they plunged down the shadowy path toward the fires housing the rites of the priests. "Quickly! Mingle with the priests! We'll have a fighting chance. Dapi can't target us as easily."

There was no argument. They reached the sandy floor and scrabbled over upended urns and amphorae of wax. They raced through clots of fleeing priests to the nearest side of the canyon. Then slunk past a low carven sphinx, with lion paws splayed into the avenue's middle. Vetra and Balir gaped at its bizarre, brooding presence. On a natural pillar of rock rearing sixty feet above the canyon loomed a strange cage, whose stone-carved bars contained a hulking bird-beast. The thing glared back with defiance through the stone mesh and was the same they had seen from a distance upon entering the canyon.

The white-faced acolyte who drew the bolt back leaped aside.

The bars of the cage swung wide. The buzzard squawked. It hopped out of its prison and bounded forth toward the edge of its oval perch. A gleeful, guttural sound escaped the thing's throat which hung with loose wads of flesh. News of Dapi's resurrection had prompted the priests to summon their god, Besirath. Another horror to plague the air, Vetra thought in grim reflection... The summoning acolyte fled in wild fear down a winding staircase. He circled the pillar, narrowly escaping the champing bill that snapped out its yellowed beak to behead him. The giant buzzard clung to the edge of the pillar's summit with its sharp talons.

It spread wings and swooped.

Down into the fray it dove, skimming over the heads of the acolytes who crouched below on the canyon floor cringing in fear and wonder. One it knocked flying, sending his brains splattering to the stone.

The devotees raised hoarse shouts of rapture at their god, hefting glinting spears. One sacrifice in a sea of others meant little to them. Much ruckus progressed for anyone to notice Vetra and his band. They half-crouched, slinking in the shadows. The buzzard god was arching and screeching while Dapi circled about, on the hunt, ruling the air like a ghoulish warlord.

Vetra saw the buzzard swing nearby and surge after the falcon like a gust of wind. The thing was one-eyed like a cyclops as if it were the inbred progeny of monstrous titans. Lifting its bald red skull to the sky, it moaned a mournful shriek then arched its yellow beak moonward with pompous authority. Dapi dipped. The buzzard dove with barbarous purpose. The gray-tipped wings barely moved at all. Yet it picked up speed. The priests must be desperate to have released this horror, Vetra thought. With determined strides, he and the others pushed past members of other cults. They caught glimpses of bear heads, amulets, weapons of steel belted at hips.

He pushed on, but Balir trailed back.

"Hurry up!" Vetra grunted at him.

Balir frowned. "One minute here, another minute gone. I want to see this fight."

"Are you daft? We've no time!" Vetra dragged him away from the sharp drop. "You want to get skewered?"

Balir cast him a sullen look. Every desire showed in his face to see Dapi die.

The buzzard god soared over the temples and was now a giant blot against the moon. It banked sharply and swooped down after Dapi who soared low over the avenue. The frenzied masses cheered. The buzzard-helmed priests clashed spears against ceremonial shields in praise of their champion—Besirath, a violent god unleashed and come to defeat the newly-risen demon prince. The thing was five times the size of Dapi. But Dapi was made of stone, while the buzzard-god was made of flesh and blood.

"Keep moving," Vetra rasped. "Let them battle it out in blood and fire, while we escape!"

A ramp directly ahead cut in the canyon's side. The narrow ledge it joined continued on, straight toward the far watchtower where the exit lay. Craning his neck, Vetra saw the ledge wind up then switch-back over the canyon. The company took the ramp, but a cry of mournful authority thundered up the valley. The buzzard and Dapi circled each other—one a looming juggernaut, the other a dark fly in comparison. But they met in a clash of thunder. Blood and feathers flew every which way and feral squawks echoed about the canyon.

Dapi went corkscrewing in a tailspin, buffeted by the larger bird's attack. It careened toward the far cliff wall and swiped a tall bull statue, shearing the head off. The shattered chunks tumbled and crashed into the boulders and sand below, crushing a half dozen priests.

Dapi rolled dizzily in midair. But it recovered, hurtling after the buzzard, circling it like some fiendish gnat before smashing its beak square in the black buzzard's feathered hide.

The buzzard swerved out of control, blind-sided, heaving an anguished croak. Dapi circled up and around it, attacking without mercy. The buzzard squawked in shrill agony.

Dapi's last strike pierced the fleshy underbelly. The maimed bird fell like a stone to the fire-lit avenue, rolling and thumping, shrieking, and it lifted itself from its broken, tumbled sprawl and limped away, croaking in miserable grunts down the *Way of Temples*. Knots of priests fled in gibbering throngs. Dapi combed the air above, a fiend of preternatural destruction. It batted aside the spear thrusts of the priests and guards with beak and wing, dodging hurled stones.

The god-bird would not let the buzzard go. The crippled thing was hopping about lamely, but Dapi smashed headlong into its face, sending its riven bulk back several feet. The stone-devil went right inside the thing's gullet.

Buzzard flesh thrashed and bucked; the beast gave a choked gurgle and in one convulsive heap fell over dead, its soul sucked clean. Dapi burst out of the thing's beak, shredding its black buzzard throat in a trail of slime and bloody feathers. It loomed larger than before, a shadow of monstrous evil. Flexing wings, it hopped about, wiping beak, while its stony, blood-soaked body gleamed with a greenish slime, its eyes blazing crimson.

Vetra and the others watched appalled as it preened itself, crouched on the ledge behind a boulder. Vetra's fist clenched on his hilt. A sour feeling rose up in his throat. To witness a god's demise in the valley of the damned was no small affair.

Shouts echoed from the ledge directly below.

Striding with grim purpose, a cult leader crowned in a massive headdress paused and studied the new development. His teeth glinted. Following him loped a band of his priestly rogues.

Rojarsh and his jackals! A murderous rage brought red mist to Vetra's vision. The death of Kalaman swept quickly to mind. His comrade-in-arms dying in agony at the hands of these devils and their kind.

The priests doubtless were revising their original plan, in light of the buzzard's fall.

Vetra dropped to his belly and pulled Balir and Laskar down with him.

The voice of the high priest came grumbling at his advisor, "If you see that knave, Vetravincus, kill him. Kill him and his crew on sight! I don't want them getting past our guard—or worse—back to that hound Caglios with those relics of ours. The bastard has caused us too much ruin." The high-priest rubbed his brow and ruffled his weighty headdress, a giant pink and white crab with wicked white pincers.

"Agreed, lord," murmured the priest's advisor. He adjusted his own feral headdress. The man was near naked, but for a pair of furred boots and a bear pelt of loin-cloth.

"The intruder must be up the old Ocelos tunnels," Rojarsh muttered. "He couldn't have gotten far from Dapi's pool. Take a team, flush them out."

"I wonder what has become of our priest, Iokru?" a cleric muttered, gazing fretfully at the winged shape. He ducked instinctively as the bird-god dipped and dove not far from their position. "Not a man from his party has returned. You saw the state of him when he came back begging for men and weapons to hunt down those swine. His face was white with excitement."

Rojarsh's features creased.

"A bad business, Rojarsh. I never trusted that smirking Iokru from the beginning."

Rojarsh eased his advisor's fears. "I've known Iokru since a boy. He wouldn't dare cross me. And yet—" the old cult leader frowned. A sullen glare showed some niggling doubt. With jaw protruding, the cruel deliberation in his face showed a man capable of formidable deeds.

Yet he seemed to stiffen at more sounds in the air. Dapi lunged in one swift fatal swoop to take down another priest, plunging beak through a pink mouth. "Curse this Dapi demon! Those filthy outlanders have loosed a hellfowl among our ranks!"

An under-priest flourished. "Our power is no more than that of ants compared to this stony fiend. What will become of—"

"Find them!" Rojarsh shouted, swatting a stave at his henchman. "The buzzardmen said they saw three rogues similar to Vetravincus and his band skulking around the hallowed ways of *Wausolo* not long ago. They disappeared into the shadows. Somehow they must have come out of the forbidden tunnels. Damn their skulking hides!"

The conch-helmed man who was the team leader ran off with

several masked priest-guards ahead to fulfill their lord's request.

"Come, Zitanger," grunted Rojarsh to his elder priest. "Let us depart this vale and take refuge in the *Cavern of the Great Clam*. We can draw the bronze portal shut. Neither Dapi's beak nor any other god's will be able to flush us out."

Vetra looked up as gravelly croaks streamed down from the winged god's throat. The horror was aiming right for him.

Sword gripped, he squared himself for instant death, but pitched sideways in time, evading a mortal strike. The rake of cruel talons passed just hair widths from his neck. He mumbled oaths and readied himself for another attack.

Dapi came fast and low. Vetra crouched, rose catlike on his feet, struck the thing full across the body. The resounding clunk of steel on stone shivered through his arms. Laskar swatted at the rising shape with his bow end, but bolts were useless against a thing of its nature. Balir notched his dully gleaming blade on the bird's rank hide as it swept by.

A bevy of spears clattered up at them. Rojarsh's crew looked below with wrath.

Vetra fell back. He danced on his toes, barely avoiding a pin-cushioning by the spears' razor-sharp tips. "Fools! 'Tis clear the bird fiend's the enemy, not us."

"They're imbeciles," Balir roared. "Let's quit this ledge, Vetra—or find some higher perch!"

Vetra prepared a defense, but the thing circled back to finish them off, its red eyes blazing.

A spear tip slid off Dapi's side. The creature swooped low at a breakneck speed and dove at the attacking priests huddled on the ledge below. The priests bleated in wonder as they keeled over or fled like dogs along the ledge. Too late. Dapi smashed into their huddle, knocking them flat on their faces, noses broken and faces gouged. Back it flew in a circle to focus on a wild-eyed Rojarsh, who stood exposed, clutching stave in hand and combing his black beard with a hand of disbelief and terror.

Vetra felt an oppressive weight grow in his pocket. Every time the bird swung close by, he could feel a throbbing against his skin. As the bird banked toward him, he saw the melted collar fused on the bird-god's neck pulse in synchrony. He pulled the collar out, shaking his fist at the sky. "It's this vile thing you want, isn't it?"

Balir gasped at the sight of the collar. "You still have that bloody thing? What in Besthra's name? Get rid of it! Why do you hold it? Are you a damned fool?"

"Don't test me, Balir! It's not me who has a mangled hand."

Balir tried to wrest the thing from Vetra's grip. But Vetra twisted away and knocked Balir off his feet. Laskar grabbed Vetra's fist before he could smack it into Balir's skull.

"Are you crazy?" thundered Laskar.

The sounds of inhuman shrieks had them all scrambling back.

Vetra and Balir masked heavy breathing. They peered down over the ledge. Bloodshot eyes scanned the carnage below as a fleet shape tossed Rojarsh's bodyguards everywhere. The protectors fought with mad desperation to keep their priest-lord from getting gored.

In the dim shadows Vetra gritted his teeth. His breath rasped in a dry throat as he searched for a solution. Pinned to this ledge by Dapi and the priests, there were not many options.

"Help me roll this boulder over the ledge," he hissed. "We can drop it on that devil."

"It would kill us more pesky priests in the meantime," agreed Balir. Wiping his split lip, he glared, looking rankled by Vetra's recent rage.

Arms and shoulders straining, the three got the stone rocking. With a rumble and clatter of pebbles, the boulder hurtled down the canyon wall.

The priests looked up in horror as a wave of spinning death smashed into their numbers and tore a half of Dapi's wing off. The creature croaked in outrage as its body was sent spinning sideways. It tumbled down the slope, a stony ball of beastly fury. In a cloud of dust it collapsed at the feet of several priests who gaped at it from the canyon floor.

The stone devil writhed—to Vetra's vast shock, a dusty form wriggled with life.

"It can't be." Vetra's mouth worked.

"No way!" murmured Balir. He shook his head in disbelief and mumbled several bitter oaths. The god half-hopped and flapped drunkenly to its feet. But it could gain no more than six feet in the air.

"Its wings are finished," grunted Vetra with some vindication. "The fiend was lucky. A direct strike would have taken it out. The thing's still dangerous..."

"But not them—" Balir pointed a finger to the ghoulish abattoir below. "Dapi has made short work of our priests."

Vetra grimaced. "Let's go."

Even as he turned, his jaw sagged. A large, dark brown shape came shambling on all fours down the ruin of the avenue. The rat creature stopped, snout lifted in the air, pointed teeth snapping at corpses.

"The rat-god of the *ratmangers*!" Balir swore.

The beast snarled a low, guttural bray. Somehow the god had broken its chains—then leaped out of its ring of fire. The matted fur was singed, pelt smoking, and the sounds that whinged from its flabby throat were chilling to hear.

The creature charged up the path where Dapi sent priests toppling to their doom.

Vetra and the others reeled, staggering up the ledge while Rojarsh's cries alerted more of his followers. Reinforcements were on their way. They surged out of the shadows. Vetra flinched as footfall pounded behind them.

He risked a glance back—some twenty determined rear guard looped around from the ledge below, scrabbling like monkeys.

Laskar loosed a bolt over his shoulder. A priest sank in a

crumpled heap. The archer paused to reload. One of Rojarsh's tall, clam-helmed giants was close behind. Evil intentions lay carved on his face. Vetra heard a knife whistle through the air. He turned, saw a gleaming blade sticking from the side of Laskar's throat. The archer sagged, gave a gurgling gasp then toppled face down, blade sunk hilt-deep in his neck.

Vetra mouthed a curse. He stooped over Laskar's twitching body. He rose in time to kick at the ogre-like priest who had skewered him.

The mercenary's ancient blade deflected the priest's murderous knife thrust. Balir dodged a fist from his enemy's companion, then he hip-checked him spinning close to the edge of the cliff. The groping man's foot slipped. Stone chips rattled as he tottered over the edge. His choked scream echoed in darkness.

Vetra elbowed his assailant in the teeth then rammed a sword into his guts. The priest sank with a strangled sob, clutching at his belly as if trying to keep entrails from slipping out. The mercenary sheathed his sword, snatched up Laskar's abandoned crossbow then pulled back the firing arm. He advanced on the throng of priests that faced them. Sour rage clouded his reason. Chest heaving, he trained his weapon, mouth curled in a vindictive snarl, ready to shoot anything that moved. The archer had been a staunch ally. He had not said much, but neither he nor Balir would be alive if not for Laskar's courage and unswerving skill.

Vetra watched the priests hang back, huddled in a knot of murmuring indecision. None were sure of their next move—or Vetra's for that matter. None dared to tempt the wrath of the mercenary's teeth-bared fury.

Balir yelled at him to get back, but Vetra held his ground. Two threw spears at him which glanced harmlessly off his mail. Others flew past when he dodged. There was not enough space on this ledge for an organized rush without bringing on casualties.

A fanatic charged. Vetra loosed point blank, catching the runner full in the face. His buzzard mask erupted in a ruin of feathers, balsam and human features. Goaded to frenzy, the rest of the horde sprang over the dead body, and lurched screaming after him.

Vetra scrambled back. He realized his options had run dry. He stumbled down a less steep section of the ledge, somewhat of a scree slope.

Balir roared, eyes wide, "Are you nutso?"

"Make your choice, mercenary," Vetra thundered, "or you're dead!"

Balir sucked in a breath. He gazed where Dapi continued to rage in a heated fang-versus-beak battle with the rat god not a stone's throw below.

"Dapi will protect us," snarled Vetra, his spit full of sardonic contempt.

Balir stumbled after him. The bloodstained god raged below. Balir gave a growl of frustration as his damaged hand shot out to balance him on the steep grade and its shattered flakes.

Vetra reloaded Laskar's crossbow. As he slid down the slope, grim retribution shone in his features. A crazed battle fever ran in his blood.

The pursuers looked down the slope at the battle between rat and falcon. Their eyes dimmed. The canyon was a litter of bodies. Fires burned, setting corpses and ceremonial banners aflame. Broken statues teetered on cracked legs while glowering under crimson firelight as screaming acolytes ran amok. Old priests stumbled pell-mell, beating tired drums tied at their bellies, wailing in wild confusion. Vats of ceremonial oil spilled over, spat and blazed. Masked men ran hither in panic, trampling their fellows and rivals who were too slow.

The rat god leapt to tear at Dapi. Its front fangs found the bird's throat and ripped at it like a wild hound. Dapi's supernatural stone was impervious to such molestations. It whipped itself free, rejecting both fang and claw alike. Straight at its adversary it flew, beak speared out like a skewer.

The rat god loosed a groan, transfixed. Dapi began sucking the life out of its mouth. The rat's squeals of horror dwindled to gurgles while blood gushed from its cloven mouth. Dapi sent a bestial cry to the nighted sky resounding about the stone canyon. More powerful than ever had the fiend grown, pulsing with a devil's spite. It wallowed in a sultry brown glow, its reward for sucking the rat's soul dry.

"This falconish devil is beyond us." Vetra murmured in contempt.

Dapi's power truly had multiplied as it consumed souls, absorbing the qualities of that which it sucked. The god hunched in grotesque squalor on its talons, face and eyes gleaming with hate. For a brief moment, Vetra thought it looked particularly rodent-like—yet then, like a man.

The priests, crushed with the demise of both rat and buzzard, decided that Dapi was unkillable. They pelted it with rocks. Stone bowls lifted in hands, ceremonial objects, anything they could get their hands on to smash the dark, gray stone god to oblivion. An act of desperation, and yet, in a brief twist of irony, it was these material objects which seemed the only deterrent against the horror.

While one would bait it, the bird would hop and croak with fury toward the stone-thrower then another priest would pelt it from a different direction. In such a way, the priests kept Dapi distracted. Fire did not seem to affect the god-bird. Broken-masked priests thrust torches up at its clacking beak only to be mowed down in a beak-and-tooth frenzy. Their resistance may have slowed the bird's advance, but it only made the falcon more aggressive.

Balir crouched, glaring up from a crumble of statues and broken bits of entablature. He had caught up to Vetra in the *Avenue*, and Vetra, gusting a curse, staggered down the broad path. He herded Balir alongside him. The columns of the Rose Temple of the Serpent towered high above them. Quieter sanctuary reigned here, for Dapi's carnage was raging in places distant and only a far thrum came drifting to Vetra's ears. Clam and rat priests had taken up the chase on Rojarsh's order, forcing the fugitives to swerve around a pillared bend and clamber into a columned court carved into the cliff.

The rebels stood motionless. A larger open worship area loomed in front of them: the *Temple of the Serpent*. While the clatter of footsteps pounded straight past them, they edged with gratitude into the dim-lit inner court and saw they were in a sanctuary with six, obsidian bull-headed gods. Coiled jade snakes hung from the walls, tongues flickering out through fanged mouths. Other grotesque shapes hunched about the tiled floor with various heads of bullfrogs, snakes, and the horns of bulls.

Vetra shuddered at the collective nightmare of forms and he lit a candle on the lintel of an altar carved rudely in the wall. The two padded on silent feet down the tapestried hall, through an incense chamber at the back.

Vetra pushed aside a tattered curtain that protected a doorway. The temple edged out onto another avenue, this one minor.

Two hundred feet up, Vetra looked upon a patch of open sky. The clouds were clearing and the sky was just starting to lighten—a patch indicating dawn. Vetra strode with grim purpose along side routes while Balir clutched at his gleaming blade. Somehow, his innate sense of direction kicked in and he managed to steer them back to the *Way of Temples*. Farther away from the slaughter, the vindictive assaults of the ratmen and clam-cult sympathizers had abated.

The mercenaries panted, their nerves frayed. Like weasels they crept along the shadowy wall and Vetra's legs burned with exhaustion. His mouth hung open, parched as a desert. In the near distance they heard the fervid beat of drums and the intense chanting of masked priests, all wishing for Dapi's demise and the quick sacrifice of the infidels who had incited the falcon god's wrath. Beads of sweat budded on Balir's cheeks. His eyes glowed. He looked wild and haunted, like a starveling wolf of the woods. Deep in his lined face, Vetra saw the gaze of a man who had survived multiple deaths, now reduced to a hunted animal. Only the threat of gruesome slaughter kept the mercenary from succumbing to shock.

Sensing no sign of pursuit, Vetra poked his head out from an alcove. He stood there blinking in the half gloom, while towering columns ranged on either side of him and squat, ram-headed statues protruded from the solid cliffs. No priests were in range—at least what he could see. Then suddenly, a shiver of movement stirred from down the *Way of Temples*. He and Balir watched as a tall priest with a ram-headed mask emerged from between the outstretched paws of a massive chimaera-like statue. The figure edged down the *Alley* toward sounds of a gathering commotion growing in intensity. The priest seemed immune to the threat, despite his peers running in the opposite direction.

What the devil was he up to? The cleric raised his arms, almost twice as long as Vetra's own, extended by thin planks strapped to his forearms. Between his extended wooden palms a red ball of flame began to grow into a whirling blaze. *A sorcerer!* It crackled and hissed and some hideous creature formed in the expanding bubble: a demon reminiscent of a smoke-wreathed gray scorpion with a flicking tail, the embodiment of his god.

A squat form suddenly hopped out of the shadows—to meet the conjured shape, cawing with distinct familiarity. *Dapi!* The gray mass of the scorpion grew to a crimson whirlwind. It lashed with its tail and fire whipped out to engulf the bird-god in flame. Like a mosquito that flies into the lantern's light, Dapi had stormed right into the sorcerer's trap.

The god rolled to the ground, smoking and cawing. But it spread its broken wings and stretched to its full height, snapping its beak. The priest stiffened and curled his lips. In a flutter of robes, he scrambled away.

Dapi hopped after him. The man, or sorcerer, recognizing that his grim god had failed him, burst away with disbelief to distance himself from the oncoming monster. He pushed aside the other priests who had come to watch, pointing and lifting his macabre hands. With magic blasts he smote them when they did not move out of the way fast enough.

The sorcerer had given Vetra the diversion they needed. In a burst of speed, they made for the farthest watchtower—the final bastion guarding the gates out of this cursed city. Thus far, they had navigated the avenue unmolested...

The walkways breasted the iron-worked tower, a path switch-backing up the steep face of the canyon like a slithering snake. Torches marked its banisters; hundreds of steps up the canyon face, the stairs crossed back on themselves above the watchtower, gleaming like white teeth.

"We have to reach that point," Vetra whispered, motioning a hand.

Balir acknowledged the truth of it. The guardpost at the tower's base led to the zigzagging stairway illumined with burning torches. To this area, Vetra crept.

Fortune was with them. They had a lighted way in front of them. No bowmen walked the battlements that they could see.

Signs of activity came to their ears: the hum of voices, a clink of cups. News of the god on the loose. It had spread to all quarters of the complex, but the men within this outpost looked as if they had been ordered to keep watch at their posts. Vetra scowled. Two sentries in the guardhouse mumbled in low tones. They peered over their shoulders, casting dark looks at the proceedings in the *Alley*. At times, one of them would throw a die or toss gaming chips on a pile. Their unicorned helms lay untended on the table.

"We may have some trouble with our friends here," Vetra

grumbled.

Balir gave an idle shrug. "So? I'm guessing it's easy to get into the canyon. But hard to get out."

Vetra shifted uneasily on his feet. He adjusted the bear's mask that made his skin itch like the plague.

"Nothing we can't handle. Move over to the side, Vetra, near that beast-headed column. Cover me when I give the signal. Watch how I handle this."

Before Vetra could object, Balir swaggered up to the two gamblers, raising a ruby stump and grinning like a simpleton from the market. "Been a hard night. A wee accident up the tunnels put a damper on my day," he bantered. "Mind you, could be worse! Could have been a leg of mine that old Dapi snipped off. Can I trouble you for a cup of arrack? Cleanse my throat and douse my wounds?" He gave them an oafish laugh then a conspiratorial wink.

The two sentries jerked to motion, knocking over wooden stools. They snatched up hooked spears and shouted at him. "Stand back, you halfwit! How did you get here?" The first sentry's eyes narrowed in confusion. "You?" he cried in lip-quivering recognition. "You're one of those damned outlanders. The ones who woke Dapi, caused us all this woe! One more step and I'll gut you!"

Balir gestured in helpless fashion. "I stand guilty as charged." He held up his sword in a gesture of surrender.

The guard came surging over to relieve Balir of his weapon. But Vetra edged out of the shadows like a panther. He brained the first guard from behind. The guard fell with a thud, his skull caved. Balir speared the other who came rushing in. The guard crumpled in a gibbering heap. Balir ran him through, thus squelching any excess noise from his writhing. He wiped the blade on the back of the guard's caftan. The two crouched over the bodies, breaths held. Vetra blinked in the flickering light, gripped his blood-soaked weapon.

Balir's face turned to the corpse in a friendly grin. "Let that be the lesson of not wearing one's helmet." He rose and squinted about.

Only the low murmur of voices drifted from the antechamber where the gamblers drank and laughed.

Vetra sheathed his sword. "It won't be as easy to get by those sods at the guardhouse, Balir," he hissed. "Let's strip these hounds and pose as them. It may not fool them for long, but long enough that we can sneak by the main force and get out of here."

Balir's nod was slow in coming. He glanced at Vetra with hesitation, his sidelong gaze speaking of how much he despised this priestly garb.

Vetra paid him no heed. They dragged the corpses into the shadows, dumping them behind the serpent-scrolled pillar.

After stripping the sentries of their white robes, belts and tanned leather breeches, Vetra doffed his own garments and put on the guard's. He bundled the clothes under his arm and grabbed a torch.

"Why take those old rags with us?" Balir mumbled.

"Because we can still change back up top—if we make it that far. We have yet to make it back to the city, remember?"

Balir grunted. His clothes-changing was a more lengthy affair given his mangled hand. Vetra helped him with an impatient flourish.

At least Balir seemed happy to toss aside his ill-smelling clam mask. He drained one of the tankards of ale left behind while Vetra grabbed a half-filled canteen of his own.

The merc peered about and saw there were roughly twenty men crammed into the ill-lit pillared guardhouse.

Lazy sods, Vetra thought gloomily, to be so holed up gambling, so inattentive while Dapi raged in the Alley. The square-topped outbuilding reeked of smoke, incense and unwashed bodies.

Together the two treaded on silent feet past the bulk of guards. They edged their way through the lingering shadows, then up the first of the stairs.

A voice called out in the torchlit gloom. Vetra froze in his tracks, gripping his sword hilt under his robe.

"Oi! What gives?" the figure bawled. "Aren't you supposed to be watching the *Alley*?"

Vetra cleared his throat. "Thought I heard something, chief. Something suspicious up the landing." He grimaced, grateful to be masked in the shadows and stationed about thirty feet away. "The gatemaster would have our heads if I let intruders in or out."

The other grumbled. "Anything to report up the *Alley*?"

"Nay." Vetra blinked while shifting nervously. "Poor old Rojarsh and his gang got blooded up by Dapi. By the blood of Dergath, the buzzards and *ratmangers* likely'll round up the infidels. Bold of the outlanders to rob the priest-king under his nose."

The man growled out a surly oath. "Let's hope they catch those wretched bastards and this be the end of this dismal business. I'm bored of hanging around this spider haunt, as nice as it is to take Ifgin's money here." He jerked a thumb back at his dull-eyed mate and tossed a coin in the air. "Yet the high priests told us to not let a man up or down these stairs on threat of death." His lips peeled back in a knowing grin. "Only a moron would be stupid enough to try to escape by this way." The priest leaned forward, frowning at the thought. "What with the double guard we have posted."

"You're right in that," Vetra said, masking a strangled chuckle. "Well, back to our watch. I'll be up and down the stairs in a flash. Keep up the good work with your game, chief. If Ifgin has any coins left, I'll be sure to take them from him."

The other gave an offhand grunt. He went back to his dice game. Vetra heard more loud shouting, fist-banging on tables mixed with obscenities.

He hissed under his breath. Balir came shuffling out beside him, a disparaging look on his face.

Up the steep ramp the two sauntered. They passed out of the line of sight of the guardhouse then bounded up the narrow flight of stairs. The steps were sunken and crudely skewed, as if long ages ago they had been subjected to an earthquake. A lone torch glimmered several paces on up. The way was flanked by repulsive hound-like gargoyles. All had elongated snouts, vampirish incisors and peculiar curled tails with three manicured knouts on the end.

"Horrid little creatures," mused Balir. "Somebody ought to give these clerics advice on stone-carving."

Vetra sighed and shook his head.

Their ruse did not last for long. Echoing shouts of angry men came stabbing out of the darkness. Then a glitter of knives and the scuff of feet pelting from behind up the hallowed, ancient steps.

"Too many of them," muttered Balir. "They'll bring us to ground."

"Help me then," said Vetra. He grasped one of the ugly dog statues. "We can roll this thing down and crush a few in the meantime."

With all their strength, they heaved. Balir wrapped his good arm under the dog's belly then put the full force of his weight behind the statue. They got the thing rolling and it tumbled down the stair. Gaining speed, it cracked off tail and paws, as the watchmen came thundering up the stair in a blade-wielding frenzy. A half dozen lay crushed in mangled heaps under its lethal weight. Others scrambled over the wreckage. Vetra seized a glowing lantern off the wall and hurled it down. The glass smashed and burst into flame. He upended the pot of replacement oil at his feet. The steps below ignited in a whoosh of fire. Vetra glared in satisfaction. Any who broke through the clotted mass of crushed bodies would be engulfed in flames.

Balir guffawed, seeing the devotees of Gyzia lit up like candle wicks. They danced like sock puppets in the wild firelight.

The stairwell was narrow but more foes scrambled up the way, hoping to catch the rebels. Arrows came skidding up at them from torchlit slits in the tower, the archers below alerted to their presence.

Vetra and Balir scrambled higher in a low, frantic crouch. Fletched shafts skittered off the stone, whining like bees. Another of the dog statues proved a tempting target. They rolled it down the steps, this one larger, and it stuck lengthwise in the torchlit stairway.

Vetra ripped a lantern off the wall and tossed its oil down. A wall of fire flared. He bounded up the switch-backing heights while Balir struggled at his heels.

They were soon out of range of the arrows. The last step was in sight. They clambered up and over it. A cool breeze brushed their cheeks as they crouched, hands on knees, panting for breath.

At last they had reached the top; the moon swung low in a ponderous arc on the horizon. Only a single, square-topped watchtower rose over the lip of the canyon, casting a faint, predawn shadow in the small walled courtyard. They plunged through an inner gate. Vetra almost ran face first into a lone sentry who gripped a two-pronged spear and torch. He glowered at the intruders while lunging with glinting weapon. Sword met spear in a shrill clangor. It was fierce as any that had clashed below in the valley. The clink of weaponry echoed off the silent stone as Vetra smote and grunted while Balir watched in the shadows in something of grinning amusement as the duel gained fire. He fingered his own blade, with an expression mirroring his expectations of the outcome. Vetra parried. At an appropriate moment, he plunged his blade into the gasping man's ribs. The guard sank with a howl.

Vetra could see the wink of torches and angry commotion far below. He wiped his dripping blade on the sentry's cloak. His lungs heaved. Both he and Balir hastily donned their original garments, keeping the others to discard later. Vetra had expected more of a fight here. There had been at least four of the unicorn-helmed priests guarding the gatehouse on the way down. Not now. No matter. He thanked Dapi for the poorly-manned outpost.

Wasting no time, the two stumbled across the court to the outer gate then onto higher ground and past a low wall and another unguarded exitway. They caught clear glimpses of the glowing lights of the city winking a few leagues east over the top of the thickets and the stunted shrubs. They took to the weed-choked path through the heath and scrub. After a time, Vetra threw the priests' bloody clothes into the brush. With eager relish, he trudged with Balir on toward Lausern.

VI

The moon was a glowering orb in the west, setting in a smoky bank of cloud. At last the mercenaries were dogging their way down a cobbled road through the precincts of the wine district, bordering the shanties of the immigrant workers, then to the outer gate.

A high wall of rough-hewn blocks surrounded the city. A sleepy guard stood atop the barbican, looking down from a crude notch with double-armed crossbow in hand.

The sentry posted below the city's West Gate uttered a challenge then approached the two. Another hefted a pike with a wicked, up-curled tip. The dwindling moonlight continued to glint off his steel morion and greaves. "Where are you going, friends?"

"Into the city," growled Balir. "Where else?"

The mace chain jangled at a hip as he cast Balir a cold glare.

Vetra cast Balir a flat warning, which Balir chose to casually ignore.

"Coming from where?" The second guard eyed Balir's bandaged stump with a frown.

"Took the long way, by the north road from Juraxton," Vetra lied.

"Juraxton, eh?" the guard barked. "Didn't realize it was rough enough to merit losing an arm." He jabbed a long spear at the bloody rag wrapped about Balir's left hand.

"Met a band of thugs there," said Vetra. "Bad luck."

"Where?"

"Where the woods meet the miller's road. Nasty place for ambushes. Went the worst for the cutthroats. We left them there in their own blood." Vetra flashed the sentry an ingenuous grin.

The man nodded, as if that was completely natural. But his expression sized Vetra up for a simpleton. "If we follow up on this story of yours and go back with a patrol to see how many of these 'bandits' you killed, we're going to find, how many of them—five? Ten?"

Vetra shrugged. "More like three. But only if you get to them before the wolves do. We heard their howls close by. Was either them or the wood elves." He gave a steely grin. "Would have made short work of those corpses by now. Fools they were."

"The elves too," corroborated Balir with a quick, snorting laugh that had Vetra cringing.

The guard stepped closer and searched Vetra while his partner pawed at Balir with somewhat less enthusiasm. The mercenary's grim scowl and twitching fingers on his sharp blade had the guard scratching dubiously at his beard.

"What's this?" the sallow-eyed watchman demanded. He snatched at the collar Vetra tucked in the pouch at his belt.

"A trinket, no more," said Vetra. "I hawked it off a blind peddler a few days back, in Nisgard. For a few talons, I figured I could trade it at the Lausern bazaar for double what I paid for it."

The other fingered the relic, tightening his lips in a sneer. "I'd get rid of this piece quick, friend, if I were you." He seemed unnerved with the way the green jewels glared back at him with lurid intensity, radiating an unwholesome heat. "It has an evil cast to it...and I'm no slack judge of omens."

"That you are, Jeral," laughed his comrade-in-arms.

"In this case, I agree," grunted Balir.

Vetra flashed him an ominous look; Balir was getting too cocky for his own good. The sentries did not follow up on the dark hint.

The tall, more heavily-built guard waved them through. The

man on the top of barbican pulled a chained wheel then the gate slowly swung open. "Move on then," he said gruffly. "And make no trouble. Steer clear of the harlot's district. 'Tis likely a lot like you will end up with your throats cut."

Vetra gave a smiling nod. He tipped his head in the traditional way of soldiers. As was second nature, he thrust out a fisted hand, a token of farewell—so habit spoke from his martial posting on the borders of Tolizia.

They ducked into a back alley and Vetra addressed Balir with approval, "Good show. Though a little surly. I thought I told you to let me do the talking?"

Balir gave a phlegmatic yawn.

"We can hole up at Suleman's, a friend of mine's down the Albion Cross way," commented Vetra. "Lie low for a while, clean ourselves up."

Balir growled. "Is that what you call it? Clean ourselves up?" He held up his three-fingered stump. "What about my hand? This is where we part ways, Vetra."

"What do you mean?" grunted Vetra in surprise. "We still have a reckoning, with Caglios, the snake. Don't you remember? We still have to get our spoils for our work."

Balir gave an explosive grunt. "What work? More a hack job. I want nothing to do with that cursed wizard and his quests and his magic collars. I'd piss down his throat first chance I got. We've nothing to show except a botched job, Vetra. No, I'll bail out of this one. Forget this ever happened. I'll slit that magicker's gullet the next I cross paths with him—" his right fist curled in a claw "—but not now."

Vetra bit his lip. "You're making a big mistake, Balir. We're a good team. We have to finish this job together. We can go far."

Balir sneered. "It's finished, Vetra. You're washed up. Bad luck. Can't say as I'll be sorry to see the end of you either."

Vetra watched him storm off, lost in the gloom and the decadence of Lausern.

He loosed a soft breath, his lip set. Turning to amble back the other way, he heard a scornful echo reaching out at him, "And get rid of that cursed collar, will you?"

Vetra shook his head and uttered a grumbling oath. "I shall, Balir, I shall." But he knew his friend could care less what he'd do. He'd likely never see the likes of him again.

A hollow emptiness ran through Vetra's gut and he gnawed at his knuckles. The pain of the loss struck him. All the toil, all the misery and blood. For what? He shook his head. A broken friendship, two comrades dead and now a few measly talons to show for it. It seemed stupid, a bloody waste. A reckoning was in order. It would not happen before the next moon. Now was not the time.

* * *

A series of killings had stricken Lausern overnight. Some strange 'night butcher', so the constabulary had said, taking random victims under the moonlight. Not surprising, none knew of a long dead god with a princely face. The killer was described as some 'beaked and clawed' monster, a hybrid form of bird and man. An entire squad of city guards fled in panic one evening, as the terror blundered after them through the dimly-lit streets, clawing down helpless victims who couldn't get out of the way fast enough. Nothing was recognizable of the bodies. A characteristic, four-toed claw mark imprinted on a back, eyes and tongue gouged out, throat distended and mangled, as if some large predator had worked it over. The killer, it seemed, stole the soul or 'soul identity' of its victims, so the local witcher said upon examining the bodies. The thing grew more powerful, more insidious, more menacing with each brutish attack—some demon, a thing from the ghoulish pits of hell, equipped with glaring red eyes that seared the darkness. Something that could fly, though not well.

The locals laughed at the impossibility of such a thing. Yet Vetra shuddered at the news. In the *Marksman's Inn* he had hid under a false name: 'Varillisus', disguising his face and age by pressing a black cap over his brow, wrapping a dirty scarf and covering his skin with ash, wax and dye. He cleverly hid his wounds, then posed as a merchant of spices and knickknacks from a far city on the River Waiin. Somehow Vetra perceived that Dapi was hunting *him*—the one who guarded the fragment of enchanted collar and who it would slay and claim the missing piece that bound it.

Vetra had to lie low for other reasons. The Rat Fang people and the members of Iokru's shell cult longed for blood. It was no leap to assume that certain members affiliated with the local temples of both cults had been informed of a renegade mercenary escaping the temples of Gyzia after defiling their fanes and loosing the god-bird Dapi.

That the god-fiend was tracking him was disturbing enough. But on a shrewd hunch, Vetra guessed the beast could not follow him when the collar was buried in the earth. There he had hid it. Securing the cursed thing in an iron-bound box, he had gone on to inter it in the graveyard on the edge of the city: the soldiers' memorial ground. Sure enough, the shadows stalking him diminished in number, and the killings lessened.

As Vetra recovered from his wounds, the arms of a willing barmaid helped ease his past hurts over the next few weeks, though his dwindling supply of coin forced his hand. The memory of the slaughter in the canyons was still fresh in his mind. He had hidden the collar in the strongbox with no plan in mind. The cemetery plot he had chosen had been a necessary precaution—in this line of work, one could never be too careful. The grave-keeper had asked no questions. As long as Vetra paid him talons on the strike of midnight under the dead oak, he could do what he liked.

Dreams, strange visions and journeys of body and mind haunted Vetra—of a beastly bird with a man's face chasing him through the shadows, seeking vengeance, ready to rip into his throat and steal the talisman that mastered it.

The thing was evil. But the object it craved was more so. The relic had power—and could sustain life in inanimate stone forever.

If it came to a showdown with Dapi, Vetra knew he would lose—under no illusion was he of his chances. Nevertheless, to resume the life he had known, confronting the sorcerer became a necessity. With vindictive determination, Vetra decided to take the broken collar with him, well appreciating the risk he faced. Things might go badly if the wizard used it against him. But it may prove a potent tool if luck was on his side.

In the hours before dawn, Vetra brewed a kettle of black coffee with cups of strong arrack added to steel his nerves. Then he dug up the relic. The sight of the collar stirred many chilling memories of terror and atrocities. A wave of nausea hit him, on recalling the wrath of the strange, bloodthirsty beast called Dapi.

* * *

Through the cobbled marketplaces and winding ways, Vetra made his way. With the throngs subsiding from their market going, and the Lausern hawkers' cries fading to thin, hoarse calls, Vetra made better speed. He heard only the brief clatter of carts jolting through the dingy streets, and saw the odd, furtive face that sought to greet him, or woman crouched miserably at the threshold of a dark household, washing frayed clothes in rusty tubs while old men sang sour songs or sat twirling prayer beads.

In the seedy district of Lo-asmar, the city dungeons kept visible presence. All the riffraff and down-and-out beggars resided in the older, poorer section. Elsewhere, dark-cobbled streets ran with filth, green puddles splashed underfoot, akin to those one might find in the slave yards of Syrn. This was the haunt of thieves and cutthroats. Where honest citizens shunned the streets at night, only the city patrols tread: thickset, sharp-eyed men clad in steel and morions, with spears gripped in gloved palms and marching in details of eight or more. One had approached and Vetra had ducked out of sight, wishing no confrontation or questions. Now, he half turned. Ears perking at a drunken shout or some shrill shriek of a man being knifed in a seedy warehouse or storeroom, he licked his lips. It was none of his business and there was nothing he could do, except maybe get his own throat cut, all for a show of some unsolicited philanthropy. Ironic that Caglios the wizard made such district his abode.

In the lower precincts of a weatherwashed tower, a metalworks warehouse made itself known. It had been converted to a workshop, a place Caglios also kept as a laboratory. Smoke rose from double chimneys high atop the old blackened brick. Vines crawled up the ancient stone like ominous snakes. Necromancy oozed from the place, judging from the heavy smelting and various signs of industry.

Vetra's face creased in a frown. He felt a strange unease at this mission. For a second time he almost turned back and thought to quit Lausern once and for all. Only a dogged thirst for vengeance kept his feet rooted on the spot. He firmed his tongue and gave the brass knocker a sharp rap, nothing more than a repugnant gargoyle with a blackened face stretched in an eerie rictus. Fitting for Caglios, thought Vetra.

His memory of dealings with the wizard were fresh in his mind. He tipped back on his heels, fingering the hilt of his sword. This time, he would be ready...

The heavy door opened and a thin, wispy-haired man of serious face and medium height stood blinking in the early morning light. His gnarled features and graying hair spoke of a man advanced in years.

"Ah, Vetra, you have returned! Very good. I see you have survived. Against all odds." He stroked his soiled overcoat of blue and white leather with special iron-studded gloves which also clutched a squirming thing, something akin to a lizard. "You have renewed my faith in the human race! There are so many treacherous dogs running about."

"Agreed," Vetra muttered. He inclined his head toward the wriggling black lizard. "I see you have acquired a new friend."

The wizard gave a prim nod. "Yes…Igor is a fine specimen! You seem to have caught me in the middle of a challenging task. A certain spell requires an 'eye of lizard'. I'm afraid there'll only be lizard stew on the menu today, much to Igor's dismay. But, on to the day's deeds! Blades be cursed, Vetravincus, you are the mercenary's dream! A delivery-man extraordinaire—a minstrel of the sword—who brings me such spoils from afar! Anything to report? How goes the quest for my piece of jade? 'Tis a dirty, amoral world out there," he repeated in an odd voice.

"Indeed, it is," said Vetra, indulging the wizard's banter. "Let us talk in private. There are wary ears in this seedy alley."

"A wise plan." Caglios beckoned him in with mirth. He led them to his workroom of many ornaments with a grand sweep of arm—up a wide staircase at the back of a dimly-lit, spartanly-furnished antechamber.

Bronze censers blazed from the walls along the upper level, cutting through the daytime gloom of an otherwise cloistered space. Scroll-worked pillars lined the walls in the style of old Monath. They lent an air of antiquity to the place. Vetra saw an old temple masquerading in the barbaric splendor here; various miniature shrines which set the columns alight with their gleaming ornaments and ceremonial trinkets. They harked back to a time when daily life was steeped in even more pagan ritual, and when he fled through the alleys of Gyzia. A thin wash of pale light streamed from a brass-worked window where the smoke breezed down from the high turrets to billow in foul clouds. Hearth and forge burned with coals; their dark iron frames were connected by metal piping to the chimneys, the source of the black fumes. A crooked stairway wound off to an upper level while a closed door led to an area at the back.

Caglios's work delved into lost arts which Vetra recalled with distaste. A hideous blend of necromancy and alchemy that captured the power of gods through the agency of rare and magical metals. Caglios considered himself a *Sorceas*, a sorcerer who strove to perfect such arts, the same which picked up on the lore of the great sage Mercifor, one of the Five Great Mages of the Ages, who wrote many volumes on the subject, all but two which are lost today. Vetra paused in recollection. As he understood it, the presence of certain metals wielded by an adept could release the magical properties of anything in their midst. That, or serve as a catalyst to channel energy from the very air. Such things were considered incomprehensible to the mind of an ordinary citizen. In such wise, Caglios capitalized on his special understanding of it.

Caglios employed sub-world imps to do his bidding, as the two hairless, nearly featureless, dwarfed figures working at the forge exemplified. These were creatures of quiet, somber disposition with tiny ears and flat, noseless faces and long bare feet, garbed in a strange mix of armor and leather. Caglios' minions forged iron and certain metallic crystals with which the wizard molded his eerie talismans.

The wizard returned his lizard to a glass bottle, then doffed his gloves and bent his nose to examine the many samples he had laid out neatly on the worktable. There were dozens to inspect, including an array of interconnecting glass tubes winding in crazy directions, and ceramic bottles, wire brushes and odd instruments of distillation. Caglios sighed in satisfaction. He moved toward the forge. "That's it, Gisryn!" he congratulated his foremost imp. "Stir the melt well! We shall forge excellent talismans!"

The creature returned Caglios a grunt of gratitude, beaming upon its master's praise.

Caglios gave it an affectionate pat on the head, straightening its leather cap. "And work well too, Peson," he advised its twin. "We do not want to suffer the pains of your erstwhile brothers. Recall how hideously they died in the smelts—burning, howling in abject agony."

The creature moaned, a weird lament and crooning gibber, which unsettled Vetra. It only prompted a chuckle from Caglios. Gisryn clutched the metal tongs with renewed zeal. He stirred the coals in the forge with a passion while Peson let sizzle some pulsing, parrot-green chunks of metal in a big metal basin of water. A child's tune lisped from his lips.

Through the open window came a breeze, carrying a scent of sour cabbage and other smells that Vetra cared not identify. He saw the spires of the Vizier's palace looming not far across the city, the wealthier end of the city. Lake Argentia glimmered here, its silver waters glistening from trace elements in the soil. Caglios had made Lausern his base of operations as certain elements, were deposited around the lakeshore. The lake had spawned a series of hopeful prospectors at one time, but the Vizier had banned miners and opportunists from exploiting it. He despised their greedy ways, and erected around its shores a fabulous park and garden instead. Farther beyond and to the west, lay the canyons of Gyzia and the accursed temples where the priests bent to their abominable rites.

Vetra caught a furtive movement in the court below. A squat, skulking shape with a beak. A shadow? The figure was gone in a flash and a cold sweat broke out on the back of Vetra's neck.

Caglios broke out in a grin of amusement. "You seem jittery today, Vetra. Is everything all right?"

"Fine," assured Vetra. "A nervous mannerism only."

"I have several herbs for you that may lend aid with this type of malaise. Nothing more than smelling salts. I sense that you have had a rough haul these past days?"

"Nothing that cannot be remedied—and no herbs today for me, thank you. What about you? You seem to be in lively spirits this afternoon…and up to your ears in industry."

Caglios smiled with an air of pride. "You are observant, and slightly dry in humor today, Vetra. 'Tis nothing." He waved a pale, gnarled hand. "Mere trifles in the overall realm of things. The great masters of the Five Ages have tallied so many phenomenal works. In the wake of their achievements we can only be humbled." With a ragged sigh, he flourished and his eyes assumed a faraway look. "Humankind is but an innocent babe in the arms of a winsome maiden, in a world rich with monsters, overlords and wolves. But I maunder on. 'Tis only the Malimon I forge here. A singular talisman. A miracle set of armor to protect its wearer. Watch as I don it! Peson, Gisryn! Fetch me my armor and strike me!"

The foremost imp whimpered with bemusement, unsure of what its master wished.

"Hurry! You know the penalties of disobedience. Tarry at your peril!"

With a squeak and a jump, the imp stumbled on short legs to take down the light, gleaming set of silver plate hanging on a trim stand. It brought it piece by piece to the master and helped him don it, where it seemed to adjust to his contours with surprising ease. Caglios, dressed in helm, breastplate and arm and shin greaves, grinned, whereby the imp coursed forward with the poker raised. The iron rod bounced off the wizard's chest as if the man wore a foot of protecting iron.

"Impressive!" grumbled Vetra.

Caglios nodded in approval. "It is." He doffed the armor and laid it on the floor, blinking expectantly. With a playful toe, he nudged the imp, who stared wide-eyed in the forge-light. He had neglected to put the armor back in its proper place. Caglios turned his attention with sharp inquiry upon the mercenary. "So, what have you brought for me today?"

Vetra paused, gauging his options. He threw down the fragment of collar on Caglios's workbench. It rolled to a stop, glowing with a lurid intensity in the pale light. "Only this."

The wizard's eyes rounded. "So! I thought your powers greater than this. I gave you an intact magic item, a legitimate relic, and you flippantly throw down nothing more than a ruined version of it. What have you done? Where is my idol?"

"Questions that surely must be burning in your mind," Vetra rasped. He glared with venom at the collar.

"And?" Caglios's voice trailed off in cold inquiry, drowned by the crackling of fire from hearth and forge.

Vetra's voice rose in an ugly snarl. "You threw me and my men to the jackals! No hope of survival on that mission. You knew it! Rojarsh, rest his rat-hearted soul, would have slit our throats in the end. But I'm curious as to your twisted motive. It's puzzled me for days now. Kept me awake, contemplating your demise."

"A shame about your insomnia," Caglios said dryly, "but daring of you to come here with nothing to show for it." He stroked his button-like chin. "Well, for your courage I will appease your foolhardy whim and fill you in on some details."

"Please do so," Vetra said harshly, swinging his gleaming weapon.

Caglios sighed. "You swordswingers are all the same. Listen! The temple city is a complex, ornate society. Many years ago, I was under-priest at the Temple of the Clam. I met Rojarsh there and discovered the art of conjuring through voice. An obscure power known as 'aural suggestion'—this among other things, including magical transference, became items of fascination for me. I also came to acquire certain knowledge of the legend of the 'Falcon Man', 'Dapi'. As you see, I am now an adherent of Dapi." He motioned a ringed finger at the small shrines set about his workroom. Various falconish memorabilia were inset in their scrollwork and designs and littered on their altars—of polished beaks, painted skulls, talons, incense vessels, candles. "These fanes are only garish props, outward manifestations of the real god, but they help me channel the god's power—and somewhat recently, a new fixation, Smarg the elephant god." He laughed. "A little aside, I am somewhat of a dilettante in this area, as you can see by the many symbols of my gods. Over there, on my altar, the ivory trunk and inset jewels are of rare quality—" Vetra's eyes darted to where the spellcaster gestured. "Pay close attention to the barbed wings and trunks of the horned elephant idol. Perhaps you encountered the followers of Smarg on your sojourn to the temple?"

"I was denied the pleasure," Vetra said.

"Pity. 'Tis truly a worthy experience. The temple is not to be missed. The sandstone palms, the ferns, the scrolled columns. But I digress."

"Iokru says the collar has power, even when sundered, having been touched by a god."

Caglios lips parted in a smile. "No doubt he did." He turned the item over in his hands. "The collar of Dapi pulses with a strange energy. Nothing is of its like. Try to touch it!" He held it out for Vetra to grasp, but the mercenary only scowled at him. "It's been tainted by the god himself in bygone days. No matter. I will use the relic, despite its damaged appearance to craft my new shield!" He tilted his head back in a cackle and curled the collar round his wrist, molding it, pressing it by some unknown means, to wear it like a bracelet.

Vetra thought the wizard slightly mad.

But his assessment was premature, for the wizard's glare grew deadly. "You were only supposed to douse the idol with the clear waters of the pool. I see by all the killings in the region and your sudden emergence that you must have failed. I required that the task be done correctly to 'wet' the sorcery, withal to maintain a measure of control. Fool! Despite the mesmeric suggestions I gave you when you were last here, you have released the demon. Through blind ignorance, chaos ensues. Now you have brought the thing here! Idiot. Or what is that queer thing I saw creeping around my courtyard?" He strode over to the open window and peered down. "Ah! I am proven correct! Dapi skulks in his most demonic form."

"My heart bleeds," said Vetra. Though his lips worked in puzzlement that the wizard seemed calmly unconcerned by the presence of the violent god lurking nearby.

"Well, the truth then," Caglios said with a sigh. Stepping away from the open window, he gave an impertinent hiss. "I knew that if by chance you managed to succeed in this mission, I would have acquired a talisman in the form of Dapi. If you failed, I would have had the last laugh. For a fact I knew Rojarsh would make sacrifices of you, leaving no witnesses. Dergath—he feeds all to his bloodthirsty god; I would have fulfilled my obligation to him for taking me under his wing at the temple. Knowing the value of the collar, he would have lusted after it, then easy for me to steal it back at a later date. He alone would know from my nature how I duped you. How I had led such innocent lambs to the slaughter."

Anger boiled up in Vetra's gut. "What of the gold you paid me?"

"The gold is nothing to me." The wizard made an arrogant flourish. "I can find crates of it in the ruins of Yaeshar not a few leagues away. Fools! All mercenaries are avaricious fools."

Vetra clenched his fists. "And what are you but an arrogant fool who has spread lies in order to recruit valiant men?"

The *Sorceas's* left eye twitched. "What you do not know is that I laid a spell on you, mercenary, with the wish or suggestion, that before you left for the temple of Dapi you would return me my collar. You were not supposed to let the collar out of your sight. Not for an instant, unless it was snapped around the winged god's neck. You failed in bridling the god and bringing me a peaceable Dapi. But you have returned me the collar—" he gazed at its broken curve with awe mixed with disfavor. "The fact that you are standing before me is a miracle." He looked at Vetra with a new curiosity. "If I had time I would perform a divination on you, then I could look deep into your soul and discover what actually went on down there in the canyon."

Vetra's limbs shook. A flood of understanding washed over him. Suddenly he realized that his compulsion to hang onto the collar all this time had been the wizard's doing. It had cost him the lives of his men. "So, the collar has been bewitched." He bared his sword, pricked by a sudden urge for revenge.

Caglios chuckled with a sad smile. "I have to protect my interests. Your gold is on the table, Vetravincus. Take it. 'Tis three bags of coin minus two. Two less for your failure. Be glad that I don't extract more than I am of mind."

"To hell with your gold!" yelled Vetra. "To hell with Dapi! And to Dergath with your blood money and your evil machinations." He threw down the handful of coins he carried in his pockets on the table. The veins stood out on his forehead. "I lost two associates and a friend. They'd have been faithful allies to me in the future."

The wizard shrugged. "So the wheel of fate rolls."

"Take your collar and eat it." On swift strides, Vetra rushed to gut the wizard. "This is for Kalaman, and Laskar!—" Gleaming steel whistled in the air, eager to cut a chunk out of the wizard's throat.

Caglios was spry and he sprang back on nimble feet. Reaching a hand for an object under his robe, he cried, "Back, I say!" His imps stepped between mercenary and wizard. "Careful, swordswinger! Lest I sic Gisryn and Peson on you."

Vetra gave a mocking snort. "All of you will die!" The imps flashed hot tongs and poker at him, their noseless faces small and sullen with pale grimaces.

Vetra was in no humor for games. He kicked out viciously and sent one of the creatures back into the blazing hearth. The other, he batted with the flat of his sword and sent it wailing on its haunches. Gisryn flung himself out of the fires, whooping and dancing like a maimed ape trying to douse the flames from his leather jerkin.

"So much for your idiot imps," grunted Vetra. "Anything else to throw at me?"

Caglios gave a sinister cackle of laughter.

Furtive noises drifted from the open window—the clacking of claws and beak on stone. The croak of a familiar creature had chills shivering down Vetra's spine. A flurry of wings became a heady beat on the reality of day as a dim form came clawing its way over the sill.

Vetra stared, rooted on spot. The thing couldn't fly, but it had managed to crawl its way slowly up the rough stone wall.

"Ah, a twist of fortune!" the wizard chortled. "The broken collar... Dapi drawn to the thing of its bondage... Well, I should have known you had tricks up your sleeve, Vetravincus. I seem to have underestimated you. No matter!" He turned with appreciation. "And what have we here? A god—or is it half a god?"

Dapi had grown and was as ugly as ever—dirty, green and bloodstained, poised on the sill like some alien baboon, with broken wings outstretched in hideous glory. Its beaked, inhuman face leered. The mournful, aristocratic features of the long-dead prince radiated in the bird-like face stronger than ever. The slightly down-turned beak was gored and caked with noxious layers of blood of untold victims. Tiny human-arms reached up and flexed baby fingers. The thing was a monstrous perversion of nature, prematurely-birthed, an aberration of the universe.

Dapi hopped down from the sill and clacked awkwardly toward Vetra and Caglios. With the briefest study of their startled faces, it shrieked a vile cry as Caglios raised his arm with the bracelet as shield. The movement seemed to ward off the beast's advance temporarily. The imps scattered, cowering behind the armor stand and the worktable.

Caglios calmly assessed the god-bird, his hand on chin, as if the five-foot-high creature with its jagged half of wing and blood-smeared beak and vaguely prince-like face were nothing more than an intellectual curiosity versus that of a force of brutal savagery.

Vetra lurched sideways. The thing flew at him with sharp stone talon grazing his temple. Vetra wiped away the stream of blood. He remembered all that the god-bird was capable of doing and with a short quick gasp, leaped back, sword whistling in front of him to avert disaster.

But now it was his turn for a cruel grin to crease his blood-dripping face. The thing launched itself at the wizard. Caglios dodged like a spider, bracelet held high. He leaped over a stool and scrabbled under the workbench, clucking curses.

Vetra had no doubt about what would be his fate if he remained locked in close quarters with that stone brute, and he began edging back, searching for any way to stay out of the thing's path. Desperately, he scrambled over to the armor stand and, on a sudden impulse, grabbed the breastplate. Would it fit him? He donned the shiny plate. It snugged around his torso like magic, courtesy of Caglios's sorcery. He fitted the helm, then snapped down the visor. The magical metal felt hot to his skin, hanging only a few yards from the hearth.

Vetra snatched up his sword and stood teeth-clenched while Dapi looked up from its advance on Caglios, assessing the mercenary with a cool, evil gaze. Vetra strode to meet it.

The bird smashed beak into his chest, knocking him back. But the armor held. Likewise the helm when the bird veered in to ram him from the side.

Vetra picked himself up and charged with bone-crunching force, slashing with blade, drawing sparks on the devil's stone. He smote two-handed—savage, brutal strikes that were the hews of gods in his strange armor. Vetra cursed the stony, bloodstained brute that faced him, his every strike taking the weight of a hundred past aggressions out on the fiend. Yet his sword could not penetrate the ghoulish jade. As strongly as it was forged, it was no match for the idol's stone, nor did it notch, but struck more sparks. Such was the resilience of its metal.

The two struggled in deadlock.

The beast croaked, words not altogether un-human.

"God-bringers...all of you must die!"

Vetra froze in midstep. The voice was that of a man's, not a bird, or demon.

Caglios panted, visibly pale with sweat and the seriousness of the situation, but still with a thin, high grin on his face. "Die?" he cried out. "What do you mean, Dapi...'die'? You are but a killjoy!"

The bird stepped up to its full height, towering like a man, croaking, its wings a-flutter.

"I am alive...only by the whim of my maker. Yet the gods shun my very existence. The prince in me that was Dapi is dead...I talk, only as a living memory of a man passed from the plane of existence, who flies with the other lost souls...I live, but only in hours of darkness. I lie stretched on the rack, the rack of life, tortured by the gods' fire and brimstone, bound by searing chains thick as pythons...I have but a dim memory of being animated by a savage god whom I know not, yet bound by a wizard's curse...I curse you, Caglios...all of you fire-setters...and I curse men, all men...and wizards throughout time...For that you will burn!..."

Caglios frowned. "Well, that's an unhappy speech to bring to a happy household." He waved a jaunty hand, as if to dismiss the god-demon's lament. "I see that you are becoming more of your old self, O Prince, what with your tongue able to frame such eloquent words. For this, I am impressed and pleased. Why don't we sit down and chat over tea in the parlor. I'll have the imps—"

"Silence your tongue!" roared the god. *"Your hosting means nothing to me. You're a dead man, wizard. Prepare to meet thy doom!"*

Caglios frowned, rubbing his chin in indignation. "Pity. I had planned to take a stroll about the shops later on."

The god gave a screech. It flung itself at the wizard with barbaric ferocity known only to a creature of its kind.

Caglios dove back under the worktable. The *Sorceas* was not so dim as to have left all his escape routes blocked off. With a smug cry, he popped up on the other side of the table, reaching for a diamond-shaped talisman.

Dapi hopped up on the table and scattered magic items every which way, making a ruin of Caglios's precious objects and assemblies. The wizard crouched, a blinking spider, to launch the talisman right at it, blasting it with his magic.

A green, glasslike smoke enveloped the leaping shape and pitched it back on its haunches. The elephant shrine came crashing down in a shower of shards and broken glass. Enraged, Dapi burst through the holding screen of pale green smoke that somehow protected the wizard.

Caglios's smirk vanished. The horrific beak came snapping at him out of the eerie cloud—in a fiendish blur that clipped off his arm at the elbow.

The wizard uttered a bloodcurdling howl. The collar fell free from his bodiless arm, clattering on the floor. The god fastened claws on the collar as if to were to tear it to bits with its beak. The magical item had a mind of its own. It tore loose from the clacking talons and, as if compelled to be whole again, the same way it had in Iokru's fist, fitted together with the fragment around the bird's neck. Dapi's small, human-like hands clawed at the hated ring, trying to rip it off.

Caglios sank to his knees, blood jetting from his arm. He cried out in agony, watching the events as a dreamer witnesses a nightmare. Wizard and mercenary stared in horror as if by strange providence, the god became whole.

Vetra's jaw sagged. Somehow Caglios's magic had failed him, and now the wizard was going to pay a price.

But Caglios had not become the wizard he was to bleed out at the feet of some fiendish god. Somewhere the collar had not lost its force, only its primal directive. With his good right hand, Caglios cupped the elbow that gushed blood and managed to cauterize the wound with whatever magic powers he still retained. The same trembling hand reached for the strange, brilliant orb cached earlier in his robe. It flashed in his palsied hand and pushed down on a hidden depression.

The orb pulsed twice, then a sudden wicked gleam of light shot out, and smote the collar about the bird's neck.

The beast clutched at its throat, gasping out choking caws. The stone around its neck grew red with heat and sizzled with noise.

The thing tried to claw off the collar again but could not. The collar had snapped on never to be released again. The relic, the thing of its dark dreams, was the binding force of the wizard Nergid who had created it for his own protection, and ultimately for Dapi's doom.

In a brilliant white wash of flame the collar exploded and flew off, taking Dapi's head with it. The iron collar blazed in a bed of fire, coals sparking to white life. The jewels in it crackled and it burst into a green flame. The headless god-bird howled like a demonic wolf while the body hopped around mindlessly. With some last intelligent purpose, it bounded toward Caglios who knelt moaning at the ruin of his arm, and his life's work.

The imps came bounding out of their hiding places, taking up pokers to defend their lord. But too late. The headless body of the bird swatted them away with sweeps of its flailing wings and fell on them, trying to tear into their necks with grasping talons.

The explosion had set fire to all combustible objects in the room: worktable, silk hangings, rags, workclothes. Such things crackled and spit and seethed with tongues of red.

Vetra stared in heart-pounding apprehension while the *Sorceas* gave a grunt of awe as the headless body of Dapi staggered to a halt. Like a candle caught in noonday sun, the god-bird melted into oblivion, leaving only a pool of molten goo. A last piercing shriek and the bodiless head emitted a gurgling hiss. Smoldering in the hearth, it flared up once and was gone.

The hearth suddenly spewed forth a tongue of red fire and another thundering blast rent the workroom as the hearth erupted in bouts of orange flame.

The last explosion pitched Caglios's lab in an inferno. Dark smoke choked the entire room. Caglios, cupping palm painfully at his elbow, rose jerkily to his feet and hobbled down the stairs, hacking and coughing. Vetra staggered after, garbed in his armor. He took a last glance back, saw that the gold was scattered, melting in the hungry flames without chance of recovery. The imps, their leather smoking, fled under the mercenary's legs and out into the pale sunshine.

"The god is dead—my minion lost, curse you!" Caglios wailed. He shook a fist as the mercenary sauntered out of the tower. Caglios uttered a high-pitched laugh, cursing the beggars and thieves and the riffraff who gathered outside his court. Many had come to gawk at his burning workshop and his misfortune, for he had never been kind to them. He screeched some expletives at his imps, gave poor Peson a boot, then pulled at Gisryn's bloody ear. Thwarted of ambition, the wizard stamped about like a bull, overcome with a rage, the work of a lifetime lost.

Vetra shook his head with disgust and marched on.

Caglios's ghastly ravings faded in his ears even as the crackles and snaps of fire leapt to new life. He wondered how hands were dealt by the gods in this card game. Of the wizard's anguish, he thought nothing as he strode from the flames, recalling the woes of past days and the many deaths he had witnessed. The wizard's ravings now turned to whimpers of lost dreams, and like so many fading screams he had heard in the past days, those of Caglios's passed from his ear like water through a sieve.

He had been fortunate to seize Caglios's magical armor. Certainly it would find its use. It had not come without price, nor was it worth the lives of his men, or any of the innocents who had fallen by Dapi's beak. His rancor could only be surpassed by his hatred of men like the treacherous Caglios.

Dergath's bane, but the fools of his trade were more honest

than the corrupt wizards and priests that haunted the shadows! Though he might be a killer himself, he only took another's life when he had to. He never relished it, nor did he rob men of their wealth or livelihood.

Feeling somewhat unstoppable in his armor, he strode through the dingy back-alleys of Lausern, a chill tickling his spine. An unpleasant grin passed over his features. Drawing the ancient sword dredged from the canyons of Gyzia, he whirled it with satisfaction, testing its grace and balance with a fighter's pride. A worthy replacement for the one he had lost. Maybe he would take a detour via the shops to the thieves' district to see what rogues he could enlist as new allies when ripe opportunity came his way...

THE LAND OF MAJA

I

The Vizier stared at his advisor, his eyes hinting at a hundred different ways to kill a man. "Tell me of Vetravincus, the mercenary."

Kalvium nodded. "He comes highly recommended, Lord Ragnum. He dealt with Parsius, the counterfeiter, and helped sort out that sordid affair with the witch burner. Word reached us he succeeded in rooting out the gang of smugglers who killed our agents. If you recall, they sent their heads back to us in snakeskin bags."

The Lord Vizier of Lvendar stroked his chin. "An unfortunate circumstance, yet this comes as a high testimonial for the mercenary. What of this other fellow, this Basineus?"

"A crass, unsubtle rogue. The lesser of the two in wit, perhaps. I suggest picking one or the other. Word is, they hate each other."

"What do I care if they do, Kalvium? You saw the deplorable state of my daughter!" The nobleman struggled to regain control of himself, his intense gaze settling on the amber-dipped skull that hung on a far wall. "I would prefer that we have two trained, proven men on this assignment. When one fails, the other can pick up the trail."

Kalvium toyed with a silver button on his doublet. He shivered at the many animal skull trophies that Ragnum found so gratifying. "That is difficult, lord. They are not a good match."

Ragnum waved an impatient hand. "I don't care. It will be as

I say, Kalvium. Assign them at once."

"As you wish, my lord."

Ragnum turned to leave, but he paused under the statue of his father poised over the lintel. "And Kalvium—this better work, or it will be your head in a snakeskin bag."

Kalvium bowed in formal acknowledgment.

* * *

Kalvium stood rubbing his temples a day later back in the Vizier's study, choosing his words carefully. In front of him, a scowling man stood feet planted apart, towering over his own spindly frame. The man's features were hard, rugged, but handsome, with no trace of a smile or leniency. Vetravincus. Even in the dim light, the man had an animal aura of energy about him. He was broad-shouldered, impassive, physically indomitable. His long weave of sable hair streamed from underneath his peaked steel helm in the style of the old Tolizian warlords. A broadsword lay sheathed in a baldric at his back; knives and an axe were belted at the hip.

Another man entered. A straw blond type, of stockier build, with similar gear, and boastful tattoos on his bared forearms typical of the mercenary thugs who controlled the docks at Syrn.

Vetravincus turned to him with a sneer. "You! What are you doing here?"

"I was just about to ask you the same thing," retorted the newcomer.

"Let me explain why you have been summoned," Kalvium said quickly. He brushed his delicate chin. "More and more people of this city are turning up addicted—to some mysterious drug, an alchemic, my witchers say. Victims turn into monsters. Ghouls, if you ask me. We believe the drug is being sold somewhere in the hills. Somewhere on the warring kingdom, Galashad's border." He flicked his fingers southward as if to indicate any destination from here to the southern sea. Vetra, the tallest of the three men, shifted in annoyance. The purported location of the drug smuggler's den was beyond vague.

Kalvium unfolded a tattered sheepskin map on the table. He pointed to a remote place on his province's southern border of Lvendar with Galashad. "This particular pass across the canyon is where we suspect the contraband is being grown and trafficked. 'Tis hard, if next to impossible, to identify the origin of the compound due to the remoteness of the region. If the trade is left unchecked, our capital Lausern and possibly all of Lvendar will be facing a ghastly horde down the road. Turned into a race of green-faced monsters! Hair and teeth falling out, violent and unpredictable behavior, craving the drug as a wolverine craves blood."

"What is the nature of this drug to cause such madness?" demanded Vetravincus. He stared with cold eyes at the other mercenary standing nearby.

"Some sort of plant oil squeezed from the bulb of a root." Kalvium frowned. "Other than that we know nothing. Where it grows, how it is smuggled, it is beyond our knowledge. Some of the poison appears in leaf form; some with oil squeezed on leaves. Others as a brown gummy wad, possibly the heart of the bulb. The poison, if termed such, is highly addictive. 'Tis said that regular eaters of the foul ichor sprout roots and vines from their skin."

The other mercenary grunted and gestured idly. "Why don't you go along the border up there with a strong force and take out the ring-leaders?"

"We've thought of that, Basineus." Kalvium scratched at his cheek. "However, the site we had been monitoring has recently been abandoned. So, we're not sure where to concentrate our forces to eliminate these scum. We haven't been able to reach the head of our operation, Tas. Weeks ago we lost contact with him and his team. Meanwhile, the bulk of the contraband flows across our southern borders, from somewhere between Galashad and Lausern."

"So, what do you want from us?" growled Vetra.

"The situation is unstable—or more to the point, out of control. We need somebody like yourselves to go in and assess the situation, get a fix on Tas. Take him out if he's been corrupted. We've lost communications with all of them. Tas's last reply, a cryptic message at best, was something about a 'savage attack', and 'we must regroup'. The message came in by carrier pigeon over a fortnight ago."

"This seems like a task for more than a few spies and two mercenaries," remarked Basineus doubtfully.

A low moaning wail drifted through the wall, followed by the scrape of heavy chain.

Vetra grunted. "What's that?" His hand sprang to his sword.

Kalvium swallowed. An uneasy frown crawled over his face and he started for the door, as if deciding whether or not to reveal a secret. "Come!" he hissed. "I'll show you something. But keep your voices down. And make no aggressive movements."

He led them to a chamber down the hall where he opened a door with a long key. He looked up and down the hall in fear, the curl on his lips more pronounced. A low growl escaped Vetra's throat as he saw what lay within that room—a young woman crouched in a feverish, semi-sprawl in a corner of the room. She wore a metal girdle around her waist attached by a chain to the wall. Her brown curls were disheveled and matted. She had about six feet of slack and only a basin of water, not much for a youthful prisoner. A feral expression infected her face. The stout rings of chain rattled to life as she sprang up and snapped at them like a wolf.

Vetra jerked back involuntarily. Basineus rounded on the Vizier's aide, snarling.

"Stand down," Kalvium ordered. "'Tis not what you think!" He pushed both palms up in awkward defense. Such gestures did nothing to placate Basineus or Vetra.

Basineus strode a step closer. Vetra moved in to squint at the girl, his lips crooking in distaste at the sight of her red welts pocked all over a haggard face and arms. Upon closer inspection he saw thin, plant-like fibers growing from pores on her naked shoulders. It cast that part of her anatomy in a strange greenish hue. It was as if her follicles had widened to permit such growths. Her garments were tattered and near stripped, as if she had been clawing at them with long, dirty nails; skin and blood clotted the spaces under them. A pot for urination lay askew, which she had beyond a doubt spilled. The acrid reek was unbearable. A lackluster gaze glazed her face, as if she were possessed.

Kalvium pointed. "She is a victim of addiction to this mystery drug. Ragnum's own daughter! I can hardly bear to look at her. Nor can her father, for she seems not to recognize him. Or if she does, she only reacts with violence, to bite, claw and hiss at him." He shook his head in distress.

Basineus hopped closer, reaching out a hand.

"Don't get too close. She—"

Basineus jumped back as claw-like nails raked his wrist, drawing blood, and he instinctively drew his sword. "Cursed bitch!"

Kalvium launched himself between the girl and mercenary. "Fool!" He slapped back the mercenary's sword arm. "Do you wish us all dead? Think twice about harming a Vizier's daughter, you brute, if you value your head!"

Basineus flashed the advisor a sinister glance. "Relax, old man. I won't harm her, as much as she looks like she wants to be put out of her misery." He inspected his wound, as if wondering if he would catch whatever the girl had.

Vetra approached with more caution, pushing Basineus back. "What grows from her shoulders?"

Kalvium gave a shivering grimace. "We think it may be the drug's doing. The castle's finest doctors have not found a cure. We have tried everything: leeching, powerful herbs, medicines, even shamanic exorcism. Nothing has helped."

Basineus's face grew pale with recognition. "Besthra's ghosts! I've seen this before. In the slums of Lausern on the west side. Beggars lolling in their own filth. Harlots, glaze-eyed, violent, clawing their clients. I thought it was a plague."

"No plague, master Basineus. 'Tis evil personified. A man-made scourge."

Vetra shook his head in bewilderment. "What inspires anyone to take something so noxious?"

Kalvium could not answer. The woman's breasts heaved, a peculiar wail erupted from her lips, a half moan and cry. Sweat sheened on her olive skin. Her breasts peeked out where she had gnawed or clawed at her own garment.

Kalvium spread his palms. "So, now you see. Who can explain the motives or practices of the addict? Tragedy has befallen this poor girl, Kealasa, and it is heart-wrenching. A sweet innocent child, betrothed to the governor of Xenses's son in a formal ceremony. Now look at her!"

"I could care less for any of your royal liaisons," murmured Vetra. "She's a human being, a child, no more, for Dergath's sake. She didn't deserve this."

"Let us quit this vile, reeking place before one of the doctors checks on her," grumbled Kalvium.

Neither offered objection. They returned to the study, Vetra casting one last look back at the maiden, who was drooling and clawing at her upper garment. He shook his head.

"Let me emphasize the delicacy of this mission," reiterated Kalvium. "Our investigators have come up with nothing—in fact, three recent spies have gone missing, presumed dead."

"What makes you think we won't end up in a similar state?" inquired Basineus sarcastically.

"You have come highly recommended. It is my employer's wish that this be done in—in secret and in haste."

"You have chosen well," said Vetra. He cast Basineus a chill gaze. "What about him? 'Tis no secret that we are sworn enemies.

Pick one of us. Not both."

"The Lord Vizier wishes—"

"I could care a whit for your *Lord's* demands, steward," snapped Vetra.

Kalvium's eyes flashed in warning. "Careful with your tone, mercenary. You do not wish Ragnum as an enemy."

Basineus gave an amused chuckle. "Vetravincus is known as the 'hothead hammer' in my circle. You would be best to leave him behind and contract my services alone."

"As much as I'd like—"

Vetra turned to leave, but Kalvium eyed him coolly. "You wouldn't let an innocent girl die, would you? Let others turn into ghouls?" He turned a frosty glance to Basineus. "And your opinion is noted, mercenary, but the decision is beyond me. Either the two of you agree to my master's wishes, or both of you walk without fat purses. I'll contract it out to the army—and gods only know what scandalous aftermath will come of that, when the truth about Kealasa comes out."

Vetra made a non-committal sound. He was unable to suppress a stir at the thought of the innocent girl suffering, and the repercussion of a rampant drug addiction. "You'll look far elsewhere for one such as myself."

"Then make a decision!" growled Kalvium.

Vetra and Basineus shot each other heated glances, the dislike clear in their eyes. The history between the two was scored with treachery and intrigue.

Vetra's powerful shoulders flexed as he heaved a sigh. His dark locks swished like a stallion's mane under his helm.

"Fine," he grumbled.

Basineus flicked fingers with rude implication at Vetra. "And if this arrogant simpleton agrees not to enact some impulsive stunt—"

"Then it's settled." Kalvium pulled two large bags of coins from a small chest and slapped them on the table. "A bag of fresh-minted gold for each of you to start. Three more to come when you return with the heads of the dealers. With proof of their complicity."

Vetra nodded, reaching for the gold, but Kalvium brushed aside Vetra's scarred, hairy arm.

"Hold up, I am not yet done," he muttered. "The leader of the original team, this Tas, is a ranger of repute, a veteran captain in our outfit for five years. He's formerly a veteran out of Varim and King Blestidarius's elite outfit, in Umbria. We hired him from a rival company—he was a guard for Grand Vizier Akhbas too and worked as an escort for Hazim of Galashad's seraglio prior."

"So?" grunted Vetra. "What should I give him, a medal?"

"We have reason to believe Tas has switched allegiance or is running an angle of his own. But he always seems to have some alibi. He hobbed together a team of at least two dozen mercenaries with Ragnum's money. You will, of necessity, be obliged to rub shoulders with some of the worst killers in the lands. It will be extremely dangerous. I bid you good luck."

Vetra gave a silent nod while Basineus growled his own acknowledgment.

* * *

Grooms outfitted Vetra and Basineus at the lord's garrisons with new coats, boots, and assorted weaponry. Hauberks too, but Vetra rejected their assistance in dressing him, preferring his own armor. Only a stable girl did he allow adjust his new garments, who had taken a fancy to him and promised free favors on his return in not so many words. Horsemasters prepared two roans in sturdy condition, laden with supplies. Vetra smoothed out his leather jerkin and the gray-gold cape slung over his shoulders. Basineus strutted about in his blue and white jupon and new, black knee-high leather boots. He tested the double-knocked high-powered crossbow at his side, grunting in appreciation. "A masterwork of Kirn design."

Kalvium shoved a map in Vetra's hand and pointed to a spot

delineated on the border. "Crow canyon is the last contact point, fifteen leagues due south on the border of Lvendar and Galashad. A no-man's land, the haunt of fierce hill tribes."

Vetra edged past Basineus roughly and hopped on his horse. He spurred the mount off without a backward glance. Basineus followed, in a jaunty mood. The two cantered through the iron gates of the castle and rode out under a cloud of dust.

For a long time neither talked, both immersed in their own thoughts. Vetra particularly was unable to get the shocking image of Kealasa out of his head.

Their riding grew more intense, as they weaved between caravans and peddlers and locals bound for southern destinations. The sun grew hotter, dipped in the sky, a blazing copper disc. More than once Vetra caught Basineus's jealous stare at his gleaming coat of mail that caught the sun's rays and reflected it in a bluish, magical glitter.

"I feel like we're being led by our noses to our doom."

"Why, going soft, Vetra, old boy?" croaked Basineus, the smirk only widening on his leathery face.

"No, we don't know what we are getting into. Kalvium is a trained spokesman, a master of words. He could have just shown us a nutcase with the pox."

"Possibly, but for what purpose? Why are they paying us so much?"

Vetra stirred restlessly in his saddle as he negotiated the long grassy hill. "I still think old Ragnum needs more men for this mission. A bad feeling I get. It's an odd thing that he only has selected two men for the job."

Basineus blew air out of his cheeks. "A covert operation. Too many bodies attract attention. What with the Vizier's daughter all poxed up like that. It's a dicey matter for these high-borns, their citizens succumbing to the zombie juice. He doesn't want to draw attention to his daughter being a user."

Vetra's sneer was less of an affirmation than a disparagement.

"The worst case is that Ragnum doesn't want witnesses after the fact. Our mission done—" Vetra made the gesture of a sword across his throat "—then so are we."

Basineus's hand gripped his scabbard. "The Lord Vizier? It's a bad business killing the hired help. I guess we'll see, come time to collect the rest of our loot."

Vetra grew disinterested in Basineus's talk. He scowled moodily at the surroundings, his thoughts restless ghosts in the trackless haze of his mind.

After a hard day of riding, the grasslands gave way to rolling, rugged hills. What little fields and passable crops on the meagre arable land they witnessed in the last leagues, came to an end. Now a dry barren landscape stretched in endless waves. Few words passed between Vetra and Basineus and the laconic exchanges they shared were in no way cordial.

The road ended in an abrupt dropoff overlooking a desolate, dry canyon. Low hills domed the space across the canyon, precursors to the mountains that ranged higher still. Vetra looked at the map. The 'x' marking a spot was west of their current location. Yet his intuition told him to put aside the map and his eyes strayed in the opposite direction—to the trail running east along the rim of the canyon.

"The end of the line?—maybe not..."

He urged his mount up the trail along the ridge, squinting in critical inspection.

"What about the map?" Basineus called after him.

Vetra ignored the question.

"I'm talking to you!" Basineus rode up to the other mount's rump in anger. He paused, puzzled at Vetra's choice of direction. He looked about him, as if the trail could lead somewhere, judging from the broken plant stems and overturned stones under the horses' hoofs. They followed a zigzagging course at varying distances from the canyon until Basineus seemed hopelessly disoriented. After a time, Vetra halted with a scowl at the wheeling of carrion birds against the sky. Tumbled masonry and fallen blocks, and patches of blackened fire pits lay strewn about an open area. Below the canyon cut a sawtooth pattern through the primordial shale. They rode up a steep lookout and rested their laboring mounts while the sun was beginning to fall.

"I'm not liking the look of that ruined outpost over there," Vetra said. He inclined his head. "Looks like barbarians took the torch to it." He gestured to the blackened stone and charred timbers piled in rough heaps. Dismounting to investigate, he strolled down a ways where he found stone and wood cold to the touch. The reek of rotting flesh was thick in his nostrils. He grimaced. A barracks and garrison joined the charred outbuildings and several carcasses littered the area, all human. Some were riddled with arrows and bolts, others looked scavenged by birds of prey, or mauled by some animal.

"Big, whatever it was that chewed them," Basineus muttered.

Vetra's boots crunched on the dry gravel. The hoot of a screech owl echoed eerily from somewhere amid the scraggly tamaracks at the foot of the adjacent hill. The agitated croak of a raven echoed high overhead.

Basineus descended from his mount and knelt, flinching. A long, two-foot print with four toes lay embedded in the soil, edges marred by rainfall, but deep enough to still be visible. He gestured at the prints that led away into the scrub, away from the ravine. Parallel scuff marks and trails of blood looked to be two human corpses dragged forth. To Dergath knew where.

"These bodies strewn about are probably three weeks old," Basineus mused.

Vetra looked around with renewed suspicion which grew to apprehension. A strange stillness hovered in the air. It did not fit well with the drowsy silence that lay thick with menace. He wondered what the hill peoples did up here, or what food they foraged. They lived on nothing but rabbits and snakes from what he had heard. He ran fingers through his tangled black hair.

Likewise, Basineus doffed his helm and wiped back his golden curls that framed his sweat-beaded brow. Vetra's leather jerkin creaked as he got up from his crouch, reflecting upon the carnage that had passed. His high leather boots trod over the pebbles underfoot. Some of the bodies were those of hill savages, with long braided hair, feathered-headdresses, and fingers locked on axes carved of bone. But many were men from the cities: tall, proud, disfigured forms with armor and surcoats hacked—Behundrians and Lvendarian stock, he guessed, whose pale, eyeless faces gaped up in horror. No doubt members of the spy party sent to infiltrate the drug operators. But so many? The sinking sun glinted on the dented helms, broken breastplates and notched swords darkened with old blood.

"Why didn't weapon mongers loot the area?" Basineus grumbled.

Vetra shrugged. "Kalvium said it was a no man's land." He chewed his lip. "No attempt to bury the corpses... Either there were no survivors, or they all up and left in a hell of a hurry."

"Probably the latter," grunted Basineus.

"Brilliant deduction," came a coarse voice jeering out of the late afternoon shadows.

Vetra wheeled. He saw a man in camouflaged leather on foot, stealthy as a panther, training a crossbow at them. Three men on sleek, black-haired horses came riding up over the ridge. Just as suddenly, their eyes cold and steel glinting in their hands. Vetra cursed as he squinted into the sun. He was too far from his mount to get the jump on either riders or footman. Basineus was likewise caught off guard. Steady hands trained bows on the two before they could draw weapons.

Vetra's blade nonetheless slid out in a rasping shimmer. He cursed himself for his daydreaming.

The lead rider snarled at him, "Who are you, rogues? Speak, or be riddled with bolts." He kneed his horse forward, his brow budded with dirt and sweat. His rooster red bristle of hair spiked up the middle of an otherwise bald scalp, and made him look like a barbarian chief of old. His flared, wide nose, flattened, broken a half dozen times was like a bull's. But what the man lacked in looks he made up for in muscle. Vetra perceived fine layers of it, judging from the bulges in his studded leather.

The rider motioned to the others to disarm the intruders. "I'll ask you again. Who are you?"

"I'm Vetravincus," Vetra said without warmth. "This is my associate, Basineus. Who are you? You in the habit of accosting innocent wayfarers?"

"Just call me the 'Enforcer' for now."

"Enforcer," Vetra mocked, his teeth bared in a sardonic grin. "We're looking for a fellow by the name of Tas."

The other barked out a coarse laugh. "Tas, is it? Well, you came to the right place. You'll see him soon enough. He'll be curious to see you too. Now move!"

They prodded the mercenaries down the crumbled path, the footman herding them along like cattle. The weapons, they examined with sinister interest, especially Basineus's fancy crossbow. The mercenaries' two horses, they towed along down a vague trail, which looked like a goat path that followed east along the ridge. The rocky canyon dropped to their right. To Vetra's eye, nothing more than a dry gulch that had seen no rain for months, if not years.

Vetra conducted swift inspection of the unwanted company. Three others were unkempt, poorly groomed, with greasy, tousled hair. Leather was stained with blood. They were quiet, sullen ruffians, gaunt men from lack of proper nutrition, as if they hadn't had a square meal for weeks. Hired bandits? No, the leader was purposeful, organized, confident, not simply an average ruthless cutthroat. Military-trained. Likely one of Tas's captains, if any of them had survived that bloodbath.

A half second of opportunity arose. A blur of movement— Basineus tripped the captor behind, but unlucky for him stumbled on an upturned stone. A boot licked out and smashed him in the face. He scrambled to his feet, spitting blood, his fists clenched in a boxer's stance, nose hooked on an unnatural angle.

Vetra lurched forward to follow up with an upward swing, but shook his head as a bow sprang up trained at his face. "None of that," the leader's henchman grunted, waving a warning finger toward the mercenary. "Little boys get themselves hurt when they play with fists."

Vetra cursed. The sod Basineus had acted impulsively. They might have had a chance if the riders were not now alert.

"Tell your underling to wise up," growled Enforcer.

"You heard him," Vetra grunted at Basineus.

Basineus shook the blood out of his nose and lunged at Vetra, but was forced back at crossbow point. Vetra felt no compassion for Basineus's bloodied up state. A fitting setback for the oaf and his arrogance.

While they navigated the steep ascent, Vetra gauged his opponents with a practiced eye. They were seasoned enough to keep some distance from him and Basineus, not foolish enough to stay bunched up. He played various maneuvers over in his head: a quick leap under the lead rider's mount, a snatch at the lax guard's axe in his belt, a scrambling rush to take down as many men as possible.

He curled his lip. Too complex—and messy—and too wide a margin of error.

With cold frustration, he marched on.

Perhaps half an hour passed of stumbling along and being goaded at sword point through winding terrain, before they came to a cleared area. Vetra caught a whiff of fried meat, acrid smoke, burning dung. Stone blocks had been dragged over to fashion a crude outbuilding, a square hovel with logs and branches placed over the top for a roof. Two score men ranged about, sharpening weapons, repairing boots, banging pots. Some bent over cooking fires, heating blades—lean, wary-eyed men in mixtures of mail.

They had rigged up a small smithy, where one man hammered on a piece of red hot metal. A pile of crude crossbow bolts lay to the side. Nothing more than a bandits' lair.

A figure dressed in a dusty hauberk emerged from the stone hut, clutching a sheaf of arrows, an axe bobbing at his hip. Vetra saw he was a big man with tawny hair under a leather cap, a relaxed stance, like some big confident cat. He was chewing on a grass stick, conversing with his men. But Vetra knew better, the man was as hard as nails.

"Hoy Kraddus, your sloth is memorable," the man called. "Took you longer to complete your rounds. Have you no shame?"

"Shame is not part of my vocabulary, Tas," came the lead rider's growl, "you should know that."

"What have we here?" the man inquired.

"A couple of birds flew in to roost, courtesy of Lord Ragnum, I wouldn't doubt."

The big man chuckled. "Are you sure of that? They look more like hill thieves dressed as nobles, strayed too far from home. Or mercenaries having come into some unexpected spoils."

"Spare me the character sketch," retorted Vetra. "Either explain to us what all this ill-treatment is about or—"

"Or what?" Kraddus jeered, his face twisted in an unpleasant grin. "How be we put steel in your guts and leave you tied to a tree for the jackals to chew on?"

"He has a surly cast to him," said another with a repellent flat face and dented steel cap. "Jackals are too good for him. I say we leave him to the trolls."

"You on about trolls again, Nurus?" croaked Kraddus, shaking his head.

Tas waved his underlings off. Frowning, he rubbed his chin, as if in contemplation, then took in Vetra's imperturbable bearing, as if he suddenly made a decision about both of them.

"Excuse the rude lodgings, but we had to relocate in haste, as you can see, farther away from the original site than we had hoped."

"After you nearly got us all killed," jeered Kraddus.

"Shut your mouth," Tas barked. He shifted his attention back to Vetra. "Your rude reception was only to err on the side of caution. One can never be too careful in such circumstances..." His eyes flicked on a fuming Basineus whose face was caked in blood. "Seems as if your aide got in a fight with the dirt, and lost. That or old Kraddus got too eager with his boots."

Vetra gave a complacent nod. "Basineus's known for his clumsiness." He smirked, pleased for once that Basineus decided to keep his mouth shut; though his face had purpled and his eyes stared at him from under a ghastly mask of bruised and disfigured flesh.

The remark seemed to appease Kraddus and crew, and a smattering of chuckles and approving grunts rose from the gathered crowd.

The leader ignored the murmur. "So, you're the fresh fish they sent from Lausern?"

Vetra bowed in mocking tribute. "None other."

"Sorry to have treated you so poorly. But we are in the middle of a 'situation' here."

Vetra frowned, struggling to bridle his irritation. "So, I've heard. Would be nice if you were to tell your employers. Would have saved us the trip up here."

"Perhaps." Tas made a negligent gesture. "Return them their weapons, Kraddus." Curiously, he stared at the two again. "Well, get yourself cleaned up. Buckets are behind the armory. A fresh spring up the hill. The armory's over there. We have weapons galore." He strode past the open fire and pulled out a battle axe from the squared stone building. Vetra saw swords and knives of various sizes and shapes, axes of bronze and some carved of bone, and a stack of crossbows, mostly serviceable, but some with trigger arms damaged.

Basineus snatched up two curved daggers to complement his arsenal. Vetra reached out a hand and hefted one of the bigger battle axes.

"Ah, a man of the axe?" Tas said with a grin. "Get yourself equipped then. The ceremonial mail you're wearing is thin as a woman's shift, though it's finely crafted. Your squire seems outfitted better than you."

Vetra grinned. "It comes well-earned, and is hardly ceremonial. It's invulnerable. Let's just say a little elf gave it to me."

Kraddus had chanced to stride up and overhear the boast. "And owls fly to the moon."

Tas shook his head in wonder. "I find it hard to believe that delicate mesh is as formidable as you claim."

Vetra shrugged. It seemed pointless to waste his breath.

"We have a meeting slated on the morrow with the drug lord, Grebu," said Tas.

"Suicide, more like it," muttered Nurus.

"Our archers will be behind us."

"What's left of them," Kraddus said with snide impatience.

"You needn't remind me, Kraddus, nor do I need your constant impudence. The plan stands for now."

"It's a dumb plan," Kraddus scoffed.

Tas rounded on him. "We made a pact, recall—with Ragnum. We'd flush out these monsters of his. If we wish to curry favor with our Vizier Lord, we cannot shirk our duty."

Kraddus yelled back, "You already have done that, by keeping them in the dark. Look at these two jackals dogging our heels." He jerked an insolent thumb to Vetra and Basineus. "Ready to put a knife in our ribs when we sleep."

One lean hireling wearing an eye patch raised his voice. "He speaks truth."

Burning eyes raked over the mercenaries; surly curses murmured under men's breaths.

Basineus took a step backward, his hand reaching for his broadsword. A wolfish snarl spilled past his lips.

Vetra likewise braced himself for conflict. His inner sense told him that some action was required. "You fool! Do you think we mean to start a war with a superior force on our heels?"

The man who had spoken stepped back, embarrassed.

"Show some respect, you dogs," called out Tas. "These men are guests—for now."

Kraddus shook his head. "Better to lie with a wolf." Others of the militia growled in agreement.

"If we're not to be hunted like outlaws for deserting, we must follow through," said Tas. "The alternatives are not pleasant. Think about a life constantly on the run, never knowing when some bounty hunter might pluck you out of your bed, or plunge a knife into your heart. I want to get Grebu to sign the agreement. Then he'll be bound to back off. Ragnum will get the rebel upstart of Galashad to sign it. Our task is then done. All of us can quit this dismal rock heap with impunity."

"What good is a signature on vellum to devils like this Grebu?" demanded Vetra.

"It's what Kalvium commissioned us for. What do I care? Three months in this wretched wasteland is enough to make a man slit his throat. Enough misery to last a lifetime."

There were mumbles of agreement.

Screams and roars suddenly filled the air. Heads turned to the howls of running men.

An axe came flying out of nowhere and brained a man standing beside Nurus. Men roared and scrambled for safety. The victim fell backward, eyes staring up, blood and brains dripping down his face.

"Damn! Get down! Dergath's hells!" cried Tas. Arrows whipped by and clattered on chipped shale.

Fierce yells rose over the mad scramble. There was a clash of arms. Vetra cursed. Rolling out of his crouch, he saw a screaming mob of ragged savages clawing their way up out of the canyon. It was at a place where it was less steep and full of gravel. Others came bursting through the scraggly larch and the tamaracks crowding the hill behind the armory; the devils had managed to cross the canyon undetected and were now flanking them.

"A chance to prove yourself!" cried Tas to Vetra. "Quick, draw your weapons on the Karkassians! After me!" He charged down the slope, axe hefted; his men snatched up weapons, in hot pursuit.

Enemies had slunk along the ridge like weasels. Slipping by the sleepy watch, they now stormed the camp, whirling axes over heads, throwing knives from white-knuckled fists.

Tas came barreling forth, a war cry on his lips.

Vetra met the raging horde. With a mighty sweep, he took out an axe-swinging warrior in a wash of crimson. Basineus slashed a yowling attacker shoulder to sternum. The Karkassians were lean, barbaric fighters garbed in camel-hair robes, leather sandals, and headbands of colored cloth. They wore no armor, making them easy prey of the heavy weapons of iron and bronze of the defenders.

The ones who had come creeping down from the hills, howled like blood-mad fiends and plunged knives into ribs and bellies. Tas's men were hard pressed, but efficient; they slit throats as , ruthlessly as butchers carve steers. Steel rose and fell in crimson waves, and Vetra and Basineus battled back to back; hewing and smiting until their surcoats ran red.

Kraddus and Nurus likewise formed a wedge, and kept the invaders from overrunning the compound. Tas's swift-footed archers ran to the canyon's rim. They dropped into a crouch and poured down arrows at the savages who still clambered up the gravelly slopes. Vetra heard men's agonized screams. The dozens that got through were met with swords and whizzing bolts.

Basineus twisted sideways, crying out in pain, as an axe gouged through his mail and caught the flesh in his side. He recovered, shifting his balance, parried a crushing arc of axe.

Three charged Vetra. A bone-carved axe smote heavily on his ribs, normally a stroke that would have cleaved a champion. But the axe head bounced off his light mail like magic, thunking back like a chunk of wood. Vetra grinned, close enough to smell the rank, animal-fat war paint on the savages' cheeks. He whirled and two-handed, smote the offenders, taking two of them out at a time. The third's head fell in a blood-spurting spray as the mercenary's sword severed it from his body.

Kraddus blinked. He shook his head, as if refusing to believe his eyes, that such light mail could stop heavy blows. For a moment he was lost in wonder and was almost brained in his stupor as the Karkassian chief came hurtling out of the fray at him, gnashing like a snarling cougar. Axe met sword. The ex-soldier was pushed back into a forest of axes.

Vetra came vaulting into the fray; Tas circled in like a vulture, using his axe like a club with an ox-like strength and resolve. But it was all over. The Karkassian leader swayed, then reeled. All around, the men's breath heaved, blades fell on flesh, as the last survivors fled with bolts and curses at their backs.

Six of Tas's men lay dead in the gravelly crumble. Two dozen of the enemy lay strewn in ghastly mounds. More sprawled dead with arrows in their throats, flung in heaps down the ravine. His men began searching the bodies for loot or hillman knives.

Basineus clutched his side. He held up a hand when Tas came hobbling over with a searching glance. "Merias! Bathe this man's wound and bandage it. There are others wounded too." He motioned a curt hand. "Swiftly!" The man so summoned, a stocky Guirite, went to fetch bitter herbs and wetted cloth.

Tas nudged a corpse with a toe, the fallen invader with his head almost hacked off. "What a sorry waste of human flesh."

"These Karkassians are stupid," growled Kraddus, spitting out blood and a cracked tooth. "Launching a daytime attack with that rabble? They must be desperate. These are not sane people.

Look! Under the influence of the maja they stormed us with senseless rage. Can you not see the green growth on their necks and arms?" He tore aside a patch of deer hide from a corpse's blood-soaked shoulder.

Nurus recoiled in a flushed daze, sucking in a breath. "Dergath, it's true!"

Vetra flinched, recalling the advanced stage of Kealasa's affliction, not dissimilar to the corpse at his feet.

Tas wearily gripped his weapon. He shook his head, as if he felt the dead warrior's pain himself.

Vetra was confused by the clear display of emotion, and he drew back with a scowl.

The bodies of the hill rogues were pitched over the cliffs. The half dozen dead Lvendar men were taken away from camp and buried under rocks far up the slope away from the clutch of carrion birds.

"Your choice of camp leaves something to be desired," Vetra muttered grimly.

"Every place here along this cursed ridge is a bad choice," grunted Tas. "The Karkassians fire up at us from the Galashad side. They think we are encroaching on their territory. The fools! We're merely trying to negotiate with that madman Grebu. What would we want of their hovels, their cacti-strewn barrens and vultures? They have little fertile land here. They have no idea the magnitude of Grebu's illicit operation."

"So, he brews this product here?" asked Vetra with incredulity. "Where?"

"Somewhere up there—" Tas flung a hand up at the mountain-mesa towering on the canyon's hither side. "Probably uses the fools who scrabble a living in this ghastly place as slaves. Easy to snatch a few of them here and there—" he kicked a foot at the eye-staring corpses. "Over a period of months, an enterprising man could accumulate a sizable crew."

Vetra shrugged. "It seems incredible."

"Grebu is an incredible man—as you will soon see."

Kraddus affirmed the claim, a saturnine grin creasing his face.

Vetra did not like the grin, nor did he like Nurus's clumsy presence, or the general level of apprehension and distrust among these fighters. Bad blood bred mishap, which in turn fostered death. He recalled the rotting bodies back at the blackened outpost as he stared over at Basineus who returned the glare. He still nursed some minor wounds from the encounter, in addition to his recent disfigurement. Conflict and petty squabbles everywhere. When would it ever end?

* * *

The sun was sinking in a veil of haze when the battle-hardened men hunched around a crackling fire, sitting cross legged or on logs. Over a meal of roasted rabbit, rattlesnake and boiled broth and home brew, the defenders celebrated their victory, in moods of mixed apathy and gratification.

"You would still have us attempt this foray of yours with six less of us?" Nurus grumbled with bitter concern.

Tas continued to munch his meal.

Glancing around the grim-eyed crew, Vetra asked, "Why don't the local Lvendarians clear out these savages who invade their lands?"

Tas muttered a gruff exclamation. "The hill people fled long ago. The Karkassians raided their territory for sheep. Then they killed them when they didn't tithe or yield to their bloodthirsty gods, on lands they believed their own."

"But they don't overrun these hills now?"

"The mountain trolls are the only thing that prevent them from invading these parts," Nurus stated.

"Trolls this far south?" Vetra frowned, trying to imagine the scenario, suddenly remembering the large prints he had seen back at the ruined outpost.

Tas rubbed his bloodshot eyes and downed a cup of spicy home brew. "I've yet to see one. A legend, no more."

Nurus took a swig from his own cup. "They're around. I grew up not far from here in Fawia, and I've seen them. The Megwans, we called them—the old hill trolls, around since the time men fought with clubs."

"But you've the mindset of a child," laughed Kraddus. "Seen the troll outside your tent this morning?"

Nurus's blade flashed out in resentment and Kraddus caught it without effort on his own. He flicked it off, grinning in sour amusement.

"Enough squabbling, you rabble," roared Tas. He sprang to his feet, upending his plate of fried snake. "I'll not have my own captains cutting each other's throats."

There came chuckles and rude cheers from the gathered militia.

"You too, you monkeys!" Tas yelled at them, glowering. They finally quieted down.

Silence spread like a wet cloak over the company. It was broken only by the sound of dull forks stabbing plates as the surly men stretched out their meager meal. There was an uneasiness about this crew that puzzled Vetra over and above what he had learned from Kraddus's and Nurus's sullen disclosures. After a period of subsequent grumbling, Vetra caught Basineus's gaze and he shifted in his seat, with a firm desire to leave.

That's when he noticed a man drinking somewhat apart from the others, a man with blond beard, flat face, small eyes, and a chiseled pattern of scars on his forearms. When the man belched and turned up the path to relieve himself, Vetra got the idea to relieve himself too.

They were far enough away from the fire to hear only the odd, lingering curses of slightly drunk men when Vetra crept up and glowered.

He waited patiently while the other swayed, the splash of urine running its course, spilling noisily on the gravel. The froth glinted under the flickering torches mantling the armory.

When the bowman turned and saw the hulking mercenary standing there, he wheeled, nearly falling back on his heels.

Vetra put out his hands and raised an eyebrow. "Easy, friend. I just wanted to ask your opinion about something—on all of this."

The man's eyes darted about in nervous circles. "What do you mean?" he hissed, as if gauging his chance to slip by the mercenary. There was little.

Vetra stared at him impassively. "You know what I mean."

The man saw Vetra was not going to stand down and he looked as if he were pondering whether he could, in fact, trust him.

He took Vetra aside, and spoke in a voice barely a whisper, "We think Tas is losing it. As a leader the man made some bad decisions and got a bunch of our men killed—thirty-eight, all hired under Ragnum's own coin. A horrible sight last month. A fan of corpses lie in open graves upon the ridge."

"I've had the privilege of witnessing the carnage."

The man gritted his teeth with a nod. "He lied to the overseers in the home office at Lausern. Said it was an accident. Accident, my eye! Human error, more like. Tas walked into a trap...like this farce tomorrow. I think he's been corrupted by the maja."

"What do you mean?" demanded Vetra.

The bowman's eyes roved as he spoke in a hushed whisper. "The man doesn't sleep. It's not natural. He stays up all night staring into space, tossing pebbles into a pot, mumbling on about 'Memju' or 'Bemju' or some daft thing. We don't know what it is. You saw his movements. Well, they're wrought with—"

"Everything all right here, Jasti?"

The crunch of boots on pebbles marked the approach of a stealthy figure.

The bowman flinched. "Mighty fine night, Tas. Stars galore," he remarked, buttoning up his pants, which he saw he had neglected earlier.

"That it is. Why don't you take a walk, Jasti? I don't think our friend Vetra here is up for some grab ass just at this moment."

Quivering in rancor, he stomped off.

When the man had shuffled out of earshot, Tas sighed and grunted without friendliness. "Men fighting in these hills frighten easily, men like Jasti. The land gets under their skin, like a chill creeping from the sea. Old legends speak of old gods, and evil bred since the beginning. 'Tis embedded in the very rock around us. Makes a person think twice about his life, that his own shadow is just a ghost haunting him, like some ghoul or venerated god, ready to snuff out his life. Even a fighting man, such as Jasti, is afflicted. I think he's gone soft in the head." He brushed his temple, as if to emphasize the point.

Vetra remained silent. He noted the dark circles under Tas's eyes, the haunted appearance of his face, as if covered by some inanimate tribal mask, his fingers twitching on his hilt, the perceptible welts standing out on his brow. For a second, the ghoulish face of Kealasa merged with Tas's.

Vetra shook off the apparition. Tas grinned, his ghoulish, devil's glare more pronounced than ever. Then it vanished and the leader was himself once more.

He gestured to the grass pallets beyond the open door of the barracks beside the armoury. "Rest up, mercenary. Tomorrow will be a tasking day for all of us—our meeting awaits."

II

By midday, a team of twenty militiamen marched grimly back alongside the canyon, crossbows at the ready. Tas and his captains rode in front followed by Vetra and Basineus, gripping their swords, but they weaved off the main trail and cantered up a hidden path, winding closer to the edge of the canyon.

Vetra peered all around at the inhospitable terrain. Below dropped a chaotic riot of boulders among twisted shrubs. Hills rose beyond, rife with crumbling outcrops and gnarled trees. These hosted plenty of places for hill folk to hide in. Basineus, armor still caked with blood, rode close at Vetra's side, too close for Vetra's tastes, and he motioned him back. "Seems like a bad place for a negotiation."

"Prey for ambush," muttered Kraddus.

Tas grunted. "Grebu agrees only to deal with us on his turf."

"And you agreed?" Vetra asked. He jerked upright in his saddle.

"We have been stalled for too long. I had to accelerate the process. Don't worry, Vetra. I've had my archers dug in behind the bridge since the morning. If things go sour, they will loose a rain of arrows on them."

"And on us, too?" sneered Kraddus.

Tas did not answer. He dismounted from his stalwart roan and beckoned for his men to follow him up the trail.

The sky blazed a deep blue. The air was chill, and a pungent scent of cook fires rode on the tails of the southern breeze— smoke curling from hill-savage camps across the canyon.

The border was crossed only by a crude wooden bridge over a dry, narrow canyon, deep and boulder strewn.

What few of them rode, left their horses tied to trees and advanced to the bridge. Somewhere back there, Vetra envisaged Tas's archers crouched in weeds and brush, noses to the dust, ready to loose arrows into enemy flesh.

The clomp of the men's boots sounded like an eerie drumbeat in the afternoon stillness, impinging on the scant chirps of songbirds, and the distant hum of insects far below. The bridge timbers trembled, causing Vetra a backward glance. Not so much out of fear, but as if wondering about those supposed reinforcements that had dug in behind the ragged shrubs. How reliable were they? He had not seen much in the way of arrows back at the armory. The man he had milked for information at the campfire, was not in their present company, nor his comrade, so he assumed that these bowmen must be part of the hidden party.

Nevertheless, the company passed safely to the other side. Vetra saw a group assembled on the barren plateau to meet them: lean, unsmiling men, dressed with steel caps, clutching axes and swords.

Halfway across the hard-packed earth, Tas warned Vetra: "Quiet. Let me do the talking. You and your man are here only as muscle to supplement our forces in case things go wrong."

"Which they surely will," Nurus croaked, hunching like a bullfrog at Tas's side.

Tas ignored him.

Vetra remained grimly silent. Kraddus flashed him a leer of amusement which Vetra had come to despise.

The parley was designated at an exposed place, windswept and deserted, on a plateau of scarred rock. In the shadow of the low crumbling mountain, the sun seemed to vanish, a shrinking blemish, already sinking past the ancient summit, though it was not far past noon. A crude stone table and rough boulders had been dragged forth on some pretense of comfort for the negotiators. A dozen men met them, on stiff legs, bearing arms. Everyone stood motionless, faces set in tight frowns. The rearguard in the black leather jerkins were central Galashadians, with square heads, fat, gnarled fingers and fresh blooded mail shirts and weapons.

The man who commanded these ruffians was stocky, just shorter than Basineus, but with an outer menace that commanded respect. A dangerous man, whose vibrant aura of malignant energy asserted itself with force and prompted Vetra to curl his lips in distaste. Wide-spaced eyes of bear-like intensity took in the men gathered before him and then dropped downward, as if having assessed their measure. The man stood, legs wide apart, draped in a long brown cape that dragged to his glossy black boots. A faint reek of rotting undergrowth preceded him.

This was not the oddest thing about the drug king.

Peculiar vines seemed to crawl on his shoulders, questing restlessly at nothing; his massive ribs bulged out with growths like tubes, yellow leaves grew in his hair like some grotesque garland and rustled when he moved. His face was utterly repulsive, but it gleamed with a preternatural energy. His three immediate henchmen to either side seemed afflicted with the same disease—part plant men, Vetra guessed. But not exhibiting the singular health of their master.

Whoever these beings were, they seemed to be in a highly advanced stage of metamorphosis—or some ghoulish alchemy at least, at which Vetra shuddered to guess. They hunched with otherworldly confidence, like strange beings from a far world rooted of their own making, and as if guarding some secret knowledge. But deadly danger burned in those carrot-colored eyes and their wavering stalks jutted out from their shoulders like spikes, as if ready to grip a man and squeeze the life out of him.

"A pleasant day to you, gentlemen," said the one called

Grebu, or the 'plant king' as Vetra referred to him. He gave Tas a sardonic bow. "Can I offer you some beverages, or maja juice, a mix with lemon and cactus?" The voice was deep-throated, matching the man's heavy-barreled frame.

Tas grimaced. He looked as if he'd rather drink rattlesnake poison. "You know why we're here, Grebu."

"A pity. 'Tis quite soothing to the palate, this beverage, quenches thirst like no other." He shrugged, took up a goblet of his own and downed it in a single ceremonious gulp. On closer inspection, Vetra saw that this man's hands seemed to have retreated into themselves, deformed, undeveloped appendages like the hands of an aborted fetus. All his minions had dark green bottles of the precious bulbs' mash at their belts, like a milky elixir for an infant.

"In good faith I agreed to this negotiation," Tas growled, his eyes cast of steel. "On your turf, even at great risk to myself."

The plant king raised his eyebrows in interest. "Where would you have us gather, in the middle of the bridge? Remember, our last meeting turned ugly after your most wanton behavior."

"Right after you started firing arrows down our throats."

Grebu sighed, a soft sad sound. "I see you are intending to inveigle more leverage out of our forces. In addition, you have brought some new faces; indeed, more men than I had specified—" he tipped his head toward Vetra and Basineus. "My band is quite spartan in comparison." He swept a plant-like hand to his immediate minions. "Meet my three lieutenants—fine fellows. As are yours, doubtless. Replacements for the men you lost on the ridge?"

Tas waved carelessly. "Just my men. Why do you ask? You would do no differently."

"I don't think so," said Grebu. "I am meticulous in these matters. Yours are well-trained men, I can tell by their disciplined stances, their hardened gazes, their well-muscled bodies, something you could do well to emulate. Not your regular stooges, like Kraddus and Nurus here."

Nurus grinned a good-natured grin but Kraddus seemed to recoil in indignation, for reasons Vetra could not altogether fathom. Why would the captain care what the mutant thought of him?

"New terms," growled the drug lord with impatience. "I continue to traffic maja to Lausern; you take your sword-swinging men and lose yourselves in the backwoods, I don't care, maybe Umbria, Mercia? In exchange, I offer you a sack of gold and fifty pounds of product, a small pittance of the spoils I intend to spread to cities of Xalgossa and Masern in the north."

Tas spoke through gritted teeth. "Your demands are unreasonable. 'Tis I who came to propose concessions. Back off Lvendar and take your miserable trade elsewhere, preferably south or east. No more flow of the accursed maja to Lausern. In return, Lord Ragnum promises not to attack you on his borders—and to join no alliances with other territories to shut you down."

Grebu looked about without humor. "Gentlemen! Does a river stop flowing because some dullard wishes it? It's all about supply and demand. I have the supply; you have the demand. You know how business goes." His face was twisted in a sinister leer and the snake-like vines on his shoulders twitched in insolent anticipation. "I think you have nothing to offer. A bit of talk, some idle threats, and much gilding of the lily thrown in for effect."

Tas compressed his lips.

Grebu smiled. "Yes, I see. Only bluster. It's the power I hanker for, Tas, command over all the kingdoms. One way or other I will have it, with or without your petty counteroffers and concessions."

Tas persisted, "Lvendar will crush you with an army, if they must."

"Where is this army then?" sneered Grebu. "I see none. The

Lord Vizier and his cowardly allies—fools and braggarts! Present a few washed up mercenaries to intimidate me?" He snorted. "It's laughable. The problem with Lvendar and its arrogant lords is they underestimate the reach of my power."

"You flatter yourself, Grebu."

"Fool yourself, Tas! I breed a new race. Didn't you know? Do they think I will shut down my enterprise at your lord's beck and call? Hardly. They have no power in my lands, not even in their own; the law of the jungle will prevail."

"They'll bring steel and fire on your heels. Does that not mean anything to you? Terror, blood and slaughter."

"All pale under the power of addiction. You can't fight that power. Once it gets in the blood it never leaves, as you readily know. It feeds on one's blood; devours anything in its path."

Tas shook his head like a savage dog. "You will not win this war, Grebu."

The mogul hissed through his teeth. "But I will!" His eyes blazed like a devil's fire. "'Tis you who do not see the light, you misguided fool." He glanced around at his audience, who were entranced by his speech, all except Vetra and Tas. The man had a definite charisma. Almost with pity, he bored eyes like snakes into Tas's soul. "The maja already runs thick in your blood. I see it, Tas. You know how it feels, don't you? Taking the soul from the inside out. Of course, your mana is now entwined, indistinguishable from the fibers of the maja. But is your desire satisfied yet?" Grebu laughed aloud in an uncontrollable rush, his head tilted back like a howling jackal.

Tas's eyes reeled about him. A mix of hopeless anger and despair washed over his face. His fists balled like iron. But he did regain his composure and spat full at the mogul's feet. "Don't try to subvert me with your taunts and deflections. I've killed men better than you."

Grebu reared up with a snarl. "Try it." Vines lashed out to take any man who challenged him. The plant king settled down quickly; his voice calm again, like flowing syrup, his tentacles inert. "It brings us to other issues." He tipped his leaf-clumped head toward Kraddus. "Well, Kraddus?"

"My lord?"

Tas's jaw dropped in stupefaction. "Lord? Is this some kind of joke?"

"No joke, 'Tas'," quipped Kraddus.

Vetra crouched on the balls of his feet, his sword flying out of the sheath.

Basineus whipped out his axe as Grebu's closest lieutenant moved on him like a panther. Axe crunched full into the lieutenant's shoulder blade, biting into his neck in a blinding sweep. The half mutant sank to his knees, shrieking, gushing blood.

"Kill him, you fool!" the plant king's fractured yell smote the air.

Kraddus's face contorted in indecision. "Gladly, lord, but the ransom—"

Grebu unsheathed his own blade. "I could give a rat's ass for any ransom. You're far too mealy-mouthed for a traitor." He bumped Kraddus aside and lunged for Vetra, whose muscled arm had begun a downward swing. The mercenary's blade cut a vine that twined close to Vetra's ear.

The plant king winced but hitched closer, like a belligerent bull, the tips of the feelers questing Vetra's skin. Vetra jerked as he saw the damaged feeler grow back gruesomely before his eyes.

Nurus's mouth worked in sick dismay. The slither of steel shivered from his sheath. Basineus sprang over the lieutenant's corpse he had dispatched, to assist Vetra. The strident rasp of men's blades echoed from all round.

The man at Tas's right fell in a splatter of blood and brains, his head cleaved by an axe hurled from the hand of Grebu's ugliest lieutenant. Arrows skittered down from the caves above from which hillmen emerged, as if by magic.

"You treacherous dog!" yowled Tas.

"What do you expect?" cried Grebu. "Now die!" He turned away from Vetra's blade and came charging in. Claw fingers clenched, nails not dissimilar to those of the Vizier's daughter. Bolts pumped from all directions. Vetra caught a glimpse of many figures swarming from beyond the bridge, Tas's archers, true to his word, pumping bolts into the fray. Swords flew in red loops hacking at both attacker and defender. Grebu's minions moved with an uncanny precision and parried, despite their ungainly looks, and they were gaining ground over the defenders.

Vetra closed with the plant king, felt a stinging lash swipe across his cheek, almost taking out his left eye. He cursed, wiped away the blood, ducked more of those serpentish feelers as he raised his blade to dice them. Grebu's other lieutenant advanced to defend his lord. Vetra took him out in a sledgehammer sweep that had the plant-man writhing on his knees.

Kraddus rounded on Tas with a wild yell.

Tas parried Kraddus's blade. "So, that's how Grebu's marksmen got through our net," he bellowed in Kraddus's ear. "I thought it was the machinations of this vicious devil." He cut sideways at Grebu. The drug lord deftly hopped aside. Tas switched back to Kraddus and smashed his blade at Kraddus's middle. "It was you!" Kraddus caught the stroke on his guard, barely avoiding a blood-letting.

Grebu laughed. Jumping back, avoiding again the hissing blade of his enemy, he ducked Basineus's sweeping axe that would have lopped off his yellow head.

"What did he promise you?" Tas cried, slashing hard at his Kraddus's exposed flank.

Kraddus moved in time with Tas's slices and forced his commanding officer back on his heels with a vicious series of cuts. "A captaincy and ten times the spoil you offered."

"You fool!—he'd have slit your throat before he gave you a groat. You'll die for your treachery and greed!" Tas drove in, whirling his blade and stabbing it like a skewer. Kraddus blocked, gasping, and darted in, spitting blood where Tas's hilt had smashed a tooth out of his mouth.

Tas let out a shrill whistle—the signal for his archers to advance, but his look back became one of dismay. They had risen minutes ago from their place of concealment behind boulders, low shrubs, some covered with sand, only to meet a horde of blood mad Karkassians streaming down the slopes to wreak their blood lust upon them. Some hurled knives or plunged daggers into their backs. Multiple arrows sung, loosed from the archers' midst. Most flew astray, clattering on stones. Above Vetra and his company, a steady stream of arrows rained down on them from the rocky sanctuaries.

Vetra roared with frustration. "Down! To the ground!"

A shaft cut into the earth at Vetra's feet. It quivered there like a snake's head.

Vetra ducked, scrabbling almost flat on his belly, to avoid a whistling shaft that would have otherwise plunged through his throat. He chopped down a vicious stroke at Grebu's last lieutenant, the ugly one, who was tensed up in fury and hate. Vetra staggered and chopped again, feeling the bite of glimmering steel connect with flesh. The attacker's mossy reek swirled in his nostrils. An arm came loose, spraying off at the elbow. The mutant laughed. The mutilation was nothing to him. Feelers from his shoulders came writhing out to grapple Vetra. The mercenary dodged, grimacing with horror that a man could endure such punishment and still be standing. A stinging sensation sank into his flesh as one of the loathsome tendrils lashed his upper shoulder and sent a stabbing pain into his nerve ends.

"Stay away from the cursed feelers!" Vetra yelled. "Don't let them touch you!"

His shout was lost in the fray. There was no getting across the bridge. They were cut off from behind. Raging hillmen flooded in numbers across the quivering timbers. Tas cried out a solemn oath. "Make for the cliff." The survivors followed his lead, plowed straight to the cliffside into the teeth of the arrows that streamed out from the caves yawning two men's heights above.

Men went down in scarlet ruin. Vetra felt a bolt bite into his mail shirt. He slipped on a pool of blood and fell to his knees. He picked himself up again and with a burst of rage grabbed a corpse and shielded himself from a spray of lethal iron. Men rounded behind him as Vetra pushed on. Basineus plucked a bolt with wincing anguish from the side of his boot and hobbled into the sheltered line.

Nurus, straggling too far back, was peppered with shafts, and staggered to a gasping halt, sinking like a straw doll. A vine curled around his throat and the writhing white mass pulled him down on his back. Grebu's massive boot stomped down on the captain's neck, crushing his windpipe. Stinging tentacles whipped from the plant king's shoulders to grapple more defenders who ran behind Vetra and Tas. Kraddus's foul mouth rang with expletives. Blood dripped from his lips down into his goatee as he cut down like wheat men he once called his own. Grebu laughed with sinister triumph, taking the carnage in with a gleaming eye, latching tentacles onto men's throats and lifting them off their feet, like man-puppets of straw, not muscle and bone.

Vetra grimaced, gagging at the repulsive scene, and raced for the hill ahead. Basineus stumbled at his heels. There were ravines to either side, dressed in cool shadow. Under no circumstance must they be dragged down by those ghoulish tentacles of Grebu.

Dark openings in the rock gaped to either side, avenues that Vetra instinctively looked to for refuge but liked not at all. Tas had dropped back to pull Vetra and Basineus aside who were scrambling for the higher, leftmost path. "Not there! Down the other ravine. I've a bad feeling about that one."

Vetra threw the corpse off his back, the weight slowing his pace, and he and Basineus scrambled into the ravine to the side that curled around the base of the hill. They watched as Tas and the others beetled into a blue-shadowed cross canyon, with dozens of shrieking hillmen pouring after them.

"Let them run!" laughed Grebu. "Like rabbits, they run. Foil us by splitting up? The maja will kill them all." His deep-throated laughter echoed like a fiendish jackal about the striated rock.

Vetra and Basineus staggered down the slope into a rocky corridor, flanked by tall, sheer cliffs, half running, half stumbling.

The canyon sported steep sides, blocking out any vestiges of the sun. A gloomy, clinging feel draped the open passage; chill drafts seeped up the avenue like wind tunnels. Shouts of men echoed in Vetra's ears. He saw crumbling stone arches to either side, and heard the whine of arrows. Bolts snapped off his mail shirt, whizzing by both their ears.

"It's a death trap," he snarled. "Run!"

Basineus needed no urging. The bulk of the enemy pursued Tas and the others. For this Vetra was thankful. Tas had disappeared from sight.

Vetra squinted ahead. He knew to stay alive they had to outwit their pursuers, or somehow slit their throats. "This way." He darted left into a cross canyon through an oval gap three men wide.

Basineus stumbled after him, fresh wounds dripping from his arms and torso.

The pounding of booted feet thundered from behind.

Vetra stopped to flatten his back against the wall of this new canyon. When the pursuers first charged through this opening, he ripped his blade into flesh and teeth. A feather-crowned Galashad crumpled with a thud. Basineus reeled in to skewer the attacker's closest comrade. Blood sprayed on the canyon wall as the mercenary's sword severed the victim's throat.

Vetra paused, snorting wrath through his teeth.

Three more charged in. Vetra felt steel rake across his mail shirt, deflected somehow as he stove in a skull and landed in a crouch to pass sword through the astounded Karkassian's loins like a skewer. Basineus thrust bloody steel up through the sternum of the remaining rogue and out through his back. The man fell in a crunching heap.

An eerie silence ensued. The distant sounds only of steel and screams of dying men.

"Hide the bodies," muttered Basineus.

"No time," argued Vetra. "We'll toss these jackals' bodies up this way a bit. Then we'll backtrack and take the other canyon. It's time for us to do the unexpected."

With a vicious sweep, he hacked the head off one of the corpses and Basineus dragged the other body and threw it up the path. The trail seemed to meander to a place up the hill. Good, thought Vetra. Make it look as if the fugitives fled up the crumbling trail. Basineus dragged the last attacker's corpse after him, and with a grimace of disgust let it fall in a ghastly heap.

"It seems obvious to say we're in a jam. What now?"

"To Dergath with that! That we ever agreed to this mission, I don't know. I should have my head examined."

They slunk down the path. The sounds of pursuit faded.

III

Through a graveyard of fallen rocks, Vetra and Basineus picked their way. They skirted boulders, sidestepped pits, crevasses, and the like. Basineus, breathing heavily, called out a halt and snatched at Vetra's arm. "Hold up, my leg's going to fall off. Besthra's teats." He gazed at Vetra's gleaming mail shirt. "Dergath, that's a fine set of mail. How 'bout we trade?"

Vetra scowled, accelerating his pace.

Basineus winced and hurried to catch up.

The canyon was stark, forbidding and the sides rose sheer out of the bedrock. They were unscalable, like the walls of a giant's tomb. A patch of clear sky loomed far over their heads. Eccentric forms seemed to grow from the rock face, the stone of which was cold to the touch where Vetra saw animal heads and demons, perhaps carved by some inspired tribesmen.

"Remember that tavern at Ajstan?" Basineus grunted at Vetra, limping in a bent-kneed hobble.

Vetra's eyes roved ahead, scouting for danger. His fingers itched to lay steel into any howling enemy that might fling themselves upon them. After a time, he sneered. "How can I forget?"

"The brawl was staged, just so you know." Basineus coughed up blood. "The slut chose you. It was just a bet. Tarkus and his men dared me but I had no idea what was going down. That it was enough to get you jailed, or that Hurdan was your enemy."

Vetra growled between his teeth. "I never forgave you for that."

Basineus smiled a grim hound's grin through his blood-clotted face. "Always a hothead, weren't you, Vetra?"

"And you, little too conniving for your own good, eh, Basineus?" grunted Vetra. "Watch your step, wise ass. If your antics don't get your throat cut, my sword will." He flourished his blade, stepping over a wide crack that oozed rank vapors from its dark depths. "I've forgotten that catty wench anyway. She wasn't worth it. I was young, foolish. Some time in the irons did me good. Taught me how prisoners think. I won them over in the end. Now the ones that walk free are my allies."

"So, all was not lost then," said Basineus with a raspy sigh. "Well, here's to better times, by Dergath!" He slapped his thigh. "Glad that's all out in the open."

"Look, if you think that fixes anything—quiet!" he warned, pulling Basineus down. "Sounds up ahead." Both strained their eyes in the blue shadows. Flickers of darting motion caught the edge of their vision. The tramp of feet echoed in Vetra's ear. "It's those damned Karkassians again."

"No...just good old Tas."

The blond-haired leader came up, stumbling out of the shadow, his eyes wild with feverish intensity. He was out of breath and his pupils were dilated, like the amber trance-stare of a rabid wolf. His soiled leather was bloodstained. Blackened lips flecked with foam, peeled back to show bared teeth.

"You look horrible," said Basineus.

"You're not very pretty yourself," snapped the ranger, hoisting his blood-dripping axe.

"What happened?" Vetra's gaze dropped to the extra bottle at his belt.

The ranger's head inclined. His hand flexed, reaching involuntarily for the glass vial at his waist. "I confiscated this from one of the scum of Grebu's rabble. I took out dozens of them. But they killed the others of our group. All our bowmen are dead." He grimaced, gripped his axe, dripping with fresh blood. "The scum followed me, but I lost them yet I fear they're not far behind."

"Then we've got to move!" gestured Vetra.

* * *

A cramped, narrow space in the canyon opened up, darkened with the sun angled low. Parallel walls of rock hemmed them in like lemmings. Vetra felt as if he scurried in an open crypt. There was no refreshing slant of sunshine to penetrate this shale-crumbled hell. The sun seemed muted by tribal magic, a place both hallowed and damned.

A cold sweat broke out on Vetra's back when he saw what lay before him. The familiar waving of stalk-like tentacles shivered out from the crevices in the sheer rock faces to either side. Vetra gaped, refusing to accept what he saw. White slimy things had engulfed the wall, giving him and Basineus about eight feet of grace to walk unhindered. The feelers had the familiar cast of Grebu's ghastly appendages exuding from shoulders and ribs. Could the wretched things pierce flesh? Vetra crabbed back in involuntary reaction. A chill familiarity struck him of their similarity to certain octopi-like creatures he had seen washed up on the western shores of Umbria. His sword fell loose in his grip.

"What are they?" quavered Basineus.

"Grebu's creation," said Tas, glowering. "I don't doubt this is his birthplace—Or his experimental grounds," he added.

"Experimental what—"

"Hush, silence!" hissed Tas. "Noise riles these creatures. It tells them there's prey lurking about."

The three slunk through the narrow defile like wary weasels. Careful not to let the things sense them, they edged by, ever fearful to dislodge a loose pebble. Basineus, the inattentive fool he was, slipped on a loose flake underfoot. Things reached out to touch him and latch onto his shin. Vetra stifled a curse; Tas cast him a dark look. Water dripped from the walls, but that was not what captured Vetra's riveted gaze and held it like a vice. It was the weird, garnet-colored globules growing from the ends of the sinister stalks. Putrid, thick liquid oozed with the yellow-brown oil from the stigma to the chalky stone underfoot. The feelers were alive with motion, writhing in synchrony like underwater anemones, ready to entangle a man with them. Vetra's blood froze in his veins.

The cackle of familiarity echoed up the ravine, followed by wrenching screams, then the chopping of flesh, finally sheathed steel.

A corpse fell tumbling to smash head-first down on the stone before them, spilling brains and blood, its limbs shattered. Vetra recognized the bloody mass as one of Tas's militia men.

"Sweet Dergath!" he hissed in despair.

Tas crept backward, his head craned upward, cursing at the enemy who lurked unseen above them.

"The cursed ghoul walks on the ledge," Basineus muttered. "Is he a spider or a baboon?"

"I wouldn't put it past him, both."

The nearby plant tentacles came to life with the smack of the falling corpse and probed the shale for warm flesh. One quested the corpse's twisted leg and dragged it. The mangled body jerked and left a foul blood trail.

The men lost all inhibitions and scrambled past the opposing walls of the white fleshy tendrils as the ghoulish feast progressed.

No sooner had they stepped beyond the swath of fiendish foliage than Kraddus came striding up, chuckling in triumph. His head was thrown back in wild mockery and a red grin shone on his face. "Ah, the wild maja!" he croaked with glee. He motioned at the writhing plants. "Do you not like them, Tas? 'Tis Grebu's pride and joy. He grows his most malevolent creatures here in this gulch—or one of them. I for one, am partial to barbarous fiends."

"Lovely," snorted Vetra. "How about a garland to twist about your neck?"

"Draw your sword, you damn renegade!" cursed Tas, rounding in on Kraddus.

Kraddus danced back, baiting him. "They're seedlings from a man-eating strain," he remarked with a grunt. "A whimsical experiment of Grebu's."

"You sicken me, Kraddus," growled Tas. "I ought to spit you like a pig." He clenched his axe, shaking his head.

"It's still not too late to join us, Tas. Show the king your loyalty. Kill these spies, show it as a token of your fealty, then the master will go easy on you. I'll see to it."

"I'd rather wash my stones in pigs' blood," spat Tas. "Prepare to die, swine. You swore an oath to us—to defend Lvendar's interests."

"Pacts are meant to be cast aside like a man sheds old clothes. You are getting old, Tas, barely able to do what you set out here to do. I'll let the master know your decision." The traitor backed away and made a signal of fist, thumb and finger. Men came creeping out of the shadows: from up the path past the tentacled area like specters.

Tas flinched, whether from the men who gathered, or the mention of the word *master*. The fierce expression on his face echoed some animated struggle, which only amused Kraddus. "I'll gut you like a fish, Kraddus, the dog you are."

"Back, fool!" bawled Kraddus. "You condemn Grebu for his bestiality, but look at yourself! You're no better than an animal. Are you not the fool who ate some experimental version of the bulb? Now you're some type of monster. I can see it in your greenish face, you've been taking the bulb."

"You lie!" Froth flecked from Tas's lips. Vetra saw the leader's fists clench into balls, his nails twitch, like the claws that depended from Kealasa's hands.

The big tawny man gave a spitting howl. He flung himself forward to brain Kraddus with his axe, but five of his thugs hitched in with swords.

"Ah, ah, ah," Kraddus chided, waving a dirty finger. "Back! Do you think I would be fool enough to let you lord over this outfit? While you were out gnawing on your bulbs, I gained control over the militia, the few that are left. I gained Grebu's trust."

"You dirty scum," Tas swore under his breath.

Kraddus thumbed his blade in an offhand manner. "Which of you dies first?"

Vetra lunged, drawing his weapon to strike.

Kraddus signaled to his men and a dozen came out to surround him.

Vetra parried Kraddus's arching blade and squared in close enough to smell the man's rank hide. He ducked a stalk's stigma which extended with a ruby-eye end. The thing's poison swept by with mere inches to spare.

Kraddus laughed. "Mind Grebu's pets, mercenary. Their sting can bring a man to tears."

"Shut your gob, cretinous oaf," Vetra snarled. He lashed out at the captain while Tas engaged foes at their back. Basineus was caught in the middle, slashing and cursing the oncoming native Galashadians, a surge of square-faces, dirty-blond hair and square steel caps.

"Ack!" A feeler raked at Vetra's throat, leaving him with a red stinging mark. He hunched and tottered off-balance, shaking his head and the sting out of his neck.

Kraddus let loose a sneering laugh. "Smarts, doesn't it?"

Tas's axe fell with a squashing thunk. A Galashad warrior with stubbled jowl rolled at Vetra's feet minus an arm. The writhing body tripped Vetra. Kraddus pounced, but Vetra rolled free, pulling his knees to his chest and uncoiled in a vicious kick, to fling boot heels first into Kraddus's gut. The movement lifted the traitor in the air and hurled him backward toward the writhing wall of stalks.

Quick as adders, the ghastly roots latched on to Kraddus's

skin and whipped him sideways, transfixing the back of his head.

Kraddus's mouth opened in a parody of a dismal scream. Another grabbed his shoulder and pierced through flesh. His white lips writhed in a bloodcurdling screech. Grunting and slashing he managed to cut some of the feelers that fanned out to grip him. But he was quickly consumed as more latched on to him, leech-like—in his mouth, down his throat. Other vine-feelers hooked into and tore at his flesh, hoisting him up like a grim, flapping puppet. On those string-tentacles he dangled like a hanged man, legs kicking.

Vetra grimaced, scrambling to his feet. He reacted in time to catch the vicious uppercut of a drawn blade. Kraddus's body began to jerk, caught in an abysmal puppet-wrenching palsy. More of the ghoulish feelers hooked onto his legs, pulling his body into the damp crevice until only his boots could be seen, kicking spasmodically. His shrieks faded into a symphony of grotesque feeding sounds.

Vetra turned his head. What hideous mouths lurked beyond that dank stone, he dare not imagine.

Basineus toiled at his sides, raining blows heavy enough to fell trees among the Galashadian guard. One croaked out a strangled howl. Tas cut into a white probing stalk, before it whipped around Basineus. With an appalling yank, the man Basineus was hewing was lifted up and pulled into the wall by the man-eating stalks. The cleft in the canyon wall was narrow, so his body was mutilated as it was forced through a hole smaller than his torso. Finally, only his boots showed, flailing.

Vetra paled, twitching, aghast at the sudden violence of the grisly attack.

Tas threw another man back into the rippling menace. A puzzled expression fled over his face as white, writhing vines gripped him in an obscene embrace. His muffled scream died in his throat as they tore apart his mouth.

Basineus struggled with his brawny contender, matching

blade for blade. Feelers whistled inches from his ears. In a sudden vengeful motion, Vetra's shadow loomed overhead and steel chopped the man's shoulder clean to the bone and the man sank to his knees in a gruesome crunch. Five enemies remained. Crimson steel struck and slashed in the dimness and Basineus's blade bit into the neck and spine of the attacker's comrade.

Tas pulled Vetra and Basineus on up the ravine. Vetra was not averse to following the blood-drenched ranger this time, knowing that it meant death to remain.

Vetra scrambled up the stony defile, Basineus stumbling and cursing all the way, the dying cries of mangled men enveloped and eaten by the carnivorous plants. Booted feet echoed on stone.

"These catacombs," Tas gasped between ragged breaths, "I explored when I was here not too long ago." He shook out the blood from his hair like a dog as he ran. "There is only one way we can hope to double around the mountain from the top." The ranger pointed up a rocky cliff face. "We can descend the canyon under cover of night, before the moon rises." He wiped the sweat from his face and spat. "The canyon is impassable for many leagues. We must navigate the bridge and cross the contested border back to Lvendar." He looked around with wary wolf's eyes. "We mustn't be seen. 'Tis the haunt of fell beasts and the Karkassian cannibals."

"What could be worse than Grebu and his ghouls?" Vetra muttered under his breath.

"Trolls, perhaps?" offered Basineus with a sarcastic sneer.

Tas snarled. "Come on!"

"What of the mission?" demanded Basineus.

"Sod the mission!" thundered Tas. "Everything is lost. Mission, honor, our life as free men while we wallow in this failure and Ragnum hears of our cock-up. We're dead men."

Vetra grumbled. "Let's go. Grebu will be on to us soon. A spider free of the web he is, spinning a web of pain for us. He knows every square inch of his lair, I don't doubt."

Through a labyrinth of stony ways open to the sky, the three groped and stumbled their way. They passed at times through a tunnel of rock, and the air would grow damp and dim, but Tas, in the grip of some disquieting trance seemed impervious to all obstacles. He had the red, staring eyes of a werewolf, the strength of five men... Vetra grimaced, remembering how he had lifted a man by the throat in one hand and tossed him into the maja creepers as if he were no more than a sheaf of wheat.

* * *

It seemed like hours that they wandered through a maze of narrow, interconnected canyons. With his throat choked with dust, Vetra could only hear the clopping echo of boots and Basineus's foul curses. Looking ahead, he saw Tas beating a swift pace, his eyes gleaming in the late afternoon light. Those eyes reflected a faraway, frenzied purpose, as if the man's mind and thoughts were not his own.

Vetra frowned. More of the grisly red bumps had broken out on the man's brow, adding to the cluster that had first appeared after the slaughter back at the ravine. Vetra's mind roved elsewhere, and he trudged on after Tas while the sun dipped lower. The heat lessened, as did the light: three men facing the press of darkness on enemy lands.

The boulder-strewn trail continued down a narrow gorge of crumbling rock. Layers of shale rose in towering folds and to Vetra's relief, not encrusted or flowered with any of those abominable feelers of Grebu's creation.

"This maze is going to kill us," Vetra grumbled to no one in particular.

Tas seemed not to hear. His wolfhound-sharp eyes trained on the shadows. Basineus stumbled on like a man sleepwalking.

At last, they came to a high, stout wooden door, brass-bound, caked with verdigris and set into the rock face. The portal was much scarred and timeworn; lock and hinges were rusted with disuse, as Vetra's keen eyes noticed. Perhaps the secret escape tunnel to some ancient fort, or defensive palisade?

The path continued ahead, winding off into dim shadows. Tas halted, tugging at his chin.

His eyes lit with recognition at what he saw, and his ears perked up, as a hound's would upon sensing some unseen foe. Either way, a smile of delight crossed Tas's face and Vetra frowned, fearing the man had started to lose his senses.

"You investigate this door," the ranger ordered. "I'll ensure there are no enemies lurking about."

"But that's a foolish—" Vetra started, but the ranger was off before he could object, and Basineus could blink an eye. "There he goes again," grunted Vetra. He threw up his hands. "What is it with these rangers?"

Basineus shrugged. "I've a feeling we're going to run into trouble soon enough." He hacked at the rusted lock that held the great portal shut. "Forget Tas. Brute force may be the only option. Hurry. There could be a well or water spring on the other side. My throat's dry as sand."

Vetra lent the butt end of his blade to the hewing, rather than ruining his blade, though he had a bad feeling about this place.

The ringing of steel on corroded iron echoed about the canyon. The stout balewood shivered. In a spray of sparks, the ancient lock splintered and they wrestled with the door, heaving and grunting. Finally it gave way with an abysmal groan. They edged down a narrow corridor, weapons in hand. A musty odor crept forth and stung their nostrils; there came the sound of shuffling further on. They crouched with instinctive wariness, staring in the sepia gloom. A tense expectancy hung in the air, as thick as drying blood.

Vetra caught his breath. Blurred shapes milled about a large open area exposed to the darkening sky. Straining his eyes, he grunted, lips parted. Human figures? Gaunt frames stooping with slow, mechanical movements. He lifted his gaze over the eccentric formations of rock. A slave colony of some kind? Curse Tas's hide—had the man led them into a trap?

A sudden realization smote him when he saw the tall maja plants. Blinking in comprehension, he willed his eyes to adjust faster to the dimness.

The place was akin to some dry seabed, a bowl-shaped cavity, a natural pit for prisoners. Strange, curved pathways wove in and among the rubble and the fluted rock carved over time. Vetra moved forward, Basineus on his heels. Doomed figures hunched in the periphery with picks and hoes in hand, chipping shale to create more arable land? Others crouched, watering plants and planting seeds in what scant soil there was. Here was water at least—

A rustle of movement to the side had Vetra spinning on his heels. In the half cave to the right, he glimpsed a long, snake-like trunk, or some fiendish stalk, as it shot back into the gloom. He advanced to get a closer look.

In that long section of pumpkin-like vine was held a large shape—akin to some horrid chrysalis.

Vetra's hand crossed blade in front of him. He gave back a short gasp of horror and disgust. Basineus stood frozen like a stone idol.

Vetra staggered back, muttering oaths. Closer inspection revealed the long stalked feeler trailing on the ground and twitching from time to time had swallowed a man whole...

The vine trembled; it was feeding on the corpse's essence. The man was days dead, his gray skin and withered features seemed only vaguely human through the filmy circumference of the transparent green stalk. It had captured the unfortunate, or contained him, in its green, pulsing housing, like some mutated pupa. The stalk was slowly devouring the victim, which was curled in the fetal position, like a fly in a web.

Vetra felt the urge to retch.

One of the emaciated captives wandered over to gaze with

curiosity at the newcomers. He held a battered hoe in hand, wiping snot from his wizened face. In crazed fury, Vetra grabbed the gawker and shook him like a rag doll. "What are you thinking? You callous idiot! Why didn't you hack the wretch free?"

The ragged man squeaked out a hoarse objection. "Are you crazy? Have that madman Grebu hack us to bits for harming his pets?" The gaunt slave blinked and struggled in the mercenary's grip. "You don't know the half of what goes on here! You understand nothing of the workings of this hell."

Vetra released him, appalled.

The slave ruffled out his tattered garments. "Grebu grows monsters in this hell pit," continued the malnourished man. "We are all part of his madness, his menagerie, destined to die in the belly of one of his fiends—like this one, when we are too old to work." He stabbed out a gnarled finger at the vile sprawl of vines, bulbs, and sucking, plant-like tendrils, the ends of which were graced with obscene lips crusted with tiny teeth.

Basineus sneered. "Seems to me as if your ghoul Grebu needs to be put down, like a sick dog." He took up his sword and hacked at the offending vine, shredding it to pieces. A hissing shriek exuded from the mini mouths of the stalks. Pus and gases flowed, causing Vetra and Basineus to gag.

Vetra stalked deeper into the open compound, holding his nose, shaking off his nausea, a man in a trance. He raked at his chin while Basineus trailed behind, a sullen frown on his face, lips slightly parted.

It was a veritable slave colony, Vetra thought dismally. Up the cliff to the right, a metal hoist and conveyor belt held a system of baskets heaped with harvested bulbs. The rig was a rudimentary apparatus designed to haul the maja from the pit to the summit. At the crest, a crude wooden crane outfitted with chains transported the cargo to a large circular vat and millstone which caught and crushed the bulbs.

Squinting against the reddening sky, Vetra could see a stone outbuilding with a long, crooked chimney, part of a roasting assembly. Likely it cured the crushed bulbs and extracted the precious, lethal oil. As to what hellish sorcery Grebu applied to his seedlings, was anybody's guess. All Vetra knew was that sorcery demanded fire. And Grebu would have plenty of it.

He gazed about with growing dismay. The cliffs were insurmountable. If not for a narrow staircase that ran a partial way up aside the conveyor there would be no access. Now the operation was inactive, as the overlords were engaged elsewhere.

Vetra gave little heed to these hoists and baskets stretching up the cliff wall. His attention was focused on the dispirited huddle who squatted listlessly about a penned-in area. A rustling field of maja buds adjoined the pen. Vetra guessed these wretches harvested the maja stalks before they became man-eaters.

Basineus motioned Vetra aside, inclining his head toward the primitive drays scattered about the fields: "Seems to me those chained slaves grow and harvest the plants, while the others cart them to the conveyor."

Vetra grunted. And as suddenly, a sharp memory assaulted him. A memory buried deep but which cut like a fiery knife. The night Umbrian slavers had stormed his father's villa and captured his sister Retia. Where she was now years later, he could not guess, if she were even still alive. The scum of slavers he had never found, but he vowed someday he would extract his revenge though the trail was long cold.

He trailed in grim silence as Basineus hopped the staked-off fence of ropes and hewed through the thinly chicken-wired pen. His crimson blade hacked some slaves free of their balls and chains. The two mercenaries stared meaningfully at the moldy potato peels and fruit rinds that lay at their feet in heaps. Haggard faces peered up at them, but in spite of the bony limbs, a fierce light shone in their eyes, inspired by the presence of the liberators and the sudden hope of escape.

"We're the sons of slaves," came the voice of the man Vetra had shaken. Vetra saw half his teeth had rotted away. His tattered garment reeked of piss and sweat. "I remember once working in a dim cave somewhere," he croaked. "Long years ago, then a harrowing journey by cart to this forsaken pit. The plant ogre Grebu told me to work as my fingers have never worked before! Otherwise Bekroma, the gluttonous plant monster you slew, would make a meal of me. Picking plants, peeling bulbs, though the oil stung my eyes and made my skin burn." He held up both hands, all raw and pink from the plant excretions. His nails were dirty as pig wallow, caked with years of grime. His eyes were sunken and his cheeks haggard, and he walked with an irreparable limp.

"So why do you not fight back?" growled Basineus.

The man shrugged his crooked shoulders. "Grebu threatens us with death—fodder for Bekroma—forces us to pick the bulbs and fill the baskets. Sometimes the plants grow large." He lifted a palsying finger to the crop at the outer edge of the compound. "Those grandfather plants, they take one or more of us regularly, for the wretched things must eat too."

"But Grebu always finds replacements," said another.

"From where?"

"From these neighboring hills. There are plenty of wandering tribesmen. But he will go as far as the plains of Galashad to get more. Sobui here, comes from the village of Urkue in a dusty valley."

Basineus asked, motioning to the primitive drays: "So these barrows—"

The man nodded with resignation. "Crude drays on stone wheels pulled by ropes. Raw contraband hauled by us to be transported to Lausern. Those who don't get eaten, at least."

Vetra craned his neck, imagining the odious process, as drug lords worked above on the flat top, curing, processing, while the slaves toiled below like ants, hauling cart and drawing stone bucket up the cliff via rope and pulley to meet Grebu's avaricious demands.

Vetra shook his head in disquiet. He struggled to grasp the madness of it all. But it was too deranged to rationalize, recalling the desiccated corpse being digested in the vine's pulpy middle.

"No matter," he said, snapping out of his reverie. "If you want your freedom, then join us! Fight this madman, though it may mean your deaths. You'll die, one way or the other, anyway."

Some shook their heads with vigorous refusal and cowered back, as if the very thought of crossing their master was unspeakable. Others ground their rotting teeth, licked blackened gums, their eyes glittering like dying embers.

"We were Karkassians and Galashadians!" cried one fiercely. He beat his hollow chest. More joined in the chant, clutching beat-up buckets: "Stripped of our humanity by a despot who reduces us to living corpses! Let us fight! Fight!"

He and Basineus pursed their lips grimly. They set to smashing the chains of those whose ankles were fastened together with a few feet of slack. A long line of them. Only a few roamed free, like the skeletal man who gaped at them, as if he were dreaming that rescue was just possible.

Vetra tensed as a crunch of boots on stone signaled the approach of a figure—Tas, who came trudging down the pebbly path, breathing heavily, his hair tousled and tawny locks matted with sweat. Something was not right about him, if there ever had been anything right about him.

Vetra motioned to Basineus. Both saw two more bottles of the dark green bulb maja oil at the ranger's belt. "Where did you go?" he demanded.

Tas shrugged lazily. "I guessed there would be more scoundrels lurking about, so I lay in wait and gutted them like fish. What's it to you? You should be thankful there're now a half dozen fewer villains to plunge knives in our backs."

"Appreciated, but unasked for. I see you got your maja juice," commented Basineus.

Tas gave a noncommittal shrug.

"Good resale value?" quipped Basineus, enjoying the rise he got out of Tas.

Tas's face burned with anger and his fists knotted. "I am collecting evidence," he growled, advancing on Basineus. "What's your beef? It'd be a waste to leave the contraband behind."

Vetra flashed an unpleasant smile. "You're a dark soul in a dark world, Tas. Or perhaps just a simpleton in total denial." He watched the ranger grit his teeth and his facial muscles tighten, but he held his ground. The ranger's fingers hovered over his axe handle. The man looked like a feral animal of the forest, hungry for blood. His bloodshot eyes scanned the brood around him with critical contempt. His breath hissed out in short wheezing pants. Judging from the half empty bottle at his hip, Vetra believed he had downed the other half. A haunted, unkempt craziness lurked about his expression, reminiscent of the plant king's.

The ranger gripped his freshly blooded axe and swung it in threatening loops. "I'd give my eye teeth to slit that nutcase's throat," he cried, glaring with contempt at the gross privation of the grime-caked beings around him.

"You may get your chance," Vetra grunted. "Look." He gestured a hand to the lip of stone above. A ponderous shadow flitted above, like some grotesque bat.

"The plant king," howled a cowering, wasted man, stumbling about the littered yard, awkward in his new found freedom.

Others of his band had drifted over and quailed in the shadow of the sinister being.

Vetra glared in wonder. He and Basineus pushed past a pile of decayed bulbs, reeking of rot and crawling with insects. A low growl burst from Basineus's throat. He kicked over a lopsided, rusted dray with one wheel missing.

Grebu's stocky silhouette hopped with spry energy on the

ridge's edge. The madman threw up his hands and some weird pods began to drift down as would lazy leaves in an autumn wind. Was he a magician?

On the high lip of crumbled rock, more figures emerged at his side and scooped up handfuls of the husk-like pods to cast them down to the slaves below. Like a predatory eagle perched on his favorite eyrie, the plant king gazed on the scene below with impassive savagery.

Vetra squinted up in curiosity, then he gaped. Some of the foolish slaves, being dependent on their master for food, reached up to grab at the floating pods and stuffed them hungrily in their maws. Their faces at once turned bright red and their eyes burned like coals. Horrible moans ripped from their throats.

"Stay clear of them!" cried Vetra. "The fiend's cursed bulbs will turn you into ghouls!"

Basineus needed no convincing. He lurched back on his heels, as one of the slaves snapped at his arm.

Tas looked on in resignation, his axe falling limp in his hand, as if part of him knew the ultimate horror that was upon them.

The slaves affected, jerked like flesh-eating marionettes and attacked their peers, taking whole chunks of their throats out with brown-gummed teeth. Their fingernails clawed and reached, elongated like a werewolf's, which they used to scratch and rend their fellow slaves' skin and flesh like badgers.

Grebu's head tipped back in a fiendish cackle as another hideous laugh ripped out of his veined throat. The echo rang off the surrounding stone. He hurled down more of the pods, and his tentacled minions at his side aped his obscene action.

The plants below which had been brushed by the pods, rustled, as if touched by an unnatural wind. The ensorcelled seedlings drove the plants mad and gave them sinister life. Roots ripped from the ground, pulling pebbly rock up with them. These maja took tentative steps in unison, like caricatures of demons possessed. To Vetra's horror, they jerked toward him, like an advancing army of corn stalks.

The figure on the ridge was gone and Vetra stared aghast, hacking at those slaves who had turned against him. As for the plant king, no doubt the fiend would be back.

"Take cover, quick—back the way we came!" Vetra yelled at Basineus who edged away from the advancing stalks and the infected slaves.

Basineus sliced the arm off a rampaging worker. The maja stalks quivered forth with fiendish energy, with a moaning whistle to stir the very demons of hell.

The stairway up the cliff face came up to a place thirty feet beside the conveyor, ending in a brass-bound door etched into the stone. Bolted from the inside, thought Vetra. Not likely a place of escape.

From this door burst a triumphant figure. Grebu! He stood squared in the doorway, his face cast in a ghoulish grin.

"Come, my pets!" he crooned. His tentacle feelers swayed in synchrony with the leaves on his head. Pushing his bulk forward, he spread his arms and slowly sauntered down the crooked steps, like the king of a twisted domain. He halted to survey the effect of his machinations.

A stream of two dozen henchmen poured out of the portal after him, hefting axes, swords and crossbows. Feral grins shone on their faces. Most were clad in mixes of leather and light armor, but a few were budding mutants like Grebu himself with tentacles rippling on their shoulders.

A portion of the slaves whom pods had touched, charged into the marching stalks which tore at their limbs, sending tendrils through their eyeballs, up through their noses and into their mouths.

Vetra's roar rose over the inhuman shrieks: "Get away from them, you fools!" He shoved one of the unaffected wretches roughly aside who would have been speared. Basineus dodged an invasive stalk that came perilously close to his ear.

Vetra turned a glance over his shoulder. The sinister maja stems shambled ever closer still, moving as one, dry leaves rustling in nightmarish warning. Behind them lay a strewn trail of mangled bodies.

At last Tas took up his axe and hewed down a row of the zombified stalks.

Strange alchemic accouterments tinkled on the plant king's jerkin, which Vetra could make no sense of. Whistles and bells carved of bone and shell to invoke spirits. Metallic emblems of colored metals he had never seen before, smoking with a strange, kelp-like reek. Doubtless, these adornments had infused the pods with life. Perhaps the same instruments the plant king used to ensorcell his man-eating strains?

With the stealth of the plant-spider, he came weaving toward them. His keen eyes swept the area with wrath. He stopped at the mangled vine. His face blazed with menace.

"Fool!" he growled at the lead slave. "I told you to guard Bekroma with your life! Now, look at her lying maimed! My oldest, most revered pet!" He took the last few steps down and flew at the gibbering idiot who backed away in jerky hops.

Vines lashed out from Grebu's shoulders and lifted the slave off the ground. The man only had time to let out an inhuman scream before a white tendril went through his ear to tickle his brain. Another curled around his eye and entered to come out the back of his head. "That will be your reward," he raged.

"And now you all shall die!" Grebu cried fanatically. The skewered man dangled inches off the ground and gave a final involuntary twitch then the mutant threw him aside in a lifeless heap.

He turned on Vetra who swung his sword with vindictive purpose.

Grebu dodged the strike. "How do you like my slaves?"

Vetra snarled, twisted sideways to unleash another savage blow. At the advancing slaves and the red welts on their brows he could not help but gape. Infection showed on their bare shins and scrawny arms.

"I have tainted them with the bulb, so that they remain enslaved to me, only to me." He leered at the pitiful opposition that faced him.

A slave frothing at the mouth raked his fingers into the eyes of one of his ensorcelled brothers. Whether in defiance of Grebu's dominance or out of self-preservation, Vetra could not tell. He lurched sideways to avoid one of Grebu's white tentacles of death.

"They're not as obedient as you think, Grebu," howled Tas, lifting aloft his axe, cutting menacing loops at the plant king's minions. "You'll lie chained ere dusk with one of your monsters ingesting you alive."

Grebu laughed. "I'll hold you to your boast, ranger."

At a gesture, a dozen swarthy, steel-helmed henchmen circled about to block the exit from the compound. The advancing stalks guarded the other flank closer to the edge of the pit. The remaining crazed slaves joined their ranks.

Vetra and Basineus crouched like panthers. Back to back, they circled, weapons gripped in white-knuckled fingers. The mass of enemies that crowded closer with each passing second eyed them like ripe lambs. Grim faces of mesmerized men, a few with vines rippling on their shoulders, grunted with the immediate pleasure of gutting men and the reward their master would give.

Tas joined their side like a hunted wolf, his dripping axe a bane for human and plant alike. His face radiated a demon-possessed glow. He ripped one of the bottles from his belt and downed it in a single gulp.

"What in Dergath's name are you doing?" hissed Vetra.

"Break through!" he snarled at them. "To the exit—don't wait up for me!"

He underwent a disturbing transformation then, as sinister

flesh formed and rippled on his face and arms. His face took on a green cast, his eyes dilated, sightless orbs into nowhere. He wobbled on his feet and rasped, "Go, I say. Fools! Slay as you've never slayed—die valiantly!" This was the last croak he made as he rushed in giddily to face the monsters approaching from all sides.

He ripped through Grebu's ranks like a storm-tossed wind, shredding vines and human flesh, while tentacles and stalks rippled out to take chunks out of him.

With wincing horror, Vetra guessed the ranger's enchantment wouldn't last long. He would be a bloody mess of flesh before the plant king could tilt back his head again in ghoulish laughter.

Yet amid Tas's bloody diversion, his strokes fell true and Vetra gave a war cry enough to chill the blood of any Karkassian warrior. Blade lifted and fell and tore into the enemy massed before him.

Corded muscle rippled; steel slashed through ripe flesh and howls came from men's mouths. Vetra braced his corded thews and swung again and again, the massive sword taking howling foes with it.

"Straight on, you rogues!" he yelled at Basineus who was at his side, scrambling and hewing and needing no prompting. Basineus's blade sliced foes like butter and he kicked bodies out of the way before dashing through the narrow rent in their ranks toward the exit.

The two cut a path side by side through the leather-armored throng dismembering limbs and slashing throats. Vetra parried and dodged; Basineus ducked and spun. Clinking steel and gut-wrenching howls filled the air and Vetra felt a sharp tug on his left shoulder, realizing an axe head had glanced off his upper arm, somehow finding a rent in his magical armor. Blood spurted from that wound and he snarled in frustration. A minor flesh wound compared to what Tas must be suffering.

The slaves, mobile at his feet, stumbled along, swinging what picks and warped hoes they had among them. Many prisoners died in that thrashing agony under the roots of stalks and by the axes of Grebu's butchers.

Vetra's weapon, notched and red started to slow; his muscled arm was splashed in crimson and gore.

Tas came clambering through, his boots slipping in blood over fallen bodies, a grisly, gore-splattered bear. The maja had lent him miraculous strength and kept him alive. He blocked the deadly cut of a Karkassian hillman then stopped another creeping at Vetra's back who would have severed Vetra's head. He and Vetra exchanged looks, knowing it was a turn of fate. They wasted no time, lunging ahead, parrying, burying steel in flesh, pushing on through the shouting throng while blood flew everywhere.

Vetra staggered through the wrenched-open door, Basineus next while Tas blundered behind. A bestial look gleamed in his eyes and his jerkin was shredded, face bloodied, but he roared laughter, spitting out blood and a few teeth.

A dozen or more able-bodied slaves clambered after the blood-soaked mercenaries. Those who were not mauled by the ghoulish horde, or the man-eating plants gaped in gratitude at their lucky escape. A few had snatched up weapons of the fallen; the rest had perished under the demonic maja stalks or the sorcerous assaults of the plant king who took up pursuit, screeching orders and flinging malignant pods at the fugitives.

The rebels fled up the ravine the way they had come—a narrow, dim corridor, now washed in sultry hues of the gloaming twilight. Grebu's shrieks tore at their backs as bolts whined by their ears, clattering on the stone around them.

Basineus stumbled off, half howling as a bolt grazed his side. He pitched forward, grimacing, picked himself up again. Vetra felt a heavy blow smash into his back, his enchanted armor taking the brunt of the hit. He wheeled about, to see, in a flush of florid anger, three ragged shapes of slaves fall shattered, riddled by crossbow bolts. The grime-streaked wretches had no chance.

Vetra fled on with Basineus, and now Tas pushed past, taking the lead. While the light grew dimmer and quivered with leaping shadows, it seemed that madness and death were all around them, that there would be no chance of escape.

CHRIS TURNER

IV

Tas sped ahead through the gathering darkness, a brawny shape lit only by the first glimmers of moonlight. Vetra kept an easy pace with the man, his eyes roving for danger while Basineus snuffled not two feet behind him.

The ranger took them on a circuitous route: through shadowy gulches, some no wider than five men abreast, then shadowy tunnels, where rock arched overhead like cathedral grottos. Rising and fading, the blustering voice of the plant king echoed behind them with sinister force.

Vetra cast a backward glance. Twenty-one men remained. Wearying fast, the slaves wheezed and huffed, struggling to keep up while the mercenaries plowed ahead.

Vetra studied them with critical eyes: a motley group, gripping broken hoes or rusty pickaxes, their eyes gleaming through the lingering starvation and hopelessness plaguing them. It was amazing these old hounds had not been culled from the pack long ago. Basineus, reading the look on Vetra's face, grunted back at the straggling pack. "The wretches will only slow us down. Get us killed."

Vetra knew it was only the slaves' desperation to escape that kept them moving at such a rate.

The clomping bootfalls and howls of the plant king and his minions at last faded, thanks to Tas's clever maneuvering. Vetra gripped bloody sword in hand, his jaw clenched. Basineus's face was a gleaming mask in the rising moonlight, his grinning white teeth shiny in the pale glow.

More often than not, some dark oval opening appeared in the rock face of the canyon which the fugitives gave wide berth. Tas's white-eyed scowls spoke volumes of what horrors and perils lurked within.

Vetra likewise sensed death stalking through these shadowy corridors. But he thrust this aside. On he loped after the tireless ranger. Tas bled as he limped, and contained his pain in a contorted grimace. How could a man endure such a beating and still be standing?

The transformation that had come over him was terrible to behold. The man seemed to have retreated into an inner hell, without bounds. He had only one bottle of his precious maja left, Vetra noted, bobbing at his waist, his eyes darting to it every few minutes. Vetra saw that his hand moved toward the gleaming vial, but by superhuman will it would go no further. The ranger somehow squelched the urge to lap it down. When that bottle ran out though... Vetra frowned. Doubtless these matters were heavy on Tas's mind.

Some minutes later, Vetra had a suspicion they were running in circles. "Didn't we just pass this wind-battered fluted pillar of rock?"

Tas scowled while Basineus blinked. Vetra mumbled an oath. What about that darker than dark entrance of a yawning cavern? All these landmarks seemed the same.

At a mouth of a corkscrew-shaped canyon, Tas paused, bringing them all to a halt.

A rustling of fiendish leaves thrust out from the gloom. On a signal from Tas, they dropped to all fours.

Vetra's muscles knotted, as if sensing life in those folds of darkness. Nothing. None dared breathe. He heard a thrum-thrum and twitching swish like spiders on rock, that could have been root-like feet invested with life.

Tas edged his bulk forward; they waited until the horror had passed. More of the marching plants! Vetra could see them in the hazy murk, quivering not a few dozen feet away. The plant king must have unleashed pockets of them to hunt down the rebels in the winding canyons with his sinister magic.

A foolish slave whimpered.

The plants halted their sinister motion and reaching to their full extent, jerked backward, like living, abominable things.

A wild and lusty curse rang from Tas's lips. "You idiot, Besthra flog you!" They all took up voice and ran. The slaves groaned and stumbled on.

Basineus trailed behind to belt the offending man in the mouth. Blood ran down his chin. The slave staggered. The lead plants bristled forward with fiendish expectation and the man slipped. The plants caught up to him and pulled him down, engulfing his frail figure in their writhing masses.

Vetra turned his head and winced. The slave's screams were as a man tortured on the rack. Leafy tendrils groped and writhed while others squeezed and tore. Roots grasped his twitching body and tore chunks of raw meat off.

Vetra grimaced. He slashed at the offending stalks whipping past to menace him. Dergath, but they were as tall as a bear on its hind legs, waving wild feelers! He scrambled back, hacking, sidling left and right like a prisoner under the lash. Basineus was at his side, slashing with no less ardor. When it was all over, the victim was indistinguishable from any of the blurred stumps or misshapen boulders that stained the woebegone place.

* * *

Far up the ravine they came to another dead stop as Tas doubled over, smitten with a coughing fit, his body convulsing.

Vetra resented halting at this exposed spot, given the horrors that wandered about these nightmarish canyons. But nothing was to be done. The ranger was beset with more seizures, his body bent over in two, quivering in an obscene paroxysm. His face was green under the ghastly moonlight. How much maja had he consumed in the last few hours? Vetra shook his head. The man's bouts were getting worse.

Tas gave a bitter laugh. Words spilled from his mouth with the spray of blood and phlegm. "I know it will kill me in the end. I've seen victims in their final stages. Slavering, monstrous caricatures of living flesh." His eyes, dilated, mirrored his face, an unreadable shaman's mask, lit with a terrible certainty.

Basineus's face was a mocking leer. "Why do you ingest it, if you know how toxic the excrement is?"

Tas's voice took on a rumble of anger. "You don't know the evil of the stuff! If you did, you would not pose such a question. A few months ago some of the oil spilled on my skin. I was leading an expedition to take out the first band of smugglers, a night job, with my recruits into our band of mercenaries. We intercepted the drug runners and we fought. We lost to the fierce mongrels—juiced on maja, their tentacles twitching like jellyfish streamers. A basket of the bulbs fell and the oil trickled out on the stones where I landed." Tas's mouth quivered at the memory.

A slave mumbled, "I know of what you speak, ranger. Ever since Grebu forced me to swallow a bulb whole, I have craved the stuff. It took everything I could to resist that sprinkling earlier Grebu fed us."

"He's right," added another. "Now that we're hooked, we're slaves to the maja. We sneak raw, unfiltered bulbs all the time— from the early crops when the guards aren't looking. Grebu dropped the snap pods on us and most of us just lifted our hands like puppets. You saw the result."

Vetra shook his head in undisguised contempt. "You're all weaklings."

"What do you know, outlander?" sneered Tas. "You've never been afflicted by the stuff. It's like a coal that burns your insides, creates the fiercest craving you can imagine. Just when I think I've conquered it, the image of the red bulb flashes in my mind, like some pulsing demon. If I've gone for a few days without it, I feel numb, chilled to the bone! Even now, I'm resisting the urge to swallow what's left in this cursed vial at my belt. I've tried to buck it, but I can't. The craving always returns, like some slug from the pits of hell."

Tas seemed to shake and shiver in an even more uncontrollable palsy.

Vetra grunted. He had seen men wracked by the yellow poppy before, but this was worse. He remembered when he was posted in the far east, in the rebel lands of Condoria. There he'd witnessed soldiers' delirium from addiction to the roots of the *Angris* bush. 'Twas was not a pleasant sight. Nor was what he had seen of Kealasa, the Vizier's daughter.

Tas sat up, coughing. "I curse that rotten hound, Grebu, for this. I curse that I was ever put on this wretched mission and crossed paths with that devil."

Vetra muttered. He shook off the tale-sharing with a shrug. The monsters would be coming soon. No time to delay the inevitable.

The slaves were flagging. They loped on, like dead men in a lost dream. Two keeled over. From exhaustion? Dehydration? Vetra would be surprised if any of them made it to the bridge. No time to bury the corpses or put up tombstone markers.

The mercenaries dragged them into a nearby cave. The less obvious for trackers to detect their passage.

Vetra was convinced they were hopelessly lost now, despite Tas's valiant efforts. He only knew that they were wandering in a land of shades and terrors.

* * *

A high cave presented itself after some tense scrabbling. They gained its mouth by a steep, winding ledge. No food was to be found in these bare confines, only some old bones dressed in cobwebs in a shadowy corner, long chewed and gleaned of gristle. While poking about for exits, Basineus discovered a small pool of water not far from the cave entrance, glimmering under the moonlight between weathered columns of shale. Perhaps it was a natural spring? Vetra was not sure. The water was brackish, or had some heavy mineral flavor to it. Though his stomach roiled to the greasy taste, he relished it as it slipped down his gullet. Some of the slaves muttered in wonder and washed away the layers of grime caked from their thin bodies. It was a luxury many had never known in the years of confinement in the pit. Their eyes gaped in the moonlight filtering through the cave entrance.

"Let's wait here, until Grebu's ghouls have passed," grumbled Tas. "We'll backtrack and brave the bridge in first light. He will not expect it."

Vetra grunted. He did not believe it, but he was too weary to argue.

Basineus muttered oaths and paced about, unable to contain his restless doubt. "Where did this fiend come from?" he demanded. "I've never heard of Grebu until a few days ago. Gods, but he has the strength of an ox."

One of the bolder slaves, a man with front teeth missing, involuntarily shuddered. "The maja bulb has given Grebu extraordinary powers. To others it brings pain, but him it feeds." He clutched at the ragged hair trailing to his shoulders.

One of his shaky-handed comrades balled a fist. "The old Karkassian legends foretold of a man with snakes not in his hair, but on his shoulders. He would be a demon among men, and create demons of his fellow man."

Basineus spat out a curse. "You speak of him as if he were a demigod." He lifted his sword in a blood-caked hand.

The slave shivered. "Rumors run rife. A wizard told a tale of stardust falling from the sky, colored specks sprinkling a mountain peak. A Karkassian witch woman, Dalkuusa, dozed by her night fire one evening. Then the stardust drifted down and set her crackling flames blazing to life. A star sprite sprang out of the hissing flames and carried her away to a cave in Gromet mountain, not two leagues from here."

"Aye, I've heard the tale too," murmured another. "From the

unholy union of witch and sprite, came Grebu—cast out of the wild tribes, for his ugliness and deformities. These were too much for the tribespeople to accept. He crawled at barely a half year old, wandered the lonely, deserted hills and learned many unusual things. Communicated with the feral animals, the jackals, the vultures. Danced with the bears, talked with spirits of the night, exploring pits and crevices not known to man in these ancient hills. It was said he discovered the maja in a high place on the mountain."

"A wives' tale, old man," crowed Tas. "No one could survive that young in the wilds."

"His sorcerous ability made it possible. From an early age it grew in intensity year by year."

A shudder passed through the ragged group. They listened to the chirps of night insects and the flit of bats echoing in the stone-crumbled canyon.

"It sounds too fanciful for me," mumbled Vetra, but part of him felt a certain truth in the slave's tale, as he did most folklore of the lands.

The company lay down on the cold stone, and slept while some traded guard. Basineus took first watch.

* * *

Vetra was jerked awake as slimy, stinging feelers brushed his cheek. He caught a glimpse of Tas cutting at the rippling vines.

Vetra lunged to his feet, snatching up his sword and slashed green shoots from the walking plants. White milky fluid ran in gobs, sizzling faintly as it sprayed on the cave floor. The ranger stood glowering. More and more maja stalks came thrashing in. Dergath! cursed Vetra. It was Basineus's watch. Had the ape fallen asleep? The plant fiends must have crept in through some secret passage in the back of the silent cave.

While Basineus was busy cleaving the tops of walking maja, Vetra joined him and they beat their way through the fiendish crop while being whipped and lacerated by the lashing shoots.

"Dergath's hells!" Vetra swore. "Is there no end to these nightmares?"

Tas's grunt was a sarcastic acknowledgment.

With wild abandon, the three slashed their way through the foliage. Spidery roots gripped the stone, questing their next step with hissing anticipation. Basineus's neck was raw with new welts; barbed leaves tore open his leg; his sword swept whistling arcs in a bloody grip. Tas grinned in feral lassitude. Madness, lunacy. That's what this place was.

Mercenary and slave crabbed down the ledge, as the plants jostled after with stiff, awkward lurches.

Outside the cave, the first blood glimmer of dawn was upon them, creeping over the rim of the world.

Down through the misty gorge they dogged their way, leaving the plants toiling behind.

The stone showed rounded, carven shapes, smoothed by eons of wind and rain. Shadows fell over the land like dew-dappled rain. A restless wind blew down the canyon, drying the wet blood on their faces.

The canyon was desolate. Some fresh animal tracks showed in the dirt—likely coyotes. A crow squawked over a trapped lizard it held clutched in its claws. A lone scraggly *marpus* tree sheltered black ravens that heralded them with baleful croaks, and hawks wheeled in the sky.

Up the ravine, they tottered, the straggling slaves well back. Tas led them in a direction Vetra thought headed vaguely west.

How much time passed, Vetra could not know, for the sun did not penetrate the mist that easily in this land of maja.

* * *

They climbed a boulder-strewn ravine choked with stunted bush, and as the pale morning light fell upon crumbled pillars of rock, Vetra's hopes soared.

Yet the reek of drifting smoke filling his nostrils prompted a sour feeling to stir in his gut once again.

The Karkassians despatched yesterday in the canyon hung from sharpened stakes like ghoulish scarecrows, as if they were grisly sacrifices of failure. Offerings to mountain spirits? Vetra had no idea. These hillmen's primitive superstitions were as foreign to him as ivory was to the Mercian peasant. Or maybe it was Grebu's ghastly doing?

They passed the corpses with silent unease. Flies buzzed on the rotting bodies; a neck hung loosely with no head, another perched with gaping eye sockets pecked by scavengers.

Up the pebbly ravine they crept in single file. Minutes passed; they entered the open space where they had once held parley so long ago. All was quiet. Too quiet for Vetra's tastes. Basineus and he traded uneasy glances.

Tas and the slaves padded forward toward the boulders and the slab where they had conversed with the plant king. A heavy mist hung like a thick blanket over the barren stone. The canyon lay like a sleeping snake below, cutting through the brume-laden rock like some titan's scythe cutting through rock and mist.

Vetra noticed small fires glimmering from the caves carved in the hill above. A lurking danger pervaded all and hung thick like a predator lying in wait. Humans had been here recently. Grebu had anticipated their destination as sure as more fiends were waiting for them, like vultures at a slaughter.

Arrows suddenly skidded from on high and clattered on the stone around them.

Vetra yelled. The slaves flung up their arms in panic. Two crumpled in anguished heaps, writhing, quivering shafts buried in their throats.

Tas gave a strangled curse. A long black-fledged shaft skidded into Vetra's mail, just below the left shoulder and knocked him back a step. He extracted it, grunting an oath. "On! Don't look back, if you value your lives! Across the gap."

Tas ducked a whining projectile. He staggered in a daze, urging them on toward the bridge. The span swept two-hundred feet across the canyon—white-washed planks built upon a timber trestle. He and Basineus ran, stumbling for the sagging structure that lay draped in mist and shadow.

Vetra gripped his sword. He faced the band of two dozen fresh Karkassians erupting from caves in the overlooking hill with fur on their backs and axes in their hands. The plant king's influence must have been large to include such fierce tribesmen on such short notice.

"After them, you fools!" Grebu rasped, as he raced at their heels.

Too many of the enemy for Vetra's eyes and he sheathed his sword and sped on with the others, heart pounding with the thought of escaping this nightmare. The bridge lay only a stone's throw away.

If they could gain the bridge, Grebu would lose his advantage. Vetra hoped the horses were still cached amid the rocks and weeds on the other side of the bridge.

But he and Basineus ground to a sudden halt. Vetra's jaw dropped. Before the first timbers of the bridge loomed a formidable shape, feeding on the fresh corpses left sprawled about from the last slaughter. The sinister shape lifted its head, wild and huge. The savage Karkassians also halted in their tracks, grunting with dismay, trading shocked murmurs at the sight before them.

The plant king hitched himself forward. "Why do you stall, you cowards? Move on!" His boot laid into the shin of a shaven-headed warrior.

"The troll, lord, it is feeding," croaked another. "It'll—"

"To fiend's hell with the troll! Slay them! I want them all dead!"

The tendrils on the plant king's shoulders flicked out in white riot. The hillmen shied away from their bristling overlord, teeth grinding, rather than choose to face the lurking troll.

"No, wait—I have a better idea. I want them alive!" cried

Grebu. "They will be fed to Zbeus, my successor grandfather maja. I'll watch these rebel scum worm in his vine-belly as his fluids eats them alive. Zbeus will seed the next generation of our plants! He needs human flesh to seed my crops!"

Ominous were the plant king's words, but more frightful yet was the formidable troll that hunched like a shadow cast by one of the great beasts of yesteryear. It was ten feet tall, hairy, and the top of its egg-shaped skull was bald and yellow while long wisps of pale, witch-like hair ran down its shoulders. On massive bare feet the thing poised, wooden club in hand, dressed in oiled leather and riveted iron. It surveyed the cringing men as if they were mere, insectoid curiosities.

A grimace froze on Vetra's face. His knuckles clenched on his hilt. There was no battling this primeval beast. It would amount to an attempt at suicide. If any of them could get by it would be a miracle. Likely the beast had been attracted by the smell of blood of the corpses from afar. Vetra had heard rumor of these creatures loping for miles to feed on fresh flesh.

Tas sought gingerly to edge around the troll, giving the creature wide berth while it continued to feed, as the slaves behind kept a sidelong course to the bridge. Vetra and Basineus made no more noise than slinking rodents on their heels. Grebu howled an order; his band surged forward.

The sudden motion alerted the beast. It lifted its bear-like snout and emitted a feral roar, blood and rotten offal trailing from its crimson jowl. The troll hitched its lumbersome bulk toward Tas who was closest, looming up in his path like a ghoulish monstrosity.

The ranger skittered for safety, axe in hand, up the bridge.

The troll caught up in three bounds. A massive paw swatted at him, sending the fleeing man careening into the bridge railing like a rag doll. Vetra rushed forward onto the bridge and laid a sword into the beast's matted hide. He leapt back in time to avoid the snapping jaws that sought his throat. Basineus charged in to hack at the troll's leg, prompting a spurt of black blood from the wound. The troll's nostrils flared as it lurched forward on its good leg. It smashed down with its club. The mercenaries ran. While the hillmen charged in, Vetra and Basineus split in either direction, leaving the hillmen exposed to the monster's teeth.

The troll threw its bulk into the fur-clad men like a battering ram, crushing limbs and heads like grapes. One victim it lifted over its head in one hand and broke his back over its knee, gnawing the man's head off. It snapped out a dripping fanged maw and tore a chunk out of another's ribs who came too close.

Grebu, grunting curses, hopped about in frustration. "Kill it! Are you imbeciles? A hundred talons for the live heads of the rebels." One of his men tripped over his own feet, only to be stomped by the creature as he tried to rise. "Bekroma's blood! Must I do this myself?" The plant king slipped around the bloody back of the fighting men and tore after the escaping mercenaries, arms and tentacles outstretched like the plant aberration he was.

In spite of their initial hesitation and devastating losses, the Karkassians were not cowards. By sheer numbers they beat the monster back onto the bridge. Each struggled to reach the greater prize, the fleeing rebels and Grebu's promise of reward.

The combined weight of troll and men set the timbers groaning. The rush of more enemy feet increased the sag. And still, the planks held.

Vetra and Basineus leaped over fallen bodies, dodging blades in their lurching scramble away from the teeming foes. They must break through the net, get past the troll and his club to cross the bridge. The straggling slaves who had not made it already, fell with bolts in their backs or reeled back with gaping sword wounds.

Tas and the first wave of slaves stood panting midway across the bridge. The ranger shambled across the remaining distance, a stretch of no more than hundred feet. But Vetra saw Tas hesitate. He had only a stone's throw to traverse and disappear into the foliage.

Vetra's eyes grew wide. The ranger came loping back to savage the troll from behind, fixing his axe head in its tough hide.

The beast turned in a shuddersome roar, lunging for him. Tas rumbled out a laugh. He ducked to skirt its swinging club, then prepared for another blow. He was an addict with nothing to lose.

Vetra watched him guzzle the last bottle of maja in a single gulp. The ranger staggered back, shaking his head like a rain-soaked dog. His eyes turned upward as an ecstatic man would, but those same eyes opened in wide, fearsome vengeance. Then his bloodshot eyes turned from red to yellow as his brow burst in a crop of red welts. His face greened like algae. It seemed as if Tas felt not his hurts from the troll. Rather, he stared down the thing, as if it were no more than a huge, overstuffed rabbit.

The troll paused, hissing out a stinking breath, not used to such boldness. Even its primitive brain seemed to struggle with the concept of a creature much punier than itself facing off eye to eye, neither cowering nor fleeing in the wake of its fierce might.

Its jaws opened wide and it threw back its head. Despite the bolts thwacking into its back, it loosed another thundering roar and charged, its breath blowing Tas's tawny hair back like straw.

The ranger did the oddest thing then. He ducked that sweep of hairy clawed arm and swung under its legs like an acrobat. Brandishing axe in bloody salute, he smote its gleaming head on into the startled Karkassians. It was as if the maja had invested the daredevil Tas with insuperable courage.

Grinning ear to ear, Vetra and Basineus sprinted forward, running right up the middle of the parted line. They hewed and roared war cries. Heads flew from shoulders while blood sprayed in crimson sheets.

Grebu charged in, shrieking orders to his slack-jawed men.

While the Karkassians recovered their wits, and trained crossbows, troll and mutant faced each other. The troll shuddered and wheeled about with a death-defying snarl as bolts thunked into its hide. It cast about, blinking at the audacity of the ant-like vermin that dared to harry it and tempt death.

Arrows buzzed like bees around Vetra. In panic, he flung the plant man to his side and shielded himself from the storm. Pale tendrils whipped out from the creature's shoulders and lanced into Vetra's ribs. He cried out in agony as one found the hole in his enchanted mail. He whipped his body around and cut the offensive festoons loose. An arrow slammed into Tas's arm and his face contorted in a grimace, but he just rained more terrible blows on his snarling, bearded foes. Basineus caught a bolt in the ankle and he blundered sideways, groaning in pain, almost knocking Vetra off his feet. The plant king's tendrils lashed out and caught Basineus's left arm, piercing leather and flesh.

Basineus loosed a howl. He slashed out at the offending shoot with his free arm. Rolling free, he staggered to a crouch, pulling the hateful, writhing shoot free from his arm.

Fire pulsed in Vetra's veins. The figures before him were like so many waxed dolls. In a dream haze, he hewed and hacked at them like a doomed avenger. In slow motion, his mighty thews laid steel into flesh and he leaped over broken bodies and pools of blood.

His blade arched scything loops. Grebu, who crouched gore-splattered before him like some grinning toad, was a monster who needed to be put down. How he would love to be the one to do it!

Grebu moved in to spring, but the troll's shadow fell upon him like a chill rain.

The creature tore off Grebu's rippling tendrils from his left shoulder and flung the offensive creepers into the canyon below.

The plant king uttered a dismal screech, as would lift the hairs on a hyena's back.

Vetra sprang in with wild triumph, dodging the troll's mallet-like hand and club and drove forth to stab through Grebu's other shoulder.

The plant king hardly felt it. The man had the vitality of a jungle tiger and he lunged in to ravage Vetra with his remaining tendrils. The mercenary ducked those lashes and dove behind the troll.

Grebu's tentacle stumps flapped in useless cords, slapping at faces and arms, leaving cuts. Victims lay on the ground, some blooded, some dazed, most crawling painfully to get away.

The troll grabbed Grebu by a leg and whirled him round then threw him headlong into the Karkassian horde. They toppled back, crushed and maimed. The plant king lifted himself up in dazed agony, shaking the black blood out of his eyes.

Tas still menaced the Karkassian throng and took them all on at once, so juiced was he on the maja. Basineus was at his side, flailing jerkily, reveling in the invincible ally he had. The ranger's axe rose and fell in red sweeps, cleaving heads, arms and shoulders.

Basineus stabbed and skewered. From time to time, he stomped boots into faces of men who fell reeling before Tas's murderous sweeps; other times he plunged axe into fallen men's hearts. Gore flew in four directions. Vultures wheeled on high, in frenzied anticipation of the ghastly feasts to come.

A shudder coursed through Vetra's body. He swung his sword in a bloody, two-handed grip and cracked a Karkassian's skull like an egg. Now it was time to flee this nightmarish carnage.

He vaulted over fallen bodies while Basineus and Tas parried enemy blades in their stumbling rush away from the swarming tribesmen and the trollish teeth of death.

A roar from behind alerted him. The bridge timbers quivered to thundering footsteps. Vetra wheeled briefly to see a godawful shape punctured by dozens of wounds, lurching in to rend them. Despite losing blood and weakening, the troll was in no way yet a dismissible threat.

The last archers among Grebu's company made the mistake of peppering the monster with more black-feathered shafts. The onslaught only angered the creature all the more. The arrows stuck in its tough gray hide but did not penetrate the pulsing organs beneath.

The troll had lost its club but it swept out a mallet paw at Basineus, who ducked, but not fast enough. The massive fist grazed his side and sent him sprawling. He lay on his back, hands clutching at his vitals. More arrows came whizzing out of the thinning mist. Still the troll came on, oblivious of its wounds.

Men it mashed like flies.

But a fierce cracking and snapping of timbers brought new cacophony to the chaotic scene. Vetra whirled, gasping as a wide crack spread under his feet.

Desperately he took two quick bounds toward Basineus and pulled the supine man along by an arm down the bridge.

"Leave me, you fool. I'm a dead man," croaked Basineus.

Vetra snarled. The planks buckled under his feet. "Never! I'll not leave you to that fiend."

"You're as stubborn as an ox," the mercenary growled.

Vetra's right leg plunged through the timbers. Cursing a venomous oath, he pulled himself up and dragged the wounded mercenary down the heaving, shuddering way. He lurched and fell again. Under the troll's weight, the planks crumbled fast, taking men and half-plant mutants with them.

Tas reached safety first and grabbed Vetra's arm. He hauled him the last few feet before Vetra slid down the buckling way. Vetra rolled on his stomach. Then swung out a hand and barely caught Basineus's wrist in time before the timbers shattered and ripped away, sending screaming tribesmen plunging to their deaths. A roaring troll and flailing plant mutant smashed on the jagged rocks far below.

Vetra roared, "Quickly, help me get him up!"

Tas grasped Basineus's blood-soaked waist and helped him

drag the injured man to safety. The mercenary lay wheezing on his back, moaning and gasping. Tas and Vetra crouched in the dirt like battered wolves, trading grimaces, panting and muttering.

The few enemy stragglers who halted at the other side, stood stranded on Lvendar territory. They stared dumbstruck at the destruction, wondering if they still owed a dead master their allegiance.

Evidently not. They loped into the wastes while a few surviving Karkassians shook fists at them from the other side of the ruined bridge. Bolts flew from this assemblage but landed without effect at the mercenaries' feet.

Vetra laughed; his vindictive wrath reached an apex. Their opposition was reduced to no more than a half dozen. He pulled a shaft from his boot; one had lodged also in his side, stuck within the leather and rings. Tas had a black-fletched arrow protruding from his upper arm, passing out the other side, but it was as if the man felt no pain. Vetra stared with incomprehension. Tas and what few slaves remained hobbled toward the wooded hillside where the horses lay tethered. Vetra hoisted up Basineus's hulk, an arm wrapped around his shoulder. He joined them, feeling the wild beating of his heart and aching in his temples subside to a dull throb. His ears were oblivious to the sounds of dying and mayhem below from those who still clung maimed to the canyon walls.

A few of the slaves managed to clear the bridge and bobbed at Vetra's side like abandoned children. "Give us food—and water, it's all we ask."

Vetra glared. "Unless you want to munch on decayed flesh, or troll's fare, there's slim pickings."

"There's food up in the outpost stores," murmured Tas, flicking a hand toward the wooded slopes. He was still in a delirium of the battle. "A league or two yonder maybe. Unless your Karkassian brothers have looted it." He scratched absently at a blackened wound on his neck.

The survivors scrambled up the broken path like starving coyotes.

"Wretches," mumbled Basineus. "You should have left them back there to rot in the slave pit."

Vetra's upper lip twitched. "Even slaves deserve a chance at life, Basineus." He moved toward the horses.

"And you, mercenary," Tas said to the wounded man, "you look in bad shape."

"You're not much better, ranger." Basineus laughed bleakly, spitting blood. "I'm glad of your insane charge back there. I don't know how you pulled it off, as you should be dead with all that maja juice and the beating you took. So what now?"

"I already am dead," groaned Tas fatalistically. "The Lvendar justice will hunt me down with their bounty hunters for this cock up."

"Why is it a cock up?" Basineus grunted with a pained grimace. "The plant king is dead."

"Yes...dead." Tas shook his head. "But like a bad weed, the trade will start up again. All that matters is that there's more maja to harvest here. There'll be others who answer the call. All the lords want is their stupid scrap of paper. Without it, they'll treat this mission as a failure, and me to blame."

Vetra shrugged as if in silent accord. Basineus admitted as much.

Tas was peppered with gashes and ugly wounds. By all odds, he should be three steps in the grave, yet the man was still standing. Vetra frowned. "Are you a ghoul or some mutant like Grebu?" He looked at the man with awe, yet not without a certain wariness.

"Let's move," Tas grumbled. He staggered up the path toward the stand of boulders where the first horses stood, while he bled from a dozen suppurating wounds. "Let's just say I have nine lives." His blood-flecked grin flashed in the sunlight, as bits of flesh still clung between his teeth, remnants of his chewing through a Karkassian's neck in a close quarter death-wrestle. Vetra shuddered, stepping a pace back.

"It would have become obvious to my lords and bosses that I'm messed up with the bulb and that it contributed to the blunders and the bowmen's deaths. I'd be court-martialed before the sun rose and strung out to dry; maybe even put to the executioner's block." He turned a bitter face toward the mercenary. "So, your job I take it, was to despatch me—or bring me in."

"Yes," admitted Vetra. Lying to the man would accomplish nothing. "But I have no desire to do so."

"What's that mean? That you'll vouch for me to Ragnum?"

"No. But I'll not speak against you. How be you just disappear?"

"As in—?"

"I look the other way."

Tas loosened the tethers. He took his roan down to the bridge where he snatched up as many of the green bottles of maja as he could from the corpses strewn on the last timbers. He led the horse back, gave a grim, grateful salute and mounted his steed and was gone.

Basineus scratched his bleeding scalp, eyes troubled. "You let him off that easy? How are we to explain to Kalvium his absence?"

"Think again, Basineus. He saved our lives ten times over. The least we can do for him is grant him his life, however short it may be." Vetra looked off into the thinning mist and shuddered, thinking of the painful road of addiction that valiant man would still have to face.

He shook his massive shoulders and the blood from his face. It was a long ride back to Lausern—it would be slower with Basineus in his injured state. Nor did he like breaking the news of the Lvendar casualties to Ragnum, but he could almost see the curl of vindication on the old Lord's face when he told him that the plant king was dead, and his daughter avenged.

Vetravincus turned his eyes northward and a grim resolve flared in his breast: to attempt once more to track down those scum of raiders who had stolen his sister so long ago...

ABOUT THE AUTHOR

Chris is a prolific author of fantasy, adventure, and science fiction. His writing spans many genres: heroic fantasy, sword and sorcery and speculative fiction.

Browse Chris's books at

https://innersky.ca/books/home

www.ingramcontent.com/pod-product-compliance
Lightning Source LLC
Chambersburg PA
CBHW032250020726
47495CB00001B/35